🍂 Praise for Charles de Lint 🍂

"There is no better writer now than Charles de Lint at bringing out the magic in contemporary life." —Orson Scott Card

"[A] sentimental, wildly imaginative follow-up to *The Onion Girl*."
—*Kirkus Reviews*

"[A] pleasing addition to the popular Newford saga . . . Inevitably recalls Neil Gaiman's *American Gods*, to which this more intimate and folksy book compares favorably." —*Publishers Weekly*

"De Lint is a master stylist." —*Romantic Times BOOKreviews Magazine*

"In de Lint's capable hands, modern fantasy becomes something other than escapism. It becomes folk song, the stuff of urban myth."
—*The Phoenix Gazette*

By Charles de Lint from Tom Doherty Associates

Widdershins

Charles de Lint

A Tom Doherty Associates Book
New York

WIDDERSHINS

Copyright © 2006 by Charles de Lint

All rights reserved, including the right to reproduce this book, or portions thereof, in any form.

Edited by Patrick Nielsen Hayden

A Tor Book
Published by Tom Doherty Associates, LLC
175 Fifth Avenue
New York, NY 10010

www.tor.com

Tor® is a registered trademark of Tom Doherty Associates, LLC.

Library of Congress Cataloging-in-Publication Data

De Lint, Charles.
    Widdershins / Charles de Lint.
       p. cm.
    "A Tom Doherty Associates book."
    ISBN-13: 978-0-7653-1286-0
    ISBN-10: 0-7653-1286-7
    1. Newford (Imaginary place)—Fiction. 2. City and town life—Fiction. 3. Magic—Fiction. 4. Man-woman relationships—Fiction. I. Title.
PR9199.3.D357 W53 2006
813'.54—dc22

                                             2005034475

Printed in the United States of America

0 9 8 7 6 5 4 3

For Honey, R.I.P.,

and all those

who shine their light

into the dark

Yesterday is ashes; tomorrow is wood.
Only today does the fire burn brightly.
—Old Inuit proverb

The music of what happens—that is the finest
music in the world.
—Attributed to FIONN MAC CUMHAIL,
from Irish folklore

God, I really hope that we just remember we
all come from the same tribe in the end.
—LILA DOWNS,
from an interview in
Women Who Rock, Jan./Feb. 2004

Contents

le Fay, on *Up She Flew*), "The Hard Road to Travel" (Kevin Crawford, on *In Good Company*), "Far from Home" (John Wood—his version is unrecorded), and "Farewell and Remember Me" (Boys of the Lough, on *Farewell and Remember Me*).

I'd like to thank Terri Windling for giving me the title for this book (and indirectly, Jane Yolen, who first came up with it), and Catherine Crowe, who first told me a version of the story of crow and the salmon, which I then proceeded to take apart and put together again in a whole different way. You can find the version she told me on her Web site at *www.imagocorvi.com* and also enjoy looking at her lovely enameled jewelry. MaryAnn and I share one of her crow pendant/pins, which hangs by my writing desk when MaryAnn isn't wearing it.

I'd also like to thank:

my agent Russ Galen for going above and beyond the call of duty with this book, and my editor Patrick Nielsen Hayden for being so patient with my tardiness at turning in the manuscript;

my coterie of friends, family, and well-wishers (too numerous to name—you know who you are), without whom writing these books would truly be a far lonelier proposition;

my readers who are so possessive about these characters, and continue to be so loyal to me and my work over the years;

those readers who continue to send such wonderful music my way, as well as all the amazing musicians who, through the years, have kept my brain fertile and my spirits lifted with their music;

and last, but never least, MaryAnn, not simply for how she still finds time in the hectic bustle of her life to work on these writing projects of mine, but for the grace she brings into my life.

If any of you are on the Internet, come visit my home page at *www.charles delint.com*.

Author's Note

After my novel *The Onion Girl,* everybody wanted to know what was going to happen next with Jilly. At least that's the message I've gotten from readers' letters and at signings, not to mention from my own in-house, first editor: my wife MaryAnn. How could I leave her in that state? Were she and Geordie ever going to get together?

I was a little reluctant to answer those questions—partly because I'd rather books not carry on with the same lead characters as my earlier books, and partly because I don't want to make readers read my books in any particular order.

Then there's also the idea that readers should be able to decide for themselves what happens after the book has ended and the story in its pages is done. If the characters feel real enough, their stories can continue in the reader's mind. There's no need for me to put in my two cents worth.

But that doesn't mean one should ignore old friends, and I realized that was exactly what I was doing. So after I wrote *Spirits in the Wires* to see what Christy and the people in his life were up to, and then satisfied my own desire for new characters by writing *Medicine Road* and a young-adult novel called *The Blue Girl,* I sat down to start the book you hold in your hands.

Except, there's another reluctance I have with going back to a character I like as much I do Jilly: Let's face it, you can't have a novel without some drama and hardship in the lives of its principal characters, and I didn't want to have to put her through the wringer yet again.

But in the end I had to agree with the rest of you. And once I'd begun Jilly's story, how could I not see it through to the end to see how she fared?

I hope you enjoy reading her story as much as I did while writing it.

The section titles come from traditional tunes. They're available on mar recordings, but these were my sources: "The Dispute at the Crossroad (Paddy Glackin, on *In Full Spate*), "Hand Me Down My Fiddle" (Morga

Widdershins

Remember how it was when we were young? It was like a dance, couples pairing up, together one month, the next everybody has a new partner, sometimes from within your social circle, other times a stranger brought in, but there was always this ebb and flow, like a tide, as though dating and love were a game of musical chairs, except you played it with your heart.

As I've gotten older, I've found that we seem to divide into two camps: the ones who keep a partner and settle down, maybe have kids, maybe buy a house; and the ones who stay in the musical-chairs dance and end up living on their own, who are on their own for longer and longer periods of time until they grow to like their solitary lifestyle—or at least accept it. Some keep a hope buried for that certain someone to fall into their lives, but nobody's really looking anymore. Or they're not looking hard.

It's hard to pinpoint exactly when that happens.

For me, hope runs eternal, even though my relationships never really work out in the long run. Maybe I set my sights too high. Maybe I'm just hopeless. I don't know. Or maybe I just never met the right woman, for all the times I thought I did.

Or maybe I did meet the right woman, but I never knew it and went out with her sister or her friend instead.

Or maybe I did know it, but I told myself it was never going to work out. . . .

The Dispute at the Crossroads

have a clue what she was doing, or what she should be looking for. Cars started when you turned the key, or they didn't. The world between the two was as mysterious as where the tunes she made up came from, though with the latter, at least, she had the faith that if she needed a piece of music, it would come. Maybe not right away. It could be late, sneaking up on her while she was in the shower, or down at the grocery store, walking down the aisles, hours or even days after she first started looking for the melody to go with a title or a feeling or the first couple of bars she already had. But it would come.

That wouldn't happen trying to figure out what was wrong with this confusing mess of wires, pipes, and engine parts. She didn't have faith, for one thing. And she certainly didn't have the mechanical background the way she had such an easy familiarity with her fiddle.

So a spontaneous solution to her problem was pretty much out of the question.

And, of course, she'd let her cell phone go dead when she could have easily had it charging while they were up on stage this evening. But she hadn't thought of that until she was in the parking lot after the show, getting into her car.

She looked up and down the dirt road she was standing on. There were no headlights visible in either direction. She hadn't seen another car or a farmhouse or pretty much anything since leaving Sweetwater and the bar where the band had played tonight. In retrospect, she should have stayed over as the others were doing. Right now they'd be hanging around in the bar, or in one of the rooms that the bar had provided for them upstairs, playing some tunes or just sharing a drink and some chat. But wishful thinking was always easier in retrospect, wasn't it? And if she had stayed, there probably would have been problems with Con, who couldn't seem to get it through that thick head of his that they weren't an item, never had been, never would be.

There was nothing really wrong with him. He was charming and good looking, easy to get along with, and while he might be just a touch too fond of the drink, he was a wonderful guitar player. She simply had her rules.

"What do you have against dating musicians?" he'd asked the last time the subject came up.

"Absolutely nothing—so long as I'm not playing in the same band as they are."

"But—"

"Oh, I know. What could be more perfect? Working and playing and loving together. Except, my somewhat drunk and certainly randy friend,

Lizzie Mahone

March 2004

The crossroads at midnight. Or at least *a* crossroads, and while it was long past midnight, it still had the feel of the witching hour about it.

If Lizzie Mahone had been superstitious, she might have been more nervous about her car breaking down as it had, here where two county roads crossed in the middle of nowhere with nothing to mark the spot but an enormous old elm tree, half dead from a lightning strike. And the thought still crossed her mind as she got out of the car and popped the hood, her flashlight beam playing over the Chevy's V-6 engine. You couldn't be a musician and not know the story, how the old bluesman Robert Johnson once met the devil himself at the crossroads. But that had been in the Delta, deep south. This was just the dusty meeting place of a couple of dirt roads, surrounded by farmers' fields and bush. Nothing mysterious here, though that big old moon lent an eerie light to the elm tree and there was something in the wind. . . .

Yes, Lizzie thought. Her imagination. Better it should concentrate instead on what was wrong with the car.

She jiggled the wires going to the distributor cap and battery, but that was about the extent of her mechanical knowledge when it came to cars, and she only tried it because it was something that others had done when the car broke down in the past. Sometimes it had even worked. She didn't really when it all comes apart, then you're still stuck playing together. Or more likely, one of you has to leave, and I want neither to start a new band nor to break in yet another guitarist."

"It didn't take that long for me to come up to speed with your repertoire."

"Exactly. You're a great guitarist, so I don't want to lose you."

"Maybe this rejection will hurt so much that I'll have to leave."

She'd smiled. "And maybe when you sober up in the morning, you'll realize that this is a great gig you have with us and isn't it lucky you didn't let your libido screw it up."

That conversation had taken place last weekend when they were in Champion, north of Tyson and on the other side of the mountains. Sweetwater, being as close to home as it was—only an hour and a half if you went by the back roads as she'd been doing—made it much easier to come up with some excuse about having stuff to do in the city tomorrow morning and get in the car, rather than have to go through it all again with him.

Except now she was stuck in the middle of nowhere at—she checked her watch—three A.M. She'd probably have to sleep in the car, because there certainly didn't seem to be anybody else on the road, which might actually be a good thing, considering. But she'd be more nervous breaking down on her own in some parts of the city than she was here. Country folk could get as rambunctious and rowdy as their more cosmopolitan cousins—more so, if some of the gigs they played were any barometer—but they usually didn't have the meanness you could sometimes find in urban centers. She felt safer watching a bar fight from the relative safety of the stage in a country bar than walking alone at night down, say, any of the streets running off Palm back in the city.

And even if some cowboy got out of hand . . . well, it never came to much. She knew how to take care of herself, as more than one big strapping lug who wouldn't hear the word *no* had found out. While she might look like "just a wee lass with too much hair," as Pappy liked to describe her—though still standing six-foot-six at eighty-two years of age, pretty much everybody was smaller than her grandfather—she was stronger than she looked. She could box and wrestle, not to mention fight as dirty as most men half again her size. It wasn't how big or small you were—Johnny, her sparring partner at the gym was forever saying—but what you did with what you had.

At least the night was balmy. There were still patches of snow to be seen in some of the fields and in the bottoms of the ditches, but the temperature was well above freezing. Typical spring weather for these parts, really: spring one day, the trees filled with the welcome calls of migratory songbirds, and the next it could snow again. But tonight was mild and the air smelled expectant, ready for spring.

She left the hood up so that if anybody did come by they'd know she was having car trouble and not just drive by while she was fast sleep in the backseat. She had a blanket, and a candle in case it got colder, though she doubted she'd need the latter. In the trunk there was also an umbrella, a collapsible shovel, a jug of water, a box of crackers, and a couple of chocolate bars. The other band members teased her sometimes about always being so prepared, though if she was really the Girl Scout they thought she was, she'd have at least charged her phone before leaving the bar.

Still, what was done, was done. She'd make her bed in the backseat and she'd get some sleep in it, too. Tomorrow morning was soon enough to worry about how she was going to get the car up and running again.

But first she had to have a pee.

She could have just gone beside the car—it wasn't as though there was any traffic, or even much chance of it—but she still felt better pushing through the old dead weeds in the ditch and going behind the elm tree.

It was when she was pulling her jeans up that she heard the voices.

She zipped up quickly, then hesitated about showing herself. There were too many voices, low and rumbling, joking and laughing. She made out four, maybe five different ones. Peeking around the elm, she looked either way down the road.

At first she didn't see anyone. Then she realized she was looking too high. Approaching from the direction she'd been heading in, before the car up and died on her, was a gang of boys, almost hidden from her sight by the weeds. She'd been looking for men, because the voices were men's voices.

As they drew nearer, she readjusted her thinking yet again. The bright moonlight showed a group of little men tramping down the road toward her. She was five-foot-six, but not one of them would come up to her shoulder. Their heads seemed large for their bodies, and they were dressed as though they were returning from some medieval reenactment—a Renaissance Faire, perhaps—with old-fashioned leather trousers and jerkins, and short swords or long knives sheathed at their belts. They all had quivers and carried bows, and three of them were carrying the bloodied remains of some kind of large animal. A deer, perhaps.

About the same time as she was able to make them out better, they became aware of her car, though why they hadn't noticed it sooner, she couldn't say. Probably they'd been too busy with joking and congratulating each other on a good hunt. But they had noticed it now.

They stopped, the two not carrying meat immediately nocking arrows to bowstrings as they all looked around.

Lizzie ducked back behind the elm.

"What's this?" she heard one of them say.

"Someone's bad luck."

That brought a round of laughter.

"Maybe good luck for us. Anything inside worth nicking?"

Oh, no, Lizzie thought. Her fiddle case was lying right there on the back-seat.

"Anybody inside worth eating?" someone added to more laughter.

Lizzie had been about to step out from behind the tree and take the chance that they were more wind than bite, but at that last comment she stayed hidden, pressed herself tightly against the bark, and tried not to breathe.

"There's food in the boot," one of them said.

"Anything good?"

"Chokky bars and biscuits . . . oh, and a jug."

"Lovely, lovely."

" 'Cept it's just bloody water."

"Now who'd waste a good jug on carrying about water?"

Lizzie had left the trunk open while she went to have her pee. Maybe they'd be satisfied with what they found in it. Maybe they wouldn't look in the car itself.

But then she heard one of the car doors open.

"Looks to be our fool's a musician. There's a fiddle case just a-lying here."

"That can't be right. Where's the fiddler who doesn't drink?"

"Better question still, where's the fiddler?"

All of Lizzie's bravery had long since fled. There was something not right about these little men.

She'd thought they were midgets or dwarves.

She'd thought they'd come from some Faire.

She'd thought that she wasn't really in any danger.

But there were no Faires at this time of year—not around here. If there was, she'd know, because her band would probably be playing at it.

And these little men . . . there was a nasty undercurrent to the jovial de-livery of their conversation. She could sense it as clearly as she could on those nights when the band just couldn't connect with a crowd, when nothing you did up there on the stage was right.

"Hiding on us, do you suppose?"

"Unless some green-brees had him for a late-night snack."

"Don't even joke about that."

"Unless he's not a *he*."

"What've you got there?"

Lizzie already knew. Whoever was rummaging around in the back of the car must have found her little knapsack with its toiletry bag and change of clothing and underwear in it.

"Nice."

"I'd like a soiled pair better."

"Where do you think she's got to?"

"Prob'bly went looking for help."

"And left her fiddle behind? Not likely."

"She carries water around instead of poteen, so she's not much of a fiddler, is she?"

"I say she's hiding."

Lizzie heard a series of wet thumps and realized that they'd dropped their loads of meat in the trunk of the car.

"Let's have a look-see, shall we?"

Oh god, oh god, oh god.

"Hello, hello, wee fiddler," one of them called out in a loud voice. "Why don't you come out and play?"

"Whisht—not so loud."

"Why not? I *want* her to hear us."

Lizzie heard the whack of someone being slapped on the head.

"Ow. What'd you do that for?"

"If you're that loud, something else might hear us, hey?"

They all fell silent. Lizzie pressed her face against the elm, wishing she had something—*anything*—in her hand to defend herself with.

But she didn't.

She had only herself.

Best defense is offense, Johnny would say. If you know you're in trouble, don't try talk. Just come out swinging.

She swallowed, her throat and chest tight, and readied herself. She'd slip from behind the tree and charge them, take them by surprise. If she was lucky, maybe they'd run off. If she wasn't, she'd hurt as many of them as she could. She had good leather boots on and the toes were hard. She made fists with either hand.

But while the little men had been silent, they hadn't been still.

"What have we here?" a gruff voice asked.

And just like that, the element of surprise was taken from her. She'd never heard them moving through the dry weeds, but here they were, all five of the little men, arrows nocked in bowstrings and aimed in her direction. They stood around her in a half circle. With the elm at her back, there was no avenue of escape.

"Pretty thing," one of them said with a grin.

She caught only a glimpse, and it was hard to tell with no more than the moonlight behind him to see by, but it seemed that all his teeth had been sharpened to points.

"But big."

"Ah, they're all big, her kind."

They were lowering their bows, one by one, letting the strings go slack. Sure they had her. Sure of themselves.

"I like 'em big," the smallest of them said.

The others laughed. Perhaps it was the way he'd said it—as though he was trying to impress his companions, more than her. One of the others gave him a light cuff across the back of the head.

"You wouldn't know what to do with her," he said.

"Bit of a laugh that hair of hers."

She'd dyed her normally black hair a brilliant scarlet a month or so ago, but the black roots had grown out now.

Go ahead, she thought. Have a good look. Get all stupid and confident.

"Only hair I'll be looking at is down below."

" 'Less she's the kind that shaves."

"Are you that kind, girl?" the one closest to her asked.

He moved toward her and she took her chance. Before any of them could react, she took a step forward. Using the momentum of her forward motion to add even more force to the blow, she drove the toe of her boot into his groin.

"How's that for between the legs?" she cried above his shriek of pain.

She didn't wait to see the result. Turning, she hit the one on her right square in the face with a cross blow. Felt his nose collapse. Turned again toward the next, right arm cocked, only to find herself staring straight at three arrowheads, bowstrings pulled taut behind them.

"Shouldn't have done that," the little man in the center said. "We were only going to play a little with you."

"Were," the one on the right said.

The one on the left nodded. "But now you're meat, girl."

"We're all meat, you little freaks," a new voice said.

Lizzie had no idea where he'd come from, a tall Native man in jeans and a checkered shirt, with long black hair and coppery skin. One moment she was alone with her attackers, the next he was standing behind the center one. But she didn't stop to work it out.

With the little men distracted, their bows lowering as they turned to the newcomer, she charged the one on her right and drove him to the ground, pounding him with her fist. She heard cries, the sound of punches. When she looked up from her own foe, the other two men were also down, the stranger standing above them. The one she'd kicked earlier was still lying in the dirt, moaning, legs pulled up, hands on his groin. The one whose nose she'd broken was pulling the long knife from his belt. Before he could get it free, the stranger stepped in and knocked him to the ground with a flurry of blows.

"The thing is," he said as his assailant dropped, "some meat fights back."

One of the men he'd knocked down earlier lifted himself from the ground by straightening his arms under himself. He spat on the ground, blood and a tooth, small eyes dark with fury.

"Eat my shite, you grand pluiker," he muttered.

And then he disappeared.

Lizzie's eyes widened, not sure she'd seen what she'd seen. But then the little man she was still sitting on vanished as well. She scrambled to her feet as though she'd had an electric shock. As she watched, the other three disappeared, one by one.

"How . . . ?" Lizzie turned in a slow circle, trying to understand.

"It wasn't magic," her rescuer said. "They just moved between."

"Between? Between what?"

"This world and the other."

Lizzie slowly shook her head. "This isn't happening."

" 'Course it's not. That your car?"

She nodded, her attention on one of the abandoned bows. It wasn't much longer than her own fiddle bow, but sturdier, and certainly deadlier. She toed it with her boot. It seemed real.

"What's wrong with it?" the stranger asked.

She looked up, confused. The bow seemed intact. What was wrong was that it was even here in the first place. It, and all those little men, and this mysterious stranger . . .

"Your car," he said. "What's wrong with your car?"

"I don't know," she finally managed.

"Let me have a look."

She trailed along behind him, stepping over the ditch and onto the road.

"Who were those . . ."

She reached for a word, still feeling lost and stupid. She had to grip her hands and hold them against her chest to try to stop them from shaking.

"Those dwarves?" she finally said.

"They were bogans, not dwarves," the stranger said. He was looking under the hood of her car without apparently needing a flashlight. "There aren't many dwarves around here and, anyway, they've much better manners. And they don't poach."

Poach? Lizzie thought. But then she remembered what the little men had been carrying when they first showed up.

"Looks like your alternator's crapped out on you, so your battery hasn't been getting any juice."

"Can you fix it?"

He lifted his head from where the was studying the engine to look at her.

"Not permanently," he said.

He put his hand on the manifold and the engine coughed, then started up. Lizzie stared at the car. The motor seemed to be running more smoothly than it had in years.

"What did you just do?" she asked as he closed the hood.

He gave her a thin smile. "Now *that* was magic. It'll hold until you get to wherever you're going so long as you don't turn the engine off."

"But—"

"Where were you headed?"

"I was on my way to Newford from Sweetwater, but maybe I should go back if the car's not really fixed."

No, it had been magicked and what did that mean, anyway? Hopefully, she'd already fallen asleep in the back of the car and was dreaming all of this. Maybe she'd never left the bar. Maybe she was actually sleeping upstairs in the room she was supposed to be sharing with her cousin Siobhan. Except, could you know you were dreaming if you were dreaming?

"What's in Sweetwater?" the stranger asked.

"A gig. We played at the Custom House tonight, and we're supposed to play again tomorrow night and Sunday."

He nodded. "I'd take your car to the garage at the corner of Willis and the highway, just after you've come into town. They're cheap and they do good work."

"I will."

"So you're a musician? What kind of music do you play?"

"Celtic stuff—you know, jigs and reels, a few songs. We also do some original material."

Although the moon was bright enough to see by, she couldn't read much on his face. His features were too still. But she got the sense he disapproved. Or maybe it was just that he didn't like her.

"Get into a fix like this again," he said, "and you should try whistling some of that music. Even bogans are suckers for anything that reminds them of their homeland."

"You called them that before. What are bogans?"

"A kind of fairy. You people brought them with you when you came in your big ships. Bogans and every kind of fairy freak."

Lizzie knew that a lot of Native Americans harboured a grudge against Europeans, and rightly so, she supposed, all things considered. So she thought she understood his anger. But all this talk of fairies didn't make any kind of sense.

"Fairies," she said.

"Oh, yeah. And as you can see, they're not all tiny little things living in flowers and sipping nectar from acorn cups."

"But—"

"I've got to go. Your car'll get you back to Sweetwater. Just remember: don't turn it off until you're actually at the garage because it won't start again until they fix it."

She nodded. "I won't. Wait," she added as he started to walk away. "I didn't get a chance to thank you."

"You don't need to."

"I'd probably be dead if you hadn't come along."

Because you can die in a dream, right?

"Maybe, maybe not," he said. "You were handling yourself pretty well."

He started to turn again.

"Wait," she repeated. "At least tell me your name."

"You don't need my name."

"But—"

"You want my advice, you get in that car. You go home or wherever else it is that you need to be, and you forget about all of this."

"God, how am I supposed to do that?"

"Not my problem."

"Look, I—"

But she was talking to an empty road. As suddenly as the mysterious stranger had appeared, he was now gone. He'd vanished, just like the little

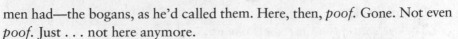

men had—the bogans, as he'd called them. Here, then, *poof*. Gone. Not even *poof*. Just . . . not here anymore.

She looked around herself. Everything seemed so damned normal.

But it *had* happened.

The soft murmur of her car engine proved it. She walked slowly around to the back of the car. The car's engine running, and the meat the little men had dumped in her trunk, because it was still there, raw and bloody.

Enough, she told herself. Wake up already.

But the dream wasn't going to let her go that easily.

Fine. She'd play it out, the way you did with a tune that you couldn't get out of your head. She'd get back in the car and return to Sweetwater. And maybe then she'd finally wake up.

Except, dream or no dream, she couldn't drive with that meat in her trunk.

Her first impulse was to simply dump it on the side of the road. She actually had a piece in her hands, meaning to do just that. It felt horrible, slick and bloody, hard to hold. A dead weight.

She let it fall back into the trunk and picked up her collapsible shovel. Unfolding it, she locked the two halves of the shovel in place, then crossed the road and went back over the ditch until she was standing under the naked boughs of the elm tree once more. She pushed around in the dirt until she found a spot that didn't have a big root and started to dig.

Ten minutes later she was ready to start hauling the deer parts from her trunk to the hole she had dug. When all three pieces were in the ground, she shovelled the loose dirt back on top, patting the rounded mound with the flat of the blade to tamp it down. It didn't seem right to stomp on the loose dirt with her boots.

She stood for a few moments when she was done, holding the shovel. The night was so quiet. A breeze rustled the twigs on the branches above her, and whispered through the dry weeds. There was a scatter of cloud, but mostly the sky was clear, the stars bright, the moon lowering to the horizon. She wasn't shaking anymore. The aftereffects of her adrenaline rush had completely gone, leaving her only tired.

Finally she went back to the car, collapsed the shovel, and dropped it into the trunk. It was a mess in there, pooled blood and dirt, but she wasn't about to try to clean it now. She got out a rag and the water bottle and washed off her hands, drying them on the rag.

The car still purred, the engine running smoothly. She had a momentary worry that it might run out of gas, but then she realized it probably wasn't running on gas anyway. She remembered her rescuer putting his hand on the engine to start it up, then saying to her, *Now* that *was magic*.

Dream magic.

The car would run until she woke up.

She looked at the elm, but knew she couldn't go yet. There was still something unfinished. It took her a moment to decide what.

She took her fiddlecase out of the back of the car and laid it on the hood, opening it. Got the bow from the lid, used the frog to tighten the hairs. Ran her fingers across the strings to check the tuning. Finally, she went back across the road to the elm and stood over the little mound of earth with her fiddle under her chin, bow in hand.

What to play?

The first thing that came to mind was a song that the band did. It was about a hare that lost its life in a hunt, not a deer, but maybe that was close enough. She started to play, slowing the tune down so that it was like an air. A lament.

Closing her eyes, she played it through three times, the notes of her fiddle weeping for the dead flesh she'd buried, for the live creature it had been, cut down by the little men's arrows. The breeze caught the music and took it away, across the fields to where a dark smudge of forest came down from the hills to meet the expanse of dried weeds and leafless bushes that lay between their trees and the road.

She held the last note, lightening the pressure of her bow on the strings until the note whispered away into silence. She tucked the fiddle under her arm and let the bow dangle from her forefinger. Opening her eyes, she regarded the little mound of dirt.

There, she thought. Now that felt right. Nothing should have to die, hard and alone, with no one to mourn their going. Not even in a dream.

She started to walk back to the car, then paused, realizing that, once again, she was no longer alone. Her pulse quickened as she turned. The moon was almost gone now, the night much darker than when her car had first broken down. At first she thought it was a huge deer standing behind her. Then she realized it was a man. Or at least the shape of a man, dressed in tunic and trousers of some kind of light-coloured cloth that made his skin appear to be very dark. On his shoulders he wore a headdress of a deer's head, the tines of his antlers rising up into the starry sky like a smaller version of the elm at her back.

There was just enough light for her to see the glisten of tears on his cheeks.

"That was kindly done," he said.

When she saw the lips move, she realized it wasn't a mask, but for some reason that didn't trouble her.

His voice was soft and warm, husky with emotion. She wondered if her dream had now conjured up the ghostly spirit of the dead animal for whom she'd played her funereal air. It didn't matter. This was far better than the horrible little bogan men, or the brusque Indian, even if he had rescued her and used his magic to fix her car.

This was like the time that she and Siobhan had gone camping with her grandfather. Pappy always went to bed late, but he was an early riser, too. "Don't need the sleep like I used to," he'd say, "and I never needed much then." The two of them were up and sitting on a log by the lake where the campsite touched the water when they heard a rustle behind them. Turning slowly, they saw a doe and her fawn stepping out across the dew-laden grass.

She'd never seen eyes so warm and deep and brown. Something rose up from deep in her chest, and she'd gripped Pappy's hand as they sat there for a good fifteen minutes, watching the two creatures feed. And long after they were gone, that feeling stayed inside her, the same deep warmth that she'd seen in the eyes of the deer. Years later, that memory could put her in a dreamy trance that helped wash away hurts or sorrows or simply the feeling that the world was all the same, one day blurring into the next.

This moment was like that, a great wash of awe that didn't make her feel small, but rather, made her feel connected to everything.

"I . . . thought he needed some kind of a send-off," she said.

The deer man nodded, antlers dipping.

"Her name was Anwatan—'calm water' in your tongue. She was my daughter and I give you the knowledge of her name as a gift for the music you played to send her spirit on its way."

"Thank you," she said, not quite sure what else to say. She'd always been bad at condolences. "I'm so sorry for your loss."

His sigh of response held a world of sorrow and hurt.

"A father should not outlive his child," he said.

"I can't imagine what that must feel like."

He dipped his antlers again. "I hope you never do. It . . . there's an emptiness in me where she once was, and moment by moment it seems to only become larger." His gaze found hers. "Sharing the gift of her true name with another helps only a little."

That made Lizzie think of her rescuer.

You don't need my name.

"Is there something special about names?" she asked.

She saw a quick flash of teeth—a smile, she realized, but it never reached his eyes. It was the smile that you saw at a funeral, when everyone's trying to be normal, but you know it never will be. Or won't for a very, very long time.

"Names are everything," he said. "If you know the full, true name of a thing, it is at your mercy."

"So it's rude to ask someone their name."

That got her another attempt at a smile. "It depends on who's asking and why. If it's someone who doesn't know better . . ."

He shrugged.

"So that's why he wouldn't tell me his name," she said.

She was speaking more to herself, but the deer man lifted his head, his nostrils working.

"I see," he said. "There were others here—aganesha and a cousin of mine."

"I guess I mean the cousin. Was he another deer man? He didn't have antlers."

The deer man shook his head. "He'd look strange with them, a bird with antlers."

"A bird . . . ?"

"He's corbae. My people are cerva. We're cousins, but not close."

"I don't understand."

"They're just tribes," he said. "His people usually sleep through the moon's rise and set. Mine wander under her stillness because her light feeds our spirits, as food does our bodies. But we're still cousins. If you need a speaking name for him, he's been known to answer to Whiskey Grey—or just Grey."

Lizzie smiled. "You make him sound like a bootlegger."

"Well, I've heard that old jay does like his drink. He has his own sorrows, they say. Old ones. I don't know the details."

Neither spoke for a moment. Lizzie looked past the deer man for a moment to see the last part of the moon slip under the horizon.

"I'm dreaming, aren't I?" she said.

"No. This is *Kakagi-aki*—your world. The dreamlands lie on the other side of the between."

"It still feels like dreaming."

The deer man nodded. "Perhaps it's better if you see it that way."

"That's what Grey said. He told me to forget about all of this. To go on with my life like it had never happened. But how can I do that if it's real?"

"I'm told forgetting can be easy, if it's what you wish. But . . ."

When he didn't finish, Lizzie prompted him. "But what?"

"You might not be allowed to forget. Or it might be better if you didn't. Not if the aganesha have marked you. It would be better to be prepared, should they decide that you owe them for your intrusion into their business tonight."

Lizzie looked nervously around them. "Do you mean the bogans? Is that what you call those little men?"

"A bogan is a kind of aganesha, yes."

"So aganesha is your word for fairies."

The deer man nodded. "It's what we call all the beings that came with your ancestors to our world."

"But you're not aganesha yourselves?"

He made an angry sound that rose from deep in his chest and spat on the ground.

"We are the spirits of *this* land," he said. "We don't steal from others."

Lizzie took a step back. "I'm sorry. I didn't . . ."

"No," the deer man said. "I should apologize. How could you know? Until tonight, it seems you knew nothing about any of us."

"So these aganesha are trying to steal your lands from you? I guess the way Europeans did from the native people?"

"Not all of them. Most are content to keep to the territories spoiled by your people. But the green and the wild, these are still ours. Until you build upon it, the aganesha have no claim to the wild places."

Lizzie gave a slow nod. "So your people stay in the forests and the aganesha stay in the cities."

"We go where we please," the deer man said. "We can live in your cities—it is still our land under the concrete and steel. But most of us don't choose to."

He looked to the sky, reading something in the position of the stars, Lizzie assumed from what he said next.

"I must go. I have still the sad tale of my daughter to tell my family, and the hour grows late."

"I really am so sorry about what happened to her."

"I know. I heard that in the lament you played for her. I saw it in the reverence with which you laid her flesh in the ground. I—my family—we are in your debt."

Lizzie shook her head. "No, I just did what anybody would have done."

"Then you don't know many people. Most would have left what they found of her alongside the road like so much refuse."

"But I don't want anything from you."

"I know that, too. But you could still have brought more trouble upon yourself from those aganesha. If they come after you, call for me and I will come. My speaking name is Walks-with-Dreams. My friends call me Walker and I hope you will, too."

"I . . . do I really have to worry about those bogans?"

"Probably not. But it's better to be careful. My daughter wasn't."

"Grey said to play music—that it would stop them."

"It might give them pause. But you'd do better to call for me."

"I travel a lot."

"Distance doesn't mean the same thing to my people as it does to yours. If you call for Walker, I will hear you, no matter where you are."

"Okay. My name's Lizzie—"

"Careful," he said before she could finish. "The night has ears, and we are too newly met for you to entrust me with your true name."

"But among my people we use them all the time."

He gave a slow nod. "And so squander the power of it. Unless the names you use are speaking names, and you simply don't know your true names."

"I wouldn't know."

The deer man nodded. "Neither would I. That's a puzzle for the shaman to worry over, not common folk like you and me." He lifted his hand. "Keep your strength, Lizzie. And thank you once more."

And then he, too, like Grey and the bogans before him, was simply gone.

Lizzie stood for a long moment, listening to the quiet night around her. Finally, she turned and walked back to the car, her head brimming with all she'd been through since her car broke down. The first part had been scary, and handling the deer meat had been kind of gross, but talking with Walker, just being in his presence, had woken a song in her heart that she didn't want to lose.

Maybe this *wasn't* a dream. And if it was, she wasn't sure she wanted to wake up from it.

Because for the first time in longer than she could remember, the world seemed to have weight to it. Everything seemed to have importance and meaning, and she felt connected to it in a way that never happened unless she was deep in a tune, lost in her music.

She made it back to Sweetwater without further incident and found the garage that Grey had recommended. There was an old and battered sign above the door to the work bay that read Tommy & Joe's. The whole place seemed sort of run-down and nothing about it really instilled much confidence in her, but she decided to leave her car all the same. Grey *had* saved

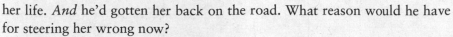

her life. *And* he'd gotten her back on the road. What reason would he have for steering her wrong now?

She wrote out a note describing the problem and where she was staying. Hesitating a moment, she turned off the ignition. The engine went quiet. She tried to start it again, just to see, but nothing happened. The car was as dead as it had been back at the crossroads.

She wrapped the key in her note and slipped it through the mail slot in the front door. Collecting her fiddle and knapsack from the car, she set off the few blocks down the road to the Custom House and hoped that Siobhan hadn't taken in a guy for the night because, until Lizzie had decided to drive back to Newford, they were supposed to share a room. That's about all these places would spring for: separate rooms for the boys and girls. Con and Andy would be sharing the other room, and she wasn't about to go knocking on their door.

The front door of the hotel/bar was unlocked, but there was no one at the desk. Lizzie stepped behind the counter, took the extra key for the room from its hook and went up the stairs. Inside the room she was as quiet as she could be undressing and using the toilet, and then finally she was lying down in her bed. In the other twin bed, Siobhan slept soundly and moments later, Lizzie was, too.

Geordie Riddell

When I stepped out of the door by the loading bays, the parking lot was empty except for my brother's old station wagon, still parked where I'd left it late last night. There was the start of a morning glow on the eastern horizon, and the cloudless sky above promised another beautiful day even though there were still patches of snow on the ground. But this was March in Newford. Some years we get more snow in this one month than we do through the whole winter. So far, we'd been lucky. The temperature was mild this morning and the promise of spring—officially here already, but yet to make an actual physical appearance—was in the air. Living in this part of the country, you took what you could get.

"Sure you won't stay?" Galfreya asked.

I turned to look at her, shifting my fiddlecase from one hand to the other.

"Not tonight."

"It's morning now."

I smiled. "So it is. But I should get Christy's car back to him."

If anybody else was here with us, they'd think I was crazy for turning down the invitation. Galfreya's gorgeous. Sloe-eyed—as they say in the old trad ballads—and tall, her waist-length hair a messy storm of braids and loose curls decorated with multicoloured barrettes, feathers, ribbons, tiny bones, and other found objects.

This morning she was wearing her usual platform high-tops and a pair of black, hip-hugging cargos, but instead of one of her skimpy midriff-baring

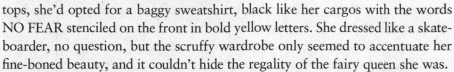

tops, she'd opted for a baggy sweatshirt, black like her cargos with the words NO FEAR stenciled on the front in bold yellow letters. She dressed like a skateboarder, no question, but the scruffy wardrobe only seemed to accentuate her fine-boned beauty, and it couldn't hide the regality of the fairy queen she was.

Okay, so she was a seer and not a queen, but that didn't change a thing except that I have to laugh as I use those words. All my life I've avoided the weirder side of life that my brother embraces, this idea that side by side with our world lies a secret, hidden world of fairies and goblins, ghosts, and other improbabilities. But the past two years have changed that. I've seen and experienced far too much that can't be rationally explained away, culminating in my showing up here at the Woodforest Plaza Mall a couple of nights a week to provide music for a fairy court's revels. I mean, once you're part of a pickup band made up of little stick people and a troll playing a stand-up bass, it's pretty much impossible to keep laying the "I don't believe in this crap" card down on the table.

So now I'm a believer, but I'm not all evangelical about it like my brother Christy, or the Professor and Jilly, wanting everybody else to see what I see. I've just adjusted these long-held, if erroneous, beliefs and carry on with my life.

I wish I could say the same about some of the other personality quirks that seem to be hardwired into my psyche. Well, not my feelings about music. I don't ever want to buy into the idea that recordings are anything more than a snapshot of a moment—especially not now, when they've got the software to tweak a bad performance so that every single element of a recording comes out sounding note perfect.

Music needs to live and breathe; it's only pure when it's performed live with nothing hidden—neither its virtuosity nor the inevitable mistakes that come when you try to push it into some new, as yet unexplored place. It's improvisational jazz. It's the jam, the session. The best music is played on street corners and pubs, in kitchens and on porches, in the backrooms of concert halls and in the corner of a field, behind the stage, at a music festival. It's played for the joy and the sadness and the connection it makes between listeners and players.

When it's played for money, it's a job. When it's played for itself, it's magic. And I guess that sums up why I'll always be living hand-to-mouth instead of making the decent living everybody thinks I should be making with it, because if a gig doesn't seem honest to me, I'll turn it down.

I've done the other kind. I've written for soundtracks. I've been a session musician on more recordings than I can count. I've played concerts. But I'm happiest sitting in a corner of the pub, playing tunes with a couple of friends, nothing planned, just seeing what happens as one tune reminds us of the next and then leads us into another.

I don't think that'll ever change. I wouldn't want it to. But I sure wish I could figure out a way to stop putting women on a pedestal—or rather, stop obsessing about the unattainable women that I've put on a pedestal. I know it cuts me off from meaningful relationships I could have, and even if I do get into a relationship with one of these pedestal women, it never works out. Partly because no one can match up to an ideal anyway, and partly because what I'm bringing to the relationship is an unhealthy devotion. I get way more concerned about everything to do with them, which makes my own life just an echo of living instead of the real thing.

But knowing all of this doesn't make me stop.

That said, Galfreya was a perfect candidate of someone for me to obsess over, but there were things about her that I just couldn't get around. For one thing, being a fairy made her somewhat promiscuous—at least by human standards. I'm old-fashioned and expect a monogamous relationship. For another, she looks like she's in her twenties, half my age, which feels strange enough. What feels stranger is knowing she's . . . well, I don't know exactly. Fairy-kind are basically immortal. For all I know, she could have been around since the beginning, when Raven first made the world. So it's weird that it looks like I'm robbing the cradle, going out with someone who could be my own daughter, but she's actually old enough to be some distant ancestor.

Then there's the fact that I can only see her on her terms. I come to her at the mall, play my fiddle at her fairy revels, stay the night sometimes in her private quarters that aren't quite in this world, aren't quite in fairyland, but some place in between the two. She doesn't come to a gig with me. To an art opening. To a movie unless it's at the mall's Cineplex. Out for dinner, except for ditto, and the mall eateries are never going to make it into the city's best culinary guidebook any time soon.

So she's not exactly an ideal life companion. She's not someone I might expect to make a life with, to grow old with.

I know, how incurably romantic of me, looking for everlasting love in a world of five-second sound bytes, where most people find it more interesting to watch the so-called reality of other people's lives in scripted television shows than to actually live one of their own.

But I do want that long-term stability. I don't really expect to ever find it, but that doesn't stop me from yearning for it all the same. That said, I also have to admit that I'm probably more scared of getting into a serious relationship than I am of living the rest of my life on my own. It's not that I'm a commitment phobe. It's just that whenever I do, sooner or later, I get left behind.

My last serious relationship really brought it all home to me—how this was something that was never going to work in my life. Because we were perfect for each other; what problems we had, we were both willing to talk about and work on, compromising where necessary—you know, all the things you're supposed to do in a relationship, though that's nothing I learned from my own parents. Tanya and I, we did everything right, but one day, there I was all the same, alone in our L.A. apartment, packing my bags to come back to Newford.

So in a way, these occasional liaisons with Galfreya—no strings attached, be together when it felt right, no hard feelings when it didn't—should have been perfect. But I, at least, am human and we're never satisfied, are we? What I had with Galfreya wasn't true love. It had no future. It had only the here and the now, and while that's obviously enough for fairy, who seem to live the whole of their lives ever in the moment, it wasn't enough for me.

"I'm sorry you can't stay," Galfreya said, then leaned close to kiss me. "Say hello to Christy for me," she added.

"I will."

I was halfway to the car when I heard the door close behind her. I reached the car, then paused, cocking my head. If I listened hard I could hear a fiddle playing—low and lonesome, coming from some far distance. I almost recognized the tune, but then the sound was gone.

I looked around, but I was alone in the parking lot with my brother's car. Or so I thought.

I opened the back door and laid my fiddlecase on the seat. As I was straightening up, my gaze became level with that of one of the small twig and leaf fairies that were regulars at the mall revels. She was lying on the roof of the car, pixie-featured and grinning, head propped on her elbows, her vine-like hair pulled back into a thick Rasta ponytail. She wasn't really made of twigs and leaves and vines—or at least I didn't think so—but her skin was the mottled colour of a forest, all greens and browns.

"Hello, Hazel," I said.

"Hello, your own self." She got up, tucking her ankles under her knees so that she was sitting cross-legged. "Can I get a lift into town?"

"Sure. What're you up to?"

She shrugged. "Oh, you know. A little of this, a little of that."

"In other words, some kind of mischief."

She made her features go very serious and said, "I don't think so," but she couldn't hold it. Laughing, she fell back onto the roof and then kicked her feet in the air.

"Well, come on," I said.

She jumped to the ground when I shut the back door. Standing, she came up to about my waist, a skinny little gamine in baggy cropped blue jeans, a sleeveless T-shirt, and a yellow bandana tied loosely at her neck. Her feet were bare on the pavement.

"You're not cold?" I asked.

She shook her head. "But I could pretend to be, if you like."

I laughed and opened the driver's door, standing aside so that she could climb in and scramble to the passenger's side of the bench seat.

"Buckle up," I told her after I got in.

"It's okay," she said. "You won't get a ticket. I won't let the policemen see me."

Handy thing, being a fairy and only being seen when you wanted to be. Unless you had the gift of the Sight, or had it given to you as I had by Galfreya, so that none of the more impish fairies could play tricks on me.

"That won't help if I have to brake suddenly," I said, "and you go flying up against the windshield."

Hazel sighed theatrically, but she already knew that I wouldn't start driving until she did as I'd asked. It was an old argument, but that didn't stop her from trying every time I gave her a lift.

"How did you get so boring?" she asked. "Did you have to practice?"

"I was just born that way."

"Boring."

I laughed. "Yes, sad isn't it?"

Once Hazel was buckled in, I started the car and pulled out of my parking spot. With the lot empty, I ignored the designated lanes and drove straight for the exit. There was already traffic as we pulled out onto the highway—commuters driving in from rural communities. They came in early to beat the rush, and subsequently were able to leave early as well, but all it really did was spread the traffic congestion over a longer space of time. Rush hour in the city was now three to four hours long, depending on the weather.

"How come you didn't stay with herself?" Hazel asked.

I shrugged. "I'm just tired. I've been up all night. I had a gig before tonight's revel, remember, and I don't exactly have a fairy's stamina. I don't think you people ever need to sleep."

"Of course we do. If we didn't sleep, how could we dream?"

I didn't see the logic of that—there were many other, and I'd say far more pressing, reasons to get one's sleep, starting with how exhausted and stupid you end up feeling when you don't get enough—but there was no point in arguing logic with fairies.

"She really does like you, you know," Hazel said.

"I know."

"It's just she—"

"I know," I repeated.

"Grouch."

"Moxie."

"I don't even know what that means," she said.

"It means you're annoyingly full of verve and pep."

She smiled. "Oh, well, that's true."

We had to slow down for a light that had turned green ahead of us, but the line of cars was just getting back up to speed.

"Oh, look," Hazel said. "Damn pluikers. Don't they just make you sick?"

I had time to note a line of three or four fairies sitting on a fence watching the traffic go by. They looked and dressed like Native Americans—jeans and buckskin, checkered shirts—but I could see hare ears and antlers, which is how I knew they were fairies. And naturally, they were invisible to everyone except for me and Hazel.

She raised her middle finger and waved it at them, sticking out her tongue.

"Why did you do that?" I asked.

She gave me a look that asked how did you ever get to be so dim.

"Because they're green-brees," she said. "Duh."

"But what does that *mean*?"

She shrugged. "I don't know. That's just what we call them. I think it means stagnant water—or the slime you find in stagnant water."

"So why don't you like them?"

I could still see the line of little figures in my rearview mirror. They seemed perfectly normal—in fairy terms, I mean.

"Why should we?" Hazel said. "They don't like us."

"They just looked like fairies to me."

"Well, they're not. They didn't have to come across the water to get here. They were already here when we arrived."

"So they're native fairies."

"They're not fairies. We're fairies. They're just pluikers."

"And what does *that* mean?"

Hazel grinned at me. "That they're great big fat pimples on the arse of the world."

"You're beginning to sound like a racist."

"I'm not a racist. I just don't like them. They keep us in the cities—right from the start they have, back when the cities were no more than a few shacks at the edge of the water. We rode those high seas for long, long weeks and looked to replenish ourselves from the green and the wild, but they kept it all for themselves and they still do."

"Well, it was their land."

Hazel sniffed. "There's so much. Did they need it *all*?"

"How would you feel if someone took something that was yours, and you didn't want to give it up?"

"I suppose. Except on the one hand they say that the wild and the green belongs to no one, it just is. Then on the other, they keep us out of what they claim are their territories. So what's *that* supposed to mean?"

"Maybe they don't want what you call the wild and the green to be spoiled the way the cities already are."

Hazel shot me a frown.

"This is a boring conversation," she told me.

She reached over and turned on the radio, stopping at a station that was playing a 50 Cent song. We listened to rap and hip-hop for the rest of the drive in, all the way to where she had me let her off downtown.

Our conversation was still bothering me after I'd dropped the car off at the garage Christy rented for it and got back to Jilly's loft. I don't know why I still called it that. After her accident, Jilly moved into the Professor's house and I took over her loft, but it's been a couple of years now. And it wasn't just me—everybody still referred to it as Jilly's place. I guess it was because we didn't want to give up the hope that one day she'd be able to manage the steep stairs of the building and move back in.

When I got upstairs, I laid my fiddlecase on the kitchen table, shed my clothes, and got into the Murphy bed that I almost never bothered to fold back into the wall. It wasn't like I ever had anybody over.

I lay there, tired, trying to figure out this enmity between the local fairies and those that had started to come over when the first Europeans landed on these shores. I didn't actually want to be thinking about this, but I couldn't get it out of my head.

I don't know how long I would have lain there, unable to sleep, but something else came to me then, the memory of that elusive snatch of fiddle music I'd heard in the parking lot, just before Hazel showed up. It teased me with its familiarity. I felt I knew it, but in a different setting, maybe at a quicker pace. But instead of keeping me awake, the memory of the music lulled me into a feeling of great peace and sadness, and I drifted off.

Galfreya

It took a moment for Galfreya to realize she wasn't alone in the central courtyard of the mall. She turned slowly to look down both of the long halls that ran east and west and south from where she stood before focusing her attention on the displays of stuffed animals that had been set up in the courtyard by the Newford Museum of Natural History. They were a sorry collection of creatures . . . wolves, bears, a bison, foxes, deer, falcons, hawks, owls, a family of raccoons . . . skin and horns, hooves and feathers commandeered to re-create a semblance of life that was betrayed by glass eyes and stances that were not quite natural. The birds fared best—at least their fur wasn't worn in places from the touch of a thousand hands—but they were still nailed to their perches.

The poor dead creatures were just as they'd been since the display had been installed earlier in the week. There were no additions. One or more of the dead hadn't suddenly become animated. She could still see no one in the halls, nor outside the front doors of the mall, nor in the shop windows closest to hand. But the presence she felt was close all the same.

"Okay," she finally said. "You're good. I'll give you that. But even if I can't see you, I still know you're here."

"What, a big shot seer like you can't find one itty-bitty me?"

The disembodied voice seemed to come from everywhere and nowhere. It was a woman's voice, smoky and low, and not one Galfreya recognized.

"I'm hardly a big shot," she replied. "Would I be living in a shopping mall if I was?"

"Who knows? The ways of a seer are mysterious. And you do have your own fairy court."

"They're not my court. This just happens to be a handy place to hold our revels. Once the cleaning staff is gone, we have the place to ourselves. And why am I telling you all of this?" she added as an afterthought.

"Guilt?" the voice asked. "To show off how important you are?"

"I don't have the need to feel one or do the other."

"Whatever. I'm curious, though. How do you keep your images from showing up on the security cameras?"

"The same way you become invisible: magic."

"Oh, I'm not magic," the voice said. "I'm just a shadow."

And then there she was, lounging on the back of the bison, a small woman in her twenties with curly dark red hair and glittering eyes, dressed in a sweater the colour of Old World heather and a pair of faded blue jeans.

"I didn't think to look for you between," Galfreya said.

Between was the border country separating this world from the spirit-world. Standing in it, you could look out on either, but not be seen if you so chose.

"Being a shadow," she added, "still makes you more than human."

"Some would say less than human, considering I'm made up of all the bits of a person that they didn't want and threw away."

"I wouldn't."

"No, of course you wouldn't," the stranger said. "You're a good fairy. So very Seelie Court and all."

"I've seen you before," Galfreya said. "But not here."

"I don't exactly haunt the malls, looking for a bargain."

"I meant in this world." She studied the stranger for a moment, then nodded. "It was at some of the parties in Hinterdale. You're one of Maxie Rose's friends."

The stranger smiled. "You see? I have a claim to fame as well."

"I don't claim any fame."

"Whatever."

The stranger slid down from the back of the bison, her walking boots making a soft thump when she landed on the fake ground of the display.

"So what's with all the dead cousins?" she asked, running her hand along the bison's flank before she stepped down onto the marble floor of the courtyard.

Galfreya shrugged. "The mall just does this kind of thing. One week it's an antique show, the next it's a display of power boats. I think it's supposed to be educational."

"It gives me the creeps."

"Me, too," Galfreya said.

The red-haired stranger frowned at her.

"Oh no, you don't," she said. "That's twice you've tried to get chummy with me and find some kind of common ground. Just be yourself."

Galfreya knew that danger came in all sizes, so the fact that she topped the stranger by at least a head meant little, but the red-haired woman's attitude was starting to seriously annoy her.

"What is your problem?" she asked, not even pretending to be friendly any more.

"You," the stranger said. "At least, it starts with you. I mean look at yourself. You've got to be a couple hundred years old—"

"Give or take a thousand."

"So there's a reason your speaking name is Mother Crone. You should dress your age—you know, robes or something instead of this skateboarder look, which is way pathetic for a woman your age, even if you do wear a glamour that makes you seem twenty-something."

Galfreya hadn't changed clothes since she'd seen Geordie off.

"What makes you think it's a glamour?"

"Oh, come on. Everybody knows that fairies go for the sleek, young look, no matter how many years they've piled on."

"Unlike shadows who are always what they seem."

The stranger looked uncomfortable for a moment, then shrugged. "Whatever."

"So the way I dress is what's troubling you," Galfreya said. "Why should that be any of your business?"

"Well, that's not all," the stranger replied. "What's with you fairies and your enchantments and how you need to have humans amuse you, no matter what havoc it might play in their own life?"

"What are you talking about?"

"Your fiddler," the stranger said. "The one you keep drawing back here, week after week, with your music and your revels and your oh-so sweet talk. Why can't you leave him alone?"

"Why do you care? If you're in love with him, you're not doing a very good job of showing it because he's never said word one to me about you or anyone else."

"Oh, please. I'm not into incest. He's my brother."

"Your brother."

The stranger nodded, a challenge in her eyes. Galfreya met her gaze with a look as steady, then slowly nodded.

"Yes," she said. "I see that he is."

"So tell me, why won't you leave him alone? I know you don't have a long-term interest in him because your kind never does. You just use people up and move on to the next."

"That's neither fair nor true."

"So, do you love him? Are you ready to give up immortality to be with him? That's how it works for your kind, right? There has to be a sacrifice. Or maybe you're trying to get him to give up his world to be a puppet fiddler in yours, always ready at your beck and call."

"Do you have to work at being so annoying?" Galfreya asked.

"You haven't seen me annoyed yet, sweetheart. And you didn't answer my question."

Galfreya stared at her, trying to keep her anger in check. The stranger was infuriating, but she was Geordie's sister, her own anger obviously born out of love. So Galfreya was willing to cut her a little more slack. But only a little.

"I love him as you do," she said finally. "As a sister."

The stranger raised her eyebrows. "Do fairies usually sleep with their siblings?"

"Fine," Galfreya said. "Then as a friend."

Now it was the stranger's turn to study her.

"Okay," she said after a moment. "Maybe you do. So then, why are you doing this? You know he'll never have a chance at a normal relationship so long as you've got your hooks in him. It might already be too late. All the glamours and magic might have already spoiled him for an ordinary woman."

"I'm hardly such a catch."

"What, are you a vampire, too? You can't look in a mirror? You're gorgeous."

Galfreya shrugged. "It's all in the eye of the beholder."

"I suppose. Is that why you dress down with the skateboarder gear?"

"I dress to be comfortable."

"And you're still not answering my question."

"I know," Galfreya said. "I don't really want to. Sometimes, speaking a foretelling aloud is the very thing that gives it life."

"Oh, please," the stranger said.

Her tone was easy, but she couldn't hide her worry.

"Very well," Galfreya told her. "This is what I saw: If I don't keep him close to me, to my court, he will be terribly hurt. Perhaps he'll even die."

The stranger swallowed, but the look in her eyes went from worried to determined. "So, what's the danger? What's supposed to hurt him?"

"I don't know. I couldn't see that. I can only see what I've told you."

"Convenient."

Galfreya drew herself up.

"So far," she said, "I've responded to your insinuations and poor manners in a calm and polite manner—more for Geordie's sake, than for yours, I might add. But one more snide comment, and I promise you will regret ever coming here."

"I'm not scared of you."

Galfreya smiled, but there was nothing friendly in her smile.

"You should be," she said.

Then she turned her back on her uninvited guest and strode down the hall, back the way she'd come.

"Wait," the stranger called after her.

Galfreya paused, but she didn't look back or respond otherwise.

"Okay," the stranger said. "So I'm an ass. I came here with a chip on my shoulder. But I've been worried about Geordie and from where I stood, it looked like you were the thing I needed to worry about."

Galfreya turned to look at her.

"Your loyalty is commendable," she said. "Your manners are not."

"I'm trying to say I'm sorry, okay?"

"You have an interesting way of expressing it."

"I don't mean before. I mean now. My name's Christiana, by the way."

"I guessed as much when you said you were Geordie's sister. He's spoken of you to me."

"Really?"

"Yes, he said you were bratty, but it's part of what he likes about you, the moon knows why."

"That's the problem with family—you have to take what's dealt to you."

Galfreya shook her head. "I don't think I agree. If the fit is wrong, you can still just walk away."

"I meant the family you choose."

"You can walk away from that kind of family, too."

"But we both care about Geordie, right?"

Galfreya nodded. "We have that in common."

"See, the thing is," Christiana said, "I've seen how happy his brother Christy is, all settled down with Saskia. And I know Geordie sees it, too.

And I also know that he'd like to have that kind of relationship with someone. The trouble is, he's made poor choices. . . ."

"Love's like that," Galfreya said. "You can't choose who you love."

"Whatever. But he's not even getting out anymore. He hasn't had a date in at least two years, and we both know why that is."

"Enlighten me."

"He's got this," she waved her arm to take in the mall. "The parties you guys have, a place to play music with people who know a whole whack of tunes that his other friends don't. And he's got you—for company and a roll in the hay whenever the two of you are in the mood. So he doesn't even look for anything else. But we both know that the relationship you guys have isn't either what he needs or really wants. He needs . . . I was going to say a real woman . . ."

"Says the shadow."

"I know—made up of all the cast-off bits of his brother. I should talk. And that's why I'm not going to say a real woman. He just needs someone who can commit. Someone who isn't the immortal Mother Crone that you are, who won't even leave this mall to go somewhere with him."

"I have responsibilities."

"And they're none of my business. But Geordie is. His happiness is. That's why I came to ask you to let him go. That's why I showed up with the big chip on my shoulder because this whole business has been totally pissing me off."

"And now?"

"Now I don't know what to say except, maybe he should have the chance to find out what's out there, even if it's dangerous. I'll watch his back, and I'm guessing you will, too."

Galfreya gave a slow nod. "For Geordie's sake, we can be allies. But we will never be friends."

"Why am I not surprised?" Christiana said. "I should have remembered. Mumbo was forever telling me that fairies never forget a slight, no matter how large or small."

"You were a student of Mumbo's?"

"She showed me the ropes when I first manifested."

"Mumbo has always had a generous nature. I'm surprised to find a charge of hers with such a lack of common sense and manners."

"Okay," Christiana said. "I deserved that. But I already said I was sorry. What more do you want?"

Galfreya shook her head. "I don't want anything. I'm just wary of the darkness you carry inside you—the shadow of a shadow that has no love for my people."

"Fine," Christiana said. "Make up a new bogeyman for yourself, if it makes you feel any better. But for the record, I don't care about fairies one way or the other, except in relation to Geordie. Cut him loose from whatever enchantment you've put on him, and you'll never have to hear from me again."

And with that, she was gone. Stepped between and disappeared, taking with her all opportunity for further conversation.

Galfreya stared at the place from which the shadow had vanished.

She hadn't handled that well.

Christiana's cocky manner had put her off, as had the shadow's insights into Galfreya's relationship with Geordie. There *was* an enchantment on the fiddler, a small calling-on glamour that kept him returning to play at their revels and of which he was unaware. Galfreya was loath to remove it, for his safety—that much hadn't been a lie—but also because she liked having him in her company. There was no spell that made him pay attention to her. Unlike other fairy women, she always insisted on her consorts having freedom of choice. That made it all the sweeter when they were drawn to her.

And Geordie's affection was sweeter still, for he could say no as well as yes, as he had this morning. So when he did stay, it was because he wanted to. Because he wanted *her*.

She sighed.

She'd known it wouldn't last. If it hadn't been this, it would have been something else, because dealing with humans was always a chancy proposition. They were unpredictable and willful—much like the shadows they could cast from themselves. Enspelling Geordie had always been only a stopgap measure, not a permanent solution. And really, she knew better than any, that a foretelling would always play out. If not sooner, then later.

The fates of men and fairies weren't inexorably etched in stone. If there were weavers, making a pattern on their looms of how lives were lived, they could only nudge and hint, not force fate to unfold on some strict schedule. And a seer's vision saw only probabilities, not truth. The only truth was now. The past was clouded by memory; the future, in the end, forever a mystery. Even to a seer.

She knew Geordie would face a grave danger once he left the protection of her court. But not when, or how it would come to him. Only that it *would* come. And by keeping it at bay, she *was* denying him the opportunity of growth through adversity. The mettle of men and fairies was tested not by lighthearted revels, but by stepping out into the dark forest of destiny.

She pulled a small leather bag from where it hung under her sweatshirt and opened its mouth. From it she took a token—a small, rough representation of a fiddle made of clay, blood, and spit, one brown hair taken from the head of a fiddler while he was sleeping in her bed, the words that encompassed his true name, and a calling-on glamour.

She regarded it for a long moment, then lifted her gaze to where the dead cousins struck their unnatural, taxidermal poses.

"I don't do this for you," she said, speaking to the shadow as though she were still present. "I do it because time can't be held back forever. I do it for him."

Then she dropped the clay fiddle to the floor and ground the broken pieces into dust.

"But I would have kept him for a hundred years, if I could."

Then she, too, stepped away into her own between, and the dead cousins had the central court to themselves for the few hours before the stores opened and the shoppers descended upon the mall.

Jilly Coppercorn

"You're breaking up with me," Daniel said.

I looked at him across the kitchen table, the remains of the Indian take-out he'd brought for our supper scattered between us. I understood that he couldn't quite believe it. I couldn't quite believe it myself. We'd been together for a couple of years and if there was ever a perfect guy, it was Daniel. But that was the problem. He was too perfect. He was so perfect I was choking on our relationship, but how could I tell him that?

"I think it's for the best," I said, which was so lame and not even close to an explanation.

"But we're such a good fit."

I shook my head. "We're not really."

"We like all the same things."

We did. But that was only because he liked whatever I liked. He didn't bring anything of himself to the relationship, and I'd known it for awhile now. I was just too lazy to do anything about it. Too comfortable in the easy familiarity of his company. And let's admit it, flattered that a guy as handsome as him, at least ten years my junior, was so into me when most people couldn't see past the wheelchair and the broken bits that define who I am. Of course, being a caregiver, Daniel saw past my handicaps to the person I was because it was second nature for him. He did it all day in his work.

"It's not you," I said, falling back on what's truly the lamest bit of break-up dialogue that's ever come out of people trying to disengage themselves from the affections of another. "It's me."

"I don't understand."

"I don't really either," I lied. "I just know it's not working for me."

"This is . . . god, it's so out of nowhere. I *really* didn't see this coming. I mean, you hear about it all the time when a relationship goes down in flames, but I never thought I'd be so blind to it."

"We're not going down in flames," I said. "We're just readjusting the parameters of our relationship." Don't say it, I thought, but the words came out of my mouth all the same: "I'm hoping we can still be friends."

He gave a slow nod. "Yeah, right."

"I know that sounded so stupidly clichéd, but it's true. I think we'd work better as friends than as a couple."

He looked at me, and I made myself face the hurt in his eyes instead of looking away. I was so bad at this, but then it wasn't like I really had a lot of experience. I've made lots of dear and close friends over the years, but you could count my serious relationships on one hand.

"I should go," he said.

I didn't say anything. I thought he should go, too, but I didn't want to make this any worse than I already had. Better to say nothing.

He stood up. I started to roll my wheelchair away from the table, but he shook his head.

"It's okay," he said. "I can find my way out."

"Daniel . . ."

He shook his head. "There's nothing more to say, really, is there?"

"No, I guess not."

So I sat there in the kitchen and watched him walk down the hall. He got his coat from the hook by the front door and put it on. A moment later, the door closed behind him and I was alone in the house. The Professor was off visiting his friend Lucius. Goon—properly Olaf Goonasekara, the Professor's housekeeper—was also out. None of my friends would be dropping by because they knew I was spending the evening with Daniel.

I wished now that I'd let one of them in on what I'd planned to do tonight. I hadn't because I was sure they'd try to talk me out of it. I'd probably have let them talk me out of it. But I knew I'd done the right thing.

At least I thought I did.

I stayed in the kitchen, staring down the hall and not moving for a long time, before I finally turned the wheelchair around and rolled it into the refurbished greenhouse at the back of the house. Sophie and I shared the greenhouse as studio space. The long work tables held a barrage of art supplies: tubes of paint, palettes, brushes, sketchbooks, pencils, charcoal. We each had an easel set up and there were canvases everywhere, leaning against the walls and crammed under the tables. The room smelled of turps and the geraniums that Goon wintered on shelves along one wall.

It was easy to tell who worked where. My area looked like a hurricane had hit it, and the paintings were all big, blocky pieces without a lot of details. Sophie's was perfectly organized, and her paintings were far more accomplished than anything I've been able to do in years.

Messy though my area was, I didn't really do that much in it because I hadn't been able to paint properly since the accident. And no, don't feel sorry for me. I was alive, wasn't I? I could still move around. I used the wheelchair in the evening because I was usually just so tired by that point, but most of the day I got from here to there by walking. Okay, shuffling, with a cane or two, but I was still mobile. A lot of people didn't even have that. I used the chair when I went to rehab, or if somebody took me out so that we weren't forced to go at the snail's pace I could manage, but I wasn't *trapped* in it.

Not like I was trapped in my inability to make art—or at least the kind of art I wanted to make. The art I once did make. Nowadays my best art took place in my imagination.

I had an art gallery in my head holding all the paintings that the Broken Girl I was couldn't paint anymore. At least not with brush in hand. The accident left me with a right arm that had no strength, and I couldn't stand for very long at an easel anymore. Trying to work sitting down was very disconcerting after a lifetime of being able to pace around my canvas. And lately my left hand, which I'd been learning to use, had developed a little tremor that the doctors couldn't explain. All I knew was it made detail work impossible. I could do broad strokes—big, painterly canvases—but the work I loved, the intricate paintings, were still out of reach.

So I did them in my head.

They took just as long as the physical ones did, but I didn't begrudge the time. What did trouble me was that I couldn't share them and that made me feel like I was talking to myself because I'd always seen the creative process as a conversation. Music needed listeners. Books needed readers. Art needed viewers. Not so much during the process. But for sure when it was done—or at least as done as art ever was. I always had to force myself to finally let go or I could fuss with a painting forever, even if the painting only existed in my head.

I know, it's weird. But I'd always had an active imagination, and my whole life I'd been out of step with most of the world. After the accident, that didn't change.

The accident.

I hated how my life was divided in two by an event over which I never even had control.

One moment, I was walking along the side of a street. The next, I'd been hit by a car. When I came to, I was in a hospital and parts of my body no longer worked as well as they once did. How was that for a wake-up call? But at least I woke up.

I didn't know what I missed the most. Dancing and bounding about, going for long rambles when the city's asleep, when it's just me and all the wild and wooly spirits of the night out there on the streets. Or my painting. My art.

It was all one and the same, I guess. I'd always lived my life like it was this great big messy canvas that was never going to be finished, but that didn't stop me from trying to experience and fill every square inch of it. Now everything felt separate. Everything took concentration. Things I used to just do without thinking. Standing up. Walking across the room. Getting dressed. And painting . . .

It was hard for me, doing these big sloppy paintings. The only way I could do detailed stuff was when I used this paint program that Mona put on one of the Professor's old laptops for me, but it wasn't the same. Nothing was the same.

I didn't know what I was doing in the studio right now. I should have been in the kitchen, cleaning up the mess Daniel and I made before the Professor came home. Or worse, if Goon came upon it before I got the chance to tidy. Goon was invariably grumbling and cranky at the best of times, so I tried not to give him anything concrete to complain about. I lived here on the Professor's sufferance and generosity, and I knew I shouldn't abuse the privilege.

But I couldn't make myself go back into the kitchen. Not just yet.

I was . . . I want to say sad, but that wasn't really it. I did feel sad, but I also felt relieved, and guilty, and kind of mean-spirited for breaking up with Daniel the way I just had. It really did come out of the blue for him.

I sighed. Well, right or wrong, the deed was done.

It was dark, here in the greenhouse. The only illumination filtered in through the door behind me, but it wasn't strong because all I had lit in the room beyond was a small table lamp. When I looked at the walls of windows, I could easily see past my faint reflection to the gardens beyond. I'd like to roll my chair out there, look at the stars and breathe in the night air, but I knew it was too chilly to go as I was and I didn't have the energy to go back inside and get a jacket. It was mild out there this evening, especially compared to the winter that was still a visible memory at the back of the garden where patches of snow vied for space with the first green shoots of tulips and crocuses. But it wasn't T-shirt weather.

This past winter had felt relentless. It started to snow right after Halloween and the snow stayed on the ground, thick and deep, until just recently. I was tired of it. Tired of the weather making it harder for me to get out of the house. Having to wait for the ploughs to come before I could take my wheelchair out onto the sidewalk.

I lifted my left hand and held it up in front of my face. The tremor wasn't so bad today. I lifted my right hand and slowly made a fist, uncurled my fingers. It was like walking was for me these days. I had to think about it.

Another sigh escaped me.

I was also tired of feeling sorry for myself, but I guess that was what Broken Girls did. They sat around feeling sorry for themselves. They broke up with boyfriends that anybody else would have been delighted to have.

I needed some distraction and considered my options. I wasn't in the mood to fight with my art, either physically or with my paint program on the laptop. I could check my e-mail, but that held no appeal. I could watch TV or a movie, but I'd done far too much of that over the winter. I could read a book, but even that was a chore. Hardcovers wore me out because of their weight. Paperbacks needed to be held open unless I broke the spine, and in this house, that was like a capital offense.

So I plugged the headset into my cell phone. Wendy was working tonight at the paper. Sophie was with her boyfriend Jeck, and Geordie had a gig. But I knew Mona would be home, and even if she was drawing or inking one of her comics, she could still talk while she did it.

I tapped in her number, and she answered before the first ring ended.

"Please be someone interesting," she said.

I laughed. "Oh, right. Put the pressure on me."

"Oh, hello, Jilly. Sorry about that. It's just that I've been getting telemarketers and crank calls all evening."

"Isn't that an oxymoron?"

"Only if you're a telemarketer."

"What are you doing?" I asked.

"Trying to ink a page that I loved this afternoon and now find spectacularly boring. Or maybe it's just that it's Friday night and even though Lyle's out of town, I still feel I should be out doing something."

"I know the feeling."

"I thought you had Daniel coming over this evening."

"I did. But he's gone now."

"Why does that sound foreboding?"

"Did it? It wasn't meant to."

"What happened? Did he get called in to the hospital?" She paused, then added before I could answer, "Except nurses aren't on call, are they?"

"I suppose they can be."

Now I paused. I looked out at the dark garden again, at my faint reflection on the windowpane, a small woman in a wheelchair.

"Except I asked him to leave," I said.

"Oh, dear."

"No, it's okay."

"I'm coming over," she said.

"You don't have to—"

I didn't get to finish because she'd already hung up.

I hadn't locked the door after Daniel left, so Mona was able to walk right in and find me in the greenhouse studio. The Professor didn't like me leaving the door unlocked when I was home alone. It wasn't so much that we lived in a dangerous neighbourhood. He just got nervous because it was me, in my wheelchair, or hobbling about with the aid of a pair of canes. It was also why he'd gotten me the cell phone, which he insisted I always keep close at hand.

"Jeez, gloomy much?" Mona said as she came into the darkened room.

She shed her coat by the door and took off her cap, ruffling her short blonde hair so that it stood up around her head. Her usual inch or so of dark roots were missing, which only meant she'd taken the time to dye her hair recently.

"There are some candles by the laptop," I said. "Along with a box of matches."

Mona smiled. "That is so you. Working on your laptop by candlelight."

"Remember my first computer?"

"An Etch-a-Sketch board attached to the back of a typewriter does not a computer make."

She found a couple of candleholders, stuck candles in and lit them.

"There we go," she said, setting them on the worktable closer to where I was sitting.

My reflection was stronger in the window now, the garden behind the panes turned into dark mystery. A faint hint of cedar rose from the scented candles. Mona fetched Sophie's chair and rolled it over so that she could sit near me.

"Do you want something to drink?" I asked.

"What do you have?"

"Tea or coffee that you have to make. Juice, pop and beer. Or we could open a bottle of wine."

"From Bramley's cellar?"

The Professor kept a decent wine cellar, though it was Goon who stocked it, coming back from the wine store with boxes of rare vintages that he happily stowed away in the basement. Goon wouldn't say a thing about me sharing a bottle with Mona, but he would know. He had such a radar for that kind of thing that he'd probably know the moment he came into the house.

"Where else?" I said.

"Red or white?"

"Red."

"Be right back."

I listened to her in the kitchen when she got back from the basement, taking glasses from the cupboard, rattling around in one of the cutlery drawers to find the opener, the pop of the cork when she pulled it out.

"To Bramley and Goon," she said when she got back, clinking her glass against mine.

"To generosity and good taste," I said.

Mona smiled. "Same difference."

We sipped our wine. As usual, it was exquisite.

"So, what happened?" Mona asked. "Or would you rather not talk about it?"

I shrugged. "There's not much to say. Daniel was perfect and so I broke up with him." I gave her a considering look. "You don't seem surprised."

Mona shook her head. "I'm only curious why it took so long."

"What's that supposed to mean?"

It came out more snippy than I'd meant it to, but she'd caught me by surprise.

"I'm sorry," she said. "That was rude of me."

"No, it was rude of me."

She smiled and offered her glass to me.

"To us, in our rudeness," she said.

I clinked my glass against hers again and we had another sip.

"But what did you mean?" I asked.

"I don't know. It's just . . . you know when you see a couple and they're so obviously right for each other?"

I nodded.

"Well, I didn't get that from you and Daniel. I mean, you're right. He is perfect. Handsome and kind and generous. But it always seemed to me that whatever light he had was reflected from what you cast."

All I could do was look at her.

"I'm sorry," she said. "It's just . . ."

Her voice trailed off as I shook my head.

"God, what are you?" I asked. "Psychic? That's exactly how I felt. Well, I don't mean the light business, but it's just . . . whatever music we listened to, it was what I was into. I chose the movies we watched. He only read books by authors I'd recommended to him. He never seemed to offer me *anything* of himself. He never even really talked about himself."

"For . . . what's it been? Two years?"

I had another sip of my wine, then tapped the arm of my wheelchair. "Well, I've been kind of distracted."

"Okay, but that's still weird," Mona said. "I mean, how could you, of all people, let that go on for so long?"

"I don't know. I just did. And then, when I started to think about it, I got lazy. It was less complicated to just go with the flow. I mean, dealing with all that I've had to, it was . . . just easier having this one nice thing to look forward to, even though it felt sort of hollow."

Mona nodded sympathetically. "I know what you mean. I've stayed in relationships that weren't bad, but they weren't particularly good either. They just were, and they kind of wear you down so you don't really have the energy to deal with them the way you know you should."

"I thought you'd think I was crazy to break up with him."

"Nope. I don't think anybody will."

"Oh, god. Did everybody feel the same way?"

"It's not like what you think," she said. "We were happy if you were happy. But we couldn't help but think you'd need more intellectual stimulation than it seemed you were getting."

"Daniel isn't dumb."

"I didn't say he was. He's just not . . ." She smiled. "One of a kind, the way you are."

"Ha-ha."

"I'm being serious here. You never could take a compliment."

I shrugged, but she was right. I don't know why, but they always seemed suspect.

"You know what the real telling point was for me?" I said.

She shook her head.

"I never told him how I'm damaged goods."

"Oh, please. You met him in intensive care. He was there when you were brought in. There's probably nothing he doesn't know about what the accident did to you."

"I mean, from before," I said. "When I was a kid. All the trouble I got into, living on the streets and all."

She didn't say anything for a long moment. Just topped our glasses and set the wine bottle back down on the worktable.

"That *is* telling," she finally said.

I knew what she was thinking.

"I was going to bring it up a bunch of times," I said, "back when I realized that we were getting serious, but then I got uneasy because he'd never talk about himself."

"It doesn't mean he was a bad guy," she said.

"I know."

"It's just . . . some people don't have interesting lives."

"I could have done without a lot of my own interesting bits."

"You know what I mean. Some people don't have a story. They just drift through their lives."

"Everybody's got a story."

Mona nodded. "But the point I'm trying to make is that they're not necessarily interesting—not even to themselves. So they latch onto somebody whose life is more interesting, or appears more interesting, because that adds some luster to their own."

"I suppose."

I didn't want to feel that way about Daniel. Not because it'd make my staying with him for a couple of years even more pathetic, but because of what it said about him. Except it seemed to be true. Unless he had some dark past like I did that he'd wanted to keep from me the way I'd kept mine from him.

It's a weird thing, and it all happened so long ago that sometimes I just like to pretend I can forget. And really, when is it the right time to tell someone how you were abused as a kid, shuffled from foster home to foster home, became a junkie, sold your body . . .

"So, what are you going to do now?" Mona asked.

I raised my eyebrows. "Well, I'm not going to get involved with another guy any time soon. It just never seems to work out for me."

She nodded. "Yeah, it's weird how this kind of thing leaves you feeling so vulnerable, even when you're not the dumpee."

"I think I'll be happier as a spinster—you know. I can be the mad old lady living in the back of the Professor's house."

Mona laughed, but it didn't reach her eyes. She didn't try to jolly me out of my mood either. Instead, she refilled our glasses, and we let the conversation drift to topics that didn't carry as much emotional weight.

I don't know when we finished that bottle and opened another, but we were well into that second bottle when the conversation inevitably came back to me and my messed up relationships, except now we were being silly and giddy about it. We started making a list of all the people we knew who were single, straight, and available.

"Well, how about Jonathan at the Half Kaffe?" Mona said after we'd already listed everyone from Bernard Colbert, the stuffy head librarian at the Lower Crowsea Branch of the Newford Public Library, to the twenty-something and way too handsome Frank Jee who delivered take-out from his dad's Chinese restaurant on weekends.

"I always thought Jonathan was gay," I said.

"I don't think so. He used to hit on me all the time when I first started going to the café."

"Okay, then what about Goon?"

"Oh, please." Then she grinned and said, "What about Geordie?"

That sobered me because of all the guys in the world, I wouldn't let Geordie be made part of a drunken joke.

"No," I said shaking my head. "It'll never be with Geordie."

"Why not? You guys are best friends and, I'm sorry, but everybody knows you carry a torch for each other. You're just never single at the same time."

I knew it was the wine talking, but she wasn't far from the truth.

"We had our chance years ago," I said, "but we didn't take it and I'm glad we didn't. You know that."

"Liar."

"Besides, he's got a girlfriend. A fairy queen, no less."

"Who lives in a shopping mall and calls herself Mother Crone."

"That's just her speaking name. Fairies all have two—their true name and their speaking name."

"So, what's her real name?"

"I don't know. But Geordie does."

"Still," Mona said, "they can't be that serious. She never goes anywhere with him."

"I don't know. We don't really talk about her."

"But if she wasn't in the picture—"

"Geordie and I still wouldn't get together," I said. "Not like that."

"But you're best friends. It's all so *When Harry Met Sally*."

I sighed. "Life's not a romantic comedy."

"More's the pity."

"And think about it. You're right. Geordie and I really are best friends. So if we did get together, what would happen when we broke up?"

"You guys wouldn't break up."

"Every relationship I've ever had has fallen apart. Every relationship *he's* ever been in has broken up."

"Except Sam."

"Who just vanished on him."

"But—"

"Mona, let me ask you this," I said. "How often do you get together with your exes?"

She pulled a face. "Like, never."

"Exactly. I don't want that to happen with me and Geordie, and I know he feels the same."

"But what if it didn't?"

"Do you ever see the girls he goes out with?" Before she could answer, I did for her. "They're all gorgeous. Mother Crone's a knockout. Tanya's a movie star. And remember Sam?"

"You're gorgeous, too."

I shook my head. "No, I'm old and broken." I lifted a hand to stop her before she could argue what was such an obvious and plain fact. "I'm not saying oh poor me. It's just how it is. And I can live without a guy in my life. Trust me. It can be a real relief sometimes."

"I guess. It just seems sad."

"It doesn't have to be. I've got a bunch of great friends. And I've gotten to the point where I'm pretty much comfortable in my own skin, even if some parts are a bit worn out and don't work as well as they should anymore."

Mona gave me a slow nod. "And you can't force love anyway."

"Nor can you plan for it. It happens or it doesn't."

Mona picked up the half-full wine bottle, but I laid my hand over the top of my glass.

"No more for me," I said. "I don't even know if I can get out of my wheelchair with all I've had tonight."

"I can help."

"You should stay over," I said.

"I'm not drunk."

"How many fingers am I holding up?"

"Which one of you?" she asked, grinning.

———

Mona fell asleep almost immediately, but I lay awake for a long time on my side of the bed, staring up at the ceiling. I didn't think about it often, but Mona had put it in my head and the wine wouldn't let it go away.

Geordie.

How different would our lives have been if we *had* gotten together all those years ago?

And if we were to get together now, could we make it work?

I wasn't ever going to find out because it wasn't something I'd ever ask him. But I couldn't help thinking about it now as I lay here, trying to sleep.

Hand Me Down My Fiddle

Lizzie

For all that she'd gotten in after dawn, Lizzie still woke up in the middle of the morning and couldn't get back to sleep. She looked over at her cousin's bed to see that Siobhan was already up. But of course her bed was made—it didn't matter that hotels had housekeepers, Siobhan couldn't leave her bed unmade. Her few belongings were neatly set out on her night table and one half of the dresser, her clothes folded and put away, her knapsack in the closet.

Lizzie smiled. Unlike her own clothes and knapsack, which she'd tossed onto the chair in the corner last night and were still lying there all in a heap. She closed her eyes and tried to sleep some more, but even with the blinds drawn, too much light crept in through them. Finally she gave up, had a shower and dressed, then went downstairs to see if any of the other band members were up and about.

She found Siobhan in Cindy's, the little restaurant/café off the lobby. The room didn't promise much from its looks: painted cement floor, Formica table tops and mismatched kitchen chairs, old faded photos on the walls that weren't hung for their artistic or historic value so much as that they'd simply always been there. But the band had eaten here last night and the food was spectacular. It was, Andy had said, as though the chef decided to go slumming after getting top marks at wherever it was that she'd studied the culinary arts, opting for this out-of-the-way backwoods café when she could have been the toast of the town at some five-star restaurant in the city.

Siobhan was sitting at a table by the window, reading a paperback. The remains of her breakfast were on the table in front of her, a plate with a few crumbs left on it and the inevitable pot of tea.

"Hey," Lizzie said, taking the seat opposite her.

Siobhan looked up and smiled. "Hey, yourself. How'd you sleep?"

"Deeply, though I didn't get enough."

"That's what you get for playing the night bird. I have to say I was kind of surprised to find you here this morning."

"What do you mean?"

"Well, the last time I saw you, you were getting in your car and driving back to the city."

"I didn't spend the night here?"

"You weren't in the room at three, which is when I turned off the light."

Lizzie buried her face in her hands. "Oh, god. I was so sure it had been a dream."

Siobhan set down her book and took off her glasses, laying them down on top of the paperback.

"What are you talking about?" she asked.

Lizzie lifted her face from her hands. "You wouldn't believe me in a million years."

Siobhan's eyebrows rose. "Now you *have* to tell me."

"I don't even know where to begin."

"Start at the beginning. Where did you go last night if you weren't going back to the city?"

"I *was* going back. But the car broke down in the middle of nowhere and then . . ."

Lizzie went on to relate what had happened, from the arrival of the bogans through to her meeting with Walker, the tall man with the deer's head that wasn't a mask. She paused only when the waitress came by to take her order, finishing up before the arrival of her coffee and toast.

"Well, say something," she said when she was done and Siobhan just sat there across the table from her.

"I don't know what to say."

"You think I'm nuts."

"No. I think you think all of that happened. But . . ."

"It couldn't possibly have," Lizzie finished for her when her cousin's voice trailed off.

"Well, it does sound like one of Pappy's fairy tales."

Lizzie nodded. Their grandfather knew hundreds of them. When she and Siobhan were small, they would sit by his knee and listen to him for hours.

And even later, when they'd outgrown the stories and were learning tunes from him, he'd find a way to bring stories of his wee folk—who weren't all that "wee" most of the time—into the origins of some of the tunes he taught them.

"Could you have fallen asleep in the car?" Siobhan asked.

"And dreamed it all?"

Her cousin nodded.

"I suppose. Only how did I get back? It was *totally* dead until Grey fixed it."

"Unless you woke up half-asleep and gave it another try, and this time it did start."

"I suppose. But the battery was completely drained because the alternator's shot. Even if I could have gotten it started, it would have died on me again."

"Unless the alternator's not the problem. Where did you leave the car?"

"At that garage he recommended."

Lizzie sighed. She'd mechanically added sugar and cream to her coffee while they were talking and had a sip of it now. Like everything else in the café, it was absolutely wonderful.

"I hate feeling like this," she added.

"If you were just dreaming," Siobhan told her, "you're not crazy. I've had tons of dreams that seemed *so* real, even after I woke up."

Lizzie nodded. She'd had them herself. Like buying some great new album only to find when she woke that it didn't even exist.

"I guess I need to go to the garage," she said, "and see what's happening with my car."

"I'll come with you."

"Thanks. Just let me finish this."

"So where are the boys?" Lizzie asked later, after they'd fetched their jackets from the room.

They were walking along Sweetwater's main street, making for the garage on the edge of the village where Lizzie had left her car last night. There were no sidewalks, but there wasn't much traffic. Lizzie had heard that there was a good farmer's market on the other side of the village, so maybe that was where you'd find whatever traffic congestion a place this size got.

"Probably still sleeping," Siobhan said. "Were you here when that Liam fellow pulled out a tin whistle, or had you already gone?"

"No, I was here. He was good."

"And he must know a thousand tunes. The three of them were still going at it when I went to bed."

"Did Con hit on you?"

Siobhan laughed. "Hardly. He's only got eyes for cute punky fiddlers who dress all in black."

"I've got red shoes and socks on," Lizzie told her.

"Hence the punky."

"I thought that was my hair."

Siobhan eyed Lizzie's mix of bright red and black hair.

"No, that's just fun," she said. She waited a moment, then asked, "So you don't fancy him even a little?"

"I'd fancy him a lot if we weren't in the same band. But that's a rule I won't break again. It's just gets too damn messy."

"And I agree with you. Though, if it was true love, I'd throw the rule book away."

Lizzie laughed. "I think it's more hormonal love."

"Nothing wrong with that."

"Nothing at all," Lizzie agreed. "Unless you're in the same band."

They reached the garage then, and both stopped to take it in. Lizzie's heart sank. It looked much worse in the daylight than it had last night. All the metal signage was fighting off an intrusion of rust, the windows were almost impenetrable from their thick coating of dust, and the building was in desperate need of a paint job. There were stacks of old tires to one side of the garage bay door and machine parts heaped in unruly piles wherever you turned. The field beyond the tires was littered with junked cars. Old gas pumps, rusting and disused, stood amidst clusters of dead weeds that had pushed up through the concrete all last summer before they'd died in the fall.

"You left your car *here?*" Siobhan asked.

"Not another word," Lizzie told her.

There was no one in the office, and considering the state of the room, Lizzie didn't blame anybody for staying out of it. There was dust everywhere and the counter was covered with tools and old engine parts. On the wall behind the counter, a bikini-clad Miss March regarded them coyly from a wrench company's calendar. But they could hear a radio playing country music in the bay and when they went inside, there was a man with his head under the hood of Lizzie's car. He stepped back and smiled at them, a slightly overweight man in his fifties, wearing grease-stained bib overalls with a T-shirt that had once been white underneath it.

"How do," he said. "This your car?"

Lizzie nodded. "Do you know what's wrong with it?"

"Alternator's shot—just like you said in your note."

Lizzie gave her cousin a knowing look.

"Can you fix it?" she asked.

"Sure can, missy. I can get a new one in from Tyson for this afternoon. But if you're not in a hurry, I could get you a used one from the junkyard—cost you maybe half the price of a new one. Trouble is, your car wouldn't be ready until . . . let's see. I guess late Monday morning."

"That's okay. We're playing at the Custom House, and we weren't planning to leave until then anyway."

"You the fiddlers?"

Lizzie nodded.

"I heard tell you put on a good show. Maybe I'll drag Joe out to see you's tonight."

That would make this one Tommy, Lizzie thought, if the sign outside was still up to date.

"I could put you on the guest list," she said.

"That's right neighbourly of you. My name's Tommy and my partner's Joe."

"I'm Lizzie and this is my cousin Siobhan."

Tommy wiped his hands on his overalls, but after giving them a critical scrutiny, he shook his head.

"Pardon my rudeness," he said, "but I got too much grease on my hands to shake."

"That's okay. Thanks, Tommy. I guess we'll see you tonight."

He nodded, then called after them as they were about to step outside.

"What made you have your car towed here?" he asked.

"Towed?" Lizzie said.

"Well, you sure weren't driving it, condition that alternator's in."

"Oh, right."

"I'm only asking 'cause most folks—'specially from the city—would take it to one of the other garages in town. They've got all them fancy computers, tell you what's wrong and what to do."

"This fellow named Grey recommended you," Lizzie said. "He's the one that, ah, got my car here."

"You're a friend of Grey's?"

Lizzie shook her head. "I wouldn't say friend. He was just nice enough to help me out last night."

But Tommy didn't seem to hear her.

"You being a friend of Grey's," he said, "I'll have your car ready for you this afternoon—no charge."

"But—"

"I won't argue about it," Tommy told her, "and that's a solid fact, missy. I'm right pleased to do a favour for any friend of Grey's."

"I don't understand."

"You don't need to. You come on back this afternoon, and I'll have that car of yours purring like a kitten."

"I really don't need it that fast."

But, "We'll see you tonight at your show," he said and turned away.

Lizzie looked at her cousin. Siobhan looked as confused as Lizzie felt, but she didn't say anything. She only took Lizzie's arm and led her away from the garage. But Lizzie couldn't let it go.

"Did you hear that?" she asked. "He knows this Grey fellow. He said the car wouldn't run with the alternator being like it was."

"I heard."

"Jaysus."

Siobhan nodded. "Yeah, it's a kicker all right. Looks like you weren't dreaming."

"But . . . that's impossible, right?"

Siobhan didn't have an answer for her.

Sweetwater got its start as a mill town at the turn of the last century when Thomas Fairburn built the area's first grain mill. The old stone mill stood where the Ashbless River fell into the Kickaha on its own endless journey down from the mountains to what was now Newford and the lake shore upon which the city was built. In recent times, the mill had become a high-class hotel and conference center, part of the ongoing transformation of the whole village into a tourist haven.

The most successful refurbishing had taken place along the stretch of Main Street where it ran closest to the Kickaha River. Although there were a few holdouts—scruffy country cousins like the old general store and a few residential properties that were yet to become commercial—most of the buildings sported a new tourist-friendly look: folksy wood fronts on the stores, old-fashioned hand-painted signs, shop windows full of souvenirs and crafts.

The Custom House was somewhere in between. Its stucco walls boasted a new paint job, and Cindy's Café had an outdoor patio for use in the summer, but inside the hotel, the guest rooms were as they'd been for thirty years and the bar room was still more of a roadhouse. Its regular patrons didn't care, neither the locals who came by for a drink after work nor the hipper crowd that showed up in the evenings for entertainment. The bar room of the Custom House provided an eclectic mix of live music that rivaled any big city venue.

The building stood on Main Street with a view of the Kickaha River, and only the railroad tracks and a thin strip of lawn separated the street from the water. Stairs led down to a wooden dock with a couple of benches on it. From the dock, one could sit and look out on the river and the foothills of the mountains that began their northward climb from the far shore.

When they got back to the hotel, Lizzie and Siobhan took the stairs down and sat on one of the benches, neither of them ready quite yet to go inside the hotel and have to interact with other people. Siobhan was still quiet and Lizzie couldn't really blame her. *She'd* actually experienced the whole weird business last night, and she could hardly get her head around it herself. And now there was this new mystery of Tommy being so deferential to Grey.

"What am I going to *do*?" she said when they'd been sitting there for awhile.

Siobhan shook her head. "I don't know, Lizzie. Maybe you should just get your car this afternoon and hope it all goes away."

Lizzie gave a slow nod. She sure didn't want to run into those bogans again. And Grey hadn't exactly been friendly. But Walker had. And then there was the whole mystery, the adventure of it all. The idea that this whole other world existed, side by side to this one, only hidden from it unless you happened to stray or were drawn into it.

"I don't think I can forget about it," she said.

"I'm still trying to understand it myself," Siobhan told her. "It's so unbelievable."

"But you heard what Tommy said about the alternator and Grey."

"I'm not saying I don't believe it happened," Siobhan said. "Not anymore, because obviously *something* did. But I'm still having trouble getting my head around it. I mean, from what you were telling me, there could be little fairy people all around us right now, and we'd never know."

Lizzie shivered. "Don't say that."

"But there could, couldn't there?"

Lizzie turned on the bench and studied the steep slope of the river bank on either side of them. The rushes and weeds were tall and brown, but thinned enough by the winter snows that a person couldn't easily hide in them. But when she thought of how the bogans, not to mention Grey and Walker, were able to just appear and disappear, stepping to and from this between place Grey had mentioned . . .

"I guess," she said.

"You said the deer man—"

"Walker."

Siobhan nodded. "You said he told you if you called his name, he'd come, didn't you?"

Lizzie saw where she was going.

"I couldn't do that," she said.

"But then we'd know for sure. And maybe he could explain what you're supposed to do."

"I don't think I'm supposed to do anything. Grey told me the same thing you did a few moments ago: I should just forget about it and get on with my life."

"But Walker said the bogans might come looking for you."

Lizzie hated being reminded of that, but she nodded.

"And I have to admit," Siobhan went on, "I'd *really* like to actually . . . you know . . . meet this guy." She gave Lizzie a thin smile. "If 'guy' is even the proper term."

"Except I got the feeling," Lizzie said, "that his offer to come to me when I called him seemed to imply that I should only do it if I was in danger."

"From the bogans."

"I guess. You'd have to have seen him, but Walker didn't strike me as the sort of person you'd bother with anything frivolous. It was like . . . I don't know." She gave a nervous laugh. "Like meeting a saint."

Siobhan smiled. "Oh, if your mother could hear that, you'd lose all the points you gained when we named the band the Knotted Cord."

Lizzie's mother, a devout Catholic, had been somewhat mollified by the band's name, because she certainly wasn't happy about her daughter becoming a professional musician. Lizzie and Siobhan had originally chosen the name because "The Knotted Cord," also known as "Junior Crehan's" after its composer, was a favourite tune of theirs. It was Lizzie's mother who'd pointed out that the knotted cord represented rosary beads, dating back to a time in Ireland when people too poor to afford them would make a set of their own out of string or rope.

"But you know what I mean," Lizzie said. "When you meet someone . . . not exactly holy, but very spiritual."

"Like the Dalai Lama."

"I suppose. But I've never met him."

"Neither have I," Siobhan said. "But I can imagine what it'd be like meeting him."

Before Lizzie could respond, they were hailed from the top of the stairs.

"There you are!"

They turned to see Andy waving down at them. A moment later he was joined by Con.

"The boys are awake," Siobhan said. "Let the revels begin."

Lizzie laughed and they got up.

"This fairy business . . . ," Lizzie began as they mounted the stairs.

"Is just between us," Siobhan assured her.

"We've been looking all over for you," Andy said when they got to the top.

"When did you get back?" Con asked Lizzie.

She shrugged. "Last night. I changed my mind and turned around about halfway home."

"You missed some grand music," Andy said. "Your man Liam McNamara—oh, he knows some brilliant tunes."

"I heard a bit before I left last night," Lizzie said.

Con fell in step with her as they crossed back to the hotel.

"So, what made you change your mind?" he asked.

"I decided I'd miss my cousin too much," she told him, smiling at the hopeful look in his eyes.

Oh, he was a handsome bugger, no question. Maybe she should kick him out of the band so that they could start seeing each other.

Geordie

Whenever I didn't stay at the mall after a revel—especially when Galfreya had specifically asked me to—I ended up carrying this pang of regret throughout the day. A kind of yearning that I could feel, but couldn't quite define. Today was no different. She was in the back of my mind when I fell asleep, just behind my concern about the conversation I'd had with Hazel. Those thoughts absorbed me until I recalled that mysterious snatch of fiddle music I'd heard in the mall's parking lot.

I slept deeply for a few hours, then woke suddenly to a feeling I couldn't name.

Loss, I realized after a few moments.

I felt as though I'd lost something, but I didn't know what.

It wasn't until hours later, after I'd fallen asleep again and finally gotten up in the midafternoon to start my day, that I realized what it was: I felt no specific yearning to go back to the mall. To play music with the fairies. To be with Galfreya.

The need was noticeable only by its absence.

I grabbed a shower and shaved, then went through the pile of clothes lying on the foot of the Murphy bed, looking for something clean to wear. I had to do a laundry soon, no question, but it could wait until tomorrow or Monday. Right now I needed coffee and something to eat, and there was nothing in the apartment.

I got myself a take-out coffee and a muffin from the neighbourhood coffee shop to see me through, then caught the subway to my brother Christy's place. I didn't have to hope he'd have coffee on. Christy was addicted to the stuff, the same as me. He *always* had coffee on.

Coming in the door to his building, I met his girlfriend Saskia on her way out. She smiled and gave me a hug. It's funny, I'm not much of a one for physical displays of affection, but it was different with Saskia—and not because she's so attractive. If whoever it was that started the whole dumb blonde thing had met her, they'd have picked on brunettes or redheads instead. She was pretty and smart, a published poet with a social conscience and a huge heart. And somehow, when she hugged you, she didn't seem to invade your personal space. She just confirmed your connections to the world around you. Or at least she did for me.

"Be warned," she said when she stepped back. "He's in a bit of a mood."

I raised an eyebrow.

"Oh, it's just that limited edition retrospective collection that Alan wants to do."

"But that's a good thing, right?"

She smiled. "You'd think. But all he can focus on is having to sign a few thousand signature sheets."

"Maybe we should buy him one of those automated signature machines."

"Except then he'd just find something else to get wound up over," she said.

She gave me a kiss on the cheek.

"Coffee's on the stove, and I'll be back in an hour," she added. "Will you stay for dinner?"

"Love to, thanks."

Then she went out onto the street, and I took the stairs up to their apartment.

I guess the biggest thing Saskia did for Christy and me was to teach us that family didn't have to be a dirty word. It wasn't something she actually talked about, or worked to convince either of us to accept. It just kind of happened. Before she came into Christy's life, Christy and I really didn't have much time or patience for each other. But once he and Saskia were a couple, she made a point of having me over for dinner, or getting Christy to take her out to one of my shows—just bringing us together with her present so that we were on better behaviour than we might have been if it was just the two of us.

It was a slow process, with lots of bristling and affronts taken on both our parts, but Saskia knew how to smooth over the rough patches without ever really letting on that she was doing so. She'd just show us how much we had in common, gentle the start of angry words, and generally refused to let us drift apart. She was such a success with us that she could probably have reconciled us with our parents if we'd let her try, but we stood shoulder-to-shoulder on that one and would have nothing of it.

I guess the reason she was so good at it was because she never had even the pretense of a family herself and was determined to make one for all of us.

"Saskia says you're grumpy today," I said after I gave a perfunctory knock on their apartment door and then went on inside without waiting for a response.

Christy looked up from where he was reading a stack of manuscript pages on the sofa.

"She's probably right," he said.

"You should be happy that your readers will pay the big bucks for a signed limited edition of your stories."

He smiled. "Oh, I am. But you know me. . . ."

"You have to pretend to at least make a credible fuss about it."

"Or something. There's coffee on the stove."

"Thanks. You want some?"

"No, I'm good."

I liked this apartment. Before Saskia came into his life, Christy used to move about once a year, and half his books were still in boxes when the time came for us to move him again. That was about as often as he and I would deliberately got together. Everywhere he lived felt temporary—the way my living arrangements still are.

But it was different now. They'd been here a few years, and the place had a warm, lived-in feel that wasn't just Saskia's touch. She'd inspired Christy to actually put down some roots—get all his books out and shelved, put up photos and art, set out handfuls of small artful objects that, to date, had spent most of their lives in boxes.

I had to admit that I envied Christy. For finding someone like Saskia. For making a real home with her.

"Were you playing at a revel last night?" Christy asked.

And there was a big reason I didn't have what he had. We'd both chosen—or had chosen for us by our respective muses—careers that didn't exactly lend themselves to stability. But Christy had put the effort into making his writing an actual career, while I just let the music take me where it would.

This past couple of years, the music took me to the mall. To the fairies and Galfreya, and neither was particularly conducive to putting down roots—either with a home or a career.

But I didn't get into any of that. I just nodded and said, "It was a good one. There was this visiting—hell, I don't know what she was. Part tree, part something like an otter. But could she play this strange little set of pipes that she had. And she knew at least a half-dozen tunes I'd never heard before."

"A whole half-dozen?" Christy asked, smiling.

I shrugged. "So I know a lot of tunes. But I don't pretend to know them all."

"I wish I had your memory."

"Then we both have something the other wants," I found myself saying.

He raised his eyebrows.

"All of this," I said.

I waved a hand to encompass his life as represented by the room we were in. Cozy, full of comfortable furniture and shelves of books, thick rugs on the floor, photos and art on the walls that meant something in their own merit, as well as their placement to each other.

"A real home you can call your own," I explained. "And more importantly, someone to share it with."

Christy gave a slow nod. "There's not a day goes by that I'm not grateful. Especially given . . . you know . . ."

He didn't have to bring up the environment in which we'd grown up for me to know exactly what he was talking about.

"Finding a partner's not something you can just decide to do," he said, "but there's nothing stopping you from making a home for yourself."

I rubbed my thumb against my fingers. "No money."

"That's not necessarily an insurmountable problem."

"Easy for you to say."

He shook his head. "No, I think I'm being reasonable. You'd just have to change a few things in your life."

"You mean like get a regular job? I think I'd go insane."

"No, I was thinking more of working with the marketable skills you already have."

I gave him a blank look.

"Your music, dummy."

"My music."

"Look," he said. "I know how you feel about recording and putting together a permanent band and all of that. And I'm not saying you should compromise your ideals. But if you want some of the things that money can buy, like a place to call your own, then maybe it's something to think about. You already accept money when you're busking and from these pickup gigs you do. It's not that big a stretch to recording and selling a CD, and doing some touring with a band to promote it."

There was a time when I heard that a lot, but considering how vocal I could be against the idea, my friends pretty much stopped bringing it up years ago. Now it was only something I'd get at a gig from strangers, caught up in the excitement of the moment. I honestly didn't think about it anymore.

I'd wanted to at one time, when I first got into playing in the early seventies, but it hadn't been feasible back then. Celtic music wasn't particularly popular in those days. There was no Worldbeat, no Pogues. The Chieftains were barely known outside of Ireland. A group like the Incredible String Band, one of the earliest proponents of mixing musical genres, weren't on most people's radar. So a recording company wouldn't get excited about recording some kid who played fiddle on street corners and in bars. And I sure couldn't afford to pay for it myself.

I still couldn't, but it was different now. These days I knew a half-dozen people who recorded everything directly into their computer. I'd done session work for any number of folks with real studios. They'd all offered, at one time or another, to help me out if I was ever interested in laying down some tracks.

"Maybe I'll think about it," I told my brother.

"Okay, that's new," he said.

I smiled. "Don't get pushy." Then, before he could press me any further, I changed the subject and asked, "What's that you're reading?"

He knew what I was doing, but let me get away with it.

"This?" he asked, tapping the manuscript with a finger. "They're transcripts of some of the interviews I've done over the past few years."

"For a new book?"

"Possibly. But mostly I'm trying to figure out something for myself. There's been a real escalation in paranormal experiences over the past few years, and I'm trying to get a fix on when it started."

"No kidding," I said. "These days you can't turn around without tripping over someone in this city who's had at least one encounter with a ghost or a fairy or a monster or *something*."

Christy smiled and shook his head. "No, it just seems that way."

"Everybody *we* know has some weird experience or another."

"That's because people who have had these kinds of unusual experiences are drawn into each other's peripheries—at least it happens to those of us who don't manage to forget the experience. Sometimes I think it's like a kind of magnetic attraction. If you've had one experience, it appears to automatically raise the possibility that you'll have another. And just having one seems to bring you into the proximity of others who've had at least one, thereby raising the probability that you'll both have another."

I just looked at him.

"But most people," he said, "go about their daily lives, oblivious—even after an experience." He smiled. "Though sometimes they really have to work at not remembering."

That was me, up to a couple of years ago when I finally had to give in and admit that all this weird stuff that kept intruding into my life was real.

"And you think it's happening more often now?" I asked.

Christy nodded. "When I first started cataloguing the incidents, they were few and far between, and pretty hard to track down. But I've had it relatively easy. It was more difficult when the Professor got into it, because he started even earlier than I did."

"And is it happening all over, or just here?"

"I don't know for sure. I doubt that this is the only pocket of increased activity, but it's definitely a lively one."

"Hence the police department actually having a task force to deal with it."

The fact that the Newford Police Department had a unit devoted to dealing with the paranormal wasn't exactly common knowledge, but I knew, because both Christy and the Professor had been tapped as consultants for it.

"Hence—" Christy smiled at the word. "—indeed."

"So what do you think is causing it?"

"I've no idea."

"I do. Newford's one of those rare places built on a nexus of time and spirit zones, which means the spiritworld rubs shoulders with this one more than it normally would otherwise."

We both looked up at the sound of the new voice to find Christy's shadow, Christiana, lounging on one of the two club chairs set across from the sofa where we were sitting. She was a small woman, all red hair and skinny limbs in a pair of black tights and a baggy sweatshirt. She grinned at our looks of surprise.

"I hate it when she does that," Christy said, "just appearing out of nowhere."

He smiled as he spoke.

"Oh, right," she said. "Like talking about me as if I'm not even here is so endearing."

They have a complicated relationship. I just accept Christiana as the sister I never knew I had until a couple of years ago, but it's different for Christy.

Supposedly, she was made up of all the bits of himself that he cast off when he was seven. When he cast those parts of himself away, they became Christiana—a seven-year-old girl as real as you or me who decided to call herself Christiana, a mash-up of Christy's name and that of his first-grade school crush, Anna. Since then, they've each grown to become their own individual person, though in a lot of ways I think they're more alike than either will admit.

Like I said, it's complicated.

"What did you mean about the city being a nexus?" I asked.

She shrugged. "Just that Newford's a funny place that draws the weird and the wonderful to it. It brought our brother here, didn't it?, and he hasn't left yet."

"I hope I'm part of the wonderful," he said.

She gave him a shocked look, as though saying, how could it be any other way?, but when he glanced away, she winked at me.

"So," she asked me, "are you still playing at the fairy revels?"

"I did last night. But a funny thing happened. I was going to tell Christy about it just before you showed up."

That got their attention. Christiana had as much curiosity as our brother, especially when it came to the mysterious and the strange, though considering her background, she probably had more of the answers, as well. I mean, she *lives* in the otherworld.

"Was it at the revel?" Christy asked.

"Not so much at it, as after."

I went on to describe the odd feeling that had briefly woken me this morning, and how I'd realized what it was when I finally got up. I looked back and forth between them as I spoke, the way you do when you're telling a story, and caught the pleased look on Christiana's face before she was able to hide it from me.

"I get the feeling you know something about this," I said.

She shrugged. "Well, I might have talked to Mother Crone this morning."

I wasn't sure if she didn't know Galfreya's real name, or simply wasn't using it because Christy had yet to be gifted with it. Fairy are very particular about that kind of thing.

"What did you talk about?" I asked.

"You. I . . ." She sighed. "She had an enchantment on you, Geordie— I've known it for ages. That's why you've been going to the revels so often."

I felt a little sick hearing that.

"You mean all this time . . . ?"

She shook her head when she realized where I was going.

"No, it wasn't an attraction spell," she said. "Whatever you and Mother Crone had going on between you was real."

"But then, why?"

"She said she'd had a premonition that if you weren't kept close to her court, you'd be in danger."

"That doesn't make any sense." I looked at Christy, then back to her. "What kind of danger?"

"She doesn't know," Christiana said. "But she believes it's real."

"So why did she turn off this enchantment?"

"I asked her to."

This was making less and less sense.

No, that's not entirely true. Learning about the enchantment did explain why I'd had this compulsion to keep going back to the revels, even when something more interesting was going on. Just last week, Whiskeycrow were in town for a gig, with the promise of a great session afterwards, and I'd really wanted to go. I hadn't played with Fanny and the rest of them in ages. But the night of the session, off I'd gone to the mall instead.

What didn't make sense was Christiana's involvement in all of this.

"Why would you do that?" Christy asked her before I could.

She shrugged. "I don't agree with coercion enchantments, no matter how well meant. And . . ." Her gaze went to me. "I felt it was holding you back."

"From what?" I asked.

She looked uncomfortable.

"Christiana?" Christy asked.

"From having a real life," she said. "Okay? And I know how that sounds." She turned to me. "It's not like I think I can run your life better than you or anything. It's just—"

"The revels were holding me back," I said.

She nodded, then cocked her head. "You don't seem mad."

"I'm not. I was kind of thinking the same thing. It just didn't occur to me until the . . . well, I guess when the enchantment was lifted."

"Oh."

"If I'm mad about anything, it's at—" I almost said Galfreya, "Mother Crone's putting it on me in the first place."

"Except she thought she was protecting you."

I nodded. "It'd still be nice to have actually had a choice in the matter." I sighed and laid my head back against the sofa. "I guess that explains why she never wanted to go anywhere. Why it was always me going to the mall."

Christiana nodded.

I turned to Christy. "See, this is why I don't like getting involved with any of this. Magics and fairy and everything weird. It makes life way too complicated. It was so much easier to just not believe in any of it."

"Kind of late for that," he said.

"Yeah, I know."

"And you kept bumping into it anyway."

I couldn't argue with that either.

"C'mon," Christiana said. "Magic's not so bad."

"Easy for you to say. You reap the benefits, living in the otherworld and all. And *you* don't have some death threat hanging over your head."

"I didn't say it was a death threat."

I nodded. "I know you didn't. But it has to be something pretty serious if Mother Crone felt she needed to put a spell on me to keep me close to her court."

"I suppose . . ."

"And how am I supposed to figure out what it is?"

"Is there anybody new in your life?" Christy asked.

I shook my head. "But why does it have to come from someone new?"

"It doesn't," he said. "But it's as good a place as any to start. Unless . . ." He looked to Christiana. "Is it a natural disaster?"

"Don't look at me," she said. "I know less than Mother Crone does, and she doesn't seem to know much of anything except that it's there and it won't happen if you stick close to her court."

Right. Like I wanted to spend the rest of my life hanging around Woodforest Plaza Mall, knowing what I did now.

"This sucks," I said and nobody disagreed.

Lizzie

The Custom House was hopping on Saturday night. Lizzie and Siobhan's twin fiddles, backed by the lilting punch of Con's guitar and Andy's button accordion, filled the bar with one driving set of tunes after the other, much to the patrons' obvious delight. They stomped their feet and otherwise kept time by clapping or banging on the tables. Directly in front of the stage, the dance floor was a thick press of valiant attempts at step dancing, with more flailing of arms and head bobbing than was usually called for.

The energy from the audience translated to the band's upping the drive of each subsequent tune set. Siobhan, so unassuming off stage, was showing off by step dancing as she fiddled and at one point, Lizzie was sure that Con was going to jump onto the nearest table and do his impression of a rock guitar hero, but it turned out he was only teasing the group sitting at that table.

Finally, they slowed things down for a song, just to make sure that the floor didn't collapse under the audience's enthusiasm and send them all down into the hotel's basement. Con stepped up to the mike and began an a cappella version of Cyril Tawney's "The Blue Funnel Line" with the rest of the band joining in on harmony for the one-line refrains. They finished with an instrumental version of the song on whistles and accordion.

The ensuing applause was enthusiastic, but the audience made it obvious that they wanted more dance tunes by returning to the dance floor and clapping in reel-time.

Lizzie took her turn at the mike.

"My car broke down last night," she said when the noise died down enough for her to speak. "Right out in the middle of bloody nowhere. I thought I'd be sleeping in the back seat, but then a Good Samaritan got me up and running again—lucky, too, or maybe I wouldn't even be able to be enjoying this night with all of you."

That brought a round of applause and Lizzie grinned at the crowd.

"Anyway," she went on, "I don't think my rescuer was a big fan of Celtic music—"

A few good-natured boos rose up.

"I know," she said. "What's up with that? But one good turn deserves another, so here's a set of American fiddle tunes we call the 'The Two Billys Set.' They're for my rescuer Grey, wherever he might be tonight."

She stepped back from the mike to let Andy count them in, then off they went into "Billy in the Low Ground," the twin fiddles growling on their low strings against the deep-throated rumble of Andy's bodhran. Three times through, then they jumped keys into "Bill Cheatum's" and Con joined them on guitar, playing a syncopated old-timey rhythm that brought out the American feel of the tune and kicked the energy up yet another notch.

They followed that with two sets of Irish reels, and then the set was over.

"Don't go away," Siobhan told the crowd. "We'll be back with lots more music right after the break."

Andy turned down the sound from the stage. When he flicked the switch that brought the house sound system up, Johnny Cash's deep baritone filled the air. That seemed enough to soothe a few members of the audience who hadn't wanted the music to stop. The band left the stage, grinning at each other.

"This is a great venue," Con said.

Lizzie nodded. "Yeah, we always seem to get exceptional audiences when we play here. It must be something in the water."

"Or in the beer," Siobhan said, "because, lord, can they put it away. You boys have fun now," she added as she walked away.

It was Andy and Con's turn to work the merchandise table, so Lizzie followed Siobhan through the door behind the stage. They took the back stairs up to their room where Siobhan fell across her bed, arms outspread, and let out a long happy sigh. Lizzie got her jacket from where she'd left it draped over a chair. Siobhan turned her head to look at her.

"Where are you going?"

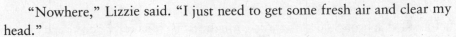

"Nowhere," Lizzie said. "I just need to get some fresh air and clear my head."

"Yeah, it's weird playing in a smoky bar again, isn't it?"

Many of the cities they played in had by-laws against smoking in restaurants and bars, but that kind of legislation hadn't yet made it to out-of-the-way places like Sweetwater yet.

Lizzie nodded. "My lungs feel like they did when I used to smoke. You want to come?"

"I'm good. You go ahead."

It was peaceful outside the hotel. She could still hear the sound of the crowd and the house music playing in the bar, but the noise was muted and distant. Crossing the road, she stood at the top of the stairs leading down to the water and looked off across the river. There were a few lights on the far bank, but not many, and none higher up in the hills above the river.

A crunch on the gravel behind her made her turn around. She was surprised to find herself face-to-face with Grey, her rescuer from last night.

"Why did you call me?" he asked. "Who gave you my name?"

No hello, how are you? Lizzie thought. But manners didn't seem to be a priority for him.

"I wasn't calling you," she said. "I just dedicated some tunes to you as a way of saying thank you for your help last night."

"You used my name."

"That's usually what you do when you make a dedication."

But it was as though he hadn't heard a word she'd said. Or maybe he just didn't care.

"Who gave it to you?" he repeated.

"He said his name was Walker."

Grey nodded. "Of course. That old interfering fool. Even after the little freaks have butchered his daughter, he still wants us to live in peace with them."

Lizzie's moment of feeling good vanished. Just like that, she was back in the weird nightmare world she'd stumbled into last night.

"He didn't say anything like that," she said. "He was just . . . sad. Wouldn't you be?"

"I'm always sad."

He didn't look it, Lizzie thought. He looked angry. Maybe he had the two confused.

He turned away and looked out across the water, just as she'd been doing before he'd approached. After a few moments, he took a tobacco pouch from his pocket and rolled a cigarette with quick, practiced ease. When he had it lit, he offered it to her.

Lizzie started to decline, but then she thought about how tobacco was a part of many Native American traditions, used in everything from calling up spirits to signifying peace between strangers. And seeing how he was a Native spirit, maybe this meant more to him than the automatic politeness of offering a smoke. Since he'd already established that he wasn't exactly a shining example of politeness, this might be his way of making peace.

She accepted the cigarette and had a puff. After returning it to him, she had to cough into her hand. There was a reason she'd given them up.

"Thanks," she said, her voice scratchy.

He nodded and took another drag on the cigarette himself.

"So how do you know Walker?" he asked.

"I don't, not really. Before I left the crossroads, I buried the remains of his daughter under that elm where we fought those weird little men—"

"The bogans."

"The bogans, right." She shivered, thinking of the horrible little creatures. "But just burying the remains still didn't seem like enough, so I played a lament for her. And then he was just there."

"One of your fairy tunes."

"No, it was a Celtic one."

"It's the same difference, Elizabeth Mahone."

She thought it was odd, his using her whole name the way he did. It was as though he was making a point. Then she remembered what Walker had told her.

Names are everything. If you know the full, true name of a thing, it is at your mercy.

So she supposed he *was* making a point. Except her name was just a name. Anybody could get it from the band's Web site, or by picking up one of their CDs and looking at the line-up. She wasn't sure names had the same impact in her world as they did in his, but it still made her uncomfortable that he'd used it. Maybe it was because when she was around him, she was already a half step into his world, where this kind of a thing *did* make a difference.

"Why don't you like Celtic music?" she found herself asking.

He shrugged. "It's too much like the fairies who first gave it to your people: busy and frivolous."

"Well, I'd argue that," she said, "but I've learned that there's not much point in trying to change people's minds when it comes to something as subjective as art. We like what we like, and words aren't going to make a difference." Especially not to someone as set in his ways as she figured he was. "But now I'm curious about what you do like."

"That's easy," he said. "The music of my people."

"What's it like?" She smiled. "I'm guessing not busy or frivolous."

"You'd guess right. It's like the beating of our hearts, which is an echo of the heartbeat of the world. It's a serious music, the rhythms are strong, the melodies deceptively simple. Whether we play it on our own, or in a group, it connects us to the whole of the world, not simply the little piece of it that we inhabit in our minds."

"That's how it is with the music I play, too," she said.

"It's different. Our music has a sacred quality to it."

"Then you've never heard a slow air played by a master musician when he totally feels the music."

He cocked his head. "I thought you didn't try to change people's minds about subjective things."

"I guess I lied."

"I know you're joking," he said, "but you should know that the truth is also something we hold sacred—both fairy and my people. Your promissory word is more valuable than gold."

"I'll remember."

Not that she planned to have anything more to do with either fairies or spirits. At least not if she could help it.

"I should go," he said.

He dropped his cigarette butt onto the gravel and ground it out under his boot before picking it up and stowing it in his pocket.

"Be careful," he told her. "This music of yours calls to fairy, and you know from last night that they're not all sweetness and light."

Thanks for that, Lizzie thought. She really needed to have it put in her head.

"It's what we do," she said. "And we've never had trouble before."

"You never interacted with them before, either."

"Well, I don't want to," she told him. "And I don't want to get caught up in any animosity between you, either."

"Sometimes you don't get a choice," he said. "And when that happens, you have to take a side."

She shook her head. "That's not going to happen."

He regarded her for a long moment, then shrugged. He was good with the shrugs, she found herself thinking.

The silence between them stretched, but not comfortably the way it did when Lizzie was hanging with Siobhan or one of her friends. She wondered why he was still here, having said he was going a few moments ago.

"So, you're like an Indian, right?" she asked just to be saying something. "I mean a Native American."

It made sense, considering his dark good looks, and his description of the music of his people, which sounded like what you'd hear at a powwow.

But he shook his head. "No, the cousins come from an older race than that."

Silence fell between them once more, but this time Grey broke it. He kicked at the gravel before turning toward her.

"I liked those tunes you dedicated to me," he said.

"Even though they were busy and frivolous?"

"Even though."

And then he was gone, stepped away into nowhere, and she was alone at the top of the stairs. She stood there for a moment longer, listening to the river lap against the shore below, before she finally turned and went back into the hotel.

It was time for their next set.

Up until meeting Grey, she'd been really looking forward to getting back on stage—the energy had been so good tonight. At least it had been so far. The way she felt now, all she wanted was for the night to be over. She wanted the gig to be done, for the band to be wherever they were playing next, for all this weirdness that had intruded into her life to go away and bother somebody else. She could think of any number of likely candidates.

The band played a few Renaissance Faires as well as festivals during the summer. Wandering around the grounds of the Faires, she'd met all kinds of people who couldn't shut up about fairies and magic and the like. Half of them dressed like they were fairies, complete with pretty little store-bought wings attached to their backs, the other half claimed to have met them—though with what she knew now, that didn't seem quite so preposterous anymore. But still. Why couldn't this be happening to them instead? They'd at least appreciate it.

Her mood hadn't improved by the time she was back on stage and picked up her fiddle. Looking out at the crowd, they didn't seem to generate energy now, as much as be a source of irritation. She sighed and turned her attention to making sure her instrument was in tune and rosining her bow. Siobhan stepped closer to her.

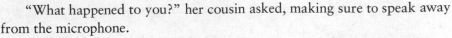

"What happened to you?" her cousin asked, making sure to speak away from the microphone.

"I met Grey again."

"What, just now? What did he—"

But before she could go on, Andy called over to them, asking if they were ready.

"Later," Lizzie told her cousin.

"I'll hold you to that."

As Andy started to count them into their opening number, they turned back to the audience and waited for their cue to begin the first reel.

Lizzie started the opening set of tunes still feeling glum, but by the time they'd finished those reels and started another set, the magic of the music pulled her out of herself—just as it always did—and the strange mood Grey had put her in faded away as though it had never crept up and taken hold of her. Soon she was grinning back at Siobhan, flirting with some of the guys on the dance floor, and generally having as good a time as she'd been having before they took their break and she'd run smack dab into another tangle of fairy weirdness.

Screw Grey, she thought. These old tunes were as valid as the music he'd been talking about. They were just as inclusive as what you'd hear at any powwow. Because, really, how many kinds of music could appeal to as disparate a crowd as they had in here tonight? There was Tommy and Joe—the two old mechanics in their coveralls leaning against the back wall—the small-town Goths happily pogoing right in front of the stage, and every sort of person in between. The big difference was that the people in here were having fun tonight. Grey didn't look like he even knew the meaning of the word.

She felt like calling his name and bringing him back to see for himself what she'd been trying to explain to him, except he'd just bring her down again, so why bother? Instead she let herself fall into the music, not coming up for air until they were on their final encore.

"Well, you cheered up," Siobhan said as they were packing away their fiddles and whistles.

Lizzie nodded. "Hard not to. God, I love this music."

"So what happened earlier?"

Lizzie glanced at where Andy was putting away his own instruments. Con was already at the merchandise table where a line had formed that was happily long and crowded. All four of them would man the merchandise table now so that folks could get their CDs autographed by the full band.

"I'll tell you later," she said. "We should go be famous."

Siobhan laughed. That was their line for the momentary buzz they got from signing CDs.

"I'm going to put out a solo CD," she told Lizzie, "so I'll get to be even more famous than you."

"I'll put out two."

"I'll write a book as well—a tell-all revealing all your dirty secrets."

"I need to have some first."

Siobhan shrugged. "I'll just make them up, then."

"Make sure one of them includes Martin Hayes."

"No way. I'm saving him for myself."

Laughing, they joined the others at the merchandise table.

It took a while to get through the line that had formed, autographing CDs and answering questions, but a half-hour after they'd finished their last song and gotten down from the stage they were finally done. Andy and Con ordered whiskeys from the bar and took them to the table where Liam McNamara, the whistle player they'd met last night, was sitting. He'd returned this evening with a few friends, but only one of them, a fiddle player named Neil Flynn, had stayed in hopes of another after-hours session.

"You're not heading off again, are you?" Andy asked Lizzie as the two women started to leave the bar.

"We're just changing," Siobhan assured him.

Lizzie nodded. "So, you can order us whiskeys, too."

But the real reason they were going back to their room was because Siobhan couldn't wait any longer to hear about Lizzie's latest encounter with the fairy-tale world. They sat down on Lizzie's bed, backs against the headboard, while Lizzie repeated her conversation with Grey in as much detail as she could manage. Siobhan was a stickler for the finer points of a story and kept interrupting to ask how Grey had looked when he said a certain thing, or had he used just *those* words?

"But in the end he said he liked the tunes you dedicated to him?" Siobhan asked when Lizzie was done.

Lizzie nodded.

"I think maybe he likes you."

"No, he doesn't give off that kind of energy," Lizzie said. "I mean, he's about as sexy as you can imagine, but he's also got this wall up about anything that doesn't relate to his own people. I get the sense he's very insular."

"With a big hate-on for Irish fairies."

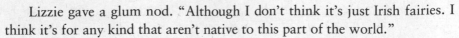

Lizzie gave a glum nod. "Although I don't think it's just Irish fairies. I think it's for any kind that aren't native to this part of the world."

"Even the Indians emigrated here at one point."

"I know. But apparently Grey's ancestors were already here when the Indians arrived."

"If not Grey himself."

Lizzie gave her cousin a surprised look. "Do you think?"

"Well, fairies are supposed to be immortal, aren't they?"

"I guess."

Lizzie hadn't considered that. Grey looked so much like a regular person, it wasn't until he did something impossible—starting up her car with a laying on of hands, stepping away into nowhere—that she'd remember he was this magical being. He wasn't like Walker with his antlers and deer head, which left no question as to what he was.

"Still, if he *has* been around that long," Siobhan said, "that's a long time to carry a feud."

Lizzie smiled. "Like the Irish aren't any better."

"We have excellent reasons for our feuds."

"Judging by these bogans I had the run-in with," Lizzie said, "I think he's got a pretty good reason, too. They really were horrible."

Siobhan shrugged. "That doesn't mean all fairies are going to be like that. There's always good and bad, and consider the source. Of course Grey is going to resent them. People always resent something new, especially when that something new is taking their land or their jobs or whatever. Remember Pappy's stories about what it was like when his dad moved the family from Ireland? There'd be signs up that said 'No Irish,' just like there were for the blacks. And while maybe some of the Irish *were* hooligans, he wasn't a bad person."

"I suppose."

"There's just a period of adjustment."

"Except, apparently, this one's been going on for a few hundred years. And I think it's different from how it is with people. It's not like fairies need jobs. And I get the sense that the whole concept of a homeland means a lot more to them than it does to human beings."

"What about Ireland and the Middle East? And that's just for starters."

Lizzie shook her head. "That's political. I think their idea of home runs a lot deeper."

"Okay," Siobhan said, laughing. "So down with all the nasty invading fairies, then. We should start putting up signs at our shows: 'Fairies go home.' Maybe we could make up T-shirts and bumper stickers."

"I don't think you should be saying stuff like that," Lizzie said as she gave a worried look around the room. "Didn't Pappy used to tell us that you're only supposed to refer to them as the Good Neighbours—or something like that—and if you didn't, you'd attract their unwelcome attention? And let me tell you, it can be pretty unwelcome. I don't ever want to see those bogans again."

"Do you think they're watching us right now?"

"I don't know. When they disappear, they go into some place called the between, but what does that mean? I'll bet they can see us from there if they want to."

"Now that's just creepy," Siobhan said.

Lizzie nodded. "I wish I hadn't thought of it."

They fell silent for a moment, then Siobhan got up from the bed.

"Well, screw them," she said. "Let's go join the boys for a whiskey and a few tunes."

Lizzie followed her cousin out of the room, pausing in the doorway to look back inside. Were there really invisible presences watching them, listening to their conversation? Pappy's stories were one thing, but having actually seen the bogans for herself . . . that put a whole new spin on how dangerous they could be.

"Are you coming?" Siobhan asked. "Or did you see someone interesting in there? Maybe tall, handsome, and Native?"

Lizzie glanced at where her cousin leaned against the wall, arms folded, a teasing smile playing on her lips.

"Hardly," she said.

She shut the door and let Siobhan usher her down the stairs. Halfway down, Siobhan made a startled cry from behind her. Lizzie started to turn, but her cousin was already tumbling into her and the two fell down the remaining stairs. Lizzie managed to grab hold of the banister and banged up against the wall, shaken but unhurt. Siobhan wasn't so lucky. She twisted as she fell and landed hard on her arm.

Lizzie got her balance and hurried down the last few steps to help her cousin.

"Ow, ow, *ow!*" Siobhan cried.

"Are you okay—no, that's stupid. Of course you're not okay. Can you sit up?"

After Lizzie helped her settle on a riser, Siobhan put a hand gingerly on her right arm and winced.

"Oh, god," she said. "I think I broke my arm."

"What happened?" Lizzie asked.

Siobhan glared up the stairs. "Someone pushed me."

Lizzie followed her gaze, but the stairway was empty.

"There's no one there," she said.

"No one we can see, maybe. But I *felt* someone push me—some invisible piece of fairy shite. Ow. God, this hurts."

"We have to get you to a hospital," Lizzie said.

She gave another glance up the stairs, nervous now. Did she hear a fading echo of mean-spirited laughter?

"I don't want to go to a hospital," Siobhan said. "I want to pound in the face of the little shite who pushed me."

But she let Lizzie help her to her feet and walk her into the bar.

They made no mention of invisible assailants when they told the others what had happened, leaving it at an unfortunate stumble on the stairs. Siobhan calmed down somewhat under the concerned attention she was getting, but her arm didn't feel any better.

"I guess the nearest hospital's in Tyson," Andy said.

Liam nodded. "But I've got a friend who's a doctor, and he lives here in town. He'll have a look at her."

"It's almost two o'clock in the morning," Lizzie said.

"It's okay. Things are different in the country. We don't follow rules and regs the same way you city folk do."

"Oh, like you're a country boy now," his friend Neil said.

"Arm," Siobhan said before Liam could respond. "Hurting a lot."

"Have a whiskey," Con told her, pushing the glass across the table to her.

Liam's doctor friend didn't seem particularly surprised to see the group of them show up on his front porch at such a late hour, though he did blink at them for a long moment. Standing barefoot in the doorway, in jeans with a T-shirt untucked, he didn't look much like a doctor. However, once they explained the situation, he woke up and became all business. Forty-five minutes later, they were all back at the bar, sitting around the table with another round of whiskeys—this round on the house, the bar man assured them before going back to closing up for the night.

"What are we going to do?" Siobhan said.

She had her right arm in a sling and wore a miserable expression.

"Do about what?" Andy asked.

"Me. Not playing. The band. Keep up here, Andy."

"We'll make do till you get better," Lizzie assured her.

"Yeah, you can work the merch table," Con said.

That actually teased a faint smile from Siobhan.

"You're willing to make that sacrifice?" she asked. Then she looked at the others. "The two fiddles is a big part of our sound—you know it's what gets us the better gigs."

"Plus the fiddlers are very cute," Con put in.

She smiled at him. "Thank you for that. But you heard the doctor. I can't play for weeks and we have a ton of gigs lined up, starting with the two shows we still have to play tomorrow. None of the people who've booked us are going to be very happy when we show up with only one fiddler and a new full-time merch table worker—" She glanced at Con. "—cute though they both may be."

"So we'll get someone to fill in till you're able to play," Andy said. "I'll take a cut in my share of the pay so that we can afford it."

Lizzie and Con both nodded in agreement.

That was the problem with the career that they'd chosen, Lizzie realized. In the best of circumstances, they made do and covered their expenses, and some months they even had a little left over to put in the bank. But they didn't make enough that they could afford medical insurance or any kind of compensation coverage for a situation such as this.

"Who would we get?" Lizzie asked.

Because she knew just how hard it would be to replace her cousin. They'd played together for so long that there was an intuitive bond between them, almost as though one musician was playing on two instruments. They traded harmonies at the drop of the hat, jumped tunes, or even keys, without having to warn the other.

Siobhan turned to Liam's friend Neil. "You play the fiddle, don't you?"

"Don't look at me," he said, holding up his hands. "There's no way I could keep up with you guys."

"So, who *do* we know that could keep up?" Andy asked.

"Who doesn't already have a gig," Siobhan put in.

They all fell silent.

"What about Geordie?" Con said finally.

Andy gave him a surprised look. "Geordie Riddell?"

"Unless there's another local fiddler named Geordie."

"No, it's just . . . he'd be booked for months, wouldn't he?"

Con shook his head. "I guess you don't know him that well. He's got this weird thing about commitment, so he really only does pickup gigs."

Siobhan gave him a surprised look. "But he's been in lots of bands. I can't count the times I've seen him around town."

"But they're never bands that tour," Con said. "Or at least, he doesn't tour with them."

"Then why would he play with us?" Lizzie asked.

"I don't know that he will, or can. But since it's just a fill-in gig, there's a good chance he'll do it. We could get him to play with us tomorrow, without mentioning the rest of our gigs. If it goes well, we can ask him then. If not, well, we've got five days to find another replacement before our next gig."

The other band members exchanged glances.

"I'd love to play with him," Lizzie said.

Siobhan gave a glum nod. "Me, too."

"He'd know all the tunes," Andy said. "Amy told me once that unless you write the tune just before you play it for him, he probably already knows it."

"And he *would* know it by the time you've gone through it a couple of times," Con said. "So, what do you think? Should I ask him?"

The rest of the band nodded their agreement.

"Then I'll call him first thing in the morning," Con said.

He lifted his whiskey and the others followed suit, clinking the glasses against each other.

"No offense," Liam said to Siobhan, "but this is going to be sweet. If you guys can get him to play, I mean."

Siobhan shrugged. "At least I'll get to *hear* some great music."

It wasn't until they were alone again in their room that the two women addressed what had really happened in the stairway.

"Oh, I'm sure I was pushed," Siobhan said in response to Lizzie's question. "I could feel the hands on the small of my back just before they gave me a shove."

They both looked nervously around the room.

"This is all my fault," Lizzie said.

"Oh, right."

"No, it is. I'm the one who got involved with them in the first place and that's gone and brought you to their attention."

"Mouthing off."

Lizzie shrugged. "They'd probably never even have heard you if they weren't already spying on me."

"It's not like you asked to be attacked by them in the first place."

"I know. But still . . ."

"Still, nothing. It wasn't your fault, and this is a free country where we can say what we want, so it isn't my fault either." Siobhan gave a meaningful look around the room. "There are other, more civilized ways of making your point in an argument."

They fell silent, almost expecting a response, but none came.

"So what do we do now?" Lizzie asked.

"I don't know." Siobhan gave another look around the room. "Keep our mouths shut and try to get along, I suppose."

Lizzie smiled. Like that would be easy for her cousin. She wasn't normally bad-tempered, but she certainly wasn't shy about speaking her mind.

"Do you remember any of the protections against fairies that Pappy told us?" she asked.

Siobhan reached into drawer of her night table with her right hand and took out the expected copy of the Bible.

"There's this," she said. "And I remember iron and rowan twigs and oatmeal."

Lizzie nodded. "None of which we have."

"We'll figure it out. I think I saw a mountain ash out back of the hotel, and that's the same diff' as rowan. In the meantime, I'm dead on my feet—well, not literally, considering I'm lying down and still breathing."

"I don't know if I can sleep."

"I suppose we could take turns standing guard," Siobhan said, "but what's the worst they're going to do? Tie our hair into fairy knots? They better have a damn light touch, because if I wake up and catch them at it, I'll have more than words for them, one-armed or not."

Lizzie nodded. Unless they'd drunk a lot—as Siobhan had last night—they were both light sleepers. It often felt like a curse, because musicians on the road didn't always get the best accommodations, but it would be useful now.

"But I'm not getting undressed," she said.

Siobhan smiled. "You'll have to at some point or you're going to smell louder than you play."

"Smells don't have volume."

"So sue me. But first help me get my top off."

Lizzie felt terrible all over again when Siobhan's injured arm was revealed in all its painful, bandaged glory.

"This sucks," she said.

"No," Siobhan said, "being dead would suck. This is just inconvenient."

"You make a much better invalid than I ever would."

"It's one of my strong points, ranked just under my humility."

Lizzie laughed. "Luckily, I got all the talent."

"I'd hit you, but I'm too tired and I only have one working arm. But consider yourself on probation."

"Yes, ma'am."

Siobhan shook her head. "Now you're just being mean."

Jilly

I was having lunch by myself in the greenhouse studio when I heard a tap on the glass pane of the side door that leads into the garden. Looking up, I saw it was Geordie and waved him in.

"Hey, stranger," I said. "You want some coffee? It's in the thermos," I added, pointing to the corner of the room by the little sink Sophie and I used to clean our brushes.

"Thanks," he said. "Do you want some?"

"No, I'm good."

There was a time when we were forever dropping in on each other, at all hours of the day and the night. That hadn't happened for the longest time. For me to go anywhere was a major production, and these days Geordie always called ahead. I suppose that small change might have reflected a much larger one, and in some ways it had. We weren't as much an everyday part of each others' lives anymore. But the good thing was that when we *were* together, it was like nothing had changed at all.

Geordie poured himself a cup from the thermos and brought it over to the empty chair beside my wheelchair. He had a sip of his coffee and grinned at me.

"This is *good*," he said.

"Don't get your hopes up," I told him. "I haven't gotten all culinary in my dotage. Goon made the coffee, just like he made this sandwich. Do you want some? Because I'm pretty much done."

"No, I already ate."

But after a moment he took one of the sandwich quarters still on my plate.

"How come you never got the nickname Stomach Riddell?" I asked him.

"Same reason no one calls you Smart Mouth Coppercorn."

"But those would be good gangster names."

He pretended to think about it, then shook his head.

"No, they're not tough enough," he said.

"Well, there you go. And all along I've been thinking that they were supposed to be silly."

"Silly would be if either of us actually were gangsters."

"I'd make a great gangster," I told him.

I gave him my tough girl look, but all he did was laugh.

"So what brings you by on a Sunday afternoon?" I asked.

"Are you up for a road trip?"

He had a twinkle in his eye that was so familiar, I actually got a little pang of nostalgia that rose up from deep in my chest. A melancholy for how things had once been when we were young and full of energy and . . . well, more mobile on my part.

"Unless you and Daniel already have plans," he added.

"No, I'm on my own today," I said. "Mona stayed overnight, but she left right after breakfast."

I wasn't sure why I didn't tell him that I'd broken up with Daniel last night. We usually shared all the details of our respective love lives. Maybe it was because I was the one who'd done the breaking up and I knew that, two years after the fact, he still carried a confused hurt over Tanya having dumped him the way she had, just like that, out of the blue. I guess I didn't want him to side with Daniel, who'd undoubtedly been as confused when I did the same thing to him.

"So, where are you bound?" I asked.

"The Custom House Hotel in Sweetwater. The Knotted Cord's playing there. One of their fiddlers sprained her arm last night, and they asked me to fill in for the matinée and evening shows."

I couldn't help the surprised look I gave him. Not that he was asked to fill in, because lord knows, he's one of the best fiddlers this city's ever produced. No, it was his asking me if I wanted to come along.

We used to do this all the time, go on little road trips to out-of-the-way towns and villages up the line where he'd have some gig. That stopped when he moved to L.A., and hadn't come up again since his return a few years ago.

"Why are you looking at me like that?" he asked.

"I don't know. This is just new . . . or rather, unexpected."

"Yeah, it's been awhile, hasn't it? But I haven't been taking out-of-town gigs for some time now."

It hadn't really occurred to me before, but now that he mentioned it, I realized it was true.

"How come?" I asked.

"There was always the revel . . ."

"Ah, the revel . . ."

He'd asked me to go a few times, back when he was first going, but I always felt like it was too much of an imposition, asking him to take care of the invalid I was at the time. After that, it just didn't come up again.

"You never did go," he said.

"You make it sound like they're not having them anymore."

"I'm sure they are. It's just that I found out yesterday that my going as often as I did was due to a . . . I don't know . . . a compulsion that was put on me."

"You mean like a spell?"

"I don't know. I guess."

"Well, what did Mother Crone say when you asked her about it?"

"She's the one who put it on me."

"What? And you haven't confronted her about it?"

"I haven't. Not yet. Christiana told me. She said she went to the mall and asked Mother Crone to lift the compulsion." He smiled suddenly. "Though knowing Christiana, I doubt it was necessarily a polite request."

I smiled with him. "Yeah, she can be feisty, all right."

"But the weird thing is the reason Mother Crone gave her for having put the compulsion on me in the first place. Apparently, she had some kind of premonition that if she didn't keep me close to the court, something bad was going to happen to me."

"What kind of something bad?" I asked, already worrying.

He shrugged. "She didn't know."

"And you're not worried?"

"Of course I'm worried. Mother Crone's a seer. But what can I do? If she doesn't know, and there's no one else I can ask . . ."

"Do we know that for sure? Maybe Bones or Cassie could help you."

"I don't know that Bones likes me all that much."

"Oh, pooh. It's your brother that drives him crazy. You he likes."

Geordie smiled—I've pretty much always been able to jolly him out of a mood, though during the fallout from the Tanya breakup it was a tough sell. He had the rest of my sandwich and washed it down with some more coffee before turning to me.

"You know about fairies," he said. "Have you ever heard of an enmity between the ones that are native to North America and the ones that immigrated here?"

"Not really. But Bramley would. He should be back some time this afternoon."

"Can't—I've got this gig, remember?"

"Right."

"So, do you want to come? I know it's short notice, but I thought it might be fun."

I thought about sitting here in the greenhouse for the rest of the day, all on my own unless I sought out Goon or Bramley for company.

"I'd love to get out," I said. "If it's not too much of a bother."

He just rolled his eyes at me.

"Okay, okay," I said. "I get the message. Yes, I'd love to come. When do we need to leave?"

He glanced at his watch. "Now?"

"Do I need to bring anything?"

"Well, depending on how we feel, we might want to stay overnight in the hotel. They'll comp us a room."

"Let me grab a few things."

I started to wheel away—I can get around now on my own two legs, but it's way slower and my balance still isn't great.

"It'll go quicker if you do the packing," I added.

He followed me into my room and got my bag from the closet while I wheeled over to the dresser and studied the clothes in the drawers.

"Have you talked to Christy about this fairy business?" I asked as I tossed a few things onto the bed.

He shook his head. "I meant to when I was over at his place last night, but then we got off on this whole other tangent of me making a CD to get the money to put down some roots. You know, actually get my own place, that kind of thing."

I paused on my way to the bathroom to look back at him. I could have told him he was welcome to keep living in my old apartment for as long as he wanted, but the idea of him actually making a commitment to record a CD—and all that would entail—took me too much by surprise.

"So, how do you feel about that?" I asked.

He shrugged. "I'm not saying no." He laughed and added before I could comment, "And yeah, I know. That *is* new. But I have to do something with my life. I look at Christy and Saskia and . . . I'm not exactly jealous. But I know I'd like that kind of stability in my life. I think I need it."

"Wow."

"I know. Took awhile, but maybe I'm finally growing up."

We'd both had troubled childhoods—it was part of what drew us to-gether all those years ago when we first met, working part-time at the post office. We didn't have real families of our own, so we had to make a new one for ourselves. He'd reconciled with Christy since then, and I was now work-ing on doing the same with my sister Raylene.

"We had to grow up too quickly," I told him, "so I think we were al-lowed to indulge ourselves with late childhoods. And really, whose business is it what we do with our lives?"

That sounded defensive, and I guess I was talking as much about myself as him, but he just nodded.

"I'd be doing it for myself," he said. "Because I want to."

"Then it's a good thing. Let me know if I can help."

He gave me a funny look, then walked over to the bed and started stow-ing the clothes I'd put there into my bag.

"Are you really going to need all of this?" he asked.

I was in the bathroom now, getting my toiletries together.

"Probably not," I called back. "But it's been forever since I've been on a road trip. Wait until I raid the kitchen."

"They have food at the hotel," Geordie said.

"Ah, but we need snacks for the drive."

It was another fifteen minutes before we were finally pulling out of Bramley's lane in Christy's old station wagon, which Geordie used far more often than Christy ever seemed to. My wheelchair was in the back. My bag was on the rear seat along with Geordie's fiddle and his small knapsack. The food I'd raided from the kitchen was in a plastic bag on the bench seat between us.

When I opened it, I found that Goon had slipped in sandwiches while he was helping me pack the food. Oh, and sensible man that he was, a couple bottles of water, too. I decided to save them for later and went straight to the road food.

"Tortilla chip?" I asked and offered Geordie the bag.

He laughed. "We're not even into the burbs yet."

"We have to do the best we can," I informed him. "It's not far to Sweet-water, so it'll be a short road trip and we've got a lot of food here."

He glanced at the bag of food and shook his head.

"You sure you're not part chipmunk?" he asked.

"Because I've brought this stash of food along?"

"Why else?"

"Well, maybe you thought my face was getting fat—though," I added as the thought came to me, "if I *was* an animal person, that's probably exactly what I'd be. Or maybe a mouse. Or a mosquito."

"As opposed to?"

"Oh, you know. The more Romantic kinds of animal people, like a deer or a wolf or an owl."

"Chipmunks are cute."

I nodded. "But they don't get any respect. And they're liable to get eaten by the wolves and owls."

"Which isn't very Romantic."

"No. Not unless someone like Robbie Burns had gotten hold of the story."

Geordie put on a thick Scots accent and began to recite: "Och, wee chipmoosie, ye dinnae hae sae lang. The warld it is a fierce auld place and . . . and . . ." He looked to me for help.

I shook my head. "You're on your own, Geordie, me lad, though you get big points for 'chipmoosie'."

"This is why I write tunes, not songs."

"Then I expect to hear 'Lament for a Wee Dead Chipmoosie' very soon."

We grinned at each other and I leaned back in my seat, happier than I'd been in a long time. I hadn't realized just how much I'd missed goofing around in Geordie's company, just the two of us, heading off to another gig where he'd be amazing and . . . well, I couldn't dance up a storm anymore, but I'd be an enthusiastic member of the audience all the same.

We weren't complete idiots for the rest of the drive, but we did keep it light, staying away from heavy personal stuff, which is why I still didn't bring up my having broken up with Daniel. There'd be plenty of time for that another day. Or maybe on the ride home. But we did talk a little more about this enchantment that Mother Crone had put on him, and then, of course, I got worried all over again about what sort of danger might be coming his way. Geordie being Geordie, he refused to let on that it was any big deal and turned the conversation to what he knew about the band he'd be playing with tonight.

I let him get away with it. I didn't want to talk about Daniel, he didn't want to talk about this. We could get to all of that later. For now, I'd rather just enjoy the drive, short though it was, because a little over an hour and forty minutes after pulling out of Bramley's lane, we were there, driving along Sweetwater's main street.

"Wow," I said, looking around. "This place has changed. It's all so . . ."

"Charming."

"Okay, I'll go with that. I was going to say touristy."

Geordie shrugged. "What are they supposed to do? The mills and mines are all closed, the logging industry's dead, and nobody's farming any more. The tourist trade is all they've got left."

"Oh, I'm not complaining," I told him. "Or even making fun. It's just a surprise, that's all. The last time I was here was with you and everything was wonderfully ramshackle."

Geordie smiled. "I'm guessing ramshackle's not so wonderful when you actually have to live with it."

"I think there's another tune title in there, but I'm too lazy to go looking for it."

I sat up a little straighter as we came up to the hotel.

"Now what?" Geordie asked.

"Nothing," I said, taking in the hotel's new paint job and the little patio out front. "It cleaned up well."

"I haven't been here for a few years myself," Geordie said. "I wonder if Eddie's still running the place."

"I remember liking him—he was so easy to tease. But why wouldn't he be there? I thought he was the owner."

Geordie nodded. "But he was always talking about moving to someplace warm." He pulled the car into a parking space alongside the hotel, then turned to me. "Shall I get the chair?"

"Not just yet, but I will need you to help me get out of this seat."

That's the problem when a chair's too low—I can't get the leverage to stand on my own. I made that mistake once on the sofa in my room at Bramley's and had to stay on it all night until Sophie came looking for me in the morning. Mostly I stick to my wheelchair. It's comfortable and easy to get out of when I need to, plus it's mobile, so I don't even have to get out of it if I'm feeling lazy.

I also use it out of the house a lot because I tire too quickly, and it's no fun walking with me when tortoises and snails are whipping by on either side. But I'm kind of self-conscious about meeting new people in it. No matter how nice they are, you're forever Wheelchair Girl in their minds and it puts this whole weird colour into your relationship.

So, while I knew I'd use it later, for now I wanted to hobble into the hotel with my canes and just be Cane Girl. When you stand upright, even when you can barely do it like I get when I'm tired, people at least see you as pretty much normal.

Geordie came around to my side of the car and helped me out. I leaned against the car while he got our stuff from the backseat and admired this young handsome guy who was walking our way from the front of the hotel. When Geordie got his head out of the car, he grinned and introduced me to Con Connelly, the Knotted Cord's new guitarist. He was the one who'd called to ask Geordie to fill in and, while I didn't know him personally, I had seen him playing in various bands over the years. I just hadn't known his name.

"Let me grab that," he said, taking my bag from Geordie.

They were both nice about pacing me to the hotel's foyer. Without me, they could easily have gotten there in a fraction of the time.

"A word of warning," Con added as we went through the front door. "Lizzie's gone all superstitious ever since Siobhan took her fall last night and is insisting we wear these little good-luck charms she's made up for us. She'll probably have one for you, as well."

He indicated something pinned to the front of his shirt, but turned away before I could have a real look at it. And then it got busy with the other band members showing up and Eddie coming from a back room to give both Geordie and me a hug. Eddie was the same jovial, balding man I remembered from years ago, and though I wasn't surprised he remembered Geordie—Geordie's played here a kazillion times, after all—I was surprised that he remembered me, too.

"Are you staying the night?" he asked.

Geordie and I looked at each other.

"I'm game if you are," I told him.

Eddie beamed when Geordie said we would.

"I love it," he said. "It'll be like old times, except there's no way you're talking me into swimming again. Not in the Kickaha in March."

"You seemed to like it the last time," Geordie said.

"No, that was the whiskey that liked it. I came down with a cold that lasted three weeks."

"How about if we say 'pretty please'?" I asked.

"Don't you dare go all puppy-eyed on me," he said, his voice stern, his eyes twinkling. "You know I can't say no to those eyes of yours."

I guess he really did remember me, because I was the one who'd actually sweet-talked him into playing polar bear that March afternoon a few years ago. In my own defense, I'd been more than a little tipsy at the time. We all had been.

He checked us into a room with twin beds and then, after introductions were made with the rest of the band, we all trooped into the bar and commandeered a table by the window. Or at least they all trooped. I was a little

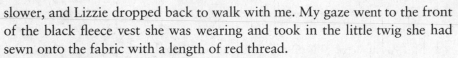

slower, and Lizzie dropped back to walk with me. My gaze went to the front of the black fleece vest she was wearing and took in the little twig she had sewn onto the fabric with a length of red thread.

"Having fairy trouble?" I asked.

She paused and got this strange look, part embarrassed, part guilty. I stopped with her, leaning on my canes.

"What do you mean?" she said.

"Con told us you were having everybody wear charms, and that looks like a rowan twig."

"God, of course," she said, and it was like a little light went on behind her eyes. "You're *that* Jilly Coppercorn."

"I didn't know there was more than one of me, though that would be handy. You know, for when I didn't want to do something, but had to show up anyway. I could just send my double."

"No, I mean, you know all about fairies, what with your paintings and everything."

"I don't paint so much anymore."

"Oh. I'm sorry. I wasn't thinking. . . ."

"It's okay. So what's with the fairy charms?"

She glanced at the table, before looking back at me.

"Can we talk about it later?" she asked. "Not everyone's in the loop. The guys'd think we were nuts if they knew what we've seen—Siobhan and I, that is. Well, I saw it, but Siobhan's the one who got hurt. . . ."

I gave her a steady look. "Siobhan was hurt by fairies?"

She nodded.

"And you have everybody wearing charms so that they won't get hurt as well?"

"I know. It sounds so stupid."

I shook my head. "It doesn't sound stupid, it sounds unfair. If your other band members are in danger, don't you think they have the right to know about it?"

"I don't think they're really in danger."

"Hence the charms," I said.

"They'll think I'm crazy."

"I've been there," I told her. "But it's better than the alternative, which is somebody else getting hurt because they don't know what's going on."

"I suppose . . ."

I left her to think about it and continued on to the table, settling happily in a chair when I got there. I was still stiff from the drive, and all the excitement in the foyer had tired me out. Lizzie took the other empty chair across the table from me.

"So, what were you guys talking about?" Andy asked.

I glanced at Lizzie and saw that she just couldn't do it. So I turned back to Andy.

"Fairies," I said.

Lizzie sighed and stared down at the table. Siobhan's head jerked up. Geordie looked from Lizzie to me with interest, while the other two men smiled.

"Fairies," Andy repeated. "Like the little fluttery things that you see on T-shirts at the Ren Faires?"

I nodded. "Although the real ones come in all sorts of different shapes and sizes."

"You're being serious, aren't you?"

Beside him, Con was grinning. He turned to look at Lizzie.

"I never thought you were into that kind of thing," he said.

"I wasn't," she said. "I'm not. But I haven't been given much choice about it."

She shot me a look that gave her words a double meaning. She didn't seem so much angry with me as a little relieved that I'd brought it up. But also embarrassed.

"I suppose you might as well hear the whole thing," she went on and proceeded to tell how her car had broken down at the crossroads, taking us through the story all the way to when a pair of invisible hands gave Siobhan a shove down the stairs last night.

Andy and Con just looked at her when she was done, waiting for the punch line.

"These bogans," Geordie asked. "Was there any indication as to what court they were from?"

"Wait a second," Con said as Lizzie shook her head. "This is all a joke, right? No one's taking it seriously."

"I am," I told him.

Geordie smiled at the men. "I know exactly what you're feeling," he said. "Trust me. I spent years pretending that there's no such thing as fairies and ghosts and monsters in the dark. Unfortunately, what we'd *like* to believe is true, and what actually *is,* can be two different things."

"No, come on." Con looked to Andy for support. "Am I the only one here who's not buying into this?"

Andy fingered the rowan twig that he had sewn on his shirt pocket.

"So that's why you wanted us to wear these," he said.

"There was no one on the stairs with us," Siobhan said. "Just me and Lizzie, a few steps down from me. But someone pushed me because I *totally* felt their hands on my back."

"But why?" Con said, shaking his head. "Even if this is possible—which I don't buy for a minute—why would fairies suddenly attack you?"

"Because," Geordie said, "from what Lizzie told us, she was badmouthing them. Normally, you can say what you want and nothing happens—it's not like the old days when people really did have to be careful about what an off-hand remark might invoke. The fairy courts are peaceful now, coexisting with our world. But that doesn't mean there aren't rogue fairies, which is why it would really be helpful to know if they're associated with a specific court."

"What difference would it make?" Andy asked.

"We could petition their queen for a hearing—settle the problem before it gets any worse."

"Oh, please," Con said. "Fairy queens? Courts? Who are you kidding?"

Andy nodded. "And even if they were real, where would you start to look for them?"

"Well," I said, "Geordie's girlfriend for the past couple of years has been the queen of a fairy court in the Woodforest Plaza Mall."

Con laughed. "Fairies live in shopping malls?"

"Mother Crone's not my girlfriend," Geordie said to me, "and she's not a queen, she's a seer." Then he turned to Con. "Fairies live everywhere. You just can't see them because they exist in—"

"The between," Lizzie said. "That's what Walker told me. Or maybe it was Grey."

"I was going to say the otherworld," Geordie said. "But they certainly spend time in between the two."

Con shook his head yet again, but before he could speak, Lizzie cut him off.

"Nobody mentioned anything about courts," she said to Geordie and me. "But Walker talked about clans or something. He said he was a cerva, and Grey belonged to the corbae."

"Those aren't clan names," I said. "They're like . . . species. Or tribes. I've never known any cerva—who are the deer people, I guess, from what you said about Walker. But we know a number of corbae." At Geordie's puzzled glance, I added, "Lucius and the crow girls, for starters."

"Oh, right," he said. "I always forget."

"So they're different from fairies?" Andy asked.

"Well, I didn't think so," I told him. "I thought they were all just spirit people. You know, kind of the embodiment of places and animals and things.

I didn't even know there was an enmity between them. . . ." I looked at Geordie. "Except weren't you saying something about that earlier?"

He nodded. "Hazel giving the finger to a bunch of cousins on the drive into the city."

"That's the word Grey and Walker kept using," Lizzie said. " 'Cousins.' I guess it doesn't mean they're related, does it?"

"Not in the same way we use the word," I told her. "It's what they call each other in general, like we'd say people."

"So these cousins you know . . . ," Con began, then he just shook his head. "I can't believe I'm having this conversation."

"It takes getting used to," Geordie said. "What did you want to know about them?"

"Well, where'd they come from? I get that fairies come from fairy tales, but I never heard stories about—what did you call them? Corb-heys?"

"Corbae," I said. "And I'm sure you have, but you didn't realize it. Their stories just aren't as easily accessible to the general populace because Disney hasn't made a movie about them, or any of the cousins, really. I don't think things like *The Jungle Book* or *The Lion King* really count because that's just anthropomorphized animals. They're not . . ." I had to think of the right word and settled for, "mythic. But you've heard of Coyote, and how Raven created the world—those kinds of things?"

"Yeah. I just don't think of them as real." He gave me a curious look. "So, are you trying to tell me that they're *all* real? Zeus and Krishna and Thor and everybody?"

"I've never met any of the more famous ones," I said. "Or I haven't, knowingly. They mostly go about their business just the way we do, and it's hard to get a take on their mythic status. You just forget. Like that fellow Lucius I mentioned earlier? He's supposedly the Raven who made the world, except you'd never know it. He never talks about it, and I don't think about it most of the time. Whenever I do, it hits me all over again how weird and amazing the world is."

"What I want to know," Siobhan said, "is what can we do to make sure they don't attack us again? Are these little charms enough? Do we just make sure we don't badmouth them?"

"That can't hurt," Geordie said.

Lizzie sighed. "But it can happen again, right? They might do something else to another one of us?"

"The charms will keep them at bay," Geordie said, trying to sound confident.

"Your problems seem to stem from having gotten on the wrong side of some pranksters," I added, "and they're not strong enough to overcome basic protections like rowan."

"I'd recommend we just do the gig," Geordie went on, "this afternoon and tonight. Tomorrow we can take a drive to the mall and see if Mother Crone can help us sort this out."

"I'd recommend we get our heads examined," Con said. "Or at least the lot of you."

"Want me to call Walker or Grey?" Lizzie asked. "Maybe that'll convince you."

"Not a good idea," Geordie said quickly. "When Walker gave you the gift of his name, it wasn't to use it frivolously."

"And from what you said about Grey," I added, "I don't think he'd much appreciate it, either."

"I know," Lizzie said. "It's just that if they could see what I've seen . . ."

Geordie nodded, returning his attention to Con and Andy.

"Look," he said. "I know exactly what's going through your heads. Like I told you earlier, I've been there before, and that was *after* I'd had the real thing rubbed in my face, and on more than one occasion. That's one of the main protections fairy have against us: we don't want to believe in them. And if we do interact with them, we'll find any kind of an explanation to convince ourselves that whatever we've just experienced doesn't have a magical origin.

"But that doesn't mean that they're not real, or that you're not in danger. So all I ask of you today is, just wear the charms and carry on the way you would otherwise. It doesn't hurt anybody, and well, better safe than sorry, right?"

"You see why I didn't want to tell them?" Lizzie asked me. "I knew they'd just think I was making it up."

"It's not like that," Andy said. "It's just . . . well, come on. It's a lot to take in, that's all."

"Wait'll some invisible little booger pushes you down the stairs," Siobhan put in.

"I think that was bogan," Con said, smiling. He turned to Geordie. "We can do what you're asking. I mean, this is about as crazy a business as I've ever heard, but I know you're a straight-shooter, and there's no way Lizzie would make stuff up just to get some attention." His gaze moved to her. "Whatever happened to you, I know that you believe it, and I'm going to leave it at that for now."

Lizzie seemed surprised, but she gave him a quick smile.

"Thanks," she said.

"Ditto for me," Andy added.

Siobhan held up her watch. "You guys are going on in an hour."

We looked around and saw that while we'd been so deep in our conversation, the bar had started to fill up. Half the tables were full and, now that we were pulled out of the little world we'd fallen into, the buzz of chatting, the clink of glasses, and the general hubbub of the crowd was so loud that I didn't know how we'd missed it.

"Do you want to freshen up?" Geordie asked me.

I nodded. "If you could get my chair, I'll meet you in the foyer so we can go upstairs together."

"No problem." He stood up, and looked around the table at others. "Just let me get ready and then maybe we can go over what you want me to do."

"I'll write up a set sheet with all the tunes listed," Lizzie said.

I smiled as Geordie shook his head.

"Don't worry about that," he said. "Just tell me the names of the tunes and how often you want to go through them before you start each set, and I'll be okay."

He wasn't bragging and probably didn't even realize how that sounded. To him, he was just telling it like it was, because he really was that good and didn't need more than that. But Lizzie and Andy appeared a little worried.

"It'll be cool," Con told them.

Siobhan grinned. "Maybe I don't get to play today, but I am going to have so much fun watching this show." She turned to me. "You want to sit with me behind the merch table?"

"You've got a date," I told her.

I used my canes to get up and happily, nobody tried to help me. I mean, I like it when people help me if I ask them to, but I hate when it's assumed that I'm useless. If I'd come in using the wheelchair, that's exactly how it might have been.

"Give me twenty minutes," Geordie said to the band members.

Then he left to get my chair while I made my way to the foyer. I actually beat him and was leaning against the wall by the old elevator, waiting for him when he wheeled in my chair. I sank gratefully into its cushion and let him push me into the elevator.

"Oh god," Geordie said, as the doors closed. "Was I sounding just like Christy out there?"

"Yes, you were very take-chargy."

"I mean with all that lecturing I was doing about fairies and spirits."

"You handled it perfectly," I assured him.

"Because I know where Con and Andy are coming from."

I smiled. "I remember. I was there, Geordie, me lad."

He returned my smile.

"Yeah," he said. "You always were, weren't you?"

Later, when we were up in our room, I had to ask him.

"So you and Mother Crone broke up?"

I'd washed up and changed into another top in the bathroom, an awkward procedure since it was pretty much the size of a small closet. But now I was sitting in my wheelchair, watching as Geordie rosined his bow and checked to make sure his fiddle was in tune. I liked the way the light came in the window and made his hair glow. It looked as though he was giving off the luminescence and I wished I could capture it in a sketch, but I had neither the necessary materials nor the motor skills to do it justice. Not anymore. Instead, I had to hold it in my memory, the way other people who aren't artists do. But did they see light the same way?

Geordie looked over at me and shrugged in response to my question.

"I don't know if we were ever really a couple," he said. "We were together, sure, but not like you and Daniel are."

"Um, we're not so much a couple anymore, either."

He gave me a surprised look.

"Oh, that sucks. Are you okay?"

"Actually, I was the one who broke up with him."

"But—"

"I know. He was perfect. But maybe that was the problem, or—not so much him being perfect, as everything between us deferred to what he thought I wanted out of the relationship, which for some people *would* be perfect."

Saying it aloud made me wince a little. It sounded so petty and ungrateful.

Geordie shook his head. "When did you buy into the whole 'bad boy' routine?"

"I didn't. I haven't. I know what it sounds like, but I wasn't looking for a bad boy. I just wanted him to bring something of himself to the relationship."

"Okay, that I get," Geordie said. "It's sort of where things were with Mother Crone and me."

"Really?"

He nodded. "But different, too. She'd never leave the mall. She wouldn't, you know, just drop by the loft, or go rambling through Crowsea late at night, or hang out in a diner, or take in a movie or a concert. Everything we did together, we did at the mall, or at her place in the between."

It was funny. All those things he'd just mentioned were things we used to do together.

But all I said was, "I guess most relationships are like that—one person always seems to be putting more into it than the other."

"Pretty much." He gave me a flash of a smile. "You'd think we'd get it right after all the years human beings have been in the world."

"We're slow learners or something, I guess."

The smile returned. "Or something."

He put his fiddle and bow back into their case and closed it up.

"So, what do you think about all this fairy business?" he asked. "Bogans attacking Lizzie, Siobhan getting pushed down the stairs."

"I don't know what to think. I just hope you'll be careful up on stage this afternoon and tonight."

"Careful doesn't make for great art."

I stuck my tongue out at him for quoting me back to myself. How many times had I given that advice? Too many to count.

"You know what I mean," I said.

"I do," he told me. "And I will."

Edgan

Saturday night, closing in on eight o'clock. The last of the cleaning staff had left by now and the warehouse-sized interior of Computer World was dark except for what light came in from the lampposts out in the parking lot and a few strategic fluorescent overheads that had been left on inside. But Edgan didn't need light to go about his business.

He was a curious little man, born a treekin—a kind of fairy about the height of a man's knee, made of twigs and mulch and leaves and moss, all held together in the shape of a human body with a weaving of braided grasses and vines. Treekin needed to replenish their body parts from time to time—when a twig got old and chipped, or when a grass braid snapped and the press of leaves and moss that gave shape to limbs began to fall away. The materials they needed for repair were easy to find, even in a city, for there were always gardens and parks to plunder amongst the tall towers of concrete and steel.

But in the past few decades, many of the treekin began to utilize bits and pieces of electronics and computer parts for their repairs, metamorphosing over time into creatures made as much of wiring and circuitry as they were of organic material. Eventually, some, like Edgan, became creatures entirely made of synthetic castoffs; each techno treekin—as they came to be called—as individual as the materials they were able to scrounge. In Edgan's case, he had a torso built up around a computer motherboard; his limbs and head were a complicated tangle of wiring and less identifiable objects, though his nose was certainly a spark plug and his eyes a pair of camera lenses.

He was in Computer World tonight because he'd recently seen another of the techno treekin sporting an iPod in the twisting snarl of wires that held her torso together, and he simply had to have one himself. He already had a PDA wired into his motherboard body—as well as a digital camera and a pair of cell phones—but its memory capacity couldn't match the sixty giga-bytes of the iPod. The iPod would be perfect for storing the data he pilfered from the Internet, but he also liked the shiny whiteness of its case for how it matched his spark plug nose.

So he wandered up and down the aisles, searching for the appropriate display, until he finally found the iPods racked with the other MP3 players in the music section of the store. He pulled one down and after opening its package, happily busied himself attaching the player to his torso, weaving the lovely white power and earphone cords into the other wiring on his arms. He stood and admired his reflection in a display case, strutting back and forth in front of the glass, swinging his arms.

Lovely. The patterns he'd knotted with the white wires looked like tat-toos amongst the darker wiring of his arms. Into the knots, he'd shaped sym-bols taken from traditional treekin tribal markings—the ancient glyphs that calendared the trees in the long ago—and had done a fine job of it, if he did say so himself.

After awhile he went looking for an electric outlet and plugged himself in to charge the batteries of his new iPod and his other peripherals. The out-let he'd chosen was near the big windows at the front of the store, giving him a view of the big parking lot. Across the lot he could see the dark bulk of the Woodforest Plaza Mall where the rest of his court were going about their business. He would rejoin them soon enough, but for now he was happy to sit beside the cash register, kicking his heels against the counter, which made a cheerful thumping sound—

Until he saw a half-dozen of the Bogan Boys go ambling across the park-ing lot.

He stopped kicking the counter and hid behind the register, hoping he hadn't been seen. It wasn't so much that he was afraid of them, as that the Bo-gan Boys were always up to no good, and the trouble that followed them had a tendency to spill over onto anyone unfortunate enough to be in their vicinity.

Over the past few years, they had become more and more like those old Irish wolves, the hard men. The hard men had been a pack of shapechanging spirits who'd once held the city under their sway until, rumour had it, the green land itself arose and swallowed them whole. But where the hard men were tall, with old dark hurts burning in their eyes, the Bogan Boys were half the size of a full-grown human and carried only spite in their small dark eyes. What they lacked in height, they made up for in muscle, stocky as dwarves, but quick and cunning. Their heads were large, their hair raggedy, their teeth sharp. And they were not at all pleasant company.

But Edgan wasn't looking for their company. He hadn't been looking for them at all and would be quite content to keep his own counsel, and let them keep theirs. Except, like any treekin, he had too much cat in his blood—a deep-rooted feline twitch that would travel the length of his nerves to tickle his mind at the faintest sign of a mystery, no matter how small. He could no more let a riddle go unsolved than he could pass by the perfect length of colourful wire without picking it up. So curiosity had him unplug himself from the outlet and then slip out of the store through a bodach door to trail along behind the little pack, his head brimming with questions.

What were bogans doing out tonight in their grey hunting leathers, knives strapped to their waists, bows and arrows in hand? Because hunts were forbidden in the city, and who was brave or foolish enough to go out into the green and wild to dare the wrath of the first people, from whom immigrant humans and fairies had already stolen so much? Not Big Dan Cockle and his little hard men for all their strutting bravado, yet here they were all the same, armed for a hunt at the north edge of the city, where protection for fairies ended unless you kept to the man-made highways and roads.

Edgan hesitated when the bogans stepped from the safety of the parking lot into the adjoining field, their footsteps crunching the dry, dead weeds underfoot. He looked across the field. In a half year, if not sooner, the bulldozers would come to clear this land, too, and some new enormous store would spring up in its place. Concrete and glass and steel. And with the man-made structure in place, it would be safe for fairies to venture out into it.

But until then it belonged to the green-brees, the native spirits of the wild and the green. Fairy-kind were not welcome in their lands—especially not to hunt. Though perhaps Big Dan and his men only carried weapons because they ventured into those chancy lands, to protect themselves in case of attack. Which didn't begin to explain the *why* of their daring the green-brees' anger.

Edgan looked across the field. A fair distance from where he stood, he could see a small copse of wintered oaks, bare limbs reaching skyward with clusters of twigs grasping for the stars. A thicket of scrub brush grew out of the jumble of rocks at the feet of the oaks. The snow that lay in patches in the field would be thicker in there, crusted with ice.

As he watched, the Bogan Boys made their way steadily across the field toward that oak copse. Edgan hesitated a moment longer, then entered the field himself, pinpricks of nervousness worrying between his shoulder blades.

Unlike the bogans, he chose his route carefully and didn't make a sound. Halfway across the field, he sensed a presence in the air above him long before he actually heard the sound of wings. He immediately dropped to the ground and crouched motionless in the browned weeds until the presence was gone.

Owl, he saw when he felt he could take the chance to look. He watched the broad wings of the bird in the sky ahead of him, though in its present shape he couldn't tell if it was an ordinary bird or a green-bree. It appeared to be making for the same copse the Bogan Boys were, but then it swerved and sailed toward the line of trees at the far edge of the field.

Of the Bogan Boys there was no sign—not until the owl had passed the copse. Then their grey bogan shapes rose from the cover of dead weeds and they continued toward the oaks, dry vegetation breaking under their boots.

Edgan hurried after them, but they disappeared in amongst the trees before he could catch up. When he reached the edge of the copse himself, he listened for a long moment. He could hear the murmur of conversation. Bogan voices and another, unfamiliar one, low and resonating.

Now would be a good time to turn around and go back, because if the bogans caught him here, they'd know he was spying on them—something that would put any fairy in a bad humour. And considering that bogans were bad-humoured in the first place and could carry a grudge forever, retreat was the sensible option.

But he'd come this far, and a secret meeting between Big Dan's Bogan Boys and some mysterious stranger, all the way out here in the wild and green, was far too enticing to resist. Gossip and stories were like coin in the fairy realms and this had the potential for a grand tale, depending on who the bogans were meeting and what they were up to. In the right ears, a tale like this could have Edgan rich in favours owed him.

And if they didn't catch him spying, then none would be the wiser, would they?

So he crept over the boulders, avoiding the patches of ice and snow as he followed a rabbit trail through the brush that took him in the direction of the voices. When he was close enough to hear what was being said, he pushed the "record" button on the PDA that was wired into his upper arm.

". . . unlikely that Grey has taken a human under his protection. He dislikes them almost as much as he does your people."

Edgan didn't recognize the stranger speaking, but his low voice seemed to wake a sympathetic quiver in the rocks underfoot. It was a voice that had to belong to an old and powerful spirit, and not one from any of the local fairy courts or he would recognize it. Sooner or later, everyone came by to see Mother Crone.

"I'm only telling you what happened, Odawa," Big Dan responded. "Are you calling me a liar?"

Odawa, Odawa, Edgan repeated to himself, trying to find a reference. Oh, if only he was connected to his database back at the court. If the name was in there, he'd know in a moment who the bogans were meeting with in secret.

"I'm not calling you anything," Odawa replied. "I'm merely making an observation."

"Well, observe this: your Grey has him a human doxie, and that's a plain fact because we took the thumps to find it out."

"It's a shame you weren't able to give as good as you got."

"Wasn't from lack of trying."

Edgan decided to dare a peek. He took one look, rising just high enough so he could see over the rocks he was hiding behind, then quickly dropped out of sight once more. In that moment he'd seen the Bogan Boys lounging about under the trees. Big Dan and the man he'd called Odawa stood together in a pool of moonlight, a few steps away from the others.

Edgan shivered in his hiding place. No wonder he hadn't recognized the stranger. He was neither human nor fairy, but a green-bree. Some old spirit of this land, tall and grim faced with a sheen like scales on his skin, his lips thin, his eyes an eerie milky-white. Those were a seer's eyes—blind in this world, seeing far into others.

A blind green-bree, Edgan thought. Powerful and with a speaking name of Odawa. He didn't need his database to tell him that this was something new. And if a green-bree was meeting and making plans with bogans, it meant real trouble.

Oh, this was big—too big to bargain with. He'd take this to Mother Crone and give it to her free. But first he needed to learn more.

"You're certain they're lovers?" Odawa asked.

"That or close friends, but who beds a friend, and what else is a woman good for except for bedding?"

That brought a chorus of snickers from the other bogans.

"Of course," Odawa said in a tone of voice that made Edgan, at least, know the green-bree wasn't of the same opinion. "And you know where to find her?"

"Oh, sure. She's a musician—plays our music, she does, the little pluiker, but licks the ass of the corbae."

"You've seen her do this?" Odawa asked, his voice dry.

"Nah, but you know she would if he told her to. Those damn blackbirds have everyone treating them like they're the kings of Shite Hill."

"I gave her a push down the stairs," one of the other bogans said, "but I got the wrong one. Her sister or something. Still, she went down hard."

The other bogans laughed.

"Why?" Odawa asked.

" 'Cause I pushed her."

"No, why did you push her?"

"She were mouthing off about us."

"Deserved it," another bogan said. "It ain't right, guttermouths like that, disrespecting us."

They should come by the mall, Edgan thought, and see what was for sale on the shelves of the toy stores and gift shops. Enough pretty little fairies to turn your stomach—as though there were only flitters and nothing else in the Fairy realm. A quick tour of such stores would show them the real meaning of disrespect for every denizen of Fairy who wasn't tiny and sweet.

"So she's a musician," Odawa said.

"And they're not bad," Big Dan told him—reluctantly, Edgan thought. "She and that band of hers. Saw her outside with Grey between their sets last night."

"What were they doing?"

"Talking. But we weren't stupid enough to get to close to *him*, so who knows what it was about?"

"When she'd be licking his ass," one of the bogans put in.

They all laughed, except for the green-bree.

"We just had us a look so we'd have something to tell you," Big Dan said. "Like you asked us to. Keeping our eyes open and all that shite."

"I appreciate your making the extra effort."

"Yeah, well, it's not like we care for any of them. The blackbirds and their like won't even let us have a ramble through their lands."

"Maybe that's because you're hunting their kin," Odawa said. "How would you feel if they hunted your people?"

"I thought you didn't like the bugger."

"I don't. I'm merely showing you how it might seem from their perspective."

"Who gives a flying shite about their perspective?"

"Point taken."

They fell silent for a moment, and it was so quiet Edgan could hear the harsh breathing of the bogans.

"Take me to her," Odawa said then.

"They're in Sweetwater and that's a ways, 'less we step between."

What a strange comment, Edgan thought. Why should stepping between matter to a green-bree? The between and otherworld were as free for them to use as for any spirit. Walking to Sweetwater would take them a few hours, unlike travelling through the between where they could be there in a fraction of the time. So why did the green-bree feel he needed to avoid the between?

"We have time," Odawa said. "And it's such a fine night for a stroll, don't you think?"

Which didn't answer Edgan's curiosity. But it didn't seem to mean anything to the bogans, one way or another.

"You know best," Big Dan said.

" 'Course he does," a bogan close to where Edgan hid whispered to his companion. "Isn't he supposed to know everything?"

They both snickered, and Edgan filed away that comment with the few other bare bones of information he'd managed to glean concerning this spirit.

When they set off, he shut off his PDA and stopped recording. He gave the group a few moments head start before he followed after them, pausing when the protection of the trees ended and there was only the open field in front of him. The others were already halfway across, making for the highway.

What now? Edgan wondered. Follow them to Sweetwater, or take what he already had to Mother Crone?

"How curious," Mother Crone said after she'd had Edgan play back the conversation for a third time. "You said he was blind?"

Edgan nodded. He turned off his PDA.

"I didn't get much more than a glimpse," he said, "but he was certainly blind and definitely—"

He almost said "a green-bree," but caught himself in time. Mother Crone didn't feel the same animosity toward the native spirits that so many fairies did, nor did she approve of negative references to them.

"—one of the spirits native to this land," he finished. "And an old and powerful one, too. I didn't dare chance taking a photo, but I dearly wanted to."

"No point in showing your hand," Mother Crone agreed.

"But maybe you would have recognized him. There's no reference in the database."

Mother Crone nodded. "It's a big land, this Turtle Island, filled with spirits and more emigrating to it every day. It would have been more surprising if you *had* found a reference."

She was right, of course, but that hadn't stopped Edgan from checking. All that was to be found there was the information he'd downloaded himself when he got back from the oak copse.

"Why do you think this Odawa won't travel by the between?" he asked.

Mother Crone smiled. "Maybe he really does enjoy walking at night."

Edgan snorted.

"But more likely he's avoiding someone," she went on. "It's not so easy to hide your presence once you leave this world to walk in another."

Thinking back on the conversation he'd recorded, Edgan said, "This is corbae business. That's who he's hiding from."

"Probably."

"Maybe we should we tell them. They would owe us a favour then."

"They would. But I'm curious . . ."

Her voice trailed off. Edgan waited patiently for her to finish her thought and share it with him.

They were in the central part of the mall, sitting on the stairs leading up from the food court. Below them fairies were dancing and gossiping, but Mother Crone looked past them, her gaze on the night that lay outside the mall's glass doors.

"If they're walking to this place . . ." she began.

"Sweetwater. Yes."

"How far is it?"

Edgan shrugged. "A few hours by foot."

He'd come back to the court when he realized he had time to give the information to Mother Crone and still catch up to the bogans and their mysterious companion before they reached Sweetwater, if she thought he should. He had no reluctance to go by the between. Truth was, like most fairies, he preferred it because it meant there was no chance he'd run into any of the green-brees on their own lands. The between belonged to no one and everyone. And while Mother Crone was right—it *was* impossible to hide your presence there—the reverse was also true. It was easy to sense the presence of others and so keep out of their way.

"I don't trust bogans," Mother Crone said. "Especially not Big Dan. And I wonder why anyone would ally themselves with them. They're hardly formidable."

"They've been trying to fill the shoes of the hard men these past few years," Edgan said.

He saw her eyes fill with memory.

"Now *they* were dangerous," she said.

Edgan nodded. "But something in the wild and the green swallowed them whole and never spat a bit of them back out."

"And you think the bogans are trying to take their place?"

"You should see the way they swagger about—they're worse than ever."

Mother Crone gave a slow nod. "I've not really been paying much attention to them. Are they feuding with the corbae?"

Edgan shrugged. "No one much cares for the blackbirds."

"They always struck me as minding their own business."

"Trouble is," Edgan said, "no one really knows what their business is, so it's easy to get on the wrong side of them."

Mother Crone gave him a sharp look.

"Have our people been having trouble with them again?" she asked.

"Not like when the mall was being built."

That had been a bad time. The developers had bulldozed a crow roost to make the mall and the corbae had been furious, doing their best to make the building process as unprofitable as they could. But the fairies had been delighted with a new safe incursion into forbidden lands and made a point of helping the builders, all of which had caused no end of trouble between the two. It took a meeting between the oldest of the local corbae and the Queen of all the Newford fairy courts to finally set the matter to rest. With the accusations and demands that flew back and forth between both sides, it had not been an easy task, even for such level heads as Lucius Portsmouth and Tatiana McGree.

Mother Crone gave a slow nod.

"Was there anything in the database about this Grey the bogans and Odawa spoke of?" she asked.

"It's a common speaking name," Edgan said, "among our people as much as among theirs."

"So we only know that he's corbae. Fair enough. Are you willing to go to Sweetwater to see what else you can learn?"

"Of course."

"And you'll be careful?"

"I'm always careful. It's how I've come to live as long as I have."

She smiled. "Only be doubly so tonight, as a favour to me."

Edgan stood up and gave her a little bow.

"I will," he said.

Then he stepped into the between and was gone.

Geordie

I'm never happier than when I'm playing music, and this gig at the Custom House was the perfect venue to simply fall into the music and let it take me away. The afternoon crowd was large and appreciative, but the room was packed wall-to-wall with people for the evening show, and they greeted us with a roar of approval as soon as we took the stage. We hadn't even played a note yet.

The kids were great to play with—okay, they're in their late twenties, early thirties, but they seemed like kids to me. Young and full of energy and sass. I'd played with Con before, but Lizzie was a revelation on the fiddle and, next to Miki Greer, I decided that Andy was the best accordion player to come out of the Newford Celtic music scene. Their arrangements were inventive, but never so far out that you lost the magic of the tune, and they kept me on my toes. Which is good, because if it's not challenging, what's the point in playing?

So I was having a good time, the band and crowd were having a good time, and even Siobhan—relegated to the merch table where Jilly had joined her—was grinning and bobbing her head, though I knew she'd rather be up here on stage. I didn't blame her. I love going to see a good band, just sitting back and letting the music wash over me, but there's always a part of me that wants to be up there *playing,* it doesn't matter how good the music is. When you're a musician, you want to play.

We had Siobhan up for a few songs in the first show—singing lead on one and harmony on the others—and again in the earlier part of the evening show. Near the end of our last set for the night, with the Corona clock over the bar reading twelve-thirty, she got up to sing "The New Doffing Mistress" with Lizzie. I stopped her before she could leave the stage at the end of the song.

"What's your favourite tune?" I asked.

She gave me a puzzled look. "God, I don't know. There are so many great ones."

"Sure. But if you were going to play a tune right now, what would you play?"

"Something fun and fast," she said, "like 'The Mouth of the Tobique,' or maybe 'The Bucks of Oranmore.' "

"Hold that thought," I told her.

I went to the back of the stage, put my fiddle in its case and got her fiddle out of hers. I gave the tuning a quick check, adjusted the E string, then brought it back to the front of the stage and handed it to her. We could have used my fiddle, but I wanted her to be as comfortable as possible. And I know, fiddles and bows all seem pretty much the same, but they're not. Every player gets used to the minute variations and idiosyncrasies of his or her own instrument.

"I really can't play," she said, "though lord knows I want to."

"You just have to do the fingering. I'll do the bowing."

She grinned. "No way."

"Come on. Aren't you game?"

"I'm sure to mess it up, but I'll give it a shot."

"You won't mess it up," I said as she got her fiddle up under her chin.

I got in close behind her, brought my arm around in front and stroked her fiddle's strings a couple of times with my bow. The crowd roared with approval when they figured out what we were doing.

"I'll need you to count us in," I said.

"Andy usually does that."

So I turned to him.

"We're doing 'The Mouth of the Tobique,' " I said. "Would you count us in? And don't hold back—she wants it fast."

Andy shook his head, but he smiled. "This I've got to see. One-two-three-*four*!"

And we were off.

Except we weren't, because Siobhan's fingers stumbled in the first couple of bars. She turned to Andy.

"Again!" she cried.

This time she got it, and we really were off, blasting through 'The Mouth of the Tobique' at hyper-speed. Con joined us on his guitar when we got to the third part of the tune, but Lizzie and Andy waited till we'd gotten through the whole tune once on our own before they came in as well.

I thought the roof was going to come off the place when we finished. Siobhan was beaming from ear to ear. She put her mouth near my ear, said "Thank you" over the roar of the crowd, then kissed my cheek.

"Couldn't let you sit out the whole night without playing a tune," I told her.

She handed me her fiddle and waved to the crowd as she made her way back to the merch table. I caught Jilly's gaze and smiled at the approval I saw in it. I replaced Siobhan's fiddle in its case, retrieved my own, and then we were off with another set of reels.

The easy camaraderie between the four of us up here on the stage got me thinking about my conversation with Christy yesterday. Maybe it wouldn't be such a bad idea to put together a real band and do some touring. I loved the music and I didn't really mind travelling. So I'd have to record a CD to get the gigs and have something to sell after the show. Was that really such a big deal? Everybody else did it, so why shouldn't I? I could even put some of my own music on it. For that matter, I had enough tunes I'd written over the years that I could fill a CD with them and still have some left over.

Con sang a song after we finished the reels, then Lizzie led us off on a truly magnificent version of "The Strayaway Child." Slow and stately, filled with heart and grace.

I switched to harmonies in the second position when we began to repeat the tune. Lizzie looked at me and smiled, then closed her eyes again, leaning into the music. I let my gaze drift over the crowd until it was drawn to a tall figure standing by the door at the back of the room. I couldn't really see much of him, what with the dim lighting and the cigarette smoke, but something about him grabbed my attention, and it wasn't because he was wearing sunglasses. It took me a moment to realize what he was. The dark glasses were a typical fairy touch, considering how they can see as well in the dark as we can in the middle of the day. But fairy like to stand out, even when they're playing at being human.

At the end of the tune, I stepped closer to Lizzie.

"Is that your friend Grey?" I asked. "Standing over there by the door— the tall guy with the sunglasses."

She looked for herself.

"I don't see anybody," she said.

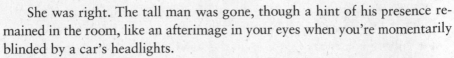

She was right. The tall man was gone, though a hint of his presence remained in the room, like an afterimage in your eyes when you're momentarily blinded by a car's headlights.

"What made you—" Lizzie began.

But Andy was already counting us into our last set for the night, and there was no time to talk again until much later. We finished the set, did a couple of encores. The band signed their CDs and chatted with their fans. I started taking down the gear, putting away instruments and mikes, coiling cables. I was almost done before any of the others could join me to help finish up. Then we commandeered a couple of tables near the stage: the band, Jilly and me, Eddie, and a few hangers-on—local musicians that the band had met over the weekend.

The others were having a rousing discussion about the merits of various single malts when Lizzie pulled a chair over to sit beside me.

"What made you think you saw Grey earlier?" she asked, finally getting to finish the question she'd started earlier.

I shrugged. "I didn't know it was him, exactly, just that it was somebody who walks between the worlds. I guess I assumed it was him because of the way he was watching you play—if anybody from the otherworld was going to be that interested in you, he seemed the best bet."

"How could you tell that's where he was from?"

"You learn to recognize it after awhile. They carry a shimmer—like there's a heat mirage pushing up against the edges of where they interact with the world."

"Is that like an aura?"

"I suppose, only without the colour. It's not something that's very obvious, unless you know to look for it."

"How did you learn?" she asked.

"Nobody taught me. It's just something I picked up. I've spent a lot of time in a fairy court over the past couple of years."

"What's that like? God, I'm so full of questions, aren't I? I must be driving you crazy."

"No, it's okay."

"So what *is* it like?"

I smiled. "The music's better on a regular basis and people generally look different. Sometimes so different, they're not even people."

"I still can't believe all these stories my grandfather told Siobhan and me are actually true."

I gave her another smile. "Well, like my brother says, 'Just because one impossible thing is true, doesn't mean they all are.'"

She gave me a slow nod. "So they all have this . . . shimmer about them?"

"Everybody does who's spent any amount of time in the otherworld. I've got it. Jilly's got it, though she has another kind of shine, too—like her spirit's too big for her body, so it escapes through the pores of her skin."

Lizzie looked across the table to where Jilly was laughing with one of the local players. I think Con told me his name was Neil.

"I don't see anything," she said.

"Like I said, it takes time to learn how to see it. And it's not of much use, except to tell when some fairy or one of the animal people is wandering around in human skin."

Her eyes got wide at that.

"Come on," I said. "You saw it for yourself the other night when you met that deer man."

"Except he had a deer head, so it was pretty obvious he wasn't human." I nodded.

"Look," I said. "Don't get all caught up in trying to figure out who's human and who's not, or what it all means. Mostly—at least when we're talking about the ones that interact with humans—they're just like us. There are certainly amoral fairies out there—and I'm talking real nightmare material—but it's not like the human race is all sunshine and light, either. Just treat whoever you meet the way you'd want them to treat you and you'll be okay."

"I don't know that I want to meet any more of them."

"Well, the bogans I can understand, but Grey sounds interesting and a deer man like Walker is just amazing."

"I know. It was totally special meeting him. But mostly, I think that kind of thing would just complicate my life way too much."

"I understand," I told her. "But the trouble is, once you start interacting with the otherworld, it's not so easy to shut it out again."

"That's what Grey said. And then he told me I was going to have to choose sides."

"Choose sides?"

She nodded. "He seems to think there's trouble coming between his people and the newer fairies—I mean the ones newer to this land."

I thought of happy little Hazel giving the finger to some native spirits when I drove her into town the other morning, the disgust in her voice when she spoke of them. I'd never seen her like that before, but then I'd never seen her around native spirits before, either.

But all I said was, "Oh, I doubt it'll come to that," except I couldn't put any real confidence in my voice.

"What are you guys talking about?" Jilly's new friend Neil asked.

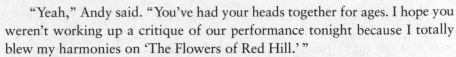

"Yeah," Andy said. "You've had your heads together for ages. I hope you weren't working up a critique of our performance tonight because I totally blew my harmonies on 'The Flowers of Red Hill.' "

I smiled at them. "I was just explaining to Lizzie why I don't care for single malts."

They all got shocked looks.

"What *do* you drink?" Siobhan asked.

I tapped my mostly untouched glass of Jameson's. "Only Irish whiskey, if you please. No water. No ice."

"My god, man," Andy said. "You need to be educated."

"Oh, please don't let them go off again," Jilly said.

But it was too late. Lizzie and I smiled at each other, then I let the conversation wash over me.

"That was really nice what you did for Siobhan," Jilly said when we finally got back to our room. "She was *so* dying to play."

"I know. She must have thanked me a half-dozen times."

"It's what I like best about you, Geordie, me lad. Your generous nature."

I smiled. "I think someone's tipsy."

She shook her head, then frowned and put her hands on her temples.

"No, someone's quite drunk, thank you."

"Then we'll have to get you to bed."

I helped her into the bathroom, waiting outside until she was done, and then walked her to her bed. She'd dropped all her clothes on the floor in front of the sink except for the T-shirt she was still wearing, but it was long enough to save her modesty. I felt sad seeing the scars on her legs because it brought everything back to mind again. How that damned hit-and-run driver had left her life in shambles. How she couldn't paint, couldn't dance, couldn't be the mad, wild Jilly I'd known for more than half my life now. But you'd never hear a word of complaint from her.

"I'm really glad you came," I told her as I tucked her into bed.

"Don't you go all maudlin on me," she said, "or I shall probably cry."

I leaned down and kissed her brow.

"Goodnight, Jilly," I said.

When she made no reply, I looked closer and smiled. She was already asleep.

I went into the bathroom and picked up her clothes, laying them down on her bag. Before I went to bed myself, I stood and looked out the window for a long time, wondering about Galfreya, what she was doing, if she missed me. I wasn't sure I missed her. There was an empty feeling inside, but I thought it might be more from knowing she'd put some spell on me. Or maybe it was me missing what the two of us had never really had—missing the potential, rather than the reality.

That made me think of what she'd told Christiana, how danger would find me if I stayed away from the court. I wondered if it had anything to do with the growing animosity between the native spirits and the fairy tribes.

Well, there was nothing I could do about it except keep my eyes open.

I turned from the window and my gaze fell on Jilly, peacefully asleep in her bed.

I couldn't believe she'd actually broken up with Daniel. With everything else that was going on—knowing what I knew about Galfreya and her enchantment to keep me going to the mall, this trouble the band was having with bogans, trying to figure out what I was going to do with my life—Jilly's breaking up with Daniel was what I kept coming back to.

I felt terrible for her. Then I felt terrible for Daniel because I knew what it felt like to be blindsided by the person you loved. But Jilly'd been my friend for longer than I could remember and when I thought of that, I felt bad for her all over again.

I knew how hard it was for her to open up and let someone into her life the way she had with Daniel. And Daniel *was* perfect. Or that was the way it had certainly seemed, looking in from the outside. Which just went to show you that nothing was ever necessarily what it seemed.

I went into the bathroom, washed up and brushed my teeth, then lay down in my own bed. Just as I was starting to drift off, I remembered the man I'd seen watching Lizzie while we were playing "The Strayaway Child."

If it hadn't been Grey, then who had it been?

Grey

It's a funny thing. Sorrow and joy are both emotions, but they couldn't be more different in how they take hold of a person. Joy's always fleeting, while sorrow runs hard and deep when it's got you in its grip. And if I'd ever needed confirmation, all I had to do was take a look down below to see just how hard and deep it can run.

I'm standing in a wide stretch of the between, outside the world where my people were born, outside the spiritlands, too. Long grey shoulders of rock fall like steps from a deep pine wood to the shores of a lake so wide you can't see its far side. Where the water meets the granite, a driftwood fire burns, bright and tall, almost smokeless. Gathered around the fire are a couple dozen cerva—male and female, some in deer form, others standing like men but with deer heads.

There are even more standing in the shadows, out of the fire's light. I see the taller shapes of moose spirits scattered here and there among them, their heads lifting from the crowd of deer men the way pine trees rise above the rest of the forest. Buffalo, too, broad-shouldered, their hair shaggy and dread-locked. Drums sound, creating the backdrop for voices raised in a sorrowful chant, feet and hooves stomping in a slow, shuffling dance around the fire.

One tall figure stands motionless, back to the lake, gaze on the fire, the tines of his antlers rising high into the night air. Walker. The sadness coming off him has an almost physical presence.

Like I said, hard and deep.

This is a blessing ceremony for a dead cousin. The first night's for family, the second for everyone whose life the departed had touched. What I'm looking at is the second night ceremony for Walker's daughter and, judging by the turnout, she'd been well loved.

"There's no body down there," a voice says from behind me.

I don't bother to turn. I'd already smelled the stranger's coyote blood, heard his approach as he came soft-stepping out from under the pines, boots almost silent on the stone. I'll admit my shoulders went a little tighter, but I didn't allow myself to be concerned. Who would bring a new death at the edge of a ceremony such as this?

The stranger joins me on the outcrop and looks down on the proceedings below. I glance at him. Tall and lean, the dog-headed man is dressed in jeans and cowboy boots, buckskin jacket. His flat-brimmed black hat has a leather band that's decorated with turquoise and silver. Two long braids frame his canine features.

"So there won't be any feed," the stranger adds.

"I know."

He grins. "Makes me wonder, then, what a corbae's doing at the good-bye do for some poor dead cerva girl."

"Paying my respects," I say. "Just like you. We're not all about carrion."

"I'm never about carrion," he says. "I can't hunt for myself, I don't eat."

"Whatever."

He takes a tobacco pouch from the pocket of his buckskin jacket and rolls a cigarette, lights it with a shiny Zippo lighter. After a couple of drags, he offers it to me.

"I'm corbae, you're canid," I say, making no move to take the proffered cigarette.

"So?"

"So, what do you want from me?"

"Not that chip on your shoulder." He gestures with the cigarette, offering it again. "I learned a long time ago to take people as they are, one at a time, not judge them by their tribe or clan or blood. You should try it—it's very liberating not to be tied down to how people think you're supposed to react to every damn thing."

I give him a slow nod and take the cigarette, draw the smoke into my lungs.

"My name's Whiskey Jack," the stranger tells me.

"They call me Grey."

His eyebrows rise. "Oh, you're *that* blackbird."

"What's that supposed to mean?"

He shrugs. "Just that I've heard of you. This black spruce jay, wandering around these parts, doing good." He smiles. "It's kind of funny, now that I think of it. My name's Whiskey Jack, and Whiskey Jack's what people call you birds. That's about as close as corbae and canid are going to get without having mixed blood like my buddy Crazy Dog."

I take another drag from the cigarette and start to hand it back, but Jack shakes his head.

"Keep it," he says and starts to roll himself another one.

"Did you know her?" I ask.

"Who? Walker's little girl?"

I nod.

"Yeah, I did," he says. He sighs and gets his cigarette lit. "They named her well: Anwatan. Calm Water. I guess it's okay to speak her true name, now that she's gone. She was a little sweetheart, always ready to see the best in everything. But I guess you know that already."

I shake my head. "I never met her."

"But here you are, paying your respects all the same."

I nod.

"So, why?" Jack asked.

I just look at him, then finally say, "You sure do talk a lot."

"Yeah, that's what everybody says. But that doesn't mean I don't listen. And man, I'm as bad as you blackbirds when it comes to being curious about just any damn thing you can think of."

I hesitate a moment, then realize that telling what I know is a way of adding to Anwatan's story. Like the songs and dancing coming up from below, it would help her spirit move on. So I tell Jack about the fiddler I rescued from the bogans, how the bogans had been out hunting, how Lizzie buried Anwatan's remains and played a lament over the grave.

"That was a kind gesture on her part," Jack says.

"She seems like a pretty decent sort."

Jack starts to pull out his tobacco pouch again, but I shake my head. I get out my own and roll us each another cigarette. Jack lights them with that shiny lighter of his.

"You sweet on her?" he asks.

"Who, Lizzie? Hardly. Like I told you, she's human."

Jack shakes his head. "You've got to get these preconceptions out of your head. Seriously." Then he smiles and gives me a considering look. "She sweet on you?"

"I wouldn't know."

"Man, you blackbirds really don't have a clue, do you? You're either all dark thoughts and deep philosophy, or you're headlong into having some fun. You need to learn to mix it up a little."

"Like the crow girls."

"Yeah, right," Jack says. "Maybe they were here when your Raven pulled the world out of the long ago, but they're all party for the moment now, man. They wouldn't know a deep thought if it came up and kicked them in the butt—though speaking of which, they do have nice ones."

"Then you don't know them."

"I know a nice butt when I see it."

"You know what I mean."

Jack shrugs. "There's more I don't know in this world than I could ever hope to get a handle on. Maybe the crow girls have this hidden deep side to them, maybe they don't. That's not the point. The point is you need to loosen up some."

"You don't know me, either."

"True. But I hear the gossip. From all I hear, you've spent a long time walking a dark road on your own."

"I've got my reasons."

"I'm sure you do," Jack says. "And I'm sure they're good ones." Then he shakes his head. "Aw, what the hell do I know? And this isn't really the time or the place to talk about this kind of thing anyway. I should just learn to mind my own business, but then I wouldn't be much of a coyote, would I?"

I can't help but return his smile. He surely does like to run on at the mouth. He's also nosy, not to mention pushy, but I can tell that none of it comes from a mean spirit. It isn't that I think he *couldn't* be hard, or even cruel. It just isn't where he's coming from at the moment.

The two of us stand there looking down at the ceremony and finish our cigarettes. Finally, Jack bends down and puts his out against the granite underfoot. I follow suit.

"So, are you going down?" Jack asks.

I shake my head. "Don't know that I'd be welcome."

"Yeah, the cerva always get skittish around predators, even when we're not hunting. Think we can't tell the difference between them and the cousins that aren't our kin."

"You going?"

"Nope. Same deal. Maybe I'll stop by that crossroads tree where your little fiddler buried what was left of Anwatan. Pay my respects directly to her."

I nod. I wait for Jack to leave, but the canid continues to stand beside me, gaze on the fire below.

"You planning to hunt down these bogans?" he asks after a time.

I glance at him. "Seems like a plan. It's not like Walker's going to do anything, and doing nothing doesn't seem right."

"Well, that's part of what makes the cerva so special. They've got these big open hearts that don't have any room for violence." He grins. "Outside of rutting season, that is."

"I suppose."

"So do you want some company?"

I raise my eyebrows.

"I've always been kind of an eye-for-an-eye guy," Jack tells me. "It's pretty much hardwired into me. Plus, I think it's time these damn aganesha were reminded of a few of the rules we have around here."

"What happened to not judging people by their tribes or clans?"

Jack smiles at me, a dark coyote smile.

"Assholes come in every size, shape, and colour," he says, "and I purely don't have any patience for them when they hurt anybody but themselves. It's that simple. I like Walker. I liked his daughter. There's plenty of deer out there who aren't of the People, and you can't tell me these little assholes with their hunting freak on couldn't tell the difference. So these bogans have just become my unfinished business, too."

"Glad to have you on board," I tell him.

"Can you track the ones that did it? Because the one thing I don't want to do is start a war by bringing justice to the wrong gang of bogans."

I shake my head. "But I'll know them when I see them."

"Maybe I can get their scent, back at the crossroads where you ran into them."

"It's worth a try," I say.

I give the mourners below one last look, tip a finger to my brow, then turn away. Jack's at my side as we disappear under the boughs of the tall pine trees.

Jilly

Once upon a time . . .

I'm having a weird dream. It reminds me of when I was in the hospital, right after the accident. When I was even more of a Broken Girl than I am now.

But back then, in amidst my pain and helplessness, I finally learned to cross over into the otherworld. Not for real, like Joe does, walking in his body. But like Sophie used to do, projecting my . . . I don't know exactly what. My soul? My spirit? Whatever it was, something crossed over from this world to the other while my body lay broken in a hospital bed. *I* crossed over, and when I was in the otherworld, it was as real to me as this world. I felt the full range of physical sensations. Better yet, I could walk. I could draw. It was as though the accident had never happened.

And not only that, I was young again, too.

Joe explained it to me, how when you cross over into the otherworld, you appear the way you want to see yourself. Life for me as Jilly Coppercorn began when I was in my late teens—in my head I've always ignored the hopeless little victim girl called Jillian Carter that I'd been growing up. I didn't have any fond memories until I started going to college, when I started hanging around with Geordie and Sophie and Wendy, and realized that life didn't have to be a horror show. That it could be something good, too. You had to work at it, you had to *make* it good, but it was possible. So that was how I always saw myself, and that's how I appeared when I finally did cross over: this twenty-something artist with a mad head of hair and more enthusiastic energy than she knew what to do with.

And it's like that tonight, too, in this dream I'm having. I'm young and I can move without pain.

I'm in a forest of immense cathedral trees—the Greatwood, where I spent most of my time when I was first crossing over. Think redwoods, but bigger. Way bigger. I've missed the deep peace to be found under their immense boughs. It's like the whole world is calm and gentle, and everybody cares for each other.

Mind you, I'm not particularly calm. I'm so full of happiness and energy, that I do a few cartwheels in between the giant tree trunks before I finally plunk myself down and lean back against one and stare up through the twilit air to how the boughs of the trees seem to go on forever.

I am so loving this dream.

And 'round about then is when I realize that I'm no longer alone. She's standing so quietly that I could almost mistake her for part of the forest. Then I realize that she *is* a part of the forest—its spiritual heart. She's the woman I met the last time I was in the otherworld, when I traded my own chance for health to bring my sister Raylene back to life. A nameless spirit who's been known as Mystery and Fate and White Deer Woman, though I wonder at the latter name, since her skin's a coppery brown, while her hair's a black curly cloud surrounding her round moon of a face.

I scramble to my feet—and how cool is it that I can be sitting on the ground and just get up like that?

"Am I really here?" I ask her as I walk over to where she's standing. "Because I thought the otherworld was closed to me after . . . you know, all that happened."

"I never said that," she tells me. "I wasn't sure. I only knew that if you came back, it would be a long time before it happened."

"Why have you let me back now?"

"I didn't do anything," she says. "You closed yourself to this world. But something else let you break through tonight."

I laugh. "Yeah, I got drunk. Which is weird because I was pretty tipsy last night with Mona, but I didn't find myself here. Maybe it's just the difference between wine and whiskey."

She gives me a noncommittal look.

"Perhaps that is it," is all she says.

"Well, it'll play hell on my liver, but it's good to know how to do it again."

Because I'll get drunk every night if it means I can dream myself back here once more. I feel alive for the first time in years. Young. Whole. Not broken. Not in pain.

"You don't need to drink to cross over again," she tells me. "Not now that you've remembered how to reopen the door."

"But I don't remember doing anything different, besides getting drunk. What if I can't do it again?"

She studies me for a long moment.

"Is it so bad for you in the World As It Is?"

"Well, yeah." Then I sigh. "No, not totally. I don't know. I try not to think about it because it's too depressing. But here in this dream, being able to put that old broken body aside and be here again . . . I haven't felt this alive in a long time."

"Then I wish I could help you be able to make the journey whenever you wish."

"Why can't you? You're like this big old powerful spirit, aren't you?"

She shrugs. "Perhaps the woman you've based me upon is, but I'm not."

"What do you mean?"

"I'm not really here," she says. "Or rather the me that you think I am, isn't really here. I'm only a memory that you've called up out of yourself, given a temporary existence while you visit the spiritworld."

"Aw, come on. Don't go all Alice on me."

"Alice?"

"You know, like in the Lewis Carroll books where everything's contradictory and screwy and confusing."

"I'm sorry for the confusion."

I give a slow nod as it starts to sink in.

"So you're not real, are you?" I ask.

"I could lie," she says, "but that would only be you lying to yourself, and that's something you've never done. You'll hide things from yourself, but you don't lie."

"Maybe I need to start. Maybe I wouldn't be living in a broken body if I did."

"The car that struck you was nothing you brought upon yourself. Nor were the unwelcome attentions of your brother and foster parents and the others when you were a child."

"Except people do bring unhappiness on themselves with their attitude, don't you think? Negative thinking brings negative energy into your life."

"I don't believe that."

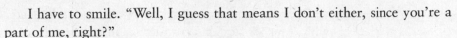

I have to smile. "Well, I guess that means I don't either, since you're a part of me, right?"

"I originated in your memories of me," she says, "but the longer I stand outside of you in this world, in this wood, the more I seem to be gaining a reality of my own." She held up a hand and looked at it. "How odd."

"You mean like Christiana—Christy's shadow self?"

Her gaze moves to my face.

"I don't know. The otherworld . . . there is so much about it that remains unknown. On the one hand, it can seem as though anything is possible here, and yet it follows its own set of rules. The trouble," she adds with a humourless smile, "is that no one seems to know what those rules are."

"So I'm here and you're here," I say, "and the longer you're here, the more real you become. Or at least until I wake up, I suppose. I wonder how long we have before that happens."

She gives me a confused look. "What do you mean?"

"Well, you know. My body's still over there, sleeping in a hotel room. At some point it's going to wake up and I'll be drawn back."

"But your body is with you."

I look down at the twenty-something girl I am, where I should be seeing an older, crippled woman.

"Yeah, right," I say. "This isn't the body I went to bed with. I was drunk, but not that drunk."

"And yet, it is your body. You are wholly here, with all that that implies."

"How's that possible?"

"I don't know."

She cocks her head and I get the sense she's looking inward.

"There's not much that I do know," she finally adds.

"Because you were born out of my memory."

She nods.

This is so way off the make-sense scale that I don't even know where to start with it. Then something else she said registers.

"What did you mean when you said 'with all that that implies'?" I ask. "What's implied?"

"Your light shines so bright . . ." she begins, her voice trailing off when she sees that I get it.

Like Joe hasn't talked to me about this a hundred times before. Like she—the real her—didn't tell me herself the last time I met her in the otherworld.

Everybody's got a light inside them—some reflection of their spirit, or soul, I guess. But apparently I've got this extra glow to my shine—courtesy of a gift the real White Deer Woman gave me when I was a kid, telling stories to a tree. See, that's how we got this connection in the first place. I treated a tree like it was a real person, and that tree was part of her. She took a liking to the sorry little kid I was and invested me with this shine, which was part gift and part burden. It draws magic to me, then helps me send it out into the world using whatever natural talents I can bring to play.

So I shine, apparently. It's what draws the otherworldly types to me, which is not a bad thing, mostly. The trouble comes from the fact that the otherworld's full of dark and nasty things, too, and this shine of mine is like a beacon to them, as well.

Joe always said he'd teach me how to protect myself—to turn down the shine, I guess, or hide it—but we haven't really talked about it since I last got back from the otherworld. No need to. The Broken Girl I am—or that I am back in the World As It Is—wasn't going anywhere. She didn't need to be protected.

"So I guess I need to wake up," I say. "If I want to be safe."

"You're not sleeping. You need to cross back over again."

I nod. Because I understand. But the thing is, I don't really want to go. Can you blame me? After two years of being trapped in a body that doesn't work properly, I want to cut loose. I want to run and dance. I want to find pencil and paper and put down all the images that have been banging around in my head, yearning to get out. I want the rush of immediate creation, not the slow pixel-by-pixel method I use on the laptop that the Professor gave me. Or the big sloppy paintings I can manage with the arm that wasn't hurt.

I want *detail* again.

I want to be like I was before the accident. Like I am now.

But I know I can't stay here. It's not just that it's dangerous for me. All of my life, such as it is, lies in the World As It Is. That's where Geordie and my friends are. That's where my sister lives. I can't just disappear on them.

God, what must Geordie be thinking? All I left behind by way of explanation was an empty bed.

No, what I need is both worlds. But to have that, I have to get back to the other one first. If the otherworld's not closed to me anymore, I can get Joe to help me learn to deal with it all. The staying safe. The going back and forth.

"I guess we have to find someone to ask for help," I say.

My companion nods.

I remember when I was here before, how I managed to make my way to Mabon, the otherworldly city that Sophie brought into being. There would be people there I could ask—I might even be able to track down Sophie. But knowing it exists doesn't really help, because my getting there before was so arbitrary. I'd go to sleep and either wake up in the cathedral wood, or in Mabon. I only travelled between the two the one time, and that was using something called door magic, which works in both worlds, apparently, but it's much easier in the otherworld.

What you do is, you open a door *expecting* the place you want to be on the other side, and if your will is strong enough, and if you're lucky—which I'm guessing is a bigger part of the procedure, at least when it comes to me pulling it off—the place you want to be in will be waiting for you.

But there are no doors here.

"Do you know where Mabon is?" I ask my companion.

"No," she says. "But I sense an end to the forest in that direction."

I look to where she's pointing. I'm not sure if I see it because it's really there, or if it's because of what she's said, but there seems to be a faint glow in that direction, as though a stronger light is pushing back the twilight of the forest. Something like the lights of a city.

"Well, I guess that's as good a direction as any," I say.

I start off, stopping when I realize I'm alone. I look back at her.

"Aren't you coming?" I ask.

She shakes her head. "No. I . . . I have the urge to find the woman you see when you look at me, though I'm not sure why. It will just . . . complete something, I suppose, even if it simply means I'm absorbed back into her."

"Maybe I should come with you. I'd love to meet her again, and I have some questions to ask her."

She gives another shake of her head.

"Though I was born from your memories," she says, "I believe we have separate journeys to take now."

"I feel funny going on by myself."

"Call one of your otherworldly friends to you. The crow girls, perhaps. Or that little man from the Greatwood who still visits you from time to time."

"You mean Toby?"

"Yes, him."

"I don't know how," I tell her. "I don't know that I can."

"You called me up, didn't you?"

"I guess. But does that mean they'll be like you? Or will they be real?"

"I think I am real now. At least here, in this place."

"You know what I mean. Will it really be them, or only my memory of them?"

She nods to show she understands what I'm asking, but all she can say is, "I don't know."

And I guess that's where we have to leave it. I don't know, and she doesn't know, and there's no one else around to ask.

She reaches out and touches my temple with gentle hands, pushes some errant curls back to join the rest of the bird's nest of tangles that's my hair.

"Be careful," she says.

"You, too."

And then she's walking away.

I stand and watch her go for a long time, until she's just a tiny figure and then finally gone, before I turn and head off in the opposite direction.

The forest is quiet around me. I know from previous visits that there's a whole other world in the topmost branches, filled with all kinds of wildlife eking out a living on boughs as broad as a county road. But down here, the stillness is absolute except for my soft passage across a carpet of mulch.

There's no undergrowth, so it's easy to make my way. If the trees' trunks weren't so big—you could hide a city bus behind some of them—it would be easy to keep an eye out for danger, too. But I don't expect danger here. There's something about these cathedral trees that won't allow it. I felt it when I was here before, and I feel it now. The last time I was here, all the trouble I got into waited until I was out of the Greatwood before it made itself known.

But even so, I'm hesitant about calling out, as my erstwhile companion suggested. I figure it's one thing to mouse my way among these giant trees, disturbing no one as I go, and quite another to be shouting out the names of Toby or the crow girls. Besides, any calling out to them probably needs to be done silently, the way I called up the echo of the White Deer Woman, because I certainly don't remember speaking her name aloud. Or even calling out to her at all. I just fell asleep drunk and then here I was, and here she was, too.

I don't know how long I've been walking, but after awhile I realize that the tree trunks are getting smaller. Over the next hour, I can start to see the upper canopies of the trees, with tiny glimpses of blue sky in between their branches. There's undergrowth now—ferns and weeds, bushes and saplings—but it's still easy enough to make my way through them. The glow that was so faint, back where I first appeared in the Greatwood, is strong now and I no longer have to guess what I means. It's obvious: I've travelled through the Greatwood into a regular forest, and that forest is now ending.

The ground starts to rise—a gentle slope—but when I get to the top, I find myself looking out at an endless array of fields. A patchwork of old farmland, separated by hedges, broken-down fences, and ragged tree lines. And there, in the far, far distance, I can see the smudge of something that might be a city.

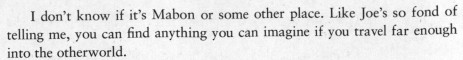

I don't know if it's Mabon or some other place. Like Joe's so fond of telling me, you can find anything you can imagine if you travel far enough into the otherworld.

I wish he was here.

I wish *somebody* was here, because I'm feeling lonely and let's face it, travelling is never that much fun when you're on your own.

And then—

Well, all I can say is, don't make wishes, because if they get fulfilled, they're not necessarily going to be filled to your expectations.

I hear something in the woods behind me. It's just a soft scuffle, like a squirrel would make, but you know how it is when you're alone. Everything gets blown up out of proportion. Except this time it's pretty much the opposite. The sound is small, but it's a bear that suddenly rears up on its hind legs from a stand of tall ferns to my left.

I don't know what kind. Brown and sort of grizzled looking, so I guess it's a grizzly, except it's at least twice my height and grizzlies aren't *that* big, are they? All I know for sure is that my poor little heart has jumped into triple time, and I'm too scared to even think about moving, never mind running away.

Bogan Boys

Big Dan and the green-bree were arguing again. Or at least, Big Dan was arguing. The tall blind spirit who called himself Odawa didn't so much talk as make pronouncements, so it was hard to argue with him. But either way, it made no difference. It was all boring and Gathen Redshanks was particularly bored.

He liked being one of Big Dan's Bogan Boys, liked the way the other fairies and even the smaller green-bree spirits gave them a wide berth when the gang went swaggering about town, liked the way they could take what they wanted from pretty much anyone without argument. They were seen as hard men now, tall in the eyes of the fearful. When they showed up at a market or a revel, people were wary of them, careful not to give offense.

But Odawa, green-bree pluiker that he was, showed no respect. Gathen wasn't even sure that he was really blind. Those milky-white eyes of his seemed to take in far too much for a sightless man. You always had the sense that he knew exactly where he was, where every bloody thing was, from Luren sitting over there on a log, picking his nose, to the small sparrow perched in the branches above their heads.

When Big Dan first let Odawa link up with the gang, Gathen thought he was meant to be their own Billy Blind, one of those household spirits who gave fealty and advice to the head man. And he'd had some good counsel at first. Like the killing of a cat and how the shaping of a rune with its entrails would steer them to the good hunting they'd had of late. It went bad the other night, but that was no fault of the ritual. That was the fault of another of these pluiking green-brees.

Teaching them how to shapechange into dogs was good, too, though none of them had quite got the hang of it yet. Rabedy Collins, who'd made the best attempt so far, couldn't get rid of his drooping dog ears and tail, which was as far into the change as any of them had managed.

But that didn't give Odawa leave to be so pluiking disrespectful.

"You stupid little men," he was saying now.

Big Dan glared at him.

"Don't be calling us names," he told the blind green-bree. "You wanted to see Grey's doxie, we showed her to you. You didn't want it, you shouldn't have asked."

Odawa gave him a slow nod. "You're absolutely right. I spoke out of turn."

Gathen looked around at his companions. Was he the only one who could see that Odawa apologized only because it was what Big Dan wanted to hear, not because he meant it?

"But did you bother to notice who else was in that room?" Odawa added.

Big Dan shrugged. "Pluikers and ass-lickers."

"Not to mention Mother Crone's favourite fiddler, and how about the woman in the wheelchair? That one is thrice blessed—I could smell the luck on her."

"I didn't smell anything. Blessed by what?"

"By corbae, canid, and an old earth spirit who walked this world before any of us were born."

Big Dan laughed. "Well, their gift of luck's not doing such a good job, is it?"

"What's that supposed to mean?"

"How'd she end up crippled if all these high-and-mightys were looking out for her? And besides, what difference does it make? You're not looking to bother her or whoever blessed her. It wasn't Grey, was it?"

"No."

"And you're only after Grey, right?"

"Yes. But I want to end this enmity between me and Grey *without* incurring new animosities."

"So, we snatch the girl he does like, he comes looking for her, and then you have him. No mess, no fuss. Nobody else involved except some fiddler girl that no one's going to miss. We can let the boys have her when we're done using her for bait."

A few of the other bogans looked up with an interest Gathen didn't have. But that was only because the human fiddler was too small and skinny for his tastes.

"Perhaps you're right," Odawa said.

Big Dan took that as agreement.

"You just let us sort this out," he said. He turned in Gathen's direction. "You and Rabedy—go fetch the girl. And bring her here."

"If I might make a suggestion?" Odawa began. He turned a bland face, full of humility to Big Dan.

"Go ahead."

"We need to keep her somewhere more secret than out in the open, where anyone with half a head for farseeing can find her in a moment. It would be better to take her to someplace hidden, such as the Doonie Stane in the Aisling's Wood."

"Except the Doonie's a bit of a do-gooder," Big Dan said.

"Not anymore. I'm afraid he's quite a bit dead now." The green-bree shrugged at the question in Big Dan's eyes. "I thought I had more need of his haven than he did, you see."

The bogans all had to smile at the way he'd put that. They respected anyone who took what he wanted and damn the consequences.

"So take her to the Doonie Stane," Big Dan told Gathen, "and let us know when you're done."

Gathen nodded, though he wasn't pleased. Like he wanted to go back to that pluiking hotel and then have to babysit Grey's doxie with no one but Rabedy for company. Rabedy wasn't any kind of a fighter, but then it wasn't like there'd be any need for more than one pair of strong arms to kidnap a human girl.

"And don't screw this up," Big Dan added.

Like you are, bringing this green-bree into our business? Gathen thought. But all he said was, "We won't, boss."

Rabedy Collins wasn't any happier than Gathen that the two of them had been picked for this task, but he knew better than to argue with Big Dan, and he certainly wasn't about to bring it up with Gathen as they left the camp and went back to the hotel in Sweetwater. He knew Gathen thought he looked the right idiot with these dog ears and tail, and who could blame him? Rabedy knew he looked like an idiot, too. All he had to do was look at his reflection in a store window. He'd been the brunt of a lot of taunting by the rest of the gang, but at least he'd made some progress in this learning

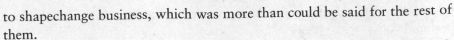

to shapechange business, which was more than could be said for the rest of them.

"Don't bark now," Gathen said as they approached the front of the hotel.

"Ha ha."

"Or go marking territory."

"Can we get on with it?" Rabedy said.

Gathen gave him an innocent look that did nothing to hide the mockery laughing in his eyes.

"It's just we need to be careful," he said, "and who knows if bits of your bogan nature have been changed along with your ears and ass."

Rabedy almost growled at him.

That was the worst thing about all of this. They made fun of his ears and tail, but he could feel other changes, inside him, as though another, simpler nature was warring with his own. He'd also noticed that while dogs still barked at him when he went creeping through backyards, it was as though they barked at something familiar now, rather than an otherworldly creature. He wasn't sure what it meant, but he didn't like it. He didn't like it one bit.

At least he didn't think he did.

But there was a part of him . . .

He shook his head.

Stop, he told himself. Just stop. That isn't bogan thinking.

"Nothing else has changed," he said.

"Then let's get a move on."

The front door of the hotel was unlocked and opened easily under Gathen's touch. Moments later they were stepping softly up the stairs and into the hall at the top. They could see closed doors along either side, but it wasn't until they were passing one on the way to the fiddler's room that they saw the glow of light coming from under it.

They both stopped, struck by the light.

"Have you ever seen the like?" Gathen murmured.

Rabedy shook his head. But he knew what Gathen was feeling. The light drew at him, too. It flickered in his eyes and went creeping down to the dark places in his heart, promising, promising . . .

Rabedy wasn't sure what. Something he'd never had, he supposed, but he already knew that he missed it terribly.

"What are you doing?" he whispered when Gathen put his hand on the door knob.

"I want to see what it's coming from."

"Big Dan just wants us to get the fiddler."

"True. But he didn't say anything about not having a look about before we do."

Rabedy sighed. Maybe Big Dan hadn't said it in so many words, but when he'd told them not to screw this up, he'd no doubt meant *just* this kind of thing. The trouble was, Rabedy knew exactly what Gathen was feeling.

The door was locked, but bogans know a hundred spells to convince a security device to open for them. There might as well not have been a lock for all that it stopped Gathen from opening the door. He let it swing all the way open before he stepped inside.

Rabedy hesitated a moment, then sighed and followed him into the room. There were two humans sleeping inside, a man and a woman, each in their own bed. The light came from the woman, a dreamy, yearning glow the warm yellow of a harvest moon, as though she was made of the radiance and her human skin couldn't quite contain it.

Thrice-blessed, Rabedy remembered Odawa saying, but this light was neither canid nor corbae magic. It was old, old. A light that had been waiting in the dark for the world to be born.

"I didn't see her shine like this," Gathen said. "Earlier, in the bar, I mean."

Rabedy nodded. He hadn't either.

"Makes you wonder about that pluiking Odawa," Gathen went on. "How blind is he? Because he saw this."

"Maybe he sees on some other level than we do."

"I'd like to shove his head up the crack of his own ass and find out what he can see there."

"Why do you say that?" Rabedy asked.

"I don't like him—I don't care what Big Dan says, or if he's the boss. I don't trust that pluiking green-bree, and I don't like him. There's something not right about the way he's gadding about with us. He's old and he's powerful—what does he need us for?"

"To be his eyes."

Gathen shook his head. "He doesn't need our eyes. He saw this, remember?"

He moved to the woman's bed as he spoke, one hand stretched out.

Don't, Rabedy wanted to tell him, but it was too late.

As soon as Gathen touched her, the light flared, blinding them both. When they both stopped blinking, the bed was empty. The light was gone, but so was the woman. Gathen stood by the bed, sucking on the ends of his fingers.

"What happened?" Rabedy whispered.

"Pluiking light burnt me."

"No, I mean, where did she go?"

"Damned if I know. Guess it has to do with that luck Odawa was on about. She must have been wearing some kind of safeguard spell that we couldn't see because of the light."

The man sleeping on the other bed made a grumbling noise in his throat and the two bogans froze in place. They waited for long moments until they were sure he was still sleeping, then crept out of the room, shutting the door softly behind them so as not to wake him and attract his attention. The man had connections to Mother Crone, after all, and there'd be hell to pay if she got involved in any of this. So they were careful now. There was no point in making more of a mess than they already had.

"You okay?" Rabedy asked his companion once they were in the hall.

"Sure. I'm fine."

But there was something new in his eyes. A resignation. A sense of loss. A sense of yearning.

"Not a word of this to anyone," Gathen said. "You're in as deep as I am. If we're lucky, nothing'll have happened to the woman. She'll come back and no one need ever know."

Rabedy nodded, though from the outset he'd tried to just get on with the task they'd been given. But it was too late now. He was in this the same as his companion, even if he hadn't had anything to do with Gathen's touching the woman. That wouldn't matter to Big Dan.

"Let's just get this done," he said.

They moved farther down the hall and, happily, there was no light coming from under the door of the room the fiddler shared with the woman Luren had pushed down the stairs. The lock here opened as easily as had the one in the other room and a moment later they were inside.

"There," Gathen said. "She's in the bed by the window."

The two of them moved forward, careful not to make a sound until they were each on a side of the bed. Then they threw back the covers and grabbed the woman's arms. Before she could cry out, they had pulled her away.

Out of the world.

Into the between.

And then farther still.

They arrived at a green sward bathed in cool moonlight and surrounded by a forest of ancient beech and oak, landing in a tumble of limbs that almost brought them right up against the tall grey Doonie Stane that stood in the center of the open space. The girl had struggled the whole of the short trip, which was what made for the untidy arrival. She pushed away from them as they hit the ground and both bogans lost their grip on her. Rabedy scrambled to his feet a moment before Gathen, but the girl was already standing, her eyes wide as she tried to take in her surroundings and guard against their next move.

Gathen grinned and held up his hands in a nonthreatening manner.

"Don't you go worrying your head about nothing," he told her. "All we were told was to bring you here. Nobody needs to get hurt now unless you do something stupid."

"Something stupid?" she said. "We're way past something stupid, you little shit."

She stood in a defensive position, hands held at the ready in front of her. It was a warrior's stance, Rabedy realized. She might look like some skinny little useless human girl, standing there barefoot in nothing but a thin T-shirt the length of a dress, but she had backbone. He remembered the way she'd fought at the crossroads. Backbone *and* skill.

"The problem with your kind," Gathen was saying, "is you don't know well enough to respect your betters."

She spat on the grass between them.

Oh, don't, Rabedy thought. There was no need for anyone to get hurt if she would just back off. But no, she had to get Gathen going.

Gathen shook his head, pretending sorrow. "Bring you here, the boss said, but he didn't say anything about what condition you needed to be in. I'm thinking you need to be taught a bit of a lesson, you pluiking little cow."

"Try me, asshole."

"Let's just leave it," Rabedy said, catching hold of Gathen's arm as the other bogan took a step toward the woman.

Gathen shrugged off his grip and gave him a glare, then turned back to the woman with a grin Rabedy recognized all too well. It was the look Gathen wore when he gave a couple of hard whacks to some miserable little treekin who happened to get in his way. It was the look he had when he cut open a still howling cat and ripped out its intestines to shape one of the runes Odawa had taught them.

Sod it, Rabedy thought. Let him make a mess of this, as well.

He stepped back and folded his arms, refusing to take part in Gathen's game.

"Oh, I'm so scared of you," Gathen told the woman.

"You should be," she told him.

After that, it all happened so fast. Gathen lunged for the woman, but instead of trying to dodge him, she stepped in close, and delivered a powerful straight-armed blow into his solar plexus that stole all the breath from him, dropping him to his knees. She danced out of his fumbling reach, turned gracefully, and kicked him in the throat, delivering this second blow with her full weight behind it.

Rabedy heard an awful popping sound as her foot connected, then Gathen collapsed on the ground. Rabedy realized that she'd crushed his windpipe.

She turned to him, falling back into her warrior's stance. But Rabedy shook his head and stepped away, into the between and back to the otherworld camp where the others waited. His last view of the woman was of her kneeling beside Gathen's body and pulling his knife from his belt, before she ran off into the forest.

Big Dan sighed when he saw Rabedy returning to the camp on his own. Something was wrong, and it didn't take a great mind to figure out who'd be to blame. Rabedy was his own nephew, but the little pluiker didn't have a bogan's instincts. Not enough backbone. Not enough bogan fierceness. Big Dan had hoped that pairing him on tasks with hard men like Gathen or Straith would awaken the little shite's natural instincts, but it hadn't helped so far and obviously nothing had changed tonight.

He didn't bother to stand up to get Rabedy's report.

"Where's Gathen?" he demanded.

"He's dead," Rabedy said. He looked at the ground, unwilling or unable to meet Big Dan's gaze. "The girl killed him. Then she ran away into the woods."

Lairds help them, Big Dan thought. Did he even realize how preposterous that sounded? A pluiking slip of a girl killed the swaggering Gathen, just like that? Like it had been nothing?

But Big Dan only asked, "What woods? Outside the hotel—in this world?"

Rabedy shook his head. "No, we took her to the Doonie Stane in the Aisling's Wood like you told us to."

"So she's still there."

"Except she's run off."

"She won't get far," Odawa said. "Except for a few glades like the one in which the Doonie Stane stands, the forest there is mostly impassable."

Big Dan frowned. The pluiking green-bree always needed to get in his own penny's worth. But Big Dan knew he only needed a little more patience and so said nothing. It wouldn't be long before the green-bree had what he wanted and then he'd have to fulfill his side of the bargain, providing the token that would allow the bogans free passage anywhere they wished to go in the wild and green.

Big Dan had been dubious when Odawa first approached them. "What kind of token?" he'd asked.

"My protection," the green-bree had explained. "No one will deny you passage."

"We'll not swear fealty to you or any other laird."

"It's not like that. If you help me, the token is yours in return. We'll neither of us owe the other any more except for our continued respect and friendship."

"And what makes you think it will be respected?"

The green-bree had turned those queer blind eyes on him and he felt the shiver of ancient power that Odawa usually kept hidden.

"Oh, it will be respected," he'd said.

So Big Dan had agreed. He kept the bargain to himself. The token wasn't anything he meant to share. He'd use it to become a bigger boss. Who wouldn't follow him if he could go wherever he pleased, extending his protection only to those who swore fealty to him?

Odawa had turned his attention to Rabedy now. "You say she killed your companion?"

Rabedy turned uneasily to face the blind man. Big Dan understood his discomfort. When the green-bree fixed his gaze on you, those sightless eyes seemed to stare straight into your soul.

"Yes, sir," Rabedy said.

"Exactly *how* did she kill him?" Odawa asked.

"In . . . in combat. She moved like a warrior, hitting Gathen only twice. Once with her fist, then she kicked him in the throat and broke his windpipe."

Odawa gave a thoughtful nod.

"It appears I've misjudged you," he told Big Dan. "There's no way some little fiddler girl could have killed a bogan without some sort of magic, and the only magic she could have gotten is from Grey."

"So he'll come looking for her," Big Dan said.

"Yes, I suppose he will. Once he knows she's missing." He smiled. "We'll have to make sure he gets word and ready a welcome for him. But first, I should think, if we're going to have a hostage, we should at least make certain she's actually in our safekeeping."

Geordie

I suppose I should have been surprised when I woke to find Jilly's bed empty, but after all the years I've known her, there was little Jilly could do to surprise me anymore. Ordinary things like hangovers didn't apply to her, so it seemed quite natural for her to have woken up without one, gotten bored because I was still sleeping, and decided to go downstairs on her own to have breakfast.

I shaved and had a shower before I went looking for her, but the only person in the restaurant off the bar was Andy. I hadn't been expecting to see anyone, considering the early hour, but then I remembered him telling me at one point last night how he was cursed with the inability to sleep in, no matter how late he'd stayed up the night before.

"Have you seen Jilly?" I asked as I sat down.

"I haven't seen anyone until now."

"She probably went out to look around. She was amazed when we drove in yesterday—at how much the town's changed since she was last here."

Andy pushed the coffee thermos over and I poured myself a mug.

"You don't seem much worse for the wear," he said.

I smiled at his bloodshot eyes. "You forget—I turned down all of your generous single malt samples except for the first one."

"When you switched back to your Jameson's."

"But only the one," I said.

"I wish I could say the same. I shouldn't have stayed up so late."

I nodded. "Good music, though."

"That's always my downfall. Good Scotch and music."

There'd been some playing around the table before Jilly and I called it a night. The others were still at it when we left.

"We never settled up yesterday," Andy said after a moment.

He pulled some money out of his pocket and offered it to me.

"Here you go," he said. "It's a quarter of what we made for the two shows. And thanks again for driving all the way out here to help us out. You really added a lot."

"It was good fun."

Andy nodded. "That it was. And we were wondering . . . we've got a few more weeks of work lined up and since Siobhan's not going to be able to play for a while, well, we were wondering if you'd consider sitting in until she's better. It'll be for the same as yesterday: a fourth of whatever we make."

I hadn't picked up the money he'd put on the table.

"What about Siobhan?" I asked.

"We're going to cover for her out of our share."

I shook my head. "No. I'll play the gigs, but for a fifth of what we're getting paid."

"That's not fair to you," Andy said. "Siobhan's our responsibility."

"We're all each other's responsibility," I told him.

Though I could tell he was pleased, I knew he was going to argue some more. And he might well have, except just then Siobhan herself appeared in the door to the restaurant. She wore nothing but the oversized T-shirt that obviously served as her nightie and had a panicked look in her eyes.

"She's gone!" she cried. "You've got to come."

"Who's gone?" Andy asked.

We were both on our feet and halfway to her when she replied.

"Lizzie," she said. "They've taken her—right out of her bed."

"Who's taken her?" Andy asked.

But I already had a sense of what she meant and said, "How do you know?" at the same time.

Andy gave me a puzzled look.

"Because all her stuff's still here," Siobhan said. "If she's gone out walking, then all she's wearing is panties and a T-shirt shorter than this. So they *must* have taken her. We have to find her."

I nodded. "And you need to get dressed."

"I'm not going back up there . . ."

"We'll be with you."

Andy plucked at my arm as I started to follow her to the stairs.

"What's going on?" he asked.

"Siobhan thinks the fairies have stolen Lizzie."

"Oh, for god's sake."

But then I realized something else and got a sinking feeling in the pit of my stomach. Because Jilly was missing, too.

"Wait a moment," I said as we got to the door of the room I shared with Jilly.

It took me only a moment to see that her clothes still lay on top of her bag where I'd put them last night. I knew she hadn't taken her wheelchair, because I'd noticed it before I'd gone downstairs. Now I saw that her canes still leaned in the corner by the head of her bed.

"They got her, too," I said as I rejoined the others in the hall.

"Now just hold on," Andy started.

But I ignored him and led the way to Siobhan and Lizzie's room. I went ahead in, but Siobhan hesitated in the doorway, blocking Andy from entering.

"I know what she has with her on this trip," Siobhan said from where she stood, "and she didn't take anything with her. Not her clothes, not her purse, not her *fiddle.*"

She said the last as though it was the clincher, and for many of us who played the instrument, it was. I couldn't imagine going anywhere without mine. Downstairs to the restaurant for breakfast, yes, but anywhere further? Not likely.

I took a closer look at the bed. It was hard to tell, but the covers appeared to have been thrown back, or pulled off roughly. Half of them were puddled on the floor.

"She was taken right out of her bed, wasn't she?"

I turned to see Siobhan standing right behind me. Andy came into the room and looked around.

"It's not possible, is it?" he said. "Tell me it's not possible."

"It shouldn't be," I said. "But it is."

Because I'd been through something too much like this before. Just a couple of years ago, Saskia had been stolen away into the otherworld—not by fairies, exactly, but it wasn't all that different, really. One moment she was talking to my brother Christy, the next she'd vanished from their apartment, just disappeared, right before his eyes. She wasn't alone, either. Hundreds of people were taken away from their homes, swallowed into a Web site that had a physical presence in the otherworld.

It was all over the news when it happened—and then it wasn't. The fact that it had ever taken place was wiped away by the spirits that live in the wires. It's this thing they have—spirits, fairies, and the like. Everything's secret, including their existence. It's an easier pretense to keep up than you'd think, because we help them in how we'll grasp at any rational explanation to account for whatever supernatural experiences we might have.

I'd been doing it myself for years, but I couldn't do it anymore once Saskia was taken. Because, as a direct result of that, I ended up meeting Galfreya and going into the otherworld myself, pretty much losing any chance I'd had of pretending that none of it was real.

"You should get dressed," I told Siobhan.

She nodded, then lifted her bandaged arm. "Except I can't do it on my own. I didn't bring anything that buttons up."

"I'll help you," Andy said. "It's not like I haven't seen it all before."

That made me wonder if they'd been a couple at some point, but the thought was fleeting.

"Look," Andy said before he followed Siobhan into the bathroom. "Maybe we should check with Con first. I mean, Lizzie wasn't in there when I went to bed, but who knows? He's been making eyes at her ever since he joined the band. She could have gone in after I went downstairs."

"And Jilly is there to make it a threesome?"

"Well, I didn't mean that . . ."

"They've both disappeared wearing only what they went to bed in," I said. "I don't think they're with Con, charming though he is."

"Not Lizzie, for sure," Siobhan said from the bathroom door. "Now come help me, Andy. I'm getting the creeps staying in this room."

I turned away and looked out the window.

When Saskia disappeared, the first person Christy called was me, not that I was much help, because what did I know about that kind of thing? He and Christiana were the experts in the family, not me. But now, when I took out my cell phone, it was Galfreya's number that I punched in.

She answered on the first ring.

"Hello, Geordie," she said.

This wasn't her being a seer. Even fairies have caller ID.

"Does this mean you're not angry with me?" she added.

"I don't know that I was ever angry," I told her. "I'm more confused and a little hurt."

"I know. I'm sorry. I didn't handle it well, did I? But I didn't know what else to do. All I knew was that I could keep you from danger by making sure you stayed near the court."

I so wasn't ready to get into this right now.

"That isn't why I called you," I said. "I'm in the Custom House Hotel in Sweetwater—do you know where that is?"

"Yes."

"We're having fairy trouble."

"What kind of trouble?"

"Bogans have kidnapped two women from their beds."

There was a long moment of silence—not the kind that comes when the person on the other end of the line doesn't know what to say and you're just getting ambient noise through the receiver, but utter silence, as though the line had gone dead.

"Are you still there?" I asked.

"Who are you talking to?" Siobhan wanted to know.

She and Andy had come out of the bathroom, and I turned to look at them.

"A friend who I hope can help us," I said, "except we seem to have been cut off. Hello, hello?" I added, speaking into the phone.

"We're here," Galfreya said. Her voice came from the receiver again. "Just in front of the hotel. I can see you in the window. Is it okay if we come up?"

I turned back to look outside and she really was there, wearing her usual baggy skateboarder pants and a tight top, standing on the sidewalk below with Hazel and Edgan on either side of her. Hazel waved when she saw I was looking.

"Um . . . sure," I said.

And then, almost before I got the words out, she and the treekin appeared in the middle of the room.

"Holy shit!" Andy cried.

He took a step back, tripping against the footboard of Siobhan's bed and went sprawling across it. Siobhan stood staring at the fairies' sudden appearance with big eyes and an open mouth.

"It's okay," I told them. "This is Mother Crone, Hazel, and Edgan." I pointed to each as I said their names. "And this is Siobhan and Andy," I added for the fairies' benefit, finishing the introductions.

"You . . . they . . ." was about all Siobhan could get out.

She backed up slowly and sat on the end of the bed that Andy had tripped over. Andy pushed himself into an upright position.

"How . . . how did you do that?" Andy asked the fairies.

Galfreya turned one of her hundred-watt smiles on him.

"Do what?" she asked.

"Just appear like that."

"We travelled through the between."

"The between," Andy repeated. "Right. Of course."

I held up my hands and made two fists.

"Look at it this way," I said. "This is our world, this is the spiritworld. They're connected by another . . . well, world's not really the best term. Let's say they're connected by a place that's wider than the whole of our world in places, thin as a veil in others, and it's called the between. Time moves differently there, just like it does in the otherworld. Sometimes faster, sometimes slower. Which can be confusing, for sure. But if you know the right paths to take, you can move almost instantaneously from one place to another by going through it.

"But the thing is," I added, turning to look at Galfreya, "to be able to do the instant travel bit, you usually have to have been to your destination before. Otherwise you could end up just about anywhere."

"I haven't been keeping tabs on you," Galfreya said. "We were able to get here so quickly because Edgan has been following some bogans for me, and they took him here last night."

Andy was staring hard at Hazel and Edgan, the one like a piece of a forest come to life with a body made out of twigs and leaves and moss, the other like an animated cartoon with his spark-plug nose and a computer motherboard for a torso.

"So Lizzie wasn't shitting us," he said. He wasn't talking to anyone in particular, just thinking aloud. "You guys are for real, just like the bogans that attacked her."

"Bogans attacked a friend of yours?"

"A couple of nights ago," I said. "We think they came back last night and grabbed her and Jilly. Why was Edgan following bogans?"

"They were acting suspicious: wandering outside our territories, having clandestine meetings with one of the native spirits of this land." She smiled. "You know me, I like to stay informed."

"So you had them followed."

She nodded.

"Did Edgan see those bogans take our friends?" I asked.

"No. It must have happened after he came back to report to me."

"I don't understand," Siobhan said. "Why would they want to push me down the stairs, or kidnap Lizzie and Jilly? What did we ever do to them?"

Galfreya sat on the other bed, the treekin scrambling up to perch behind her. That left only me standing, so I sat beside Andy.

"You need to tell me what's been happening," Galfreya said.

So we did. Not as clearly, or in as linear a fashion as maybe Christy would have, but Galfreya was patient and we got the story out. Then she told us what she knew. After she had Edgan play back the conversation he'd recorded last night, he turned on one of the PDAs that was attached to his torso to show us a picture he'd snapped of this Odawa that the bogans were with.

It was a side-shot, not particularly clear. The small size of the PDA's screen didn't help, either. But looking at it, I remembered the tall man I'd seen at the back of the bar last night, staring at Lizzie.

"I think he was at the show last night," I said. "I saw a man in sunglasses at the back of the room during the last set who seemed awfully interested in Lizzie, but when I went to point him out to her, he'd already done a fade."

"But what does he *want* with her?" Galfreya said.

"I don't think he wants Lizzie at all," Siobhan said. "She only just met this Grey guy so she hardly knows him. They're talking about someone who's his girlfriend."

Galfreya nodded. "Except they think *she* is."

"Bogan logic," Hazel said, then snickered. "As if they had any."

"What did you see last night?" I asked Edgan.

"Little enough," the little techno treekin replied. "They were by the riverbank when I got here, Big Dan and Odawa watching the hotel, while the others were drinking beer, which they probably stole from somewhere. I couldn't get close enough to hear what they were saying before they all went off into the between where I couldn't follow."

"Wait a sec'," Andy said. "I thought you guys just used this between to get here."

"We did," Galfreya replied. "But it's hard to go unnoticed in it. Everything has more presence over there. If Edgan had gone after them, they would have quickly realized he was following them."

"So that's why this Odawa guy wanted to walk to Sweetwater," Siobhan said. "He didn't want to draw attention to himself."

"So it would appear," Galfreya said. "I would dearly like to know what he's up to, why he's stolen away your friends."

"It doesn't really matter why they were taken," I said. "Or whatever's going on between you fairies and the native spirits. What we need to do is figure out where Jilly and Lizzie are and get them back."

"Of course," Galfreya said. "I'll need a bowl and some water—preferably from the river."

"I'll get it," Andy said.

"I'll go with him," Hazel added.

"But . . ."

"Oh, it's okay, silly," she said, taking his hand. "No one will see me unless I want them to. Can I ride on your shoulders?"

"Um . . . sure."

He hoisted her up and off they went, Hazel ducking her head under the lintel and laughing because she was now at such an improbable height that she had to.

"I'll need to know something about your friends," Galfreya said. She reached out a hand to me. "Will you share some memories of them with me?"

I'd seen people come to her for help at the mall often enough to know what she wanted. I was supposed to think about Jilly and Lizzie and from my thinking of them she could get touchstones she could use to find them. But that made me think of something else.

"We haven't talked about payment," I said.

Because fairies didn't do anything without a bargain of some sort.

But she gave me a sad look and simply shook her head.

"Did you ever require payment for the affection you gave me?" she asked. "Or the music you gifted our court?"

"No, of course not. I'm sorry. It's just that whenever I've seen you use your gift . . ."

"That's different," she said. "Those petitioners are neither kith nor kin."

"I wasn't thinking . . ."

Her only response was to reach out her hand. I did the same, concentrating on Jilly when her fingers closed around mine.

It's funny. I never really thought about what this would be like. I started when I felt the presence of her mind inside my own. Not because it was a bad feeling. It was just nothing that I'd ever experienced before—having two people in my head, me and her. I had a moment's panic at the thought of every private part of myself being open to someone else's scrutiny. I knew it didn't work that way. At least, Galfreya had told me it didn't—she only saw what the other person allowed her to see—but that didn't change the feeling of utter vulnerability.

If it had been anybody else, I would have just closed down my thoughts and shut her out. But this was Galfreya, and alien though the sensation of having her inside of me was, I trusted her. And I knew I had to do this for Jilly and Lizzie. Especially for Jilly. Because as my memories rose up—

There. The first time we met, two scruffy part-timers working in the post office, thrown together because we were the only oddballs amongst our very straight coworkers. We literally bump into each other in the door to the cafeteria, and I find myself smiling at this small woman who seems to be all wild curly hair, looking up at me with those electric blue eyes of hers, wearing this huge, oversized sweater that hangs almost to her knees. She looks as scared and out of place as I feel, and we have this weird, unexpected moment of frisson where we know, without question, that we'll always be safe in each other's company. If she hadn't asked me to go for a coffee with her after work, I would have asked her, and asking girls to do anything—even something so innocuous—wasn't something I really did back then.

There. We're outside a subway stop on Lee Street. I'm busking, playing my fiddle, and she's sketching the passersby. We're still scruffy, still the odd ones out when it comes to the rest of the world, but we have our own little world together where none of that matters. She turns to me and says, "Geordie, me lad, if I'd never met you, I'd have had to make you up, because I couldn't live without you."

There. Coming home from a late gig—it's maybe three in the morning— I see the light on in her loft and go up the stairs to knock on the door. The pure pleasure on her face when she opens the door wakes an answering joy in my heart, a familiar treasure that I never take for granted.

There. I'm on stage at a folk festival in Fitzhenry Park, Amy on pipes, Matt on guitar. The audience is having a great time, bobbing their heads, some of them step dancing with more enthusiasm than skill, while right in front of the stage, there's a small pack of whirling dervishes flinging themselves about with an abandon that few people seem to manage without drink or drugs. And in the middle of them is Jilly, grinning up at me whenever she whirls about to face my direction.

There. A poetry reading of Wendy's, where we're sitting through some terrible poets before it's Wendy's turn to read. Jilly keeps pressing her thumb on the table, pushing an imaginary button that will open an equally imaginary trapdoor under those well-meaning souls who are boring us from the stage.

There. The wistful joy on Jilly's face as we lean on a chain-link fence in a playground, watching her goddaughter Jillian being pushed on a swing by her foster mother.

There. At the opening of one of her shows, grinning and giving me a thumb's up when another painting is sold.

There. At Zinc's funeral. Her hand holding tightly onto mine as though I'm all that can keep her in this world.

There. Sitting in a diner at four in the morning, watching her eat a massive breakfast of pancakes, bacon, and eggs—the sheer happy gusto with which she puts away her food.

There . . .

And there . . .

And . . .

—I realized that I couldn't imagine living in a world without her.

One of the hardest things about moving to L.A. with Tanya had been having my relationship with Jilly relegated to only phone calls and letters.

I was suddenly cut off from my best friend. But we hadn't been that close since I got back, either, and I could feel the ache of that in me now. It was always there. I just hadn't realized *what* it was until this moment.

But this wasn't what I was supposed to be focusing on.

I looked into Galfreya's eyes and saw surprise and understanding there, but I wasn't sure what she was surprised about, or what exactly she understood. Surely she'd already known what good friends Jilly and I were?

"And the other woman?" she asked, her voice low.

I didn't have much for Lizzie, having only just met her, but I called up what I did. Mostly it centered around the joy of our playing together last night, the music of our fiddles entwining with such easy familiarity that we could have been doing it for years instead of just one night.

"Maybe you should get some memories from Siobhan," I said, as Galfreya gave my hand a squeeze and then let go.

"No, I have enough," she said.

Andy and Hazel came back then and I realized that, while the memory-sharing had only seemed to take a few moments to me, it had actually gone on for much longer. Hazel was still riding on Andy's shoulders, little legs kicking against his chest, her arms wrapped around his forehead. Andy carried a soup bowl from the restaurant filled with murky water. He put it on the floor and sediment began to settle.

Getting up from the bed, Galfreya sat cross-legged on the floor in front of the bowl. She moved her hand above the water and a ripple echoed the motion, back and forth—across the surface, following her hand. The sediment rose up again. When she moved her hand away, the water went still and she leaned forward to study something only she could see.

I could tell that Siobhan and Andy were dying to ask if it was working, but they seemed to know enough to not interrupt. I wanted to know, too, but I'd seen this many times before and had already resigned myself to being patient. When she knew something, Galfreya would tell us.

"How curious," she murmured.

We all leaned forward, but the water didn't look any different until Galfreya put her hand above it once more, setting new ripples in motion. She watched the movement until the water went still, then repeated the whole process a third time before she finally sat up straight and looked at us.

"You didn't have any luck, did you?" I said.

I knew her well enough to notice the frustration that Siobhan and Andy wouldn't spot.

"I can't see them in this world or the other," she said. "It's as though they have simply vanished from existence."

Siobhan blinked tears from her eyes.

"Do you mean . . . are they . . . are they dead?" she asked with a quiver in her voice.

"No. Even death leaves a trace." She looked to me. "There are places, of course, hidden pocket worlds on the other side of the between that can't be seen into, but by that token, you'd expect the bogans to be there as well."

"They're not?"

"No," she said. "I found Big Dan and his gang easily enough. They're camped in the bush on this side of the river—north of town—which might seem bold of them, trespassing in cousins' territory, except we already know that they have a cousin in their company."

I gave a slow nod. "Right. So we get the information from them, however we have to."

Galfreya held up a hand before I could get up.

"That cousin I mentioned," she said. "I had only a momentary glimpse of him, but it was enough to see that he is an old and powerful spirit. Not one of us here—not all of us together—could make him tell us anything he didn't want to."

"So we get backup," I said. "I know a lot of the fairies in your court enjoy a good tussle. If we make enough of a show of force, they'll probably cave in without anyone having to raise a hand."

Galfreya shook her head. "We can't go to war over this. We have to find another way to track your friends."

"Who's talking about war?" I said. "We're just dealing with some bogans and one native spirit who—I shouldn't have to remind you—started all of this in the first place."

"You don't understand," Galfreya said. "The lives we fairies live are forever in an uneasy balance with those who rule the wild and the green. A simple skirmish such as you propose has the potential to escalate to such a point where it would be years before we could find peace again—even as uneasy a peace as we have at the moment."

"So it's all politics."

"We're not unique in this. Unfortunately, you have only to look at the trouble spots in your world to see how common this sort of a situation is."

"So what do you plan to do?" I asked.

"Talk to the Queen. I'll ask her to intercede for us."

"Okay."

"Wait a minute," Siobhan said. "We can't just—"

I turned to her, shaking my head.

"We're out of our depth here," I said. "Trust me on this."

"But Lizzie could be—"

"I *know*. Jilly's out there, too. But we need to let Mother Crone handle this her way."

"Which we'll see to immediately," Galfreya said.

She beckoned to Hazel and Edgan, then the three of them stepped away into the between. All that remained of their visit was a porcelain soup bowl on the floor, filled with river water.

"I can't believe we're just leaving it at that," Siobhan said, once she and Andy got over the surprise of the fairies' sudden disappearance.

I understood. It's not easy to get used to.

"We're not," I told her. "But there was no point in arguing—fairies don't ever see themselves as wrong. We'd never have convinced her not to deal with this the way she felt she needed to."

"But what *are* we going to do?" Andy said. "She seemed to think we wouldn't have a chance against the bogans."

"Maybe, maybe not," I said. "That's why I'm going to call in the big guns—someone who's got power, but will also have a personal stake in all of this."

"So long as you know what you're doing," Siobhan said.

"I don't. But Joe will."

I took out my cell phone again, this time punching in the number of Joe Crazy Dog.

"Who's he?" Andy asked.

"A friend of Jilly's that I don't think anybody wants to get on the wrong side of."

My call connected, and I could hear it ringing on the other end.

"Is he . . . human?" Siobhan asked.

I had to smile. I hardly knew what the question meant anymore. For the past year or so I just thought of those I met as sentient beings, because they sure came in all shapes and sizes.

"Not really," I told her. "He looks like a Kickaha, and he's lived on the rez, but he's supposedly one of those rare mixes you don't find much among the animal people. His father was pure-blooded corbae, his mother pure-blooded canid."

"Which means?"

"Crow and dog. Hang on. Someone's picking it up."

But it was Cassie, Joe's girlfriend, who answered, not Joe himself.

"Joe's already on it," she said without any preamble.

Cassie was a seer, like Galfreya, only she was human and used cards instead of a scrying bowl. I guessed Christy had been right the other day. You didn't have to scratch far under the skin to find that pretty much everyone in Jilly's periphery has some connection to the world most people don't even know exists, never mind sees. So I knew about Cassie's gift, but I was still startled at how she'd answered the phone.

"How did you know?" I asked.

"Joe put some kind of mojo on Jilly after that last time people were messing around with her. I don't know exactly what—I mean, it's Joe, right? But whatever it was, he set it up so that when something dangerous is threatening her, it would take her out of danger and send a warning to Joe. And that's what happened last night."

"So you know where she is? She's okay, right?"

"No, that's the problem. It was supposed to take her to the Greatwood—that place in the otherworld she used to go when she was in the hospital."

"Yeah, she told me about it."

"Except it didn't," Cassie said. "He had me lay out the cards before he went looking. One of them showed you. One showed that old woman of the woods—you know who I mean?"

"No."

"She's got a hundred names. Joe calls her the White Deer Woman, or Grandmother Toad."

"What was the third card?" I asked, because Cassie always laid them out in threes.

"The Greatwood."

"But you said she wasn't there."

Cassie sighed. "I know. Your card was clear, but the other two weren't quite right. It was like there was a mist on them, or a veil. I think the cards were trying to look into some piece of the unknown, and that's all they could give me."

"Is Joe coming here?"

"No, since he can't get a bead on Jilly, he's gone looking for the old woman. He figures the confusion's got something to do with her. The last I heard from him was when he called me from the pool hall on Palm Street to tell me he's got some folks helping him out."

"I hope they figure this out quickly," I said.

"Me, too. What happened anyway?"

So I explained about the bogans and what Galfreya had told me.

"You're still in Sweetwater?" she asked when I was done.

"We're at the hotel."

"I've never been there, but I'll see if I can get someone to take me up there."

She meant going by the between, which was way quicker than her driving here, or me going to pick her up.

"Maybe there'll be something I can pick up from where the other girl disappeared," she added. "Wait until I come, okay?"

"I've got nowhere to go," I told her.

"Don't worry," she said. "Jilly's tough."

"I know." Then I had a thought. "That protection Joe put on her—does it still hold?"

She hesitated for a moment, then said, "Not until he's had the chance to reset it. But don't worry. Joe won't let us down. You just hang in there, Geordie."

"We'll be here," I said and cut the connection.

There was nothing more to say. Sure, Jilly was tough, but she was also physically limited so it wasn't like she'd be able to do much on her own. And while I knew Joe would do his best, I was too worried to be comforted by that.

Con came into the room as I relayed my conversation to the others, putting the positive spin on it for them that I couldn't muster for myself. I let them fill him in on what was going on while I went back to the room I'd been sharing with Jilly.

I sat on her bed and picked up one of her canes, holding it across my knees.

"Where are you Jilly?" I asked the empty room. "What did those freaks do with the two of you?"

There was no response, but I hadn't expected any.

I hated feeling so useless.

I wanted to break something. I wanted to go out into the bush, track down these bogans, and pound the answers I needed out of them with this cane of Jilly's.

But I knew Cassie was right. This was taking place in Joe's world and he knew how to handle it. And unlike Galfreya, he wouldn't care what it took to get Jilly back. Whatever was needed, he'd do it.

The others came drifting into the room then. I set the cane aside and schooled my face to not show how depressed I felt, doing my best to bolster their hopes.

I guess I didn't do such a bad job because, after awhile, I almost started to believe it myself.

Lizzie

As soon as she was in among the trees, Lizzie dropped to the ground and threw up.

Oh, she'd talked brave back there, facing the two bogans. Acted brave, too. But she hadn't been. What she'd been was furious. And when the bigger of the bogans started threatening her, she hadn't even stopped to think. She'd simply put all those lessons with Johnny back at the gym to good use. Except . . .

She threw up again, dry heaving now because there was nothing left in her stomach. Dizzy and weak, she sat up slowly, pressing her face against the rough bark of the nearest tree trunk.

Except she hadn't simply defended herself the way Johnny had taught her.

She'd killed him. The bogan. Miserable excuse for a creature though he was, he'd still been a living, breathing, thinking being.

And she'd killed him.

The memory of the wet sound as her heel struck his windpipe made her feel sick all over again.

She leaned against the tree for a long time until she became aware of something else. Or rather a lack of something. The forest around her was utterly silent. Not an animal sound, not a breath of wind.

Shivering, she got to her feet and looked around.

Where was she?

All she remembered was waking in her bed, the two bogans grabbing her and dragging her . . . *elsewhere*. One moment they were in the hotel room, the next here, in this strange and silent forest.

It was fairyland, she realized. The otherworld. And she had no way of getting back home. Unless there was something in that glade.

Her gaze went to the knife she'd taken from the dead bogan. Reluctantly, she picked it up. This was a whole new world. Who knew what she'd need the knife to defend herself against? She might still feel sick from killing the bogan, but her sense of self-preservation was too strong for her to turn her back on a weapon.

Knife in hand, she started back toward the glade, but had to stop when she came up on an impenetrable wall of undergrowth and thorns. A machete the knife wasn't. It would be no help here. Turning, she tried going in the opposite direction and found herself on the edge of the glade. She stayed hidden at the tree line, studying the moonlit view. The dead bogan was there. So was the tall grey stone in the center of the glade. The other bogan didn't seem to have returned yet, either to take the body or to come after her.

No, she thought. He wouldn't do that on his own after she'd killed his companion. He'd probably gone back to wherever to get the rest of them before coming after her.

Steeling herself, she stepped out into the glade. She walked once all around it, then stopped to study the standing stone. If there was a door or a gate back into her own world, she couldn't see it.

She kept her gaze away from the dead bogan.

Okay. So there was no way home, nothing to help her here. But maybe she could summon help.

She tried Grey first, calling his name. Her voice seemed feeble, as though something about the air was swallowing its volume.

And there was no response.

So much for his help, she thought. But then, he hadn't promised to help her. Not like Walker had.

She called his name next, over and over, until her throat felt rough.

When she stopped, the silence was oppressive. Nervousness went skittering up her spine and she began to shiver again.

She was too much in the open. At any moment, the bogan could return, a pack of his friends in tow.

She retreated to the tree line, then went deeper in amongst the trees until once again she was stopped by the wall of underbrush and thorn. Dressed only in panties and a T-shirt, there was no way she could get through it unscathed. She wasn't sure it was passable even if she had been properly dressed for it.

But she couldn't just stay here, waiting for the bogans. So she began to follow the wall of tightly-knit branches and thorns, hoping to find a place where she could get through. Get through to where, she had no idea, but she didn't want to still be here, where the bogans would have no trouble finding her upon their return. There was no real place to hide. The lowest tree boughs were well out of her reach, and she wasn't much of a climber—not enough so that she could shimmy up a trunk in bare legs.

She wasn't sure how far she'd gone when she was suddenly struck by something odd on one of the trees ahead of her. She couldn't make out what it was, just that it was a white blotch against the dark of the tree's trunk. Knife held out before her, she walked slowly toward it. The moonlight was faint by the time it got through the boughs above and her gaze had long-since adjusted to the dimness, but she had to get right up to the tree before she was actually able to see what it was.

And then she felt like throwing up all over again.

A little man—two, no more like three feet tall and with skin the white of alabaster—hung from the tree. He was held in place by spikes of wood that had been driven through the palms of his hands to keep him aloft. His head lolled against his chest, and he was dressed in a ragged tatter of clothing all browns, moss greens and greys, his hair a bird's nest of matted dreads.

She wanted to look away, but her gaze was drawn and locked to the pitiful figure. She'd thought he was a child at first, a thought too horrible to comprehend, that someone could do this to a child. But when she realized he was full-grown—some sort of fairy man, she supposed—his fate seemed no less awful.

The tears that hadn't risen for her own situation—torn from her bed, killing the bogan, abandoned in this eerie silent wood with no way home—now filled her eyes. She wept for the little man, tears streaming down her cheeks.

That the bogans had done this, she had no doubt. And just as she'd known that she couldn't leave the remains of Walker's daughter on the side of the road, she couldn't leave the little man hanging from this tree, either.

She dropped the knife to the ground. Catching hold of one of the spikes, she worked it back and forth, trying to get it loose. It was slick with tacky blood and hard to grip, and her hands and shoulders were aching by the time she was finally able to pull it free. Getting that first spike out turned out to the easiest part of the task. To get at the second one, she had to step in close, supporting the dead weight of the little man, while she worked on the spike. She could have let him dangle from it—that would certainly have been easier on her—but she couldn't bring herself to let him just hang there while she tried to get his other hand free, even if he was dead and couldn't feel anything anymore. It just didn't seem right.

So she supported the weight of the dead man, holding his cold body in place with her own torso pressing him against the tree while she worked the bloody spike back and forth, her tears still flowing. When the spike came free at last, pulling out quickly with a final hard jerk, she lost her balance and collapsed at the foot of the tree. The little man tumbled to the grass beside her. Sitting up, she drew him onto her lap. She cradled him in her arms, and brushed the dreadlocks from his pale face, her tears dropping onto his skin.

She was no longer sorry she'd killed the bogan. She only wished she could have killed the other one, too. She'd like to give them all a taste of their own medicine.

Her gaze was blurred by her tears, her ears filled with the sound she was making, so the first indication she got that something had changed was when she realized that she could no longer feel the cold that had been emanating from the dead little man. He was warm now to her touch. She sniveled, wiped her eyes and nose on the shoulder of her T-shirt, then looked down.

The little man's pale skin had changed. Now the pure alabaster of it was mottled with varying shades of brown.

Where it was wet from her tears, she realized.

She had no idea what it meant, but she dabbed her fingers in the wet areas and spread her tears to where they hadn't touched the little man's skin. Wherever she touched the white skin, she left behind brown, as though she'd dipped her hand in mud and was smearing it on him.

Then suddenly his eyes opened, and she was looking down into a gaze as dark and warm as Walker's. Deer eyes. They were unfocused, seeing through her or beyond her. She went still with shock, unable to move, unable to even breathe. Slowly the little man's gaze focused, found her face.

"Why did you kill me?" he asked with a calmness Lizzie couldn't begin to feel. "Why did you kill me and then bring me back?"

"I . . ." She had to clear her throat, remember to breathe. "I didn't kill you. The bogans did."

"Bogans . . . I don't remember bogans."

"It must have been the bogans. There's nobody else here. There's *nothing* here. I've never heard a forest so still."

The little man studied her for a long moment.

"Can I get up?" he finally asked.

"What? Of course."

He'd been lying with his head on her lap all this time, having to look up at her. She put a hand under his head and helped him to sit up beside her. He held his hands out in front of himself and gave his fingers an experimental wriggle, then touched his face and his chest. The wounds were gone.

"I think I remember a blind man," he said, his gaze returning to her face. "He smelled like a fish."

Lizzie shook her head. "I don't know anybody like that."

But the little man didn't appear to be listening. "He spoke my name and I couldn't do anything. Couldn't move, couldn't speak, couldn't slip away. And then he . . . then he pulled my soul out of my chest with another word and cast it away . . . far into some darkness . . ."

He smiled as he told her the last.

"That's awful," she said.

She was a little thrown by his obvious delight in what had happened to him.

"You don't understand," he said. "You're human. You know you have a soul. They've always told us that we don't have souls, but still that blind man took *something* out of me that can't be measured or held, and you called it back into this body of mine. If that's not a soul, then what is?"

Lizzie didn't know what to say. "I guess . . ."

"So what made you think it was bogans that attacked me?" he asked.

"I don't know. Because they brought me here and that seems to be what they do. Hurt people, I mean."

She went on to tell him a little about what had happened to her over the past few days: the death of Walker's daughter, Siobhan being pushed down the stairs by invisible bogans, being kidnapped from her bed, killing the bogan before it could attack her again in the glade by the standing stone, and how the other one had fled.

The whole time she spoke, she couldn't get rid of the weird, dislocating sensation of talking to someone who'd just come back from the dead. The fact that he was a little fairy man—the size of a child, but with the brown wrinkled face of an old man—didn't feel close to unusual, not compared to that one fact.

"They shouldn't be able to come here," the little man said. "Not them, nor the blind man. This is a private place, *my* private place that I made here for myself in the Aisling's Wood."

"What do you mean?"

"I'm a doonie," he told her, as though that explained everything. "Timony Twotot is what folk call me, at your service. I was freed from mine, and this is where I chose to . . ." He thought for a moment, then settled on, "This is the place I made to live out my days."

"All alone?"

He shrugged. "I spent a lifetime with people, working for them, being around their noise and bustle. I like my solitude. And I can always go visiting if I want."

"But there's a barrier of thorns . . ."

He grinned. "And spells, too, to keep my stane secret and safe." But his humour fled. "Except it's not so safe anymore, is it?"

"What's a stane?"

"How could you miss it? It guards the glade for me. Without it, the forest would reclaim the land I cleared. The Aisling's Wood is riddled with hidey-holes like my own, each protected and kept hidden by its own charms and spells like the ones in my stane."

He meant the tall standing stone where she'd killed the bogan, Lizzie realized.

"Is it broken?" she asked.

Timony cocked his head and was quiet for a long moment, then gave a slow shake of his head. "No. The blind man is just stronger, it seems. The bogans must be in his service, for bogans alone don't have the power to outwit the safeguards of a doonie's stane."

Lizzie gave a look in the direction of where she thought the stone was. The stone with the dead bogan lying near its base.

"We should find a place to hide," she said. "Because they'll probably be back."

"Why would you think that?"

"Well, they brought me here for some reason."

To nail her with wooden spikes to a tree the way they had Timony?

"And I did kill one of them," she added.

"Ah, yes," Timony said. "You must be much fiercer than you look."

"I could say the same of you, coming back from the dead and all."

The doonie nodded.

"What was it like?" Lizzie had to ask. "Did you see the light and the tunnel that they talk about?"

"I don't remember anything," Timony told her. "I have only a vague recollection of the blind man, and then there was you, drawing me out of the dark with your tears. I'm lucky you knew the spell to bring me back."

"The spell?"

"Washing me with your tears. The genuine tears of a human hold a potent charm. All human secretions have a gift to some degree or another."

Lizzie pulled a face.

"Thanks for putting those images in my head," she said.

Timony gave her a puzzled look.

"Never mind," she told him. "It's not important."

"Yes, it is," he said. "I owe you my life. Ask me anything, and if it's in my power, I will give it to you."

"You mean like a magic wish?"

He nodded.

She shook her head. "No, that wouldn't be right. I didn't know that my tears would bring you back to life, but even if I had, what kind of a person would I have been to just leave you lying there like you were dead? You can't trade on that kind of thing."

"That doesn't change my debt to you."

Lizzie shook her head. "Let's just concentrate on how to get out of here. Or at least find someplace safe."

"I have a house," Timony began, "under the ground . . ." But then he shook his head. "Except that's where I was when the blind man pulled me out with a binding word."

He gave Lizzie a considering look.

"What?" she said, feeling self-conscious.

"You're not really dressed for any kind of a journey," he told her.

"That's because I'm dressed for bed. God, do you think I just walk around like this? I'm a fiddler, not some pop tart."

"Let me see if I have something that will fit," he said.

And then he did that disappearing thing that all the fairy people seemed to be so good at, like they were walking through a door that only they could see. She moved her hands in the air where he'd been standing, but there was nothing there that she could either sense or feel. Before she could start to worry "What if he never comes back?" he appeared back in front of her, stepping out of nowhere with a huge armload of clothes that he dumped on the ground between them.

"See if any of this appeals to you," he said.

Like anything that belonged to somebody half her height had the remotest chance of fitting.

But when she picked up the first item—a pair of pants made of some sort of thick cotton, dyed a greenish brown—both the waist and inseam looked to be about her size. When she tried them on, they were a perfect fit. There was also a cream-coloured jersey with three-quarter sleeves, a long-sleeved shirt made of some sort of soft blue material that was like flannel, socks, and a pair of boots that all fit as though they'd been tailored for her.

"You can turn around," she told Timony, who'd been sitting with his back to her to offer her some privacy.

"Do you like your new clothes?" he asked.

"Anything'd be better than wandering around the forest in just a T-shirt," she said, "but these are wonderful, thank you. They're all so comfortable. Not really my colours, but I'm totally grateful."

"What's your colour?"

She smiled. "Not really a colour, per se. Just your basic blacks."

Timony made a motion with his hands, as though he was writing something in the air, and just like that, everything she was wearing changed to a black as deep as a moonless night. It gave Lizzie a shiver, as though they weren't clothes on her skin, but some living thing.

"Okay, how did you do that?" she asked. "Not to mention how did you find me a wardrobe that's such a perfect fit?"

It was his turn to smile. "That's a doonie's gift. Our magics are of a helping nature—unless you cause us offense. But when we take a liking to you, we can call up the small changes that bring comfort against common hardships."

"So magic just lets you do anything?"

"No. All I did just now was to ask your clothing to be a different colour and happily it agreed."

"So it *is* alive. I got this creepy feeling when you made it change colour." Then she realized what she was saying, so she held up her arm and told her sleeve, "No offense."

The doonie laughed. "It's only alive in the same sense that everything is alive with a spirit of some sort. But your clothes can't get up and walk off on their own."

"Then how can you ask it to change colour? Who are you talking to?"

"The great dream of the world—that's how my granddad put it. Everything is connected, so when you ask the whole of it all for a favour—with the right words, and the right amount of respect—oftentimes, it will do as you ask. So your clothes changed colour, while the clothing itself was made from root and leaf and briar, convinced to take another shape."

"Is that how the blind man caught you?" Lizzie asked. "You said he used a binding word."

Timony gave a glum nod. "The great dream of the world grants favours through its grace, but if you know the true name of a thing, and if you have power and the will to use it, you need ask no one. You simply take and do."

"So, even though you don't know him, the blind man must know you." Then she had another thought. "You told me your name."

"I told you my speaking name—it's not the same."

"Oh."

She was vaguely disappointed in that. But then it made perfect sense. Why should he trust her? They'd only just met and hadn't some other stranger gone and nailed him to a tree with wooden spikes?

"I should have remembered," she said. "Somebody else told me about the whole business with names."

"But it's a cold soul who uses such advantages against another," Timony told her.

As though responding to a cue, they heard a sudden hubbub of voices from the direction of the glade.

Oh god, Lizzie thought. The bogans were finally back. She looked around for where she'd dropped the knife.

Timony dropped to his hands and knees.

"Quick!" he whispered. "Stand above me."

"*What?*"

"If you want to live, you'll do as I say. Now, without question."

Lizzie hesitated only a moment longer before doing what he'd told her. She swung a leg over so that she was straddling the crouching doonie, then gasped as he *changed* under her, transforming into a small brown pony that was still large enough to lift her feet from the ground. She grabbed onto his mane to keep her balance.

Hold tight, a voice said inside her head.

"But . . ."

Too late. Before she could register the shock of his changing shape, of his voice inside her head, the pony that had been Timony dashed toward the wall of thorns and briars. Lizzie stared wide-eyed, wanting to jump off, too scared to let go. She heard a cry from behind them, then everything went grey, the forest dropped away, and they were somewhere else. A place of thick mists, filled with the salty smell of the sea.

Crap, she thought. I forgot the knife.

Bogan Boys

The bogans appeared by the Doonie Stane in a jostling crowd, a half-dozen plus one of them, followed a moment later by Odawa and Big Dan who arrived at a slower pace. The bogans cursed loudly when they found Gathen, his body sprawled near the stone, head bent at an awkward angle. Big Dan stepped over to where it lay and frowned.

Lairds help them, there was no doubt about it. Gathen was as dead as the doe they'd taken down in that hunt the other night. But it made no sense. How could this pluiking slip of a girl have killed him with only her bare hands? Big Dan had been there at the crossroads. He'd seen her tremble and shake, for all the brave stance she took. She had no magics. She had no power. There was nothing special about her except for her relationship with Grey.

"She's there," Odawa said, pointing to a section of the woods.

Big Dan looked up, his gaze moving from Odawa's face to the direction he was pointing. The blind man appeared to be taken off guard by something, but whatever it was, he wasn't sharing it.

Fine, Big Dan thought. Keep your secrets. You won't have them forever.

He turned his attention back to his men.

"Well, you little shites?" he said. "What are you waiting for? Go fetch her."

The bogans ran off in the direction Odawa had indicated. Big Dan heard one of his men shout in surprise as he followed them.

Bother and damn, he thought as he picked up his pace. However she does it, don't let her kill another one of my boys.

But when he and Odawa caught up to the others, it was only to see the girl disappear, riding bareback on a pony as she shifted out of this world. He caught a flash of her unnaturally bright red hair, a flick of the pony's tail, and then the pair were gone. All that remained behind were a discarded T-shirt and the knife the woman had stolen from Gathen's body.

Big Dan turned to Odawa. "That was a doonie she was riding."

"So it seems."

"I hate the stink of those do-gooders," Big Dan said. He waited a beat, then added, "I thought you'd killed him."

"I did," the blind man said. "This woman has power indeed if she can raise the dead."

Unless you never killed him at all, Big Dan thought. But all he said was, "She didn't seem so powerful at the crossroads. We could have had her easy if Grey hadn't shown up."

Odawa nodded. "But he did, and you lost her, and now we've lost her again."

"We can track her," Big Dan said. "Rabedy's got a nose like a Church Grim."

Rabedy flushed and the other bogans snickered.

"Not to mention the ears and tail to match," Scantaglen said.

Big Dan glared at him. When Gathlen was still alive, he and Scantaglen had made it their personal crusade to torment his nephew, and it seemed Scantaglen planned to continue the practice. Big Dan had thought it might build Rabedy's character—make him stand up for himself for a change—so he'd let it go on, but Rabedy had yet to stand up for himself and Big Dan grew tired of the endless baiting. And after all, while there might not be much to his nephew, he was still family.

"At least Rabedy's learned some part of the shapeshifting spell," he told Scantaglen, before turning his dark gaze on the others. "That's better than the rest of you pluiking lot. I don't know why I bother with any of you."

Scantaglen cast his gaze to the ground, apparently cowed, but Big Dan knew he was unrepentant. It was a bogan's way to give ground to the more powerful, biding a moment of weakness. And there was always a weakness. The trick of being a boss was to never show it.

"You and you," Big Dan said, pointing to Luren and Geric. "Go with Rabedy and see what you can find."

The three bogans stepped away, out of this little pocket of a world. Big Dan toed the girl's T-shirt with his boot, then walked over to the trunk of a nearby tree. There was blood on the bark, wooden spikes on the ground at its base, holes in the trunk from which he assumed the spikes had been pulled. Odawa joined him, his passage as unerring as always. Just once Big Dan would like to see him stumble.

"He was dead when I hung him on that tree," the blind man said.

Big Dan nodded. Maybe it was true, maybe it wasn't. It didn't matter anymore. The doonie was alive now.

"How did you find this place anyway?" he asked. "A doonie's hidey-hole is supposed to be impenetrable."

The blind green-bree shrugged. "I came upon it while I was swimming."

"Swimming? There are no rivers near here."

"There are always rivers," Odawa told him. "If you know how to see them."

Big Dan gave another noncommittal nod.

"Your water clans probably have the same ability," the blind man added.

"I wouldn't know," Big Dan said. "You're the first I've ever spent any time with and you're not even close to kin."

He was just a great big pluiking green-bree, maybe blind, maybe not, but for damn sure too full of his own importance.

Big Dan looked over to where his men were lounging against the trees while they waited. He was suddenly tired of all of this. What had started as a kind of game to relieve boredom and perhaps raise his standing among the fairy clans was turning more sour than he'd ever admit to anyone but himself. The truth was he didn't care for either Odawa or Grey's problems. He didn't care about this girl. And he was sick and tired of feeling like no more than an errand boy for the blind piece of shite who'd gotten him into all of this.

Happily, Odawa kept his own counsel while they waited for Rabedy and his companions to return. As soon as they did, Big Dan walked over to get their report.

"Well?" he asked. "I see you don't have the girl. Do you at least have any news?"

"She's gone," Luren said, picking his nose as he spoke. "Both of them— like they never were. Rabedy tracked them to a beach on some grey sea, but they were already gone when we got there. The pony's tracks started nowhere, then ended the same, but we couldn't find a way through to wherever it was that they went."

Rabedy nodded. "We hunted up and down the beach, but it was all grey sand, and then a fog came rolling in from the water and we couldn't see anything anymore anyway, so we came back."

"Where was this beach?" Odawa asked.

Rabedy shrugged. "Somewhere in the otherworld."

"Could you see the sun? The moon or stars? Was the water east or west of the land?"

Rabedy and the other two bogans took a step back under the blind green-bree's sudden barrage of questions. Luren shot Big Dan a questioning look, but Odawa spoke before Big Dan could.

"Answer me, you stupid little men," he demanded, his voice booming between the trees. "Surely your tiny brains will let you do that much."

"Hold on there," Big Dan said.

The green-bree turned, his blind gaze fixing on the bogans' chief.

"This is *my* business," he began.

His voice had gone soft, dangerous, and low now.

"And these are my men," Big Dan said before he could go on. "So you'll be respectful to them, or you won't speak at all."

"This from the one who constantly berates them himself."

"What I do or don't is none of your pluiking business. While you're working for me, you'll do as I say, or you'll take a hike up your own arse."

"Working for *you*?"

Big Dan gave him a dangerous smile. "Well, I'm sure as shite not working for you."

"Why you—"

"And before you go on," Big Dan added, finally enjoying himself for a change, "think on this: Piss me off enough and I'll speak a name you won't want to hear, and then you will *have* to do as I say."

"You're bluffing," the blind man said. "You know nothing about me but what I've chosen to share—certainly not my name."

"So try me."

The blind gaze lay on Big Dan for a long moment, then Odawa shrugged and smiled.

"Why are we arguing?" he said. "We're allies. Partners in this endeavour. We each have everything to gain if we're successful."

Big Dan nodded. "So, why do you think the doonie took her to your *croí baile*—your heart home?"

The green-bree was unable to hide his surprise.

"How could you know?" he asked.

"This land is full of stories," Big Dan replied. "Do you think we don't hear them, just because we came to its shores later? One of them tells of a corbae who pecked out the eyes of a salmon on a night it was so cold he froze half in and half out of the water. We have a story like that back in the

Isles—on Achill Island. The difference, it seems, is that on this side of the ocean that corbae was a grey jay instead of an old crow."

Odawa said nothing.

"This new version I've heard," Big Dan went on, "took place long ago on the western shores of this land—coincidentally, the same place you and Grey are from. A landscape of grey shores and tall pines. The story names the salmon by his true name, if not the corbae."

"I don't know that story," Odawa finally said.

"Of course you don't. But that place the doonie fled to with the girl— you suspect it's your *croí baile,* don't you? That little piece of our own true home that each of us carries inside us. I'm guessing you left a bit of it in the doonie when you killed him."

"It's possible. Now you see why I have to track him down."

"Sure," Big Dan said.

He wouldn't want anyone to have access to the place where his own heart home manifested in the otherworld either. No one would.

"And why I have to do this by myself," Odawa added. "The doonie owes me."

"What? Now you've got a vendetta against him, as well as Grey?"

"He owes me an explanation as to how he survived the death I gave him."

"You said it was the girl that brought him back."

Odawa nodded. "She'll have some explaining to do also."

"Fair enough," Big Dan said. "Can you get there on your own?"

"To my heart home? Of course. But not this other beach your men found. I'm not entirely convinced they're the same place."

Big Dan turned to Rabedy. "Show him the way and then come right back. It's time we got back to some real bogan business."

"You're dissolving our partnership?" Odawa asked.

"Nah. But I'm getting tired of all the pussyfooting about we're doing when it comes to this pluiking corbae. These complicated schemes of yours—that's not a bogan's way. When you're ready to finish the business proper, let me know and we'll lend you the help we promised."

"You don't think I will deliver what I promised?"

"I didn't say that. I just know I've got a man dead, and we've been doing a lot of running around without much profit to show for our efforts. What am I supposed to tell Gathlen's mam and da? I should have something fine to offer them for their loss. Gold. Silver. Or at least a death they can brag about. But all I've got is the story of him dying the way he did, killed by some pluiking little girl while we're running around playing fetch for some green-bree. How do you think that's going to wash?"

"I understand," Odawa said.

He seemed to take no offense at the derogatory term. Maybe he didn't know what it meant.

"But let me ask you this," he added. "Will one of your company travel with me to be my eyes?"

"To be your servant, you mean."

"No, I will treat him with the respect you rightfully demanded of me."

Big Dan didn't speak for a long moment.

"Only if somebody volunteers," he finally said.

He looked at his men, but none of them were interested until Rabedy stepped forward.

"I'll go, Uncle," he said.

Big Dan hid his surprise. What was this? The little pluiker actually showing some backbone?

"Fair enough," he said.

Then he took Rabedy aside and whispered a name in his ear. He studied Odawa as he did it and saw the twitch in the blind man's cheek. The other bogans hadn't heard, but when your true name was spoken, even as the tiniest whisper, you always knew.

"You didn't have to do that," Odawa said. "My word is good."

"I know," Big Dan said. "And so is the name I gave him. But promises made or not, I had to do it. His mam'd have my hide if I let her boy head off into the unknown without my giving him the best I could to keep him safe."

"You surprise me," Odawa said.

"What? That I care about family?"

But the blind green-bree only shook his head.

"Come, Rabedy," he said. "Show me this beach, if you would."

Then the two of them stepped away.

Big Dan stared at the place they'd crossed over, then shook his head. There might be no good to come of this, but the boy had volunteered and he'd given him the best protection he could.

He turned away.

"Let's go fetch Gathlen," he told his men, "and bring his body home."

When he started for the Doonie's Stane, his men fell in beside him.

The Hard Road to Travel

Jilly

What do they say about meeting a bear in the woods? Oh right, you shouldn't. And to make sure you don't, you should make a lot of noise so that they'll know where you are and keep their distance because, supposedly, they're as nervous of us as we are of them. Which is all good, except this bear doesn't seem the least bit nervous. He's giving me a look like I'm Goldilocks, ate his porridge, broke his chair, slept in his bed, and now it's payback time.

Don't look him in the eye, I think. That'll only make it worse.

Or is that just for dogs?

Maybe you're *supposed* to look them in the eye?

I can't remember. I'm pretty sure you're not supposed to run—not that I could anyway. My legs are shaking so badly I'm surprised I'm still standing.

"I'm really not good to eat," I say.

I don't even know why I'm talking. But that's me, I can never keep my mouth shut.

"I mean, look at me. I'm just this skinny girl who seriously wouldn't taste very good."

God, he's big. Really, *really* big. And doesn't it just figure? For years people have been warning me about the supernatural menaces to be found in the otherworld, but nobody ever said anything about gigantic bears.

I keep waiting for him to attack, but all he does is glare at me. I'm totally surprised that I'm still alive.

Maybe he likes the sound of my voice.

Maybe he's not hungry.

Maybe he's one of Joe's cousins and just *looks* like a bear and now he's pissed off at me because I'm acting like I think he wants to eat me.

But maybe he *does* want to eat me and he's just trying to decide on the best recipe.

Skinny girl with a honey-nut glaze.

Roasted flank of Jilly with a side of roots and berries.

Or perhaps the ever-popular and simple to prepare Jilly Tartar.

I'm babbling, if only in my own head. I stand here shaking like the proverbial leaf, moths of morbid nonsense banging around in my brain, and I can't stop either.

And then she shows up, stepping out from behind the bear like wandering around in the woods with a giant bear is the most natural thing in the world to be doing and hello, where's yours?

She looks like a little girl, eight or nine years old, barefoot and dressed in a baggy green-brown shirt and Capri pants. Her face is sweet and open, her thick blonde shoulder-length hair spilling out from under a loose rusty-red cloth cap that trails off down her back to a point at its end. But I'm not ready to take appearances at face value. This is the otherworld, so she could be a thousand years old and only wearing the shape of a young girl with innocent eyes. Unless you've got a built-in magic detect-o-meter like Joe does, there's no way to tell.

And the really funny thing is—funny strange, not funny ha ha—is that I feel like I've seen her before only I can't remember where. I just have the feeling that the memory's not a good one.

"Don't be scared of him," she says. "He's just a big old teddy bear."

"Right."

The bear looks no less menacing and grim, but I feel a bit of hope at her words. I mean, she's standing right beside him and he hasn't mauled *her*, has he?

Except then she says, "It's me you should be scared of."

Nothing changes about her. The innocent eyes don't suddenly show red coals glowing in their depths. Her features don't go all dark and broody. But it doesn't matter. I don't doubt her for a moment, though I can't begin to explain why. Instinct, I suppose.

"If I've done something wrong . . ." I begin.

She gives a merry little laugh that makes me shiver.

I've always hated those movies where little kids are possessed by some powerful spirit that makes them do horrible things totally out of keeping

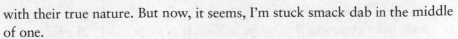

with their true nature. But now, it seems, I'm stuck smack dab in the middle of one.

"Maybe everything about you is wrong," she says. "Maybe those ferns and plants you've been tramping on are my feelings. Maybe I'm allergic to your pheromones. Maybe I'm offended by the way that light in you shines so bright."

Again with the light. I'm tempted to look down at myself, but I know I won't see this light everybody's always saying I give off. I never do.

"Look, I'm sorry," I say. "Really. I had no idea I was trespassing on your private territory. I'm just lost."

"No, you're not. I found you, didn't I?"

Some smart-alecky remark almost jumps out of my mouth, but I remember the bear, still hulking over my little blonde tormentor. I remember the fact that I'm in the otherworld, where nothing is necessarily the way it seems.

"Yes, you have," I say. "And if my being here's a problem, I'll be happy to get out of your hair. I just need for you to point me in the right direction."

"Don't you want to stand up for yourself? Don't you want to protest your innocence some more?"

I don't know why it took me so long to twig to the red hat she's wearing, but I suddenly realize that she must be a fairy, a Redcap. Except according to folklore, they were supposed to be these wicked little goblin men. They're usually described as short and wizened, with long teeth, big red eyes, fingernails like an eagle's talons, and long greasy hair. Their caps are red because they've been soaked in the blood of their victims.

So she doesn't have their look. But their whole purpose in living's to make life miserable for anyone around them and she certainly seems to have that much down pat, not to mention a really good vocabulary for a little kid.

There are milder Redcaps, almost like brownies, but they're invariably described as little men, too. I'd never heard of a Redcap appearing as a small blonde child with a bear for a companion, only that doesn't mean anything. I'm sure the otherworld's full of things and beings that I've never heard of.

"I'm just trying to be polite," I tell her, because one thing I do know is that fairies expect a good dose of respect.

"Hmm," the little girl says. She cocks her head like a bird. "So what's your name, polite girl?"

Right. Like I'm going to fall for that.

"Jilly," I tell her, which is enough to be true and respectful, but not enough for her to work some mojo on me. "What's yours?"

"Today it's Emily."

"Well, I'm pleased to meet you, Emily."

"Are you? Are you, really? Because I just have to say the word and Grath will eat you in two bites. And maybe I will and maybe I won't, but since you don't know which it will be, how can you be pleased?"

"Except you told me not to be scared of him," I say. I tell myself to be brave and face the bear. "I'm pleased to meet you, too, Grath."

"How do you know that's Grath?" Emily asks. "Maybe Grath's a dragon who's hiding just out of sight, waiting on my word to appear and wreak terrible havoc, not to mention eating you."

"I guess I don't," I tell her. "I guess no matter what I say or do, you'll find something wrong with it."

"Ha ha."

"No, seriously. You remind me of these friends of mine, the crow girls. They're just as—" I'm about to say "illogical" and amend it quickly to "—quirky."

"Well, I don't like them."

"I didn't expect you would. What do you like?"

"Oh, the usual." She counts them off on her little fingers. "To be left alone. To not have strangers tramping around my woods, pretending to be polite. Daggers made of sugar and left-handed pinwheels. Songs that only make sense when they're sung backwards. Anything with a clock mechanism in it."

"Well, I don't have a dagger or a pinwheel. I don't have that sort of song either, or anything with a clock mechanism in it. But I can leave you alone and not tramp around in your woods anymore. I just need to know which woods are yours so that I can leave them and not accidentally intrude on them again."

"They're all mine," Emily informs me. "Every last stick, twig, and leaf of them."

"Oh. I guess we have a problem then."

She shakes her head. "I don't have a problem. Only you do. Once Grath eats you, everything will be fine again."

I make a point of keeping my gaze on her face and not looking at the bear.

"Is there anything I can do so that Grath won't eat me?" I ask.

"Can you stop them from coming to my bedroom late at night and hurting me?"

Oh no, I think. How can that kind of thing exist here as well? But then I realize that if human dreamers can appear in the otherworld, they're not necessarily always going to be nice people. Pedophile freaks are going to have dreams just like everybody else.

"I know about being hurt like that," I tell her.

"No, you don't," she says. "Nobody's cut off your nose. Nobody's made a necklace out of your fingers and toes."

"Nobody's done that to you, either. At least, you seem to still have your nose and all your fingers, and they're very pretty, too, I might add."

"I don't want to be pretty."

"Well, the world's full of stuff we don't want. We just have to make do with it as best we can."

"They won't let me make do. They just want me to do what they say. They just want to hurt me, and they'll hurt me even more if I tell."

I've been concentrating on her, but as she gets more agitated, the bear looming at her side growls and stands taller. I steal a glance at him and wish I hadn't, because the shaking in my legs starts up again, worse than before.

"And now I've told you," Emily says.

"No, you haven't," I assure her. "Everything's going to be okay."

I want to calm her down, because if she calms down, then hopefully the bear will, too. But I have a sinking, horrible feeling inside me that nothing's okay at all. Because a memory is pushing into my consciousness from deep inside me, rising up from somewhere lost and hidden. A memory that I don't want to recall.

No, it's not the sorry story of my own childhood horrors. I think I've pretty much worked my way through them as best as I can by now. It's the how and why behind Emily's having had to experience the same nightmare.

"How can it be okay?" she asks. "It's never okay and now I've told and there's never going to be an okay again."

"Emily . . ."

"Do you *want* them to cut off my nose?"

"No, of course not. But I don't think it will happen. I don't think it *can* happen. Not anymore."

Because I know who she is now. I remember.

Like I've said, the otherworld is full of all sorts of beings. There are the spirits who make their home here and stray into our world on occasion: fairies, animal people, and all the rest of the magical and odd beings that we've put into our myths and fairy tales. There are humans visiting in physical form, though they're rare; mostly we visit in our dreams. Some say this is where the ghosts of the dead come, too, but I don't know about that.

But I do know about another sort of being that's particular to the otherworld: the Eadar. These are beings created from our imagination: characters from books and paintings, and even daydreams, who exist only so long as there is belief in them. I think the Eadar are where the whole idea of fairies needing our belief to exist comes from.

That's what Emily is. She's an Eadar. Only she's not Emily. She's Mattie Finn from "Prince Teddy Bear," a story in *The Wandering Wood,* which was this fairy tale collection illustrated by Ellen Wentworth that I read and reread as a child. I had it even before I knew how to read and got comfort just from holding it and looking at the pictures. I'm not sure where it came from— probably from some uncle or aunt before my parents alienated everyone in our family—and I didn't realize it at the time, but half the stories in *The Wandering Wood* were original. Mixed up with old classics like "The Matchstick Girl" and "Little Red Riding Hood," you'd find other stories such as "The Scarecrow That Couldn't Sleep" and "Prince Teddy Bear" that were written by Wentworth herself.

Emily looks exactly like the painting accompanying the text of "Prince Teddy Bear." In the story she was a precocious little girl living Cinderella-style with a stepmother and stepsister, only she didn't have a fairy godmother, and there was no royal ball waiting for her to attend and lose a glass slipper. All she had was a toy teddy bear she'd found in the garbage, missing an eye and so old and used up that all its plush was worn off. But she loved it. She called it Prince Teddy Bear, and in the end, her love brought it to life like the Velveteen Rabbit and it rescued her from her life of drudgery and toil.

I know, I know. I never said Wentworth wasn't above borrowing the best from other stories to use in her own. But that's not the point. The point is, I had it worse and I didn't have a magical teddy bear. I didn't have anything. I was all on my own, this little kid trying to deal with crap that no one should have to, but especially not a three-year-old whose family is supposed to protect them, not abuse them.

When my brother first started coming into my room at night, I used to pretend that the things he was doing weren't happening to me. They were happening to Mattie—the girl in the picture book. *She* was the awful little girl who made my brother do the things he did, not me.

I didn't know about the Eadar then.

I didn't know that I was creating one.

I never knew until right now, until I'm facing her here in the otherworld and understand what it was that I did all those years ago. How I'm responsible for the nightmare she's been living—trapped in these memories of abuse that were my experiences, not hers.

"None of that happened to you," I tell her. "Your name's Mattie Finn and you were born in a story. Your bear is just a version of Prince Teddy Bear, your companion in the story. All those awful things happened to me, when *I* was a little girl. I just pretended they happened to you so that it wouldn't hurt me so much."

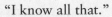

"I know all that."

"You do?"

"Why do you think I hate you? Why do you think I'm going to let Grath eat you?"

"But I didn't *know* what I was doing."

"So that makes it okay."

"Of course it doesn't. Nothing can make it okay. Just like nothing made it okay for me."

"It doesn't matter," she says. "You still have to feel the pain I had to feel."

"But I already *have*. Those things all happened to me first."

Mattie turns to look up at the big bear by her side. When she looks back at me, she seems confused.

"I'm so sorry I did what I did to you," I say. "I know that saying I didn't know what would happen isn't an excuse. And neither's the fact that I was just some scared little kid. But take comfort in knowing that it can't ever happen to you again. Those days are long past and over."

"Maybe for you."

Now it's my turn to be confused.

"What do you mean?" I ask. "It all happened a long time ago. It's been years and years since I was that stupid little kid, projecting my hurts onto you."

She gives a sad shake of her head. "This is the otherworld, where everything's always happening at the same time. Past, present, future. And he's still here, in this part of the otherworld."

I feel a shiver of dread, like I'm that little girl again, waiting for the creak of my bedroom door as it opens.

"Who's here?" I ask.

"You know."

"But . . ."

That's impossible, I want to say, except I know it isn't. *In this part of the otherworld,* she said. Joe's told me about these places—the pocket worlds that make up part of the otherworld. Special places we make for ourselves that other people can't access unless we let them in. But normally, they're places of safety and wonder—a heart home where everything is good, insofar as you're concerned, at least.

Trust me to create a horror show.

I don't need to ask if this is where I am. If this is why I met a version of White Deer Woman, who told me she was born from my memories—a copy of the real one. She knew, but I don't think Mattie does. I want to ask her, but I know it wouldn't be right to lay that on her, as well. It would be bad enough if she was only an Eadar, still existing because of the terrible memories I invested in her when I was a child. But to tell her she might only be some figment of my imagination, made real by the power of the otherworld, existing only in this place and unable to roam anywhere else the way my friend Toby can . . . that was too unfair.

But it explained a lot. It explained how the battered toy bear from the story had become this powerful creature standing at her side. And it raised some horrible questions in my mind.

Was my brother Del really here as well, perhaps transformed into some even more monstrous version of himself, made gigantic and even more fierce, the way that Prince Teddy Bear had been changed?

And what about my body? White Deer Woman said I was here in my body. That it wasn't still lying in a bed in that hotel in Sweetwater. Did that mean I was somehow trapped in my own mind?

I can't even start to understand how that would work—how it would even be possible.

"Mattie," I say.

But she shakes her head before I can go on.

"I need to think about this," she says. "About what we're going to do to you. Maybe we can give you to him, and he'll leave us alone."

"No," I say. "We need to face this together."

But I'm too late. She and the bear are gone, and I'm alone in the woods again.

I look around myself, starting at every sound. Bird calls make me turn my head quickly, looking for the source. Because Del used to be able to mimic bird calls.

The rustle of a squirrel in the underbrush sets my pulse into quick time.

This is crap, I tell myself. I'm a grown woman now. I can deal with Del. My brother's just your everyday human freak with a yen for abusing his sisters, not some otherworldly monster. These days he's nothing more than a fat old drunk, arms covered with jailhouse tattoos, living in a trailer park where, according to my sister Raylene, folks call him Bottle.

Except, Mattie's still scared of him, and she has a giant protector at her side.

And I don't have to work too hard to call up the way I saw him as a little girl: big as the world and twice as mean. If that's the way he is here, no wonder Mattie's scared of him, even with Grath to protect her.

I don't have anyone to protect me.

I don't have anything.

Grey

After a fruitless night of walking Newford's streets, dawn finds us on Palm Street near Vine, standing by the entrance of Jimmy's Billiards. Officially, the pool hall on the second floor there above us would have closed at three, but looking up, I can still see light spilling from its windows. That's the way it is—it's always open for cousins.

Jack leans against the brick wall of the building as he rolls himself a cigarette.

"You want to grab a beer?" he asks.

"Sure, why not. It's not like we're doing anything useful on the street."

He gives me a look and I'm afraid I've given him the wrong idea, like I don't think he can do the job. But I know that he's more than capable. We might not have found the bogans yet, and he talks way too much for my liking, but his skill as a tracker and his instincts as a hunter are astonishing. Where I couldn't see a thing, Jack found the traces of the bogans' trail that led us straight back to the city. Okay, so then it finally got lost in all the fairy traffic this place supports, but no one could be expected to sort through it all to find the one trail we were following.

Jack has an eye for an ambush, too, and while there were never bogans waiting for us at any of the likely sites, I have to admire the way he sifts through the possibilities. And let's face it. I'd rather he errs on the side of caution than for us to walk unsuspecting into a firefight.

I don't think these skills are necessarily just canid traits. I've met others of the dog clan who don't have near his smarts. I figure it's because he can be so single-minded when he puts his mind to it. Sure, it's obvious that he likes to talk and joke—there's always humour dancing in his eyes—but he also seems to know just when and how to get a job done, and then follows through.

"Look," I start to say.

But Jack just claps me on the shoulder. "Patience. You blackbirds don't know how to hunt. Mostly it's a waiting game."

"I can wait."

"Yeah, but are you patient when you're waiting, or are you chomping at the bit? See, that makes all the difference. Now, I'm not the most patient canid you're going to meet—I mean, Cody can take a hundred years to make sure a deal plays out just the way he wants—but I've learned that calm persistence gets a man a lot further than a lot of aimless running around."

"Which is what we've been doing all night," I have to say.

Jack shrugs and holds the door open for me.

"Except," he says, "we also paid our respects to Walker's daughter, and we now know a lot of places where these bogans aren't."

I smile. "I could name you a thousand off the top of my head."

"Sure. A thousand *unlikely* places—but unless you actually check them out for yourself, you'll never know for sure. Now, are you coming in, or do I have to hold this open for the rest of the night?"

"I'm coming."

I follow him up the steep stairs to the second floor. The door to Jimmy's is closed, but it opens when Jack gives the wood panels a push and then we step into the pool hall.

Jimmy's turtle-blood. I've heard it said that he carries the world on his shoulders—you know, like he's *that* turtle, took on the weight back in the long ago, when Raven brought everything into being. Maybe it's true. Maybe the good-natured owner of the pool hall was actually there when time and the world began and accepted the responsibility from Raven. I don't know. What I do know is that for as long as I can remember, there's been a pool hall, an inn, a tavern—some establishment where the cousins can gather that's called Jimmy's. And waiting inside, there's always this same thick-set man with a half-smoked cigar sticking out of the corner of his smile.

He says hello to us with a nod, like he just saw us yesterday, and starts to draw two pints without our having to order. But that's not magic. This time of night, what else would we be here for?

"There's my friend Joe," Jack says. "Remember I told you about him?"

He nods toward the other end of the room where a tall man in jeans, cowboy boots, and a leather vest is talking to a half-dozen men who all have

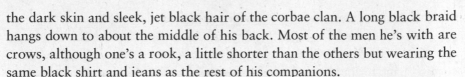

the dark skin and sleek, jet black hair of the corbae clan. A long black braid hangs down to about the middle of his back. Most of the men he's with are crows, although one's a rook, a little shorter than the others but wearing the same black shirt and jeans as the rest of his companions.

Jack reaches into his pocket to pay for our beers, but Jimmy waves the money off.

"First one's on the house tonight," he says.

"Thanks," Jack tells him, then turns to me. "Let me introduce you to Joe. Hell, he might even have some information for us. Sooner or later he hears about pretty much anything that happens in this city."

So I follow him to the back of the room where we come in on the tail end of something his friend Joe's saying. We're too late for the details, but it's enough for me to pick up that he's looking for someone, too.

"Who'd you lose?" Jack asks.

Joe turns. He nods a vague greeting in my direction before answering the canid. I hardly register what he's saying for a few moments, because I'm still adjusting to that momentary weight of his gaze on me. Now I know why Jack calls him Crazy Dog. I never saw eyes like that: part clown, part I don't know what. Spooky and dark. I've seen my share of that kind of cousin, but never anybody like this.

"Jilly's gone missing," he tells Jack. "I was just asking the boys here to keep an eye out for her in their travels. You haven't heard anything, have you?"

"No, but we weren't looking for her. This connected to what happened the last time with that wanna-be canid?"

Joe shakes his head. "No. How many times do I have to tell you? Her sister's cool now."

"So what happened?"

"I don't know. I'd laid a safeguard on her awhile back, and something sprung it, but it didn't take her back to the Greatwood like it was supposed to."

The corbae he's been talking to begin to drift away. A couple who'd been playing a game rack their cues, then they all head for the door. The rook picks up a beer from one of the side benches, downs it, then pauses before he follows the others.

"We'll get the word out," he tells Joe.

"Thanks. I owe you."

The tall, dark-haired rook flashes his teeth in a humourless smile and shakes his head.

"We don't keep a tally for this kind of thing," he says.

Joe nods. "Thanks."

Jack leans against one of the wooden support pillars scattered throughout the pool hall and takes a sip of his own beer as he watches the corbae leave.

"You should've let that woman of yours set the spell on Jilly," he says, turning back to Joe. "You always screw that kind of thing up."

"I'm not really in the mood for jokes," Joe tells him. "I've been in and out of the otherworld all night, trying to get a lead on either Jilly or the Old Woman, and I haven't had much luck with either."

"How'd Nokomis get involved?"

"I don't know that either. She just came up in the cards Cassie drew for me." He looks at me before returning his attention to Jack. "Can you give me a hand on this?"

"We're on a hunt of our own," Jack says. "Trying to track down some little bogan freaks that thought it'd be funny to use Walker's daughter for target practice and a Happy Meal."

"Aw, crap. Did she pull through?"

Jack shakes his head. "Tonight was the second night of her blessing ceremony. You know the cerva—they aren't going to do anything—so we thought we'd bring a little justice to the problem."

"I understand," Joe says. "Thanks anyway."

"I didn't say we wouldn't help," Jack tells him. "What you've got seems like it's a bit more time sensitive than our gig. It's not like those bogans won't be around tomorrow."

He turns to me to see if I agree.

I hesitate. I think about what had happened to Walker's daughter, what might happen to somebody else who got in the way of this pack of bogans.

"Who's Jilly?" I ask.

"A human with a shine on her like you wouldn't believe," Jack says before Joe can answer. "And she's got friends in high places: Raven, the crow girls, us. Not to mention the Old Woman herself, or at least the aspect of her that people call the Mother of the Wood."

"Who'd mess with someone carrying that kind of medicine?"

Joe's gaze goes flat and hard—the clown in his eyes completely gone.

"Somebody who's tired of living," he says.

"They go way back," Jack explains to me. "Jilly and Crazy Dog here. You've never met a woman like her. The world can't seem to stop throwing crap at her, but all she does is shrug it off and keep on trucking. Always has the time and a kind word for anybody that needs it. Sort of like Walker's daughter—you know, that deep, peaceful nature the cerva have down pat— except Jilly's proactive, too. She'll try and fix anybody's unhappiness, if it comes to her attention. And if it can't be fixed, she'll comfort."

"Sounds like a saint."

Jack shakes his head. "No, she's just a person who lives her life the way we all should." He smiles, then adds, "Short version: she's a big story in a little package."

That actually wakes an answering smile from the grim-faced Joe.

"I know I promised I'd help you," Jack goes on, turning back to me, "but I'm wondering if we can put a hold on tracking down our little bogan freaks—just until we get this business with Jilly resolved."

I guess I don't really have to give it that much thought. It's not hard to weigh the fate of someone still nameless that the bogans *might* hurt against that of someone who needs help right now. And like Jack had said, it's not like the bogans won't still be around tomorrow, or the next day.

"What can we do?" I ask.

"Let me check in with Cassie," Joe says. "See if she's got any news."

As he walked over to the bar to use Jimmy's phone, Jack puts a hand on my shoulder.

"I appreciate this," he says.

I shrug. "Like the rook said, nobody keeps a tally for this kind of thing. It's what sets us apart from the ones that came after."

"Humans aren't all bad."

"I know. Just like cousins aren't all good. But our word still means something."

Jack looks like he has something he wants to add to that, but then Joe rejoins us.

"Anything?" Jack asks.

"Nada," Joe says.

"So, what do you want us to do?" I ask. "If we split up, we can probably cover more ground, but you'll have to tell us where you've already looked."

Joe shakes his head. "I've already checked all the obvious places."

"Sounds like us and our bogans."

"So I figured to try something different," Joe goes on, "and I could use some backup—just to put up a stronger front."

I'm not sure where this is going, but Jack seems to have an inkling.

"Just what are you saying?" he asks.

"I want to petition the fairy courts for some help. They see places we don't."

"Why would they help?" I have to ask.

Joe turns to me. "Don't know that they will. But Jilly's got ties in their world, too. That might make the difference."

"Jilly doesn't see any difference between people," Jack explains to me.

"Fairy, cousin, human—she takes them all at face value. But the interesting thing is, they reciprocate. I don't know any place she isn't welcome, except for some of the Unseelie Courts."

"I've got to meet this woman," I say.

"I'm hoping you'll get the chance," Joe tells me.

"Who do you want to try?" Jack asks.

Joe shrugs. "Hell, why not start at the top and see what Tatiana McGree has to say?"

I just shake my head. I might not spend any time in the city, but even I know that name. Like the Queen of all the Newford fairy courts would even grant us an audience.

"You sure you don't want to call in a few more bodies?" Jack asks. "Maybe grab us a flock of those blackbirds like you were talking to? You know, show her we're really serious."

"Nope. Then she'll think we're trying to force the issue."

"And we're not?"

"First we're going to play nice," Joe says.

"You know if fairies are involved," Jack says, "she's never going to give them up."

I nod in agreement. Fairy are all about keeping their skeletons to themselves. They've got this big colonization mentality—the way they see it, only fairy can lay judgment on another fairy.

"We don't know fairies are involved," Joe says.

Jack shoots back a sudden fierce grin.

"But this is as good a way as any to find out," he says. "I get it."

I do, too, though of the three of us, I think I'm the least happy with the idea. Because if fairy are involved, what exactly does this pair of canids think we can do?

But all I say is, "Count me in."

I've already made the commitment, given my word. I'm not like some humans, ready to take it back the moment the going gets a little tough. But I'm wondering about Jack's earlier caution about not wanting to start a war by taking out the wrong pack of bogans. This Jilly must be something really special.

I'm looking at Joe, not letting any of that show, and he gives me a nod, those crazy eyes of his glittering like he's ready for anything.

I get the feeling he probably is.

"Let's do this thing," he says.

Geordie

By the time Cassie arrived, I was a jumble of nerves. It was only forty-five minutes from when I'd talked to her on the phone—not even ten o'clock yet—but it felt like it had been hours. Hours of rattling around in this hotel, wanting to be doing something, *anything*, only there was nothing I could do but wait. It got to where I couldn't be inside anymore—not in the room I was sharing with Jilly, not in one of the other band members' rooms, not in the café or the bar. So I went outside, walking up and down Main Street a couple of times before I finally took the stairs across from the hotel and went down to the waterfront.

The others checked in with me from time to time, but mostly I was there on my own, looking out across the water, worrying. Con had just left when Cassie arrived with the crow girls, who'd given her passage through the between. It wasn't that Cassie couldn't navigate the between herself—it's just not the same for humans as it is for spirits. We really need to have been, at least once before, to the place we're going, otherwise we'd take just as long to make the trip as if we'd gone by more conventional methods.

I've never learned the trick of it myself.

They made quite the sight and would have cheered me right up if I wasn't so worried about Jilly. Cassie was her usual flamboyant self: bright yellow T-shirt which set off her dark skin and dreads, even brighter pink baggy cotton pants, purple running shoes. The crow girls were dressed in plain black T's and jeans, but their hair was done up with what looked like a hundred barrettes and Zia was doing a handstand when they suddenly arrived on the pier beside me. Zia almost went off the edge of the pier, but she caught herself just in time. Maida clapped when she did a perfect flip to a standing position.

Most people can't seem to tell the pair of them apart, but I always have, right from when I first met them. I can't tell you what the difference is because they sure look identical. I just know.

All three had big smiles for me, though in Cassie's eyes I could see a trace of the worry that I was feeling. I couldn't tell what the crow girls were feeling, but then who can?

"Hello Geordie-Pordie," Maida said. "Don't you worry anymore."

Zia nodded. "Because we're helping."

"We're looking everywhere."

"And then at all the theres all over again."

"Thanks," I told them. "I appreciate it."

"Of course you do," Maida said.

"We're the sort of people that should be appreciated."

"Because we're so helpful," Maida explained, just in case I didn't get it.

They looked at me for a moment, heads cocked like the birds that were their natural shapes.

"Well, it's been nice talking to you," Zia said.

"But we can't stay."

"We're busybusy, you know."

"Veryvery."

"Looking and all."

"Being ever so useful, don't you think?"

Before I could respond, the pair of them were gone, and it was just Cassie and me on the pier. I took a deep breath, feeling as though I'd just run up a flight of stairs. Talking to the crow girls always did that to me.

"How are you holding up?" she asked me.

"Like crap. Do you have any news from Joe?"

She shook her head. "Not since he called me from Jimmy's. He's got Whiskey Jack helping him out and a corbae named Grey."

I gave her a sharp look. "Did you say 'Grey'?"

She nodded. "Do you know him?"

"No. But I think he's involved in all of this."

I gave her the longer version of what had happened to Lizzie the other night, all the details I hadn't gotten into when we'd talked on the phone. The business with Grey and the cerva hadn't seemed relevant then.

"From what you're telling me," Cassie said when I was done, "it doesn't sound as though he's got it in for Lizzie, and he doesn't even know Jilly—does he?"

"Not so's I know. But doesn't it seem weird to you that Grey should be helping Joe, when Jilly was kidnapped by the same bogans that he had the run-in with a couple of nights ago?"

"Maybe. Joe doesn't know about the bogans—or he didn't when I was talking to him."

"We should tell him."

Cassie nodded. "Except since I can't get him to carry a cell phone, I have to wait for him to call me back." She paused for a moment before adding, "Maybe this Grey doesn't know what happened either."

"I guess."

It didn't take a genius to see how discouraged I was feeling.

"Let's go see the room that they took Lizzie from," Cassie said. "I'm not nearly as good as Joe is with this sort of thing, but I might be able to pick up a trace of where they've taken her."

Except when we went back to Lizzie and Siobhan's room, the only thing Cassie could confirm was that bogans had been there. The other members of the Knotted Cord joined us before we could leave the room and I made introductions.

"What about the cards?" I asked.

"It's hard when I don't know the person I'm laying them out for."

"Can't you use that mind-meld thing the fairy woman did?" Con asked.

Cassie raised her eyebrows.

"Mother Crone was scrying earlier," I explained. "You know how she can tap into your memories by taking your hand?"

Cassie nodded. "It's a good trick, but not one I ever mastered. You probably need fairy blood to be able to pull off that sort of thing. But maybe if you've got something of hers that she was particularly fond of, a favourite shirt or—"

"Her fiddle," Siobhan and I said at the same time.

"Normally she wouldn't go anywhere without it," Siobhan added, "and she played it every day."

"That might work."

Siobhan got Lizzie's fiddle case from the corner of the room and took it over to her bed. Sitting down, she put the case on her lap and opened the clasps.

"Is it okay if I touch it?" she asked. "I mean, it won't throw off whatever you're going to do, will it?"

"No, it'll be fine," Cassie told her.

She took the fiddle from Siobhan and sat cross-legged on the floor. Closing her eyes, she put the fiddle on her lap and rested her hands lightly on its wooden top. Siobhan, Andy, and Con watched wide-eyed and expectant, and I had to smile. I don't know what they had in mind, but some vision wasn't going to suddenly appear in the air before us. Although to be fair, this was all so new for them, they could be forgiven for thinking that anything really might happen.

But all Cassie was doing was getting a vibe off the instrument, making a connection between herself and its owner. After a few moments she handed the fiddle back to Siobhan and pulled a pack of cards out of her pocket that were held together with a rubber band.

Cassie's a street fortune-teller, and she's got this amazing pack of Tarot cards: large, with beautiful art on the back pattern and individual paintings for each card's front. When she takes them out of their silk bag for a customer, you can't help but be impressed and expect an accurate reading—which is the whole point of them, of course. But this old pack she pulled out now were her real working cards, battered and worn with a plain pattern on their backs. She'd apparently gotten them from some old witchy woman years ago, long before I met her and Joe.

She shuffled the deck once, twice, three times, then laid three cards down on the carpet by her knee.

"They're all blank," Siobhan said.

They were. The fronts of the whole pack were blank. But that would change, now that Cassie had put her mojo on them.

"Watch," I said. "Pictures will show up."

A long moment passed with no visible change, but I, at least, could feel something in the air. It was like the static charge you get when you walk across a carpet in the winter and the air's so dry; like a promise, except instead of a static shock it was the promise of magic.

"Are we all supposed to believe in this for it to work?" Andy asked.

Cassie responded with a wistful smile.

"If magic required any kind of widespread belief to exist," she said, "there wouldn't be any left in the world at all—not in this day and age."

Andy looked like he wanted to ask something else, but then the images began to form on the blank fronts of the cards, rising up from the white surfaces the way a picture develops in a darkroom, and we all leaned forward.

"Jesus," Andy murmured.

I didn't pay attention to anything the others went on to say as I studied the images.

The first showed a number of small figures doing something in what looked like an empty lot surrounded by abandoned buildings and rubble—I thought it might be the Tombs, that part of Newford that's fallen into the worst kind of urban decay. I needed a closer look to see who the figures were, and what they were doing, but first I turned my attention to the next card.

It had Lizzie riding a small brown pony that was walking along a deserted shoreline. Sand, sea, and sky all appeared leeched of colour, which made the bright red shock of her dyed hair really jump out.

The third . . . I caught my breath. The third showed Jilly, but not the Jilly who referred to herself as the Broken Girl. This was the Jilly I remembered from when we were in our twenties—a vibrant and young Jilly who didn't need canes or a wheelchair. She was in a forest of some kind, but it wasn't the Greatwood—at least not the way it had ever been described to me. It looked more like the bush country up around here or over in Tyson, where Jilly was originally from.

I looked up to meet Cassie's gaze.

"It doesn't look like they're together," I said.

She shook her ahead. "But they seem unharmed."

"Who are these people?" Con asked, pointing to the first card.

I got down on the floor so that I could get a better look. I could see now that they were bogans, but not just a marauding pack like Lizzie had described. There were old and young ones here, male and female. An extended family, maybe. And then I realized what they were doing.

"That's a bogan funeral," I said. "See the figure on the pyre? Why are the cards showing this?"

"I think it's the Tombs," Con said. "That building back there is the old Charleton Mill."

He was right.

Siobhan pointed to the third card. "And that could be anywhere between here and Tyson."

"Damn Joe," Cassie said. "Because," she added when we all looked at her, "he'd know where these places are. He could *take* us to wherever they are. And if he'd carry a cell, we could call him right now." ·

"Can you get hold of the crow girls again?" I asked. "They could take us, couldn't they?"

"Probably," she said. "But I don't know to get in touch with them. I was lucky to run into them in the first place and just like Joe, they don't have phones."

"Fairies don't use phones?" Andy asked.

"They're not fairies," I said, "and they're just like us. Some of them have no use for technology, some can't live without it."

My gaze returned to Jilly's card and I went away for a moment, remembering. We'd been such good friends in those days, seeing each other every day. We could have been more, too. I remember trying to build myself up to broach the possibility of that with her, but then we took a road trip to Tyson and on the night when our relationship could have slipped into a more physical intimacy, we'd shared war stories instead, sorry tellings of how bad it had been for each of us growing up. Hers were worse. Somehow, that night changed the possibility of our being lovers to the certainty of our being best friends instead.

I'd never want to not have Jilly for a best friend. But they were times over the years when I wished it could have gone differently. That we could have had both.

"What do we do now?" Siobhan asked.

I blinked and looked away from Jilly's card.

"Mother Crone said that the bogans who've been bothering us are camped nearby," I said. "Along with a cousin she thinks is pretty powerful. So I don't understand why we're being shown this funeral."

"You know how it is," Cassie said. "It's never completely clear if the cards are showing us the present or a possibility. And sometimes it's . . ." She looked for a word. ". . . more like a metaphor, rather than something we should take as literal."

"But we could go the Tombs, couldn't we?" Siobhan said.

Cassie nodded. "Except if those bogans *are* there . . . well, for one thing, they outnumber us, and for another, they're not exactly prone to talking to humans in the first place."

"I don't understand," Andy said, still looking at the cards. "Why aren't Jilly and Lizzie together? And if this is a metaphor, then what is it saying? Jilly in a forest, Lizzie riding a pony along some shoreline. She doesn't even ride, does she?"

He looked to Siobhan.

"We both did some riding when we were kids," she said, "but that was a long time ago."

"Whatever. It still doesn't explain what this means."

I tuned them out, trying to pin down something that was creeping around at the edge of my thoughts. And then I had it. Walker had told Lizzie to call his name three times if she needed his help.

"You don't need a phone to call Joe," I told Cassie. "You can just speak his name three times, can't you?"

She shook her head. "I'd have to use his true name."

"Oh, right."

"What's wrong with that?" Con asked.

"Joe wouldn't be the only person to hear it," Cassie explained. "It would give his name away to anyone who might also be listening—the bogans, for instance, or that cousin camping with them."

"So what?"

"So it would give them a power over him," Cassie said, her voice sharper than she probably meant it to be.

"Having the gift of someone's name like that," I explained, "isn't something you can take lightly."

"This isn't anything light," Siobhan said. "Who knows what kind of danger Lizzie and Jilly might be in?"

"The cards say they're not," I told her.

I didn't want to say it. Just like her, I wanted to get Joe here *right now*. I wanted Jilly and Lizzie back. I wanted all these stupid problems to go away.

But we couldn't do it like that.

"It wouldn't be fair to give up Joe's name unless it was a real crisis," I added.

"And if the cards showed that," Cassie put in, "I'd be the first to call him to us."

I could tell Siobhan didn't understand—or at least she didn't agree. I sympathized, but I still wouldn't do it. I didn't know Joe's real name, anyway. I'd heard him referred to as everything from Bones to Joseph Crazy Dog, depending on who I was talking to.

And I trusted the cards enough to believe that wherever Jilly and Lizzie were, their situation wasn't critical. Lizzie was just riding that pony. Jilly leaned against a tree and was looking out over a landscape of rolling forested hills. Neither seemed in any immediate danger. We were the ones obsessing and worrying.

"Well, what about that other guy?" Con asked. "Didn't Walker say Lizzie could call him for help? She didn't say anything about having to use a secret name with him."

Cassie and I looked at each other.

"You never know," she said. "If he made that offer to her, he could respond to us as well. And Walker was the name he gave her to use—or rather, Walks-with-Dreams."

I gave a slow nod. "I guess we could try. Although we might be taking the risk of having a seriously pissed off stag show up and complicating matters even more."

Siobhan stood up from her bed. "Well, I say we try it. What do we do—just call the name?"

"I suppose," I said. "But not in here. We can't just call him into this room because what if he shows up in his stag shape? We need to go somewhere else, like the woods behind the hotel."

Siobhan looked around at each of us, then started for the door.

"Well?" she asked. "What are you waiting for?"

Andy and Con walked over to the door where Siobhan stood. I waited for Cassie to put away her cards before joining them myself. A little reluctantly, I might add. I had an uneasy feeling about this. The trouble with the spirits of the wild was that unless you'd gotten a promise from them before, you never knew how they'd react to being summoned.

But like Siobhan, and for pretty much the same reasons, I was willing to take the chance.

Lizzie

The landscape was a dreary grey for as far as Lizzie could see, which wasn't all that far because of the banks of fog that shifted with the winds. Sometimes a hole appeared in the fog and she caught glimpses of the water that she could hear lapping against the shore, or the grey dunes that disappeared into the distance opposite the water. But mostly the fog hung close, blocking her view. It made the air damp and cool, waking a chill in her.

The new clothes the doonie had provided didn't help, nor did the warmth of his pony body under her as he walked along the drab shore. To add to her discomfort, she was also feeling a little motion sickness from the sudden passage they'd taken between the worlds. They never mentioned that in stories. How come the crew of the *Enterprise* didn't throw up every time Scotty beamed them somewhere?

She took a deep breath of air—it was bracing, with a bit of a salt fishy smell to it—and tried to focus on something other than the damp cold and the queasiness in her stomach.

"What is this place?" she asked Timony. "*Where* is this place?"

I'm not sure.

Lizzie grimaced and put her free hand against her temple. The other was wrapped in the doonie's mane.

"Do you have to talk inside my head like that?" she asked.

Only so long as I keep this shape, and I need to keep this shape until we can get someplace safe.

"This place isn't?"

No. It's . . . connected to the blind man.

"So why are we here?"

When I had to shift us away from my hidey-hole, this was the only place that was open to me. He hesitated a moment, then added, *That's never happened to me before. I've always been free to come and go through the other-world as I willed.*

"Maybe . . . um . . ."

My dying has something to do with it, Timony finished for her. *Yes, I'd already thought that.*

"So can you take us away from here?" Lizzie asked.

And the sooner the better, so that she didn't have to have the soft burr of his voice resonating inside her head. It didn't hurt or anything. It just felt way too creepy.

I've been trying from the moment we got here, Timony said, *but I can't find one single point of exit in my mind.*

"Well, we can't just wait here for them to show up."

No, we can't. That's why we need you to find us a way out.

"Then we're screwed," Lizzie told him. "Because when it comes to all this magic and stuff, I have zip. The only reason I'm here is because I spoiled the bogans' fun a few nights ago."

You don't need magic, Timony assured her. *You just need to focus on a safe place and then hold on to the thought of it. I'll do the work to take us there.*

"You mean like back to the hotel where the others are?"

If you mean your friends, then, yes. That's as good a place as any, and we'll at least have the safety of numbers.

"I hate to break this to you," Lizzie said, "but we're just musicians. Musicians and two incapacitated women. We're not exactly the National Guard or anything."

It doesn't matter. At the moment, the most important thing is that we get away from here. I don't know exactly where we are, but I do know it belongs to the blind man. His smell is all over it.

Because he smells fishy to you, Lizzie thought, and that's what it smells like here, what it always smells like around the ocean. But she was as ready as Timony to leave the place. It was depressing and just didn't feel *right*.

"So, what do I do?" she asked.

Concentrate on a safe place, Timony said. *On safety. I'll do the rest.*

Safety, Lizzie thought. So far the hotel hadn't exactly proved to be a safe place, between Siobhan getting pushed down the stairs and her being kidnapped.

What was safety?

She thought of Siobhan and the other band members. Andy and Con were great guys. She liked them both, and she knew if it came to it, they'd try to protect her, but they weren't exactly bruisers. And then there was Siobhan with her arm in a sling, already hurt because of all of this.

If only they knew more about the bogans and the blind man—what they wanted, what their weaknesses might be.

That made her think of Geordie, but more of Jilly. Yes, she was in a wheelchair, but she still exuded this air of calm efficiency and knowledge. And courage. Just knowing what Jilly had gone through in the past couple of years . . . if it had happened to her, Lizzie thought, she'd have curled up in her hospital bed and just waited for the world to go away instead of facing it head-on the way that Jilly did. And Jilly certainly seemed to know *all* about fairies.

I don't think we have much time, Timony said.

"It's okay," she told him. "I've got it."

She focused on the hotel, but only because that was the last place she'd seen Jilly, gaily waving goodnight to them all in the bar while Geordie helped her up to their room.

Hold it firm in your mind, the doonie told her.

"I am."

Jilly. That great welcoming grin of hers and those startling eyes, the blue of sapphires.

I can feel it, Timony said. *Hold on. Here we go.*

Lizzie grabbed his mane with both hands and the world dissolved around them. As it did, the nausea rose up her throat once more.

Grey

First time I heard about the fairy courts I was like anybody else, expecting castles and turrets and dainty little pennants fluttering high from towers. There'd be fairy knights in spiffy armour, ladies in gowns, all that kind of thing. And maybe it's like that, back in the old countries where they came from, but here, they mostly go around dressed like humans and set up their courts in shopping malls and theaters, hotels and apartment buildings, all of it a step sideways from *Kakagi-aki*—you know, the human world.

So, humans can't see these courts, but to tell you the truth, there's nothing much to see. Fairies live pretty much like humans. The only difference is they don't look right. Oh, they seem human enough. It's just that everything about them is too much. They're too handsome, too beautiful, sometimes too ugly. Too tall, or too short. And if they don't look human, then they kind of run the gamut from what they call the treekin—little creatures that look like they're made of twigs and leaves and the like—to shapeshifters like us. But while they can turn into birds and horses and dogs and all, it's not the same. They don't have the animal blood in their veins. They're not cousins.

Anyway, Tatiana McGree's the big deal in the fairy world, so her court's housed in the Harbour Ritz, that fancy place on the lakefront whose main claim to fame is that it once housed Mickey Flynn, the last of the old-time Irish mobsters. Those days are gone now, though they're not so long gone—especially not how we see time. But these days the place is strictly for the up-scale rich, or CEOs coming to town on business trips, with a few penthouse apartments on the top floors for the seriously connected, money-wise.

Jack, Joe, and I get the once-over from the hotel staff when we come in the door looking like three braves down from the rez, but the fairies know who we are and step in quick, moving us sideways to Tatiana's court where, if there's going to be a problem, it won't spill over into the human world. There's a lot of talk between Joe and the fairies then—these tall, slender blonde guys in nice tailored suits. They argue about protocol and crap like that, but Joe won't budge and they finally shuffle us off to a waiting room and have somebody bring us tea when we won't take them up on their offer to partake of something stronger. Oh, I can see that turning down some of that strong fairy home brew is hard on Whiskey Jack, but he's ready to follow Joe's lead. Me, I'm only along for the ride, and I've got no problems doing the same.

"Now remember," Joe tells us when we're left alone with our teas, centering his attention mostly on Jack. "We're not here to play cowboy. We just want to get some help, so we're going to be reasonable and polite."

I nod my head in agreement. Jack does, too, but he also gives Joe a grin.

"I'm serious," Joe tells him.

"I know you are," Jack says. "You've got my word—I'm here to follow your lead."

"Then why are you grinning like that?"

"I'm just thinking of when the fairies turn us down and who's going to be the cowboy."

Joe shakes his head. "Never going to happen."

"Maybe, maybe not. I just know that I've dealt with fairies a lot more than you have, and they can be seriously irritating. Now, normally you're a patient man, but someone takes a run at one of your family . . ."

"What are you saying?"

"Nothing. I'm just here to back you up. But don't tell me I can't enjoy the show, too."

"There's not going to be a show."

"Whatever you say, Joe."

We've been cooling our heels for the better part of an hour before there's finally some motion at the door. We look up, expecting Tatiana to finally show up, or at least someone who'll take us to her, but it's only some more fairies. A tall woman and a couple of those treekin. One of them's standard fare, all roots and leaves and vines, but the other one looks like it broke into a junkyard and built itself out of salvaged parts. It's the woman who holds my attention.

I've had her pointed out to me before, and she's a perfect example of everything I dislike about fairies. A thousand years old, probably, but she dresses like some punky skateboarder, playing at being with it and now, but then she goes by a speaking name of Mother Crone. Her "court" is a damn shopping mall.

She and her little friends aren't directly affiliated with Tatiana's court, but they still have to answer to her, just like all the smaller courts in Newford.

I play it cool, not letting my dislike show, but they're probably picking up on it all the same. Jack just leans back in his chair, smiling at Mother Crone like she's going to come sit on his lap or something. Joe's the one who makes nice, asks her how she's doing, fills the silence with small talk.

Turns out she's having bogan trouble. She doesn't get into any details, but Jack sits up and there's a considering look in his eyes now.

"What kind of trouble?" he asks before I can, his voice more casual than mine would be.

She shrugs. "Oh, the usual. What about you? It's not often that the cousins come to any of our courts."

"We're hoping to get a lead on a friend of ours who's gone missing," Joe says. "I figure that Jilly's built up enough good will with your people that maybe Tatiana will give us a hand."

"Jilly," Mother Crone says. "Do you mean Jilly Coppercorn?"

Joe nods. "Do you know her?"

"I've certainly heard of her. She's good friends with a human fiddler who visits our court."

There's a funny look in her eyes and something—I can't say exactly what—in her voice. Fairies always seem to think they can put one over on anybody, but none of us here are buying what she's selling right now.

"You know something," Joe says.

"I don't know what makes you think—"

"Ten to one it's got something to do with those bogans," Jack says.

Bingo. There's a flicker in her eyes. The smile she's been offering us goes just that little fraction tighter.

"Talk," Joe says.

His voice is quiet, but there's a dark promise in those strange eyes of his.

"I thought that's what we were doing," she says.

Joe shakes his head. "Easy or hard, you're going to tell me what you know."

Mother Crone gets up out of her chair and gives him a hard look.

"I think you're forgetting where you are," she says.

Joe stands up as well and takes a step closer to her. Jack and I exchange glances, then he shrugs and we both get to our feet.

"I don't forget *anything*," Joe says.

"Well, good for you. But if you have a problem, take it up with the queen. I'm not the one you should be—"

"You want Cody in on this?" Joe asks.

It's not an idle threat. We cousins don't have hierarchies the way the fairies do with courts and kings and queens and crap like that. But we have old ones that everybody walks a little carefully around—especially if you're not related to them. In my clan it's Lucius Portsmouth, because he's the Raven who brought the world into being, though I've never heard of him actually admitting to it. With the canids . . . well, Cody's the original Coyote, carries all the canid medicine in one dark-eyed package. And sure, he can mess up on a grand scale, but that doesn't mean he's ineffectual. He's just got bad judgment sometimes.

But Mother Crone doesn't seem to be worried—not by Cody, not by Joe smiling at her with those crazy eyes of his, which I figure should make anybody feel uncomfortable.

"Oh, like suddenly Cody's your best friend," she says.

"No, I wouldn't say we're close at all. But Wendy is."

"Who's Wendy?"

"One of *Jilly's* best friends. Remember Jilly? The woman some little freaks of yours have probably stolen away?"

"I never said—"

"You see how complicated this is getting?" Joe goes on, talking over her. "Jilly's real close to Lucius Portsmouth, too, which isn't that bad for you, I guess, seeing how you can usually count on him to be reasonable. But the crow girls . . . now that's a whole different story. They might act all goofy and sweet, but I've seen them take on a couple of dozen gangbangers and not even work up a sweat. Did I already mention that they're Jilly's friends, too?"

"Look—"

"And then there's Nokomis. Funny thing. The old woman's taken a liking to Jilly, did you know that? You ever wonder why you weren't kicked off Turtle Island the day you arrived? Right or wrong, that was her decision. Now what do you think she'll do to you when she finds out you're messing around with somebody under her protection?"

Joe's lining up all the big guns, and I can see Mother Crone's heart sinking as she begins to realize just how bad a situation she's in. Sure, she's got her little treekin with her, and I don't doubt there are guards right outside the door, but the treekin can't do much of anything and Joe's the one right in her face, not the guards.

"And then you've got me," Joe tells her. "Now I'll be the first to admit no one's going to count me in among the ranks of Jilly's more powerful friends, but all the same, you really don't want me going all Jack Daw on you and your little fairy courts. But believe you me, I will if you don't start telling me what you know right now. We clear?"

Mother Crone actually takes a step back from him and I don't blame her. Jack Daw was a corbae who, back in the eighties, single-handedly took out the whole local cuckoo clan, and they weren't exactly pushovers. Joe's got a look in his eyes right now that's twice as fierce.

"You need to deal with Tatiana on this," is all she's got to fall back on.

Joe shakes his head and steps right up to her, backing her against a wall.

"Time's wasting," he says. "Whatever you know, you're telling me *now*."

None of us see the tall fairy come gliding into the room until he's already grabbing Joe's arm and trying to pull him back. Fairy are strong, everybody knows that, but this guy can't even budge Joe.

Joe turns to look at him.

"You want to lose that hand," he says, "just leave it right there where it is."

Jack turns to me. "We're not here to play cowboy, remember?"

Then he steps up and delivers a sucker punch in the kidney to the fairy who's got a hold of Joe. When the fairy drops Joe's arm, Jack grabs him in a neck hold that brings the fairy to his knees and keeps him there.

"Get the little ones," he tells me, as Mother Crone's two treekin start for Joe.

I grab each of them by the nape of the neck and hold them at arm's length with their legs dangling. They struggle in my grip, but they're not going anywhere.

"I figure we've got ten, maybe fifteen seconds before all hell breaks loose," Jack tells Joe, "so you might want to speed up your conversation there."

"This isn't helping anything," Mother Crone starts.

Joe cuts her off. "You don't understand. We don't play by your rules. We don't go around pretending to be human and tying up our lives with all this pretentious crap about courts and procedures and diplomatic conventions. Mess with us, and all you do is bring hurt down on yourself. Now, tell me what you know."

But we don't get the ten or fifteen seconds Jack thought we might. I don't know if Mother Crone was going to go all martyr on us, or break down and talk, but right about then the door bangs open and we're looking at a half-dozen guards, bows in hand, arrows nocked and aimed at us.

Jack lifts his captive and holds the fairy in front of himself like a shield. I do the same with the squirming treekin I've got in either hand. Joe grabs Mother Crone's arm, and slips around her, twisting her arm behind her back to put her between himself and the guards.

"You better hope you kill me with your first shot," Jack tells the guards, "because you're not getting a second."

"*What* is the meaning of this?" a regal voice demands from behind the guards.

They never shift their aim, they never look away from us, but the guards move slightly aside so that the owner of that voice can step into the room. I'm guessing this is Tatiana. She might be standing there in jeans and a blouse, tawny hair pulled back in a casual ponytail, but she's got the air of someone who doesn't just expect her every command to be obeyed. She can't even see how it could ever be otherwise.

Behind her I can see the hall filling with more guards.

I figure we've got seconds to shift into the between. I consider which guards I'll throw the treekin at. That's saying Joe doesn't want to stay and fight. I give him a glance and see that those eyes of his are just filled right up with a crazy, feral light and realize we're not going anywhere.

"Well, it's a funny thing, your Majesty," Joe says. "We came here, polite as can be, hoping to get some help on tracking down a missing friend of ours, and what do we find out while we're waiting? Turns out she's not so missing after all. Turns out your people are involved. Turns out you just bought yourselves into a whole mess of grief."

"I have only to say the word," Tatiana says, "and the three of you will be dead."

"Maybe. We'll just have to see how that works out for you."

I can see the queen studying him, expecting to read the bluff, but eyes like he's got tell her that he's pretty much capable of anything. So she turns her attention to Joe's captive.

"What do you know about this?" she asks.

"What I have to tell is for your ears," Mother Crone says.

Joe just shakes his head. "Well, isn't that a shame. Guess none of us are going to know."

The queen sighs. "I thought better of you, Joseph. Haven't you always been the one preaching calm mediation rather than threats of violence?"

"Everybody makes mistakes, your Majesty. Guess I was just too damn trusting."

I've got to give it to him. Those eyes of his are crying for some old-time blood and fury, but his voice is just as polite as can be.

The queen looks away from him, her gaze moving from Jack to me.

"Will someone please tell me what this is all about?" she finally says.

Interesting. She's asking, not commanding.

"You shouldn't have let your people go after my family," Joe tells her. "And if you didn't let them, but any of you knew something about it, you really shouldn't have been trying to stonewall me. That makes for bad neighbours, your Majesty."

Jack grins at that play on how the humans used to refer to fairy as the Good Neighbours. Tatiana doesn't miss it either.

"If you know something about this," she tells Mother Crone, "you will inform us of it now."

Oh, she doesn't want to talk. Not in front of us. And we soon find out why.

"Big Dan Cockle is responsible," Mother Crone says.

"And you couldn't tell Joseph this?"

Mother Crone shakes her head. "It's not just his friend Jilly. They've kidnapped another woman, a fiddler named Lizzie Mahone, and pushed her cousin Siobhan down a flight of stairs. But worse that that, they've apparently been going into the wild and the green, hunting cousins."

"This is the same damn bunch we're tracking," Jack says before I can. "There's no 'apparent' about it. They killed Walker's daughter a couple of nights ago and would have had themselves a roasted cerva feed if Lizzie and Grey hadn't stopped them."

Joe gives Jack a look.

"Hey," Jack says. "We told you about it. We just didn't know there was a connection."

"And what were you planning to do to these bogans when you found them?" the queen asks.

"What do you think?" Jack tells her. "Somebody comes into our territories and starts hunting cousins, they've signed their own death warrants."

The queen sighs and gives a slow nod.

"Would you let my people go," she says. "Please. You have my word you won't be harmed. Stand down," she adds to her guards.

The bows lower, arrows are removed from their bowstrings. Joe lets Mother Crone go, and she takes a few quick steps away from him before turning to give him a glare. Jack dumps his fairy unceremoniously on the floor. I put the treekin down more carefully, but the female—she's the woody one—turns and gives me a sharp kick on the shins. It hurts like hell, but I give her a pass on it. This time.

"There's more," Mother Crone says.

That gets everybody's attention.

"Big Dan's gang has a cousin running with them," she tells us. "They call him Odawa. He's old and powerful."

And all of a sudden, everything becomes very personal for me.

"Tall blind guy?" I ask. "From the salmon clan?"

She nods. "Tall and blind, but I don't know his clan."

"You know him?" Joe asks me.

"We go way back, and none of it's pleasant. Nothing he'd like better than to stick my head on a pole."

"Why's he so pissed with you?" Jack asks.

"I pecked out his eyes."

"That's a little harsh. What did he do to you?"

I shrug. "Nothing. I thought he was dead at the time. But the point is, if he'd come after *me,* I'd have had no problem. It was his right."

"But he didn't."

"No. He killed my wife instead. He'll kill anybody I get close to."

"You mean lovers?" Even talking about something serious like this, Jack can't help giving me a wink and adding, "Which would explain why you're giving that sweet little fiddler the cold shoulder."

"I mean anybody."

Jack nods. "Well, thanks for that little late tip. I'll make a point of watching my back."

"But this doesn't explain what he's doing with the bogans," I say, "or why he's kidnapped these two women."

"Well, Lizzie spoiled their party the other night," Jack says. "Maybe they were bringing the meat back to him."

"And Jilly?" Joe asks.

No one had an answer for that, least of all me.

"We will find out," Tatiana says. She turns to her guards. "Fetch me Big Dan and his followers. And bring a gruagagh with you, in case this Odawa offers any trouble."

Half the guards hurry off with the queen's gaze on them before she turns back to us.

"There will be a reckoning," she tells us, and I'm not entirely sure if she means with the bogans or with us. "Until then, you are welcome to stay as our guests. I will have food and drink brought to you. Mother Crone will remain with you to answer any further questions you might have."

"But—" Mother Crone begins.

Oh, she doesn't like it, being stuck here with us. Truth is, I'd just as soon she leave with the rest of them, but I guess Tatiana's making a point of some kind with her.

"There is a problem?" the queen asks.

Mother Crone shakes her head.

"Fine. Is there anything else you require?" she asks of us.

Jack and I wait for Joe to answer.

"Just to be clear," he says, "if we were to walk out that door, you wouldn't try to stop us?"

"Of course not. You are my guests, not prisoners. But I'd prefer you to wait here so that we don't have to go looking for you when we have Big Dan in hand. My guards won't be long."

Joe nods. "Then if someone could bring me a phone, we're good."

"It will be done," the queen says.

Then she sweeps out of the room—which is a good trick when you don't have some big dress or a cloak, but she pulls it off all the same. The guards all leave, the door stays open, and it's just us, Mother Crone, and her treekin.

Joe looks at Jack and me, then settles back in his chair, ignoring the fairies. The two of us take our seats as well, but the fairies stay on their feet.

"Do you have any further questions?" Mother Crone asks.

You can tell that asking us that took something from her. But I guess she's a good soldier, following her queen's orders.

Joe just shakes his head.

"This antagonism to my people's a new thing for you," she says to Joe. "And especially for you, Jack. Half the court has been out drinking and dancing with you and would name you a friend."

"Respect's something that has to be earned," Joe says. "And it has to be maintained. You folks have just let me down, big time. First going after my family—yeah, yeah. You don't have to argue about how you had nothing to do with it. You tried to stonewall me and let's get one thing straight. Jilly gets hurt coming out of this, and it's coming out of somebody's hide."

"You keep talking about family," Mother Crone says. "But Jilly's not related to you."

"You wouldn't understand," Joe tells her. "Relationships don't have the same meaning with fairies as it does with my people. Or even humans."

"What's that supposed to mean?"

Joe just shrugs. "Things are different outside of the fairy courts. People have passion. They're not these cool customers registering zero on the emotional scale when it comes to things that matter, like a relationship."

Mother Crone gives him a withering look. "Oh, would you give that tired old spiel a rest? We have passion."

"Right. Which is why you referred to Geordie Riddell, your lover for the past couple of years, as this 'human fiddler who visits our court.' Why, if someone hurts one of your own, it's a problem of honour and respect, not the deep ache you should feel when someone you care about is in pain."

"You don't understand," she says. "Human lives are so fleeting compared to ours."

"You're right," Joe agrees. "I don't understand, and I don't particularly want to. Because what's important is now. What's important is the faith and trust and love you build with your relationship to someone else. What's important is that you take care of your own and make sure wrongs are righted. That's why Jack's here at my side, ready to take on all comers even though he's got casual drinking buddies and lovers in your court. Because we're friends. Because he's got a big heart that won't stand for innocents being hurt. It's why Grey over there—a guy I've never met before—is willing to stand shoulder to shoulder with me to make sure the sister of my heart is brought back safe and sound."

"But—"

"And, see, that's where you really don't get it. Because Jilly *is* family to me. Just like Jack is. Just like it seems Grey is. We're bound by the way we take care of each other, no matter the personal cost."

"We're not so shallow as you'd like to make us out to be."

"I know you're not," Joe says. "You're self-centered."

Mother Crone glares at him, but before she can speak, one of the guards returns with a cell phone that he tosses to Joe.

"Hold that thought," Joe tells Mother Crone. "I need to make this call first."

Jilly

I'm scared and I hate it. Ever since I broke free of the terrors of my childhood and teen years, I've prided myself on being fearless. I promised myself I wouldn't let myself get scared again. At least not this kind of scared.

I mean, everyone gets scared. Or maybe cautious is a better word.

I'm like most people in that regard. I don't do things that are foolhardy or take unnecessary risks just for the sake of taking them. But I'll stand up to anybody—for myself, for my friends, for whoever needs me to. I don't abide bullies and when I finally broke free of the cycle of abuse, I vowed that I'd never let myself fall into it again.

But talking to Mattie, being here, all my brave words and stances have been stripped away and I find myself sucked into the mindless, abject terror that held me as a little kid, waiting in my bedroom to be hurt again. I hope you never have to know that kind of fear. It's not even the knowledge of the pain to come. It's being so helpless. So powerless. It's knowing that no matter what you do, no matter what you say, it's not going to make any difference, because the person hurting you is bigger than you, and way stronger, and they just don't care. Or rather, they care for the wrong reasons. Your whimpering and crying makes it better for them.

I'm not quite in that head space yet, alone here in this forest, imagining some aspect of my brother Del about to appear from behind any tree, but I'm close. Way too close.

And I really, really hate it.

I hate how my mind's betrayed me, reverting me back to a helpless child like this.

And it's not even real. All of this . . . Mattie, the bear, Del—if it *is* him terrorizing Mattie—none of it's even real.

Except that's the kicker, isn't it? Here in the otherworld, it all *can* be real. And I'm stuck dealing with it.

And there's no point crying about how it isn't fair. Just like when my body betrayed me after the accident.

Oh, I don't mean I should have recovered more than I have—not when you consider the damage I sustained getting hit by that car. Given how badly I was hurt, I'm doing better than the doctors expected.

But I know people in magical places, by which I mean healers. Big-time magic workers. They *could* have helped me recover so that I'm not this Broken Girl the way I am back in the World As It Is. But my body won't cooperate with them because it turns out that where I'm really a Broken Girl is *inside*. All these healers, Joe told me, can't do a thing until I fix the thing that's wrong inside of me.

I thought I had. When I reconciled with Raylene. When I came to terms with my having run away from that house of horrors and leaving her to take my place. I didn't know that was going to happen, but I should have.

Now I find out that wasn't the real problem. Or only a part of the real problem.

The real problem is that locked away inside my head are two little girls who are still dealing with the nightmare: the girl I created from a fairy-tale book, and the one I was. Mattie and me. Poor Mattie, made real by me when I didn't even know what I was doing.

So there's that, and then there's this place where Del's still running free, where all my hard-earned bravery and courage have just drained away, turning me back into a victim.

This must be what blocked the healers from helping me.

And the thing is, I haven't even *seen* Del yet. I don't have a shred of evidence that he's actually here. All Mattie said was "he" and I just assumed it was Del. "He" could be anyone. But I know who he is. Del was only the first of many for me, but he was Mattie's first and only, so who else would be here?

I look around myself.

I could wait here for Mattie to come back and tell me if she's decided to turn me over to Del. Or for Del himself to show up.

I walk off instead. Not to avoid the problem, because how can you avoid what's locked up in the deepest part of your own head? It's just that I need to be moving. Doing something.

So I press on through the woods and they start to seem familiar. I don't realize why until I see the house.

It stops me cold. I haven't seen that place since I went back to Tyson with Geordie, but I couldn't forget it if I tried.

That's where it all began.

In an old clapboard house without indoor plumbing on the edge of Tyson—the part of town that people called Hillbilly Holler when I was growing up. A shabby, unkempt place, the overgrown yard dotted with junked cars, machinery debris, and other rubbish half-swallowed by the vegetation. It looks as abandoned as it did when Geordie and I came here years ago in the World As It Is. Maybe it always looked abandoned, even when my family lived there. It's not like anybody ever took any care of it except for me, and what did I know about gardening or the upkeep a house needs? But at least I tried.

The county road still runs by it, here in this world inside my head, but the house stands all alone, the neighbouring houses and shacks gone like they never existed.

I guess in this place they never did.

I wonder if this is where Del's holed up. I study the windows, their screens hanging awry, curtains in tatters. It's impossible to tell if there's anyone in there or not. Then I catch a glimpse of movement—not inside the house, but along the side.

Nothing's changed, except . . .

I blink and take a closer look. The figure I thought I saw has either stepped out of sight or it's just me, projecting more of my fears. But I swear I caught a glimpse of a priest in his black habit, standing at the corner of the house before he slipped away.

I step back deeper under the trees, hoping I wasn't seen.

Does this mean they're *all* here? *All* the freaks that made my life such a horror show?

Del, the priest, my old boyfriend Rob, my foster parents . . .

I feel nausea rise up my throat and I have to sit down. I lean my head against the trunk of the tall birch behind me, wishing I could stop the flood of memories. But I can't.

Del was the worst betrayal—because you expect your family to protect you, not to hurt you—but Father Cleary came pretty close. When the church preaches love, you don't think they mean it so literally.

I had my first communion when I was six, which followed hard on the heels of my first confession. I knew what I had to confess, but I also knew what Del would do if I ever told anybody. That line Mattie had about having her nose cut off and a necklace made of her fingers and toes—that came from Del. I'd only ever tried to tell anyone about it once, when it first started happening. All it got me was a slap in the face from my mother for being such a filthy little liar. And later Del made his own point: he burned me with the end of his cigarette, then claimed I'd walked into it. Naturally, they all believed him.

So I couldn't confess to the priest because I wanted to keep my nose and fingers and toes, and I didn't want to be burned again. But it started eating at me because I knew I was lying during confession by not telling about it.

I realized that not only was Del hurting me, but when I died I was going straight to hell.

Still, it was another two years before I finally got the courage.

There I am, this little eight-year-old girl trying to tell the priest what's been happening to me, and he says that I have to go to his office after I leave the confessional and wait for him there.

"This is very serious, Jillian," he told me. "We're going to have to pray hard and long together to make things better between you and the Lord."

Who knew that "praying" was just Father Cleary's euphemism for dealing with something else that was hard and long? Not the little kid I was. Not until we were in his office later. Not until he closed the door and started to unzip his pants.

Del was waiting for me outside the church to walk me home. I don't know if he was psychic, or if it showed all over my face, but he knew right away what had happened. He slapped me hard across the back of the head, just like Mama always did, and told me I was going to pay for this.

I guess he didn't like to share his toys.

That night when I was asleep he scattered broken glass on the floor beside my bed, like my water glass had fallen over, and when I got out of bed in the morning, I stepped right on it with my bare feet.

Oh, it was a mess, me bawling my head off, blood all over the bottoms of my feet and dripping on the floor. It hurt so bad.

Mama came in and started yelling at me about how could I be so stupid as to not clean up my glass when it broke last night. I saw my younger brothers, Jimmy and Robbie, standing in the doorway, eyes wide. Del was in the hallway behind them, just grinning away and we both knew why.

Mama threw a rag at me.

"Now, you just clean that up, missy," she told me. "And don't you go tracking blood all over the floors, neither."

I was hobbling around for days, my feet wrapped in rags, trying not to cry with every step I had to take as I did my chores. But I learnt my lesson.

I didn't go tell anybody else. And I knew there was no god. Or at least, if there was, I hated him for letting this happen to me.

After that, I expected people to betray me. So I wasn't surprised when I got abused again in one of the foster homes I was put in after I ran away from home. I wasn't surprised when my boyfriend Rob—another runaway like me—got me strung out on junk and started me turning tricks.

By the time Lou—who was a patrolman at the time—got me off the streets and into his girlfriend Angel's recovery program for kids like me, I'd been betrayed so many times I don't know how I ever learned to trust again.

I guess Lou and Angel started the process with—when I look back on it—their infinite patience.

Sophie and Wendy made it real, befriending me, teaching me what it could mean to have people in your life that you can count on.

And Geordie . . . Geordie was the first guy I ever met who didn't betray me, who wouldn't even *think* of betraying me. I mean a guy my age, because Lou'd already proven to me there were decent men in the world.

But they're not here. Lou and Angel. Sophie and Wendy. My dear lad Geordie.

There's only a made-up girl and her monstrous bear who hate me.

Del, and it looks like the priest.

Maybe Rob and Adrian L. Brewer, the pasty-faced freak from the last foster home I was in. I remember him the best because he was the worst that child services sent me to.

Maybe they're all living together in the house, all my enemies under one roof.

If I had a can of gasoline, I could burn it down with them in it.

I sigh. No, I couldn't. Oh, I could burn the house down, no question, but I wouldn't want the deaths of even such monsters weighing down my soul.

It's funny. Whenever I talk about this kind of thing—in my art, in outreach programs like Angel runs—you get these people saying things like how it's all old hat, movie-of-the-week, tearjerker crap. They're tired of it and wish that people would just shut up and get on with their lives instead of going on and on about it. Well, we're tired of it, too, those of us unfortunate enough to be Children of the Secret. But that didn't stop it from happening to us and screwing up our lives. Way too many of us weren't lucky enough to find support like I got to help me pick up the pieces of my life again.

And as being here makes it all too clear, the reality of it never really goes away, does it? It's always there inside us, an unhappy ache that we can't completely ease no matter how deeply we bury it.

It's not something I think about all the time or anything, but I still wake up sweating from bad dreams where I'm that kid again, trapped in an endless cycle of being hurt. Or something I see or hear will trigger a rush of panic before I remember that I'm not there anymore.

Something like the beat-up old house sitting down there on the other side of a county road that, in this world, probably goes from nowhere to nowhere.

I have to look away. I have to get away, but I don't know what to do, where to go, until I remember the tree. My magic tree that listened to all my stories and gifted me with her light. The one that Raylene burned down in the World As It Is.

Maybe it's still standing, here in this world inside my head.

That's where the magic started for me, I guess. Not in a book, because I didn't know what I was creating from its pages. I thought I was only taking comfort from those fairy tales and Wentworth's illustrations, not creating a walking, talking version of Mattie, full of hurt and pain.

That tree and Raylene are the only good things I remember from Hillbilly Holler. In the World As It Is, one's burned down, and the other tried to kill me before we made our peace. But maybe it'll be different here. Maybe, even with everything else that's so awful here, the tree will at least be here.

I circle around through the woods because the tree's in the fields behind the house, and I don't want anybody to see me making my way toward it. It was always a private place before and maybe my enemies don't know about it.

I'm in a curious state of mind as I walk, weaving my way through the underbrush. I start at every sound, my nerves all a-twitch. Anticipation's running high that I'm going to see the tree again. But I'm also dreading that it'll be like it was the last time I saw it: nothing more than a charred ruin of a stump. Overgrown. Dead. Gone.

When I finally get to the field where the old tree stands, I let out a breath I wasn't aware I was holding. It's still here, as big as ever. I thought it might be smaller than I remembered, the way the things from your past usually seem, but it's still huge. It'd take three or four of me to touch hands reaching around the base of its trunk, and the canopy has an enormous spread, bigger than any of the oversized infill housing that started to appear in Lower Crowsea during the mid-nineties. They'd jam these monster homes onto a tiny lot with no regard for the look of the neighbourhood.

But the neighbourhood here is just fine. That old oak. The apple trees at the other end of the field, growing up out of a mess of thorny thickets. The field itself, grasses and weeds swaying in the light breeze that's coming from the woods behind me.

I take the time to study the edge of the forest surrounding the field, longer still to check out the second field that runs up to the back of the old house. I can't see anybody. And I can't stop grinning as I walk slowly through the tall grass and weeds to where the tree's waiting for me.

I wonder if she's here, that aspect of the White Deer Woman who told me she used to listen to my stories when I sat under its branches and poured out my heart. Or if she's not here . . . well, maybe I can call her to me through the connection we have to the tree. Because *she* found a way out of this world inside my head. If I call her back, maybe she can take me out of here, too.

I don't sense her presence when I'm under the tree, but then I never sensed it when I was a kid, either. Or rather, I sensed something peaceful and comforting, but it's what I always feel in a place like this.

I lay a hand on the trunk.

"I'm sorry about Raylene," I say. "She was getting back at me, and you shouldn't have had to suffer because of that."

Sometimes it feels like that's always going to be the way of the world. The innocent get hurt, and no one really pays any attention unless it happens right in their face and they can't possibly ignore it. But even then they manage to forget pretty damn fast.

Why does it have to be like that? Why does wishing we could all just get along and take care of each other have to be a naive, innocent hope instead of something we could all actually work toward?

I guess I'll never know. Because the people who do the hurting don't care, and they're not about to explain themselves in terms that would make any kind of sense to a normal person.

I still have my hand on the rough bark of the tree. I move closer and hug it, the bark scratchy against my cheek and catching in the tangles of my hair. I can't possibly get my arms all around it, but it feels good to stand here, holding onto something this full of comfort.

I don't know how long I would have stood there—looking, I'm sure, like some bad editorial cartoon of a die-hard environmentalist—but there's a sudden crash in the branches above me. I look up and see a woman and a pony. Impossibly, a woman riding a pony has suddenly *appeared* in the branches above me, but I don't get the time to puzzle it out. The woman manages to grab onto a branch, but the pony comes barreling down toward me, changing into a little man along the way.

I jump aside and he just misses me—all little man now, nothing of the pony left except that his dreadlocks are the same colour as was the pony's mane. He lands on his feet like a cat, expelling a sharp *whuft* of air from be-tween his lips, and we stare at each other. He looks as ready to bolt as I am.

"Some help up here," a voice calls down from above.

We both look up.

After all I've been through in the past little while, I would have said that nothing could surprise me anymore. But I would have been wrong.

"Lizzie?" I find myself saying. "What are *you* doing in this world?"

Her familiar face looks down at me from where she's clinging to a branch as fat around as her own torso.

"So," she says, "I'm guessing this isn't Kansas, or even Sweetwater."

I shake my head.

"Great. And here I am, stuck up in a tree."

"Just let go," the little man beside me tells her.

"Oh, right. Like I'm going to do that and break my neck. I'm neither cat nor doonie."

"It will be fine," he tells her. "I'll take your weight."

"Nope."

"Trust me."

She gives me a look but I have no words. I'm still trying to process the fact that she's here with a little man who can turn into a pony.

"Oh, crap," she says and lets go where I'm pretty sure I wouldn't have.

But instead of falling, she comes floating down. I shoot the little man a look and see that he's got this serious look of concentration on his face. I guess by taking her weight he didn't mean he was going to catch her, but that he was go-ing to literally take her weight so that she doesn't tip the scales more than a leaf.

When Lizzie's feet touch the ground, she loses her balance and I catch her arm.

"You see?" the little man says.

She gives me a quick smile of thanks and puts a hand out to steady herself against the tree. Then she looks at the little man and shakes her head.

"I saw all too well," she says. "What did you do? Talk to my fat cells and ask them to be air for a few moments?"

"Something like that, although you're hardly fat."

I have no idea what they're talking about.

"What are you *doing* here?" I ask.

"Same as you," she says. "Bogans kidnapped me into the otherworld—or at least some part of the otherworld. The forest where we were was a lot darker and scarier than it is here. You did say this is the otherworld, didn't you?"

I nod. "It's sort of the otherworld, except bogans didn't bring me. I just kind of appeared here."

"And look at you—you're like twenty years old and all, you know . . . healthy and everything."

I give her another nod. "Apparently the way we appear here has everything to do with how we perceive ourselves to be."

"Sweet."

I look from her to the little man.

"Oh, this is Timony Twotot," Lizzie says. "And this is Jilly," she adds for his benefit.

The little man and I regard each other. Then he sticks out a little brown hand, and we shake like we're meeting at an art show opening or something.

"Pleased to meet you," he says.

I nod, but before I can say anything, Lizzie's talking again.

"So then, where exactly *are* we? Timony told me to concentrate on somewhere safe, so naturally I thought of you because you know all about this kind of thing, right?"

"Not really."

"Just tell me there isn't some pack of bogans waiting around the corner."

"None that I know of, but—"

"I thought we'd end up back at the hotel, but obviously *that* didn't work out." Then she gets a worried look. "What did you mean it's sort of the otherworld?"

"It's complicated," I tell her. "I think we're in a world that's inside my head."

She just looks at me.

"I know. I can't really explain it myself."

"I can," Timony says. "We're not exactly in your head. We're in your *croí baile*—your heart home."

"My what?"

"*Croí baile,*" he repeats. "Everyone has a place like this in the otherworld, but most people only visit it when they're sleeping or dreaming. It's a place personal to just you."

"Like some kind of pocket world?" I ask.

Joe's told me about them, but all I can remember is the term 'pocket world,' none of the details. It's like the place that Geordie's sister Christiana has in the between, though I guess she's not really his sister. Or at least she wasn't born his sister.

I shake my head and concentrate on what Timony's saying.

". . . a term as any. They're often set up so that only you can visit them. Anyone else needs a specific invitation."

"But I didn't invite . . ." I start to say.

But then I realize I did invite them. Not them in particular, perhaps, but I was desperately wanting *someone* to be here with me.

"So, can we go back home now?" Lizzie asks.

"I don't know the way," I tell her.

We both look at the doonie, but he shakes his head.

"This world is closed inside and out," he says. "Nobody can get in or out without permission."

"Well, I give you permission," I say.

That gets us another shake of his head. "It seems more complicated than that."

"Are you saying, we're stuck here?" Lizzie asks.

"So it would seem."

"Well, at least there aren't any bogans." She looks to me. "You said there weren't any, right?"

"I think there's something worse," I tell her.

They both look at me, waiting for me to explain.

"It's a complicated story," I say. "And not a very happy one."

"We don't have anywhere else to go," Lizzie says.

I give the house a look, but there still doesn't seem to be anybody stirring there.

"Has that place got something to do with this?" Lizzie asks.

"It's where it all started," I tell her.

Then we all sit down in the grass under the tree and that old oak of mine gets to hear my story all over again.

Rabedy Collins

The mists had drawn back a little when Rabedy arrived on the seashore with Odawa at his side, but otherwise the beach was much the same. A grey and dismal place that smelled of fish and algae. The doonie's hoof prints still began abruptly and ended as they had before, although this time there was the addition of the tracks that Rabedy and the others had left. In time, no trace of them would remain, for the tide was coming in and already washing onto the prints, softening their edges.

"Take me to where their trail ends," the green-bree said.

He put a hand on Rabedy's shoulder, as he had when they crossed over from the Aisling's Wood. Rabedy shivered, disliking the touch as much now as he had before. And why was it that Odawa hadn't needed this sort of help before?

"Are you really blind?" Rabedy asked.

"Yes. But I'm old and my medicine is potent. It allows me to compensate. While I can't physically see as you do, and I can't sense details, I can usually get by."

"Medicine . . . that's what we call magic."

"It is and it isn't. There are parts of it that reside in ourselves, that come with our blood, but mostly it's power we borrow from the spirits."

"This is where the trail ends," Rabedy said.

Odawa let go of the bogan's shoulder and moved his hands back and forth in the air, feeling for the doonie's trail.

"What do you sense here?" he asked Rabedy.

The blind gaze turned to look at the bogan, finding his face with no trouble.

Rabedy closed his eyes, as much to not have to look into those milky eyes as to concentrate.

"Access to anywhere," he said. "A thousand roads."

"And the doonie? Where did he go?"

Rabedy concentrated again.

"He's just gone," he said, surprised.

Normally a passage between the worlds left some residue, some hint of where one's quarry had gone. But here, there was nothing.

"I get the same," Odawa said. "They've vanished into a hidden world, and there'll be no following them now."

Rabedy waited a moment, then asked, "Does it really matter that much?"

"Who's the blind one here?"

Rabedy shrugged, then realized the green-bree couldn't see the gesture.

"I understand vengeance," he said, "but unlike some of my kind, I don't understand cruelty."

"You think me cruel?"

"What would you call what you do?"

"He blinded me."

"When he thought you were already dead. And then you killed his wife, and others close to him, too, if all the tales are true. You should have taken your battle directly to him. That would have been the honourable course."

Odawa gave a slow nod. "And probably the wiser, too. She cursed me before she died. She cursed me to wander forever, but never reach my destination."

"So that's why you needed our help. If you were to hunt him directly, you would never get near to him."

"That was my thought, to use you as a bridge to reaching the damned jay. But it seems that the curse holds true even when I use intermediaries, for I'm no closer to Grey now than I've ever been."

Rabedy looked down the long grey sands of the beach to where it disappeared into the mist. He sighed.

"I can take you to him," he said.

"And yet you thought me cruel."

"Hurting the people around him—that's cruel. Finishing your business with Grey . . . that's just between the two of you."

"And for a reward," Odawa asked. "What do you require?"

Rabedy spat on the sand between them. "I don't want anything. I just want this done so that we can go back to doing what bogans do, and you can go back to whatever it is that you are."

The blind gaze never left Rabedy's face.

"Big Dan wanted safe passage through the green and the wild," Odawa said. "For him and anyone in his company."

"I'm not my uncle."

"Then perhaps I could show you how to complete your shapeshifting one way or the other so that you don't have to walk around the way you do, caught between dog and bogan."

He started to reach for Rabedy, but the bogan backed out of his reach.

"I told you," he said. "I don't want anything, and I don't want to be beholden. I'll figure this out on my own."

"I meant it to be knowledge, freely given."

"Do you want Grey or don't you?" Rabedy asked.

The brow above the green-bree's milky eyes wrinkled into a frown, but then he forced himself to smile.

"I want him," he said.

"Fine. Then let's finish this."

Rabedy stepped closer, but paused just out of reach before the blind green-bree could put his hand back on the bogan's shoulder.

"Remember," Rabedy said. "I have your name."

Odawa moved so quickly, Rabedy never saw him coming. One moment the green-bree was standing in front of him, the next Odawa had him in a headlock, arm around his neck so that neither air nor words could escape his throat.

"Don't threaten me, boy," he said in Rabedy's ear, his voice conversational and soft, which felt all the more deadly. "You need to get that name out into the air for it to be of any use and I am not entirely infirm."

Rabedy fought the grip, but to no avail. The green-bree held him long enough to show that, had he wanted, he could have caused some real pain— could have snapped Rabedy's neck, could have held him until he choked— then he let go and gave the bogan a push away from him. Rabedy staggered on the sand and only just caught himself from falling. He turned, glaring, a name forming on his lips.

"I could have killed you, boy," Odawa said before Rabedy could get the name out. "I could have snapped your neck like a twig. But I didn't. Will you now kill an unarmed, blind man?"

Rabedy lifted a hand to rub at his throat. He wanted to speak the name Big Dan had given him. Wanted to drive the pluiking green-bree's face into the beach and choke him on the wet sand. And he wasn't fooled by the mild tone of Odawa's voice. He was wary now, and if the truth be known, more than a little nervous. How could a blind man move that fast?

Odawa's milky-white gaze remained fixed on him, waiting for a reply.

"I'm not a boy," was all he could find to say.

"No, you're somewhere between a bogan and a dog. Hold," the green-bree added, lifting his hand when Rabedy was about to speak. "I know what you meant and I'll offer you this promise: I'll mind my manners and call you by the speaking name you've given me. Can I expect the same consideration in return?"

"Or what?"

Odawa sighed. "Or nothing. Or you'll go your way and I'll go mine. Or you'll speak my true name and my will becomes yours. Why must everything be a confrontation with you people?"

Rabedy could only look at the green-bree. His neck was sore. He remembered the ease with which Odawa had put him out of action.

"After what you just did to me," he said, "you still expect me to help you?"

"I expect nothing. I am only asking. The decision is entirely yours."

"And if I help you, you'll go away and leave us all alone?"

"I'll leave you alone even if you don't help me," the green-bree said. "Haven't you been listening? I offer you no threat. I need help and I'll be grateful to you if you provide it, but I am not here to force my will on anyone."

"Except for Grey."

Odawa shook his head. "No, not even him. I just mean to kill Grey. I'm done with games and threats and all the childish nonsense that has filled my life for too many years. It's time I simply dealt with Grey and got on with my life."

"Corbae don't die easily," Rabedy said.

The doubt was plain in his voice. True, Odawa had dealt effortlessly with him, but he was only a poor excuse for a bogan, as his uncle liked to say. Grey . . . Grey was a corbae in his prime. In his veins ran the same blood as that cousin of his who had brought the world into being in the long ago.

"No," Odawa agreed. "Especially not when he's aided by the curse of his dead wife that keeps misdirecting me whenever I try to get near him. But I guarantee you this, Master Rabedy. Put him in front of me, and you'll see how easily a corbae can die."

Rabedy gave a slow nod. And then the world could go back to the way it had been before Big Dan brought the blind green-bree into their lives. Odawa would go away. Grey would be dead, and they wouldn't have to worry about his coming after them for the killing of his cerva cousin. Fairy and the spirits of the wild and the green could go back to ignoring one another, and life would be so much less complicated than it had become.

"I'll bring you to him," he said. "But then you'll be on your own. I won't add to the troubles between our people."

"All I ask," Odawa assured him, "is for the chance to stand face to face with the man who blinded me. Give me that and I won't need your help or that of anyone else."

"Fair enough," Rabedy said.

He took a piece of string out of his pocket and knotted it once, twice, and then a third time.

"Here," he said, putting the knotted string into the green-bree's hand. "Think of Grey as you undo one of these knots, and it should guide you to him."

Odawa fingered the string. "There are three knots."

"So you'll get three tries. I can't fit more onto that bit of string. But surely that should be enough."

"Depending on how well they work against his wife's curse."

"I can't help you with that."

"I could still use your eyes until I find him."

Rabedy sighed. He wanted to be done with this *now*. But if he was to get rid of the green-bree once and for all . . .

"Fine," he said. "So let's go and get it done."

He stepped closer to Odawa and allowed the green-bree to grip his shoulder. When those strong fingers found their hold, Rabedy led them away from the dismal grey shoreline of this unhappy world that was Odawa's *croí baile*.

Geordie

I wondered what Eddie would think to see the bunch of us go trooping off into the woods behind his hotel, but we didn't run into him on the way out, so I was spared the need to come up with some plausible excuse. That also meant that I didn't have to introduce him to Cassie and explain what she was doing all the way out in Sweetwater without a car or a ride to get here. I liked Eddie and didn't particularly feel like lying to him, but telling him that we were off to call up a stag spirit, or that Cassie had gotten here by crow girl express would only make things way more complicated than they already were.

We tramped through the bush, avoiding the clumps of hard, icy snow that had yet to get the message that spring was here, until we found a small meadow that was out of sight of the hotel or any of the other buildings in Sweetwater. On any other day I'd have been happy to hang out and play some tunes under one of the beeches or elms that rose up above the cedars and scrub trees. But although the weather was warm enough, and I did have my fiddle with me, the case hanging from my shoulder by a strap, we were here on more serious business.

"So, who's going to do it?" Siobhan asked.

Now that we were out here, she didn't seem quite so sure about what we were getting into. If she knew what Cassie and I did, she'd probably be more nervous still. Sure there are native spirits like the crow girls or Cody who seemed to thrive on getting involved in human affairs, but most of them just want to be left alone and don't take kindly to being drawn into our messy lives. Especially not when those calling them up are strangers to them, and we'd certainly be strangers to this Walker.

But we were here now, and I really didn't want to get back into another discussion about calling Joe here by using his true name.

"I'll do it," I said.

"Is there anything we should know?" Con asked.

Cassie replied before I could. "You'd be smart not to draw any more attention to yourselves than simply being here is already going to do. Let Geordie do the talking unless either of them asks you something directly."

"So . . . is this dangerous?" Andy wanted to know.

"Any dealings with the otherworld can be dangerous," Cassie told him. Then she smiled. "Hell, being alive is dangerous. But in this case, just be quiet and things should be okay."

I looked around to see if anybody else had something they needed to say, but they were all quiet now, waiting on me.

I won't say I wasn't a little nervous myself. I know. I've spent all kinds of time with Galfreya and her fairy court, but this was a whole other ball game. I'd heard enough stories about people getting on the wrong side of a hot-tempered cousin not to approach a situation such as this without a healthy dose of caution. But while you can worry forever about what might go wrong, and make all the safeguards in the world so that it won't, in the end you still just have to do it.

So I took a steadying breath and called the cerva's name, or at least as much of a name as we had for him. I hoped it would be enough. Without his true name, we could only hope to get his attention. Maybe he would be curious enough to see who was trying to summon him. Maybe not. All we could do was try.

But I tried to feel positive as I sent his name out into the forest.

Walks-with-Dreams.

Once, twice, three times.

And we waited.

I have to admit I felt a little self-conscious yodeling "Walks-with-Dreams" off into the woods at the top of my lungs—like a low-grade version of one of those dreams where you're up on stage playing a tune to a huge crowd and suddenly realize you forgot to put your pants on before the show. Here in the meadow, everybody was just looking at me and nothing much was happening in response to my call. It wasn't that big a surprise to me because I know that the otherworld has never been about answering to our beck and call. Normally, you'd have about as much of a chance attracting the attention of a cousin as you would teaching a mouse to play a jig.

But then I sensed a change. In the air, in me—I'm not sure. I just became aware of a difference. It took me a few moments to realize that it was the forest going quiet all around us.

I'm not sure the others felt it. Or at least they weren't showing it. Glancing at their faces I saw that they were starting to get that look of boredom people develop when they have to wait too long for something to happen— even when they are in a dangerous situation. But I knew that Cassie heard what I heard—or rather the lack of what there was to hear. The normal sounds around us were withdrawing. I could still hear birdsong, the chitter of squirrels, the droning of insects, but they seemed far away now. Muffled, as though they were coming to us from the other side of a window.

Con turned to me. "So, how do we know that anything's even going to—"

"Shh," Cassie told him.

And then the cerva was here, and no one wanted or needed to speak. Not even me, and I was supposed to be our spokesperson.

It's funny. I thought I'd be fine, that my time in Galfreya's fairy court, that knowing Joe and some of the other cousins, would have prepared me for this. But Walker was different from any of them. Fairies, depending on their affiliations, were by turns whimsical, grotesque, heartbreakingly beautiful, or stern. Joe and his cousins were mostly earthy and scruffy . . . and just a little scary. Or at least the ones I'd met were—barring the crow girls.

But Walker . . . Walker was tall and composed in demeanor, an inspiring figure with the long face of a deer, a massive rack of antlers and deep brown eyes that were like dark pools hiding all the forest's secrets in their depths. Looking at him, I started thinking about all those murmurs and hints of the Horned Lord of the Hunt that sometimes come twisting through the ballads and tunes that make up my repertoire. If Walker's presence was anything like what Cernunnos was supposed to be like, it didn't surprise me that he'd been so revered back in the old countries—you know, before the priests in their robes made worshipping him yet another sin.

Standing here in his presence, I understood the reverence people had felt for that European lord of the forest. Here, in our own woods, I wanted to go down on my knees in front of Walker and ask for a blessing.

But that wasn't going to happen. Not so much because I couldn't find the voice to ask, but because I realized those calm eyes of his also held dark fires in their depths. There was a set to his jaw and shoulders that told me he was nowhere near pleased to meet with us here.

"I don't know you," he said, his voice deep and resonant, "and you have the stink of fairy on you. Why did you summon me, and who gave you my name?"

A threat lay heavy in the air, carried on the shoulders of his words. Not the threat of violence. For all that he was so tall and broad-chested, I didn't get the impression that he dealt with his problems in a might-makes-right kind of way. The threat I sensed was subtler than that. A promise that he could close doors inside us that were open at the moment. And the doors he could close were . . .

I don't know what the others were getting from him, but for me I understood that the door he could close was on my music and my connections to the fairy realms. I could live with losing magic—it always just seemed to bring complications and trouble anyway—but not my music. I couldn't live without my music.

That made me think of Jilly, having lost her art because of the accident, and I gained a whole new sympathy for her. Jilly, who was lost somewhere in the otherworld.

"Are you all mute, as well as foolish?" Walker asked.

No one had said a word, and then I realized that was because we'd all agreed earlier that I was going to do the talking. I wanted to turn to the others and tell them that I'd changed my mind, but for Jilly's sake, I found the courage to step forward. I tried to remember all the things my brother Christy had told me about situations such as this. I knew that being respectful was right near the top of the list. Foremost was, don't get involved in this sort of thing in the first place, but it was already too late for that.

"I . . ."

I had to clear my throat.

"I'm sorry if we've disturbed you, sir," I finally managed, "but we're here on Lizzie Mahone's behalf."

He gave no sign of recognition, and I didn't think the name registered at first.

"Lizzie," he repeated.

"You told her she could call your name if she ever needed any help."

Walker surveyed our small company.

"And yet *she's* not here," he said.

"I know. She's—"

"And it doesn't explain the reek of fairy. This is not a time when aganesha or their friends should be coming uninvited into our forests. And as things stand at the moment, that invitation would be a long time in coming."

"We understand, sir," I said. "We offer our condolences to you on the loss of your daughter."

"Do you now?"

I swallowed thickly and nodded. That deep dark gaze of his studied me for a long moment.

"I thank you for that," he finally said. "My daughter will be much missed."

His gaze lifted to take in the others before returning to me.

"So, you are friends to Lizzie *and* to fairy," he said.

"To Lizzie, yes," I replied. "And I have often played music in Mother Crone's court, but we seem to have gotten on the wrong side of the fairies—or at least some bogans. Nothing like what you've had to endure, but Lizzie's cousin—Siobhan here—was assaulted by them, and now they've stolen away Lizzie and our friend Jilly."

"Bogans," Walker said, and there was a world of menace in his use of the word.

I nodded. "Possibly the same gang that has brought so much sorrow into your life."

Walker gave a slow shake of his head and looked off into the woods.

"What can they possibly hope to gain with all of this?" he said.

I figured the question was rhetorical and waited until he looked back at me.

"There's something else," I said when he did. "We've been told there's a cousin with them. An old and powerful one from one of the fish clans—blind, but still formidable."

Walker's brow darkened. "Who?"

"The only name we have for him is Odawa, and I don't believe he's local."

"I can find out," he said.

He looked like he was about to go and do just that.

"Sir?" I said.

He waited for me to go on.

"Will you help us track down our friends? We know they were taken into the otherworld, but none of us are that familiar with travelling through it on our own."

"Do you know where in the otherworld?"

I shook my head. "No one can seem to get a trace on them."

"Do you have any idea how big the otherworld is?"

I was about to tell him that I did, that it was world upon world, vast and confusing, but then a cell phone went off. The tone played the opening bars of *The Flintstones* theme.

"Crap," Cassie said.

Trust her to have that on her phone. Her preferences have always ranged from the tasteful to the tasteless.

She pulled out her phone and looked at its screen.

"It's Joe," she told us.

Walker gave her a considering look as she spoke. It was as though he was seeing her for the first time.

"I know you," he said.

"I'm sorry," she told him, "but I really need to take this. He might have news about Jilly."

Walker turned to me. I thought he might be angry, considering how Cassie'd just blown him off, but he only looked thoughtful.

"And Joe is?" he asked.

"Joseph Crazy Dog."

"Ah."

He looked as though he was going to say something else, but stopped himself.

". . . behind the hotel," Cassie was saying. "With Walker. Uh-huh."

She turned to us to say, "He's going to be right here," but she needn't have bothered because hard on the heels of her words, Joe came stepping out of the between, a cell phone in his hand. He gave Cassie a quick hug and nodded to me before turning to face Walker.

"Is it just me," I heard Andy say from behind me, "or does none of this seem so weird anymore?"

I didn't bother to respond. I was more interested in what news Joe had. But Walker spoke first.

"I should have realized," he said, "that one of Cody's people would be mixed up in all of this."

"Well, first off," Joe told him, "I'm not one of Cody's 'people'—whoever the hell they're supposed to be—and the reason I'm involved is that somebody's made the mistake of messing with my family."

"Your . . . family."

"Her name's Jilly. She's like my sister, or my daughter."

Emotion flickered in Walker's eyes.

"Oh, crap," Joe told him. "I'm really sorry about what happened to Anwatan. I only just heard."

Walker nodded. "Thank you."

"Now, I don't want to be crass," Joe went on, "but unless we want a repeat of that, we need to track down these women. What do you know?"

"Only what I've just been told by your friends," Walker said.

That crazy gaze of Joe's turned to me, and I couldn't repress a shiver. There was always something going on in his eyes, but today they looked positively feral.

I gave him a quick introduction to the others and after I'd filled him in on what we knew, he told us what he'd learned at the fairy court.

"I'm sorry about your girlfriend," he told me, finishing up, "but she shouldn't have tried to stonewall me like that."

"She's not my girlfriend."

"Whatever."

"And," I added, "I'm not particularly happy with her at the moment, either. She seemed way more concerned about the politics of the court than in helping us find Jilly."

Joe shrugged. "She's a fairy—what did you expect?"

Walker nodded in agreement. His reaction was expected, all things considered, but I was a little surprised by Joe's attitude. I'd never gotten a sense of animosity towards fairy from him before. But I guess I understood. While I felt a little guilty, siding with them instead of with Galfreya, she'd brought this on herself. My first loyalty was always going to be to Jilly, not to the fairies or their court.

"Do you trust them to actually help us?" Cassie asked.

"Don't know," Joe said. "But I'm not hanging around to find out. I left Jack and Grey back at Tatiana's court. If something comes up, Jack knows how to find me."

"Last night," Walker said, "we held the second blessing ceremony for Anwatan."

Joe nodded. "Like I said, I only just found out what happened to her."

"That's not why I'm bringing it up. I just thought you should know that cousins from the buffalo clans were in attendance. Many of them."

"I'd heard she was close to Pijaki-tibik's son—he still their chief?"

Walker shook his head. "He got voted out at their last clan gathering for being too moderate. Minisino's their chief now and he's more hard-line—like the Warrior's Society up on the rez."

"Considering what happened to your daughter," Joe said, "they've got my sympathies."

"I know I should be feeling the same," Walker said. "Moon knows, I want those bogans brought to some kind of justice. But with the buffalo clans mustering under Minisino . . . this could lead to a war."

"Maybe, maybe not," Joe told him.

But Walker wasn't finished.

"I don't think Anwatan would want her death to be remembered as the start of another conflict between our people and the fairy courts."

"The way your daughter died," Joe said, "that wasn't the first time the aganesha have murdered one of us in the last few years. It's time the fairy courts learned that we're only going to take so much of their bullshit."

"But if there's war, even more will die. Cousins and fairy both."

"I know. But it's not up to us, and right now I'm more concerned with getting Jilly and her friend back." He turned to me. "Can you show me the place where she was taken from?"

I nodded and we all trooped back to the hotel. By the time we reached the building, Walker didn't look a whole lot different from Joe—black braids, jeans and a flannel shirt, cowboy boots. The antlers were gone, though I thought I could still see ghosts of them when he was in my peripheral vision. We met Eddie in the foyer and I made introductions. If he was surprised at how our little company swelled by three, he didn't ask about it, sparing me having to make something up.

"Are you staying another night?" he asked.

I knew he was trying to find a polite way to tell us that any extra nights we might stay wouldn't be comped.

"I think so," I told him. "But don't worry. We know we've used up our freebie nights."

I shot a glance at Joe and saw he had no patience for any small talk right now. He just wanted to find Jilly. We were on the same wavelength, so I left the other band members with Eddie and took Cassie and the two cousins up to the room Jilly and I had been sharing.

"I can't believe I slept right through them taking her," I said when we were inside.

"Don't beat yourself up about it," Joe told me. "They'd have been in and out so fast and quiet, you probably wouldn't have seen them if you'd been awake."

He and Walker made their way around the room, looking for I don't know what, because there wasn't anything to see. After a few moments, Joe turned to Walker.

"I had a protection spell on her," he said, "and it seems to have worked just fine. It took her away before they had a chance to grab her."

Walker nodded. "Only where? All I see is a dead end. The trail leads into the between, then nothing."

"I know. It wasn't supposed to work like that. It was supposed to take her into the Greatwood."

"The last cards I drew showed her in a forest," Cassie said, "except it looked like something around here."

"And she seemed safe," I added.

"At least that's one small blessing," Walker said.

Joe nodded. "Heavy on the small. I want to know *where* she is."

"So," I said, "even if the fairies get the bogans to talk, it won't help, will it?"

"Not to find Jilly," Joe said. "But what about the other girl? Nobody put any kind of a mojo on her, did they?"

He looked at Walker. When the cerva shook his head, Joe turned to me.

"Let's see her room," he said.

As soon as we walked in, Joe and Walker obviously got something.

"Well, they sure as hell grabbed her," Joe said.

Walker nodded. "I've been where they've taken her. That's an old, almost impassable wood with a few inhabitable glades. But I don't sense that she's there anymore."

"Neither do I."

I wondered how they could do that, just stand here, looking into the air, and know what was going on a world away. But it wasn't the time for questions like that.

"Maybe we'll get a better take when we're there," Walker said.

Those crazy eyes of Joe's went dark with a feral humour.

"Yeah," he said. "And maybe there'll still be a few bogans hanging around that we can convince to tell us more."

"I'm coming with you," I said before they could leave.

Joe looked from me to Cassie. "Someone needs to stay here in case something comes up while we're gone. And no offense, but I don't think your friends downstairs could necessarily handle what might be coming down."

I knew what he was thinking. What did I have to offer? Cassie was the one with the mojo.

But Cassie weighed in on my side.

"I'll stay," she said. "Geordie needs to be doing something more useful than waiting around."

I guess Joe didn't want to waste time arguing the point because he just nodded, gave Cassie a quick kiss, then turned to me.

"Stay close," he said.

He started to cross over, and I hurried to where he was already vanishing from the room as though stepping through an invisible door. He was gone by the time I got there. But Walker put his hand on my shoulder.

"Come on," he said.

And the hotel room dissolved into a forest glade with tall trees rising up all around us.

I got a little lurch in my stomach from the crossing over, but not like I had when I'd first done it a couple of years ago. I still had a sour taste in my mouth, though, and my heart was beating way too fast.

Walker dropped his hand from my shoulder, and we walked over to Joe. He was in the shadow of a tall standing stone, crouched down with one knee on the grass. Something in the vegetation had obviously caught his attention. He ran a finger through the grass, and it came up with some sticky liquid on it, dark and red. He held his finger under his nose, then nodded. It took me a moment to realize it was blood.

"She's a fighter," he said to us.

"What do you mean?"

"She killed at least one of them."

I remembered the other card of Cassie's, the one that showed a bogan funeral in the Tombs. When I told Joe, he just nodded.

My gaze went back to the bloody grass at his knee.

"And Lizzie . . . ?" I asked.

"There's only bogan blood here."

"The Tombs," Walker wanted to know. "That's in Newford?"

Joe nodded. "But let's see where this trail takes us first."

He wiped his finger clean on the grass. Standing up, he led us across the grass and into the forest. We didn't get far before we ran up against an impenetrable wall of thorns and undergrowth.

"She went through that?" I asked.

Joe shook his head. "There's a smell here I don't recognize. Fairy, but it's not one of the bogans."

"Look at this," Walker said.

While we were studying the wall of vegetation, he'd wandered over to one of the nearby trees. He pointed out the blood on the bark of its trunk, the wooden spikes on the ground at its base. When we joined him, we saw the holes in the trunk from which the spikes had obviously been pulled.

Oh god, Lizzie, I thought, but Joe seemed to be reading my mind.

"It wasn't your friend. The bogans had somebody else nailed up here. One of their own—or at least some kind of fairy."

"And there was someone else here, as well," Walker said. "I don't know the scent, but it's definitely a cousin."

"Maybe it was the blind man that Mother Crone saw," I said.

"Maybe," Joe said.

He took the scent from one of the spikes, then let it fall back onto the grass.

"A cousin handled this," he said, "and so did Lizzie. I guess she was taking down whoever they'd nailed up."

Walker shook his head. "So, now it's fairy against fairy, cousin against cousin. This gets worse all the time."

"Unless it's not a racial thing," Joe said. "Maybe we've been coming at this all wrong. Every race has its assholes. Could be all we're dealing with is a bunch of freaks who just happen to be fairy *and* cousins. Could be the targets are all random—just whoever happens to get in their way."

Walker frowned. "I thought it was only humans I didn't understand."

"Hell," Joe said. "Most of the time I don't understand *anybody*."

"But why these senseless killings?"

Joe shrugged. "Who knows? Until we actually track down one of these little freaks and—"

He broke off, lifting his head to look back at the wall of brush where Lizzie's trail ended.

"Incoming," he said.

Walker hadn't needed his warning. He was already moving to the trail's end, Joe right behind him.

"What is it?" I asked, bringing up the rear.

But then I didn't need anything to be explained to me, either.

Two figures stepped out of the between—a bogan and a man almost twice his height who, with his milky-white eyes, had to be Odawa. The bogan made a cry of warning, but the blind man didn't seem to have needed it. His sightless gaze went right to us.

"Grab the bogan!" Joe called to me, as he and Walker moved in on Odawa.

I was willing to give it a shot, but I never got a chance. Before I could get my hands on the little man, before Walker and Joe could tackle Odawa, the blind man changed his shape. One moment he was a man, the next an enormous salmon was writhing there between the trees. It was the size of a shark, and when its tail shot out we were all swept from our feet. I banged up against the wall of brush, lost my fiddle case in the tangle of thorns, and had the breath knocked out of me. Walker hit a tree headfirst and went down hard. Joe managed to roll with the blow, coming to his feet almost as soon as he went down.

But he was too late to do anything. The salmon turned a blind gaze toward the bogan who—reluctantly, it seemed to me—caught hold of its dorsal fin and swung himself onto the fish's back. Then up the salmon went, swimming off into the air, moving in and out of boughs and tree trunks like it was avoiding stone outcrops in rapids.

I got to my feet and all I could do was stare, slack-jawed at the impossible sight.

The salmon was maybe twenty, thirty feet away from us when a large crow rose from the ground where I'd seen Joe moments before. When I say large, I mean it was twice the size of a normal crow, but it was still no match for the salmon. As soon as it got near to the fish, the salmon gave a flick of its tail and knocked the crow from the air. It went tumbling, head over talons, and fell into the branches of a tall pine.

By the time it got itself free, the salmon and its rider were long gone.

The crow sailed back to us, changing into a man once more when it was on the ground.

"Goddamn," Joe said. "I should have had him."

"No, he was too strong for us," Walker said.

He was sitting up against the trunk of the tree he'd hit, one hand on his head. I went over to help him up, then went and untangled the strap of my fiddle case from the thorns and brush. I was moving mechanically, trying to get my mind off what I'd just seen.

I'd forgotten that Joe had both corbae and canid blood in him. Man into crow, crow into man. That had been weird enough, but I couldn't get the image of our last view of Odawa out of my head.

"Tell me I didn't just see a giant fish go swimming off through the air," I said.

Joe just looked at me.

"No, come on. I know you're all shapechangers, but he was *swimming* through the air."

"There's water in everything," Walker said.

"Yeah, but—"

"When someone from one of the fish clans is powerful enough, he can swim through anything."

Joe wasn't interested in any of that.

"I didn't know that guy at all," he said. "Not the look of him with those blind eyes, not the smell of him."

"I've seen him before," Walker said. "From a distance. He's been through these woods more than once, but he always kept to himself. He moved with such assurance, I would never have guessed he was blind."

"I guess he's like Daredevil."

From the look they both gave me, I realized that neither of them got the reference.

"He's a character in this movie," I explained. "It's based on a comic book where a guy loses his sight, but all his other senses are intensified."

"I suppose . . ." Walker said.

"We need to make a decision," Joe said. "Do we backtrack their trail to see if we can find Lizzie, do we follow them, or do we go back to see what Tatiana's found out?"

"I don't see much success in the first two," Walker told him, "and I'd rather avoid the latter if I could. Maybe the two of you should go to the fairy court, and I'll see where Lizzie's trail leads me."

I'd just as soon have done the same, but I waited to hear what Joe had to say. I figured I was here by his good graces, and it'd be up to him whether I came or went.

Joe looked away into the forest for a long moment before turning back to us.

"Maybe there's a fourth choice," he said. "Something that didn't occur to me until right this minute. There's somebody else that might help us. At least she's helped me find Jilly before. She's got this connection with Jilly—something to do with what they both had to go through growing up. Thing is, I already owe her a favour and she hasn't called in the marker on it yet. Asking for another might be pushing things—like I was trying to take advantage of her good nature—and I wouldn't want to piss her off."

"You make it sound dangerous," I said.

"Guess it could be, depending on her standing in the pack. I used to see her more often, but not so much in the past few months. Could be somebody else has gone all alpha, and she might not even be running with them anymore."

"She's one of your canid cousins?" Walker asked.

Joe shook his head. "Sort of. The blood's thin, but the heart's big."

"What's her name?"

Joe turns to me and gives a slow shake of his head. "She doesn't have a name—none that I ever heard her give out or anybody else ever used." He gave us a humourless smile. "She can't talk, you see."

I thought about what Joe had said, how Jilly and this friend of his had shared certain experiences growing up.

"Somebody . . ." I couldn't bring myself to say cut, though I couldn't erase from my mind the image of a man slicing off some little girl's tongue. "Took away her voice?"

"She never had one—I mean, not like we do. She's a pit bull. I found her in some freak's backyard, chained up with the rest of her pack. Fighting dogs, born and bred to kill each other in the ring. So I let them go. Showed them the way into the otherworld where they could make a new life for themselves. And before you ask: no, she doesn't owe me anything for doing the right thing. I made that clear to her when I tracked her down later and asked for her help."

"But if she can't talk . . ."

"Then how can she help us? That last time she took me right to Jilly."

"So what are we waiting for?"

"Nothing. Except I'm going alone—it's safer that way. You and Walker check out where that trail leads, see if you can't get a line on your friend Lizzie."

"And Odawa?" Walker asked.

Joe looked up between the trees where the giant salmon had swum away through the air, a bogan clinging to his dorsal fin.

"Damned if I know how we're going to deal with him," he said.

Without wasting any more time, he stepped away into the between and it was just Walker and me.

"Are you ready for another trip into the between?" he asked.

"If it gets us any closer to finding Jilly and Lizzie . . . just bring it on."

Grey

Joe's concise with whoever he's got on the other end of the phone, just laying out the main facts with none of the details. He listens for a moment, then looks over to us.

"Cassie's with Geordie," he says, "and they've got something that I need to check out. Can you hold the fort here?"

He steps away into the between before either Jack or I can respond.

Mother Crone gets up from her chair, heading for where Joe disappeared. I don't know if she's planning to follow or what, but Jack grabs her arm as she passes by him.

"I didn't hear an invitation," he says.

"It's just—"

"And according to Tatiana, we're free to come and go as we like—or did I get that wrong?"

"No," she says. "But I'm concerned about Geordie."

"Then maybe you should have been helping him instead of running to the queen to see what you're supposed to do. Do you have to check in with her to see if it's okay to blow your nose?"

"You don't—"

"Yeah, I know. You like me as much as you don't like Joe. Feeling's mutual, darling. But right now, you need to keep being a good little fairy and sit down and wait with us like Tatiana told you."

Her face is dark with anger, but she shakes her arm free of Jack's grip and returns to her chair. Her two little treekin glare at us from where they're sitting, but Jack only grins at them and comes back to me.

I turn so that I'm facing away from them.

"You're being a little harsh," I say, soft, so only he can hear.

Jack motions me out of the chair with a nod of his head. When I get up, he walks me to the far side of the room.

"I'm just playing the card Joe would want me to," he says, pitching his own voice so low that I have to lean in to hear him. "Until we know where everybody stands on this, we need to act a little hard-core. Don't forget—they outnumber us something like a hundred to one in this place."

"I hadn't thought about it that way," I tell him.

Jack nods. "But just for the record, I want you to know that Joe's normally an easygoing guy. You look up patience in the dictionary and there's his mug, grinning up at you. And he's not one for getting all messy and physical, either—that usually falls to me. But there's certain things you don't do to him and messing with his family's the big one. That's when the promise in those crazy eyes gets real."

"I got that," I tell him.

"So what's with this Odawa guy? He really so powerful?"

"Hard to say. You know the story of the first salmon? The one that sleeps in a pool at the beginning of the world and how when he wakes the world will end?"

"Aw, come on. Don't tell me this is him."

I shake my head. "No, but they're kin. They share the same gifts of knowledge and . . . I was going to say wisdom, but that's something Odawa lost along the way."

"Maybe it's got something to do with you plucking his eyes out."

I can tell from the tone of his voice that Jack's just trying to get a rise out of me, but I answer him seriously.

"Maybe," I say. "But remember, I thought he was dead at the time, frozen half in, half out of the water. The thing you need to keep in mind with Odawa is that he's got a one-track mind and an indomitable will. That combination's hard to make peace with."

"Hard to fight, too," Jack says.

"Hard to fight," I agree, "and impossible to reason with." I wait a beat, then add, "Look, if this is really about me, I should just stop trying to avoid the problem because it's obviously not going to go away, and I don't want anybody else to be hurt because of me. Let me track him down and we can finish this once and for all, just the two of us."

"How's his helping bogans hunt cerva supposed to hurt you?" Jack asks.

"I don't know what you mean."

"The point is," Jack says, "this isn't just about you and him anymore. He's crossed the line and needs to be taken down."

"I said I'd do it."

Jack nods. "But he's old and powerful—you said so yourself. And if he's in bed with bogans, who knows what else he's been up to. You could go face him on your own, only to find he's got an army and you don't even have one person to cover your back."

I shrug. "That's the chance I'll have to take. Anyway, if they kill me, it'll still be over."

"I don't think so," Jack says. "This has gotten too big for that now. You think Tatiana would be so concerned if it was just some little skirmish between a few bogans and cousins? You can bet that somewhere out there in the bush cerva are mustering."

"What do you mean?"

"You were at the blessing ceremony—you saw the buffalo soldiers there."

"Do you really think they would break the truce?"

Jack shrugs. "Anwatan's not the first cousin to be killed by aganesha in the past few months. And the buffalo have a new leader—a hard-line warrior type. You know the kind."

I do. The buffalo lost more than most of us when the aganesha landed on our shores to start their long, bloody march inland.

"The funny thing is," Jack adds, "I'm not sure I want to stop them."

I know exactly what he means. I don't want to pretend that everything was perfect before the aganesha's arrival, but things only seem to have gone downhill since then. Maybe what this world needs is a good cleansing.

"But see," Jack says, "that's where we'd be wrong. We'd be letting our personal feelings get in the way of what's really important, which is that we take care of each other and this messy old world we're living in. Because that's why Nokomis put us here, right?"

I give a slow nod.

"Even," he goes on, "when we feel we could really do without some of the people who are making the mess."

I nod again, more reluctantly this time.

"So that's why we need to get this business of Joe's settled, because we need Joe on this. But he's not going to be worth a damn while he's worrying about Jilly."

"And if we're too late to help Jilly?"

Jack shakes his head. "Then we're screwed because you don't want to see the hurt that'll go down if Joe loses it."

"I don't get it," I say. "He's not one of the original People. He's not like Cody or Raven. He's not even of one blood."

"Canid and corbae," Jack agrees. "But he's got something old and dark in him. Some piece of the long ago that Raven didn't use when he made the world. Don't know what it is, and I doubt Joe does either—that's even saying he'd admit it's there—but if he gets turned around and goes all hard and looking for payback, that piece of the dark's going to come roaring up through his soul, and we won't have Joe to deal with anymore. We'll have something new and a hundred times more dangerous."

I give Jack a long, considering look.

"And this is who we need to make peace?" I finally ask.

Jack grins. "Well, that's the thing, isn't it? Whatever that old power he's got sleeping inside him is, if it wakes for a just cause, it's going to be shining the light instead of bringing on the dark."

"You ever heard the term 'playing with fire'?"

"Sure. But none of that's got to happen. We get him working on this—with his mind free of other worries—and nothing needs to wake up. It's as simple as that. Joe's got big-time peacemaking skills. Who do you think negotiated the last truce between us and the fairy courts?"

"I thought that got worked out between Tatiana and Raven."

Jack nods. "And who do you think kept them talking?"

I glance over at Mother Crone and her pair of treekin. They're pretending not to care what we're talking about, but who are they trying to kid? I'd be wanting to know if I were in their shoes.

"So maybe," I say, "we shouldn't be taking such a hard line with the aganesha right now."

"Maybe. But I want Joe in front of me telling me to back off before I do."

"Except—"

"Yeah, I know." He glances at the fairies and sighs. "Do you have any tobacco left? I'm a little short."

I nod and pass him my pouch. He takes half of what I've got left and puts it in his own pouch, then rolls a cigarette one-handedly—showing off for the fairies, I suppose, since it's sure not going to impress me—and lights it with his Zippo.

"Obliged," he says, handing me back my pouch.

He has a drag, then returns to where we were sitting and offers the cigarette to Mother Crone. She looks as surprised as I am, and maybe she's pissed off with us, but she knows enough protocol to understand what Jack's doing. Nodding her thanks, she takes the cigarette from him.

They smoke it in silence. The little treekin are still glaring at us—or at least the one that looks like a walking shrub does; it's hard to tell about the one with the spark plug nose—but you can feel the tension leaving the room. I'm not sure where we would have gone from there, but there's movement in the doorway right then and we all look up.

It's Tatiana. And this time she's only got one guardsman with her. He looks totally worse for the wear—his clothes torn and dirty, face bruised and swollen, and he's favouring one leg.

"Where's Joe?" she asks.

"He got called away," Jack tells her. He gives the beat-up guard a pointed look before adding, "What's up?"

Tatiana looks the way Mother Crone did earlier, when Joe was grilling her—she really doesn't want to tell us. But she doesn't make Mother Crone's mistake.

"We've got a problem," she says.

Jack and I stand up.

"What kind of a problem?" Jacks asks.

His voice is mild, but he's not fooling anybody. He's alert and ready for trouble now, just as I am.

Tatiana glances at her guard.

"Maybe I should just let Corin tell you," she says.

Jilly

It's harder than I expect to tell my story, mostly because of the doonie's reaction to what I have to say. He stares at me in disbelief as I talk about my brother and the priest and all—experiences that are all too common in the world Lizzie and I come from.

"Humans really do such things to their own children?" Timony asks, unable to hide revulsion.

And I haven't even gone into any real detail.

"That and worse," I say.

"I can't imagine it. Not even trolls or Redcaps would treat their own in such a way."

What a great world it would be, to live where the kinds of things that happened to me are impossible to contemplate.

"Welcome to the real world," Lizzie says. Then she turns to me and adds, "I knew you had a rough time growing up, but I had no idea it was anything like this."

"It's not important—" I start, but Lizzie cuts me off.

"How can you *say* that?"

"I just mean I'm not telling you about it to make anyone feel sorry for me. But you had to know the background because it's the reason we're here. Or at least, it's the reason this place is here, that it exists."

I go on to tell them about Mattie and her teddy bear that can turn into a giant version of the real thing, about the house two fields away and how I came to realize what this world is.

"I'm not so sure I like magic," Lizzie says. "All it seems to bring is grief."

I shake my head. "Oh, no. This isn't the fault of magic. It's us. People. And what we bring to it. Magic . . . the otherworld . . . it all exists as we shape it. And I guess if you've got a lot of baggage, it gets messy like this."

"So we created the bogans that killed that poor deer girl and have been making my life so miserable?"

"No, there's good and bad in the otherworld, same as in ours. And while the bad's pretty extreme, so's the good."

I'm thinking of some of the experiences I've had, especially those in the Greatwood. I'm thinking of Joe and the crow girls and the gemmin, these lovely spirits of a place that collect stories and have the most amazing violet eyes. I've had all sorts of wonderful encounters with spirits and magic, but I don't suppose this is the place to get into it. But I can't entirely let it go, so I settle for:

"It can fill you with such joy and awe," I tell Lizzie, "that it feels like you can't possibly contain it."

"Well, I wouldn't mind a shot of some of that right about now," Lizzie says.

"You've seen some of the worst," Timony tells her. "When we get the chance, I'll show you the best, as well. But first . . ."

"First, we have to figure a way out of here," I say, "and let me tell you, I'm totally open to suggestions."

"Well, it's your world," Lizzie says. "Can't you just make it let us go?"

I shake my head.

"And there's nothing I can do, either," Timony says when he looks at her. "No matter where I push or prod, the way out is closed to me as well."

I guess it's because we're so into our conversation that we don't realize that we're not alone anymore. We don't know until a sweet child's voice suddenly says:

"There they are."

We look up to see Mattie pointing at us. Her giant bear is just a raggedy plush toy, held against her chest with her other arm. Beside her . . .

My heart goes still. I can't breathe.

Beside her is Del.

Del and the priest I caught a glimpse of earlier. Dear old Father Cleary.

But it's Del who grabs my gaze, and I can't look away.

Raylene told me she cut him with a knife the night she ran away from home, cut him bad enough in the leg that he was still walking with the trace of a limp when she saw him years later. He was also a fat, alcoholic loser, living in a trailer park.

But that was her Del. The one that lives in the real world.

Mine's from before, when all of Tyson County was still his playground and nobody'd dare give him a hard time. Tall and lean, that lick of hair hanging down on his forehead. Dark-eyed and mean, even when he's smiling. Maybe especially when he's smiling.

"You did good," Del says, and he rubs the top of Mattie's head, mussing up her hair.

She beams up at him.

All the guilt I was feeling, for what I did to her when I was a kid, for *making* her . . . it all just drains away. But it's not replaced by anger. There's only fear.

No, fear's too tame a word.

I'm terrorized.

"Is that him?" Lizzie asks from beside me.

But I can't answer. I can't move.

Lizzie and the doonie get to their feet, neither of them quite sure what to do. It's not like there's any apparent threat. It's just a good old boy and a priest and a cute little girl, holding her teddy bear.

"They're so old now," the priest says. "Why does the good Lord let sweet little girls grow up, anyway?"

Del grins. "What, they're too old for your tastes? Well, you old perv, like the old saying goes, I may get older, but my girlfriends never will. 'Cept here we don't have to go looking for new ones. I can just make 'em younger."

He doesn't move, doesn't say a thing, but I feel something happening to me. I can't tell what until Lizzie speaks.

"What the fuck?"

It's a little girl's voice. I glance at her and see that she's small now. Younger. Eight, maybe nine years old. I lift my hands and they're a child's hands. I'm still the me I always was, but now I look like a little kid, just as Lizzie does.

What has Del *done* to us?

"Fight this enchantment," the doonie says. "It's up to you how you appear in the otherworld—what shape you wear."

My gaze goes to him. He's unaffected by what's happened to us.

What enchantment? I want to ask him. Since when did my white trash brother become some kind of wizard?

But my tongue's still stuck to the roof of my mouth. Paralyzed with fear, I can't speak, can't move.

"I can't do a lick with that boy," Del says. "You wanna give it a try?"

Father Cleary shakes his head. "He's just going to want to do dirty things with our little girls."

He makes a brushing away motion with his hands and just like that, Timony's gone.

They're *both* wizards?

What kind of sick world have I made inside my head?

At that moment Lizzie rushes forward, but the two men sidestep her rush. Del sticks out a foot, and she goes sprawling in the grass.

"Somebody needs a good spanking," the priest says.

Del laughs, but his gaze is on me.

"Knock yourself out," he tells Father Cleary. "Me, I've got some unfinished business with little Jillian here."

He takes a step closer, and I cringe back against the trunk of the tree.

"I hear you've been telling tales," he says, "and you know what happens to little girls with big mouths, right?"

My gaze darts right and left. But there's no help, no escape—even if I could get my muscles to work.

I see the priest pick up Lizzie. He laughs as she bats ineffectually at his big hands holding her. Mattie's watching it all with this small, awful smile tugging at the corner of her mouth.

"Well, toodle-oo," she says.

"Don't you stray too far," Del tells her.

She doesn't answer. She just walks away. He doesn't turn to see her go. He's too busy reaching down for me.

Big Dan

Big Dan knew he shouldn't have let his nephew go off with that pluiking green-bree. He didn't doubt that Rabedy would handle the blind man—not after he'd given his nephew Odawa's true name. No, that wasn't the problem at all. The problem stood beside him, smelling like she hadn't washed yet this week, although that wasn't stopping her from leaning in close to speak in his ear with a hoarse whisper.

"Is this what you have in mind for my boy?"

Gretha Collins was unattractive even for a bogan—a squat barrel of a woman with a nose like a ski slope, wide-set eyes, and lips so thin they might as well have been nonexistent. Her hair was always greasy, hanging down her back in long untidy braids, and she dressed like a ragpicker who was too fond of her own wares.

She was also Big Dan's sister, Rabedy's mother.

They were attending the funeral for Gathen Redshanks in an empty lot, deep in the Tombs, with abandoned buildings rising up all around them. It had proved to be a far more sizable gathering than Big Dan had expected. All the Redshanks were in attendance, which was only to be expected, but at least two-thirds of the other local bogan clans had gathered as well, including a sizable showing of Flynns and Burtons, both of whom had been feuding with the Redshanks for about as long as anyone could remember.

But it had been a long time since a bogan had fallen in battle. At least that was the story Big Dan had told. How they'd been attacked by a pack of canids in the otherworld, how Gathen had fallen in that struggle, but not before he'd driven the canids off through the sheer ferocity of his own assault.

Perhaps it hadn't been such a good idea—not if the ugly murmurs and whispers he'd been hearing among the crowd were any indication. All they'd need was for a gang of pluiking Redshanks and their kin to go looking for revenge against the green-brees. That would bring the whole business right to Tatiana's attention, and then there'd really be hell to pay.

But at the moment Big Dan's main concern was Gretha, worrying over the son she only paid attention to at times like this, when it gave her a chance to rag on Big Dan.

"Rabedy's in about as much danger as you are," he told his sister.

Less, really, he added to himself, because he was in no mood for her games today and if she kept it up, he'd see how a good whack across the back of the head might set her straight.

"Oh, no," she said. "Off in the otherworld with some murdering greenbree. That's safe as plucking flitter wings afore you bite off their little screeching heads. Safe as rooting for food in a garbage bin instead of stealing it off a table the way a good bogan would. Safe as—"

"We're at a funeral," Big Dan said, interrupting her. "Could you show some respect?"

"What? For a Redshanks?"

"He was one of my men."

"Aye, and much good that did him."

"Give it a rest," Big Dan told her.

She had something to add to that as well, but the look in his eye made her keep it to herself.

Big Dan turned his attention back to where Gathen's body lay on a pyre of scrap wood, newspapers, and whatever inflammable items could be found on such short notice. It wasn't like the old days, when they could go into the forest and get what they needed. Here they had to scrounge through the city streets and back alleys to find any sort of fuel at all. The whole mess had been doused in gasoline to ensure a quick ignition and the smell of the gas drifted throughout the empty lot where they had gathered for the funeral.

Stourin Redshanks, Gathen's grandfather, stood in front of the pyre, a flaming brand raised high in his hand. Though he cut a fine figure for an old bogan, Big Dan was more mesmerized by the sparks that came from the brand as Stourin waved it back and forth above his head. Any moment, Big Dan expected one of those sparks to land in the cloud of Stourin's frizzled grey hair and set the whole hairy bush on fire.

"He was a good lad, Gathen was," Stourin said, his voice ringing and clear. "He had many years left in him. But those stoogin' canids didn't see it that way. Oh, no. Cut him down and leave his kith and kin to grieve the loss while they go laughing on their way. And for what? What crime did Gathen commit 'sides being a bogan?"

Many of those gathered had staves which they pounded on the ground in response. Those that didn't, stamped their feet.

That brought Big Dan's attention away from the sparks and Stourin's hair.

Oh, he thought. Maybe he shouldn't have made up that story. He'd meant well, but he hadn't wanted this. Even his own men—who had been there with him and heard Rabedy's tale, who'd seen Gathen's body without a dog or wolf bite upon it—were getting caught up in the anger against the canids. They *knew* how Gathen had really died. Taken out by some pluiking slip of a girl. But here they were, getting carried away by the elder Redshanks' speechifying.

"Tatiana will tell us we need peace," Stourin went on. "That we must maintain the truce. But what do we tell her?"

"No!" almost a hundred bogan voices cried in return.

It made a sound loud enough to be heard halfway across the Tombs.

This wasn't good. This wasn't any bloody good at all.

Big Dan had only meant to give Gathen some measure of respect in how his life had ended. A tale of a battle with canids seemed so much more noble a death than the truth.

"And if she sends her guard to tell us different?" Stourin demanded.

"We'll send them back in pieces!" someone shouted to a general roar of approval.

This was truly, pluiking bad, Big Dan thought. But it was too late to own up now. Better the anger be turned on the court's guard and the canids than on him. And besides, by the time Tatiana actually sent anyone to look into this, all the hubbub would probably have died down, just the way it always did. There'd be no pack of bogans heading off into the wild and the green to hunt down Gathen's supposed murderers. That was too much like work. A more likely scenario was that the next canid some of these bogans ran into here in the city might have himself a bit of a hard time. But so what? Big Dan's sympathies had never run with canids, innocent or not.

He let himself relax and concentrated on the moment at hand. He thought of the good times he'd had with Gathen, the stupid little bugger. Lairds, but he was a bogan's bogan, always into something and none of it good.

When Stourin stopped for a breath in the middle of a particularly descriptive rant against the canids who'd murdered his grandson, Big Dan let himself get into the spirit that the others were showing.

"We'll hunt the pluikers down like the dogs they are!" he shouted.

That brought him a response of thumping staves and stamping feet as loud as any Stourin had received. Big Dan let himself look stern, hiding the grin that was building inside him. Maybe this was a better way. Instead of making deals with some pluiking green-bree, to just take what they wanted from the green and the wild. Bugger them all.

But then the guard had to arrive, twenty strong and with a gruagagh in tow, and everything went very bad indeed.

The guards all had bows, with arrows nocked and ready. They fanned out when they saw that they were outnumbered five-to-one, and if their captain had had any sense at all, he'd have withdrawn and come back another day.

But they had a gruagagh with them—a tall, gangly wizard with dark eyes, who was too full of his own importance the way gruagaghs inevitably were. He ignored the numbers and the anger of the crowd, and called out the names of Big Dan and his boys, their true names, so they had to come stepping out from where they stood with the others, ready to be magically marched back to the queen's court to face whatever pluiking business she might have with them.

And even then it might have been all right.

Big Dan had no idea why they were being summoned—no specific idea, at any rate. It could be for any number of things. But what was the worst that could happen? They might be banished from the city for a year and a day and have to carve out a territory in some smaller town away from the queen's influence for the duration. It wouldn't be the first time for him.

But Stourin had primed the crowd with his incitements. They surged forward with a roar, their staves lifted above their heads. Others pulled slings from their belts and loosed rocks against the guards.

The gruagagh, already standing straight-backed and grim, lifted himself a little taller still.

"You *dare*?" he cried.

Mage lights flickered around his fingers and who knew what he might have done. But before he could call up his magics, a stone from one of the slings struck him on the side of the head and down he went.

The guards loosed a volley of arrows, aiming for legs to bring the attackers down, for fairy didn't kill fairy. But it wasn't enough and it was too late. The crowd fell upon them, breaking their bows, knocking them to the ground with their staves where they could be punched and kicked by those not carrying weapons.

It was over in moments. The guards made a hasty retreat, dragging their wounded fellows and the gruagagh with them into the between.

The bogans laughed and stamped their feet in victory, and if there were a half-dozen that needed attention from a healer, they were also heroes and were borne up by the crowd to be treated as such.

"*That's* how we see a warrior off!" Stourin cried.

He cast his flaming brand onto the pyre and the gasoline caught with a huge *whuft* that had the crowd cheering madly.

Big Dan cheered along with the rest of them, but he, at least, knew this wasn't over. Lairds knew what the queen had wanted with him and his boys, but whatever it was, this had just made it worse. By the time the guard came back with reinforcements, he planned to be long gone from this place. This place? He'd quit the pluiking city itself and make himself scarce for as long as it took for all of this to blow over. Just step off into the between and—

Except then he heard the drums.

They were faint, lying just under the raucous cheers and shouts of the bogans seeing old Gathen off in proper style. But Big Dan could hear them all the same.

He looked around, past the crowd that surrounded him, but there was nothing to see. Only the empty lots and abandoned buildings of the Tombs.

That was when he realized that the drumming came from the between.

He shook his head, realizing what that meant.

For it to be so loud . . .

He had himself a look, peeking through the veil that hid this world from the lands that lay between it and the otherworld, and near shat his pants from what he saw.

"Away!" he cried. "Away!"

Those closest to him heard and looked confused.

"Turn your pluiking eyes into the between!" he shouted.

They did, one after another, the word spreading like a wave through the crowd. And once they'd looked, there was no more talk of brave battle, of showing the pluiking green-brees and court both that they meant business.

The crowd fled to a bogan, scattering in all directions.

Moments later, there was only Gathen's pyre in that empty lot of weeds and rubble, burning hard and bright as it sent a streak of black smoke trailing high up into the sky.

Honey

It was good now, she thought. Smells were deep here. Pure. Like the inside of a thing, not just what was on the fur. Game was plentiful.

And there were no men.

Up in the mountains, the air was cool under the drooping boughs of the Ponderosa pines. Lower down, here among the cacti and desert shrubs, it got cool at night, but the days were gloriously warm. The view was open and wide, and there were quail and doves to give warning if her own senses should miss the approach of danger—unlikely as that might be.

Motionless under a mesquite tree at the top of a dry wash, the pit bull was invisible, her honey-blonde fur blending in with the washed-out dirt, stones and cross-hatch of branch shadows. She lay with her forepaws stretched out in front of her and watched a small pack of pups playing with each other in the loose sand at the bottom of the wash below.

They weren't her pups. Hers were a year and a half old now and didn't need watching anymore. She'd been particular in choosing a mate, settling on a passing wolf who hadn't stayed to raise the litter with her. She hadn't expected him to. He was a handsome old loner, but her choosing him had more to do with the spirit voice that was so strong in his head. His blood, combined with hers, had made sure that her offspring had strong voices, too.

Cousins, they called themselves, these creatures with the spirit voice like she had in her head, like her wolf. Or sometimes they would say the People, which seemed funny, since most of them were like her—unable to shift to a two-legged, five-fingered shape. But while they couldn't walk upright, there was more to them than the beasts who had no spirit voice. What set them apart came from that old blood of theirs—not solely from the air of the otherworld, although the very air here was potent as well. The longer she stayed in these lands, the more she felt the changes.

Her spirit voice was stronger than it had ever been. She could shape words with it now so that anyone could understand her, not simply the pack. The voice had also created a new kind of wisdom inside her, a knowing that filled her mind with concepts beyond survival and simple physical comfort, and then allowed her to articulate them. She was fascinated with these new concerns—concepts of right and wrong and her place in the world, as well as the responsibility she owed the world for the gift of her own life. They were things that she had already known before, but they had simply been a part of her being. What had changed was that now she understood the reasoning behind them. When she made an ethical choice now, it was informed rather than by instinct.

And it wasn't only her voice that had changed.

She should have been past her prime, not so quick on her feet and stiff from the years she'd fought in the ring and the wounds she'd sustained. Instead, she felt young and vital, her muscles firm, powerful. She could run for hours without tiring. She could bring down prey many times her size in the hunt.

It was very good now, but it had been hard at first.

The pack could have gone wild, loosed in these lands as they had been, a world beyond the world they knew, where they were born. And they would have, if she hadn't had the voice in her head. The voice wasn't strong. She didn't have many words. But she could always speak a little, and she'd already known the basic rights and wrongs, enough so that she'd held their wildness in check. She made sure that other creatures with voices—hare, squirrel, deer—did not become prey unless they were old or infirm, those voices of theirs calling to predators for release from their ailing prisons of flesh.

The pack hadn't understood—except for her own offspring, they still didn't—but they obeyed her. Her leadership carried over from the old world, from the fighting ring where her sire and dame had fallen. Where the rest of her litter had died, too—brothers and sisters sacrificed for the amusement of men.

She knew in her old world that there were bonds between some men and dogs, though it wasn't something with which she'd had any lasting experience. She could remember the Boy when she was a pup, the Boy who'd loved her and called her Honey. But her time with the Boy was short. She was soon taken from him by the Man, beaten and made to fight in the ring. Tooth and claw and blood. Always the blood.

She was undefeated, but the victories were hollow. They meant nothing to her except for how they left her scarred, especially around her neck and chest. Her victories pleased the Man, but why should she care? Her only reward was a cuff on the head, the cage in which she was transported, and the chain that held her in the yard, winter and summer, storm or shine.

The Man was careful with her. He had a thing that spat pain to keep her in check—a small black box he could hold in his hand. When he touched it to her, her muscles jumped and went slack and her mind went spinning, spinning . . .

She had no interest in pleasing him. Their bond was formed of hate and pain. She was only a tool to him, nothing more, while he . . . he was the chief monster in a world of monsters.

She had sneered at the dogs who cozied up to men, who thought they could be a part of men's lives—the part that held comfort and joy and contentment. When the Boy was gone, she understood that dogs and men could only be enemies. The bond was a lie. A hateful lie to make her stare at the moon and pine for what reason told her was impossible.

Her heart had hardened. Her life revolved around the ring, being transported to and from it, being chained in the yard, always waiting for that one single opportunity to tear out the throat of the Man. Time and again she vowed that this night she wouldn't fight. She'd let her opponent kill her and be done with the prison of her life. But in the ring, all the anger she felt toward the Man arose, and she took out her rage on whatever hapless dog had been thrown into the dirt ring with her.

And then she met Joe.

She could still remember how he'd treated her as an equal, right from the first, when she was still chained in the Man's yard. He carried a strange, unrecognizable scent—man, yes, but also that of dog and bird. Not that he'd been in contact with either, but that they lived under his skin with the man. His presence made her whiskers twitch and woke a tickle in that part of her mind that housed her spirit voice.

When he approached her he was cautious, but fearless. She'd heard the words spilling from his lips, but she also heard his spirit voice in her head. She'd never met any man or beast with that voice before. Voices had come to her before, but they were always distant, beyond the confines of where she was chained, or in passing, when she was in a cage in the back of the Man's pickup on the way to or from a fight.

But here was a man with that voice. A man offering friendship with no bargain attached. Who'd freed her and the rest of the pack without the fear that they would then turn on him.

It was only later that she understood why. When she saw he could wear more than one shape. Dog, man, blackbird. He offered friendship and freedom because he was one of them. From another pack, but he was still kin. Or at least kin to her with the voice in *her* head.

That voice.

When he came to her a couple of years ago and asked her to help find a friend, she'd done so willingly. He'd come as he had when he set the pack free and showed them how to step into the otherworlds: Fearless. Without guile. Expecting nothing. As a friend. The way, she realized, that he'd go to another to ask help for her if she were in trouble and he couldn't help her on his own.

She felt like part of two packs then. The one she led. And the one . . . his . . . in which she . . . this was hard. The one in which she neither led nor followed, but in which she was an equal. The feeling was alien and uncomfortable, but not altogether unpleasant.

She'd seen him numerous times since they'd gone off to help his friend, coming upon him suddenly in some part or another of the otherworld. They would run together for a time, playing and roughhousing like littermates.

When she was with her pack, he took on the role of the other members, letting her lead, happy to follow. When it was only the two of them, neither led.

He hadn't come for a while now. Not since her voice had gathered strength inside her. She wanted to speak to him of everything that ran through her mind, but she was too shy to approach him. His life, she knew, was busy and full. Who was she to push herself into it?

But sometimes she went to his world. Late at night, she would sit outside the building where he lived with that woman, that woman with her spirit so big her dark skin couldn't seem to contain it. From across the street, she would watch the flicker of candlelight in their windows. Sensing his presence. Wondering if he sensed hers.

Movement in the dry wash below caught her eye, bringing her up out of her reverie, but it was only one of the pups straying too far. She gave a sharp bark and he turned his head in her direction, trying to outstare her until she barked again, sending a command with her spirit voice at the same time. He hurried back to where the rest of the litter had paused to watch the exchange and jumped on the nearest one to prove that he still had backbone.

She smiled to herself, then made a quick turn away from the wash, suddenly aware that she and the pups were no longer alone. A growl awoke deep in her chest as she lunged to her feet. Below the puppies scattered for shelter as they'd been taught. But as though her thinking of Joe had called him to her, there he was, sitting on his haunches a half-dozen paces from where she stood.

"Hello, darling," he said. "Didn't mean to startle you. Been awhile, hasn't it?"

He bared his teeth and her hackles began to rise before she remembered that this was how men showed their good humour.

It's good to see you, she replied.

She used her spirit voice, speaking mind to mind, employing images as well as words to get her meaning across.

His eyebrows rose and he showed more of his teeth.

"I thought this might happen," he said, "if you stayed in the otherworld for long enough. Could be, pretty soon you'll be able to walk around on two legs—if you want, that is."

???

"Yeah, I know. Why would you want to? But it can be useful."

No. I meant . . . how would it be possible?

He shrugged. "I never could figure out the exact physics, if that's what you're asking, but somebody tried to explain it to me once. What I got out of it is that there's all these little subatomic particles that make up everything. You go looking down far enough and eventually you can see that everything's just energy, not one thing or another. It just is. If you can put a name on it, you can make it be or do anything you want. It's how we change our shapes and why we don't stand around buck-naked when we shift from animal to human. Hell, it's why everything looks the way it does, because of Raven putting a name to it in the long ago.

"See, there's a reason names are so important in all the old stories. Put a name to something and you don't just control it, you can create it."

As she absorbed that, his gaze drifted down into the dry wash where the pups were cautiously making their way out of their various hiding places.

"They yours?" he asked.

When she shook her head, he studied them a little more closely.

"Yeah," he said. "I can see now that they don't have your blood." His gaze went back to her. "How are those kids of yours?" he added.

Strong. Smart.

"No surprise there. They'd pretty much have to be, with you for their mother."

Flatterer.

"Just telling it like it is."

Incorrigible flatterer.

His eyebrows rose again.

"You're waking all the way up, aren't you?" he said.

What do you mean?

"The way you're dealing with intangible concepts. You're becoming a full-blooded cousin."

Can you teach me to walk on two legs? To fly?

"You don't have any bird blood, darling, so flying's out. But taking a human shape? Sure. It'll take a little while, but I figure you aren't scared of some hard work."

No. But it might be . . . useful to learn the trick of it.

He bared his teeth again—smiled, she corrected herself. That was what they called it. Smiling.

"Can be," he says. "Makes life more complicated, too, but hell. Complications build character, right?"

When can we start?

"I'd say right now," he told her, "except I'm in the middle of a crisis. It's why I've come to you. You remember that sister of mine you helped me with before?"

She had to think for a moment before she found the name.

Jilly.

"That's the one. Well, trouble's found her again, and I sure could use your help in tracking her down."

She hesitated for a moment and he misread her.

"I'm not saying the one's dependent on the other," he told her. "But I need to deal with this first. Whether you help me or not, soon as she's safe, I'll come back to work on it with you."

No. I was thinking of the last time. How that woman died. . . .

"Wasn't your fault. You just knocked her down. Might as well blame the rock she cracked her head on."

If it hadn't, I would have torn out her throat.

Joe gave her a slow nod. "Yeah, I can see how knowing that would be a burden. But if you hadn't, my sister'd be dead. I know how the teachings go— every death diminishes us and all that—but give me a choice, and I'd rather it was my family that lived than somebody who was trying to hurt them."

What do you need me to do?

"Just find her—like you did the last time. I figure the two of you have got some kind of special connection, you know, with . . ."

How we were hurt when we were young?

He nodded. "I don't know how it is for you, but that's still sitting hard and deep in her—a dark ache that's always right there under everything else in the life she's made for herself. I don't think it's ever going to go away."

I know.

"Yeah. I guess the sad truth is, you do."

When do you need to go?

"Yesterday."

I'll need to get someone to look after the pups.

"I appreciate this," he told her. He waited a beat, then added, "We should see each other more than just when there's trouble. The times we've had together were good."

She nodded, pleased that he remembered them as fondly as she did.

"Thing I'm wondering," he added. "All those times you were outside the apartment . . . how come you never stopped in to say hello?"

You knew I was there?

"After the fact. I'd catch your scent when I stepped outside."

I just . . . I don't know. I wasn't sure I'd be welcome in that other life of yours.

Joe regarded her for a long moment.

"I guess that's more of the baggage from when you were a pup, because I'll tell you right now, my house is always going to be your house, too. If I'm not there, you can bet Cassie'll give you the same welcome I would. Guaranteed."

She had trouble meeting his gaze.

Let me get someone to watch out for the pups, she said, *and then we can go.*

"I appreciate it," he said.

She shook her head. *There are no debts between friends and kin.*

He smiled again, but she was beginning to get used to it.

"I'd be honoured to have you as either one," he told her.

She nodded.

"You want me to watch the pups while you go get a babysitter?" he asked.

I've already sent for one of my boys.

"Slick. I didn't *hear* a thing."

She couldn't help herself. Her tail gave a flicker of a wag under his praise.

While we wait for my pack brother, she said to cover up her awkwardness, *tell me what happened. When did you last see Jilly?*

"A couple of weeks ago," he said. "But I'd put this safeguard on her . . ."

He went on to explain how he'd woken when the safeguard had been tripped, and Jilly had subsequently disappeared when she should have been sent to the Greatwood.

"And now it's like she's not even in the world anymore," he said. "Not in *any* world."

I can see that, she said. *This will be hard. I'll have to go by the inside of her.*

"I don't understand."

It's hard to explain. She's not in any world as we know it. She's some-where else—somewhere inside herself.

"Inside herself?"

She nodded. *And someone's hurting her . . .*

It was always like that with men, wasn't it? If they couldn't hurt a stranger, or some poor mute beast, then they'd hurt one of their own.

Joe's eyes, always unusual, flashed with strange fires in their depths, and she could smell the sudden surge of adrenaline in him.

"Who's hurting her?" he said in calm voice that promised anything but calm.

I can't tell. Someone she knows well.

"Is that boy of yours going to be long?"

He's almost here.

Joe nodded, giving nothing away. But he was like a hunter, poised to launch himself at his prey.

Don't worry, she told him. *We'll get to her in time.*

They had to, she realized, or Joe would go rogue, and she was just be-ginning to get an inkling of how dangerous that would be. Not just to his prey, but to himself as well. She'd seen it before in the ring. If he let himself go, he might never get back to himself again. But he wasn't some fighting dog, thrust into the ring. Power surged behind his eyes, old and dark and stronger than she'd ever imagined until this moment.

Once it was loosed, he wouldn't be just a danger to himself and those around him.

Worlds could fall.

Geordie

When Walker took me through the between, we ended up on some dismal seashore with nothing going for it but its eerie desolation. There was little to see because the fog was thick, but I could hear the crash of waves close at hand, and the smell of fish and brine was all around us, strong, almost overpowering. Underfoot, it was all sand and pebbles, wet weeds, shells and bits of driftwood—everything pretty much one shade of grey or another. There didn't seem to be any colour here at all, and I felt like I was standing in some old postcard, except it was totally depressing instead of quaint. The air itself seemed to have too much mass so that just standing as we were I felt weighed down with some unhappy and heavy burden.

"What is this place?" I asked Walker.

He was too busy trying to make out what lay inside the fog to look at me.

"I'm not sure," he said. "This was simply where the trail led. Some small unwanted world, it seems, grey and abandoned by whomever . . ."

His voice trailed off and he cocked his head.

"No," he said.

I didn't know if he was talking to me, himself, or someone I couldn't see.

"Who are you—" I started to ask, but I never got to finish.

"I *won't* allow you to do this in her name," Walker cried.

He spoke loudly, his eyes flashing with anger. I backed away from him, but it became quickly obvious that he wasn't talking to me because the next thing I knew, he was gone, stepping away through the same invisible door that had brought us here.

"Hey, wait a minute!" I cried.

But I was alone on the beach now and talking to myself.

I hurried over to where he'd disappeared and moved my hands through the air, but there was nothing there that I could feel or see.

I couldn't believe it.

Jilly and Lizzie were the ones who were lost. *We* were supposed to find *them.* So what do I do? Get lost myself.

I looked around the beach, but I couldn't see much of anything because of the fog. I got the sense that even if the fog wasn't here, there still wouldn't be anything to see. My gaze went to the ground, which was the only part of this world that I could actually make out with any clarity, but there were no clues there either.

I kicked at a piece of driftwood in frustration.

This was it. I'd totally screwed up. Now what was going to happen to Jilly and Lizzie? I'd barely gotten started in the search and now here I was, already defeated.

My gaze lingered on the tracks Walker and I had made in the sand, and I realized that there were too many of them. I looked beyond where we'd appeared. The sand there was undisturbed. Turning the other way, I saw a busy trail of footprints leading off into the fog. Their edges were soft from the incoming tide, but still clearly visible.

Shrugging, I decided to follow them. It seemed like a plan, though it turned out to not be a very good one because about thirty yards along, they ended as abruptly as they'd begun.

I moved my hands through the air here as I had at the spot where Walker and I had appeared, not expecting to feel anything. But no sooner had I started, than someone crashed into me, and we were both sent sprawling onto the wet sand. I scrambled to my feet a moment before the strange little man who'd knocked me down did, but I didn't see that it gave me any particular advantage. The only thing it did was leave me standing with my fiddle case in the sand a half-dozen paces away where it had been thrown when the little man knocked me down—happily, beyond the reach of the incoming tide.

I still wanted to check that it was okay. Instead we just stood there, studying each other warily.

He was an odd little bird, but I'd seen stranger at Galfreya's court. He had the matted dreadlocks and very bright eyes that so many fairy did, stood no taller than my waist, and wore raggedy clothes in a mottle of earth colours.

I could never decide if wearing those kinds of things was a fashion statement, or just that clothing didn't mean that much to them so they let them get all threadbare and worn.

Mind you, I should talk. I doubted I cut much of a figure myself after having been banged around the way I had been in the past couple of hours.

"So . . ." I said.

The sound of my voice broke whatever spell had been keeping the little man motionless. He took a step back.

"No, wait!" I added, speaking quickly when I realized he might be about to abandon me the way Walker had. "Please don't go. I won't hurt you. I . . ." I searched for something that would let him know that I was harmless and settled for, "I'm a musician—at Mother Crone's court in Newford."

He nodded. Apparently that was enough for him to hear me out, though he didn't seem any less wary.

"I don't much hold with the courts," he said.

So he was one of the solitary fairies. He probably spent the majority of his time in the otherworld.

"That's cool," I told him.

He gave me a confused look.

"I mean, I understand. The courts can be a pain. Even a casual one like Mother Crone's has all these levels of hierarchy, and it's a total pain keeping track of them all."

He nodded.

"My name's Geordie, by the way," I went on. "Not that I expect you to tell me your name," I added quickly, knowing how fairy felt about being asked that kind of thing. "And I'm kind of stuck here. You wouldn't know a way out of this world, would you?"

"That seems to be a common problem lately."

"What do you mean?"

But he ignored my question to ask his own. "How did you get here?"

I started to give him the abbreviated version, but as soon as I mentioned Jilly and Lizzie's names, he interrupted me.

"I know how this story goes," he said. "I've met your friends."

"You *have*? Where are they? Can you take me to them?"

"Yes, it's hard to say, and no."

It took me a moment to realize he was simply answering each of my questions in turn. I focused on the middle response.

"Why is it hard to say where they are?" I asked.

"Are you familiar with the term *croí baile*?" he replied. "It means the home of one's heart."

I nodded slowly. I'd heard my brother and Christiana talk about them in the past.

"Those are the places in the otherworld where you're most comfortable or something, isn't it?"

"It's a little more thorny than that," the little man told me. "A better way to put it would be that your *croí baile* is that part of the otherworld that most closely reflects what lies inside your heart."

I nodded to show that I understood him so far.

"But your friends are in a place that seems to reflect the opposite of that. The place where they are mirrors Jilly's darkest and oldest fears and is peopled with those who brought such hurts into her life. What makes it confusing is this place shouldn't exist. At the heart of each of us, no matter how desperate or bleak our lives might seem to be, is a flicker of light and hope—a small echo of the Grace working its light against the dark. That is what our *croí baile* reflects, and only the dead are without it."

I felt my pulse quicken.

"Wait a second," I said. "You're not telling me she's—"

"No, no. She's not dead."

"But—"

"I can't explain it," the little man said. "Even by the capricious laws that govern the otherworld, I wouldn't have believed that such a place could exist, because we all carry the blessing of the Grace inside us—even those of us with the darkest hearts. And your friend Jilly carries a bright reflection of the Grace's light. But still, given that bounty of light, this place exists inside her. I think because she believes it does."

"She's inside her own mind?"

He nodded. "The three of us were trapped in there until I was pushed out by one her phantoms. And before you ask, I can't get back in."

I hardly heard the last thing he said. I was too busy trying to work through the concept of being physically trapped in your own mind.

"Is that even possible?" I found myself asking. "Being physically trapped in your own mind?"

Just because it was nothing I'd ever heard of before didn't mean it couldn't be true. I knew next to nothing about magic, even after having hung around in a fairy court for a couple of years. I'd just played music there. I'd never gotten into the philosophies of magic. But still. You'd think something this odd would have come up in conversation before—with my brother, with *somebody*.

"Somewhere," the little man told me, "anything is possible."

"Why is that not comforting."

"And less so for those I was forced to leave behind. Your friends are in a terrible place. The things Jilly told us about her childhood . . ."

I nodded slowly. "Yeah, she really had it rough."

The little man gave me a shocked look.

"You knew?" he said. "You knew and you did *nothing*?"

"Hey, I was just a kid myself at the time, and I hadn't even met her yet. We didn't meet until we were in our twenties, and all that crap was behind her." I hesitate a moment, then add, "Well, it seemed to be behind her. You had to know her to understand that it was always going to be an issue."

"I don't understand you people—how you can let such things be."

"I don't understand why we treat each other the way we do either, but right now I don't much care. I'm more concerned about how we can get to wherever it is that you left Jilly and Lizzie."

"There is no way back to them," the little man said.

But I could hear Jilly's voice in my head, repeating something I'd heard her say a thousand times . . . to me, to herself, to anyone who came up against the wall of "I couldn't ever do that":

"There's no such thing as impossible; there's only not trying."

I repeated it now to the little man.

He shook his head. "It's a pretty sentiment," he said, "but one can't do what can't be done. That brother of hers has changed the two of them back into children and closed the road into her mind. There's nothing we can do. Only she can stop him, but she has to believe that she can."

"Changed them into children?" I asked. "You mean physically?"

The little man nodded. "They might be children in their minds, as well—I wasn't there long enough to tell. I tried to tell them that he doesn't have the magic himself—that he only has it if they believe he does—but I don't think it took. And then I was cast out."

"But you said you had to believe he has the power. If you didn't, how could he cast you out?"

"I don't believe, but she does. So long as Jilly believes, he *does* have the power."

"And there's nothing we can do?"

The little man shook his head.

"This sucks," I said.

He gave me another of those blank looks that told me he didn't catch the idiom, but I didn't bother to explain it to him. My mind was too busy trying to figure out a way out of this mess. Then I had a thought.

"You know where they are, right?" I asked. "I mean, you can't get to them, but you do know *where* they are?"

"Yes, much good that it does us. As I told you, I can't get back to them."

Maybe he couldn't, but we weren't completely alone in this.

"That's okay," I told him. "I've got a friend that might be able to take it from here."

I was thinking of Joe. If anybody could get to Jilly, it would be him.

So I explained to the little man how I'd gotten here and who we needed to find if we were going to help Jilly and Lizzie.

"This is the man who left you here?" he asked.

"No, that was Walker, the deer man. And I don't think he did it maliciously. He was just looking off into I don't know where and then started talking to someone I couldn't see. The next thing I knew, he was gone and I was stuck here."

"I wonder what he saw," the little man said.

He got that look in his eyes then that Joe so often had, that Walker'd had just before he vanished on me, as though he was seeing into an entirely other world—which, come to think of it, was probably exactly what they were doing.

After a long moment, the little man's gaze cleared and he focused on me.

"This isn't good," he told me.

I was *so* not ready for more bad news.

"What is it?"

"See for yourself."

I was about to tell him that I didn't have access to whatever trick he knew that let you look out of one world into another, but before I could, he laid a hand on my arm and suddenly I could *see*. See and hear.

"I don't understand," I said as I studied what he showed me. "What does it mean?"

"War."

Grey

Corin—the guard that Tatiana brought to where we're waiting with Mother Crone and her little treekin—really is a mess. One eye's almost closed and there's a cut above the other. The left side of his face has swollen, rounding out his once-chiseled cheekbone. His suit's torn and dirty, he cradles one arm that's obviously giving him pain, and he's favouring his right leg.

It all becomes clear when he tells how he and his men tracked the bogans down to a funeral in the Tombs. Vastly outnumbered, they still tried to bring Big Dan and his boys in and got the crap beat out of them for their effort. I feel bad for him, but my heart sinks for an entirely other reason as he tells his story. I look at Jack and I know he's thinking the same thing I am: This isn't good. It's not just that Tatiana's guard was routed and the bogans have now scattered from here to who knows where. It's that when Joe finds out about it, there's going to be all hell to pay.

Corin's voice trails off and for a long moment nobody has anything to say. Finally, Jack turns to the queen.

"So, basically, you've got nothing," Jack says.

"It's not like we didn't *try*," Tatiana tells him. "I sent a dozen guards *and* a gruagagh."

Jack nods. He starts to roll himself a smoke and looks at the guard.

"How many died?" he asks.

The guard and Tatiana are seriously taken aback by the question.

"None," Tatiana says. "Fairy don't kill their own."

Jack just looks at her, then he gives a slow nod.

"That's right," he says. "You save the killing for my people."

"We don't condone—"

"Yeah, yeah. But you don't do much to stop it, either."

Jack lights his cigarette without offering it to Tatiana first. I'm not sure she picks up on the insult.

"I've gotta say," he goes on, "I'm surprised at how this turned out, though if I'd stopped to think about it, I guess I wouldn't have been."

"You're not being fair . . ."

"And your people aren't dying. No offense, Tatiana, but we've played it your way about as long as it's going to go. We'll handle things from here on out."

"You can't just—"

"But I've got to tell you," he says, cutting her off, "you'd better hope we find Jilly in one piece or you're going to have more to worry about than what we'll do with a few renegade bogans."

"Threatening me won't get your friend back any more quickly."

"I'm not threatening you. It's just a friendly warning because you just really don't want to be in the firing line when Joe gets this news."

He glances at Mother Crone and tips a finger to his brow, then turns to me. "You ready to hit the road, Grey?"

I nod, but before we can go, we're interrupted by the sudden appearance of an odd little man who comes running in through the door. He's the first of the aganesha I've seen here in the court that actually looks the way I've always imagined fairies did—I mean, before they showed up here and started mimicking human clothing and mannerisms. He's a wizened little fellow with sharp features and pointed ears, dressed in a pale blue robe, the hem of which he's holding in his hand to make it easier to run. His hair's a pale cloud of frizz and his eyes are that steely blue of chicory flowers.

"Your Highness!" he cries as he bursts in the room. "You must come and see . . ."

His voice trails off when it registers that we're here, a pair of cousins. He stares at us wide-eyed. The hem of his robe drops from his grip and his bony ankles are hidden under its folds.

"It's all right, Muircan," Tatiana says after a moment's hesitation. "You can speak freely in front of our guests."

Jack and I exchange glances. Muircan waits another beat, plainly unhappy—either with his news, or his queen. Probably both.

"You must look into the between," he finally says.

So we all do. I'm expecting some kind of fairy business, something of major concern to them, and I guess it is, but it's really a big deal on all fronts: fairy, cousin, and maybe even human, depending on the fallout.

The first thing to hit me is the sound, because all that's initially visible is an indistinct ocean of brown. I can't make out what it is we're looking at. But the sound . . . the sound is huge: the boom of a multitude of drums combined with hooves stamping on the ground, dancing in place, pounding like thunder when it's rumbling directly overhead, playing a heartbeat rhythm—a single, cadenced pulse that immediately awakes an echoing response in my own chest.

At that moment, my brain separates the ocean of brown into individual shapes and I realize we're looking at an enormous gathering of buffalo. I'm talking multitudes here. There are thousands upon thousands of the horned cousins assembling there on an open plain, drumming and dancing as more, and then still more, join their already swollen ranks.

Jack gives a low whistle.

I know he saw this coming—we were just talking about it not that long before Tatiana came in—but the actual moment seems to have come upon us way faster than I ever thought it would. And on a far larger scale.

"There must be thousands of them," Tatiana says in a quiet voice.

Jack gives a slow nod. "And that's just for starters."

"What do you mean?"

"I see both living spirits and the ghosts of their dead, which tells me that they're calling in *all* the buffalo tribes, past and present."

"I still don't know what it means."

Jack gives her a look that says Who are you kidding?, but he only says, "Do you have any idea how many buffalo got displaced or killed when the humans you followed over here made a grab for their lands?"

"We had nothing to do with that."

"Maybe not. But you still took advantage of their misfortune and moved right into their territories wherever you could."

When Tatiana doesn't respond, Jack adds, "Come on. You had to know this was coming. Sooner or later, there had to be a reckoning."

"We settled that with Raven."

Jack shakes his head. "You settled a local problem. And then you let your people go out and hunt cousins."

Tatiana doesn't look at him. She can't take her gaze from the gathering buffalo.

"You have to get Joe back here," she finally says. "He has to talk to them."

When Jack doesn't respond, she turns to look at him. He just shrugs.

"I can do that," he says. "Soon as you bring Jilly and her friend back to us—safe *and* sound—I'm sure he'll be happy to give it a shot."

"So he's just going to let the buffalo overrun the city because of two missing humans?"

"You know it's not about that."

"But it's awfully convenient that they should all show up just when he thinks he needs some bargaining power."

Jack gives her a hard look. "Joe had nothing to do with this. You called it down on yourselves by not keeping your bogans in check."

"Maybe we could have kept a better eye on them," she says, "but this is still overkill."

"Fairies don't much care for cousins," Jack tells her. "Cousins don't much care for fairy. It's been like that since you first showed up on these shores. Sometimes we get along, sure, but that's only been the easygoing among us. Back in the hills there have always been individuals, waiting and brooding and planning. It's just your bad luck that one of them got elected war chief at the same time that some of your people decided it would be entertaining to kill a few cousins."

"You know it's something we don't condone," she says, falling back into royal speech and repetition.

Jack sighs. "But you didn't control it, either."

"So because of that, Joe's going to make us suffer."

Jack shakes his head. "No. Joe's so focused on his family that he probably doesn't care one way or the other what goes down. None of this'll mean anything to him until his sister's safe."

"But we don't *know* where the humans are."

"Then you know Joe's not going to be helping you."

"In the time it would take for us to track them down, we could lose everything to that army. Tell him we'll do whatever he wants if he first helps us stop this."

Listening to the two of them talk, I feel for her. Once those buffalo start to move they're going to wipe out pretty much every fairy they find in the city. And once they have the taste of fairy blood, I doubt it'll stop there. After all, so far as a lot of cousins are concerned, there's a whole continent to take back.

Yeah, I feel sorry for her, but I empathize with the cousins, too.

"And in the time he takes to help you," Jack is saying, "Jilly and her friend could be killed."

"You don't know that."

"We don't know *anything*," Jack says. "That's a big part of the problem."

"But—"

"And I doubt it'd make that much difference to him anyway. You know Joe. He looks at the little picture first. Until he knows his family's safe, you'd have better luck whistling up the wind to help you."

It's pretty obvious from Tatiana's face that she already knows this, but I guess she had to try.

"How about you?" she asks Jack. "Can you talk to them?"

"The buffalo wouldn't listen to me. You need someone way up on the respect ladder, or at least someone who's got the gift of calm, the way Joe does. I wouldn't know where to start with that trick of his that has people putting down their weapons to listen to him pretty much as soon as he opens his mouth." He shoots a glance at Mother Crone. "Barring one or two exceptions, that is."

Tatiana lets the veil that separates the between from her court fall closed once more. We can still hear the buffalo, but it's like a distant thunder now.

"So, what do we do?" she asks Jack.

"I haven't a clue," he says. "All I know is you've got a problem."

"You can't seriously not care."

"What I feel's got nothing to do with it."

"You could at least try."

"I'm telling you right now, they wouldn't listen to me, and I'll be damned if I'll let them pound me into the ground under a few hundred hooves just to prove that to you."

"But—"

"You're just going to have to find your own way out of this," Jack says, cutting her off. Then he turns to me. "We need to get out of here."

I hear Tatiana calling Jack's name, but we're already on the move, shifting from the world the court is in to the between that lies next to it. The sound of the buffalo is louder once more. We're not exactly on the plain where they're gathering, but close enough to hear them. Really, how could we *not* hear them? Thousands of drums. Hundreds of thousands of hooves pounding on the dirt. A line of trees blocks our view, but we can see the dust from their dancing rising up above the topmost boughs.

"You were a little harsh back there," I say.

Jack shrugs. "We were wasting time. There's nothing you or I could do to help, in the court or with the buffalo."

"But the queen was right. We could have tried."

"We're not going to try, we're going to do."

I raise my eyebrows.

"Here's how I see it," Jack says. "This whole show is Minisino's doing and though I don't entirely disagree with his reasons, I don't believe that everybody should pay for the sins of a few. Trouble is, all that war chief of the buffalo is going to listen to is someone with a bigger gun."

"Which we don't have."

"Nope. But maybe we can find us one or two."

"Now you've lost me."

"You ever hear of Ayabe?" he asks.

I nod. People talk about wolves and bears—maybe elk—as being the lords of the forest, but the most powerful beings you're going to find in the deep woods are the moose spirits. Like the buffalo, they don't have a whole lot of give to them. Unlike the buffalo, they don't have a herd mentality. They're solitary by nature, but that doesn't make them easy prey because *nobody* willingly takes on a moose. They weigh in at over half a ton, can have an antler spread of six feet, and they're not the most even-tempered of the cerva. Easy to piss off, and impossible to shake if they get it in their heads to come after you.

Ayabe's the oldest of the moose spirits in this area and his range takes in everything from the Kickaha Mountains down to Newford's lake.

"You think he'd be interested in helping us?" I ask.

"If I can convince him it'd be in the best long-term interests of his people, yes."

"Well, let's go."

Jack shakes his head. "No, I'll go. I need you to talk to Lucius."

He means Raven, the big gun of the corbae, my people. I've never met him, but from all I've heard I know what his reaction would be.

"I can already tell you what he'll say," I tell Jack. "He'll say that the fairy brought this problem onto themselves, so they can fix it themselves. That's pretty much his response to anybody who comes looking for him to get involved in something."

And while I hate to say it of one of my own, he'd probably rationalize the whole thing along the lines of not wanting to be seen as pro-fairy when the buffalo run them over, but he also wouldn't want to join them in case the fairy pull something out of a hat at the last minute. He's always the mediator, the old stories say.

"I still need you to try," Jack says.

"I'll try. I don't know if he'll even hear me out, but I'll give it a shot."

"That's all anyone can ask."

"And if he won't help?"

Jack grins. "Then stick around. There'll be plenty of pickings for a carrion bird."

With that, he steps away and I'm alone in the between with the sound of the buffalo ringing in my ears and echoing the drum of my own heartbeat, deep in my chest.

I find myself wondering what I'm doing here, going out on a limb for a people I don't even like in the first place. All I was interested in doing was seeing that some justice was done to Anwatan's murderers. Then that got complicated in this search for Lizzie and Joe's sister Jilly. Now here I am, going off to petition the head of the corbae clan to intercede on behalf of what I've always pretty much felt were my enemies.

And none of this even comes close to dealing with my own problems with Odawa.

I listen to the buffalo for a little longer, let their righteous anger rise up and fill me.

But it won't hold.

I've given my word.

So I step back into *Kakagi-aki*—Raven's world—and set off to find its creator. Who knows? Maybe he'll listen to me. Maybe he'll take out that old pot of his, the one he stirred that brought the world into being in the long ago. Maybe he'll stir it again and re-create the world. Make a place where we can all start over and do it right this time.

Jilly

My paralysis lasts right up until the moment Del actually touches me . . .

And then all hell breaks loose.

Maybe I'm just a little kid, but I only *look* like a little kid. I'm still the grown-up me inside this nine-year-old body. I'm tough. I'm resilient. I've survived a lifetime of good and bad, and while maybe the good was really good, the bad was worse than bad, so it's not like I'm a pushover.

What I know for sure is, I don't have to take his crap anymore—not like the little kid I used to be had to.

Am I still scared? Sure I am. I'd be stupid not to be. In my present circumstances, he's at least twice my size and way stronger. And he's always been way *meaner*.

But I don't give up.

Through the hardest times I've been through, I never gave up except for once—that day when I was out of dope and out of money and three-days hungry, when Lou found me and took me to Angel. And even then, I still sassed him. But I just didn't have it in me to care anymore.

I care now. I care big time.

What's happening to me right now is something I've fought against ever since I got myself off the streets. Not just for myself, but for other people, for other kids. I've worked at raising awareness. At standing up when standing up was needed. Being the shoulder to lean on. Working the soup kitchens, the crisis lines, whatever was needed when it was needed, not only when it was convenient.

Until my accident, I was always out there on the front lines, cutting out a chunk of every week to be there. To be doing something. To fight the injustice and wrongs that we seem to do so casually to each other.

So how can I not fight for myself?

As soon as that big brother of mine gets close enough, I give him a solid kick in the groin with all the power of a little girl's leg behind it. And it hurts him. I *know* it hurts him. I can see it in his eyes. I can see it in his body language.

But he doesn't buckle. He just stands there, and I watch the pain leave his eyes. I see him grin at me.

"You just don't get it, do you?" he says. "You might have put this world together in some little dark place of your mind, but it was never yours. It was always mine, little sister. What I say goes and *only* what I say."

"Bullshit."

He gives me a casual swat with his hand that sends my little child's body tumbling to the grass.

"Don't you sass me, little sister," he says. "I purely don't have the patience for it."

My head is ringing, but I force myself to sit up. I can feel the heat of a welt burning on my cheek. But I'm too mad to pay attention to either. Too mad to consider the consequences of fighting back, if only with words.

"You don't have the patience for it?" I say, getting to my feet. I feel dizzy and my voice sounds so weird—thin and childlike. "You arrogant piece of—"

He hits me again—still with an open hand, but harder now, enough to make me cry out and send me sprawling once more. Before I can even think of getting up, he's standing over me—towering, larger than life. He puts a boot on my shoulder and pushes down until it feels like my shoulder is going to snap.

"Where'd you get all this fight in you?" he asks.

He leans down, peering into my face. The motion puts increased pressure on the weight of his boot. Tears of pain leak from my eyes.

"Not that it matters none," he tells me. "It all comes out the same in the end. You do whatever the hell I tell you, when I tell you, the way I tell you. Or I just break you like a twig."

The weight of his boot lifts for a moment, then he brings it down hard and bones snap in my shoulder. He grins as I cry out.

"And here's the fun part," he says.

He grabs me by my hair and hauls me to my feet. My arm dangles limply from the broken shoulder and pain flares in sharp, dark waves until I can barely stay conscious.

He grabs my shoulder and squeezes it. I shrink in anticipation, but it's all gone. The broken bones are mended, the pain is gone except for the memory of it.

"Whatever I break," he tells me, "I can fix, too. Isn't that a comfort, little sister? Knowing that no matter what I do to you, I can bring you back just with a snap of my fingers and we're ready to start all over again."

He waits for me to make some smart remark but I've got nothing. I'm too numbed by the enormity of this hell I've made for myself.

He laughs, knowing just what's going through my head. Knowing he's got me beat. Then he picks me up and throws me over his shoulder.

"Time we were getting back to the house," he says.

He sets off across the field, my head bouncing against his back. He smells of sweat and cigarettes and something else, something vile and awful that's rotting there in the dark void of his soul.

"We've got *so* much catching up to do . . ."

Lizzie

Before the priest carried her away, Lizzie saw enough of what was happening to Jilly to break her heart. But there was nothing she could do to help her. She had her own problems with the priest. But whether the priest simply wasn't as strong as Del, she was more determined or stronger than Jilly, or he simply hadn't been expecting her to bite his arm, she was able to break free of his grip. He grabbed at her as soon as she got loose, but she scrambled out of his reach.

She glanced over to where she'd last seen Jilly. Del had her slung over his shoulder now and was already carrying her away—to the house over in the next field, Lizzie assumed. She took a step in their direction.

She wanted to help Jilly. She wanted to knock that smirk off Del's face and show him what it meant to be helpless. And she would have, too—or at least she would have tried—but then the priest was lunging at her again, and she had to dodge out of his way.

This was so insane.

Surely, when her car had stalled at that crossroads, she'd fallen asleep and was only dreaming all of this.

The bogans and Grey. Siobhan's tumble down the stairs. Being kidnapped into some fairy world. Killing a bogan and meeting the doonie.

And this.

This.

It couldn't be real, not any of it, but especially not this.

Stuck in a world inside Jilly's head. That hateful little girl who had led Del and the priest to them, then ambled off like she was on a Sunday stroll. Del's manhandling of Jilly. And now Jilly was so still, slung over her brother's back, not even struggling anymore as he carried her to that dilapidated old house in the distance.

And, of course, the priest.

Maybe she was the size of some little kid, but if he thought that meant she was easy pickings, he had a whole world of hurt coming to him.

"Child," he told her. "Denying your holy duty is a cardinal sin."

"So's fucking little girls."

She wasn't sure which stopped him. The coarse language coming from an apparent child's mouth, or the simple truth that what he did was wrong in the eyes of both God and man.

He gave a sad shake of his head.

"I'm afraid you need to be taught a lesson," he said, then he smiled. "And there will be smiting."

If that's what you want to call it, Lizzie thought, but she didn't bother replying.

Instead, she backed away from his careful approach, waiting for an opening. She knew she couldn't count on much power from this child's body she was stuck in, but that didn't mean she couldn't hurt him. Just so long as he didn't use his mojo on her.

The weird thing here was that she couldn't get past his being a priest. Oh, she knew all about how so many of them were old pervs—sometimes it seemed like a new scandal showed up on the news every second day. And she sure knew the dark side of the church's black-robed pep squad. She and her cousin had gone to an all-girls Catholic school where the nuns worshipped the priests maybe more than they did God, and they certainly believed that a ruler on the hand or the back of the head was a far better behaviour modifier than ever a kind word might be—never mind the Bible's teachings. And there had always been talk of which priests and nuns to avoid seeing when you were by yourself.

So, she wasn't exactly naive about the so-called sanctity of a priest's vows.

What was it her granddad used to say? Something about how the two main problems of the Irish were black with white collars: one you found in the church, the other in a pub in a pint of Guinness.

But none of that stopped her from this feeling of . . . uneasiness that came over her whenever she saw a priest. It was like seeing a policeman. She couldn't help but feel guilty as soon as she came into their periphery, even when she'd done absolutely nothing wrong. It was so stupid. And priests . . . well, being around a priest made her think that God's eye was upon her because she was in such close proximity to one of His chosen. That she should go to confession, say a few "Hail Marys" and ask for the priest's blessing.

All bollocks, she knew. At least it was for her, more power to those who still got comfort from the church. But even feeling this way, respect for the clergy had been so ingrained in her from before her first communion that, while the passing of time had faded the edges on any number of her memories, the expectation of being respectful still reared up inside her, sharp and clear, whenever she saw a priest's collar.

Even now. Even in this stupid place that shouldn't exist, with a priest who made a mockery of everything he was supposed to believe in.

He made a sudden grab for her, and she dodged under his arm. She kicked him in the back of the knee as he went by—cursing this weak little body she was in as she did—but he still went down. While he was off-balance, she kicked him again. Once, in the side of the head, but that didn't do more than shake him up. He turned to her, and she kicked him a second time, in the solar plexus. All the air went out of him. She watched his face go white as he tumbled to the grass, turned and gave him one last satisfying kick in the side of the head.

She stood in a defensive position, ready, for long moments, watching his still body. When he still didn't move, she let herself relax a little. If she ever got out of this and back to the gym, she was going to have to give Johnny a big thank you, since he was the one who insisted she learn footwork as well as the hand-to-hand and defensive techniques she'd been more interested in. In this body, a blow from a little hand couldn't do nearly as much damage as a foot with the weight of her body behind it.

Carefully, she went over to the priest. With the toe of her shoe, she lifted his head from the ground. When she pulled her foot away, his head fell limply back to the grass.

Okay, she thought. So, either he didn't have the time to work the mojo, or he didn't have it in the first place, either of which pointed to Del being the really dangerous one.

She looked toward the house where he'd taken Jilly.

"Is he dead?" a voice asked from behind her.

Lizzie turned to see that Mattie had come back. She still held that teddy bear in her arms like a little kid would, but Lizzie wasn't sure how much of a kid she really was. Her eyes were anything but a child's—too old, too calculating. And from what Jilly had said, the teddy bear wasn't exactly an innocent little toy either.

"Well, is he?"

Lizzie shrugged. "Who cares?"

"He will."

Lizzie knew the girl meant Del, not this sorry excuse for a priest that lay at her feet. She looked across the field to the farmhouse, then turned her gaze back to the girl's.

"Only if you tell him," she said.

Mattie smirked. "You can't stop me."

"I guess that's true."

Because she'd seen the bear twitch in its mistress' arms, Lizzie loaded her voice with discouragement, letting Mattie think she was beaten. It was still only a plush toy, threadbare and floppy, but seeing that twitch of movement made Lizzie believe Jilly's description of how the toy could turn into a giant grizzly bear. She wasn't going to give it a chance to transform.

She let her shoulders sag and cast her gaze down when Mattie started grinning. But she looked at the little girl through her lashes, chose her moment, then lunged forward.

Mattie cried out as Lizzie snatched the toy bear from her hands. Before she could recover, Lizzie started to twist off the teddy's head.

"No!" Mattie screamed.

She charged forward. Lizzie stepped aside and gave the girl a boot in the rear to send her reeling off-balance as she went by. Mattie tripped over a root and went sprawling in the weeds. Lizzie returned her attention to the teddy bear. In her hands she could feel the toy swelling in size, changing. The plush sprouted coarse hairs. The sawdust stuffing took on a spongy feel, like flesh. Grimacing, she gave a final twist and the head came free, happily spraying sawdust rather than blood.

Whatever spell had begun to animate the teddy was gone and now it was simply a broken toy, head held in one hand, body in the other. Mattie sat in the weeds, staring in horror, tears streaming down her cheeks.

"No!" she cried. "No no no no . . ."

Lizzie pushed down the sympathy that rose up in her at the pitiable figure the little girl made.

"Now it's down to just you and me," she said. "Are you ready to bargain?"

Mattie stared daggers at her. She wiped at her cheeks with her sleeve, then blew her nose in the fabric.

"Why should I?" she asked, her voice gone flat and hard. "You've killed him."

Lizzie shook her head. "Give me a needle and thread and I can have him back, ship-shape, in no time. But first you have to make me a promise."

"I won't promise anything. I hate you!"

"I'm sure you do. But I can fix your bear. Just swear you won't hurt or help anyone hurt Jilly or me or any of our friends."

"I won't. I hate her. I hate both of you, but I hate her more."

There was no point in arguing that Jilly had never meant to hurt her. Mattie was a child, with a child's one-dimensional concept of right and wrong. Shades of grey in terms of circumstances or remorse simply didn't enter into the equation.

"I don't care if you do or don't," Lizzie told her. "Swear, or you'll never get your teddy back. I'll tear it up into so many small pieces no one will ever be able to put him back together again."

Mattie started to cry again and once more Lizzie almost gave in. The little girl's tears were so heartbreaking. But she remembered how Mattie had led Del to them earlier, and from what Jilly had told her, the bear was extremely dangerous. They couldn't chance Mattie sending it after them—just saying they managed to escape Del in the first place.

"Swear, on your true name," Lizzie said.

A cunning look came into Mattie's eyes, but Lizzie shook her head.

"Don't think for a moment that I don't know your true name, Mattie Finn," she said.

Jilly had told her that as well.

"So . . ." Mattie said. "If I help you and promise not to hurt you or Jilly or any of your friends, you'll fix Grath and give him back to me?"

Lizzie nodded. "You don't even have to help. Just promise not to hurt us."

"Okay, then. I promise."

This seemed a bit too easy, Lizzie thought. And Mattie still had a bit of a smug look, hiding there in the back of her eyes. She also had her hands behind her back.

"Say it again," Lizzie said, "and let me see your fingers this time. And it doesn't count to cross your toes or your eyes or any other part of your body you might be able to cross."

Mattie glared at her.

I was right, Lizzie thought.

It was so easy to forget that although they both looked like children, Mattie still *was* a child. To a child, forget ethics. Crossing your fingers while making a promise truly invalidated the promise.

"I won't," Mattie told her.

"Won't what?" an all too familiar voice asked.

Don't let it be, Lizzie thought. But turning, she saw that Del really had come back and her heart sank. She remembered how easily he had dealt with the child Jilly was. What were the chances she'd have any better success?

Mattie had turned as well, but as soon as she saw him, she looked away and stared at her shoes.

"I won't promise not to hurt them," she said in a small voice.

Del shook his head. "I don't like my girls squabbling. And you know what I do when things I don't like start happening."

Mattie kept her gaze on her shoes and nodded.

"How about you, little girl?" Del asked Lizzie. "Can you guess what happens?"

Lizzie shook her head. "But go ahead. Do your worst."

Del laughed.

"Little girl," he said. "You can't even imagine my worst. Say, what's your name, anyway?"

Lizzie let the moment draw out. She was figuring out the distance between them, the best way to take him down.

"I asked you a question."

"Yeah, and I don't feel like answering. So bite me."

He swung his hand at her, but he'd telegraphed the attack with his eyes and Lizzie easily dodged the blow. While he was off-balance, she spun around, putting the force of the movement behind the foot aimed at his knee. After all, it had worked on the priest. But Del recovered faster than she'd expected and grabbed her leg. He gave it a jerk and she went tumbling to the ground.

Before she could get up, he had a boot on her chest, exerting pressure until she stopped struggling.

"Feisty little thing, aren't you?"

"Fuck you!"

"Potty-mouthed, too." He glanced at Mattie. "And we all know what happens to potty-mouthed little girls, don't we?"

"Oh, Christ," Lizzie started, "would you give it a—"

But then her mouth stopped moving. She . . .

Del laughed. He lifted his boot and stepped away from her, allowing her to get up.

Lizzie lifted shaking hands to her mouth, but there was nothing there. Only smooth skin from the bottom of her nose down to her chin. She tried to move her jaw, but there was nothing there to move. Under her fingertips she could feel that it was all solid bone beneath her skin. No jaw. No jaw muscles. No mouth.

"See," Del said. "I don't need to know your name to work my mojo on you. That's how it works here. Asking your name—that was just me being sociable."

Lizzie couldn't look at him. She couldn't stop moving her hands over the bottom of her face. A huge, gibbering dark panic was starting up in the pit of her stomach. When she finally turned in his direction, she couldn't stop the pleading in her eyes.

Don't do this. Fix this. Please . . .

But he wasn't even looking at her anymore. There was only Mattie, staring at her with big eyes and a smile twitching in the corner of her mouth. Del had walked over to the priest who still lay where Lizzie had dropped him.

"Well, aren't you a piece of work," he said to the unconscious man. "Letting an itty-bitty girl like that knock you flat on your arse and out cold."

"He's just a big stupid," Mattie said.

Del nodded. "It's not like we didn't know that. All we really needed him for was to help discombobulate our little Miss Jillian, and he did a fine job of that. But now . . . well, I guess we don't have much more of a use for him, do we?"

He glanced at Mattie who only shrugged. He shifted his gaze to Lizzie.

"Guess you can say goodbye to the priest," he told her, then he grinned. "Oh, wait. You can't say anything anymore, can you?"

He turned back to the priest and waved his hand casually over the supine body. Instead of vanishing the way Timony had, the priest simply dissolved. Flesh and vestments turned into a dark, gooey liquid. Moments later, all that was left of him was a dark stain in the grass. The horrific and impossible sight was probably the only thing that could have taken Lizzie's mind from her own awful predicament.

"Mattie and I are going back to the house," Del said, drawing her attention back to him. "You can come or stay, I don't care. But little nameless girl, don't you forget for one sweet second that I'm the rule here. What I say goes."

He seemed to be waiting for some kind of acknowledgement, so she nodded. She was too scared not to respond. What else might he do to her?

"That's a good girl. Maybe there's hope for you. Maybe I'll give you back your mouth before you starve to death."

He took Mattie's hand and they started across the field, back to the house. Lizzie stared at the stain on the grass, trying to get her mind around how the priest had simply *melted* away, then her gaze drifted to Mattie's stuffed toy, the two pieces lying abandoned on the grass where Lizzie had dropped them. She lifted a hand back to where her mouth should be.

The panic started up again, deep inside her, swelling.

She quickly dropped her hand and took a deep breath through her nose, trying to calm herself.

This wasn't real, she told herself, remembering what Timony had said just before Del sent him away.

She and Jilly had been transformed only because they'd *let* it happen to themselves. Because they believed it was true.

It was all lies. That they could be trapped in the bodies of little girls. That Del was all-powerful. That a teddy bear could become a full-size grizzly.

But something didn't fit.

She didn't really believe in any of this.

Even with what her senses were telling her, she hadn't fully accepted anything that had happened to her since the moment the bogans dragged her out of her bed. No. From before that. From when she first saw them at the crossroads.

So, if she didn't believe, why was she still here, stuck in a world inside of Jilly's head in the body of a nine- or ten-year-old girl?

A horrible thought occurred to her.

Maybe Timony hadn't been talking to her specifically. Maybe it was only so long as *Jilly* believed.

She turned to look at the distant farmhouse. Del and Mattie had almost reached it now.

She had to get the message to Jilly. How she was supposed to do that without being able to talk, she had no idea. But she had to try.

If there was a moment of bravery for her in all of what had happened, this was it. Everything else, from killing the bogan, knocking down the priest, attacking Del . . . all of that had just been her acting on instinct. Standing up against what she knew wasn't right without stopping to think.

She lifted her hand once more, caressing the strange smooth expanse of skin the way she'd run a finger over a scab, or tongue a sore on the roof of her mouth—hardly even aware she was doing it.

Her gaze remained fixed on the farmhouse. Del and Mattie had gone inside now.

This time, Lizzie realized, she knew exactly what she was getting into. Until she could get Jilly to understand how everything was dependent on what *she* believed, Del could make anything happen. *Anything.* She was sure that taking away her mouth was only the least of the horrors he could come up with.

His voice echoed in her head.

Little girl, you can't even imagine my worst.

No, she probably couldn't. Because she wasn't some insane sociopath with the power of a god in his hands.

But she got up all the same. She brushed dirt and grass from her pants, then slowly started across the fields herself, aiming for the farmhouse.

Rabedy

Rabedy was sure he was going to throw up, if he didn't first fall off the salmon's back and break his neck on the ground below. The ground far, *far* below.

Their route through the forest had been bad enough, weaving and bobbing to avoid the trunks and boughs of the trees, leaves slapping him in the face, branches almost knocking him from his precarious perch. But then they broke from the trees and up Odawa took them, up and up, high into the sky, to where the clouds lived and bogans weren't supposed to go. If they were, the Moon-mother would have given them wings. But she hadn't, so that was fairly clear, wasn't it?

Nevertheless, here they were, a salmon swimming through the air with a bogan clinging to its back and his stomach crawling up his throat.

Until that moment, Rabedy hadn't known that he had a fear of heights.

Or maybe it was just a fear of clinging to the back of some giant pluiking fish while soaring through the sky.

There were probably worse things that could happen to a bogan, but Rabedy couldn't think of one at the moment. It was all he could do to hang onto the salmon's dorsal fin, knees clamped as tight as they could be against the slippery scales of its body. He knew he should just keep his eyes closed, but he couldn't stop himself from staring at the ground speeding by below.

He really was going to throw up.

The terrain changed under them as they passed through various worlds, from forest to desert, large frightening expanses of deep, dark water to endless sweeps of tundra that went as far as the horizon until the passage into yet another world put those desolate lands behind.

Rabedy had no idea where they were going. He didn't care.

"Let me down, let me down!" he kept shouting.

But all Odawa would reply was *Patience,* his voice ringing in Rabedy's head, resonant and most unpleasant.

"Bugger your patience," Rabedy finally cried. "Let me down *now!*"

Fine.

Their descent was fast and sudden. Rabedy held on so tightly that by the time they were finally near the ground, it was all he could do to pry his hands from the salmon's fin and drop the last few feet. He lost his balance and fell to his knees. For a long moment, he kept his head close to the ground, waiting for the contents of his stomach to come roaring up his throat. For the pounding in his head to stop.

The vertigo passed, if not the thunder in his head. He pushed himself to his feet, swaying because his legs felt all rubbery. He put one hand out for balance, the other against his temple in a vain hope to stop the pounding. His gaze searched for and found Odawa, standing in his own form at the edge of a cliff, looking down at something below.

Supposed to be pluiking blind, he thought as he stumbled over to join the green-bree, so what was he staring at?

"What do you see?" Odawa asked when Rabedy was beside him. "My senses tell me one thing, but this once, I don't trust them."

"I see . . ."

Rabedy's voice trailed off. He stared down at the thousands of buffalo warriors gathered on the plains far below and let his hand drop from his temple. The pounding wasn't in his head. It came from them, from hundreds of thousands of hooves stamping and war drums beating. The buffalo filled the land below, from one horizon to the other.

"Cerva," he said after a moment. "Impossible numbers of them."

Odawa nodded. "The living, with the spirits of the dead swelling their ranks."

Rabedy didn't bother to ask how he knew that. He just suppressed a shiver and wished they'd landed somewhere else, anywhere else, so long as it was far, far away from here.

"This part of the between opens onto the city," Odawa said. "Where the fairy courts lie."

"Do you think they mean to attack?"

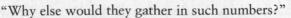

"Why else would they gather in such numbers?"

"But why—" Rabedy began, except he knew.

This was the price for bogans going off into the wild and the green, hunting what was forbidden.

"We did this," he said. "You and I, and pluiking Big Dan with all his grand schemes."

The blind man turned his sightless gaze in the bogan's direction.

"Now, why would you say that?"

Rabedy hated the look of those milky-white eyes that seemed to see too much, but he didn't turn away.

"Think about it," he said. "You're the one who's helped us to go out into green-bree territories where we've been killing cerva. Why else would they be going to war?"

"I can think of a hundred reasons."

"So can I," Rabedy said. "But have you ever heard of the straw that broke the camel's back? That's what this business of ours has been: those last few ugly straws."

Odawa studied him for a long moment, then finally said, "You're not much of a bogan, are you?"

Rabedy was sick of this. Bad enough he had to take it from his own, without some pluiking green-bree throwing it in his face as well.

"You try growing up with a mother like mine," he said, his voice bitter. "Always the butt of every joke, including hers. It doesn't take too long before you come to understand meanness and the yearning for a kind word. You learn how kindness *means* something, but it's not something anyone will ever let *you* experience."

"Then why did you want to learn to shapeshift—if not to hunt, I mean?"

"For the freedom."

"I don't understand."

"People'd look at me and they'd see a dog, not a bogan. They wouldn't be suspicious of my every word and action anymore. They'd take me at face value—for who I am."

"And the other bogans don't?"

Rabedy shook his head, then realized the motion was useless to a blind man.

"Bogans think only of themselves. First themselves, then their family, then their clan. And sometimes, though more rarely, of fairy as a whole."

"And you?'

"I don't like bogans." He paused, then added, "You see what that says about me?"

Odawa didn't respond for a long time. Then finally he laid a hand on Rabedy's shoulder.

"There are days I'm not too fond of myself, either," he said.

Rabedy shook off the green-bree's hand. He didn't need anyone's sympathy. Certainly not Odawa's.

"Don't pretend you understand me," Rabedy told him. "You don't know me and we're not friends."

"I only . . ."

"You only nothing. I've watched you from the beginning. Watched you play on Big Dan's greed. I don't know what your game is, but I know that whatever you do for anyone else, it's only for your benefit."

"Then why didn't you say something?" Odawa asked him, his voice cold.

"Because who'd ever listen to me?"

"How sad."

"Right now," Rabedy said, "I'm not important. You're not important. All that matters is that we do something to stop this."

The blind gaze regarded him for a long moment, then the green-bree smiled. There wasn't even a hint of warmth in that smile.

"That, my little high-minded friend," he said, "is something you'll have to do on your own. I have a corbae to kill."

And with that he stepped away and Rabedy was left alone on the cliff top, looking down at more buffalo green-brees than he could ever have imagined existed.

Geordie

It was an astonishing sight, this view that Timony showed me of thousands of buffalo gathered on the plains below. It was like a sea of brown waves undulating softly as the individual cerva stomped and pounded their drums.

This, I thought, was what it must have been like in the old days, when the early explorers first reached the prairies and came upon the vast herds that lived there. The difference was, the European hunters immediately started butchering the buffalo for their hides, leaving the skinned carcasses to rot on the ground by the hundreds of thousands, while Timony and I would just as soon stay off their radar completely.

Thinking of those killing fields, I didn't have to ask Timony what he meant by his simple reply of "War." But then something else occurred to me.

"Fairy followed the buffalo hunters, didn't they?" I said.

Timony shrugged. "I suppose. I wasn't here in those days. I came on the later boats, after one of those big wars where you people killed each other."

"So when you said war, did you mean with humans or fairy?"

"Fairy," he replied. "But if they're successful in that endeavour, I don't doubt that they'll turn their wrath on your people."

It was weird, his constantly saying "your people." I didn't feel the remotest connection to those early explorers who only saw the Americas as a source for monetary gain—no more than I do now with the big companies that run roughshod over anyone and anything that gets in the way of their profits.

I returned my gaze to that vast gathering of buffalo cousins. Their numbers seemed endless.

"There's nothing we can do about this, is there?" I said.

"A doonie and a human? Hardly."

"Then maybe we should concentrate on what we *can* do and try to find Joe."

The doonie nodded. I didn't see what he did next, but the view into the between disappeared, and we were back on that lonely grey shore once more. After what we'd just experienced, this place seemed even more desolate and lost, reflecting my mood. I tried not to get absorbed by the feeling it woke inside me.

"So, how do we start?" I asked.

"Concentrate on your friend," Timony told me. "If you can bring up a strong enough essence of him in your mind, I should be able to use that to start my own search."

Fairy magic's mostly about will—I'd learned that from Galfreya. Oh, there are spells and magical talismans and all the usual baggage you hear about with magic, but the clarity of your vision and the strength of your will are what underlies everything.

Well and good in theory, but it wasn't anything I'd ever put into practice.

Have you ever noticed how when you don't want to think about something, you can't get it out of your mind? Conversely, when you're trying to concentrate, holding a particular person or place in your head seems impossible. No matter how well you think you know them, the familiar keeps sliding away and all you're left with are ghost traces of these things you thought you knew so well.

It was like that when I tried to envision Joe. He was the kind of guy who made a serious impression on you—those crazy eyes, for starters—but I couldn't seem to hold onto an image of him. So I tried thinking about the times I'd been around him, which were usually in Jilly's company, and that made me think of Jilly instead. I had no trouble calling up an image of her. She's hardwired into my head and has been pretty much from the day we first met, working as part-timers for the post office that Christmas so long ago.

It's funny. I was in my early twenties at the time, but it feels like I've known her all my life. Sometimes when we're talking, I'll bring up things from when I was a teenager—swimming at the sand pits, being chased by that bull on the old Haile Farm, playing fiddle tunes on a granite outcrop out behind my parents' house—and I'm surprised when she doesn't remember them. She'll give me a look and then I realize, well, *of course* she wouldn't.

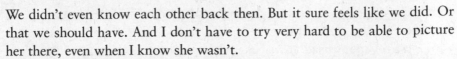

We didn't even know each other back then. But it sure feels like we did. Or that we should have. And I don't have to try very hard to be able to picture her there, even when I know she wasn't.

Jilly says that's because we must have known each other in past lives, "You know, like when I was a teapot and you were a kettle. Or there was that time we were both mice in a Victorian travelling circus. Ah, those were the days, Geordie, me lad. It was all cheese and applause."

The memory brought a bittersweet warmth, but it also reminded me of what I was supposed to be doing: concentrating on finding Joe. Because if we didn't find Joe, then we might never find Jilly and then these memories would be all I'd have.

I needed more than memories.

I needed her.

I tried again, but if anything, I was getting worse at bringing Joe clearly to mind. He became this elusive butterfly, always hovering just a few steps away, no matter how carefully I approached. This happened again and again until I started to get frustrated, which is pretty much the last thing you want to do in a case like this.

Frustration, worry, anger . . . these are the things that totally muddy our thinking. Not that I've ever been a clear, linear thinker, which is another reason that Jilly and I get along so well because she's anything but linear.

Jilly . . .

I went back to trying to hold onto Joe in my mind. I remembered him coming to visit me one time at the apartment I had on Lee Street. I'd lived there pretty much forever—this was before the disaster of my moving to L.A. to be with Tanya. There wasn't much to the place, but then I've never needed a lot. If you need proof, consider how long I've been staying in Jilly's studio loft and how little of myself you'll find in there. Most of my things are still boxed up and stored in the basement of my brother Christy's apartment building.

But back at the Lee Street apartment, I'd taken the time to make the place look nice. I had posters and art on the walls—mostly courtesy of Jilly and our various artist friends. There was a stereo set up with all my albums organized in old milk crates. Brick and plank bookcases for my tune book collections. And then all the instruments, of course, leaning in corners, hanging from the walls, the better-quality ones stored safely away in their cases.

It was easy to call the place up. I could remember the smallest details, from the row of figurines and knickknacks lined up on the windowsill and the odd patchwork quilt on the bed, to the way the red neon light from a sign on the street outside crept in under the bottom of my blinds. That night . . .

I felt a tug in my head. It was like when you have something on the tip of your tongue, something you know backwards to forwards, but you just can't put it into words at that moment.

I suppose it should have made me feel more frustrated—this new little intrusion added to my inability to grab and hold a strong memory of Joe—but instead, it brought me the oddest feeling of comfort. And then . . . and then . . .

I was back there in that memory. In my Lee Street apartment. Or at least my every sense told me I was. I looked to the window. The blinds were still up and a gentle snow was falling, just as it had been the night Joe came by.

This is good, I thought. I'm going to have that memory for Timony now.

Except there were a hundred other snowy nights that I was living there when Jilly dropped by. And this time, when the door of my apartment opened, it was Jilly who was standing there with snow dripping from her unruly hair, not Joe.

She had a bundle under her arm. Unwrapping the brown butcher's paper, she took out a painting, and I saw the familiar flower fairies cavorting in a junkyard. That let me place exactly the when of this memory. It was the night after one of her shows at the Green Man Gallery. Throughout the show there'd been a "sold" sticker on the painting she was offering to me here in my apartment. Now I realized that the sticker had only been there so that she could show the painting and then give it to me after.

Because I'd loved it so much. The two little gnomish guys in one corner, playing fiddle and bodhran, using old tin cans for seats. And the flower fairies dancing to their music—like Cicely M. Barker's, but still very much Jilly's own, wearing the accoutrements of their naming flower, only punky, kind of raggedy versions of how Barker painted them.

But I could hardly look at the painting.

I'd forgotten all about Joe, I was so relieved to see Jilly again.

Or at least I was until I realized that this wasn't real. This was a memory. I remembered it so clearly. In those days I never locked my door, and she'd come right in without bothering to knock to find me sitting at the kitchen table with my fiddle on my lap as I was transcribing a new tune.

She'd grinned at me and said, "So what do you think, Geordie, me lad? Can you find a place to hang this old thing?"

Except this time she didn't. This time she laid the painting on the table and stood there looking at me with the saddest expression.

"Oh, Geordie," she said. "I've done a terrible thing."

I couldn't seem to find my voice.

This wasn't how it had happened. I've never forgotten that night. We were all so poor in those days—not that we ever got much richer, but at least we weren't scrabbling from hand-to-mouth as we had been back then. The money she could have gotten for that painting would have paid her rent and art supplies for a month, but she'd insisted I accept it and wouldn't take no for an answer.

"But I had to see you again," she said. "If just one last time."

"Juh . . ." I had to clear my throat. "Jilly, what's going on here?" I finally managed. I laid my fiddle on the table and got up from the chair. "What are you doing in my head?"

"I'm not in your head," she said. "You're in mine."

And when she said those words, that old apartment of mine faded from around us, and we were standing in some empty bedroom with a roof that made a sharp forty-five degree turn halfway across so that the wall on the window side was only half the height of the wall on the other. There were no furnishings except for a bed frame holding a ratty old mattress. The floor was some kind of hardwood, scratched and scuffed, and paint was peeling from the plaster walls. A single unlit bulb hung from the ceiling with a pull chain dangling below it.

"Your . . . I don't understand . . ."

My voice trailed off as I turned back to her because she was different now, as well. A child stood in front of me, recognizably Jilly, but a Jilly I'd never known. She was ten or eleven, even smaller and thinner than she normally was.

The child gave me a sad shake of her head.

"I know," she said. It was Jilly's voice, but a little higher pitched. "It's all preposterous and stupid and confusing, but somehow I've managed to pull my physical self inside my own head and . . . you know how you used to say—when I was carrying on about some mad thing or another—that I must have this happy attic of a brain, just brim full of interesting things?"

I gave a slow nod.

"Well, it turns out it's not like that at all. It turns out it's this weird little world where everybody hates me, or just wants to hurt me, and there's nothing I can do about it."

"Jilly, you—"

"Oh, I know. I sound pathetic, don't I? But you don't know, Geordie. I always thought that with pluck and perseverance, we could all make it through our dark woods to the other side and safety. But that was before I realized that my dark woods are right here inside me. I can't get away from this, because it's a part of me and it won't ever let me go."

"Everybody carries their past inside them."

"Yeah, but not literally. It's not memories we're talking about here. This—" She waved a hand to take in the room. "This is all real."

"No, it's not like that," I said, remembering what Timony had told me. "It's only like that if you believe it to be true."

"Oh, how I wish that were true. But I know better. I . . ."

She broke off and turned to the window. It took me a moment to hear the voices that had distracted her. Outside I saw unkempt fields, choked with high weeds and brush. Beyond them was a forest—mostly dark cedar, maple and pine. It all looked vaguely familiar—as though I'd seen it before, just not from this particular perspective. In the closest field, I could see a man approaching along a path that wound through the weeds. He had a loose, lanky stride and held the hand of a little girl who trotted to keep up with him. Behind them another little girl followed, redhaired and trailing a half field back. They were all too far away for me to make out any real details.

I turned back to look at Jilly. Her face was scrunched up, eyes closed, brow furrowed.

"Jilly, what are—"

"Shhh," she told me. "I'm trying to concentrate on sending you back."

"I don't want to go back. I've been looking for you ever since you disappeared. I'm here to help you."

Her eyes opened and her gaze met mine. Her eyes held an unfamiliar sadness.

"There's no one in the world I'd rather see than you," she told me. "But that's just me being selfish. Every moment you're here is more dangerous than the last. You *have* to go back."

"Not without you."

"This is no time to be brave, Geordie, me lad. It's a time for running away and hiding."

"Then run away with me."

She shook her head. "I can't. Everything that's horrible and dangerous comes from inside of me. How can you run away from yourself?"

I'd never seen this Jilly before. I don't mean the child she now was, but the defeatist attitude she wore like a huge weight on her shoulders. The Jilly I knew had no patience for resignation or any sort of unhappy acceptance to whatever obstacles the world could throw at a person. And she'd had some serious problems, both as a child and an adult, from her brother's mistreatment of her to the accident that had left her sitting in a wheelchair most of a day.

But regardless of their severity, she'd always met her difficulties head-on, often with a cheerful smile that was surprisingly genuine.

"Ms. The-Glass-Is-Half-Full," she'd say. "That's me."

But now she stood in front of me, lost and vulnerable with a hopeless look in her eyes.

I didn't know what to do, so I did what you always do in a situation like this. I put my arms around her and pulled her in close, letting her know that she was loved and creating at least the illusion that she was protected. It's not that I wouldn't give up my life for her. It's just that I don't know that it would even help.

It was weird. I could see that I held a child, but she felt like the grown-up Jilly I knew. It was as though whatever enchantment made her appear young was only working on my eyes.

I'd forgotten how perfectly she fit in my arms. I'd been away to L.A. and then when I got back she was always in a wheelchair, which just didn't feel the same as holding her at this moment did. It was like old times, like the hugs she always had for me when we met somewhere.

I was facing the window and could see the two little girls in the overgrown yard below, one with hair so bright it had to be dyed. The man who'd been accompanying them was nowhere to be seen. I started to look away when I realized two things:

The second little girl with the bright red hair looked a lot like a young Lizzie.

And she had no mouth. There was only smooth skin between her nose and chin.

"Jilly," I said into the hair of the child I was holding. "Is Lizzie here with you?"

She pushed away from me to look out the window. Her hands went up to her own mouth as she stared down.

"Oh, god, oh god, oh god . . ."

She turned to me, her face a mask of anguish.

"I did that to her," she said. "If it wasn't for this sick little world I've made, nothing would ever have happened to her."

I tried to hold her again, but she pushed away from me.

"You have to go before something horrible happens to you, too," she said. "You can't help me. Nobody can help me."

"You can say that again, sugar."

We turned at the sound of the new voice. The man who'd been with the girls outside now stood in the doorway. He leaned casually against the door jamb, grinning at us.

This had to be Del.

My hands clenched into fists at my sides. This was my chance to finally do what I'd been wanting to ever since Jilly'd told me about the horror show he'd made of her childhood.

"Now isn't this sweet," Del said. "I was thinking you might need a little further convincing so I let you bring your best shot here to give you a hand at escaping. But, little sister, that's never going to happen." His gaze went to me. "So, what do you say, boy? You going to show me what you've got?"

And then he laughed at me.

I knew what he was thinking. He had weight on me and reach, and he could probably fight better, too. But I had the Riddell temper on my side. Christy and I had both learned to keep it in check, determined we weren't going to be like our father. Our brother Paddy hadn't been so lucky. He'd ended up in prison where he'd finally hung himself. But before that, he'd been a crazy man. He'd had Dad's temper and his own brawn, and he liked to fight pretty much more than anything. It didn't matter the odds, because once his temper kicked in, he didn't feel the pain anymore. He just kept on coming until either his opponents went down or he did.

That was what was going to happen here. It didn't matter what Del threw at me or how much it hurt, I was going to keep on coming until he couldn't touch Jilly again.

But I didn't get to lay a punch.

He did a little wave of his hand before I could reach him and something happened to my body. I felt a mild shock—like from static—and a high-pitched ringing in my ears. I could taste something odd in my mouth, like mulch, or dirt, and felt a spreading warmth go through me. I looked down and saw myself collapse onto the floor, changing and shrinking until all that was left was a small mess of leaves and mud and dead twigs, lying on the floor in the shape of a human being. Somewhere I could hear a child screaming.

At first, I was only dimly aware that the terrible cries came from Jilly. All I could do was stand and stare at what had become of my body. Then the incongruity struck me: how could I be standing and also looking at my body? The answer wasn't hard to figure out, but I shied away from accepting it. Instead, I turned my attention to Jilly, whose gaze was locked on the mess upon the floor that had once been my flesh and blood.

Tears streamed down her cheeks. The wailing had subsided into a deep sobbing that shook her shoulders.

"It's okay," I told her. "Really. I'm still here. I don't know what the hell that thing on the floor is, but it's not me."

She made no sign that she'd heard me. I stepped closer and tried to touch her. That's when the awful truth I'd been trying to hide from myself couldn't be pushed away anymore. My hand went through her. No. What I *felt* was my hand going through her. But there was nothing to see. I *had* no body. I was just some kind of disembodied spirit.

Del had killed me. Turned my body into a mess of forest debris on the floor, and all that was left of me was a ghost.

I turned to him. He still leaned against the door jamb, still grinning.

"Now do you see what happens when you don't listen to me?" he said to Jilly.

Her tear-strained face slowly lifted to face him.

"Guh—go ahead and k-kill me, too," she told him.

Her brother just laughed. "What? And spoil all the fun? We've got forever to get reacquainted, little sister. We can't come up on the finish when the good times are just starting."

She charged at him, but all he did was wave his hand again and her trajectory took her crashing into a wall. She collapsed on the floor.

I went after him too, except in my case, I went right through him and found myself out in a hallway that was as run-down and derelict as the room I'd just quit.

"You just think on that awhile," Del told Jilly in the room behind me. "I'm going to play with my new friend outside and when I come back, I want to see a whole change in your attitude. You got me?"

I drifted back into the room to see Jilly still lying where she'd fallen.

Del banged the heel of his boot on the floor. "I said, you *got* me?"

She lifted her head. Her cheeks were still wet with tears, but her eyes were dull as she gave a slow nod.

"That's my girl," Del said.

He went back into the hall, banging the door closed behind him.

I went to Jilly and crouched down beside her.

"Jilly," I said, trying to touch her, wanting to hold her.

But I couldn't give her any comfort. She didn't even know I was there. Her gaze went to the small man-shaped mess of mud and debris on the floor, and she began to cry again.

Timony Twotot

When Geordie vanished, Timony blinked in surprise, then quickly tried to follow the fiddler. But instead of crossing over as Geordie had, the doonie ran up against the impenetrable shell that enclosed the small pocket world he'd been so abruptly cast out of earlier. It would no more allow him entry now than it had before.

"Well, that's that then," he said to no one in particular.

He had no idea what had just happened. For all his efforts, Geordie's disappearance had nothing to do with anything he'd done. He'd needed the clear picture in Geordie's mind and that had never come. But nevertheless, he'd certainly felt that closed world of Jilly's open long enough to pull the fiddler in, slamming closed before he had the chance to follow himself. They hadn't found this dog crow named Joe, but now it was no longer necessary. Geordie was with Jilly and . . . and . . .

And nothing, he realized.

So long as Jilly believed in her brother's authority, he would remain all-powerful. And Geordie wouldn't be allowed the time to convince her otherwise. As soon as he appeared, the brother would cast him out of the world once more. Or worse.

Timony sighed.

What were the times coming to? Bogans and a green-bree killing a doonie who'd never done them a lick of harm. Buffalo gathering to lay ruin to the world of both fairy and men. A literal world held inside the mind of a young woman.

None of it was right. And there was nothing he could do about any of it. He couldn't even help Lizzie, and that was a responsibility he was unable to shirk. She might not accept the truth of it, but that still didn't change the fact that he owed her his life and had no choice in the matter. He had to help her. He couldn't—no, *wouldn't*—give up until he had proof that she was dead, however long that would take. And then he would see that retribution was paid, and paid in full.

But he wasn't ready to give up hope just yet. If Geordie had gotten through, then the opportunity might arise for him to cross over as well.

He would wait.

Doonies were patient. He could wait forever.

He would keep his senses open to any change in that strange hidden world, but he wouldn't remain idle.

He sat on the sand and shaped the outline of a dagger with his finger.

"What do you think?" he asked the sand. "Would you care for a change in life? I need weapons, and my, but would you would make a fine blade. Sharp and sleek. So dangerous."

He moved his hands upon the sand as he spoke, cajoling the sand to take the new shape. When the first blade was done, he began anew, making another.

Doonies had a knack for knife-throwing—something the bogans and their green-bree would have discovered if they hadn't caught him unawares. If the opportunity arose, Jilly's brother would not be so fortunate. This time Timony would be prepared and ready. Give him half a chance and the brother would find his chest decorated with the knives this beach was so kindly providing for him.

"Thank you," he murmured to the sand as he set a second blade aside and began working on another. "This will be an adventure for all of us."

Honey

Under clear blue skies, with a hot sun no longer quite directly over-head, the two dogs trotted through the desert scrub. One was a honey-blonde pit bull, the other a narrow-hipped short chestnut-haired mongrel like you might find on any rez. They were bound for a nearby hilltop of red stone that reached up tall from the desert floor. It had a flat top with Ponderosa pines climbing up its red rock sides.

It's one of those places where medicine swirls in never-ending circles, the honey blonde explained to her companion as they wove a trail through the cacti and mesquite toward the small mesa.

A vortex, the greyish red dog told her. *That's what they call it.*

Hmm.

What?

I thought the name would be more resonant, Honey replied. *Vortex. It sounds like a puppy gagging.*

The dog that was Joe gave a sharp bark of laughter.

Why are you laughing?

I'm sorry, he said. *It's just that you're so new to language, but already you have such a strong opinion about it.*

Is that a bad thing? Voicing strong opinions?

I don't know that it's bad or good, but it's very human.

They'd left the pups behind in the arroyo to be watched over by one of

Honey's sons before setting off for the mesa. Honey tried not to worry about them as she led the way up through the red rocks to the top. There was nothing nearby to hurt them, but she carried a dread inside her from having reached out to Joe's friend Jilly earlier. She hadn't been able to make a strong enough connection, which was why they were on their way to the vortex, but it had been enough for her to want to be with her family at this moment, not chasing across the desert and into the worlds beyond.

She loved her boys, and had confidence in them, but at a time like this, she would only be able to relax if she was keeping the young ones safe herself.

To distract herself, she thought about what Joe had just said.

Being human, she said. *I don't know if that's a good or a bad thing, either.*

Welcome to the confusing world of the five-fingered beings who walk on two legs.

Now it was Honey's turn to bark a laugh, and she could feel some of her tension draining away.

I think "human" is an easier way to say it, she said.

Joe grinned at her. *If not as accurate.*

But at least it's shorter.

But is shorter always best? That makes me think that—

Here we are, Honey broke in as they crested the mesa and came out onto its flat top.

There was a jumble of stones on the north side, watched over by a tall saguaro cactus and tangles of prickly pear. The rocks had petroglyphs scratched onto their surfaces—relics of long-gone hands carving old symbols, speaking ancient prayers to the spirits as they worked the stone. Honey gave the markings only a passing glance, her attention taken, as always, by the invisible churn of medicine that came spiraling up out of the stones and dirt under their paws.

Joe came to a stop in the middle of it, and she could see all the hairs on his back stand upright and shiver in the invisible stream.

It is strong here, he said, turning to her.

Shhh. I still need to concentrate.

The dread had returned.

It had nothing to do with the hilltop on which they stood.

She understood what the word sacred meant when she was in a place such as this, a place where the earth itself gave up medicine prayers to the sky. What she couldn't understand was it being used when medicine was locked up between four walls and a roof, with no way to reach the sky except through intermediaries. But here, on this mesa, she could never feel anything but awe when she experienced the spiritual force of holy groves and hilltops, of secret canyons and sea-bound grottos.

No, the dread came from what she would find when she reached out to Jilly. But she couldn't turn back now. She'd told Joe she would try, and that was the same as giving her word.

So she reached out, hard and far, the earth medicine filling her spirit and allowing her the strength to push, and push, and push again, further than she ever could have without its help. But it was still no use.

It was hard to explain it to Joe.

It's like a nut, she told him, *where the seed is also the shell which is also the seed. Jilly is the seed inside that world, but that seed is also the barrier that keeps us out.*

Joe had taken human shape again and sat cross-legged in the dirt, leaning back against the petroglyph stones. There was a furious look of concentration in his gaze as she tried to make him understand.

"Tell me that again," he said.

He nodded when she repeated it.

"So it's like she's trapped inside herself," he said.

I hadn't considered that. Honey had to think about it. *Is that even possible?*

"This is the otherworld. Anything's possible, if someone can think of it. Can you show me what you're seeing?"

I don't know how.

You know how when you "talk" to me, you're really just sending out short bursts of thought?

Honey nodded.

It's not a lot different from that, Joe explained, *only this time, don't break the connection. Reach out to me and hold that thread of thought open between us. Then, when you look again, I'll be able to see what you're seeing.*

Does this work with anyone? Honey asked.

Sure. So long as you can find a mind to connect to. Why do you ask?

It would be a great way to communicate more clearly with the rest of my pack.

Joe grinned. *Not to mention keeping rambunctious puppies in line.*

That, too.

Joe got serious then. *Show me what you're seeing.*

His instructions had seemed so simple, and they proved to be just that when she put them into practice. She reached out to him with a thought and held the connection. But as soon as his mind caught hold of her thought and began to follow it back into her own mind, she shied away.

Shivering, she broke contact.

I'm sorry, Joe said. *I grabbed on too hard.*

No, it's me, she told him. *I wasn't expecting it to feel so . . . intimate.*

You don't need to worry. I won't actually have access to your thoughts and memories.

She nodded. *I understand.*

What she couldn't explain was how it was hard for her to open up to anyone, even someone she trusted as much as she did Joe. Companionship, helping each other as they had and what she was doing now, searching for his friend . . . that was one thing. But this . . . this felt too much like baring her very soul, and she wasn't sure he'd like what he saw if he got a glimpse of it. She wasn't nearly as brave as the face she put on to show the world, and lying deep inside her, as deep as Jilly's hidden world must lie in her, was a raw red place of anger and hate that she could only keep in check, not erase.

Who could like her once they'd caught a glimpse of that? Whenever she touched it, she didn't even like herself.

All this does is let me ride your senses to see what you're seeing, Joe added.

I believe you. I just didn't expect it to feel the way it did.

We don't have to do this.

Yes, we do, she told him. *If we're going to help your friend.*

I just don't want to put you in a position where—

I'm fine. I know what to expect now.

Using the medicine gift that rose up from the vortex to reinforce her courage, she sent another thought to him, a strong cord, easy for him to follow back to her mind. She couldn't help but shiver again as he began the journey along her thoughts, but this time she held the contact. Still fueled by the vortex's medicine, she showed him the strange world that both held Jilly and was inside her.

It was all the same as before. They could view the world—or rather the space that the world occupied—but entry was impossible.

If anything, Joe said, his voice a quiet murmur in her mind, *this is even stranger than I imagined. I can sense the space, but at the same time it's like it's not there.*

But it is there, isn't it?

It was such an odd phenomenon that Honey wasn't entirely convinced of what her senses were telling her. How could something both exist and not exist at the same time?

Well, something's *there,* Joe told her. *I just can't figure out what—*

He broke off as they both became aware of a sudden change. They were no longer alone in the strange interior landscape in which they drifted. There was another presence, here with them on the outside of that world of Jilly's. While Honey couldn't tell who or what it was, through her connection to Joe, she knew he could almost recognize it.

But there was no time for discussion. Whatever the presence was, it had found an entry into Jilly's world. Honey darted after it, moving so quickly that she lost her connection to Joe. She reached back for him, but she was moving too quickly. A moment later, she was inside the hidden world and Joe was left behind.

The presence she'd been following was gone, and she went sprawling to the ground. She smelled dirt and a forest around her, but the forest was as still as a mere photograph. She scrabbled to her feet, reaching about herself with her senses.

The new world surrounded her with no possibility of escape back to the mesa from which she'd so recently come. There was no escape to *anywhere* else. There was only this world of Jilly's, and at its heart, a dark malevolent presence that made her bare her teeth.

And in the heart of that heart of darkness, she found Jilly.

She lifted her head and searched the woods in which she'd found herself.

There, she thought, facing the direction where the feeling was strongest. That was where the darkness and Jilly were.

And that was where she had to go.

Joseph Crazy Dog

Joe tried to keep up with Honey. He moved as fast as thought and should have been able to enter along with her, but he banged up hard against an invisible wall.

It didn't make sense. He could see the crack that Honey had gone slipping through—was right there with her—but the damned thing slammed shut before he could get through. His impact with the barrier broke his contact with her and was enough to knock him out. Unconscious, he went spiraling through the dark reaches of his own mind, his body dumped back onto the top of the mesa.

When he came to, his face pressed against the stones and dirt, he wasn't sure how long he'd been out. He sat up, weak and disoriented, his head spinning. He spat out a mouthful of fine grit and brushed the dust from around his eyes. It took him a few moments to catch his bearings, and then it was only because of the medicine twisting up out of the ground he was lying on. Without it, he didn't know how long he would have been out, and he certainly wouldn't be recovering as fast as he was.

He stood up finally, waited a moment for his sense of balance to settle, then looked around himself.

He was definitely here by himself.

This wasn't how it was supposed to go down. He'd only wanted Honey to point him in the right direction, not take his place in whatever was to come. But he was here and she was gone, following that elusive, half-familiar presence that had cracked the protection surrounding the world Jilly was trapped in.

That presence . . .

His head snapped up when it came to him who it had been.

Geordie.

No wonder it had seemed familiar. But how was that even possible? Of all Jilly's strange and curious circle of friends, the Riddell brothers were the most human. They had no animal blood. No trace of the old ghosts of fairy haunting their genes. The two of them were forever surrounded by the inhabitants of the otherworld and the world between, but they themselves had no medicine. No magic.

He had to be mistaken. It had to have been someone else.

He sent out his thoughts, searching, searching, but there was no trace of the fiddler left anywhere. Like Jilly, he was gone from all the worlds except—he assumed—for the one that Honey had discovered, the one she said was inside Jilly's own head. And there was no way he could look into it.

He didn't need to. Contrary to what he knew about Geordie, that had definitely been the fiddler breaking through into that world, with Honey hard on his heels. The big question was *how* had he done it?

The last time Joe had seen the fiddler, he'd been in Walker's company, unable to even travel from one world to another on his own. So either he'd suddenly acquired abilities he'd never shown before, or Walker had—

Walker.

Again Joe sent out a questing thought. Unlike Jilly, and now Geordie, the cerva was easy to find. Joe almost wished he hadn't.

"Jilly . . . Honey," he said to the silent air on top of the mesa. "I'm sorry, but I've got to deal with this right now."

Then he stepped away from Honey's desert world and the mesa was empty once more.

Cassandra Washington

Cassie was tired of the hotel room with its folk art paintings on the wall, the gingerbread moldings, the hooked rug on the floor, the quaint bedspreads, the decorative basin and pitcher on the dresser. It was all so *Country Living*, which was fine for those who liked it, she supposed, but too much of it put her teeth on edge. She didn't care much for the view out the window either, all that forest running up into the Kickaha Mountains. Very picturesque, but she was a city girl. Too long away from the city's urban sprawl and its familiar background noise of traffic and sirens, and she always started to get antsy.

But what really wore on her was having to listen to the remaining members of the Knotted Cord as they worked through the thorny issues of having to see the world through this new view that had been forced upon them by Lizzie and Jilly's disappearance. It wasn't that she disliked the three musicians—they seemed nice enough and were actually taking all of this rather well. And she certainly couldn't blame them for their endless conversations circling around what had happened, what might happen, how could any of this be real? It would have been stranger if they *hadn't* been so caught up with all these questions.

But it wore on her. It really did.

And she was worried about Joe—more worried than she'd care to admit. She should be with him, not cooling her heels babysitting these musicians. She knew that wasn't the real reason for her staying behind. It just felt that way. It made complete sense to have her here in case Lizzie or Jilly returned, or if some fairy or cousin showed up making ransom demands, but she didn't think either was going to happen.

It wasn't that she believed their friends were dead—she shuddered to think of what Joe would do if that was the case. But she doubted they'd be coming back on their own. If they could have, they would have by now. Especially Jilly, because she'd know how much they'd all be worrying about her.

After awhile, the musicians finally fell silent. Siobhan sat by the window, staring through the pane, her eyes bright with unshed tears. The two men were on the other bed—Con leaning against the headboard, Andy sitting on the end, leaning on his elbows, his gaze on the floor.

Cassie considered pulling out her cards and taking another run at what they might tell her. She'd already done it once since Geordie and Joe had gone off with Walker, but the images on them hadn't changed and there was no reason to think they would have by now. That was just how the cards worked. When you asked a certain question of them, they'd only give the one answer, it didn't matter how many times you asked. She knew that. But that hadn't stopped her from trying anyway.

"This *so* sucks," Siobhan said out of the blue. "Did I say that out loud?" she added when everybody turned to look at where she was sitting by the window.

"Loud and clear," Con told her.

Siobhan sighed. She wiped her eyes on her sleeve.

"Well, it does," she said. "I feel so useless. And don't anybody make any jokes about how's this different from any other time."

"I wasn't going to say a word," Andy said.

Con gave her a half smile. "Although you're very good at the merch table."

"Oh, shut up." Siobhan turned to Cassie and asked, "Is there any news?"

Cassie blinked in surprise. "I've been here with you the whole time. How could I have any news that you don't?"

"I don't know. I thought maybe there was some magic way of talking in your head or something."

"There is. But no one's contacted me so far."

"Crap."

"I hate this waiting, too," Cassie told her.

"How about those cards of yours?" Con asked. "Can't you check with them again?"

Andy nodded. "So that we can at least know that everybody's still okay."

"The cards don't work that way," Cassie said without bothering to go into why.

"Figures. That'd be too easy."

"I don't know that it's a matter of easy or hard. It's more the innate capricious nature of any and everything that comes out of the dreamlands. The otherworld," she added at their questioning looks. "The place has a hundred names. I often think of them as dreamlands because it's where we go in our dreams."

"We go to a real place?" Con asked.

Cassie nodded. "Except, usually, *we're* the spirits there. And most of us don't remember the trip, or at least not clearly."

"I have some really weird dreams," Siobhan said.

"There are some really weird parts to the dreamlands. Joe says that anything we can imagine exists there, and more. Lots more."

"So," Con said, "anything can happen there—just like it does in a dream? There's no structure or—I don't know—natural laws?"

"There are both, but they're not readily apparent. Which is why it's so dangerous for humans like us to go there."

The three of them fell silent for a long moment, but Cassie could see where their thoughts were taking them. Andy was the one who started to voice the question.

"So then Joe," he began.

Cassie nodded. "Isn't like you or me."

"Who isn't?" a familiar voice asked from the middle of the room.

"Jesus!" Andy cried.

He fell back onto the bed and banged into Con's legs as he tried to get away from the man who'd suddenly appeared in the room with them. Siobhan and Con just stared wide-eyed, but Cassie jumped up from where she was sitting and flung herself into Joe's waiting arms.

"You aren't," she said into his shoulder and hugged him tightly. "You'll *never* be like anybody else."

"I'm going to take that as a compliment."

She gave him a harder squeeze. "I'm glad you're back. I was getting so worried."

He pulled back, the trace of a smile touching the corner of his mouth.

"And bored," he said.

"That, too."

It was only then that she realized Joe was on his own.

"Where's Jilly?" she asked, stepping back to look around the room. "And the others?"

"It's complicated," he told her. "And right now we've got bigger problems."

"But—"

"See for yourself."

He opened up a view of the between and the rhythmic sound of drums and stamping hooves filled the room, loud as thunder. Cassie and the musicians could see the massing buffalo, facing a glow that Cassie knew was how the city manifested in this place between the two worlds. Standing on the plain, between the buffalo and the city, was a lone figure, the many tines of his antlers lifting high from his brow.

"Is that . . . ?"

"Walker? You bet."

Joe did something to the opening he'd made into the between so that the roar of sound was gone, but they could still see.

"He's there," Joe went on, "standing all on his own—the only thing between the Newford courts of fairy and way more pissed off buffalo soldiers than anybody's got the time to count."

"What does it mean?"

"War."

Cassie shivered. "Oh, god. Why are they *doing* this?"

Joe shrugged. "What have they got to lose?"

Cassie turned to look at him.

"Everything," she said, her voice soft.

Joe gave her a slow nod.

"I suppose you're right," he said. "Revenge starts out tasting sweet, but dealing in hurt is always going to leave a mark on your spirit. Still, I've got to tell you—if someone killed you to make clothes out of your skin, or just to cut a steak from your thigh, I wouldn't be taking the time to worry about the state of my soul. I'd just be taking them down—any and everybody who had a hand in it."

"And then?" Cassie asked. "It wouldn't bring me back."

"Then I'd deal with the fallout. But the thing is, at a moment like that, you don't have time to work out the details of what's wrong and what's right, or how what you're going to do makes you no better than them. You just want your payback."

"Except they've had a lot of time to think about it."

Joe nodded. "And maybe all that time just makes it worse. Makes it build up to a point where you just don't care about anything anymore except bringing the hurt to those who hurt you."

"So, what are we going to do?"

"Try to stop it."

Cassie shook her head. "You know that's suicide."

"Can't not try."

"You're not going without me."

"Didn't expect I would. Something like this, everyone has to make their own stand and we have to respect their decision, even if we don't like seeing them put themselves in the line of fire. But I've got to tell you, I was hoping you'd stay someplace safe for the duration."

"Then why did you come to me first?" Cassie asked.

Joe smiled. "I had to see my girl. Isn't that what knights do when they go into battle?"

This was so Joe. Keeping it light when everything was so dark and pressing down on them.

"What about Lizzie?" Siobhan asked. "And Jilly?"

Con nodded. "And what happened to Geordie?"

Joe turned to the musicians. "They're all some place I can't get into. If this hadn't come up, I'd still be there, banging on the figurative walls and trying to get in—you can put money on that. But this . . ." He waved a hand to the window he'd made into the between. "This can't wait."

"You made it sound like you won't survive," Andy said.

"The odds aren't good," Joe told him, "but I've got enough Cody and crow in me that I've got a chance. And see, the thing is, we don't deal with this, there won't necessarily be a world for Jilly and the others to come back to."

"But they're safe enough for now, right?" Siobhan asked.

Joe couldn't hide the unhappy look that came into his eyes.

"I won't kid you," he said. "It looks bad. But a friend of mine got in there before the place closed down on us, and if anyone can help them, it's her. Honey got in," he added, turning to Cassie.

"So, what do we do?" Con asked.

"There's nothing you can do," Joe said, "except sit tight, and if you've got a god, send up a prayer for all of us."

Joe gave the musicians what he probably thought was a reassuring smile, but with the fierce light in his eyes, it was more like a wolf baring its teeth as it confronted an enemy. Except, Cassie thought, this enemy was made up of cousins. Cerva, but still Joe's kin. He wasn't letting on, but she knew that was the hardest part of this for him—maybe even harder than leaving Honey to look out for Jilly.

Joe could be as fierce as any predator, though in situations such as this, he was usually the mediator. But with the way those buffalo were revving themselves up, she doubted they'd even be capable of listening to reason anymore.

He turned and took her hand. But before they could step away into the between, Siobhan moved forward.

"I'm coming with you," she said.

Joe and Cassie paused to look at her. Cassie expected Joe to argue with the fiddler, if he didn't just shut her flat down. Instead, he nodded in agreement.

"This is going to spill over into your world," he said, "so you've got a stake in it, too. But I've got to tell you, I don't see us making much more than a statement here, and then we lose our lives."

"But you're going."

He nodded. "My problem is I'm an eternal optimist. I always figure something'll come up at the last minute."

She smiled back at him. "Me, too."

"Then let's go and give it our best shot."

In the end, they all went, leaving behind an empty hotel room.

Christiana Tree

"Remember those kids who asked if they could use one of my stories for a film school project?"

Saskia and I were sitting on cushions on the floor of Christy's study, leafing through an old photo album and smiling at all the pictures of the Riddell boys when they were young. At the sound of Christy's voice we lifted our heads and looked over to where he was sitting at his desk, reading e-mail on his laptop. It was such a nice quiet day: the sun shining outside, the three of us in here, just hanging out like the family we'd come to be. I cherished moments like this.

So, why did I feel this sense of foreboding, creeping around under my skin, burrowing deep in my bones?

Saskia nodded in response to Christy's question.

"I remember," she said. "You told them it was okay."

"I know. For a school project. Except now—" He pointed a finger at the screen of his monitor. "—Bernie tells me that they've made a DVD out of it and are selling it on the Internet. He found a link for it on eBay while he was doing a search on my name."

"Your friends need to find better things to do with their time," I said.

"Ha ha."

"Or maybe it was really *you* doing the search."

"This is serious, Christiana."

Beside me, Saskia was frowning.

"They can't just do that, can they?" she asked.

"Apparently, they think they can."

"But—"

She broke off and I could feel her stiffen beside me, but there wasn't much I could do because it hit me at the same time. I don't know what it felt like for her, but for me it came like a sharp pain riding up through the back of my head, leaving in its wake a spreading wave of irrevocable loss. It was as though a little black hole had opened up inside me, sucking I don't know what into itself. But whatever it was, it felt like it was gone forever.

Saskia was the first to put a name to what I'd lost. Her anguished gaze met mine.

"It's Geordie," she said.

As soon as she said his name, I knew she was right. That was what I'd felt—Geordie pulled out of the world. This world, the otherworld, *any* world. The little subconscious fishhook of connection I kept attached to him was gone. The line holding it tethered to him, severed.

Christy got up from behind his desk and hurried over to us, worry plain in his eyes.

"Are you okay?" he asked. "What happened to you two?"

Saskia looked up at him.

"It's Geordie," she repeated. "He's just . . . gone."

"Gone? What do you mean 'gone'? Gone where?"

"I don't know. It's like he doesn't exist anymore."

Christy dropped to the floor in front of us.

"I don't understand," he said. "What's happened to him? *Where* has he gone?"

Saskia wore a pained expression. "There's no way I can tell."

"But I can guess," I said, getting to my feet. "This stinks of magic, and magic means fairy is involved. I *told* her to leave him alone."

"Told who?" Christy asked.

"Mother Crone."

"But she's—"

"His girlfriend? Don't kid yourself, Christy. Fairy don't have relationships the way we do. It's all about how useful we are at a given point in time."

"But she wouldn't have . . ."

"Hurt him?" I said. "That's what I'm going to find out."

"Christiana!" Saskia called before I could step away into the between.

"What?" I asked. "Don't beat the crap out of her?"

"No," Saskia said. "Don't lose your temper."

I didn't realize how tightly I was clenching my fists until she said that. I forced my hands open and took a steadying breath.

"Okay," I said. "I'll let her tell her side of the story."

"Thank you."

"And if she's to blame, *then* I'll beat the crap out of her."

"You'll have to wait in line," Saskia told me.

We held each other's gaze for a long moment. I saw everything that was boiling away inside me reflected in her eyes: my worry, my love for Geordie, the fierce need to protect those I loved. Then I nodded my head to her and stepped away.

Galfreya

Tatiana's court lay one step sideways from the Harbour Ritz Hotel in the world of men, but this afternoon the court's council was in one of the small conference halls of the hotel itself, its members gathered around a large round table set in the middle of the room. Guards stood on either side of the door to keep outsiders at bay. Inside, the small group sat around a table uncluttered by paperwork or any of the paraphernalia one would find in the business meetings of men. The only commonality was a plastic bottle of spring water in front of each individual.

We're like Arthur's knights, Galfreya thought, except while everyone gathered here could certainly fight, they were none of them warriors. And perhaps, it could also be said, they weren't nearly so selfless and clear of heart as those knights of old. Or at least as the knights were remembered and revered in legend. Humans always fared better in Story than they did in real life. Story allowed them time to polish their better traits and cover up their baser ones with a glitter of words and edited takes on truth.

Fairy were probably more particular than humans when it came to their reputations, but they were only concerned with how they were perceived in the ever-present now, in the footprints they left on the world itself, rather than how they were remembered in Story.

Fairy were rarely interested in participating in Story. When it caught you up in its pages, especially here in the real world, it was a messy and dangerous business. And there were no guarantees for a happy ending. It was too much like History, dusty volumes stuffed away in some dark corner of a library, and fairy had no patience for anything so cut and dried.

No, Galfreya decided, their only resemblance to the Pendragon's men was how they were gathered at the sacred circle of a wooden table to consider the fate of their world. In their company, they had no knights errant, no ambitious purveyors of their place in Story. All they wanted was for this crisis to be over and done with so that they could return to their normal lives.

Except that wasn't going to happen. Not unless they came up with a miracle.

Looking around the table, Galfreya didn't see the makings for such in the grim faces of her fellow councilors.

When she'd first come into the room, she'd been surprised at the small size of the council Tatiana had called. Were they really so few now? she'd thought. But then she realized exclusions had had to be made.

They couldn't have most of the gruagaghs present today because too many of the court's wizards had some long-standing personal quarrel with one or another of the local spirits. For that reason, only Muircan and Kimiad were at the table, neither of whom spent enough time outside the court to have become embroiled in animosities.

The bogans and their various trollkin were absent for the very good reason that it was individuals from among their ranks who were the source of the problem now at hand. Arguing rights or wrongs, or attempting to assign blame, was an impossible task when it came to the Unseelie fairy. Even the most evenhanded of bogans immediately became impossible in what anyone else would consider a reasonable discussion.

Though they *could* fight, Galfreya thought. Perhaps Tatiana had been hasty in excluding them. It was far too late now for the pointing of fingers. First they needed to survive, and whatever else they might be, the Unseelie fairy were survivors.

But the queen, it appeared, had another course of action in mind.

"As queen of these courts," Tatiana said, "this is my responsibility. I never condoned the hunting of the local spirits, but I should have done more to keep the hunters in check."

"Your Majesty," Kimiad argued, "*no one* can keep bogans and their like in check."

Unlike her fellow gruagagh Muircan, whose garb wouldn't be out of place for a wizened little wizard man in some nursery tale, Kimiad was a tall, attractive woman, sensibly dressed—considering the circumstances—in jeans and a cotton shirt. A worn leather jacket hung from the back of her chair. If they needed to take to the field, she'd be ready, unlike Muircan in his robes and silly pointed hat.

"Regardless," Tatiana told her, "I must take full responsibility for what they have done."

Kimiad shook her head. "We're beyond simply taking responsibility. Those cerva want blood."

"Which is why I will deliver myself to them for judgment. If the moon is with us, perhaps that will be enough."

For a moment, no one could speak. Then Swanson, Captain of the Queen's Guard, stood up from his chair and banged a fist on the tabletop.

"This is madness," he cried. "I won't allow it."

"*You* won't allow it?" the queen said.

"Please, your Majesty. Reconsider this—if not for your own sake, then for that of your people. They will take your life, then still fall upon us. But we will have no leader, no rallying point for our people."

At two o'clock from where Galfreya sat at the table was another of the court's seers: Granny Cross, young, black-haired and even-tempered, her speaking name no more representative of her appearance than Galfreya's Mother Crone.

"I see no good coming from this," Granny Cross broke in before Tatiana could respond to her captain. "There is only darkness ahead." Her dark gaze went to Galfreya. "Can you pierce it, sister?"

Galfreya looked down into the small scrying bowl set in front of her on the table. She spoke a word and the water began to eddy, but before an image could form, she felt as though a knife had been plunged into the back of her head. She cried out, falling back into her chair, her hands going to her temples where the sudden flash of pain had lodged.

Tatiana was closest to her. Rising quickly, she put her arm around Galfreya's shoulders.

"What is it?" she asked. "What did you see?"

Galfreya grimaced and massaged her temples.

"It's not anything I saw," she said. "It was . . . it was Geordie."

"Geordie?"

"The human fiddler at my revels."

Tatiana nodded. "Oh, yes, him. Your lover."

"He's not my lover."

"But you've—"

"Yes, we've been intimate on many occasions, but his heart belongs to another. It belongs to a woman he thinks he can't have."

"I see," Tatiana said, although she obviously didn't.

"That woman is Jilly Coppercorn, one of the women Joe Crazy Dog is trying to find."

Tatiana returned to her seat and said nothing for a long moment.

"Tell me what just happened," she finally said.

Galfreya wasn't given the chance. A figure appeared on the conference table directly in front of her—a small red-haired woman, sitting on her haunches. Swanson rose so quickly his chair fell behind him. Two throwing knives appeared from under his jacket, one in each hand. By the door, the guards lifted their crossbows, aiming at the woman. It took Galfreya a moment to recognize her as Christiana.

Christy Riddell's shadow. Geordie's sister.

Christiana pointed a finger at the guards without ever taking her gaze from Galfreya.

"Don't even think you can use those on me," she said, her voice conversational and pleasant. She pointed with her other hand at Swanson. "Nor you—the big boy with his knives. The first person to try is going to find out just how hard it is to walk around with his weapons up his ass." Then she smiled at Galfreya. "See how calm and reasonable I'm being? Did I come in here kicking ass? No. But I warned you what would happen if you screwed around with Geordie, and unless you've got a damn good explanation for what just happened to him, you're going to find out that there's a lot more to a shadow than some bit of darkness you can roll up into a corner and forget about."

"Your Majesty?" one of the guards by the door asked Tatiana, looking for direction.

"Do you know this woman?" Tatiana said.

Galfreya nodded. "Unfortunately, yes."

"Then stand down," she told her guards.

Galfreya wasn't so certain that was the best idea. Not with that dark look in Christiana's eyes.

Christy's shadow turned a little and studied the queen from over her shoulder.

"Now I see where your people get their fashion sense," she said. "How old are you? A thousand? Two thousand? And you're dressing like a teenager?"

Tatiana regarded her coldly. "You do understand that I have but to say the word, and you'll be dead."

"Well, you could give it a try," Christiana said, as though she were Joe's sister, not Geordie's, "and we'll see how it works out for you."

"I will not have yet another—"

But Christina turned her back on the queen and focused her dark gaze on Galfreya.

"I'm still waiting for an explanation," she said. "I know something just took out Geordie and there was the stink of fairy in the air when it happened."

As soon as the words were spoken, Galfreya realized their truth. There *had* been the sense of a fairy present at the moment of Geordie's—she found it too hard to consider the word death—disappearance from the world. But whether it had been a Seelie elf, or some Unseelie bogan, she couldn't tell from her fleeting memory of the moment.

"Would someone please tell me what's going on here?" Tatiana demanded.

Christiana shook her head without looking in the queen's direction.

"Uh-uh," she said. "This is between me and your little skater seer."

"We're in the middle of a crisis here," Galfreya told her.

"You betcha. And if you don't start coming up with some answers—"

Before she could finish, Galfreya opened a view into the between, and the thunder of drums and hooves pounding on the dirt filled the air. Christiana stared at the gathering cerva clans, her face expressionless.

Galfreya was unable to resist a dig: "Didn't you even *see* them on your way here?"

"Didn't come that way," Christiana said after a moment. She turned to Tatiana and added, "What did you do to them?"

"What did *we* do?"

That damned shadow girl just lifted an eyebrow.

"I know the cousins," she said. "Sure, you'll get the odd hothead, determined to right all the old wrongs, and everybody agrees, but it never really comes to much of anything. Getting cousins to agree to something is just about as hard as getting fairy to dress their age. But this . . ." She pointed to the ever-growing herd of buffalo soldiers. "To get that many of them riled up, all at the same time, you had to really piss them off."

Galfreya let the view into the between close, but didn't respond. Around the table, the others remained silent as well, waiting for Tatiana to speak or not.

Christiana gave the queen a considering look before turning back to Galfreya.

"So, does this have anything to do with what happened to Geordie?" she asked.

"What makes you ask that?"

"Just answer the question."

Galfreya let her gaze go to the queen for guidance and Tatiana shrugged.

"We don't know for sure," Galfreya said. "Part of what's happening here is tied up in a problem we've had with a gang of bogans. So far, we know that they've been hunting cerva and kidnapped a pair of human women—one of them being Geordie's friend Jilly."

"And now they've got him."

"We don't know that. The first I realized something had happened to him was a few moments before you arrived."

"And now we must ask you to leave," Tatiana said. "We have business to conduct that concerns only us."

Christiana shook her head. "Hold on a minute here. You're still not telling me *what* happened to Geordie."

"He's *gone,*" Galfreya said. "And *that's* all we know. He's either . . . dead or disappeared into some world that we can't access."

Christiana gave a slow nod. "And you have to deal with these cerva before you can try to find out."

Galfreya almost laughed. The shadow girl spoke of the problem at hand as though it were simply a matter of adjusting the bass and treble controls on a stereo system.

"Yes, that's about it," she said, rather than trying to explain the sheer volume of complications that were involved.

"So what's your plan?"

"As I've already told you," Tatiana broke in, "this is our concern, not yours."

Christiana glanced at the queen and cocked her eyebrow again.

"You don't think I could help?" she asked.

"I don't see how anyone could help us at this point," Tatiana told her.

Christiana smiled. "See, that's where you're wrong. Minisino's the new war chief of the buffalo cerva, right?"

Tatiana gave her a slow nod.

"Well, he and I go way back. Stop treating me like some lower life form and maybe I'll talk to him for you."

"And then what?"

"Then you'll help me deal with whoever hurt my brother Geordie."

Tatiana studied her for a long moment before giving a royal nod.

"Help us with the cerva," she said, "and we will do all in our power to help you in return."

"Fair enough."

"You really think you can just talk to Minisino?" Galfreya asked.

Christiana smiled. "I might not have to."

"What's that supposed to mean?"

"Well, there's something you all seem to be forgetting here."

Rabedy

Long after Odawa had left him on the cliff top, Rabedy remained behind, staring down at the monstrous gathering of buffalo soldiers. Just looking at them started him trembling until he had to sit down on one of the slabs of granite at the edge of the drop-off, he was shaking so bad. He drew up his knees and wrapped his arms around his legs. He wanted to look away, but he couldn't.

This was horrible, horrible, horrible.

He'd known bad things were going to happen when Big Dan first had the gang take up with Odawa. He'd just *known*. But he could never have guessed it would be this bad.

And who was left to deal with it? Not Big Dan. Not any of the gang. Not Odawa, for sure.

There was just him.

And what was he supposed to do? Go down and wave his ears and tail at the buffalo and say, look at me, I'm part animal, just like you. Listen to me.

They'd stomp him under those hooves of theirs like he was a bug, and that would be the end of him.

He sighed.

Well, it wasn't as though there was anybody who would miss him. Too bogan for most fairy, not bogan enough for his own clans.

He tried to pick out individuals in the mass of stomping brown figures below, but it was impossible. They were too far away and moving too much. From this vantage point there was only the carpet of brown.

Would any of them listen to him?

What could he even say if they did?

There was no excuse for what the gang had done. No explanation that would justify killing those cerva, and certainly nothing that would bring them back.

It was hopeless.

Hopeless, hopeless.

Unless . . .

It suddenly occurred to him that there were an awful lot of buffalo gathering down there in the valley below him. And if some of those warrior cerva were spirits, called up from their graves, or the ground where they had fallen . . .

He stood up.

Maybe there was someone he could talk to. Somebody who might listen. Somebody who would agree that the responsibility for the recent deaths lay not with all fairy, but only with one gang of bogans.

He needed to go, and he needed to go quickly. Much more quickly than two short bogan legs could take him. As quick as salmon swimming through the air. Oh, where was that damned blind green-bree when he was needed?

He lifted a hand to his flopping dog ears.

Four legs were quicker than two. But he was too stupid and useless and just couldn't master the change . . .

Odawa made it sound so easy. He said it wasn't changing into something you weren't, so much as remembering something you'd never been, which made absolutely no sense at all. How could you remember something you hadn't known in the first place?

"Figure that out," the blind green-bree had said, "and you'll have the trick of it. The change is in your blood. It remembers, even if you don't." And when someone—Rabedy thought it had been Luren—asked how that was supposed to be possible, Odawa added, "Anything's possible . . . if you want it badly enough."

Rabedy considered that.

If you want it badly enough.

He hadn't wanted to go hunting cerva. He'd wanted to be able to change, yes. *That* he'd wanted badly. But clouding that desire was the sure knowledge that the new shape would be used for killing. Big Dan had made that plain, right from the start.

Maybe that was what had stopped him partway, turning him into a bogan with a dog's ears and tail.

It was different now. Now he wanted to help. Now he wanted to do whatever he could to make up for the wrongs in which he'd played a part. It didn't matter that he hadn't wanted to do it. He hadn't spoken up loudly enough to stop it. He hadn't really spoken up at all. He'd just gone along with the others, following Big Dan's lead.

He needed to make up for that.

And *that,* he realized, he wanted more than anything he'd ever wanted before.

He closed his eyes and tried to ignore the thundering sounds of the buffalo in the valley below. When that didn't work, he used the sound. Breathed in time to it. Twinned his pulse to the rhythm of drums and hooves. Concentrated. Focused.

If you want it badly enough.

He didn't want this. He *needed* it.

The change is in your blood. It remembers, even if you don't.

Yes. It wasn't something strange and different. It was something he'd always known, even if he hadn't realized he'd known it.

It was . . .

The change is in your blood.

He could do this. He could. He wasn't some useless bogan. He was . . . he was . . .

When it happened, it was almost anticlimactic.

One moment he was a bogan, eyes shut, brow furrowed, as he concentrated. The next, his clothes became air and blew away on the breeze. He fell forward onto his hands, propelled by a sudden twist of his spine. Except his hands were paws. Fur covered his body. Everything smelled and felt and looked different, but so familiar.

He lifted his head, laughing, meaning to shout, "I did it!" It came out as a yelp and a bark and a joyous howl. He chased his tail for a moment, spinning in a wild circle, then remembered the why for this change and sped off into the forest, heading to the place where a gang of bogans had ambushed a deer, bringing her down with a flight of barb-tipped arrows.

South of the Kickaha Mountains, but already deep into the acres that made up the Kickaha rez, the dog that was Rabedy burst out from a shadowed forest in the between to pad across the meadow where Big Dan and his gang had killed the doe. He followed the slope of the meadow down to the bed of a creek and cast about for scent, his ears attuned to the approach of anything that didn't belong here.

Belonged any less than he did, Rabedy corrected himself, then put that thought away. He wasn't here to hurt anyone. He was here to make amends as best he could. Except he couldn't help but be nervous, all the same, seeing how he was out here on his own in the green and the wild. But either the green-brees were too occupied with their own business to spy him here in their territories, or wearing a dog shape made him seem more like a green-bree himself, less like a bogan.

He found the bones first—already stripped clean by crows and foxes and other scavengers. Their scent was everywhere. But under it, the smell of the doe's blood could still be found, an echo of scent clinging to the brush and stones. It grew stronger under the old beech tree where they'd butchered the carcass.

But the spirit of Walker's daughter wasn't here.

He hesitated for a long moment, knowing what he needed to do now, only nervous about attracting attention other than that of this one spirit to himself. But he had no choice.

He changed back into his bogan shape—it was so easy, once you knew the trick—and stood barefoot in his proper shape. There were no lingering bits of dog. His ears didn't droop, but rose to their proper height. There was no tail slapping against his buttocks.

He wore no clothes either. He remembered Odawa explaining how they were drawn from one's surroundings, molecule after molecule convinced to take another shape. Unable to master the change into animal shape, none of the bogans had really paid much attention to that part of the instruction, including Rabedy.

He was pretty sure he could puzzle it out now, but he couldn't spare the time. He didn't need clothes anyway, not for what he was here to do. He called out—across the meadow, up into the branches of the tree, down by the creek, anywhere a spirit might still be lingering. Over and over again, he made his apologies and explained why he was here.

When there was still no response after another few minutes of this, he became a dog once more. He exulted in the powerful muscles of this shape and sped off across the meadow and into the woods, heading for the crossroads where the fiddler and her corbae had stood up to Big Dan and taken the doe's remains away from them.

There he went through the whole process again, with no better results.

That left only one other place she might be . . . if she hadn't already travelled on to wherever it was the spirits of the green-bree went when they were done with this world. But he didn't think she was gone yet. Spirits were never so quick to leave when their deaths were as unexpected and violent as hers had been. It was why there were ceremonies for the dead.

To comfort those left behind, certainly, but also to allow the dead to let go and travel on.

The cerva would have had a ceremony for her. The question was where?

He started casting for scent once more and quickly found Walker's. The thought of coming face to face with the tall grim cerva was more than Rabedy could easily contemplate. He'd only ever seen Walker from a distance, and he'd like to keep it that way. But Walker's trail would take him where he needed to go.

He gave a nervous look around himself, ears cocked, nostrils flared, before finally following the cerva's scent into the between. The trail was old, but his dog's nose was keen and he had no trouble staying with it. He went cautiously, every sense attuned to his surroundings so that he wouldn't run into the cerva, or another green-bree, without having a chance to hide first.

Because it was an old trail, it took him some time to finally reach the shore of a lake where he was sure that the ceremony had taken place. Here, the faint traces of Walker's trail disappeared into a maelstrom of cerva scents. Hundreds of different ones, but no one was here now. The beach was deserted. The water was dark where it lapped against the shore, though not as dark as the charred remains of a fire that lay halfway between the water and the rocks where he hid.

This was where the war against fairy must have been conceived, Rabedy decided. The leader of the buffalo clans would have realized that he could use this sorrowful occasion as a fulcrum to convince the others to follow his lead. Not immediately. Not here, at this ceremony. But soon after, while the sorrow and anger still ran hot in the blood of the cerva.

But what of the spirit herself?

Was she still here? Would she listen to him?

He stepped out from the rocks and padded across the granite slab to what was left of the ceremonial fire. The fur at his neck and along his spine began to prickle when he got close. He stopped and looked around. Lifting his muzzle, he searched for scents. He was still alone on the shore.

But when he turned back to the charred remains of the fire, a slender figure stood barefoot in the ashes. Her hair hung in long brown braids along either side of her narrow face, decorated with cowrie shells, feathers, and coloured beads. There were more beads woven into patterns around the throat and on the shoulders of her cotton dress. In her eyes burned a strange, unworldly light.

Though there was nothing threatening about her, Rabedy felt a sudden chill.

"Dog that is not a dog," she said in a low voice. "What do you want from me?"

Grey

Having promised Jack I'd talk to Raven, I make my way across town to the Rookery on Stanton Street where he lives. I don't expect much of anything to come of it. These days, Raven might call himself Lucius Portsmouth and look like a man, but he's still not exactly engaged with the world around him the way the rest of us are. It's just him, in that big house of his, living inside his head. He's not supposed to be as bad as he once was, but from all I've heard, he firmly believes that people should handle their own problems.

"That's how you grow," is what I've been told he says when people come to him looking for help.

I know it seems harsh, but I guess when it gets around that you've made the world, everybody must come by asking for just this one little favour, or maybe just that one, and there's not enough time in any one day to deal with it all.

Or at least that's the argument I use when I'm speaking outside the cor- bae clans. Personally, I believe that if you can make a difference, it's your re- sponsibility to do so. *Especially* when you're responsible for the world the rest of us find ourselves in. But it's not like Raven would listen to that com- ing from me any more than he'd stop whatever he's doing to come talk to the buffalo.

I found myself wondering if he even saw the world anymore. When he stepped outside the Rookery, did he ever stop to appreciate this big old sprawl of dirt and green and stone for the grace and beauty that could still be found in it, or did he only see the parts we'd messed up?

I'm guessing he only saw the mess, or he'd be more proactive.

But I was still going to talk to him, so I keep on walking.

The oak trees lining the street are filled with cousins, marking my passage as I follow the sidewalk to Raven's tall house, my boot heels clicking on the concrete. Though they're mostly crows, I catch the white flash of a magpie's tail and spy a few rooks and jays. I can hear them gossiping about me, but they don't call out to me directly, and the business I have is for Raven's ears alone, so I don't try to start up a conversation.

I get about a half block from where Raven's house rears up above the treetops when suddenly all those birds take to the air and fly off in a burst of black wings and raucous complaints.

I turn to see what's disturbed them and just shake my head. Now *there* was something you didn't see too often, a great big lunk of a salmon swimming through the air like he's making his way through deep water.

I stop and wait for him to approach.

I suppose I should be more nervous—on my guard and ready to fight—but I'm really tired of how long this has dragged on, of listening to the ghosts of all the people who've gotten hurt through the years because of this stupid enmity between the two of us. Lizzie wasn't the first; she's just the latest. I'm ready for this to be over. It's long past time we finished our unhappy business with each other. But as I stand there waiting for him to come down, I find myself thinking mostly about how Odawa's timing sucks, the way it always does.

He changes from salmon to man just before he reaches the ground, landing way more gracefully than a blind man should have been able to. He should have gotten all entangled in that robe he'd taken to wearing. He should at least have had to put his arms out for balance, the way we corbae use our wings on our final descent to a roost. But I've learned over the years that you never get what you expect from Odawa.

It's no different now. I can't get a reading from him. No way to guess his emotional state. No sense of what he has planned, how he'll attack.

"Your wife cursed me before she died," Odawa says as he approaches me, his voice conversational. "She cursed me to wander forever, but never reach my destination."

If he's willing to talk instead of fight, that's fine with me—I don't see violence as a solution, though I won't back down from it if it comes looking for me. But I can't shake the clock ticking in my head. I need to get in to see

Raven as quickly as I can, so that after he turns me down, I can rejoin Jack while I can still lend him some help.

"Your destination," I repeat.

The blind man nods.

"Which was me."

He nods again.

That explains a lot. I've wondered why Odawa has never mounted a direct attack against me in all these years. He always comes at me from the side, slipping out of the shadows to hurt the people I've come to care for the most. I'd always thought it was just some cruel streak of his, wanting me to feel the loss over time, rather than having it all over with at once by killing me. My wife Mira had been the first he'd taken from me, but she wasn't the last. That's why I prefer a solitary existence now. It's lonely, this life I lead, but it's far easier on my conscience.

I'd never guessed it was because of a curse that he'd been kept from me. Trust Mira. Even dying, she'd been looking out for me—the same as I would have done for her.

Mira.

She died so long ago, but right now it feels like yesterday.

Thinking of her, of what Odawa had done to her, I want to rip his eyes out all over again, along with his heart. But I make myself pretend the same calm he's projecting.

"And now . . . what?" I ask. "Your destination's changed?"

"Hardly. I had help." He holds up a piece of string with two knots tied into it. The thing stinks of fairy magic. "And here I am."

I nod. "You're here, your bogan pets are out killing cerva, your buffalo army is about to lay waste to this city. You've been a busy little fish, haven't you?"

I can tell the barb cuts. He pretends differently, but I know him and his pride, which is why I'd called him a little fish. I hoped to put him on edge, annoy him enough that he might make a mistake. It isn't likely, but it's worth a try, because I need some kind of advantage here. He's an old spirit and undoubtedly much more powerful than this corbae jay.

"I had nothing to do with the gathering of buffalo," Odawa tells me, his voice stiff.

I shake my head, then realize he can't see the movement.

"You have everything to do with it," I say. "But then you don't own up to your mistakes, do you? Any more than you take the time to think a thing through before you set it into motion."

The blind gaze stays on mine, leaving me with the disconcerting impression that he can actually see me.

"After all these years," he says, "you still know nothing about me. My clan is the clan of wisdom, and what you took from me was the ability to study the ancient texts as they are laid out in the visual patterns of the world. I can feel them, but thanks to you, I can't *see* them."

"No," I tell him. "Salmon are the clan of knowledge, not wisdom. It's easy to acquire information. Wisdom comes from knowing how to use that information. So using me as the reason you stayed stupid is no excuse."

If his voice was stiff earlier, now it's positively frosty.

"I don't make excuses," he says. "Just as nothing I do is unplanned. If I'd wanted to orchestrate a war, I could have easily done it. But this nonsense the cerva have put into motion is their own doing, not mine."

I don't know if he's trying to convince himself or me, but I'm not buying it. One thing with cousins: we know the connectedness of everything, so it's easy to see where one thing begins or another ends. He might be blind, but he shouldn't be blind to that.

"However it got started," I tell him. "I have to stop this thing."

"Since when are buffalo your concern?"

"A friend asked me to help. Besides, it's what I do."

"You stop wars," he says, sarcasm thick in his voice.

"No, I try to help people. It's just usually not on such a large scale."

"Like you helped me."

I just look at him for a long moment.

"We both know how that really went down," I say finally. "And I take responsibility for it. But you've either got to let it go, or we really have to deal with it here and now. Today."

"What about your *mission*?"

He's good with the sarcasm, I'll give him that. Just the right sneer of superiority in his voice. But I'm not going to play into it, and I decide to take what he's saying at face value.

"Why would you care?" I ask.

"What makes you think I do?"

I sigh. "We're not high school kids, Odawa, so can't we let go of the posturing here for just a minute? I need to talk to Raven, to see if he'll help stop the buffalo. Will you let me do that before we finish this business between us? The Grace knows, you've waited long enough that another few minutes shouldn't kill you."

Until now, I've never realized how much I use a person's eyes to read what they're thinking. I can't get anything from Odawa, obviously, not with that milky-white gaze, but I do get the sense that he's genuinely curious and serious about what he asks me next.

"That's really all you've been doing?" he says. "Helping people?"

It's not something I like to talk about. It always strikes me that if you talk about it, you're not doing it for the people you help anymore. You're doing it for yourself.

"You've been following me long enough," I say. "What do you think?"

There's a long pause before he finally gives me a slow nod.

"I never really thought about it," he says.

"So what's it going to be?"

"You want to talk to Raven?"

"It's more that I promised I would."

"Fine," Odawa says. "But I'm coming with you."

I have to look at him for a long moment, trying to figure out if he's actually being reasonable, but I still can't read him. So I take the chance, and turn my back on him, heading for Raven's house. I hear his footsteps fall in behind me.

Whiskey Jack

North, in the Kickaha Mountains, Whiskey Jack stood on a high slope where a break in the trees created by slabs of granite gave him a long view of the valley that lay below his vantage point.

Wetlands stretched from one end of the valley to the other. They'd begun as a small lake, fed by a natural spring, but beaver had damned the stream that drained from the valley, the backed-up water slowly rising to swallow all of the land except for a few small islands supported by granite outcrops. Cedars stood throughout, tall, grey and dead, returning to life and green only on those islands and the surrounding slopes where they rose up out of the waterlogged valley. Where it wasn't choked with swamp grass and reeds, the surface of the water was still as glass, reflecting back the sky, the cedars, the immediate hills.

Jack sighed.

He wasn't fond of this swampy land. All those dead cedars depressed him, and he didn't like getting his feet wet. He also didn't like all the little mosquito and deer fly cousins who made such places their home and eagerly fed on intruders. But he supposed he had to go down there.

He turned back into the woods and worked his way down through the trees until he reached the edge where solid ground grew marshy. He was just mapping out the route he'd take to reach the largest of the islands where Ayabe was supposed to make his home, when a deep voice came to him from the forest to one side of the lake.

"So, do you have that thousand dollars you owe me?"

Jack turned to see Ayabe leaning against the trunk of a tall dead cedar. In human form, he still stood almost seven feet tall, big and broad-shouldered with an impossible rack of antlers rising from his brow. He didn't seem to feel their weight.

"You do remember that poker game?" he added.

"You must be thinking of my brother, Jim," Jack said.

"I happen to know that you don't have a brother."

"Then somebody's been feeding you lies. My litter had two boy pups and one girl. I'm the youngest, and I'm telling you now I couldn't possibly owe you any money."

"And how's that?"

Jack shrugged. "When it comes to poker, I don't lose."

"I wonder if it's only with poker."

Jack didn't see where the knife came from. One moment Ayabe's hand was empty, the next it held a twelve-inch blade. The cerva smiled humourlessly as he threw the knife.

Jack moved his head just enough so that the blade went by his ear, imbedding itself in the trunk of a cedar behind him with a dull *thunk*. It would be so easy to pluck it out of the wood and throw it back. He'd aim for the chest, though, not the head. Head shots were always tricky, but it was hard to miss as big a target as the cerva's chest.

It took all his will power not to retaliate. Instead, he schooled his features to remain calm and took a steadying breath.

"I'm guessing you weren't actually trying to hit me," he said.

"Why would you think that?"

"Would you have missed?"

Ayabe laughed. "You're a cocky one, I'll give you that." He waited a beat, then added, "Are you going to show me some respect and offer me a smoke?"

"Sure," Jack said. "Why not. It wasn't like you were trying to kill me."

Taking out his tobacco and papers, he rolled a fat cigarette and lit it with his Zippo.

"Nice lighter," Ayabe said as he accepted the proffered cigarette and took a drag.

"I won it from Cody in a game. Like I said—"

"You don't lose."

Jack shrugged. "Though gambling's probably the only area in my life where that applies."

Ayabe had a second drag and offered the cigarette back to Jack.

"That's okay," Jack said. "I'll roll myself another."

Ayabe looked across the lake while Jack built his own cigarette. The cerva absently rubbed his antlers against the cedar behind him as he smoked, creating a steady snowfall of bark flakes that fell to his shoulders.

"I'm guessing you're here about the buffalo," he said, once Jack got his own cigarette lit.

Jack nodded. "So you've heard about it."

"A cousin would have to be dead and long in the grave not to have." He paused, then added, "Though come to think of it, Minisino's managed to swell his ranks with a great many spirits of the long dead, as well as the living that make up his own clan."

"Yeah," Jack said. "He's got himself an army, so you know this is going to be a mess. A lot of innocents are going to die."

"You know where my sympathies lie. A lot of innocents are already dead."

"I know, but—"

"I'm surprised you don't feel the same."

"I suppose I have a problem with laying the sins of the fathers on their children."

"The aganesha who have been killing cerva aren't exactly innocents," Ayabe said.

"No, of course not. It's just . . ."

"What exactly do you expect of me?" Ayabe asked.

Jack knew he had to play this exactly right. He was only going to get the one chance to make his argument.

"I don't expect anything," he said. "But I'm hoping for a favour."

"You want me to stop them."

There was the hint of amusement in Ayabe's voice, but it didn't show in his eyes.

Jack shook his head. "I'd like you to convince them that we can work this out another way."

"And what would that be?"

"The guilty will have to pay for what they've done."

Ayabe fell silent. He finished his cigarette, his gaze on the distance of the lake's far shore. Jack didn't push for an answer. He simply followed the cerva's lead and finished his own smoke.

"And you can make this happen?" Ayabe asked finally.

Crap, Jack thought. He should have known it would come down to this.

"I can't promise that it will," he finally said, "but you've got my word that I'll do whatever it takes to see this through."

"Even if it means your life?"

Jack hesitated a moment, then nodded.

"These aganesha mean that much to you?" Ayabe asked.

Jack shrugged. "Truth us, I couldn't give a damn about most of them. But I know war isn't the way to work this out."

"Sometimes the board needs to be cleared."

"Except this isn't a game," Jack said.

"Which means you might lose."

Jack shook his head. "It's not about me. In the long run, everybody's going to lose. I don't want to see that. And I'm hoping that even you, living here in the back of nowhere, might feel the same way."

Ayabe fell silent and the minutes ticked by.

"Do you really have a brother?" he finally asked.

"Ask around," Jack told him. "He gets some kind of kick out of pretending to be me. I think it's because I was the runt of the litter, but in the end, I turned out stronger and smarter than he could ever hope to be."

"And more humble, as well."

Jack shrugged. "I know my limitations. But I know my strong points, too. I'm just stating the facts. I've never met you before. I don't owe you anything. But if collecting what my deadbeat brother owes you is what it'll take for us to close this deal, you've got it."

"No, that's all right," Ayabe said. "I can collect my own debts."

"So, will you help me?"

"I can try. But I don't hold the sway over the cerva clans the way you might think I do, and Minisino's never been one to take advice."

"All I can ask is that you try. I've got a friend getting the word to Raven. Maybe the two of you together can convince him to let us find a better solution to the problem."

"Raven, you say?"

"Is that a problem?"

Ayabe slowly shook his head. "No. I'm just . . . surprised to hear that he'll be involved."

"Don't know that he is—not yet. But we're working on it."

Ayabe pushed himself away from the tree he was leaning against and straightened up.

"Well, if nothing else," he said, "this should at least prove interesting."

It's not about whether or not it's interesting, Jack thought. It's about saving lives.

But he kept it to himself. At least Ayabe was on board. With any luck, maybe they could actually defuse this whole situation before it exploded and took all of them down.

Far from Home

Lizzie

That couldn't have been Geordie, Lizzie thought, staring harder at the second-floor window of the battered old farmhouse where she thought she'd seen his face. How could it have been? Except, what was so implausible about Geordie suddenly appearing here? Hadn't she already been shown that anything could happen in this place? *Anything.*

Real, not real. How were you supposed to know anymore?

She might have actually seen Geordie, or it might have been just another piece of this freak show she was stuck in—trapped in this stupid dream world inside Jilly's head.

If you were looking for unbelievable, how was *that* for unbelievable? Not to mention totally unfair.

How had she ended up here anyway? Better yet, *why* had she ended up here? She'd never wanted very much out of life: the chance to play her fiddle, the companionship of travelling with her friends, trying to be a good person, maybe someday finding that special someone. But she'd have settled for just getting along without any particularly dramatic crises.

Instead, the only thing she'd managed to do with her life was getting lost in this horrrible world, all her twenty-seven years scrunched back into a child's body. Worse, she had only an expanse of smooth skin where her mouth should be. Under the skin, a solid piece of bone. No teeth, no muscles, no jaw. She couldn't talk. She couldn't eat or drink.

Ignoring Mattie, she moved a little closer to the house, trying to get a better view of what was inside. Maybe she could find Jilly and figure out a way to tell her they could escape. Then Del appeared in the doorway with a grin on his face that made her wish she'd just stayed in the field with the goopy mess in the grass that was all that was left of the priest.

"Isn't this sweet?" Del said, his gaze moving between them. "Two of my best girls, wanting to know if I can come out to play."

Beside Lizzie, Mattie giggled. Lizzie turned to look at her. She wanted to punch the little twit in the face, break her nose and make it bleed. She even got so far as clenching her fists when she realized what she was thinking.

God, when had she become so violent? Was that going to be her new answer for anything she didn't like or couldn't make go away? Kill it, or at least try to hurt it? And it wasn't even Mattie she was mad at. It was her own helplessness, and Del, who'd made her weak.

"Our little nameless girl looks mad, doesn't she, Emily?"

Lizzie turned back to face him. Her hands fell limply open at her sides.

Don't, she wanted to say and felt more disgusted with herself than ever for being so helpless that she'd be willing to beg like this. Don't hurt me. Whatever it is you're going to do to me, please don't make it worse.

She had no voice. She had no *mouth*. She couldn't speak. But Del could read the fear in her eyes.

"You'd better be scared," he told her. "Emily knows why."

He doesn't know Mattie's real name, Lizzie thought. She had no idea what that meant, if it meant anything, but she filed it away all the same. Know your enemy, Johnny had been fond of telling her when they'd worked out at the gym. He'd meant the way the enemy moved, how he might be telegraphing his moves, but Lizzie figured that anything she could add to the little she knew could only help.

"Everything belongs to Del," Mattie said. "And everybody is here to do what he says."

"Think you've learned that lesson yet, little nameless girl?"

Lizzie gave a quick nod. Was he going to give her back her mouth?

She tried not to let the hope rise, but it was impossible to stop it. She knew better. She really did. But she couldn't stop it.

Del grinned at her and shook his head, and all her hopes went crashing down again, just as she'd known they would.

"No, I don't think you really believe," he told her. "You still think there's some way you can get out of this."

"She's so stupid," Mattie said.

"That's right, Emily. She's just not as smart as you." He cocked his head and studied Lizzie for a long moment, before adding, "But maybe she can learn. What do you say, little nameless girl? Do you want to learn how to be smart?"

Lizzie nodded. She didn't really. She knew that whatever he was talking about was only going to be worse than things already were. But she couldn't seem to stop herself.

"Then you better come inside," Del said. "Both of you. Emily can show you how to make me happy. You'd like that, wouldn't you, little nameless girl? You want to know how to make me happy, don't you?"

Lizzie was spared the need to answer. There was no question but that she was going to agree, only she never got the chance. Before she could nod, before either she or Mattie could take a step toward the house, a dog burst out of the long weeds behind them and came to stand between the girls and Del. It was a broad-shouldered pit bull, its short fur the colour of honey.

Lizzie felt no hope at its appearance. It wouldn't be able to protect her. Del would see to that.

"The hell?" Jilly's brother said. "I don't know where you came from, but you're sure not squatting your ugly ass anywhere around here."

He made a wave with his hand in the direction of the dog. Lizzie tensed, waiting for the dog to disappear, or turn into black goo, or maybe just explode. But nothing happened.

The dog growled, low in its chest, and took a step forward.

Del waved his hand again. Dirt spat up around the dog as though the ground had sustained a powerful blow, but the dog was untouched. Unmoved. It growled again, lower, angrier, and then something wonderful happened. Lizzie saw fear in Del's eyes.

She had no idea why he couldn't deal with the dog the way he had had Timony and the priest. She was just so relieved to see that he *wasn't* all-powerful.

Was Jilly finally waking up to the fact that Del could only have power over them if she believed that he did? Maybe there was hope after all.

The dog suddenly charged Del, leaping high. Del vanished before the jaws could close on his throat. The dog's trajectory carried it toward the open door of the house, but the door slammed shut before the dog could reach it. The dog banged into the wooden slats and fell to the porch, off-balance. It was on its feet almost immediately, turning this way and that, searching for Del.

As soon as it realized it was alone on the porch, it returned its attention to the door. Standing on its hind legs, the dog tried to work the doorknob, its claws sliding from the smooth metal.

When it turned back to them, Lizzie and Mattie both took a step back.

Can one of you open this?

The voice rang in Lizzie's head—a weird and awful intrusion. It took her a long moment to realize that it had come from the dog.

Mattie was quicker on the uptake. Not bothering to reply, she turned and bolted back into the fields behind them. Lizzie tracked her as she fled through the tall weeds, then her gaze went up to the second-floor windows. In the one where she thought she'd seen Geordie earlier, Del was framed, looking down at them. It was hard to tell—what with the distance and the dirty windowpane—but he didn't seem scared anymore. He just looked mad.

Girl, the voice said in Lizzie's head, bringing her attention back to the dog. *I asked if you can open this door for me.*

You . . . you can talk? Lizzie thought, trying to focus the question and send it to the animal. *In my head?*

She thought that if the dog could speak in her head, maybe it could read minds, too.

In a fashion. Why do you look so surprised? You should know. Without a mouth, how else do you speak?

Del stole my mouth.

Ah.

Why couldn't he hurt you? Lizzie asked.

He doesn't have power over me.

But why not?

No one will ever have that kind of power over me again, the dog replied.

There was something dark and dangerous in its voice that told Lizzie this wasn't an area she should be trying to explore any further, and at any other time, she might have respected the dog's privacy. But if it knew a way to get around Del's control, she needed to know it.

Yeah, but how does it work? she asked. *I thought he was like . . . I don't know, God. At least until Jilly stops believing in him.*

Jilly is here?

You know her?

I've come to find her, the dog said.

It figured, Lizzie thought. There weren't all those magical stories about Jilly Coppercorn for nothing.

Have you seen her? the dog went on. *Do you know where she is?*

Lizzie pointed to the house behind the dog.

She's in there.

The dog didn't turn around.

And so I repeat, it said. *Can you open the door for me?*

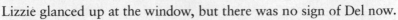

Lizzie glanced up at the window, but there was no sign of Del now.

I don't know, she said. *I guess I could try.*

The dog moved aside as Lizzie came up the stairs and approached the door.

So, what's your name? she asked.

I don't have one, the dog replied. *But I've been called Honey.*

Was that why Del had no power over her? Did he need to know your name before he could do all these horrible things to you?

But then she remembered what he kept calling her. Little nameless girl.

He didn't know Lizzie's name, but he was still able to steal her mouth.

Can you teach me how to stop Del from having power over me? she asked. *I'm a full-grown woman trapped in this child's body. I want my real self back. I want my* mouth *back.*

You must be the fiddler Joe told me about, Honey said. *Lizzie.*

That's me.

She tried the door knob, but it wouldn't turn.

It's locked, she added.

Honey nodded. *Then we have to do this the hard way.*

Before Lizzie could ask what she meant, the dog took a run down the porch, then flung herself at the window, head tucked down to protect her eyes. She went through in a crash of breaking glass.

All Lizzie could do was stand and stare until the dog's face appeared back in the window, her paws on the sill. Blood trickled down her forehead and onto her muzzle from the cuts on her head.

Are you coming? Honey asked.

Lizzie hesitated a moment longer, then nodded and ran to the window.

Geordie

I was still trying to comfort Jilly—a hopeless endeavour since she could neither see nor hear me—when Del suddenly reappeared in the room. He stalked to the window, then turned away, the fury plain on his face. For a moment there, I thought I'd seen a trace of fear in his eyes, but it was gone now.

"Goddamn it," he said. "Where did that dog come from?"

Jilly never looked up. So far as she was concerned, he was no more here than I was. But then he kicked at the man-shaped pile of debris on the floor that had once been me. Leaves and twigs and dirt went flying across the room.

Jilly screamed.

"Shut up," he told her. "Just shut up. You want to lose your mouth like your lippy friend did? Because I'm the man can make it happen."

The Jilly I'd always known was back now. The fearless Jilly who wouldn't back down for anyone. Tears still wet her cheeks, but her gaze was cold and hard as she looked up at her brother.

"I don't care," she told him.

She got to her feet, ready to pit her child's body against him.

"Oh, you care," Del said. "You say you don't, but bottom line, everybody cares. Everybody's looking out for number one."

"That's where you're wrong. Do whatever you want to me. It doesn't matter anymore."

"And why's that, little sister?"

Her gaze went to my transformed remains, scattered the length of the room now.

"You've already taken the only thing I care about away from me," she said. "What does it matter what else you do?"

I don't know why, but it took me a few moments to realize that she was talking about me. Then I understood. I might have thought I hadn't heard her right, but I'd already realized the same thing myself: she was the most important thing in the world for me as well. I'd always known that. I just hadn't *known* it, if you know what I mean.

How was that for a kicker? Here it was, too later for either of us now. I was dead, or at least a disembodied spirit with no body to return to, and she was locked in this monstrous nightmare taking place inside her own head where it was impossible to escape. And *now* we admit this to ourselves?

"You really think I'm going to believe that?" Del said. "Everybody cares what happens to them."

"Sure they do. But at what cost? Everything I believe and am stands against freaks like you. I won't let you control me again. If I give in to you, you win. But if you hurt me and I don't give in, then I win. If you kill me, I win. No matter what you try to do to me, so long as I stand against you, you can't really hurt me."

"Jilly, no!" I cried. "Look what he did to me. Don't push him like this."

But she couldn't hear me any more than he could. My words rang only in my own ears. I don't think it would have mattered even if she could have heard me. This was Jilly in full fierce mode.

"Bullshit," Del said.

Jilly's gaze was steady, unflinching. "Try me."

They locked gazes for a long moment until Del shook his head.

"I still don't buy it," he said. "But it doesn't really matter. I don't need to hurt you to make you do what I say. I can just tear apart your red-haired friend instead."

"That's right. And I can't stop you."

"But you can, little sister. All you have to do is say the word and I'll leave her alone. But if you don't . . ." He moved a finger across his throat. "Well, then she's just history."

Jilly shook her head.

"I'm not responsible for what you do," she said. "I never have been. Only you are. We all make our own karma."

"Your friend's going to be real happy to hear you say that."

"I doubt anybody could be happy around you."

"You've got that much right, little sister. We may be in your head, but I'm the one in charge here. I've always been the one in charge."

Jilly shook her head again.

"No," she said slowly. "I don't think that's true."

Del laughed. "Jesus Christ, you just never learn, do you? I guess I'll just have to—"

He broke off when the sound of a breaking glass came from downstairs.

Del stalked back to the window and looked out. That flicker of fear was back in his eyes when he turned away, gaze on the doorway. A shotgun appeared in his hands.

"That dog's not going to help you," he told Jilly.

"What dog?"

"Yeah, right."

With the shotgun at the ready, he stepped out into the hall. I gave Jilly a last look, then let myself drift down through the floor to see what was going on downstairs.

Honey

The cuts she'd sustained going through the window stung, but they were only superficial. Though they bled, the glass hadn't severed any major artery. All they did was help her focus her rage on the man tormenting her sister.

Some might question that designation. There was no bond of blood between them. But they were both Children of the Secret, hurt and abused, betrayed by those who should have been protecting them, and that kinship made a bond stronger than the ties of blood. Del was only another version of the Man who'd beat her as a pup. Who'd let her family die in the ring.

Stay behind me, she told Lizzie as the child clambered in through the window.

Then she padded towards the stairs.

She heard his step on the landing, the creak of the wood under his weight. She was halfway up when he appeared at the head of the stairs, the shotgun in his hand.

The weapon gave her only a moment's pause.

This world appeared solid and real. It had substance and dimension, smells and weight. It might be inside Jilly's head, but to all intents and purposes, it was genuine. By that argument, the weapon in his hands was probably real as well. It could fire, the shot coming out of its barrels could tear her apart.

But it didn't matter.

There came a point when nothing mattered except the ending. This was Del, but it might as well have been the Man, whipping the pup she'd been. Leaving her in the metal cage to nurse her wounds after a turn in the ring, when the fever shook her. Laughing as she chewed at the mesh, trying to get at him. Banging a stick against the crosshatched metal wire to make her retreat.

She was here to bring Jilly back.

But she was also here to put an end to the piece of the Man that lived deep inside her own head, the way that Del lived in Jilly's. If she died doing it, so be it. She'd die with her jaws on his throat, and not even death would be able to pry them loose. Not magic or power or whatever it was that let Del rule in this place.

Because he didn't rule her.

No one would rule her again.

So as Del tightened his finger on the triggers of the shotgun, she charged up the last few stairs separating them.

The shotgun went off with a roar that sounded like the world ending.

Grey

The woman who opens the door to Raven's house looks from me to Odawa. She knows my grey jay blood the same way I know hers is raven—for cousins, it's as quick and familiar a form of recognition as looking at somebody's face. She also knows Odawa belongs to the salmon clan, but I don't think that's what makes her frown before her gaze returns to me. At least it's not the only thing.

"Lucius will see you," she tells me after I explain why I'm here, "but the fish man can't come in."

Though I've never met her, I assume this is Chloë Graine, Raven's long-time companion who looks after him those times when he withdraws from the world. She's elegant and tall, dark-haired with strong, stern features and midnight-dark eyes that warm somewhat when she faces me, but go flat and cold whenever her gaze turns in Odawa's direction.

Something's off here, I realize. Exactly what, I can't tell.

"Why not?" I ask.

"Think about it," she says. She brushes her hair back from her eyes, and I catch the faint scent of anise. "I'm surprised you even have to ask."

Beside me, I can feel Odawa stiffen. It could have been with tension, it could have been from anger. I can't tell. I just know that the last thing I need is for him to cause some kind of a scene now, just when I'm going to get my chance to talk to Raven.

"I'm really in the dark here," I tell her.

Chloë gives me a look that seems to ask, are you a moron?

"Well, for starters," she says, "he murdered Lucius's goddaughter."

"His goddaughter . . . ?"

"Your wife Mira."

"She was *Raven's* goddaughter?"

"She never told you?"

I turn to look at Odawa. He's already backing off the porch, but he's making his escape too late. Before he can step away into the otherworld, or even change shape, a tall black man appears from further down the porch and grabs his arm with a big meaty hand. I don't know the newcomer by name but he has the scent of a rook about him. Odawa tries to pull free of his grip, but the rook's as unmovable as a stone cliff.

"Don't even think of changing shape, Odawajameg," he says.

I can see Odawa deflate at the use of his full true name, obviously having been planning to do just that. But I can barely concentrate on Odawa's problems. I'm still trying to get around Mira's connection to Lucius Portsmouth. She'd been Raven's goddaughter? *The* Raven who'd brought the world into being?

"How could you not have known?" Chloë says.

"I . . . it just wasn't something we ever spoke of," I tell her. "I knew her parents were dead, but she never wanted to talk about her past. I had to respect that. I assumed she'd tell me when the time was right, but we never got that time."

Chloë nods. "She and Lucius certainly had their differences. I suppose I shouldn't be surprised that she never mentioned him."

I look to where the rook's still holding Odawa. I feel no guilt at having led him into this.

"What's going to happen to him?" I ask.

"There will be a trial, I suppose. Considering the clan affiliations, we'll have to call up some of both the water and air cousins to arbitrate. Brandon will keep him safely until then."

I nod. "But I don't understand. Why would Raven wait until now to deal with this? Mira's been dead for years."

"The fish man's never been stupid enough to actually come knocking on Lucius's door before. You know how it is. Lucius is the last one to create a problem between the clans over a personal matter. But he can't ignore this."

Not to mention that Raven has been withdrawn from the world for most of the long years since Mira had died, but it would be impolitic to actually come out and say it.

"Maybe Odawa's here because he didn't know," I say.

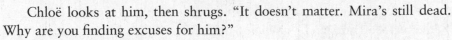

Chloë looks at him, then shrugs. "It doesn't matter. Mira's still dead. Why are you finding excuses for him?"

"I'm not. It's just—"

I don't know what it is that I'm feeling. I want Mira's killer brought to justice as much, or more, than anyone. I guess I just can't shake the guilt of having plucked out his eyes and starting all of this in the first place. I'd thought he was dead—an honest mistake, anybody knowing the circumstances in which I'd found him would say, and after all, cleaning up carrion is what we corbae do.

But I should be the one avenging Mira's death and all the unhappiness that Odawa had created for me over the years. Instead, as unknowingly as I'd first blinded him, I'd led him to Raven's justice instead. Odawa's quick to point the accusing finger at me.

"This is all your doing," he tells me before Brandon leads him away. His voice is dark with the unhappy promise of what he'll do to me if he ever gets free and finds me again. "You had this planned from the beginning."

I shrug, but don't say anything as he's taken away because there's nothing left to say. All things considered, I don't really owe him an explanation. And he wouldn't listen if I tried to give him one.

I watch Brandon strong-arm Odawa down the stairs and march him across the lawn toward the back of the house. The oaks are full of black-winged cousins once more, taking in the proceedings with great interest.

Not until he's gone do I turn back to Chloë.

"I keep telling Odawa," I say, "that the salmon clan has the gift of knowledge, not wisdom, but he doesn't seem to have either or why would he have come here with me? Even if I didn't know Mira's connection to Raven, he should at least have made the effort to find the names of the kin of the cousin he killed."

"He obviously didn't. And why he didn't doesn't really matter."

"I suppose. But you'd think he'd have been able to see that I didn't know anything about any of this."

"Maybe he thinks you're just a good actor."

"I don't know how much he actually *thinks*. You know he's caught up in this business that has the cerva on the warpath?"

"Why doesn't that surprise me? He's as conniving as a cuckoo and easily as dangerous."

She was referring to the long-standing enmity between corbae and cuckoos that had finally been laid to rest a few years ago by the deaths of most of the local cuckoo elders. I'd first arrived in the area not long after, and the air had been filled with cousin gossip about the events.

"He's also involved in the abduction of a couple of humans," I say. "A fiddler named Lizzie and a woman named Jilly that Joe calls his sister."

Chloë eyes go darker still. "Jilly Coppercorn?"

I nod. "It's all got to do with—"

But she cuts me off. "Don't tell me about it now. Save the story until we're with Lucius so you only need to go through it once."

When she leads me inside the Rookery, it's like stepping back into a Victorian household. There's an umbrella stand just inside the door with a cloak rack on the wall above it, all brass and oak. Wooden wainscoting runs the broad length of the hall at about waist height, setting off a willow leaf pattern of Morris wallpaper. There are paintings in ornate wooden frames, old-fashioned oil landscapes, mostly, though I do see a couple of more contemporary pieces, also in oils. One in particular catches my eye. It shows a pair of dark-haired teenagers with a hint of crow heads surrounding them like auras.

Chloë allows herself a small smile when she sees me looking at it.

"That's one of Jilly's," she says.

I'm surprised. It's really good. But then I don't know all that much about Jilly beyond the fact that she seems to have some very powerful friends.

"So she's an artist?"

"She was." Chloë seems to catch herself. "No, that's not right. She still is. She's just been limited in how much she can express since the accident. I can't tell you how worried I am, having heard your bad news."

"I'm sorry to have been the one to bring it."

She shakes her head. "No, it's something we needed to know if we're going to be able to do anything about it."

"To tell you the truth," I say as we continue down the hall. "I didn't think Raven would even see me."

Chloë smiles. "First, he prefers to be called Lucius. 'Raven' has too many connotations that he'd just as soon let lie. And secondly, we always have time for kin."

"I'll remember that."

But I don't feel any more comfortable as we go on. I catch glimpses of a stately dining room, a living area with sideboards and fat comfortable furniture, and then Chloë leads me into the library to meet the owner of the house.

There are more books in here than I've ever seen before outside a public library or a bookstore. Fat, leather-bound volumes fill the shelves from one end to another. The shelves themselves cover the walls, floor to ceiling, with library ladders on rails to reach the higher ones. The only breaks are the door through which we've entered and two bay windows that look out on to the garden at the rear of the house. An immense desk stands in one half of the room. Two fat club chairs share a marble-based reading lamp and side table in the other half. The floor's polished wood, the ceiling's high, and my nostrils fill with the pleasant, if slightly musty, smell of old books.

After a quick view of the room, I turn back to the door, expecting Raven to be following us in. Chloë touches my arm and directs my attention to one of the two bay windows. I blink when I see the vast bulk of a man standing in front of it, then realize that Raven has the gift of so many cousins: that trick of not being noticed until you want to be. I'm good at it, but not this good. I'd looked right at the window and hadn't noticed a thing, which, given his presence now that I do see him, impresses me even more.

Raven's the biggest and blackest man I'd ever seen. He's tall and rounded like an enormous Buddha, bald and dressed in a simple dark suit, with a gaze so dark and bottomless it makes Chloë's midnight eyes appear like pale twilight.

He places his broad right hand over his heart and offers me a nod of welcome that's almost imperceptible in its movement.

"Wisskatjon," he says. "I'm pleased to finally meet you, though I do wish it were under better circumstances."

I start at the use of my true name and almost say You know of me?, but then I realize, of course, he would. I'd married his goddaughter. Everybody knew that, it seems, except for Odawa and me.

"People just call me Grey," I say.

He nods. "And I prefer Lucius. Come. Sit down. You have a story to tell me."

He crosses the room to shake my hand, then directs me to one of the club chairs. I wait until he sits down—holding my breath to see if the chair can actually take his weight—before I take the other chair. Chloë leans against the front of the desk, facing us, her arms folded.

"I don't think we have time for stories right now," I say. "Or at least, not long ones. Not if we want to stop a war."

"Then keep it short," he says.

I do. I tell him about my first meeting with the bogans and Lizzie's rescue, and then how she and Jilly disappeared from the hotel in Sweetwater. He sits up straighter at the mention of Jilly's name.

"I'm sorry to be the one to be telling you this," I say.

Instead of responding, he first gives Chloë a questioning look.

"I didn't know until only a few moments ago," she said.

Nodding, he turns back to me.

"Please, go on," he says.

I try to be quick about it, telling them how I'd met first Whiskey Jack and then Joe, of going to Tatiana's fairy court and discovering Odawa's involvement with the bogans, though I'm still not sure exactly what it had been. Safe passage through cousin territories is the easy guess, but I'm sure there was more to it than that.

"I'll have to have a little talk with Odawa about Jilly's disappearance," he says when I'm done.

"But the war . . ."

Lucius sighs. "You know I've been through this before."

I nod. "With Joe, the last time the local cousins had a problem with Tatiana's court."

"That was only the most recent crisis of many. If it's not the aganesha hunting cousins, then it's one of the clans taking out some fairies. It doesn't matter. We get it all smoothed over and have a few calm years, then everything just starts up again." He pauses before adding, "I'm truly tempted to sit this one out."

"And there's Jilly to consider," Chloë says.

Lucius nods. "Yes, there's Jilly."

"But so many innocents will die," I say.

That old, dark gaze of Raven's settles on me.

"Nobody's innocent," he tells me.

"You know what I mean."

That gets me another sigh.

"But some," he agrees, "are more innocent than others."

"It wouldn't take you long, would it?" I try. "To have a word with Minisino, I mean. To stop this."

"I've only to wave a hand and everything will be set right? After all, I made the world."

Something in his voice, in his eyes, tells me it's not that simple. He's amused at my naiveté, but there's a sadness, too. And under that, an anger, though it doesn't appear to be directed at me.

"I don't know," I say, feeling I still have to be careful, though I'm not sure exactly why. "It's just . . . you're Raven, aren't you?"

"I am and I'm not. Raven the World-Maker, the Creator, the one who pulled a world out of the darkness . . . somewhere inside me . . . somewhen . . . I suppose I was him. But now I'm just Lucius Portsmouth. An old corbae who's perhaps outstayed his welcome in this time and place."

"But . . ." I start.

My voice trails off because I don't know where I'm going. Questions fill my head, but they fall silent before they leave my lips. I can almost understand what he's saying. Once, there was a Raven who made the world. Once, it might have been the man sitting in the chair beside me. But that was in the long ago. There might be a piece of that Raven still hidden somewhere deep inside him, somewhere in his blood, in the deep of his bones, but it wasn't something the man he'd become now could readily access.

Because we diminish, we spirits.

I remember a conversation I had a long time ago with an old woman by the coals of a campfire, in a place that's no longer a part of this world. That's what she told me: We diminish. Not because we're dependent on people's belief, the way it's said the Eadar are, but because time moves on and nothing stays the same. Mountains are ground down, continents change their shape, glaciers withdraw. Time moves and everything changes.

We diminish because it's simply the way of the world.

"It's funny, isn't it?" Chloë says, her thoughts obviously travelling a similar road as mine. "No one ever wonders why the Raven who made the world would be living in an old house on Stanton Street. Why Cody, the Great Trickster, wanders the world like a hobo, when he's not spending his time in pool halls or playing poker. Why even Nokomis can be met and spoken with, for all that she *is* the spirit of all these worlds, made manifest."

"It's because we're more than the stories," Lucius says. "And less than them. Reduced only, perhaps, because there isn't room in the world for beings of such mythic proportions. So the stories stay big, but the subjects of those stories . . . we become cousins and dreams and old men living forgotten in old houses."

"Doesn't it bother you?" I ask.

"Not even a little. Perhaps I did bring the world into being, but so what? I don't see it as my having done anything more marvelous than someone opening a box to see what's inside. The world goes on the way it will. It doesn't follow my wishes and I wouldn't want it to. That, it would seem to me, is a responsibility that would break anyone."

I don't mention the stories I've heard about his withdrawals from the world—breakdowns, some might say.

"So there's nothing you can do?" I ask instead.

"I didn't say that. I still have a voice. I can still be heard. The old mysteries rest somewhere in my blood and things still happen when I speak. But I don't control those mysteries. I don't know that I ever did. They come and go of their own choosing. Mostly they seem to leave us to muddle through our lives as best we can."

I nod.

"But I will speak to Minisino," he says. "Perhaps he will listen. Perhaps it will make a difference."

"That's all I can ask," I tell him.

I see Chloë smile.

"You seem disappointed," she says.

"I'm not. It's just . . . I'm hearing things I didn't expect. They make perfect sense, of course, but it's just . . ."

"Here's something to remember," Lucius says. "Respect the old spirits. Even venerate them. But don't set them above you. The world in which they lived and the one in which we do are no longer the same."

But a funny thing happens while he tells me that. The room seems to swell with a presence too large to be held by these book-laden walls. Too large to be held by a cousin's mind.

Then the moment's gone and it's only Lucius in the room with me once more. Still massive. Still a big presence. But the scale is so much more normal.

He rises from his seat with a lightness and grace that belies his size.

"Let's go see the buffalo," he says. As I get up, he turns to Chloë. "Can you look into this business with Jilly while we're gone?"

"I will."

"And Odawa . . ."

"I'll have Brandon talk to him."

"I want him alive enough to face trial."

Chloë nodded, a grim look in her eyes. "That's why I won't do it."

At my upraised eyebrows, Lucius explains, "Chloë was very close to your wife at one time and is deeply resentful that she didn't live long enough for them to be reconciled once more."

I want to ask what the rift between them was, but this is neither the time nor the place. For now, I keep my mouth shut and simply follow Lucius as he leaves the library. But when this business with the buffalo is over, I'll have questions for him.

Instead of taking me back through the house, Lucius leads me down another hall that brings us into a large kitchen. He opens the door and after we go through a summer kitchen and another door, we step out into the Rookery's backyard. He looks up at the trees, still filled with all those gossiping blackbird cousins.

"I know you were listening," he says to them. "Now make yourselves useful. Find those bogans for me."

They rise in a noisy cloud of black wings and fly off in all directions. He turns to me and smiles.

"I might only be the memory of that Raven of old," he says, "but they refuse to believe it. Sometimes that can be useful."

"I can see how it would be," I tell him.

But I'm still not completely buying it myself. The way we all feel in his presence, that natural ruling charisma of his . . . there has to be more of a reason behind it than simply his being a memory of the Raven of old.

Those dark eyes of his are studying me, then he smiles again.

"Show me where the buffalo gather," he says.

Christiana

"Okay, here's the thing," Christiana told the fairy court. "At tops, there are maybe fifty actual buffalo soldiers out there looking for your scalps. The rest are all ghosts. Meet them in the between or the otherworld, and they'll cream you—that's a given. But if you make them come to you here, in the human world, you'll only have that fifty to deal with. The others can cross over, but so what? They'll be wraiths in this world. Spooky, yeah, but they can't touch you."

"Are you sure about this?" Tatiana asked.

"I didn't spend all that time in the libraries of Hinterdale just partying."

"I've no idea what that means."

"It means, yes. I'm sure." She paused to give the council a once-over. "You can muster more bodies than you've got gathered here, right?"

"Of course. I'm just not . . ."

The queen's voice trailed off and Christiana nodded.

"You don't trust me," she said.

"It's not so much a matter of trust," Tatiana said, "as that we are in the wrong, not the buffalo."

"Haven't you already said that you didn't have anything to do with it?"

"Yes. But this is still my court. I rule. I am responsible for what my subjects do, even when they do it without my knowledge."

"Okay," Christiana said, "but you can't go to them. You need them to come here."

"You obviously don't understand."

"Oh, I do. You want to take responsibility. You feel you need to tell them that even though it wasn't you, you should still have known and stopped the deaths before they happened."

"Exactly."

"But you don't need to be a martyr to do that," Christiana told her. "You can tell them the same thing here in this world, where they'll number fifty or so instead of in the thousands. The whole martyr thing is really overrated, trust me. It doesn't work for anyone, except maybe Joan of Arc, and she still had to die." Christiana paused a moment, head cocked as she studied the queen. "You don't have a death wish, do you?"

"She's annoying as hell," Mother Crone said before Tatiana could respond, "but she's right."

Around the table, other heads were nodding in agreement. The queen took a moment longer, then gave in to their consensus.

"So, what do you suggest we do?" she asked Christiana.

"Let me go talk to Minisino," Christiana replied, "and see if I can't get him to come into this world to meet with you. What's a common ground close to here?"

"Fitzhenry Park," the queen's captain immediately said. "It's in the city, so we have access to it, but there's enough of the wild and the green in its borders for the green-brees to feel comfortable."

The queen nodded.

"A word of advice," Christiana said as she rose from where she was sitting on the table top. "Don't call them 'green-brees.' You might think you're being clever, but everybody knows it's got something to do with cesspools back in your old country."

"I think we can manage to remember that," the queen said with a dry tone to her voice.

Christiana shrugged. "Whatever."

And then she was gone.

Jilly

When Del steps out of the room, all the anger I feel toward him drains out of me and leaves with him. I watch until the doorjamb blocks him from view, then my gaze turns and settles on Geordie's remains. There wasn't much left of him in the first place, just a mess of dirt and leaves and twigs that had once been a human being. A manlike shape on the floor.

Until Del kicked it apart.

I stare at the scattered pieces with a morbid fascination, but for some reason the anger doesn't return. There's only a deep, painful sadness, swelling up inside me once more, creeping up on me from someplace just out of sight.

This can't be right.

How can Geordie just be *gone*?

But I saw it with my own two eyes. I watched, trapped in this child's body, while the sick freak that is my brother waved his hand and Geordie was gone. Transformed like fairy gold into forest debris.

Once upon a time . . .

If this were a fairy tale, I could get him back. I would have befriended a sparrow, a spoon, an old woman by now, and one of them would help me sew a sweater from nettles, or climb down into the underworld to bring him back.

But it's not a fairy tale. It's just this sick place inside my head, where women are changed into little girls, and little girls have their mouths erased.

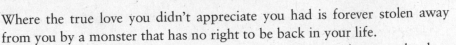

Where the true love you didn't appreciate you had is forever stolen away from you by a monster that has no right to be back in your life.

I get up from the floor where I've been crouching and go out the door into the familiar hall beyond. I know this house so well. Too well. It's been decades since I've set foot in it, but I know its every inch. I can detail every horror that happened to me in it and where it took place.

I see Del at the head of the stairs with that shotgun in his hands.

I see a little red-headed girl . . . Lizzie, I realize, putting the name of the adult woman I knew to those child-sized features. Lizzie at the bottom of the stairs, a blank expanse where her mouth should be.

Between them, I see a yellow dog. Some kind of bull dog—no, pit bull. Charging up the stairs toward Del.

Del aiming the shotgun.

I have a flash of recognition when I see the dog. No, it's more like I know I *know* that dog, but I can't remember where.

It doesn't matter.

Right now, all that matters is that I wasn't lying to Del. I really don't care anymore. I'm not scared of him because there is no worse he can do now that he's taken Geordie away from me. Poor, sweet Geordie, always there, my best friend, my soul mate through thick and thin, my should-have-been true love except we were both too stupid—maybe just too scared—to recognize it.

I'm right behind Del. I know he's about to shoot the dog. I know he can turn around and work his ugly mojo on me with a wave of his hand, with a word, with a look in his eye, and I'll be changed into dust, or deformed like Lizzie, or simply killed like Geordie was.

I don't care.

I'm not scared.

I give Del a push, just as he fires. His shot goes wild, spraying a blast of buckshot into the walls. There's no time for a second one. He doesn't turn on me to work the mojo. He doesn't turn the dog into a newspaper, or mushrooms, or a pile of dirt.

My ears are deafened by the blast of the shotgun in this confined space.

In an eerie silence, filled with the ringing of bells, I watch the dog tear out his throat. Blood sprays everywhere. The two fall on the stairs, man and dog. The shotgun goes clattering down the risers. Del's body follows, blood fountaining from his throat, splattering on the walls, the dog, the risers, Del's clothes.

The dog stumbles, but catches its balance.

Together we watch Lizzie scramble out of the way as first the shotgun, then Del land at the bottom of the stairs where she was standing. The dog turns to me, its muzzle and honey-coloured fur splattered red with my brother's blood, and I remember where I've seen it before. Not it—her. It was in the dense acres of brush and forest that grow along the edges of the Great-wood. She was there to save my life once before, from another human with a gun, except that time it had been Pinky Miller, my little sister's best friend.

There hadn't been any blood then. Just the sick wet sound of Pinky's head cracking on a rock when she fell, knocked down by the dog.

I wouldn't be able to hear that now. My ears are still ringing from the blast of the shotgun.

"Did Joe send you?" I ask.

I can't hear my voice, so I doubt she can either. But I guess I'm thinking the words as I say them, and she seems to be able to talk and listen without the need for sounds, because she answers me all the same.

He asked me to bring him to you, she says inside my head, *but we got separated.*

I sit down on the top riser. When she comes near, I do the thing Joe said I should never do with her because she's not a dog, a pet, she's a person, just wearing a different shape. But I lay my hand on her head all the same and brush her fur with my fingers, trying to get the blood off, but getting comfort from touching her, knowing that she's real and here to help me, not hurt me.

She doesn't seem to mind. She doesn't move away. Instead, she leans in closer to me and then I start to cry. I burrow my face against her bloody fur, sobbing.

I don't notice Lizzie until I feel a small hand on my shoulder. I look up, then away from the smooth expanse of skin where her mouth should be.

Like everything else that's gone wrong, what happened to her is my fault. It doesn't hurt me like the black hole in my chest where the pain over Geordie's death is lodged, but it's there all the same. Another ache of sorrow. Of anger at myself that I let all of this happen.

But I'm done crying now. I'm not done with the pain—I don't think I ever will be—but the tears have stopped.

I sit up straighter, wipe my eyes with my sleeve, then blow my nose on the piece of cloth that Lizzie hands me. I'm not sure what it is. A piece of some old T-shirt. A rag. It doesn't matter. It does the job.

It's okay, the dog says. *It's over. You're safe—at least for now.*

"Safe?" I say. "What does it matter? Geordie's dead and look at Lizzie. Nothing's ever going to be okay again."

Geordie's . . . dead . . . ? Lizzie says.

I can feel the weight of sorrow swelling inside me again and can only manage to give a slow nod. But then something occurs to me.

"Unless . . ." I say. "This is all happening somewhere in my head, right?"

The dog nods. *So it appears.*

"So maybe it's not real. Maybe we'll just wake up and Geordie will be fine and Lizzie gets her mouth back and we'll be free of Del . . ."

My voice trails off as she shakes her head.

It's not that easy, she says. *Not as long as you leave the memory of your brother sitting in some dark, hidden place of your mind.*

"But what am I supposed to do? How can I stop that?"

My hearing's coming back because my words are now louder than that weird sound like bells ringing in my ears.

I don't know.

I make myself look at Lizzie.

"I'm so sorry," I tell her.

She shakes her head. *You didn't bring me here.*

I suppose I should be surprised that she's got the talking-in-your-head thing down, too, but I don't think anything can really surprise me anymore. But the fact that she can still communicate, even without a mouth, makes me feel a little hopeful until I realize that she still can't eat. What's she going to do if we ever manage to get back? Spend the rest of her life on an IV just to get nourishment?

This is the bogans' fault, she says. *If it wasn't for you and Honey, who knows what that monster would be doing to me now.*

So that's the dog's name. Honey.

My arm is still around her and she stays close to me, making no sign that she wants me to remove it.

I look down the stairs to where Del still lies in a pool of blood.

"I keep expecting him to get up again," I say.

He probably will, Honey says. *Unless . . .*

Her voice trails off, and I think of all the well-meaning advice about forgiveness, usually delivered by someone who's never had my kind of life, who only sees the world through rose-coloured glasses.

"Unless what?" I ask. "This isn't going to turn into some bullshit after school special, is it? You know, where I'm just supposed to forgive him and everything'll be fine."

No, she replies. *You're supposed to forgive yourself for thinking you were to blame for what he did to you. For thinking you deserved it.*

"Oh, man. You don't think I feel like that, do you?"

The dog turns her head so that she's looking right at me.

I don't know, she says. *What do you feel?*

Lost. Hurt. Broken. Brokenhearted. Scared, but not of Del or anyone like him. I'm scared of having to face the rest of my life without Geordie in it.

But I don't want to talk about that. I don't think I *can* talk about it. But I feel I need to talk about something or the black hole of Geordie's loss is going to rise up again and swallow me whole. So I change the subject.

"How come Del didn't have any power over you?" I ask the dog.

I will not let anyone have power over me, she replies. *Not ever again. I refuse to believe it.*

"So it's a matter of willpower."

Belief certainly plays a part.

"I have willpower. Ask my friends and they'll describe me as willful."

I feel a smile in my mind that comes from her.

"So why didn't it work for me?" I ask.

She looks away. I wait, but she doesn't answer. I guess she's already told me once and sees no reason to repeat it.

It's because I think I deserve it.

"Then what about Lizzie?" I ask. "And . . ." It's so hard to say his name. "And Geordie?"

They believe this place is true.

That can't be true, Lizzie says. *I don't believe. I didn't believe in any of this.*

This what? Honey asks.

All this weird stuff that's been happening to me. Not at first. Not even when I got here inside . . . inside Jilly's head.

"It's totally weird to me, too," I assure her.

Lizzie looks back down at the bottom of the stairs to where Del is lying. Her hand reaches up to touch the smooth expanse of skin between her chin and nose.

But then . . . , she says. *Then, when he turned us into kids and did this to me . . .*

It's difficult, Honey agrees. *And confusing. I can feel the wooden stairs under me. I can smell the world around me. The dust, your bodies, the blood. And if Jilly hadn't thrown off his aim, I would have felt the impact of that shotgun blast. I would have been hurt. I'd probably be dead.*

"So it's only you yourself that he couldn't touch," I say. "He couldn't *manipulate* you the way he did us."

Honey gives me a slow nod.

"This is all so sick and weird. I can't believe it's coming from inside me."

It's not coming from you, Honey tells me. *It comes from the piece of your brother that's still inside you.*

I give a slow nod. "But I don't know how to get rid of it. I know it's not my fault, what he did to me, but still . . . I don't know. All my memories of that time are so messed up and confusing . . ."

I look at Honey, look into her eyes, and see a clarity that I wish I could have. I know she had it just as bad as I did—Joe told me about it, how it made a connection between us. Two Children of the Secret. It was what let her find me the last time, when no one else could. But she's dealt with it.

We should go, she says. She gives Del's body a meaningful look. *Before he comes back.*

I know she's right. Del *will* come back. He'll get up and be just the same as he was. Or maybe he'll come back all bloody, his head dangling from a broken neck like some zombie in a horror flick.

"Go where?" I ask.

This world was closed until he . . . died. It's open now. I don't know how long it will last, but right now, we can leave.

"And then what? Nothing will have changed."

I don't know. Maybe Joe will be able to figure something out. But we need to leave.

"I can't," I say, even as I'm nodding in agreement.

I know she's right. But I can't leave the pieces of what had once been Geordie scattered across the room where he'd died.

"Not without Geordie," I add.

You want to bring his body? Lizzie asks.

"I can't leave it here. If we—" No, that's not right. I amend it to: "*When* we find a way to put everything back to normal, we'll need it."

Because that's the little thread of hope that I'm hanging on to. Without it, I've got nothing. Without it, Geordie's dead and gone forever. But there's magic in the world.

Once upon a time . . .

We just need help.

If we can find someone to give Lizzie back her mouth and return us both to our proper ages, then they'll be able to bring Geordie back, too.

It *has* to work that way.

Once upon a time . . .

Is he a little kid, too? Lizzie asks.

I shake my head. "Not exactly."

I take hold of the banister and pull myself to my feet. I give Del's body a last glance—still dead—and lead the way into the bedroom. Lizzie and Honey follow me, Honey's nails clicking on the wooden floor.

I know what they see when we step inside. An empty room except for the old bed with the mattress on it. And the mess of dirt and leaves and twigs that is all that's left of Geordie.

Where . . . where is he? Lizzie asks.

I point to the debris.

But . . .

"Del turned him into this thing made of leaves and dirt and then kicked him apart."

Lizzie just stands in the doorway, staring. Honey pads slowly into the room, her gaze taking in the mess that Del left on the floor.

This is impossible, she says. *We can never gather it all up.*

"We can," I tell her. "We have to."

Once upon a time . . .

They try to talk me out of it, but in the end I go down to the kitchen, sidling past Del's body, expecting him to sit up and grab me as I go by. The blood is congealing, and there are flies all over him. I find a pail, a dustpan, and a hand broom and take them back up the stairs, where I spend the next fifteen minutes sweeping up the debris that was once my Geordie and transferring it into the pail.

When every speck of dirt, every bit of leaf, that I can find is removed from the floor and put into the bucket, I work at the bristles of the broom, making sure everything's in there. The whole time I'm working, Lizzie kneeling on the floor beside me to help, I'm trying not to think of what the debris represents. I try not to think of Geordie, but how can I not?

Every time I start to despair, I repeat the words in my head—

Once upon a time . . .

—and keep on working.

Now I lay the broom down. I lay the rag that Lizzie gave me earlier across the dirt and leaves to keep them from coming out and pick up the pail. I turn to Honey.

"I'm ready," I say. "Can we still get out?"

She nods. *Put your hands on my shoulders. Keep contact with me.*

Lizzie had stepped out into the hall. She rejoins us, lays her hand on the honey-coloured fur beside mine. Two tiny hands. Children's hands.

He's still dead, she says.

I think she means Geordie, but then realize she's talking about Del.

Get ready, Honey tells us.

I tighten my grip—one hand in her short fur, the other around the handle of the pail. I see—feel—the world dissolve around us.

Just before it's gone, I hear a voice.

An awful, familiar voice.

Del.

Shouting.

I can't make out what he's saying, but then it's gone, the old farmhouse and world it was in, are all gone. We stand blinking in bright sunlight. We're on some kind of plateau, looking out over mile after endless mile of red rock and badlands. I let go my grip of Honey's fur and step away, my legs a little wobbly. I look at my free hand—still child size. When I turn, I see Lizzie's still a little girl, too. She still has no mouth.

Where are we? she asks.

In some part of the otherworld, Honey replies. *I don't know if it has a name. It's where I was when I crossed over to the world I found you in.*

She looks around, nose lifting to smell the air.

I thought Joe would still be here, she adds.

"Joe was with you?" I ask.

She nods. *But something happened just before I got into your world, and I lost hold of him.*

"But he's okay?"

I can't imagine losing anybody else.

It's Joe—what could happen to him? *But I thought he'd be waiting . . .*

She's still looking around, still trying to get some scent from the air.

"What is it?" I ask. "What are you looking for?"

I'm not sure. It felt like something crossed over with us, but it's gone now. I can't sense it anymore.

I swallow nervously, remembering what I'd heard just as we were leaving.

"Did it feel like . . . my brother?" I ask.

No. It was more . . . gentle.

She gives herself a shake, as though to wake herself up.

We should get down from this mesa, she adds, *and see if we can find out what happened to Joe. Once we get to the bottom, I can take us more quickly to where you can rest and have a drink.*

Why can't you do it right away? Lizzie asks.

I want to check for signs of Joe on the path first.

She starts to trot down what appears to be a faint trail of some kind, coming back when she realizes that we aren't keeping up.

Are you all right? she asks. *Were either of you injured in that other world?*

We shake our heads.

"We're just little kids," I say. "Physically, I mean. We can't go as fast as you in this heat."

The pail with Geordie's remains is totally weighing me down as well, but I don't want to bring that up and have another discussion about how I should just leave it behind.

I'll take it slower, Honey says.

Lizzie falls in behind her and I take up the rear, switching the pail's weight from one hand to the other. It's so dry and hot here. I was already tired from all we had to go through with Del, and I'm thirsty now, as well. Lizzie must be, too. That makes me worry about how she'll even be able to take a drink.

I've been staring at my feet, being careful of where I step. Looking up, I see that I've fallen behind, so I try to pick up my pace. That's when I trip and lose my balance. I try to hold on to the pail, but it falls from my hand and goes tumbling down the steep slope, clattering and banging against the red rock, spraying the debris that was all that was left of Geordie in its wake.

I scrape my knee, but manage to grab on to a rock and not follow the pail down the slope. I watch it go until it finally hits the ground far below. My vision blurs with tears.

Once upon a time . . .

I see a painting in my head, a big red-dirt desert stretching as far as the eye can see, and everywhere there's little pieces of Geordie scattered. The twigs and leaves, rattling across stone outcrops and dropping into arroyos. The dirt turning to dust and blowing from one end of the horizon to the other.

The painting's real. It's there whether I close my eyes or not.

Once upon a time . . .

I was going to do better than all the king's soldiers and put him back together again.

I was going to spin straw into gold and buy him back from the underworld.

I was going to weave a nettle coat and wear it until the end of my days in trade for his life.

I would have done anything.

Once upon a time . . .

But that hope's gone now. I can't possibly gather up all the debris that went skittering down the side of the mesa. The dirt and leaves and twigs.

I'm not aware of Lizzie and Honey coming back to where I've fallen until Lizzie touches my arm.

Oh, Jilly, she says.

I can't speak. I can't do anything but stare at that tiny pail far below. Some of the dirt that spilled from it is close at hand, dark and moist where it lies on the red sand and rock. The heat's so intense that I can watch it dry out and turn into dust while I crouch here, one arm around the rock that saved me from falling as well.

We need to keep moving, Honey says. *We need to get out of the sun.*

She's right. We do. Or at least they do.

I don't care anymore.

I could take being the Broken Girl and losing my art. Just like I took the horrible years of Del hurting me and the foster homes and then my running away and living on the streets. I could even take the nightmare of being stuck somewhere in my own head, reliving it all over again.

But I can't take losing Geordie.

Not like this.

If he were in love with another woman again, or had just moved away . . .

But he isn't and he didn't.

He came to rescue me and got turned into dirt and crap that I've now managed to dump all over the side of this mesa.

Once upon a time . . .

Fairy tales saved my life as a kid, but they can't help me anymore.

Rabedy

Rabedy managed to change back into his bogan shape, fully clothed, though the clothes were a poor fit. The trouser legs were too short, the shirt tight around the shoulders, its tails far too long. But for the moment, it was the best he could do. It was much harder to speak. He couldn't even get one word out to respond to the cerva spirit's question, to explain why he had summoned her.

"Uh . . ."

Seeing her in her human form, her killing seemed far more a murder than it had when she'd been a deer.

He knew there were bogans who would as happily cut a flank steak from a human as they would from an animal, but he wasn't one of them. Even Big Dan wasn't. Truth was, Rabedy would just as soon live on vegetables and fruits and nuts. He rarely ate meat and never cared for hunting. But he'd been out there in the green and the wild all the same, out with Big Dan and the rest of them, Odawa's protection keeping them safe, though the same couldn't be said for the green-brees they'd been hunting.

"There is something familiar about you, little man," the cerva said.

Anwatan, Rabedy remembered hearing somewhere. Her name had been Anwatan. It wasn't some nameless beast they'd murdered in the forest, but a cerva with a name and a family and a spirit that lived on.

"*Why* are you familiar?" Anwatan asked.

"I . . . I . . ."

Now was the time to use his new-learned talent, to change into a dog and flee, flee, flee . . .

Except he couldn't. He couldn't think of himself or his fear or what was going to happen to him. He could only try to set things right before he had to pay for his part in her murder.

"I killed you," he said.

The cerva spirit frowned and studied him for a long moment.

"I don't remember you," she finally said. "They were little men like you, but their scents were different."

"I didn't shoot the arrows—at least not any that even came close to hitting you. But I was there. I was in that stupid company of murderers."

She continued to study him, then slowly nodded.

"I remember now," she said. "You stood back from the others when they ran in to finish me off. But you lifted no hand against me."

"I was still with them."

"And if you were," she said, "why do you call me up now?"

"To . . . to make repayment."

"You can bring me back to life?"

"No, I . . . did you know that the cerva are going to war over your murder?"

She gave a slow nod. "Not all the cerva. Only the buffalo clans."

"A lot of innocents will die—your people, as well as fairy."

"I know."

Rabedy couldn't tell from her simple response if she thought that was a good or a bad thing.

"It doesn't seem right," he quickly went on. "Killing them won't bring you or anyone else back. It'll only make things worse between fairy and your people."

"And yet amends must be made."

"That's why I'm here."

"You said as much," Anwatan said. "So tell me, how were you planning to make amends?"

"I was there," Rabedy told her. "I was part of it. I want to give myself up to your people so that they can hang me or stab me or do whatever it is that your people do to your enemies. That way, justice will be served, and there'll be no need for a war."

"But you didn't kill me."

"It doesn't matter. I was with them. I didn't stop them. And you weren't the first they killed."

She nodded. "And what part am I to play in this?"

"I thought you could come with me. I know they won't listen to me. They'll probably just kill me before I can explain, and the war will still go on. But if you speak for me, they'll listen. They have to listen to you."

She looked away, her gaze going beyond him into the dark woods above the cove where they stood.

"What makes you think that will be enough?" she asked.

"I . . ."

"We would have you, but the rest of you little men—the ones who actually killed me—they would continue to run free, able to kill again."

Rabedy shook his head. "The Queen will see that they're punished. She must know by now and no matter what you think, she would never let something like this go unresolved."

"You can promise this?"

How? Rabedy thought. Even if he could ever gain an audience with the Queen, nothing bound her to the promise of some Unseelie bogan. And besides, he'd already be dead anyway.

"You seem uncertain now," Anwatan said.

"It's just . . . I'm nobody. I know the Queen will do the right thing when she has the facts—she's not stupid or malicious—but I can't *make* her. No one's going to listen to this bogan. I can only promise what I'm already doing: offering myself up to your people so that justice of some kind can be done."

"What is your name, little man?" the cerva spirit asked.

Rabedy shivered. Give her his name and she could command him. But for this he didn't hesitate.

"Rabedy Collins," he told her.

She repeated it after him, then nodded.

"Thank you," she said. "That is your true name."

She fell silent and Rabedy waited for what she would do to him now. He got a nervous tick in his cheek, and he had to plant his weight on his right leg to stop it from shaking. It didn't help.

"This is my death," she said, "so I should have some say in how amends are made."

She looked at Rabedy as though expecting a response, and he quickly nodded.

"So this is what we will do," she said. "We will go to my kin and your Queen. We will give them the names of the guilty. If we can make Minisino see reason, there will be no war, but there will be justice."

"Will the buffalo wait?" Rabedy asked.

"We won't know until we ask them, will we?"

Oh, this didn't feel good, Rabedy thought. Maybe this hadn't been such a good idea. Why should the buffalo listen to some useless bogan's story any more than the Queen would?

But Anwatan was right. It was her death. So it should be her decision to make.

"I'm ready to take my punishment," he said.

"I don't include you in this," she told him. "If I have my way, your punishment will be to live with knowing how you stood aside while evil was done. It's not a mistake you'll make again."

"No, I won't. But—"

"I won't argue this," Anwatan said. "Yes, you stood by while I was killed, but you raised no hand against me, and you have enough honour to come to me to make amends."

"No, I was going to say something else. You should know that while it was bogans who killed you, it was one of your own who gave us safe passage through the wild and the green."

"Was it now."

"His name is Odawa—Odawajameg, of the salmon clan. He appears to be blind—I think he really is—but he doesn't seem to have much trouble getting around when he needs to."

"He gave you safe passage?"

Rabedy nodded. "And taught us to shapechange the way your people do, although I was the only one with any luck at actually learning the trick."

"Show me again," she said.

So he did. He changed from bogan to dog, as he had done earlier from dog to bogan when she'd spoken to him. Effortlessly. So effortlessly he couldn't understand why it had ever seemed hard.

Anwatan nodded when he stood before her as a bogan once more. This time he'd managed to get his clothes to fit better.

"There's no scent of fairy on you after you changed," she said.

"Really?"

"This makes it worse."

Rabedy knew just what she was thinking. With this knowledge, bogans could go where they wanted in the wild and the green. They could creep up on unsuspecting cousins without the need of being shielded by someone like Odawa.

"We will deal with him, too," Anwatan said. "But first we must find my father."

"Your father?"

"He is the clan chief of the deer."

"I . . . I didn't know that."

Rabedy's heart sank. So, not only had he been a part of murdering a person, now it turned out she was also a princess. No wonder war was on the horizon. He was only surprised that her own clan wasn't standing shoulder to shoulder with the buffalo clan.

Carefully—because he didn't want to appear to be slighting her kin—he asked her about that.

"We are a people of peace," she said. "My father would have seen that reparation was made, but not this way. The buffalo have always been the warriors among the cerva, and they have old grievances with your people that go beyond the death of a few of the deer people."

"I didn't mean—"

"I took no insult from your question," she said. "They have their way and we have ours. We are not without anger or defenses. But we prefer the peaceful solution. Two wrongs will never make a right."

"But still . . ."

She nodded. "Yes, amends must still be made so that those such as your erstwhile companions won't feel that they can do whatever they wish without fear of punishment."

"People can be so horrible, can't they?"

"But they also have the potential inside them for great good, too, Rabedy Collins. It's true we cannot *make* them turn from doing wrong. But we can set an example by how we live our own lives."

"Do you think it makes a difference?"

"Everything we do makes a difference," she told him. "The onus is upon us as to whether the difference we make is for good or evil." She paused a beat, then added, "I will go find my father. Wait for me here."

And then she was gone.

Rabedy stared down at the fire, then let his gaze drift out across the open water of the lake.

He knew they were doing the right thing. Giving up Big Dan and the others would stop so many innocents from dying. But if he was doing the right thing, why did he feel so guilty? Why did it feel so wrong?

Timony

After he had called up a half-dozen knives out of the sand, Timony knew it was well past time to stop. He looked at the weapons lined up in front of him, six razor-sharp blades that gleamed brightly, even in this dull light. Six of them were enough. More than enough, considering that he only had two hands. But cajoling and teasing the sand to take these new shapes had at least kept him busy while he waited. Now there was nothing to occupy him except the enveloping fog, his own worried thoughts, and just out of his view, the morose sound of the waves falling upon the shore.

None of them was particularly appealing, so after awhile he let himself doze. There was no cozy hedgerow at hand, nor a warm tree to wrap him in its deep roots, but he was still able to forget this cool, foggy beach on which he'd set up camp to wait for either Lizzie or Geordie to return—at least he could forget it enough to drift off. He didn't fall into a deep sleep like the one in which the fish man had caught him unaware, back in the Aisling's Wood. It was more a light dreaming, a half-awake wander through a dreamscape where the sun shone cheerfully bright, gleaming on the white caps, and the rhythm of the waves on the shore was comforting rather than sullen. Gulls wheeled and dipped above, and there was only one cloud in that otherwise clear blue sky.

He studied it, vaguely considering its shape. Was it like a turtle—if you ignored that big bit on the left—or more like syrup pooling on a stack of pancakes in some goodwife's kitchen?

Hunger woke a faint rumble in his stomach, and he considered convincing some of the seaweed draped upon the sand into becoming something more to his liking. Scones, perhaps. Or a fat slice of ham. Perhaps both, with plenty of syrup and a side dish of—

His eyes snapped open and he jumped to his feet, a knife held ready in each hand, before he realized what had brought him out of his half-sleep to stand here, awake and alert upon the sand.

Lizzie.

She'd escaped that locked world. In fact . . .

Yes, the world was open now, but that didn't matter because Lizzie was free of it.

He let his mind range wide, focusing on where she was, but before he could step away to join her, he realized he was no longer alone on this shore.

He turned slowly around, trying to pierce the fog. Though he didn't sense danger, he held the knives by their blades, locked between thumbs and fingers, ready to be thrown.

"Who's there?" he asked after a moment.

He got no response, but he sensed confusion in whoever was hiding from him.

"I know where you are," he lied. "If you don't step out where I can see you, you'll be trying to tug one of these blades out of your throat, see if you won't."

Though there was still no response, he didn't throw the knives. There was no point. Because now he realized that floating out there in the fog was a spirit. Bodiless. Voiceless. The spirit of what, he had no idea. All he could sense from it was the confusion and a sadness. No malevolence.

And it was beginning to drift away from him, losing itself in the fog.

"Wait!" he called after it. "Don't go. I can help you find a voice, and then you can tell me what you need."

Because when they were left behind like this, spirits always needed something.

Usually, if the will was strong enough to keep them from going on to wherever the dead went when they were done with their bodies, they were also strong enough to give themselves a shape and make their needs understood. But some were helpless. They existed more in the next world than in this, but were unable to move on.

"Come to me," he said.

He let the knives drop onto the sand and began to gather driftwood and seaweed, shells and whatever other flotsam he could find upon the sand. When he had as much as he needed, he pushed it all together in the rough shape of a man.

"You see?" he said. "You can wear this and tell me who you are, what you need."

Then he began to use that gift of his, convincing the spirit to enter his makeshift man, the changeling shape to hold that spirit and allow it to take on a semblance of life.

This was an old knowledge he worked with. Normally, one wouldn't make room for a spirit in the changeling. It was only meant to last long enough to replace the child or human that had been taken away. The poor twig and leaf creature was expected to die quickly, leaving the survivors something to bury.

This was different, but not so different that he couldn't see the way to bind the two together. Not permanently—nothing could be permanent with a body such as this—but certainly long enough for him to speak with it.

"Yes, yes," he said softly. "That's it. There's nothing to hurt you in this body I've made for you. It's all found debris, washed up on the shore. Natural. No spells on it. Nothing to bind you to it, just here for you to use while you will."

Spirits like this were such funny things. They wanted to be bound back into the world, but at the same time they couldn't abide the binding.

"There, there," he said, as first an arm twitched, then a foot. "See how comfortable it is. Made just for you, and you can cast it off any time you like. You don't need my promise to know I speak true. You can feel it in the changeling, can't you?"

It was a thing of his making, but Timony still took a step back when the creature sat up.

Oh, it was a marvel, this calling up magic. Wasn't it just?

I . . . feel really weird . . .

Timony blinked. He knew that voice echoing in his head.

"Geordie?" he said.

Its two seashell eyes looked down at its body, then lifted to the doonie's face.

What . . . what did you do to me? Geordie asked.

"Gave you a body and a voice," Timony told him. "That's all. I . . . oh, lad, who did this to you? Who killed you?"

I'm . . . dead?

Timony nodded.

But . . .

Geordie held his arms in front of his face, seaweed wrapped around pieces of driftwood. He tried to touch his fingers to each other, but the doonie hadn't made them particularly flexible. He hadn't been trying for an exact anything, since he'd had no idea what the body that once housed the spirit had originally been. Mostly, he'd concentrated on the changeling's head, giving it sight and hearing and a voice.

"I'm sorry, lad," he said. "This is the best I could do with what I had at hand."

Geordie didn't reply. He let his hands drop. It was impossible to read an expression in that grotesque face of his, but the doonie could feel the continuing waves of confusion and despair coming from him.

"What happened to you?" Timony asked.

Geordie told him. It wasn't a long story. He'd arrived in the bedroom of some old farmhouse where he'd had a few moments to be with Jilly before her brother had changed him into a creature much like the one Timony had just built to hold his spirit. And then Del had kicked *that* changeling apart.

But do you know what she said? he added. *She said I was the only thing she ever really cared about.*

When he spoke of Jilly, he gained a strength and an inner glow.

This was the thing that was keeping his spirit here, Timony thought. Except . . .

"Tell me again what he did," the doonie said. "When he made that changeling of his."

There wasn't much to it, it happened so fast. He just appeared in the doorway . . .

Timony listened carefully as Geordie repeated that part of his story, interrupting him a couple of times to make sure had the details right.

"Maybe you're not dead," he said. "That world you found her in is still open. We can go back and put together the changeling Del kicked apart. If he could convince your body to turn into the creature, I can make it go back to what you were."

It's not there anymore, Geordie said. *Jilly scraped it all together into a pail and took it with her.*

"And she's with Lizzie?"

Geordie nodded. *With Lizzie and the dog. Her name's Honey.*

"That's still good," Timony told him. "We'll go to them."

And you can do this?

The doonie nodded confidently.

"So long as she gathered up all the parts of the changeling her brother made," he said.

Geordie stood up and teetered for a moment on legs made of driftwood, held together with seaweed.

Then what are we waiting for? he asked.

Walker

In the beginning, there was only Walker standing alone on the plain, a solitary bulwark to protect the courts of fairy from the buffalo army that Minisino had raised against them. The worst of it was that Walker didn't even want to be here. His sympathies, if they were to be counted, lay with the buffalo, to the clans with whom his own people were kin. Not to fairy.

It was his daughter that was dead.

It was he who should be seeking vengeance.

But not like this. Not through war. That was never the way of his own clan. For them, all life was sacred and the taking of it—even from an enemy—left a scar on the soul that never went away, even after the prescribed cleansing and healing ceremonies had been undertaken.

There were no exceptions. Not even in the defense of one's own territories and life. The scars remained forever—in this world, and in the next.

Walker wouldn't allow it—not in his daughter's name.

The stomp dance, the drumming, the chanting, the thunder of the buffalo didn't stop, didn't even pause, when he took up his defensive position. But he knew they were aware of him. He knew they saw the tall tines of his antlers scraping at the sky, the determination in the set of his shoulders, the stillness in him when everything that defined them at this moment was sound and movement. They didn't call for him to join them, but they made no threatening move toward him, either. He wasn't sure if it was out of respect for his recent loss, or because they knew that one antlered forest lord standing against so many buffalo soldiers would make no difference when they finally marched on the fairy courts.

After a time, Minisino stepped out of the crowd to face him. Walker wore the shape of a man, tall and broad-shouldered with the wide spread of his antlers rising high, but the buffalo war chief still loomed over him, taller, broader of shoulder, shaggy as only these plains cousins could be.

They faced each other in a long silence until Minisino finally raised a hand and silenced the war dance. The ensuing quiet seemed as loud as the thundering drums and stomping hooves had earlier and left a ringing in Walker's ears. He could still hear the drumming, but soon realized it was the sound of his own pulse, still keeping time to the rhythm of the now silent stomp dance.

As the quiet lengthened, deepened, the two cerva studied each other, neither speaking.

There was something wrong here, Walker thought. No, not exactly wrong, but not exactly right, either. He knew the politics behind this move of Minisino's, how it was time for all the injustices against the cerva clans and tribes to be set right, beginning with Anwatan's death and stretching back to the great herds of buffalo that had been slaughtered with the coming of the Europeans and the aganesha who stowed away on their great ships as they crossed the ocean. Trolls and bogans, hidden deep in the holds. Fairies riding invisible on the rigging.

A reckoning was not only required, it was long past due.

It was an old, unhappy argument.

At one time, when he was a young buck, Walker might have been swayed to join Minisino's army. But while he'd seen too much of the hurt and trouble of the world, he'd also seen the good in it. And he knew the spiritual leaders of the cerva spoke the truth when they named all life sacred, even that of one's enemy.

So, while yes, Walker agreed, it *had* been better before the Europeans had come, that was many, many moons and seasons ago. The world changed, whether you wanted it to or not. It had changed from when Raven first called it up out of the long ago, and it would continue to change. The great tribes of buffalo could not be brought back. Anwatan, and those who had died these past few months as she had . . . they could not be brought back, either. Attacking all humans, or all fairy, would change nothing except to leave a dark stain on the soul of any cousin who took part in this war.

Minisino obviously disagreed. With the count of recent deaths mounting, more and more of his clan came to side with him until finally Pijaki-tibik, the old war chief, was ousted and Minisino claimed the title.

There had always been coals of anger smoldering deep in Minisino's eyes, but today Walker sensed that anger was older than the injustice of Anwatan's death and had little to do with vengeance for the thousands slain by the Europeans with their rifles and knives, who left their bodies to rot on the plains, taking only their skins.

But Walker couldn't work his way through to the source of that anger, and now was not the time to try. With the army listening, he could only use the argument to which he had an undeniable right.

"You need to step aside, old man," Minisino finally said.

Walker glared at him. "I will not allow you to do this in Anwatan's name."

"Perhaps you haven't noticed: you are only one and we are many."

"You have no right to take my vengeance," Walker told him. "It is mine to take. Mine to decide the when and the where and the how."

"Of course," Minisino said. "But this is not for Anwatan, though we could certainly include her vengeance in ours. We do this for all the cerva the aganesha have butchered. The time of reckoning has finally come."

"This is wrong. When one of the herd breaks a leg in a prairie dog's hole, do you declare war on all prairie dogs?"

Minisino shook his head. "Except these aganesha are not innocent. Have you forgotten so quickly how they butchered your daughter?"

Walker had to take a breath to steady himself, but it was still hard to keep his sorrow and his own anger in check.

"Bogans killed Anwatan," he said finally. "A handful of them. You declare war on all fairies."

"I repeat: they are none of them innocent. Those who haven't raised a hand against us have still stood aside while the damage was done. They treat us like vermin in our own land. I say again, a reckoning is long overdue."

"I won't allow it."

Minisino nodded.

"Except standing there alone as you are," he said, "there's not a damn thing you can do to stop us."

"Do you want me to beg you?" Walker said. "Is that what it will take?"

"No," Minisino said. "I want you to—"

But he was cut off by a stranger's voice before he could finish.

"Or maybe you want me to beg," the newcomer said.

They had appeared out of nowhere, the two men who approached them now.

No, not men, Walker realized. But cousins. The collective surprise of the gathered buffalo echoed in his own chest when he realized who the larger of the two was.

Ayabe, the moose lord.

And with him . . .

An instinctual nervousness tracked up his spine when he saw the coyote in Ayabe's companion—a cerva's natural response to a predator—and he immediately looked for the rest of the pack. But the two were alone and Walker made himself relax. What could one canid do in such a gathering of cerva? And after all, he was in Ayabe's company.

Ayabe.

Walker could count on one hand the times he'd seen the elusive cerva lord. There were always stories of his carousing in far-off places, of week-long poker games and story sessions that went on longer still. But the only glimpses Walker had ever had were from a distance, the proud moose lord ghosting through the cedar woods, or spied in the shallows of a lake, high in the mountains, seen one moment, gone the next. Walker couldn't *ever* remember hearing of Ayabe involving himself in a situation such as this. By winter fires, when the stories were told, if a hero went to Ayabe for aid, he was told that whatever trouble you got yourself into, it was up to you to extract yourself from it.

Walker turned his attention back to Minisino. The buffalo war chief had already recovered from his own surprise.

"An admirable show of concern," he told Ayabe, "for one who, by all accounts, otherwise expresses so little interest in the welfare of his people."

Ayabe frowned. "You are not my people. I rule no one."

"Yet here you are, expecting us to forget hundreds of years of murder and death, because your views differ from ours."

"You have no idea why I am here," Ayabe told him. "I have yet to speak."

"I think it's quite clear. You expect us to defer to—"

"I am an individual," Ayabe broke in, "just as we are all individuals, though you seem to forget that, or why would a herd mentality have you all following the foolishness of whoever has the loudest voice?"

"You—"

"I don't agree with this war and I am here to explain why. But I don't rule you. Each of you must make up your own mind as to why you are willing to go to war."

"We have concerns—"

"Everyone has concerns," yet another new voice said, "though most of us don't express them in war."

If Ayabe's appearance was a surprise, Raven's was a complete shock. Walker couldn't remember the last time he'd heard of Raven leaving the neighbourhood of his roost, little say involving himself in the business of others. He came with one corbae for a companion, but he didn't need a show of force to command attention. He had such an imposing authority that even Ayabe was overshadowed by his presence.

Walker looked from one to the other and couldn't understand how two of the most powerful of the cousins, two known to distance themselves from the troubles of the world, had been brought together in this place, at this time. Then yet another group appeared on the plain—a handful of humans led by a cousin, part dog, part crow—and Walker began to get an inkling.

Joseph Crazy Dog.

He knew those crazy clown eyes. Everybody did. The stories surrounding this crow dog cousin were endless—mostly tall tales, Walker had always assumed. Now he wasn't so sure, because this was just like one of those improbable stories told late at night around a campfire. Who else but Crazy Dog would find a way to bring both Ayabe and Raven here? And while this was unlike either of them, it was classic Crazy Dog, considering how each story told of him began with his involving himself in everybody's and anybody's business. At least, he did so if he thought there was a wrong that needed to be set right.

So it had to be Crazy Dog's doing. And if Walker needed more confirmation . . . while he didn't know Raven's companion, he now recognized the canid that had come with Ayabe: Whiskey Jack, a well-known companion of Crazy Dog's.

But power didn't always equate control. One look at Minisino's face told Walker that neither the presence of the two great cousins nor the potential threat they represented would be enough to stop him.

They would have to physically move against him.

They would have to spill his blood.

And if it came to that, the buffalo army would not stand idly by.

If these were all the game pieces Crazy Dog had to bring to the board, they were no closer to ending this problem than they had been before their arrival. In fact, by bringing Ayabe and Raven to argue his case, Crazy Dog might have made things worse.

There were few as stubborn as Minisino. With such great cousins standing against him, he would only be all the more determined to see this through in his own way.

Joe

Joe was in an excellent mood. Just before he led Cassie and the remaining members of Knotted Cord into the between to confront the buffalo army, he'd suddenly lifted his head and a big smile creased his features. That earned him a puzzled look from Cassie.

"I know they call you Crazy Dog," she said, "but what can you possibly find to smile about right now? And if you give me that old 'it's a good day to die' line, I'll whack you so hard you'll wish you were dead."

He turned and kissed her, then said, "Honey came through. She got Jilly out of that damned place. Can't you feel it?"

As soon as he spoke the words, he could see that she did and her smile matched his own.

"What about Lizzie?" Siobhan asked. "Is she okay?"

Joe turned to look at the fiddler with her arm in a sling and her eyes full of hope.

"I'm sorry," he said, "but I don't know her well enough to be able to sense if she's with them. But someone's there, and I know she's female."

"It's got to be Lizzie, right?"

"We can hope," Joe told her. "But we've got other business right now."

With that he stepped into the between, the others following on his heels. He'd expected that they'd be alone with Walker—just the handful of them facing off against the buffalo army—but when he got there, he grinned again. Good old Jack. He and Grey had brought in the big guns.

Maybe this was going to work out after all. Maybe nobody had to get hurt.

"Well, what do you know?" he said as he strolled over to Walker. "The gang's all here."

He heard an unhappy sigh come from where Lucius was standing, but he ignored the old corbae doing his Buddha thing, just as he did the impressive moose lord, standing tall on his right. He gave Walker a friendly nod, then met Minisino's glare with his crazy clown gaze. Knowing Jilly was safe, all his worries were channelled into so much energy he felt like grabbing a drum from one of those buffalo soldiers and doing his own dance. But while he couldn't crank down the mad light in his eyes, he managed to stand still and keep his voice calm.

"So, what do you say, Minisino?" he asked. "Can I take up a moment of your time?"

He rolled a cigarette as he spoke, had it made and lit in less time than it would take someone else to shake a Lucky Strike out of its pack. He blew a wreath of blue-grey smoke and offered it to the buffalo war chief.

What's the situation, Jack? he asked, speaking mind to mind and narrowing the focus of his thoughts so that only Jack could hear him.

Pretty much a mess, Jack replied. *This thing's like a powder keg that's about to explode. Minisino's got a stick up his ass the size of a redwood, and he's not interested in listening to anybody—not even the powerhouses we've got lined up here.*

Got it, Joe sent back.

Minisino made no move to take the proffered cigarette.

"There will be no peace smoke between us, mongrel," he said.

"It's not a peace smoke," Joe told him. "Just an offer of respect before we start in on this thing. I mean, you've got to know a whole lot of people are unhappy about how it's playing out."

"What happens here today is cerva business," Minisino said, his voice flat. "It concerns no one else."

The war chief gave Raven a pointed look before letting the dark anger of his gaze settle on Joe once more.

"Yeah, see that's the thing," Joe said. "If it was only you and the bogans going at each other, I'd agree with you. But you're setting a whole other thing in motion here, something that's going to affect everybody for a long time to come. So all of a sudden, it's other people's business."

"Will someone remove this mongrel from my sight," Minisino said, "or must I do it myself?"

"That's twice," Joe told him before anybody could move.

The buffalo soldiers who'd been about to move forward held their place, waiting for their war chief's response.

"Twice what?" Minisino asked.

"Twice you've insulted me. Why would you want to go and do that?"

Minisino shook his head. "I speak only the truth—how can that be an insult? You're a half-breed. Canid and crow. *Neither* of whom have any business here."

Careful, Joe, Jack said.

I hear you, Joe sent back. *I'm cool.*

But after taking another drag on his cigarette, he flicked the butt at the war chief's feet.

"I guess we're done being polite," he said.

He heard Lucius growl a warning, "Joe," to him, but he never let his gaze stray from Minisino's. He understood everybody's concern, but he wasn't being jackass prideful here. It was all a matter of respect. If Minisino didn't offer him some respect, then the war chief wasn't going to listen to him. And if he didn't listen, then this whole situation was going to come crashing down like crow boys playing football with a bird's nest.

So it had to come down to them going at it one-on-one. Joe had no idea if he could take the war chief or not, but that wasn't the point. The point was that he was going stand his ground and, whether he liked it or not, Minisino would have to respect that.

The war chief ground out the butt with a hoof. The faintest trace of a smile touched his lips.

"I'm going to enjoy this," he said, stepping forward.

Well, I won't, Joe thought, but he couldn't back off now.

He'd fought big men before. The main trick to it was to not get yourself killed. You didn't let them connect a solid blow, and you for sure didn't let them get a hold of you. The only weakness you could find with a trained warrior like Minisino—sometimes, if you were lucky—was that they were so sure of their own ability, and so disdainful of yours, that they came into the fight feeling cocky.

Minisino was going to come in hard and fast, that was a given. His eyes gave away the first lightning fast blow. Joe was able to duck under it and land two of his own on the war chief's broad chest. It was like pounding his fists against a stone wall. Minisino batted a big hand—the way you might an insect flying up into your face—and caught Joe a glancing blow that sent him sprawling back in the dirt.

The war chief came in quickly, following up on his advantage, but before he could land a real blow, before Joe could get up, an apparition took shape in the air between them. Minisino dodged to one side so as not to knock her down, his eyes widening. For the moment, Joe was forgotten. Joe himself froze in the act of getting back on his feet before he slowly stood up. His gaze, like everybody else's, was on the spirit of the dead woman who now stood between him and the buffalo war chief. In this place she had the same solid substance to her as did the spirits of the buffalo dead in Minisino's army.

"Anwatan," Walker said, the first to name her.

There was no happiness in the cerva's voice. Only surprise at her unexpected appearance. And sadness for her death. Perhaps a touch of worry that she was here, instead of moving on into the next world.

So this was the girl the bogans had killed, Joe thought.

"How dare you decide on the manner of my retribution?" she demanded of Minisino.

The war chief actually retreated a step from her, but that, Joe decided, was involuntary, because it soon became apparent that he wasn't backing down from his plans.

"This isn't about you, Anwatan," Minisino told her. "This is for all the cerva the aganesha have slaughtered."

The spirit shook her head. "The dead see through the lies of the living," she said. "Why don't you tell this army you have gathered the truth, since they seem to be conveniently blind to it?"

"That's because he wouldn't have an army if he did," another woman's voice answered before Minisino could speak.

She didn't take shape the way the deer spirit had. She'd stepped out of nowhere—the way you did in the between, when you come from the world that Raven made, or from the otherworld—a small woman with long tangles of red hair, dressed in baggy green cargo pants and a tight black T-shirt. There was something familiar about her, but Joe couldn't quite place it. What he did know was that she wasn't human or fairy, a cousin or a spirit.

Cody's balls, Jack said in his head. *This is turning into a regular variety show for freaks and misfits.*

No kidding.

Minisino looked at the newcomer, and Joe saw something change in his eyes. Whoever the stranger was, the war chief knew her. Knew her and didn't want her to be talking.

"Don't even start, Christiana," he said. "This is neither the time nor the—"

"Hey, speak for yourself," Joe broke in. "Me, I'm all ears."

Because now he knew who she was. Jilly'd spoken to him of her. She was Christy Riddell's shadow.

"Yes," the spirit of Anwatan said. "Let her speak, or I will."

Minisino glanced back at his army.

"Drum," he commanded. "Dance."

But not a hand touched drum skin, not a foot moved, not a voice was raised in the stomp dance chant. Like Joe, the gathered buffalo knew that their war chief was afraid of the stranger's words, and while they would readily follow their leader wherever he might lead them, whether it be battle or a strategic retreat, they would not follow a coward.

"Speak," Anwatan repeated.

"Well," Christiana said. "You all see a war chief standing here at the head of his army—and damn, he really looks the part, doesn't he?"

"Christiana," Minisino said softly, the threat plain in his voice.

The red-haired woman ignored him. "But we go way back, Minisino and me. Or should I say, Wininotawag—Fat Ear, because that's how I knew him then."

As serious as the gathering was, a rumble of soft laughter rose up from the buffalo army. A smile touched even Walker's lips.

"Anyway," Christiana went on, "I originally came here at the request of Tatiana McGree, Queen of the Newford Fairy Courts. She wanted me to set up a meeting with Fat Ear to see if, between the two of them, a peaceful solution could be found. And I was willing to do that because then they'd owe me a favour. But since this young woman—" She waved a hand in Anwatan's direction. "—has brought it up, maybe it'd just be easier for you all to decide if Fat Ear should even be leading anybody in the first place."

"This woman," Minisino began, pointing at the red-haired stranger, his voice loud, "is—"

"Telling the truth so far," Anwatan said. "So why don't we let her continue?"

The war chief glared at Christiana. She's just made herself a serious enemy, Joe thought. But it didn't seem to bother her in the least.

I like this girl, he told Jack.

Do you know her?

She's Christy's shadow. The question is, how did she get involved with all of this?

Who cares? Jack replied. *She's doing great so far.*

No kidding.

Plus she's got a nice ass, Jack added.

Stay focused.

Oh, I am.

"So, as I was saying," Christiana continued, "Fat Ear and me, we used to pal around, back in the once upon a time when we were young. Even then he was real serious—already the warrior—and ambitious as hell. He was going to lead the buffalo tribes back into glory, he told me, it didn't matter what it would take. He'd chosen this new name—Minisino. Warrior. It's got quite the ring, doesn't it? Better than Fat Ear, anyway. I mean, who's going to follow a war chief named Fat Ear?"

"Get to your point," Raven said.

"Right." She turned to face Minisino. "What you're doing here isn't right. It wasn't right when you talked about it way back when, and it's not right now when you're actually doing it."

Minisino hadn't stopped glaring at her.

"You know the history of my people," he said, his voice stiff with anger. "It's long past time that we—"

"Oh, spare us all the bullshit. You're doing this for one reason and one reason only: you want to be in charge. You want to be remembered—and not as Fat Ear. Pretending that you're doing this for Anwatan, or for any other victim of injustice, is just low."

"You—"

"And here's the thing," she went on, turning to look at Ayabe and the others. "Did you never wonder why this stomp dance is going on for so long? It's because Fat Ear needs the Court's army to come to him. Here he's got the numbers. Over there . . . well, what does he have? Forty flesh and blood warriors? Maybe fifty? Because you do know that spirits of the dead can't do much of anything once they cross back over to the world Raven made, don't you?"

Her gaze went back to Minisino and his army.

"Here," she said, "he's got a sure victory that'll live on in stories told around the campfires for a hundred years. Over there he's going to get his ass handed to him on the end of a fairy spear, because if you don't think Tatiana can field enough fairy to deal with fifty buffalo warriors, you're living in a whole other reality than I am."

Damn, she was right, Joe realized. Why hadn't anybody else figured that out?

It was such a basic thing—all, or at least one of them, should have remembered.

"Tatiana's already promised to see that Anwatan's murderers are punished," Christiana went on. "And I'm sure she'll be open to hearing any other concerns. But this is the kind of thing you deal with at a council table, not on a battlefield. Not unless you want your asses whupped. Or—" She fixed her steady gaze on Minisino. "—you're out to make some kind of a name for yourself."

There was an uneasy shuffling in the ranks of the buffalo army. Minisino turned to them.

"You don't actually *believe* this crap, do you?" he asked. "Why are you even listening to her? She's not one of us. What do you even know about her?"

"You tell us," one of the buffalo warriors said.

"We don't have to know anything about her," another added. This one was a spirit of the dead, the holes in his chest where the bullets had struck him were plainly visible. "We can see through the lie to the truth she tells."

A third buffalo warrior—another of the spirits—nodded. "We should have seen it from the first, but we were too eager to be avenged."

"We still can be!" Minisino cried. "If we guard the entrances of the otherworld against the aganesha, they'll *have* to meet us here or the dreamlands will be closed to them forever."

"What do you have that needs to be avenged?"

"You're my people. Your deaths weigh on *me*."

The buffalo spirit who had last spoken slowly shook his large shaggy head.

"No," he said. "Anwatan spoke the truth. We let ourselves be blinded. But now we do see through the lie. All that weighs on you is your ambition. Our deaths . . . hers . . . they were only something you planned to use to reach your goal."

One by one the spirits of the buffalo dead faded away until finally there was only the army of the living left. The ghost buffalo went silently, their drums silent, their hooves insubstantial and raising no dust with their passing. The few dozen buffalo soldiers that remained also turned their backs on their war chief, stepping away, out of the between.

When the last of them were gone, there was only Minisino standing on the plain. Minisino facing the handful of cousins and humans who'd had the courage to stand between his army and the fairy courts.

"Why did you do this to me?" he asked Christiana.

"I didn't do it to you," she said. "You did it to yourself. Truth is, I make it a rule never to get involved in this kind of crap, but I need a favour from Tatiana and stopping you's the only way I'm going to get it."

"You could have asked me for help."

"Yeah, right."

She turned to look at the others.

"That was well done," Raven said.

She shook her head. "You heard me. I wasn't doing this to help anybody but my brother. Now Tatiana has to find him for me."

"Who is your brother?" Walker asked.

"Nobody you'd know. Just another human who got caught up in your fun and games."

She tipped a finger against her brow and just like that, she was gone again, stepping away as suddenly as she'd come.

Jilly

Lizzie and Honey work at getting me up on my feet—Lizzie physically trying to pull me up, Honey whispering encouragement in my mind—but I can't rise. I can't do anything. All I can do is relive that moment when I dropped the pail and so threw away any chance of getting Geordie back.

We can't stay here, Honey is saying. *We need to get out of the sun. And we need to find Joe. He'll know what to do.*

Not even Joe's going to have an answer for this one. How do I reclaim all the dirt and debris that spilled out of the pail and went scattering down onto the rocks below? If I've doomed Geordie, I'll be damned if I'll do anything to help myself. I deserve to just die here. I should stay here until that burning sun overhead turns me into dust and the wind blows all the little bits of me away.

Let me be Dust Girl.

"You go on," I say. "Just leave me here. I need to stay here."

We can't do that, Lizzie says. *We won't.*

"Sure you can. You just put one foot in front of the other and away you go."

Honey gives me a soft bump with her muzzle. *Jilly . . .*

I turn to look at her. She knows what I'm going through. She's failed the ones she's loved as well. I remember Joe telling me about it, how her family all died in the dog fighting pits and there was nothing she could do about it.

How did you get past that? I want to ask her.

Geordie wouldn't want you to be doing this, she says.

She's right. Geordie wouldn't. But the world doesn't go by what we want. I didn't want Geordie to die, but he went ahead and got killed anyway, didn't he?

Still, I let Lizzie pull me to my feet. Poor Lizzie, trapped in a child's body just like me, except the lower part of her face is like a crash test dummy's. She has no mouth, no jaw. She can't eat, she can't drink. She can't speak.

But I suppose if she can still have hope, the least I can do is pretend that I do, too. And what does it matter? If I die here or someplace else? At least if we get away, we might be able to find someone who can fix Lizzie.

So I let her help me to my feet. I rub the tears from my eyes, making muddy streaks in the dust on my cheeks. I think of how Geordie would smile to see the mess and that just makes me want to cry again. But I can't seem to cry anymore. Everything's too dry, me included.

We hardly get started down the vague trail we'd been following before I fell, when Honey suddenly stiffens at my side. She turns, a threatening growl rumbling deep in her chest.

I remember what happened to Del and wouldn't want to be whoever's on the trail behind us.

There are two strangers there, obviously having just stepped out of nowhere the way we did earlier. For a long moment, we're all transfixed. The monster holds our gaze first, a shambling thing in the shape of a man, made of seaweed and driftwood and shells. Beside him is a small fairy man the size of a child, but with the face of an old man. He's dressed in a ragged litter of clothes, brown and dull green and grey, and his hair is a nest of matted dreadlocks.

Fairy and monster. Probably sent to us by the bogans.

At my side, I can sense that Honey is ready to attack. One wrong move on the part of the strangers is all it'll take.

But Lizzie's voice rings in our heads and stops her.

Honey, no! she cries. *That's my friend Timony.*

Then I remember. I'd seen the little man before. I'd seen him changing from a pony into a man, falling out of a tree with Lizzie. She said he was a doonie. That he'd helped her.

Del made him vanish with a wave of his hand. But that doesn't explain where the monster came from.

Then the monster speaks. It looks right at me with those weird seashell eyes and says, *It's me, Jilly.*

All I can do is stare.

That was Geordie's voice I heard. It's so improbable that I'm sure I didn't hear it right.

"Geordie . . ." I say anyway, and hope flickers inside me.

Finally you can hear me. I kept trying and trying before, but it was like I was just a ghost.

I'm having a real problem equating my dear Geordie with this shambling thing put together from seaweed and shoreline debris.

"But you're . . ."

I can't say the word. Dead. He's dead.

It's really me, the voice says in my head.

Hope changes from a flicker into a bright light inside me.

He's here.

While he might be inhabiting some freaky seaweed creature, it's still him, speaking in my head.

But I'd seen what Del had done to him. And then I'd gone and dropped his remains off the side of this mesa.

"But aren't you a ghost?" I have to ask.

I . . .

The thing that claims to be Geordie, that has Geordie's voice, looks to Timony, but the doonie only has eyes for Lizzie.

"What have they *done* to you?" he cries.

He doesn't give Lizzie or any of us a chance to answer. Running over to her, he puts his hands on her temples. It's the strangest thing to watch—like when the Nature Channel shows you a flower opening in slow motion. One moment, she and the doonie are of equal height. In the next, he has to reach up to keep his hold on her as Lizzie returns to her normal size. Most wonderful of all, her mouth reappears.

Just like that, everything's back to normal.

"Oh," she says.

Then she puts her hands to her mouth and starts to grin. Grabbing the doonie, she gives him a big hug and dances him around, laughing, her mouth wide open. When she finally lets him go, he comes up to me, a question in his eyes.

I don't say anything, but I guess he reads that as my agreeing because now he's got his hands on my temples. I feel the oddest sensation, a tingling from head to foot as though a static charge is running through me, but nothing changes in me. We're still at each other's eye level.

His brow furrows as he concentrates harder.

The tingle is sharper now, but still nothing.

"Something's blocking me," he says. "Every time I begin to feel my way to how you should be, something pushes me away."

"It's Del," Lizzie says.

I'm sure she's right, but I don't really care.

"Never mind me," I say. "Can you bring Geordie back?"

He nods. "I just need his body—or rather the changeling that he was turned into."

Of course he does.

There was an accident, Honey says.

"I was carrying the bits and pieces in a pail," I explain, "but I tripped and fell and the pail . . . the pail went over the edge . . ."

The doonie stares down at the jumble of red rock, all the way to where the pail lies far below.

"He . . ." I start, then I have to try again because the words choke in my throat.

I touch some of the dirt that's still on the rocks where I fell. Moist and dark, when I was carrying it. Now it's just dust.

"That's all that's left," Lizzie says. "The rest went down the mountainside."

Timony gives a sad shake of his head.

"Don't say you can't do anything," she adds.

I look at the seaweed creature, but I can't read an expression in its features and Geordie doesn't speak in my head.

Maybe that's a good thing. I don't know if I could bear the hurt that would be in his eyes. The disappointment that I couldn't even do this one thing right.

"Living creatures are different from things like clothes and food," Timony says. "I need a substantial amount of the actual being to have anything to work with. I can make a semblance of him—better than what we have here. But I can't bring *him* back without . . ."

His gaze goes back to where I let the pail go tumbling down the mountainside.

"Please," I say. "Please try."

"Can't you just make him a new human body?" Lizzie asks. "You know, the way you can make clothes and stuff out of nothing?"

The doonie shakes his head. "As I said, bodies are more complicated. You need the actual substance of the original to work with."

"So . . ." I say. "If we could gather some of it up . . ."

"Perhaps."

"How much do you need?"

Timony lifts his hands and cups them, indicating more than we could ever gather together. The rocks below are way too steep, and how could we ever tell the difference between his dirt and the dirt that's already there? It's all dust now.

It's not your fault, Geordie says.

I turn to the seaweed changeling. It doesn't look like a monster anymore. But it doesn't even remotely look like Geordie.

"How can you say that?" I ask him. "I was the one who was too stupid to be able to hang on to a simple pail."

It was an accident.

"But that doesn't *matter*. Not if we can't get you back."

The seaweed head turns to Timony.

Maybe there's someone who can get down there for us, he says. *Mice, or birds, or something.*

"This isn't a campfire story," the doonie replies. "There are no magical beasts to ask." He turns to look at Honey. "Unless Mistress Honey knows of some?"

I know enough not to hunt the little cousins, she replies, *but I've made no friends among them.*

"But we know someone," I say to Geordie.

I'm thinking of that time after my accident, when I was still in the rehab. The crow girls left me two locks of their dark hair that turned into crow feathers when they laid them on my bed.

If you ever think we can help, they told me, *hold these in your hand and call our names.*

I still have those feathers. Or at least I had them back at the Professor's house in Lower Crowsea. In Newford. They're in my room, in the drawer of my night table.

They might as well be on the other side of the moon.

Except . . .

Once upon a time . . .

I turn my attention to Honey and Timony.

"Can either of you get back to Newford?" I ask. "You know, do your walking between the worlds thing and just step over there?"

"You want one of us to take you back?" Timony asks.

I shake my head. That wouldn't work. I'd be the Broken Girl then and sure to screw something up. And I refuse to go if Geordie's still here.

I look at him again. The seaweed that's holding all the bits and pieces of him together is starting to dry out. Whenever he moves little pieces flutter to the ground. There's already a pool of dried-out debris lying around him.

"I need one of you to go back and get something for me," I say, turning back to the others. "Two crow feathers in the drawer of my night table. Can you do that?"

I've never been there before, Honey says.

"Neither have I," Timony tells me. "But I can take the knowledge from your mind, if you'll let me."

"Go for it."

He puts a hand on me again, just the palm lying against my brow. I feel the tingle again, but it's different this time. Softer. Like anticipation.

"Picture it," he says.

I do.

And then he's gone.

I blink. I know I've seen a lot of magical comings and goings in my time, but it still surprises me every time.

I start to say something reassuring to Geordie, but before I can even open my mouth, Timony is back. Lizzie and I both jump. I don't know that Geordie can in his seaweed body and who can tell what he's feeling? Honey just regards the doonie with a considering eye.

He's holding the two crow feathers in his hand.

"Are these the ones?" he asks as he gives them to me.

I nod.

Please let this work.

Once upon a time . . .

I'm not asking magic for me.

This is for Geordie.

My sweet and gentle friend Geordie, who doesn't deserve having his life turned into a horror show. Who doesn't deserve to lose that life just because he tried to help the Broken Girl who can't be fixed.

Once upon a time . . .

I hold the feathers tight and call their names. Maida and Zia.

But nothing happens.

"With fairy," Timony says, "everything is in threes."

With the cousins, it's usually fours, Honey adds.

So I repeat their names again, calling those crow girls to me. A second time, a third.

I don't have to do it a fourth.

As their names are pulled away by the wind for a third time, they drop from the sky. Two black crows, changing into two black-haired girls as they reach the ground. Skinny in their black jackets and jeans, faces brown, eyes laughing.

Once upon a time . . .

I let out a breath I wasn't aware I'd been holding.

Thank you, I think.

I don't know who I'm directing my thanks to. The crow girls. Nokomis. The spirit of life itself. Or maybe magic.

"Hello, hello!" Maida cries.

Zia spins in a slow circle, arms held out wide. She stops when she sees Geordie.

"Oh, look," she says. "It's a seaweed man."

Maida smiles and waves at the changeling that Geordie inhabits.

"Hello, hello, seaweed man," she says.

Zia turns from him to look at me.

"And Jilly's gone all small and girly," she says.

Maida grins and shrinks down until she's a small dark-haired girl, my apparent age and size. Clapping her hands, Zia follows suit. Then the two of them dance around me, singing some nonsense song.

I lay a hand on each of their shoulders and make them stop.

"Please," I say. "This isn't a time for joyful prattle."

Zia looks at me with this serious expression in her eyes that transforms all her lightness and silly humour into something old and wise and just a little dark.

"Sometimes," she says, "that's exactly when you need a dose of joyful prattle."

"Yes, but—"

"We've just come from watching crow boys tear apart a gang of bogans," Maida says, looking as serious as her companion. "Bits of flesh and blood and bone spraying everywhere."

Zia nods. "Because Raven said find them, but those crow boys saw what happened to Anwatan and when they're angry, mercy's not a word in their lexicon."

I have no idea what they're talking about, but apparently I'm alone in that.

"They're dead?" Lizzie asks. "*All* of them?"

"Veryvery dead," Maida replies.

"Though not each and every one of them," Zia adds. "There was one they couldn't find because he doesn't have enough blood on his hands."

Lizzie's eyes are clouded, unhappy, and then I remember her telling me about how all the trouble she got into was because of some Unseelie fairies.

"These are the bogans that you met at the crossroads?" I ask her.

She nods. "The ones that killed Anwatan—the deer woman. They also killed Timony—or at least this fish guy who travels with them did."

My gaze goes to Timony. Incongruously, I wait for him to pipe up in a Monty Pythonesque voice, "But I got better."

"I *was* dead," he says instead. "Lizzie brought me back."

"And I killed one of them," Lizzie says.

Maida gives her a wicked grin. "Oh, you'll have crow boys mooning over you when they find out."

"It's not . . . I don't . . ." She sighs and tries again. "What the bogans did was wrong, but I don't know that killing them solves anything."

"It stops them from doing more harm," Zia says.

Maida nods. "And it will make the others think twice before they try the same."

"I suppose. It's just . . ."

Zia cocks her head when Lizzie's voice trails off.

That every life is sacred, Honey says.

That's a funny thing for her to say, I think, considering how she so recently tore out Del's throat. But then I remember how upset she was after she'd killed my sister's friend Pinky. When I asked him about it, Joe told me that while she knew it had to be done, she also knew she'd have to carry the weight of it with her forever. She hadn't liked it, but she'd gone into the situation accepting the responsibility for her actions and knowing what she'd have to take away from it.

"But she eats other animals," I had said to Joe. "She kills them."

"It's not the same," he told me. "That's a whole different wheel of life and death."

Lizzie's nodding in agreement with Honey while all that's going through my head.

"Are you sure you don't have any cerva blood in you?" Maida asks. "Because they're all about finding peaceful solutions."

"And you're not?" Lizzie says.

The crow girls look at us, one by one, their gaze finally resting on me.

"If we'd known they'd tried to hurt our friend Jilly," Zia says, "we would have led the crow boys in their attack."

They can be so fierce and hard. It always shocks me, even though I've seen them like this before. But it's never easy for me to equate what they really are to the pair of silly corbae girls that I usually know. Except they're not really like that, are they? Goofy and dancing and always talking about candy. They're not like that at all.

Joe says that they were here before the long ago, that they watched Raven make the world. When I asked him why they act the way they do, like a pair of goofy little crow clowns, he told me that most of the time they live in the present. They don't think of the future, they don't remember the past. They just are. Because the more they remember, the darker and grimmer they can get.

Like they are right now.

Zia's words hang in the air, and no one says anything for a long moment.

I look at them all, my gaze settling on the seaweed creature that's got Geordie inside of it.

I remember a time, not so long ago, when all I had to worry about was getting around on my canes. About feeling trapped in my wheelchair. About wanting to paint, so desperately, but not ever being able to recapture the way I used to make magic with pigments on canvas.

For the past couple of years, the one thing I've really wanted is to be freed of all those chains on my life.

Now I wish those days were back. I'd trade them in a moment for how everything's gone all dark and horrible.

And Geordie, my Geordie . . .

No, he's not my Geordie. Maybe he could have been, but I never opened my heart to him and now it's too late, unless the crow girls can make a once upon a time happen for me.

They must feel the need in me because they turn back to me.

"How can we help you?" Maida asks.

Zia nods. "Yes, because we promised we would and crow girls always keep their promises."

"It's something we're good at."

"We're veryvery good at it."

"Except when we're not."

"But not today."

"Oh, no no no. Today we're the opposite of not."

"We're the can-do crow girls today," Zia assures me.

As they fall back into their familiar ways, it feels like the sun coming out from behind a bank of dark clouds. Even depressed as I am about Geordie and what I've done to him, I can't help but smile.

As I tell them what happened, they peer over the edge of the drop.

"Is that all?" Zia says.

"How much of him do you need?" Maida asks Timony.

I expect them to go clambering down the rock face like a pair of monkeys, magically picking up all the little grains of dirt, the bits of twig and leaf. Instead, they hold hands and sing some nonsense song that trills and rises like morning birdsong, when it's not squeaky and shrill like the cries of mice and other rodents.

I'm about to ask them to please stop fooling around and *help,* when something magical *does* happen.

Once upon a time . . .

I don't know where they come from, these hundreds of birds and animals and bugs. Pink-winged flickers and spiny lizards. Cactus wrens and little white-throated woodrats. Ground squirrels and sparrows. Shrews and mice and toads and beetles. Tarantulas and a whole column of harvester ants.

I lose track of them all and can only stand there with the others, watching as the animals and birds swarm over the rocks, or fly from one to another, collecting little unrecognizable bits that they drop in a growing pile at Timony's feet. The crow girls laugh and clap and egg them on.

"That's it, that's it!"

"Every changeling bit."

They look at each other, giggling at the impromptu rhyme.

And when the growing pile seems to encompass every little bit and piece that spilled when my pail went tumbling off the edge, Timony moves his hands over it and mutters something just under his breath. I watch as the seaweed creature falls apart, collapsing into a mess of drying weeds liberally sprinkled with driftwood and shells and other debris. While there, in the pile collected by the wild creatures the crow girls summoned, something stirs.

I realize I'm holding my breath, but I can't seem to let it out and take another.

Something stirs.

Once upon a time . . .

The debris rises in a ghostlike shape of a man, then slowly solidifies.

Once upon a time . . .

And Geordie's standing there, blinking in the bright light.

"Oh, my god," I hear Lizzie say.

"Ta da!" Zia cries.

"La di da di da ta da!" Maida adds, so as not to be outdone.

Their little army of helpers scamper and fly away as quickly as they came, and then the crow girls are birds again, flying loop-the-loops in the air above us.

You see, you see? I hear in my head.

We promised and we did.

Because we're the can-do crow girls.

Then with a dip of their wings and a chorus of bye-byes, they're gone, too, sailing away from the mesa on currents of wind, casting two shadows on the red dirt of the plain before them. But I hardly see them go. My whole world narrows to the fact that Geordie's back. He's in his own body and he's okay. Grinning at me.

I don't have words for what swells inside me.

I close the distance between us and hug him as tightly as I can, my head pressed into his lower chest, because I'm still a child's size.

"This is weird," he says. "When I look at you, you're just a kid, but when I feel you, it's like you're an adult. You know, taller and everything."

I step back from him and look up into his face.

"Really?" I ask.

He nods.

"It's what Del has done to you," Timony says. "Geordie sees the illusion, but he can't feel it."

I look around at the others, my gaze settling on Honey.

"Do you see through it?" I ask.

She shakes her head. *But only because you don't.*

"So is it real, or not?"

"I think it's both," Timony says. "Just as the world inside your head doesn't exist, yet at same time, it does."

"This is too weird."

I turn away and give Geordie another hug. I'm being greedy because I know what's still to come, even if no one else has figured it out yet. And then I tell a little white lie.

"We need to have a long talk when this is all over," I say to Geordie. "You know, about you and me."

It's not a complete lie because if there is an after, I'm definitely going to want to have that talk.

"I know," he says. "I'm looking forward to it."

"What do you mean when this is all over?" Lizzie asks. "Aren't we done here? And talk about anticlimactic. Not that I'm complaining, but after all our struggling, just like that, everything's okay."

I don't know where she gets the "just like that." Has she so quickly forgotten the Del-world inside my crazy head, and what we had to go through in it? It had taken Honey to rescue us. Timony to restore her and Geordie. The crow girls to bring in their wildlife troops to find all the bits and pieces of Geordie's changeling self. And these crow boys that Maida and Zia mentioned—they'd killed the bogans that had caused all of this.

That didn't seem like much of "just like that" to me. But I understood what she meant.

"Everything *is* okay, right?" she adds.

Then she turns to me and her hand goes to her newly-restored mouth.

"Oh, god," she says. "I was so totally not thinking."

"I understand," I tell her. "There's been a lot going on."

"I think you can be restored, too," Timony says.

"How so?"

"I think when you return to your own world again, the spell your brother put on you will no longer have power over you."

"Would that have worked with Lizzie and Geordie, too?"

He gives a slow nod. "Probably. If you'd had all of Geordie's changeling parts in one place."

"So we can go now, can't we?" Lizzie says. "We're all done here."

This is my home, Honey says. *I'll stay here and go back to my family. Unless you think you still need my help.*

I hadn't even thought of her having a family. It hadn't occurred to me that the crap of my life had spilled over not only onto her, but her family as well.

"No, we're good," I say. Then I turn to the others. "We should go back, except . . . I can't go with you."

For once Geordie reads me wrong. I can see it in his face. He thinks I'm scared of going back to being the Broken Girl again, but that's not it. That's not it at all. I'm a little scared of that, sure, after having had the freedom of not being the Broken Girl. But the problem is, I'm the Broken Girl here, too. It's just not so easily seen. I'll always be broken—until I face the monster that's set up house in my head.

"I have to back and . . . you know. Deal with Del. Just me and him."

Everybody's shaking their heads.

"You can't face him again," Timony says. "The moment you reappear, he'll have you under his thrall again."

"I don't think so," I tell him.

Translation: I hope not.

I look to Honey. "You understand, don't you?"

I do, she says, *but I still think your going alone isn't the wisest of decisions.*

"But if I don't go alone, nothing will have changed. I'll still be dependent on others for my safety from him."

Is it so bad to accept the help of others?

"No. Of course not. But if I don't deal with it myself, how do I get him out of my head?"

I know. But—

"I think I've got it all figured out. You know, what you were telling me about not believing in his power. I can do this."

She just looks at me.

"What?"

If that's true, she says, *then why are you still a human pup instead of a grown woman?*

"I . . ."

I look around at them. No one wants to let me go.

I've been blessed with friends—ever since the day I stopped living on the streets. Real friends. True friends.

That's never seemed a liability until this moment.

I can't let any of them come with me. I just *can't.*

I can go, Honey says. *He can't hurt me.*

We both know that's a lie. If I hadn't shoved Del, if she'd caught that shotgun blast, she'd be dead. He might not be able to manipulate her the way he did the rest of us, but he could still hurt her. He could kill her.

I shake my head.

Lizzie and Timony both want to help, but I know I can get them to stay. Geordie's a whole other matter. Even with what he's just been through, that Riddell loyalty won't let him allow me to face this by myself.

"You're not going alone," he says. "I won't lose you again."

"You don't understand. I have to do this alone. I *can't* do it if I have to worry about anyone else."

"But he's—"

"I know what he is. I know how powerful he can be. I just have to be stronger. I have to really believe that I'm stronger. That no matter what he does to me, it's only real if I let it be real."

"But I could be your Tamlin," Geordie says. "You know, holding on to you no matter what he changes you into."

"Except he'll change you first."

"Well, what about you?" Geordie asks Honey.

There's some disagreement as to how safe it would be for me, she says. *And I would argue it more, but in the end, Jilly's right. I can't do what needs to be done. No one can . . . except for Jilly.*

"It's true," I say. "Everybody's been telling me this from day one. Joe. Nokomis. The crow girls. This is the thing I've got to deal with before I can work on anything else."

"I don't like it," Geordie says.

I have to smile. "I don't like it either, Geordie, me lad. What's to like about it? But it's what has to be done."

I look away from him across the badlands. The combination of the red rocks vibrating against the complimentary greens of the pines, with the wide blue sky above it all, does a funny thing to me. It makes me feel physically small, but big inside. I understand now why Sophie is so enamoured with this landscape—escaping to it whenever she can, not just to paint it, but to be a part of it.

The religions have it wrong. God isn't in holy books and churches. God's out here where the sky feels like it goes on forever.

Unfortunately, I have to go back to the close woods and the claustrophobic confines of the house I grew up in.

I turn to look at Honey and Timony.

"Can one of you send me back?" I ask.

"I could," Timony says, "but it would send you back to what you've just left behind. It would be better for you to make your own way, to choose your own time and place to meet him again."

"I can do that?"

Timony smiles. "It's your mind."

"But I don't know how to go."

"The easiest way to enter the fairy realms," he says, "is to walk widdershins around a place or object of power. I sense one at the top of this mesa."

Joe called it a vortex, Honey says. *It's what we used to try to get to you.*

Widdershins, I think. Which is counterclockwise, the opposite way of how the sun moves.

It's like how I finally opened my heart to Geordie, coming at it all backwards. But then I've spent the better part of my life coming at things from an unexpected direction, so why change now?

"Okay," I say. "I can do this."

I give Geordie another hug, then put a finger across his lips when he starts to speak. Honey gets a pat. More hugs for Lizzie and Timony. Then I go back up the trail to the top of the mesa, the others trailing along behind me. My gaze is drawn to the petroglyphs and I wonder how I'm going to walk around the big stones that they've been scratched into, but then I realize that the vortex is right in the middle of the open ground.

I don't know why, because I've never been sensitive to this kind of thing before, but I can almost see the flow of energy rising straight up in a glittering column of amber and smoky green. Maybe this time in the otherworld's changed me. Maybe it's responding to something in me—this light inside me that Nokomis keeps telling me I have.

Whatever it is, I know exactly where the vortex is and all my doubts flee.

I start to walk backwards around it, giving Geordie and the others a last wave.

I can do it, I'd said cockily, because that's usually me: the I-Can-Do-It Girl. But you know what? I *can* do it.

I do.

There's a weird shifting under my feet, the bright desert fades into the cool green of an Eastern forest, and then I'm back in the world inside my head, standing in a copse of cedar and spruce. A squirrel, startled by my sudden appearance, scolds me. I glance in its direction, then look out across the field. The house rears up out of the weeds and grass at the far end, worn down, shutters askew, ugly.

I don't want to go there—not for a moment—but I know I need to finish this.

I won't pretend that I'm not scared. You want to know the truth? I'm terrified. I'm sure this is the hugest mistake I've ever made.

But it's too late to turn back now.

I don't know how to get back, and the only things waiting for me there are all the arguments that brought me here.

So I do what I have to do. I set off across the field to find my brother Del.

Galfreya

Galfreya could only shake her head in admiration as, from the safety of Tatiana's conference room, she and the other council members watched Christiana work the war chief of the buffalo. After her first meeting with the shadow back in the mall, Galfreya'd had Edgan find out what he could about her. So she knew Christiana was physically capable of carrying out the threats she'd made to the queen's guard earlier. Now she realized that the shadow was smarter than most would give her credit for—at least those who didn't see past her brash and cocky manner.

"How did she do that?" Tatiana asked as the buffalo army dispersed. "Minisino wasn't going to listen to any of them. Not Anwatan's father or Joe. Not Raven. Not even Ayabe—and when was the last time anyone saw *him*? But she just waltzed in there and the next thing I see is Minisino standing alone on that plain and the threat gone."

Galfreya shrugged. "I don't know."

"She's a shadow," Granny Cross, the other seer said. "They're both more and less than the rest of us."

Tatiana turned to her. "How so? I can see how there might be more to them, but in what way are they less?"

"Consider their origin," Granny Cross replied. "Born from what another has cast off, they carry inside them the conviction that they were never meant to be, and that what they are will always be of less worth than their twin. It's why so many of them fade away like the Eadar, except what they need to sustain them is a belief in themselves, rather than the belief of others."

Tatiana nodded, her gaze going back to the scene playing in the between. "That one will never fade," she said.

Granny Cross made no reply, but Galfreya could see in her eyes that she wasn't as certain herself. Unless Granny Cross's seer vision had shown her something the rest of them couldn't see, Galfreya tended to agree with the queen. This shadow was so sure of herself that it would take a battalion of self-doubt battering away at her night and day for a year, and even then she would probably prevail.

As Galfreya returned her own attention to the between, she was just in time to see Christiana's approach. A moment later the shadow appeared back in the fairies' conference room as suddenly as she'd left. She stood on the middle of the table once again, her arms spread wide and grinned at how every one of Tatiana's guardsmen had either a sword or crossbow pointed at her.

"What?" she asked. "No parade? No 'All hail the returning hero!'?"

The guardsmen didn't lower their weapons until Tatiana made a dismissive movement with her hand.

"How did you do that?" she asked Christiana. "How did you get the army to disperse?"

Christiana shrugged, which was no answer at all, then got straight to the point.

"I delivered what I promised I would," she said. "More, really. So now it's your turn to deliver. Where's Geordie? And if you can't give him to me, then where do I find these bogans?"

"I didn't say we had either," Tatiana replied. "Only that we would help you find them."

"That's not good enough."

"It's all we can offer because we don't *know*."

"Fine," Christiana said, though it was obvious she was anything but appeased.

Galfreya understood. Throughout the drama of what had unfolded in the between with the buffalo soldiers, her own mind kept returning again and again to worry at the mystery of Geordie's disappearance. If he'd been killed, they should at least have been able to sense his spirit slipping out of his body. But he was just *gone*.

"Get those seers of yours to start working on it," the shadow went on, as though she were the queen of this court, not Tatiana. "Get your gruagaghs and seekers and finders and whatever it takes. I made your problem go away

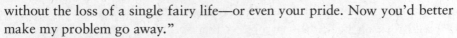

without the loss of a single fairy life—or even your pride. Now you'd better make my problem go away."

Tatiana sat straighter, her eyes flashing.

"We are not servants," she said stiffly, "to jump at your beck and call. I have said we will do all we can to help, and so we will."

Christiana glared right back at her. "Then what's the hold up? If you think I'm just going to—"

She broke off before she could finish her threat and lifted her head. Everything about her changed. The anger drained away from her features and she grinned. It was such an abrupt and startling transformation. A moment earlier and one only wanted to slap some manners into her. Now her good humour filled the hearts of everyone in the room with an echo of her joy.

Though the others were puzzled at her sudden change of demeanour, Galfreya understood it immediately. Because she felt it, too.

Geordie was back.

She didn't know exactly where he was, but that wouldn't be hard to figure out. What mattered was that he was back.

"You," Christiana said, pointing at Galfreya. "Can you call up an image of where he is? Something sharp and clear—none of your murky fairy riddles. I can't cross over to someplace I haven't been before unless I have a clear picture of it."

"Here," Granny Cross said, before Galfreya could consult her own scrying bowl. "I have it."

As Christiana walked across the table to where the other seer was sitting, Galfreya rose from her own chair.

"I'm coming with you," she said.

The shadow turned to look at her. "You? Why would you want to come?"

"Because I love him, too."

"Right. With spells and enchantments to keep him at your side."

"You *know* why I laid those."

"So what are you going to do?" Christiana asked. "If you don't use spells, do you think you can actually hold him? It means going out into the world, you know. It means making a commitment to living, instead of holing up in that mall you've made into a fairy court for yourself."

"I know."

"And what makes you even think he'll listen to you? He knows what you did."

"It doesn't matter. I still need to see him. To talk to him. I need to tell him how I feel."

Christiana cocked her head. "You really do care, don't you?"

Galfreya bit back the sharp retort that sprang to her lips. What was it about this woman that made her constantly want to slap her?

"I thought you said he loved this other woman," Tatiana said.

Galfreya nodded. "Jilly."

"So then . . ."

"They circle and dance around each other," Galfreya said, "neither able or willing to commit. But I am ready. I can give him what she can't."

"And being this immortal seer in skater gear?" Christiana asked. "How does that play into a normal relationship?"

"I would give it up for him."

Galfreya ignored the shocked response of Tatiana and the rest of the court.

"Wow," Christiana said, then she smiled and nodded. "Cool. And you know what? If you're on the level, I'll even make sure he hears you out."

Galfreya blinked in surprise. The shadow was going to *help* her? What sort of game was she playing now?

But Christiana's eyes were guileless. She reached out a hand to Galfreya.

"Come on," she said. "Time's a-wasting."

With her hand still proffered, she turned back to Granny Cross and her scrying bowl.

"Show me that picture you've got." She put on a pretty smile to make it sound less like a command and added, "If you please."

Galfreya shook her head, but she walked over to where Christiana was waiting for her, red curls falling in her face as she bent over the image in the bowl.

Tatiana caught Galfreya's arm as she walked by her.

"I have to do this," Galfreya said. "I should have done it a long time ago."

"But to give up your heritage . . ."

"We'll see. Maybe it will need to come to that, maybe it won't. But I'm determined that this time, I'll do it properly. That we will share our lives. If he'll have me. If he'll listen to me."

"Oh, he'll listen to you," Christiana said. "Unless you keep lollygagging, because then I'm just going to leave you behind."

Tatiana dropped her hand from Galfreya's arm.

"Good luck," she said.

"I don't need luck," Galfreya said, her gaze going to where the shadow waited impatiently for her by the bowl. "I've got her with me, don't I?"

Grey

There's a long uncomfortable silence after the red-haired girl leaves, neither cousins nor humans quite sure what's coming next. I figure the situation's under control now, and we can just go and get on with the rest of our business, but I'm taking my cues from Jack and he shows no sign of leaving. He winks at me and lights a cigarette, then lifts his eyebrows and offers it to me. I shake my head and look back at where the buffalo war chief is standing.

Minisino seems unrepentant, a tall, formidable figure, even without his army at his back. He has one hand on his hip, the other around the handle of a weighted club that's stuck in his belt.

"Is it over?" I hear one of the humans ask, pitching her voice low.

You'd think it would be, but something's still going on. Whatever it is, it's all under the surface where I can't access it.

I glance over to see that it was Lizzie's cousin who spoke, her arm still in a sling. She's leaning close to Cassie who, in her bright yellow T-shirt and even brighter pink baggy cotton pants, is pretty much the only splash of colour in this place.

I don't know what Siobhan and the other members from Lizzie's band are doing out here on the plain with us, what they thought they could possibly do against the buffalo army, but I have to admire them for taking a stand like this. If the red-haired girl hadn't come through the way she did, it would probably have meant their deaths. You don't see that kind of commitment much anymore—the realization that the world is everybody's responsibility, so we've all got to do our part, no matter how tough that might be sometimes.

Oh, who am I kidding? Hardly anyone's ready to stand up and be counted anymore, not cousin or human. But here these humans are, nevertheless. Siobhan with only one arm that's of any use and the other two: the guitarist and the accordion player. Musicians, not fighters.

I feel like I owe Lizzie an apology. I guess I owe her a lot of things. If I hadn't been so brusque with her at first, if I'd stayed around and kept watch against the bogans, none of these friends of hers would be here. Hell, I probably wouldn't be here.

But this apology would be for being so dismissive of the music she and her band play. If they've got enough heart to be here when it matters, in a fight that's not even really their own, then there's got to be more to that diddle-dee-dee music I've heard them play. I guess it comes from the heart, too, but I just wasn't listening. I'd already made up my mind as to what both it and they were like.

Anyway, because it's so quiet, everybody heard Siobhan's question, and she looks embarrassed at the sudden attention directed her way. Before Cassie can answer her, Minisino stomps a hoof on the dirt and opens his big mouth.

"No," he says. He points at Joe. "This one and I—we have unfinished business."

I don't *believe* this.

But Joe sighs, then stands straighter, shoulders going back.

"You think?" he says.

Minisino's only response is his fixed glare.

Joe gives another sigh. "I suppose we do. You know, I was hoping I wasn't going to have to whup your sorry ass, but you're not leaving me a whole lot of choice here."

"You've already stolen all my choices," Minisino says. "Why should I leave you with any?"

Joe shrugs. "I don't know. For the sake of common sense? Maybe for the fact that this is over, and we both know it, but you still figure you need to hit something?"

Minisino responds by letting his hands fall to his sides and assuming a combat-ready stance.

"Don't play into his game," Cassie pipes up. "You don't need to do this anymore."

Listen to her, I think.

But, "Yeah, I do," Joe says without turning to look at her. "You know how it goes. If we don't finish this now, we're just going to have to go through it all over again another time. And maybe the next time it won't end so pretty."

Keep this up and it's going to end anything but pretty, I think. I don't know what he plans to do, but it's painfully obvious from what happened earlier that if they go at it again, the buffalo war chief's going to pound Joe into a lot of little pieces. Cassie's right. There's no need for this kind of posturing crap anymore. The army's gone and maybe Minisino's big and tough, but all we've got to do is stand together, and we can take him down. Just Jack and Joe and me, if it comes down to that.

I give Jack a meaningful look, but he shakes his head.

Let this play out, he tells me.

C'mon, Jack, I tell him. *He's going to kill Joe—just out of spite.*

You don't know Joe like I do. He's got resources he can call on. Ones he couldn't use when he was trying to be diplomatic.

Diplomatic? I repeat, remembering the things Joe told the war chief earlier.

Yeah, diplomatic. The one on one was for the benefit of the army. But now the army's gone and Joe doesn't have to play fair anymore. I figure he's about to let Minisino see his real face . . .

I have no idea what Jack's talking about, but then I look back at where the pair of them are facing off. There's something wrong here. Minisino had towered over Joe, but now they're about the same size. No, Joe's bigger, and he's still getting bigger as I watch.

I sense the crackle of power in the air—an old, dark power.

"Joe," Raven says.

There's a warning in his voice, but he sounds nervous, too. I look at Walker and Ayabe and they're both backing up a little. Walker motions to the humans for them to move further back as well.

What the hell's going on here? I ask Jack.

Joe's a bit of a wild card, Jack says. *Everybody talks about him being the clown crow dog. They point at his mixed blood, like it makes him less, but it only makes him more.*

I still don't get it.

Joe's got something old inside him, something that came down from the long ago through the mixed blood of a red dog and a black crow. Wake it up too much and you could have some serious world-shaking on your hands.

But—

Yeah, I know. Look at him most of the time and he's just some raggedy cousin with crazy eyes. But it's like all the old powers.

He starts counting them off on his fingers. *Raven and Ayabe here. Cody and Grandmother Toad. Old Man Hummingbird and you don't want to forget Turtle, who bears the weight of us all. They don't walk around with that old power hanging from them like a cloak for anybody to see, but that doesn't mean it isn't there.*

I remember that moment in Raven's study, when he was suddenly *more.*

And the thing is, Jack adds, *if Joe plays this right, he doesn't even have to kill Minisino. He just needs to take it to where that cerva knows that he'd better be walking the straight and narrow in the future, or he'll have* that *on his ass, looking for the reason why.*

He nods with his chin, and I look over to see that Joe's the one towering over Minisino now.

I have to give it to the cerva. He knows he's screwed, but he's still not backing down. Or maybe he isn't brave. Maybe he's just stupid, because I sure as hell would be trying to smooth things over right about now. Either that, or running like hell.

That feeling of some old, dark power's continuing to build. It's like we're standing in the middle of an approaching thunderstorm that's about to let loose a torrent of rain on the back of a swath of lightning bolts that'll be as thick as the old redwoods back home. One of those wild storms that has no conception of friend or foe. It just takes down everything in its path.

Isn't this . . . dangerous? I ask Jack.

Sure it is. Why do you think Raven and Ayabe are so nervous?

But you'd think the two of them would be enough to keep Minisino in check.

Jack shrugs. *If it was only about power. But you know them. Like most of the old spirits, they just stop paying attention to the world after awhile. But Joe's always in the world.* Jack shakes his head and smiles. *And you know what's funny? He won't even remember this when it's over. He'll just remember Minisino backing down—or at least I hope that moron's going to back down. But that won't stop Joe from taking that buffalo man down hard if he* forgets *and tries any of this crap again.*

We never get to find out which way it's going to go, because Anwatan speaks then. I guess she doesn't know what's going on, the way Raven and Ayabe do, or the way I do now, since Jack's just explained it to me. She's been standing there like her father and the humans, knowing that something bad could be coming down, but not knowing exactly what. And since no

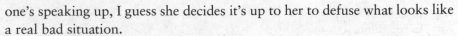

one's speaking up, I guess she decides it's up to her to defuse what looks like a real bad situation.

"There's something else," she says.

For a moment it seems as though no one's going to listen to her. Then slowly Joe changes again. He's back to his own size and turns from Minisino to look at Anwatan. None of us seem to know we've been holding our breath until we let it out in a collective sigh. There's some foot shuffling as people adjust their weight. One of the humans—I think it's the guitar player from Lizzie's band—coughs.

"What's that, darling?" Joe says, sounding more like Cody than himself.

I guess it's the widening of her eyes that warns him. I never saw it coming, and it seems no one else was looking either. Only Anwatan. But we all see it now: there's Minisino taking a swing at his head with a weighted club he's pulled from his belt.

Joe turns, but he's not quick enough. The business end of that club catches him in the back of the head—hard—and he goes down.

The rest of us aren't much quicker than Joe in our reaction times. Cassie got out a late warning cry, but too late. The other cerva and humans don't seem aware of what's happening until it's over. Raven and Ayabe stare, motionless, too surprised to immediately respond.

I understand perfectly.

There are a lot of things I don't admire about Minisino, but the last thing I expected from him was such a cowardly attack.

Only Jack's instincts are good. He doesn't think, he just acts.

At the instant the club connects with Joe's skull, a big grey coyote is already closing the distance between himself and Minisino, launching himself at the war chief's throat. Minisino manages to turn just enough to protect his throat, but the coyote gets a hold of his shoulder and his weight throws Minisino off-balance. The two go down. Minisino closes a big hand around the coyote's throat and raises his club.

But that's as far as he gets.

We've all started forward, but Raven gets there first. He just picks Minisino up, like the big buffalo has no more weight than a child, and gives him a shake. We all hear the sharp crack as his neck snaps.

Raven drops the body and turns to Jack. The coyote's gone and Jack gets up, brushing dirt from his clothes.

"How's Joe?" Jack asks.

We turn to find Cassie kneeling beside him, cradling his head on her lap. She has her hand on the open wound and blood streams from between her fingers.

It might look worse than it really is, I try to tell myself. Head wounds always bleed a lot.

But his brown complexion's got a grey cast to it and there's a bad feeling in the air. I reach out to send him some positive thoughts, but they just dissipate in the air because there's nothing there to receive them. Like there's no one home.

Cassie lifts her head to look at Raven.

"Do something!" she cries.

He lifts his head and roars the word into the sky: "Healers!"

I put my hands on my ears, but it doesn't diminish the howling call because he's sending a thought demand that's louder than the physical cry.

"Oh, crap," Jack says at my side. "This doesn't look good."

Jilly

I make my way toward the old house, step by reluctant step, pushing through the tall weeds, circling around the tangled thickets that are too dense for me to negotiate. I know why I'm dragging my heels. I want to get this over with, sure, but I don't know that it's actually going to happen—at least, not in a way that will make things any better for me. But hope springs eternal and all that, and whatever else I might be, I'm so not Quitter Girl, though right now I'm certainly Pokey Girl.

It's hot in this field, but not like it was back on the mesa where I left the others. The air's humid and close here. It makes my hair frizz and my skin feel damp and sticky under my clothes—in other words, typical Tyson County summer weather, which is pretty much my least favourite. But why should the weather be any more pleasant than anything else here? This whole place seems to have been designed to make me as miserable as possible, and so far—between the last visit and this one—it's been doing a pretty good job.

But at least no one else has to suffer this time. There'll be no mouthless Lizzie, no Geordie getting killed. No chance of Honey getting shot. Nobody else will get hurt because it's only me in here and either I finish this, or I stay here. Either way, Del won't be able to hurt anyone else again.

Okay, so that's all it's got going for it, and everything else is just a horror show, but it's enough. And who knows? Maybe I'll get lucky. Maybe I'll figure out how to circumvent this hold Del's got over me. Maybe I'll actually beat him, instead of just running away like I did when I was a kid.

But I don't know where to start.

I will not let anyone have power over me, Honey told me.

I know exactly what she means. Ever since I got off the street, I haven't backed away from either a problem or a bully. It didn't matter if I was in the hot chair, or if it was somebody else—I stood up and dealt. I made the same vow Honey holds to, and I've stayed true to it.

So what's the problem here? What's the hold Del has on me besides fueling the occasional nightmare that I still wake up from in a cold sweat? Those days—the days when I was just a kid and he was in control—are done and gone. Del's just a fat old drunk living in some trailer park now. I know that for a fact because Raylene tracked him down a couple of years ago, looking for payback for what he'd put her through, but when she finally found him, she decided he just wasn't worth the bother. Instead, she came away with a lost soul that needed her help—taking up the rescuing of strays just like her big sis.

So it's not Del. It's me.

You're supposed to forgive yourself for thinking you were to blame for what he did to you, Honey told me. *For thinking you deserved it.*

Except I honestly don't believe it's that. I'm not stupid. I *know* I wasn't to blame. I was just a little kid being hurt by someone who was supposed to be protecting me. I didn't deserve it—no one does—and I don't think that. So what's to forgive?

But Honey seems to think it's still sitting here inside me, and she's not alone. All those healers Joe consulted, back when I first had the accident, they all said the same thing. That I have something inside me that needs to be fixed before they can help me with my physical problems.

I guess that something is this place, with Del ruling the roost. Del in control again, only amp that up a hundredfold because the old Del, the brother I grew up with, didn't go around wielding magical powers. He was just a redneck pedophile—bad enough for any kid to deal with, of course, but nothing like what he is here.

Which brings me back to, what am I supposed to do?

If this is all in my subconscious, then I need to find some way to tell my subconscious that it's over. Del's not god. He's not even the devil. He's just a loser that *I've* managed to raise to these huge supernatural proportions, here, in this world that sits inside my head.

I actually have to smile then, because that gets me thinking: If this world's inside my head, then what's inside my head when I'm here, physically in the world inside my head? It's a confusing piece of Escher logic—or illogic, depending on how you view that kind of thing. Me, I appreciate the odd riddling mystery it provides. It's like holding a mirror up to a mirror where the reflections get smaller and smaller as they go on into infinity.

It's a once upon a time, and if you can have that, then you can still have hope, because however a fairy tale turns out in the end, the once upon a time beginning at least sets you up with the hope of a happily ever after. In a world of angst and irony, that's actually a precious thing. At least it is to my way of thinking.

How would my story go?

Something like:

Once upon a time, there was a girl who lived in an old house in the middle of the woods . . .

I realize I've come to a full stop at the fence between this field and the one that runs up to the back of the house. I study the windows, trying to see if there's any movement in them. Looking for Del's face to be staring back out at me through the dirty panes.

I don't see anything, but that does nothing to lighten my sense of disquiet. I don't know that there's a single solitary thing in this place that could, but just as I'm thinking that, I've turned away from the house to look around myself and I see it. The tree. My old friend and confidante.

Here, it's not a burnt down stump. Here, it's still tall and majestic with a full canopy.

Once upon a time, there was a girl who lived in an old house in the middle of the woods and her only friend was a big old tree . . .

So, even though I've left everybody behind, I'm not alone in this place. Just as I wasn't when I was a kid. Because she was always there for me, the White Deer Woman, her tree my haven from the darkness.

Now it's the two of us again, and I don't have to worry about what Del might do to her. Those old spirits exist on a whole other level from the rest of us. Del going after her would be like a flea or gnat going after us. Annoying, sure, but nothing you can't just swat and be done with.

I'd like to go over and press my face into the bark like I did before. It would be cooler under her heavy boughs. Safe.

But the sight of her's enough to bolster my courage. I clamber over the fence and start across the last field. The house rises taller and taller in front of me, the clapboard walls stained with mold and covered, on one side, by dead kudzu pretending to be decorative vines before it all died off. I guess that says something about the evil in this place that not even a parasite like kudzu can survive in its presence.

I can't really see inside the windows—they're too dirty and dark, the sun's too bright out here—but I don't get the sense that anybody's watching me. I look at the back porch. The door to the summer kitchen hangs ajar so it'd be easy to go in, but I circle around to the front instead.

I want to know right away if the body's still lying there at the bottom of the stairs. I want to just push the front door open, look inside, and *know*. I don't want to have to go creeping in from the back of the house to find out.

Except when I get to the front of the house I now have this urge to go back to the rear again—just to put off the moment. But I know I'm just being stupid, like I've turned into Anxiety Girl, and that's so not my style. I'm a doer, not a worrier.

So holding my breath, I step up on the porch. I wince when a board creaks underfoot, but cross to the door and push it open.

It takes my eyes a moment to adjust to the dimmer light, and then I let out that breath I've been holding.

The body's still there. Del lying in a pool of blood. Flies buzzing around him.

I give a nervous look into the open door of the parlour, down the hall to the kitchen, up the stairs to the second floor. Nothing. It's just me and the body.

So I step inside.

I approach the body and study it. The open eyes, staring at nothing. The awkward angle of the neck. The torn flesh between his chin and chest where Honey ripped out his throat. The blood, coagulated and thick with the flies.

I'm repulsed and fascinated at the same time. And truth to tell, half-expecting the corpse to sit up.

Because this isn't the real world. Nothing here plays by the laws of physics the way I know them. Here a man can be turned into a changeling of twigs and leaves. Women can be turned into children. Their mouths can be erased. Here anything can happen.

So I *am* half-expecting it to sit up, but when it does, I still give a shriek and jump backwards.

It doesn't lumber to its feet like a George Romero zombie. Instead, it's like watching a movie playing backwards. The blood runs back into the body, then the body goes bouncing back up the stairs, banging back and forth between the banisters and the wall, sucking the smears of blood into himself, until there he is, at the top of the stairs once more.

Del.

Unhurt.

Holding that shotgun, just like he had been before I pushed him.

Looking down at me with a grin.

"Gotcha!" he says.

He starts down the stairs and I back away from him. I thought I was backing out the front door, but I got my trajectory wrong and find myself backing into the parlour instead. He follows me in, the shotgun dangling from one hand.

"Man, you should have seen your face," he says. "I thought you'd piss your panties." His grin broadens. "Now tell me the truth, did you? You can tell your brother something like that."

"You can't hurt me," I tell him.

"Can't I? I'm thinking different. But we both know for sure you can't hurt me, though I got to say, I'm disappointed that you'd try."

"You're a monster."

"Nothing you didn't make."

"Bullshit! I didn't make you. A child doesn't make an adult want to fuck her—especially not her own brother."

Del shrugs. "Mama thought different."

"Mama was as sick as you."

"Father Cleary told me you confessed to him."

"Yeah, and then *he* did me."

"Can you blame him?" Del asks. "Hot little thing like you, who's already proved she'll put out?"

"Goddamn you!"

A funny thing happens then. I step towards him, swinging a little girl's fist, but by the time I reach him, I'm my normal size and instead of hitting him in the chest, my fist connects with his cheekbone. He staggers back, then does that wavy thing with his free hand, and I fly back and hit the wall behind me.

It knocks the breath out of me, but I get up as quick as I can. My back hurts from where I banged up against the wall and I nurse my hand. The skin's all broken across the knuckles.

Then I realize that I'm still full-grown.

"Now this is interesting," Del says. "Turns out you've got a smidgeon of backbone still left in you."

"You—"

"Oh, shut up," he says.

He waves his hand at me again, and again I bang up against the wall. This time I'm a little girl again.

"There," he says. "You see? What did that get you? Two seconds of freedom from my will?"

"I don't—"

"I can do any damn thing I want to you," he says. "But you know what? If you want things to be like they really are, then why don't we just do that."

Another wave of the hand and I'm full-grown again, but not the twenty-something I see myself as in the otherworld. Instead he's returned me into the Broken Girl: frail and brittle, tottering on weak legs, half my body numb. It's all I can do to keep standing.

"Now there's my little sister that the world knows and loves, though what in goddamn hell anyone sees in you looking like that doesn't make the first bit of sense to me."

"You know what?" I tell him. "I don't care."

He lifts the shotgun. "I could shoot you."

"Go ahead. Knowing my luck, I'll just come back to life the way you did."

"Oh, yeah? What makes you so brave all of a sudden?"

"It's not all of a sudden. But right now, it's just you and me. There's no one else for you to hurt in my place and that's the way it's going to stay."

"Oh, come on," he says. "You must have some big rescue in mind. Some trick to play."

"I don't."

"Then why the hell would you come back? You didn't really think I was dead, did you?"

I have to lean against the wall. That helps some, but it doesn't stop the trembling in my bad leg.

"I had hopes," I tell him.

I think back on that moment when I hit him. When I changed back into who *I* wanted to be. Was it just being as angry as I was? God knows, that shouldn't make a difference because I was angry before.

What did Honey say?

Something about focusing. About believing.

That was what was different, I realize. For that one moment before I hit him, I wasn't uncertain anymore. I was completely focused on hitting him. I *believed* I could hurt him, and he couldn't stop that. He didn't get back control until after, when the uncertainty hit me again.

"Well, you hoped wrong," he says. "Get this straight, little sister. No matter what happens, I'm *never* going away. You're always going to have this piece of me inside you. So you might as well get down on your hands and knees and pray to me, because in this place, I'm God."

"You're probably right."

"Goddamned right, I'm right. So let's see a little respect from you. We can start with a little begging."

"No," I say. "I meant you're right about me always being stuck with a part of you inside me. Memories don't go away. We can lock them up and shut them away so that we think they're gone forever, but even when we can't see them, they're always there."

"What the hell are you on about?"

"You. Me. This curse you've put on me because, even though I got away from you, I'm always going to be carrying a piece of you around with me."

"Damn straight," he says.

I can tell he's just mouthing the words. That he doesn't really understand what I'm talking about. I'm only just getting it myself.

Bleeding hearts would think I need to forgive him.

Honey thinks I need to forgive myself for ever thinking I was to blame, that I deserved what happened to me.

But that's not what it's about.

It's about acceptance.

It's about me accepting that I had no control over it, that it happened, and that all I can do is not allow myself to fall back into a situation where it might happen again.

And you know what? I don't need to do the rest of it by myself. Maybe I need to find the conviction and belief in myself on my own, but dealing with Del? Nope.

"You ever think of Raylene?" I ask him.

Raylene went through everything I did. She ran away, too. But before she did, she stood up to Del. She cut him with a knife, and that's why the fat drunk in the trailer park still walks with a limp.

"Why do you want to talk about her?" he says.

He's still all cocky and full of bluster, but I caught the momentary flicker of uncertainty in his eyes when I mentioned her name.

"You know what?" I tell him. "I think we need to have ourselves a little family meeting."

Lizzie

"Okay, somebody explain this to me," Lizzie said.

She'd been sitting on her haunches, staring at the spot from which Jilly had disappeared. Now she lifted her head to look at her companions. Honey was the closest. She lay on a nearby stretch of flat red rock, mouth open, her tongue lolling as though she was simply an ordinary dog. Timony perched on the petroglyph rocks, legs dangling, while Geordie studied the distant mountains. Geordie turned at the sound of her voice.

"Explain what?" he asked.

"How does it work? This world where Jilly's gone—it's inside her head, right? So, if she's gone there—you know, inside herself—shouldn't her body still be here with us? How can she physically go inside her own mind?"

"Who knows?" Timony said. "How do the Walking Hills of Tremaynse travel without legs?"

Lizzie just looked at him. "You know that doesn't make any sense either?"

I think that's his point, Honey said. *Many things are possible, here in the otherworlds. In some parts you can find anything. You only need to go deep enough.*

"Everybody keeps saying that, but it just seems too weird."

"Weird?" Geordie said. "Sure. But too weird? I don't know. These are also called the dreamlands—the place we go when we dream. And I don't know about you, but I've had some weird dreams in my time."

"So if I dreamed I went to a place where fish breathed air and had arms and legs and lived in skyscrapers . . . that place would actually exist somewhere in here?"

The otherworld is infinite, Honey said.

Timony nodded. "It has to be, to fit everything in."

"I guess."

Honey stood up and stretched.

It's time I returned to my family, she said. *You will be safe here until Jilly returns.*

Like that was a given, Lizzie thought. None of them wanted to talk about it, but they'd all been there. They'd all seen the power Del could wield. What were the chances that Jilly was even still alive at this moment? The world she was in had immediately closed behind her so that neither Honey nor Timony could get a reading on how she was doing.

But if Geordie and Honey weren't going to talk about it—and they were way closer to Jilly than she was—Lizzie certainly had no intention of bringing it up. It didn't seem right for her to dash their hopes.

"Yeah, we should be fine," Lizzie said.

"Thanks for everything," Geordie added. "You totally saved the day."

I only did what Jilly would have done for any of us.

The trace of a smile touched Geordie's lips. "She is a going concern, isn't she? It doesn't matter what's going on in her life, she's always ready to drop everything to lend a helping hand."

The dog nodded. *She thinks the light she carries was a gift from one of the old spirits, but all it does is illuminate the largeness of heart that was already there.*

They were using the present tense, Lizzie thought, but the things they were saying still felt like eulogies.

If you should need me, Honey said, *you have only to call for me.*

She turned and started down the trail.

"Honey!" Lizzie called after her.

The dog turned.

"I was wondering . . . how come you don't just, you know, teleport to where you're going?"

Tele . . . oh, I see. I understand how you got that idea, but what we have been doing is walking between worlds. It's not quite the same thing. There are still distances that must be travelled by foot.

"Bummer. Teleporting would be cool."

I suppose. Though I like to take the time to feel the dirt under my feet when I travel.

"Time," Timony said, "runs differently in different parts of the other-world. Some places it passes more quickly—where a day for you would be a year for those you left behind."

"Like Rip Van Winkle," Geordie said. "Or True Thomas."

The doonie nodded. "In others, your year is another's day. It's why the otherworld is so dangerous—for anyone unfamiliar with its reaches, but especially for mortals. But it's even dangerous for fairy and the First People—what you call cousins."

"Except you know your way around, right?" Lizzie asked.

"Somewhat. But I'm no expert."

Joe is, Honey said.

She'd been sitting through the conversation, but she stood up on all fours once more.

Until later, she added. *And Timony—you might consider fetching your companions some water.*

Turning, she padded down the trail and was quickly lost from sight.

"Water would be good," Lizzie said.

The doonie smiled. He gathered a pile of dirt and bits of stone onto a stretch of flat red rock and sat down in front of it. Bunching it together, he began to speak over the tidy mound. His voice was low-pitched, but Lizzie already knew it was in some fairy language so she wouldn't understand it anyway.

Geordie came over to stand with her.

"What's he doing?" he asked.

"Asking the dirt if it wants to be water, I guess."

Except it turned out that Timony wasn't summoning water. As he continued to speak over the mound he'd gathered on the rock in front of himself, the dirt began to take on the shape of a pot. A moment later, and he had a wide-mouthed clay bowl. He grinned at them when Lizzie clapped, then cupped his hands above the vessel. This time his voice woke water that rose up to the tops of his fingers and overflowed into the bowl under his hands.

"Good trick," Geordie said.

The doonie shrugged, but Lizzie could tell he was pleased so she clapped again.

When he offered the bowl to them, Lizzie took it first and had a long swallow. She couldn't remember the last time anything had ever tasted so good. The water was cool and fresh, as though it had just been dipped from a mountain stream.

"Not too much," Timony said. "At least not all at once."

Lizzie had another mouthful, then reluctantly passed the half-full bowl to Geordie. While he drank, she walked back over to the place where Jilly had disappeared.

"I still think it would be cool to know how to—"

She didn't get to finish. Two strangers suddenly appeared in the spot and she scrambled back.

"Whoa," she said, then took up one of the defensive stances that her old gym-mate Johnny had taught her.

"Easy," Geordie said.

Lizzie had time to see that the newcomers were both young women—one red-haired with a feral tangle of curls, the other dark-haired and dressed like a skateboarder. Then the red-haired woman flung herself at Geordie and wrapped her arms around his neck. They were obviously old friends.

"How could you *scare* us like that?" she demanded. "We thought you were dead."

"I think I was."

The woman pushed back to look him in the face. "What?"

Geordie smiled. "This is my sister Christiana," he said, introducing her to Timony and Lizzie.

"And I'm Mother Crone," the dark-haired skateboarder said.

"That's Timony," Lizzie said. "I'm Lizzie and I've got to say, you don't look like a crone."

"Oh, you'd be surprised at how old she is," Christiana said.

The dark-haired woman shot her a look, but Christiana only shrugged and offered a sweet smile in return.

"I'm . . . surprised to see you," Geordie said to Mother Crone.

"You shouldn't be. I've never meant you any harm."

"I know. You sure were right about the danger. But . . ."

"But I should have let you decide for yourself what to do about it," Mother Crone said. "Believe me, I know that now."

Okay, what was going on here? Lizzie wondered. She hadn't even known that Geordie had a sister. Now who was this other woman going to turn out to be? His mother? Too young. But there was obviously history here.

"But I'm fine now," Geordie said. "I guess you didn't see that I'd get past dying and come back."

Christiana hooked her arm in his. "I need to hear this whole story."

But Mother Crone wasn't done yet.

"First I owe you an apology," she told Geordie.

"No, it's okay. I understand why you had to keep me at the court."

"Well, for that, too, but I meant for something else."

Geordie's eyes narrowed. "You had another enchantment on me?"

"Moons, no. It has to do with our relationship over the past couple of years. Or rather, the mess I've made of it."

"You don't have to explain."

"I think I do. I want to."

"But—"

"Hear her out, Geordie," Christiana said. "For my sake."

She unhooked her arm from his and gave him a little push toward Mother Crone.

"You guys need to talk this out," she said.

She walked away from them and made a show of having a great interest in the petroglyphs on the rocks. Geordie and Mother Crone waited a moment, then moved away as well, going to stand by the edge of the mesa. Lizzie watched them talking until she realized she was staring. Turning away, her gaze went to Timony, who was still looking at the pair with big eyes.

It took her a moment to realize that he was starstruck.

"Okay, what do you find so interesting in all of this?" she asked him.

"It's—she's a *seer*. I wasn't sure at first, because she looks different than I remember from the last time I saw her, and people called her by a different name, but I'm sure it's her."

"Which means—what?"

"Well, she's like royalty, isn't she?"

Lizzie smiled. "So what? Do fairy have their own version of *E!*? Is this like the fairy version of *Entertainment Tonight*?"

"I'm not sure what that means."

"Do you like to follow the gossip of the rich and famous?"

"Well, surely. When was the last time you saw a seer? It's like being allowed into the inner workings of one of the courts."

"Not judge and jury, I'm guessing."

"No, no. The fairy courts. That's where I saw Mother Crone before. It was at the wedding of Tatiana's daughter Saireen to the Prince of the Golden Court in Demaskendale. Of course, being a doonie, I wasn't a member of the court, but I had a good seat in the second hundreds."

She gave his arm a little tug. "Well, let's get closer so we can hear what they're saying."

"Oh, no," he told her. "We must allow them their privacy." He gave a slow shake of his head, then added in a tone of voice that Siobhan might have used after meeting some admired musician such as Johnny Doherty. "When Geordie told me he was a fiddler at her court it never really registered."

"I think there was more going on than fiddling," Lizzie said. "Or at least fiddling that didn't involve musical instruments."

Timony's eyes went wider. "Do you really think?"

Lizzie laughed. The sound of it was odd in her ears until she realized that she couldn't remember the last time she'd been able to laugh.

She gave the doonie a hug.

"You know what?" she said. "I think everything's going to be all right."

"I hope so."

He gave Geordie and Mother Crone another look that seemed wistful.

"*Now* what is it?" she asked.

"It's just . . . I never had a wife or even the possibility of one. I always thought it would be nice."

"Oh, I don't know. I think they're overrated."

Timony gave her a surprised look.

"Or maybe it just never works out for me, either," she said. "I always seem to fall for musicians. But if they're in my band, it usually gets awkward. And if they're in another band . . . well then, they're never around, because either they're travelling, or I am."

"Maybe you need to look for someone with a different sort of job."

"You don't exactly get to choose who you fall for."

"But surely you've met other intriguing men," Timony said. "What about that Grey fellow?"

Lizzie laughed. "Oh right. Hook up with a guy who hates the music that's my life—not to mention that he hates humans, period. No, if I was going to get involved with anybody I know right now, it'd be Con—the guitarist in my band—but that would just be a big mistake."

"Well, if it can't work out for us," Timony said, "I hope it works for them."

He nodded to where Geordie and Mother Crone were still talking.

Lizzie shook her head. "I don't know what their deal is, but did you not catch the way Geordie and Jilly were looking at each other?"

"But Mother Crone is a seer."

"Doesn't matter, if they don't have the sparks."

"I don't know about that."

Lizzie turned to see what he was looking at in time to see Mother Crone give Geordie a kiss that was anything but chaste.

Geordie

Galfreya and Christiana are pretty much the last people I expected to run into out here in the middle of otherworld nowhere, but I suppose I shouldn't have been surprised. At least not with Christiana. By all accounts—her accounts, mind you, related over lazy Sunday afternoons at Christy and Saskia's place, or after-hours at some bar where I've been playing—she's in and out of the otherworld all the time. She's had more adventures than a character in one of those old movie serials, and some of them were seriously strange.

So it's not such a stretch to find her here, out in the middle of nowhere. I've had her pop up in places almost as unexpected.

But Galfreya . . .

Galfreya rarely strays far from her court in the mall. It's enough of a way to define her that it was certainly a point of contention in our relationship, even if I never pushed her on it. It'd just sit there in my head. A minor annoyance, most of the time, because I liked the music in the mall. I liked being with her in her own space. But there were times when I'd just want to be with her in some of my old haunts—the places that I felt defined me. The Lee Street Market. Fitzhenry Park. The clubs in Crowsea and Lower Foxville. The sessions at the Harp.

She'd always have some reason not to come with me. It got to the point where I thought maybe she *couldn't* leave the mall. Like if she ever did, she'd burst into flame the way stories say a vampire will when it steps into sunlight.

Or maybe she'd live up to her speaking name and turn into a hag, or she'd dissolve into water, or *something*.

It wasn't something she'd ever talk to me about.

Hazel and Edgan would tell me not to take it personally.

"All seers have inexplicable eccentricities and habits," Hazel said. "It's not something they choose, or the price for their gift. It just seems to work out that way."

"Like pipers."

She gave me a confused look.

"They're all a little crazy," I told her. "It just seems to come with the territory."

She nodded. "That's it. It comes with the territory. In Mother Crone's case, she remains here, in the court."

Edgan's explanation was more like a parent dealing with a problem by saying "because I say so."

"She's the seer," he told me. "So she can do what she wants. Who are we to question her?"

"Would it kill her to come out with me once in awhile?"

He shook his head. "That isn't the point. The point is that this is how she is. You can either accept it or not. It has nothing to do with you. She leaves the court at no one's bequest, and she is not required to explain why."

"Because she's a seer."

He nodded gravely, obviously happy that I understood. But I didn't. I just didn't see the point in arguing it with a couple of treekin—especially since Galfreya herself wouldn't discuss the matter. I had to either accept it or not.

And for the past couple of years, that's just what I did. I accepted it.

So finding her here, this far from the court—not to mention in the company of my brother's shadow . . .

It was confusing, to say the least.

But as she continued to talk, I realized I wasn't about to get an explanation now either. That wasn't why she was here.

When I did understand what she wanted, I shook my head.

"There's Jilly now," I said.

She nodded. "There's always been Jilly. I know how you feel about her and I respect those feelings. But we have something special, too, and what we have can be real."

"It's not that."

"I have to earn your trust again. I understand that."

I shook my head. "It's not just that. You say you had me under an enchantment and I believe you, but the truth is, you almost didn't need it. Deep down inside, all I wanted these past few years was to not be locked into a re-lationship with any woman—even one as gorgeous as you. I know that sounds crazy. But really, for all my trying to get you to commit more, I wanted it casual, too."

"But you were always pushing for more."

"I know. I did want more. It just took me forever to figure out who I re-ally wanted it with. It took me learning she feels the same way that I do. It took me dying and her crying over the changeling mess that was left of my body—and if that doesn't bring the point home, I don't know what could."

"I'm not going to just give up," she said.

"We can't choose who we love—or who we don't."

"Don't you think I know that? Why do you think I'm here? I'm ready to give it all up. The court, magic, everything."

"You shouldn't have to change who you are to be with the person you love."

"No, that's just the way it works when a fairy falls for a mortal."

"Galfreya . . ."

She didn't let me finish. Instead, she just kissed me—a hard and passion-ate kiss filled with magic, but the magic of a woman, not a fairy. It was de-manding and expectant, but yielding, too. And I admit it was a long moment before I finally pushed her away.

What can I say? I'm a guy and she's a gorgeous woman. We have history. My body responded to her because of it, because it knew the familiar way we fit together. Because it felt right, just the way it always did.

But I did push her away.

"You can't say you didn't feel anything," she said.

"That's not the point."

"I think it's the whole point."

She stepped toward me again, but I backed off a step.

"I'm sorry," I said. "But it's too late. Everything's changed. I want to be with Jilly now."

She folded her arms across her chest.

"And where is Jilly?" she asked.

"She's . . ."

I didn't even know how to begin to explain the world inside Jilly's head. I settled on, "She has some stuff she needs to deal with."

"Without you."

I wasn't particularly happy about it myself, but that was neither here nor there.

"It happens," I said.

I glanced away from her across the mesa top. Christiana was leaning against a pile of rocks that were covered with petroglyphs. Lizzie and Timony were farther away, the doonie studiously trying to pretend that he wasn't watching us. I turned back to Galfreya.

"There's not a whole lot else to say," I told her. "Maybe we should rejoin the others."

Her gaze met mine, and I saw the world of hurt sitting there in her eyes.

Why now? I couldn't help but wonder. After all the time we'd been together and she'd never said anything, why had our relationship suddenly become so important to her?

She looked as though she was going to say something else, but then she simply nodded and we started back toward the others. Christiana immediately bounced up from where she'd been sitting.

"How did it go?" she asked.

"It didn't," Galfreya said.

And then she disappeared. Took that step from this world, away into another.

Christiana looked confused. "What'd I say?"

"Nothing," I told her. "But if you were aiming for a career as a matchmaker, you might want to consider some other options."

"But you guys are so great together."

"I guess we were. In our own way. But . . . everything's changed."

"She only did what she did to keep you safe," Christiana said. "Because she loves you. Granted, she should have talked with you about it first, but come on, Geordie. Give her a chance. I know she's sincere."

"I want to be with Jilly," I said.

"You . . ."

"And she wants to be with me."

Christiana's eyes went wide and then she grinned.

"You have got to be kidding me," she said.

"Why is that so strange?"

She shrugged, still grinning.

"It's just—well, according to Christy, the two of you have been doing this dance for pretty much ever, but no one ever thought you guys would get your heads out of the sand long enough to realize how perfect you are for each other."

I smiled. "So you approve?"

"Approve? What does what I think have to do with anything? But yeah. Since you're asking. I totally approve. Jilly's going to be the coolest sister-in-law."

"I didn't say we were getting married."

"I know, I know. It's just a figure of speech. Everything's good. In fact, it's great."

"What's great?" Lizzie asked as she and Timony came up to join us. "And where did Mother Crone go?"

"Who cares?" Christiana told her. "Geordie and Jilly are finally going to be a couple."

Lizzie smiled.

"But speaking of Jilly," Christiana went on. "Where is she? And what was all this crap about you dying and coming back?"

"It's a long weird story."

"And we're in a hurry to go where?"

So we all sat in the shade of the petroglyphs and got caught up with each other's stories. But the whole time I couldn't stop worrying about Jilly. I knew—better than anyone, maybe, considering I was the one who'd died—just how powerful Del was. I wanted to be full of hope, but the longer Jilly was gone, the heavier my heart grew.

Joe

There was something solid underfoot—dirt, he thought, though he couldn't see it. It just had that rough and uneven texture against the soles of his boots. And he could hear the sound of moving water. A river, maybe. Or waves lapping against a lake shore. There was an echo, so it was hard to tell what it actually was, or where it was coming from.

Everything else was mist. An oddly dry mist that was of no particular temperature, but it certainly wasn't cool.

Joe didn't know where he was, but he knew it couldn't be good. The last thing he remembered was turning, but not quickly enough. That club of Minisino's caught him on the back of the head and then . . . and then . . .

There was this.

Whatever this was.

Mist. Silence, except for the sound of that water. Nothing to smell. Nothing to see.

All things considered, he could guess where Minisino's club had sent him. There were stories about a place that lay between the world of the living and wherever the dead go when their time was finally up and done. A kind of holding ground. Supposedly, everybody paused here on their journey. Most went on, took the next turn of the wheel. Those that didn't . . . they stayed here, or haunted the world of the living. Restless. Unhappy. Unable to go back, unable to move on.

The key here was, you had to be dead to reach this place.

Funny. He'd always thought he'd be looking death straight in the face when his time came. Instead, he'd been taken down by a coward's blow from behind.

It was his own damn fault.

He should have stayed on track. He should never have let himself get involved in a war that wasn't going to happen anyway. He should have realized that the ghost buffalo couldn't cause any damage if they crossed over to the world of the living, and let the fairy courts and buffalo sort it out between themselves.

It didn't help that nobody else had seen it, either. Not Tatiana or Jack. Not Ayabe. Not even Raven. None of them.

Only that slip of a shadow of Christy's had her eyes open wide enough to actually see what was going on.

Being distracted as he'd been was no excuse, but what he should have done was forget the buffalo and concentrate on his own business. Family business. The kinds of things that buffalo war chiefs and fairy queens didn't care about and certainly wouldn't lend a helping hand to fix because they were too busy creating endless crises of their own.

But it was too late now. He wasn't going to see either Cassie or Jilly again. Wasn't going to hunt with Honey, carouse with Jack, shoot a game of pool at Jimmy's, or have any more arguments with old Jack Whiteduck back on the rez.

That wheel had turned all the way to the end and let him off here.

He turned around in a slow circle, trying to decide where to go. Heading for the water seemed like a good bet. At least it would be a start. Trouble was, he just couldn't pinpoint where it was. It sounded like it was coming from all around him.

Maybe it was. Maybe he was on an island.

Then he heard something else—the scuffle of a footstep in the dirt. He faced that direction and then there was Minisino, stepping out of the mist.

"Which one of them killed you?" Joe asked him.

The buffalo war chief stopped and studied him without expression for a long moment.

"The big fat black man," he said finally. "Picked me up with one hand and gave me a shake that broke my neck."

"Raven."

Minisino nodded.

The thought that Lucius would avenge him surprised Joe, considering how everything Joe did seemed to annoy him.

"I thought it'd be Jack," he said.

"The coyote? He tried."

"You didn't hurt him, I hope."

"Didn't really get a chance."

"Good." Joe waited a beat, then added, "So was this the outcome you were looking to have?"

He couldn't help the dig. Hell, the buffalo's stupidity had gotten him killed, so Joe felt he was entitled to say pretty much anything he damn well felt like saying.

Minisino glared at him. "Things would have gone just fine if you and your friends had minded your own business."

"What makes you think it wasn't our business?"

"You're a half-breed, but I don't remember hearing that there was any cerva or fairy blood in that mix."

"See, that's where you screwed up," Joe told him. "You have no respect for anybody but yourself. If you had half the heart you think you do, you'd understand that everything that happens is everybody's business. You see something wrong, you do something about it. You don't turn and walk away."

"What the hell do you think I was doing? Cerva were being killed. I was going to stop it."

"You know you can't lie in this place, don't you?" Joe said.

"I'm not—"

Joe shook his head. "No, don't even try. Christiana had it right. You just wanted to be the big shot in the campfire stories. Anything you did was for the sake of power. To be looked up to. To be remembered. Tatiana cares more about those poor dead cerva than you ever did."

"You think you know all the answers, don't you?"

"No, just a few of the little ones."

Minisino shrugged. "It doesn't matter. You died with me today. Maybe you've got some big scary spirit power hiding there inside your half-breed body, but in the end it didn't do you any more good than my army did me. I can still count the coup for your death."

Big scary spirit power? Joe thought. What the hell was he talking about?

But all he said was, "I don't think a coward's blow from behind counts as taking coup."

"Who cares? You're still dead."

Minisino turned away then.

"I'll see you in the hunting grounds," he said over his shoulder. "And when I do, I'll kill you again." He paused long enough to give Joe a grin.

"Maybe that's what eternal bliss means. I get to kill little pissants like you, over and over and over again."

And then he disappeared into the fog.

Joe listened to him go. There was the sound of footsteps. Then something being dragged on the dirt. A splash. A creak of wood. More water splashing, this time against something hollow. Then nothing.

He'd launched a canoe. Joe realized. And now he was paddling off into the next turn of his wheel.

He waited a moment, then set off in the direction Minisino had taken. When he came to the place where water met land, he still couldn't see either. But he did see the bow of a second canoe.

This one was his, he supposed.

He touched the rough cedar of its side, but he didn't launch the craft. He had no intention of stepping on any new wheel just yet. That mystery could wait. He had unfinished business with the living. He wasn't sure if he could interact with them—some spirits could, some couldn't—but he had to at least see them one more time. Cassie and Jilly. Jack. Honey.

He turned and retraced his steps through the mist. Twenty paces later, he stepped in water and only just stopped himself from losing his balance and falling in.

Maybe this *was* an island. Except . . .

He reached forward and there it was. The bow of a canoe. It was either the same one he'd just left behind, or so similar it might as well be.

He turned and set off a third time, and again after twenty paces or so, he was stopped by water and found a cedar canoe.

Interesting.

If there was one thing Joe had a knack for, it was finding things. His sense of direction—whether in the world Raven had made or the otherworlds—was uncanny. It was like he had a compass hardwired into his brain. He never got lost.

But here . . .

He smiled. Well, life was complicated. Why should death be any different?

He looked through the mist, over the water. There was nothing to see. No sound came to him except for the water. Lapping against the shore by his feet. Washing softly against the end of the canoe that was in the water.

He backed off a few steps and sat cross-legged on the ground. Taking out his tobacco pouch, he rolled himself a cigarette. He tossed a pinch of tobacco to each of the four directions, then lit the cigarette and repeated the offerings with the smoke.

Half-breed, the buffalo war chief had called him. Like it was an insult.

Funny how some people took this idea of racial purity so seriously. Like everybody's spirit wasn't pulled out of that same pot of Raven's, back in the long ago. No matter how different people looked—cousin, human, fairy—inside they were all the same. It was only what you did with the spirit that made a difference.

Big heart or sour twist.

Generous spirit or miser.

You had a choice.

But you had to make that choice, or the circumstances around you would make it for you. People would decide for you.

He remembered when he first came to the Kickaha rez. When asked his clan, he'd say Red Dog, after his mother's, a clan of gangly rez dogs, but they'd hear Crow. He had the blood of both, only the elders—the aunts and old Jack Whiteduck, who'd been the new young shaman back then—focused on the Crow and likened it to the tribe's guardian spirits. Except when they said crow, they meant corbae, because crow in the old Kickaha language translated into any kind of blackbird or jay: crow, raven, rook, blue jay, grackle. All the corbae cousins. The guardian spirits of the Kickaha.

That was the way of the world. People met you and they either looked for how you were similar to them, and welcomed you into their circle, or focused on how you were different, so that all you could be was a stranger at best, an enemy at worst.

Trouble was, if you didn't have a clear enough idea about your own identity, you could become what the people around you decided you were.

Good man, bad man.

Crazy man, brave man, thief.

Living man, dead one.

Right now, he was lying on that plain where the buffalo had gathered. Head probably bleeding from the blow he'd taken from Minisino's club. Not breathing.

They were going to say he was dead.

If enough of them believed it, it could come true.

Or at least stay true.

But it didn't have to be that way.

Because that was the part of this holding ground that wasn't talked about as much. Sure, spirits stayed here for a time before they either moved on, or returned to haunt what they'd left behind. But it was a place of more possibilities than the next turn on the wheel or the ghost road.

Supposedly, you could also find your way back into your own body. Have a second chance on your old wheel. All you had to do was get back.

It should be a piece of cake, for an old crow dog with his talents.

Trouble was, Joe didn't have the first idea where to go.

Every direction looked, sounded, smelled the same.

Every direction led back to water and the canoe that would take him on.

"What do you say, spirits?" he asked the mist. "Is there one of you out there willing to lend me a hand in this? Or have you decided that this part of my story's well and truly done?"

There was no reply, but he hadn't really expected one.

It looked like this was something you were supposed to figure out on your own.

Grey

My ears are still ringing from Raven's summoning cry when a pair of crows appear in the sky above us. They come spiralling down at a dizzying speed and change into a pair of teenage girls just before they touch the ground. I'm impressed with their balance. Neither of them so much as stumbles in her landing.

As soon as they touch the ground they turn to Raven and start jabbering away, the two voices intermingling so that it seems like it's only one person talking.

"We didn't kill them."

"Not even one."

"I know we didn't try to stop them."

"But you never said stop them."

"You never said anything."

"You just said find the bogans."

"You never said what to do when they were found."

"And you know crow boys."

"They can be all sharp beaks and talons."

"So they're all dead dead dead."

"Veryvery dead."

"And in lots of little pieces."

Raven holds up a hand, and the pair immediately fall silent.

"Crow girls," Jack says from beside me, his voice soft, the tone implying that it's a big mistake.

I glance at him, but he only shrugs.

Raven points to where Cassie's holding Joe.

"I need you to fix this," he said.

The crow girls look at Joe's body, and they seem surprised.

"Who did this?" one of them asks.

Raven jerks a thumb in the direction of Minisino's body.

The other girl shakes her head. "A little buffalo man killed Joe?"

Her—sister? It must be, they look so similar. She nods and says, "How did a little buffalo man get so powerful?"

It's odd the way they keep referring to Minisino as little. The pair of them are so skinny and small themselves. If Minisino were alive and standing, he'd be twice their height.

"He didn't," Raven says. "He struck Joe down from behind."

I've been finding myself agreeing with Jack. Why has Raven brought in a couple of little girls to help us with this? But when he tells them how Joe died, something changes in their eyes. They go dark and old and more dangerous than anything I've ever seen before. And then I remember a story that's sometimes added to the one about the beginning time, about how a pair of crows were already here in the long ago, watching Raven make the world.

"If we bring Joe back," one of them says, "what will he do?"

The other one nods. "Will he go all Jack Daw on us and start a clan feud with the buffalo?"

"I don't know," Raven says. "It's Joe. Anything could happen. But right now I need you to heal him."

The girls nod. They study Joe's body for a long moment, then start to talk in tandem again.

"We'd like to," one of them says.

"But it's too late."

"He's already gone on."

"Into the mists."

Raven's frown isn't one I'd want directed at me.

"Can't you go and bring him back?" he asks.

One of the crow girls nods. "But you'll have to kill us to do that."

"It's true," the other says.

"But we don't mind."

"We've never been dead before."

One of them drops a switchblade from the sleeve of her jacket and thumbs it open with a loud *snikt*. She flips the knife so that she's holding it by the tip of the blade and offers it to Raven.

Raven shakes his head and turns to Cassie.

"I can't ask that of them," he says.

The girl then offers the blade to Cassie, but before Cassie can say anything, Anwatan steps up.

"Nobody else has to die," she says. "Not when I'm already dead. Just tell me how to find him, and I'll go."

Jilly

Before Del even knows what I'm doing, I reach out.

Out and out and out.

Away from this world inside my head.

I'm making another once upon a time.

Once upon a time, there were two sisters and whatever one felt, the other did, too.

That's a good start.

Once upon a time, there were two sisters and whatever one felt, the other did, too, so when one of them called to the other, she always heard, and she always came. No matter how far away she was. No matter what.

And just like that—here in the world inside my head, in the house from hell where Raylene and I grew up—she's here with us. My little sister. His, too.

She appears with her back to me, facing Del.

"The fu—" she starts.

Except then she sees that Del's already lifting the shotgun. So she does what Raylene always does. Acts, without thinking. Instinct.

She steps right up to him, knocks the barrel of the shotgun aside, and drives her knee into his groin. He drops the shotgun, and it vanishes before it hits the ground. She shoves him back. Her hand goes into the pocket of the jacket she's wearing and comes out with a flick-knife that she snaps open.

But she doesn't have to use it.

Del stays where he's fallen, staring at her with confused, scared eyes.

"She's not supposed to be here," he says. "I'm in charge here. *I'm* in charge!"

"In your dreams," Raylene tells him.

Then she finally turns and sees me leaning against the wall. She backs up so that she can keep an eye on Del, but still see me.

"Hey," I say.

She shakes her head. "Christ, you look like hell."

That's Raylene for you. Always the diplomat.

There was a time when we looked enough alike that we could be mistaken for each other. But that was before the accident. We don't stand at all the same anymore. And she's done something new with her hair. It's short and she's had it straightened. It looks good on her and I say as much.

"Yeah, yeah," she tells me, but she smiles to take the sting out of it. "I'm a regular prom queen. You mind telling me where we are? Because I've got an idea, and I don't much care for it."

"It's the old house," I confirm.

"And we're here with that piece of crap because . . . ?"

She indicates Del with the blade of her knife.

"It's a long story," I say.

"Well, considering I was sleeping peacefully in my bed a few minutes ago, so I'm probably dreaming now, I'd guess we have all the time in the world."

I nod. "Just a sec'. I want to try something."

When I reached out for Raylene and brought her here, I could feel myself tapping into the essence of this place—the way that Del does, I guess, to make the things he does happen. So I try it again.

Once upon a time . . .

Once upon a time, there was a girl who looked Broken, but she'd always left out milk and honeycakes for the good spirits, and so one day they took pity on her and made her whole again.

"Whoa," Raylene says.

I smile and straighten up from the wall. I'm like I was when I first entered the otherworld what feels like centuries ago. Has it only been a day? But I'm unbroken again. Twenty-something and strong. If we had a mirror, I'm sure that Raylene and I would look almost the same except for our hair.

"Nice trick," she says. "I take it we're not in Kansas anymore."

I shake my head. "No, we're definitely in Oz. Or at least the Carter version of Oz."

"I'm still waiting on that explanation," she says.

"I know. Just let me do one more thing."

I look at Del.

Once upon a time, I think, there was an evil brother who made life miserable for his sisters. But one day they defeated him and whenever he had a bad thought after that, leather cords appeared and bound him hand to foot so that he couldn't move and do anybody any harm.

And there Del is, all tied up.

I could get so used to this.

"I think you can put your knife away," I tell Raylene.

She studies Del for a long moment, then slowly nods. I see her thumb push the release button, and she flicks the blade back into its handle. She stows it in the pocket of her jacket.

"Stop stalling," she says. "I want to know exactly what the hell's going on here."

Joe

She made no sound, but Joe still looked up at her approach. She seemed taller and more regal than he remembered, but maybe that was only because he was sitting cross-legged in the dirt while she was still standing. He started to get up, but she sank gracefully into a position similar to his, facing him, their knees almost touching.

"Now I know for sure I'm dead," he said as she smoothed out the fringes dangling from the hem of her dress.

"But you don't have to be," Anwatan told him. "I can take you back."

"I like the sound of that. You're not what I was expecting when I called out to the spirits, but I'm happy to see you all the same—don't doubt that for a moment."

She cast her eyes down for a moment and looked—not exactly nervous. Just uncertain.

"But I have to ask you a favour first," she said.

Joe took out his tobacco pouch and started to roll another cigarette.

"The thing with favours," he said, not bothering to look at what his fingers were doing, "is that they should be just that, no strings attached. Maybe you don't know me well enough, but I don't trade in favours. But if you have a need, if I can help you and no one gets hurt in the process, all you've got to do is ask."

"I didn't really mean it like that. It's just . . . really important."

Joe put the cigarette between his lips, lit it with a match, and took a drag, before offering it to her. She hesitated a moment before taking the cigarette from his fingers and bringing it up to her own lips. Joe stowed his tobacco pouch away, then took the smoke when she handed it back to him.

"It's all truth between us now, right?" he said.

She nodded.

"So, tell me what you need me to do."

"I . . ." She sighed, started again. "I need you to hide a bogan for me."

Joe's eyebrows went up.

"A bogan," he repeated.

"Yes."

"One of the ones that killed you?"

She shook her head. "But he was with them. He was there. I promised him safety, but I know if the crows find him, they'll tear him apart the way they did the others. And if they don't, somebody else probably will."

"Whoa, back up a little there. The crows have been killing bogans?"

"Raven called the crow girls to heal you," she said, "and they told him that the crows he'd sent out to find the bogans had indeed found them, but then they'd torn them apart."

"I'm having trouble working up any sympathy." He held up a hand to stop her. "I know. Every death diminishes us. But there are times you need to bear the weight of the killing so that worse things don't happen further down the road."

"That isn't our way," she told him.

"Usually isn't mine, either."

He offered her the last drag from the cigarette. When she shook her head, he ground it out in the dirt, then pocketed the butt.

"The crow girls couldn't revive you," Anwatan went on. "You had to be found and brought back, they said, but they couldn't do it without being dead themselves. They were willing to do it, too. To die, I mean."

Joe shook his head. "Today's just one damn surprise after the other."

"But then I said I'd do it."

"You already being dead."

She nodded.

"Nobody could bring you back?" he asked.

"I didn't have a body to come back to—not in one piece like yours is."

"More or less."

Joe touched the back of his skull, but there was nothing to feel there. No lump. No blood. But then this wasn't his actual body, was it?

"More or less," she agreed.

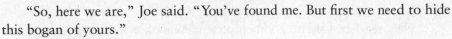

"So, here we are," Joe said. "You've found me. But first we need to hide this bogan of yours."

"No, you need to be alive to do that."

Joe nodded. "I'll do it, but not because you're helping me. I'll do it because I can and I want to. Are we clear on that?"

"Yes. Thank you. But . . ."

She hesitated.

"But what?"

"Why is it so important that it not appear that we're trading favours?"

"Why do you want this bogan kept safe?"

"He's not evil," she said. "He didn't even want to be with them in the first place."

"He still had a choice."

"Were you never young and stupid?" she asked.

Joe smiled. "I don't know that I was ever young, but I'm still pretty good at being stupid. It's what brought me to this place when I should have been off helping my sister. But I get your point."

"His name's Rabedy Collins. He can take the form of a black dog—will that make it easier?"

Joe nodded. "Nice trick for a bogan."

"Those bogans had a cousin helping them—giving them safe passage through our territories and teaching them how to shapechange. I'm told his name is Odawajameg—Odawa of the salmon clan."

"I think I heard something about that. Do the others know about him?"

"I'm not sure," she said. "I was about to mention it when Minisino . . . attacked you."

"I'll make sure the word gets out." He cocked his head. "Unless you want him to be hidden as well?"

Joe wasn't sure he could do that—this cousin had already caused too much damage—but he had to ask.

"I don't know him," she said. "I don't know if he's a good man or bad."

"Considering he was behind the bogans' little killing spree, I'd be guessing he's not someone you have over to your place for a beer and a laugh."

"I suppose . . ."

"It's out of your hands now, anyway."

She nodded. Looking down, she plucked at the fringe of her dress before finally lifting her gaze again.

"You never did answer my question," she said.

Joe shrugged. "It's just this theory I have that there's not enough goodness in the world. And we need more of it."

"I don't understand the connection."

"Well, see," he told her, "if you do somebody a favour, expecting something in return, it's not as pure as just doing it with no expectations. Doing it just for the sake of doing it, because it's the right thing."

She nodded again, but he got the sense that it was only to tell him that she was hearing him. Not that she understood.

"It's a funny wheel we're on these days," he went on. "Sometimes I feel it wobbling so much I get worried it's going to go right off track, and then where the hell would we be? The best way I know to keep it running smooth is make sure the acts of kindness outweigh the bad. I can't do it for the whole world, but I can do it in my own life, and I figure every little bit helps."

"So if I didn't bring you back, you would still do me this favour?"

"Depends," Joe said. "On whether it's righteous. And whether I could. But if it was clear on both counts, then, yeah. I would."

Anwatan smiled. "Minisino said you carry a mix of crow and dog blood. Are you sure you don't have some deer in there, as well? Because I was just telling my bogan much the same."

"That's the thing about being a mutt. Go back far enough and who knows what you've got in the mix."

"I like your attitude better than Minisino's."

"It's all in the delivery," Joe told her.

He stood in one smooth motion and offered her a hand up.

"I wish I'd known you when I was alive," she said.

"All the spirits say that."

She smiled again. It was a good smile. It took away some of the shadows in her eyes.

He started to let go of her hand, but she held his tighter.

"Hold on," she told him. "I'm taking you back. And later . . . when you are done with your business with my father and the others, I will show you how to find my bogan."

And then they were gone from that place.

Jilly

"You know how all this sounds, don't you?" Raylene says when I've given her the *Reader's Digest* version of what's been happening.

We're sitting on the front porch, leaning against opposite porch pillars at the top of the stairs. The toes of my shoes are close enough that I could tap the toes of her boots. Del's still safely tied up in the parlour. The humidity's gone now. I look away from Raylene, across the fields. A soft breeze makes the tall grass and weeds sway like they're keeping time to an old-fashioned waltz. Above them, the sky is that perfect summer blue with a couple of fat clouds lazing on the horizon.

Positive thinking and all, I think. That's what makes it this way.

Once upon a time . . .

I turn to look at my sister.

"Well, *you're* here, aren't you?" I say.

"I could just be dreaming. In fact, I *was* just dreaming before I suddenly found myself fully dressed and staring our monster brother in the face. Who's to say I'm not still dreaming?"

"You know better."

She doesn't say anything for a long moment, her gaze locked on mine. Then she slowly nods her head.

"Yeah, I guess I do," she says.

We both sit and look at the fields for a while longer before she adds, "So, do you think it's all okay now?"

"What happened to us will never be okay."

"I meant the way you've been carrying Del around in your head. Are you done with that crap now?"

I nod. "They say that the final closure is to forgive. Not to condone or forget, but to forgive, because if you don't, you end up carrying the cancer of resentment around inside you forever. I heard it described somewhere as taking poison and then waiting for the other person to die."

Her eyebrows go up. "So, do you forgive him?"

I shake my head. "But I'm okay with that. I don't feel like there's a poison inside me. I just feel . . . I feel like I'm finally done with it."

"I know what you mean," she says. "That's what happened to me. When I tracked him down in that trailer park—the real Del, I mean, fat and drunk—I was ready to cut him a new asshole in the middle of his face. But once I saw him, I knew I didn't have to do a damn thing. He was the one with the fucked up life. I realized that mine didn't have to be that way—but it would be, if I took him down."

"So, are we bad people because we can't forgive him?"

Raylene just laughs. "Well, we're not nuns. Or at least I'm sure not walking around with a rosary saying my Hail Marys. But are we bad people? Who knows? Does it matter?"

"It matters to me."

"That you forgive him, or that we be good people?"

"That we're good."

"*You're* good," she says. She answers immediately, like she doesn't even have to think about it. "Me, I'm still working on it."

"I think that makes you a good person."

She does that thing with her eyebrows again—part question, part ironic comment.

"When you know the difference between right and wrong," I explain, "and you choose to do the right thing, even when it's usually harder, that's the sign of a good person."

"I guess . . ." She waits a beat, then adds, "So, are we really inside your head? Because I've got to tell you, that kind of freaks me."

"Me, too."

"I think maybe we're not. I think all the crap in your head made some new little pocket world here in the dreamlands and *that's* where we are."

"I guess that's possible . . ."

"Let's go with probable."

I nod. "Okay. I suppose it makes more sense. Like anything makes sense in this place."

"Everything makes sense," she says, "if you study it enough. We just don't know the right physics to explain this place because it's all different once we cross over. If we could ever find the manual, we'd be laughing, but I think it's pretty much the kind of thing you have to come up on from behind. You know, catch it by surprise."

I keep forgetting how smart she is. Unlike me, she's got a real head for maths and sciences. And she totally gets computers. Me, I know how to turn them on and work the software, but she can get right inside to the mechanics of the circuitry and wires. She used to do it just for fun—because she could—but now she makes her living getting people's machines up and running, and keeping them that way.

No more stealing and scams and running wild and crazy. Like I told her, she's a good person now because she knows the difference and chooses to not break the law anymore.

" 'Course that's a problem for me," she goes on. "This being the dreamlands, I mean. Those wolf boys find out I've been back, and they're going to seriously kick my ass."

"No, I think it'll be okay. I brought you here. You didn't force your way."

"Yeah, but I don't think that'll hold much water with them, Jill. They were pretty damn clear when they told me to get out and stay out."

She's got some kind of canid connection, which seems funny to me because we come from the same gene pool and I don't have cousin blood. At least, it's never shown up and that's what everybody tells me. She made her own way into the otherworld, dreaming herself here in the body of a wolf. The trouble came when she started running with a pack of other dreaming wolves, hunting and killing.

She didn't know better. She thought she was just dreaming. But she knows now, and she would never do it again. But I doubt those friends of Joe's who gave her her walking papers would take the time to see that. Whiskey Jack and Nanobozo. If it hadn't been for Joe, they would have killed her then and there and been done with it.

"They'd have to go through me first," I tell her.

She smiles. "What would you do? Once upon a time them into kinder, gentler canids? Somehow I doubt that'd take. I think it only works here, on the things that you've been carrying around in your head."

"I guess."

"So, what are you going to do now?" she asks.

I give her a blank look.

"With Del," she says. "With this place. Are you going to shut it down and make it all go away?"

"I don't know that I should."

"You're kidding, right?"

I shake my head. "All of this is a part of who I am. I already tried to cut it out of my memories and hide it away. And you see how well that turned out."

"So you're just going to let him run free in here?"

"No. Him I'll once upon a time into something better. But this place, the memories . . . I'm just going to accept that it all happened. That it wasn't my fault. And get on with the real business of my life."

"Living."

I nod.

"You ever wake up in a cold sweat, thinking you're back in those days?" she asks.

"That never went away. It probably never will. But if it happens again, I'm not going to pretend it never happened. I'm going to hold it up to the light and tell myself that it happened, but it's done now."

"I hope it works."

"It has to," I say.

She smiles. "Yeah. And you're a tough little cookie. If anyone can make it happen, you can."

"What about you?"

She shrugs. "Like I told you. I've been done with it since I saw him in the trailer park. Sometimes I still wake up from the bad dream that I'm just a kid again and he's coming into my room, but I deal."

"You're the tough one," I say. "If you'd been here before I figured out how to stop him, you'd have just shut him down with a look."

"And a good kick in the balls."

"That, too."

She stands up. "We should go. I think we're done here."

I nod. "I've just got a couple more things I need to clean up before I go."

"Do you need a hand?"

"No, I'm good."

She cocks her head. "So, are you really going to hook up with Geordie?"

"I hope so."

"Well, whenever you talk about him it's pretty damn obvious you're head over heels."

She catches me off guard with that.

"What do you mean?" I ask.

But she just laughs. "Good luck, sis."

I start toward her, and she shakes her head.

"Don't go getting all mushy on me," she says.

Except she lets me hug her. She even puts her arms around me and sort of pats me on the back. But she seems relieved when I let her go.

"Call me when you're home," she says.

"I will."

She just stands there.

"Well?" she says after a moment. "You brought me here—aren't you going to send me home?"

"Oh. I didn't think about that."

"I was dreaming about Johnny Depp, if that helps. We were about to—"

I give her a smile. "I don't think I need to know the details."

Once upon a time, I think.

And then she is gone, and I'm alone on the porch.

I stay for a moment longer, looking out over the fields. I watch a hawk slowly circling above, following its flight until it sinks below the far trees. Then I turn back into the house, the boards of the porch creaking under my feet.

Joe

Coming back to the plain where the buffalo had gathered didn't work the way Joe had expected it would. Instead of Anwatan putting him back in his body, they were a pair of spirits, invisible to all except each other.

Joe's gaze lingered for a long morbid moment on his body, his head cradled in Cassie's lap. The blood from his wound had made a mess of her clothes, but she didn't seem to care. She just held him in the crook of one arm while she stroked his hair with her free hand, avoiding the area that had been bashed in. Zia and Maida sat on either side of his body—more still and serious than he could ever remember seeing that pair of crow girls. Raven stood behind Cassie, his gaze fixed on the cliffs on the far side of the plains. He, too, was still, but in him, it was as though he'd turned to stone. He seemed more statue than corbae.

Beyond Raven he saw the humans—the three musicians he'd met back at the hotel in Sweetwater when he went to find Cassie. They stood in an uneasy group, the two men on either side of the woman, protective, though there was no longer a threat in evidence. But that was from Joe's own viewpoint.

Their anxiety probably came from the cousins that still remained. Unlike Raven and the crow girls, the cousins wore their animal heritage on their human shapes. Walker and Ayabe both had their tall racks of antlers, lifting up into the sky. Jack was a coyote's head on a man's body, his dark, unblinking gaze on Minisino's body as though he expected the dead cerva to get up at any moment.

"This is depressing," Joe said, turning to Anwatan.

It was too much like watching his own funeral.

The deer woman nodded. "I'm sorry, I wasn't thinking. Go ahead. Just climb back into that body of yours."

"Climb back into it, huh? Just like that."

She gave him another nod. "Can't you feel it reaching for you?"

That immobile, dead thing? Joe thought. It wasn't reaching for anything. It just lay there with its head in Cassie's lap, a limp, lifeless thing.

But as soon as she'd said it, he realized Anwatan was right. He *could* feel a pull and then he saw the loose, silvery thread that ran from where he stood to the corpse Cassie was holding.

He glanced back at Anwatan.

"You'll get back to me on this business with your bogan?" he asked.

"Soon," she told him. She looked past him to where her father stood. "Will you . . . will you tell him goodbye?"

"You don't want to do it yourself?"

She shook her head. "It's why I brought us here like this. I don't want him to see me again. It hurts him too much, and I feel every ache that lies in his heart."

"It hurts him not to see you, too."

"I know. But he has to get used to it."

"I'll give him your message," Joe said.

And then she was gone.

He stood for a long moment, staring at the dead body in Cassie's arms. *His* dead body.

It was funny, he realized. He could accept it. He didn't feel any personal need for another chance at life.

But his time on this wheel wasn't done. He could feel it straining to turn. He could sense all the connections, all the lives that were a part of this turning that needed him to be here before he could go on to see what the next world held for him.

Never thought getting killed could be a selfish act, he thought.

And then he let himself go. The silver thread went tight and reeled him back toward his body. A moment later and the corpse shivered in Cassie's arms. He opened eyes that were caked shut with dust and salt. The first thing he saw was the blurry image of Cassie's face as she leaned down to kiss him.

"Don't you ever scare me like that again," she whispered.

He sensed movement on either side and realized it was the crow girls dancing around when he heard their voices.

"He's back, he's back!"

"Should we fix him, Lucius?"

"Should we, should we?"

"Oh, say we can!"

And then there was Raven's gruff voice: "Didn't I bring you here to do just that?"

"Well, yes."

"But what if you'd changed your mind?"

"Then there'd be shouting."

"It'd be all bad Maida. Bad Zia."

"Would you just get to it," Raven told them.

Cassie's face left his field of vision, replaced by the merry faces of the crow girls.

"Hello, crow dog," Maida said.

Zia nodded. "Hello, hello."

They put their hands on his head, running their fingers through his hair to where his scalp was split open. He winced when they touched the open wound.

He was about to complain. He heard Cassie warning them off. But then he felt the wound close, the flesh knit. The sharp ache in his head vanished.

He didn't just feel healed. He felt renewed.

His vision cleared and the crow girls came into sharp focus above him. Zia winked before they pulled their faces away.

"Careful," Cassie said as he started to sit up.

"Don't have to be," he said. "There's not a damn thing wrong with me anymore."

Zia smirked.

"Better than new," Maida said.

Joe sat all the way up and nodded. "No kidding. What did you do to me?" His gaze went from one to the other.

"Filled you with a bit of Grace," Zia said.

Maida just stuck out her tongue. The pair of them bounced to their feet and did a little stomp dance around him and Cassie, then they leapt into the air and two crows sped off, vanishing before they'd gone more than a few dozen yards into the sky.

"You really okay?" Jack asked.

Joe stood and gave Cassie a hand up. He put his arm around her shoulders.

"Like Maida said: better than new."

Jack wore a man's face again, and a big grin like he'd just drawn a fourth ace to match the three in his hand.

"Man," he said. "I could've used those girls that time Zella's old man beat the crap out of me. It took me weeks to get back on my feet."

"Zella's that puma girl Jack can't stay away from," Joe said to Cassie.

"I remember."

But the desire to crack jokes fled Joe when he saw Walker approaching him.

"Did you see my daughter?" he asked.

Joe nodded. "She showed me the way back to my body, but . . ." He hesitated, then added the lie: "She's gone on. She told me to say goodbye for her and to give you her love."

The cerva sighed, the ache plain in his eyes.

"There's blood between us now," Joe told him. "You, your family— they're my family now. You ever need anything, all you have to do is say the word."

"Goes for me, too," Jack said.

"I just want my daughter back. I want to see her running with the herd. I want to hear her voice."

Joe glanced at Raven.

It was too late for her, the gruff voice said in his mind. *You know that.*

Joe turned back to Walker and put his hands on the cerva's shoulders.

"That's the one thing I can't do," he said, "though it's the one thing I would do if I could."

Walker nodded. "I know."

There was so much hurt in his voice, in his eyes. Joe felt a pang of guilt. Why should he come back when she couldn't? But he knew the answer. Never mind whether your time on the wheel was done or not. If you had to die, do it while helping power players like Raven and Ayabe who could see that you were brought back again, better than new. Anwatan had died alone, and there hadn't been enough left of her body before anyone knew she was dead.

Thinking of the cerva spirit who'd shown him the way back reminded him of what she'd told him when they were still in the holding ground.

Joe returned his gaze to Raven.

"Anwatan told me something on the other side," he said. "She says there was a cousin running with those bogans—giving them safe passage through our territories and teaching them how to shapechange."

Raven nodded. "I know. Odawajameg of the salmon clan."

What, now he chose to be omnipresent? Why couldn't he have played that card before all of this began?

"How'd you know?" he had to ask.

"Grey brought him to us. I have him in custody at my roost. He will go up before a council of air and water cousins."

Standing beside Joe, Jack started to roll a cigarette, pulling out that Zippo lighter of his when he was done.

"How do you think that's going to work out?" Jack asked.

"It's not for me to say," Raven said. "But if I had my way . . ." He sighed. "There's history between Odawa and the corbae—old, unhappy history in which we're not entirely blameless. But it should have been finished by now. And I should probably learn a cerva's ability to forgive, but I can't find it in me."

"Everybody's got their own nature," Jack said, "and what you're talking about, well, right there you've got the big difference between herbivores and carnivores."

It looked like Raven was going to argue the point, but after a moment, he simply nodded.

"We need to close the door on this," Jack said.

He put the cigarette he'd rolled between his lips. A flick of his Zippo got it lit. Taking a drag, he passed it around, sharing the tobacco smoke, sealing the moment among them all. Everybody had a drag, even the humans who probably only had the barest inkling of what it meant. But Joe knew he shouldn't be too hard on them. They'd come here to stand with Cassie and him when none of them thought they'd survive the day.

When the cigarette was done and the butt stowed in Jack's pocket, Ayabe put his arm around Walker's shoulders.

"You should come with me," he said. "There are quiet places of retreat by my lake—places to let your sorrow run its course without interference or distraction from the world at large. You can stay on any of them for as long as you need."

"I . . ."

Walker's gaze went to Minisino's body, then returned to the moose lord's face. He straightened his shoulders and nodded.

"Thank you," he said. "I'd appreciate that."

Ayabe pointed a finger at Jack.

"You'd better have a brother," he said.

Then he led Walker away, and the pair of them were gone.

"What was that about?" Joe asked.

"Long story. The short version is my brother Jim's left me holding the short end of the stick again."

"You should let him take your place the next time Zella's old man comes looking for you."

Jack smiled. "Yeah, my mother'd really like that. You know how she is about Jimmy."

Joe nodded. Jack's mother doted on his brother. It was that old "the kid could do no wrong," even when the proof was staring her in the face. He supposed there were worse things than loyalty, even when it was misguided.

"I have to see about this council," Raven said.

"I won't be coming," Joe told him before there could be any talk of him showing up as a witness. "I've had my fill of this business."

Raven smiled. "I think we'll manage without you."

Before he could step away as the cerva had, Grey moved toward him.

"I'd like to come with you," he said. "If it's okay. That old history between Odawa and me still needs to be resolved."

Raven nodded and then the two of them were gone, as well.

"Well, that's that," Jack said. "But tell me. Am I the only one who thinks we shouldn't have to go through this kind of crap in the first place?"

Cassie smiled. "If that were the case, the two of you wouldn't be who you are."

"What's that supposed to mean?"

"Let me put it another way," she said. "You'd die of boredom."

"Right now, I'll take a little boredom," Jack said. "Hell, I'll take a lot."

Joe glanced at where the humans still stood in a cluster together. Hearing everything, understanding maybe a third of it, just wanting to go home and get back to their lives.

"We should get them home," he said.

Cassie nodded.

"What about that sister of yours?" Jack asked. "Aren't we going to look for her now?"

Joe couldn't believe that he'd let that slide. That's what happened when you died and then got brought back to life again. You lost all perspective on the things that mattered.

He lifted his head, casting for scent, though it was more Jilly's familiar presence he sought. It was something that had nothing to do with physical senses, but he could always find it.

Except for now.

"Damn," he said. "She's gone again. Cassie . . . ?"

He looked at the humans, knowing they couldn't just be left here to their own devices.

"I'll take them back to the hotel," Cassie said. "But you'd better be careful."

"I'm just going to see Honey—find out what happened."

"You want company?" Jack asked.

Joe nodded, but he glanced at Cassie. She came up to him and gave him a fierce hug.

"Just go," she said when she stepped back. "Both of you. And—"

"We'll be careful," Joe promised her.

"Don't worry," Jack added as they stepped away out of the between. "I'll have his back."

"Why does that not comfort me?" Joe thought he heard Cassie mutter. But by then they'd already left the plains behind.

Geordie

I had the mesa to myself.

I thought the time alone would help me feel a little balanced, but it wasn't helping at all. The problem wasn't my being here, in the middle of nowhere and farther from home than I'd ever imagined I could be. I won't say it wasn't dislocating and strange, but it ran deeper than that.

The problem was inside me, and being alone just made me focus on it without distractions.

I was on my own because Jilly still wasn't back, Honey hadn't returned, and Lizzie and the doonie had gone to fetch my fiddle from that fog-bound seashore where he and I'd first met. When I was pulled into Jilly's world, it had happened so quickly that I hadn't been able to bring it with me. I didn't even know I *was* going anywhere until I was already there. Later, when we came to the mesa, Timony hadn't thought to bring it along with us and it wasn't exactly a priority for me, considering I was nothing more than some changeling creature made up of seaweed and flotsam at the time.

It was a very odd feeling, when I realized that I'd left the fiddle behind. Considering how I've been pretty much inseparable from the instrument for as long as I can remember, you'd think it would have occurred to me much sooner, but I hadn't even missed it.

I was that worried about Jilly.

It had taken Lizzie's mentioning that it was too bad we didn't have our fiddles for me to remember my own, and even then it didn't seem nearly as important as Jilly's continued absence.

I wasn't going to say no when Timony offered to get it for me, but neither was I about to leave the mesa until Jilly got back. Lizzie went along to keep him company—though I'm sure it was as much from her wanting a change of scenery.

So off they went.

While they were gone, I tried to focus on my surroundings in an attempt to shut up the panicked voice of worry yammering away in the back of my head. It should have been easy. The landscape around me was stark, but incredibly beautiful. No matter where I turned, ranges of mountains lifted from each horizon, with a gorgeous light show starting up in the west as the sun began to dip below those distant peaks.

All I could do was worry.

And when I wasn't worrying about Jilly being away for so long, I worried about what would happen when she got back.

We'd made promises to each other before she left. I know we said we had to talk, but we both knew it meant more than that. Now I couldn't help but wonder: did we do the right thing? If it was going to work with us, wouldn't we already have been together by now?

What if it had only been something born out of the heat of the moment? She'd thought I was dead. People say things—feel things—in times of crisis that don't necessarily hold when the real world comes back into focus.

God knows I loved her. She was my best friend and weren't best friends supposed to make the best couples? I can't remember how many times I've heard of a pair of old folks celebrating some incredible anniversary—you know, they've been together for fifty years, sixty years—and when they're asked how it lasted so long, as often as not, the answer was that they're each other's best friend.

So we've got that totally going for us.

But I've never been able to hold a relationship together, and neither has Jilly. So what happens if we break up? Do I lose my best friend?

I can't imagine a life without Jilly in it.

I know we've drifted apart these past few years—we used to see each other every day. We did that for years. *Years*. And if for some reason we weren't in the same city—like when I moved to L.A. with Tanya—we'd write. There'd be phone calls.

Granted, it hadn't been quite the same since she had the accident and I got back. But the thing was, even these days, whenever we did get together, there was never any awkwardness. We'd just fall back into our old comfortable ways with each other as though nothing had ever changed.

That wasn't any big surprise, because inside each of us, nothing had changed. We still cared for each other.

But now we were going to make a change, and the truth was, it scared the crap out of me.

I sighed and turned to look at the spot where she'd disappeared.

After awhile, I got up and wandered down the trail that Honey had taken, collecting bits of wood and lengths of dried up cactus. It was going to get dark soon and we'd probably want a fire.

I managed to kill a half-hour with that and had a good pile gathered by the time the sun went down. Then I realized I didn't have either a lighter or matches to get a fire started. Hopefully Timony could work some of his magic.

But it wasn't as dark as I'd expected it to be. Back home, if you were anywhere beyond the city's light pollution, you could have trouble seeing past the length of your arm. Unless there was a moon.

There was no moon here—at least not yet—but the stars were peculiarly bright and cast a cool light by which I couldn't have read, but I could still see well enough to get around. I could even make out the petroglyphs.

I ran my fingers along their patterns, then sat down with my back to the rocks that held them. The view was still spectacular—more so, or maybe just differently so in this eerie starlight—but all I did was stare at my shoes and start running all my worries through my head again.

I know. A pointless endeavour. But did you ever try to not think about something?

I was so caught up inside myself that I never heard Lizzie and Timony return until Lizzie spoke.

"Earth to Geordie," she said.

I started at the sound of her voice. Then the words sank in, and I realized she must have called me a couple of times before I'd finally heard her.

"You're back," I said, looking up.

"And successfully, too," she said. She held a fiddle case in either hand and lifted them to emphasize her point. "We even got food that Timony didn't have to make."

I dredged up a smile. "What? Somebody opened up a pretzel stand on that impossibly desolate seashore?"

"No, we went back to the hotel. I wanted to get my fiddle, too, and let the band know we were doing okay."

There was enough light for me to see the worry crease between her eyebrows.

"What happened?" I asked.

"They weren't there. Eddie couldn't tell me where they'd gone except that the last time he'd seen them, they were with Cassie."

"Then they'll be okay," I told her. "Cassie'd never let them get into any trouble. They're probably out in the woods, still looking for us."

"I guess. Eddie got weird about the rooms, so I put another night on my charge card for all three of them."

I nodded. "That's good. I'll give you some money when we get back."

"Don't worry about it. Are you hungry?"

I wasn't, but I knew I should eat. The way things were going, who knew what was going to happen next? Better to eat while I could to keep up my strength.

"Sure," I said. "What have you got?"

Timony opened the paper bag he was carrying and the smell of fish and chips filled the air. He handed us each a package of them, then reached into the bag again and brought out a large Styrofoam cup of coffee.

"Lizzie said you'd like this," he told me as he handed it over.

"You," I told her, "are an angel."

She smiled. "Aren't I, just?"

Timony lit the fire I'd laid—I've no idea how because I wasn't watching—and we sat around it, eating the meal they'd brought. Lizzie wanted to play some tunes then, but I begged off, telling her to go ahead. Instead, she poked at the fire with a stick and looked at me across the flames.

"I take it you're not holding up so well," she said.

"That's an understatement. I can't stop worrying about Jilly—she's been gone so long."

"That might not mean anything," Timony said. "Time moves differently in different parts of the otherworld."

"I know. But then I'm also . . ."

I hesitated a moment, but knew I had to talk to someone. It might be easier with folks I didn't know so well.

"I'm also worried about what happens when she does get back," I said.

Lizzie and Timony both waited for me to go on.

"It's just we've been best friends forever," I explained, "only it was always just that. Friends."

"I have to tell you," Lizzie said. "When you and Jilly showed up at the hotel—and doesn't *that* feel like a million years ago?—I thought the two of you were *already* a couple. I didn't know any different until your sister got all excited."

"Christiana's pretty much an 'in the now' person, and she tends to wear her emotions on her sleeve."

"From the way you say it, I take it that's not the case with the rest of your family."

I hesitated a moment. Where did you even begin explaining Christiana?

I settled for, "She didn't really grow up with the rest of us."

"She's not even . . ." the doonie started to add, but broke off and gave me an embarrassed look. "I'm sorry," he said

"It's okay," I told him. I looked to Lizzie. "What Timony started to say is that she isn't human."

I gave her the short explanation, the one Christiana had given me, how she was my brother Christy's shadow: all the bits of himself that he hadn't liked when he was six or seven that he somehow rolled up into a bundle and cast off. Except she ended up having a life of her own. Took a name that was part his and part that of a girl he'd had a crush on in grade school, and there she was. Christiana Tree. She used the surname because that's what Christy called her for years, before she'd tell him who she really was. To him, she was Mystery. So, she liked to call herself Ms. Tree.

"If you'd tried to tell me this a few days ago," Lizzie said, "I'd have thought you were nuts. But now it almost doesn't seem weird."

"Tell me about it."

"So, do we all have these shadows?"

"Fairy don't," Timony put in.

"Well, you'd know," I said. "As for the rest of us . . . I guess. But I don't think it's the same for most people. I'd say you have to be pretty intense to start off. Christy certainly fit that bill. He was a bad-tempered little kid, but one day he just changed—like someone had thrown a switch inside him. He didn't suddenly start liking our parents, but he didn't bother battling them anymore. He just kind of shut himself off from everybody. At least, that's what our older brother Paddy told me."

"You have another brother?" Lizzie asked.

I nodded.

"Let's see," she said. "You're a musician and Christy's a writer . . . so he must be an artist. Or an actor."

"No, he's dead."

"Oh, I'm so sorry. I didn't mean to make a joke of him."

"I know. And I'm sorry, too. After I learned to make an effort to get along with Christy and found out that, what do you know, I actually like the guy, I wished I'd been able to do it with Paddy, too. But I never got the chance."

"What about your parents? Did you reconcile with them, too?"

I shook my head. "I didn't even try. They've always been a lost cause."

We fell silent for a few moments. Timony added some more wood to the fire—he'd taken on the role of caretaker for it, and I was happy to leave him to it. There must have been some mesquite in the new wood he'd added because its distinctive scent was soon wafting over to me.

"So, was Mother Crone really your girlfriend?" Lizzie asked.

"I think it was more that I was her boy toy. Except she surprised me today. Now she wants to get serious."

"*After* you've hooked up with Jilly."

"Isn't that always the way? But nothing should surprise me when it comes to Mother Crone. She . . ."

I broke off when I saw Timony leaning close, eyes wide. Lizzie laughed.

"You have to dish *all* the dirt," she said. "Timony's kind of like the royalty junkies back home when it comes to court fairies."

"I am not."

"You are so," Lizzie told him.

I think he blushed, though it might just have been from the way the firelight fell on his features.

"Well, there's not a whole lot to tell," I said. "I was at her court a lot—you'd have liked it, Lizzie. Fairy musicians have tunes you just *never* hear anywhere else. But you'd never get her out of the place."

"And where was Jilly during all of this?"

"She had a regular boyfriend. That's the way it's always been. When one of us isn't in a relationship, the other's been seeing someone else."

"And now neither of you is," Lizzie said. "So what's the problem?"

"Neither of us is very good at keeping a relationship going."

"Maybe you were just never in the right one."

"Maybe. But what if it doesn't work out? I'll lose my best friend."

Lizzie gave a slow shake of her head. Her gaze met mine across the fire.

"And what if it does?" she asked.

Timony nodded in agreement.

"Love is the great gift all creatures can share," he said. "It's our only chance to be a part of the Grace."

"The Grace?" I asked.

I heard a capital when he said the word and instinctively found myself repeating it the same way.

"I learned that from the First People," he said, "who call themselves the cousins. Like our friend Honey. Fairy would say it's the blessing of the moon.

It might not last, but to not dare her gift . . ." He shrugged. "One might as well not be alive."

"I understand what you're saying. It's just . . ."

"Don't let fear choose the outcome," Timony told me when my voice trailed off.

"I suppose."

"You need to distract yourself. Too much heavy thinking's not good for human or fairy."

"We should play some tunes," Lizzie said. "You could show me one of those fairy ones you were talking about."

I was afraid that would only remind me too much of Galfreya, but music's always been my way out of my head. When I'm playing, the rest of the world dissolves away. I might be unhappy, or broke, or lonely, but music could change that. It didn't so much make me forget, as give me a new perspective, and lord knew I needed a new perspective right about now.

I pulled my fiddle case closer and opened the clasps.

"Sure," I said. "Why not?"

"Music has a magic of its own," Timony said. "Maybe your playing will help Jilly return more quickly."

I already liked the doonie, but when he said that, I felt a real warmth toward him.

Lizzie and I rosined our bows and checked the tuning of our fiddles against each other.

"Okay," I said. "I got this from a troll whistle player, if you can imagine that. It sort of feels like 'Shenandoah' when it starts, but then it gets into this funny modal section that really gives it a lift. Let me show you."

I played it through, slowly, smiling when she started to pick it up by the second time around.

Rabedy

The only thing that saved Rabedy from sharing a fate similar to that of his uncle and the other bogans in Big Dan's gang was a bad case of nerves.

Anwatan had told him to wait for her here by the lake's shore, but without her to protect him, he'd been afraid that some other cousin might come along and discover him. So he hid himself away in a cave-like overhang that had burrowed its way almost ten feet into the limestone cliffs. For good measure, he'd also changed back into the shape of a black dog.

He'd hardly been in there a half-hour, when he heard the crows arrive.

At first they kept to their bird shapes, filling the air with hoarse caws, but they soon landed on the beach and took human shape. Rabedy listened to their footsteps and the snatches of conversation that drifted in and out of his hearing.

". . . can smell him. He was here."

"But he's not here now."

"Maybe, maybe not."

"He might come back."

"Or he could be hiding."

That brought a croak of laughter in response.

"Where? In a crack in the rocks?"

"Ha ha. But there might be caves in that cliff face."

Oh no, oh no, Rabedy thought. Don't look here.

But it was too late. He could hear their footsteps approaching.

What should he do, oh what should he do?

He looked like a black dog, but he was sure they'd see through to his true shape. Crows were just too smart. That's what Big Dan always said. Don't get on the wrong side of a crow, because they never forgot and were far too ingenious when it came to retribution. That was if they didn't simply call up a murder and swarm you, beak and talon.

How far back did this overhang go?

Except that would do no good. It was too hard to move backwards in this shape—at least not without making too much noise—and he wasn't about to turn around and have his back to them.

Perhaps he should simply emerge from his hiding place and brazen it out. Oh, good plan.

Here was a better one: why not simply turn back into a bogan and cut his own throat?

But then the decision was taken away from him.

"Oh look, crow boys," a familiar voice said. "Have you come to pay your respects to my departed spirit, or were you hoping for some carrion overlooked by others of your kin?"

It was Anwatan, Rabedy realized.

He could feel his whole body relax—though not enough for him to emerge just yet.

"Can't help what we are," one of the crow boys said.

"That's true," Anwatan replied. "But this place has nothing for you."

"We're here on Raven's business."

"Ah, Raven. That's true. He's not too happy with you boys just now."

"What do you mean?"

"I was just with him when he got the news about the bogans you slaughtered. You have a strange way of defining the word 'find.' "

Slaughtered? Rabedy thought. The others were all dead?

"They killed you," a crow boy said.

"They did. But cerva don't believe that more killing is a solution. The Grace holds all life sacred."

"But—"

"And carrion-eater though Raven is," she went on, "he doesn't seem at all pleased to have only bits and pieces of bogans with which to approach the fairy court. It won't make negotiations easy."

"He said that?"

"Not in so many words. But you know Raven. He can say more with the look in his eye than you or I might in ten minutes of talk."

"We thought he'd be glad . . ."

"Well, he's not. Now, shoo! Get away from here. This place is sacred to those who follow the path of nonviolence."

"We're sorry . . ."

"It's all right, cousin. I know you thought you were helping. But now it's time for you to go."

Rabedy leaned closer when there was no response to that. What was happening out there?

But then he heard the sound of wings, and he knew they were leaving. He let out the breath he'd been holding.

"You can come out now," Anwatan said.

Still nervous, he crept forward until he emerged from under the overhang. But Anwatan was alone on the beach.

"Keep that shape," she said, "or you'll bring them back. I've had enough of death and vengeance."

Rabedy cocked his head and looked up at her. There was an unhappy light in her eyes.

Are you all right, mistress? he asked.

"No," she replied. "How could I be? I'm dead. Minisino is dead. Your friends are all dead. Soon Odawa will be, too. And what has anyone learned from all this killing and death? Nothing."

I'm so sorry . . .

She reached down and ruffled the fur on the top of his head.

"I know you are. Why do you think I kept them from you?"

But maybe I shouldn't be allowed to go free. Maybe I should give myself up to—

"Weren't you listening to me? I think there's been enough 'justice' served as it is."

But—

"No. Preserving your life . . . that's all I have left."

Only I'm the enemy.

"Are you? Is that how you feel?"

No. But I was with them. I'm a bogan.

"And there are stags that kill, but so what? We all have our natures, but that doesn't mean we should use them to excuse what we do. We *choose* what we do. You chose not to be a part of the killings. I choose not to take vengeance."

The more he got to know her, the worse Rabedy felt about not having tried to stop the others from killing her. She was so strong of spirit—nothing like an Unseelie fairy.

If I could trade places with you—

"I wouldn't let you," she said before he could finish. "My time on this wheel is done—yours isn't. But if you want to honour me, then choose to add to the Grace, not degrade her gifts."

I don't know that I'm brave enough to be as good as you. I don't know that I could ever find the courage.

"You might surprise yourself," she told him. "But I won't leave you alone."

You'll stay to teach me?

She gave him a sad smile. "No. I told you. My time is done. But a friend has promised to help you. I think you'll like him. He's part crow, but part dog, too."

Rabedy began to get a bad feeling. If this was who he thought it was, every Unseelie fairy did their very best to not attract his attention.

What's his name?

"People just call him Joe."

Do you mean Joe Crazy Dog?

She nodded. "Do you know him?"

Everybody knows of him. He's . . . How to put this diplomatically? *He's not exactly patient with the likes of me. And if he was to find out that I was a part of your death . . .*

"He already knows," Anwatan said. "And he's promised to help you. But now it's up to you."

Up to me to what?

"To prove that I haven't made a mistake in hiding you from the corbae's too-fierce justice."

But . . .

"I have to go now, Rabedy Collins. I won't ask you to promise to be the best you can be. I only ask you to promise that you will try."

I . . .

She ruffled the fur on his head again.

"Don't worry so much. There is a reason for everything. Perhaps the reason for this was for you to claim the chance to truly be yourself."

It's too dear a price.

"Then perhaps it was to stop Minisino before he did any real harm. I don't pretend to understand fate's plans."

She bent down and kissed the top of his head.

"Wait here for Joe. He won't be long."

I will. I . . .

She went down on one knee so that she could look him in the eye.

"What are you trying to say, Rabedy Collins?"

It's just . . . thank you for believing in me. No one's ever done that before.

She shook her head. "Knowing how we can treat each other—that's not something I'll miss from this world."

She stood up.

"Goodbye, Rabedy Collins. Perhaps we'll meet again in the world beyond."

She stepped away before Rabedy could reply.

Rabedy studied the beach, looking one way, then the other, before returning to the hidey-hole he'd found under the overhang.

Joe Crazy Dog was coming for him.

He only hoped that the crow dog cousin would keep his faith with Anwatan.

And if he didn't?

He was still held by the memory of Anwatan's calm presence and didn't even shiver. Instead, her calmness seemed to have settled inside him as well, as though she'd left it with him as a final gift.

Well, you don't even deserve a second chance, he told himself.

So if he got one, then blessings to the Moon. And if not, he would finally have to pay for running with Big Dan's gang.

He'd never believed in fate before. But now he felt firmly held in its grip, and all he could do was wait.

Jilly

Del's exactly where Raylene and I left him. Lying against the wall, the leather cords holding him captive. He looks up when I come into the parlour and glares at me.

"So, it's just you and me again," I tell him.

"You'll be sorry once I figure a way out of this."

I shake my head. "You still don't get it, do you? It's over, Del. We're done here."

But he doesn't get it, and why should I be surprised? This isn't the old drunk Raylene tracked down in a Tyson County trailer park. This is the Del of our childhood, full of piss and vinegar. The one who figures everything's always going to go his way because the world owes him.

"I can wait," he tells me. "I'm patient as hell, little sister. Sooner or later, you'll let down your guard."

"The trouble is, it's got nothing to do with whether I'm paying attention to you or not."

I crouch down on the floor so that we're seeing eye to eye.

"See," I go on, "I know I can't get rid of you. You're always going to be in my head."

"Damn straight."

"Except it's no longer on your terms. It's on mine."

He shakes his head. "That's not the way it works. And as soon as I get myself untied, you're going to see."

"Yeah, about your being tied up," I say. "That's not going to work for me either. I don't like the idea of leaving anybody like this, unable to move, lying on the floor in an empty room for the rest of their lives—especially not when that room's in my head."

"So let me go."

He tries to use what he thinks of as charm, looking at me from lowered lashes, dimple in his cheek from the touch of a smile. Maybe that worked on the girls back in Tyson—though I'm guessing not, or why'd he have to come sniffing after his little sisters?—but it's sure not working on me.

"Yeah, right," I say. "As if that's going to happen."

"Hey, we'll let bygones be bygones. You go your way and I'll go mine. No hard feelings."

"Oh, there's always going to be hard feelings," I tell him. "Don't you doubt that for a moment."

And just like that, the phony charm switches off and there's that familiar look in his eyes. Feral. Calculating.

"I'll see you in hell," he says, "before I—"

"No," I break in. "Here's the new deal."

Once upon a time, I think, and build a fresh story in my head.

Once upon a time . . .

"Every time you have one of your mean-assed thoughts, you're going to shrink to half your size. Have too many . . . well, you're just going to mean-ass yourself into nothing. Bad news for you, but it's all good for me."

He spits at me, but I saw him building up the wad of saliva in his mouth and was expecting it. I move my head so that he misses, though bits of spray still spatter on my cheek. I wipe it away with the back of my hand.

"Because, see," I tell him, "even though you deserve it, I don't want anybody's death on my hands. This way, you're just going to be small and useless and unable to hurt anything."

I stand up and step back, finishing the story in my head.

Once upon a time . . .

And just like that, the leather cords are gone.

He lunges to his feet and immediately shrinks to half his size—contracting from that towering six-foot-something to no more than three feet tall. The top of his head only barely reaches my waist.

"Oh, you're going to pay big time for this," he says.

But almost before he can get the words out, he's half his size again—no more than a foot-and-a-half tall now.

"Goddamn you."

It would almost be funny, if there wasn't so much hurt wound up in my just having to look at him. Even now, when he's less than a foot tall and still shrinking because I guess he just can't stop thinking mean thoughts.

Finally, he's shrunk down so small I can't see him at all.

I look down at the floorboards where he was standing, but there's nothing to see. He's probably mean-assed his way right down to molecular size.

I don't feel any satisfaction. Only a sense of relief.

I back carefully out of the room—he's so small I could accidentally crush him and not even know it. I close the door behind me.

It doesn't matter if he stops thinking bad thoughts and starts to grow again, because he still won't be able to hurt anything or anybody without having to go through the whole shrinking process all over.

I turn away from the closed door of the parlour and step out onto the porch.

There's only one thing left. One loose end.

Mattie.

And I think I know what to do now.

I walk back into the house, up the stairs and into my old bedroom. It's still ratty and abandoned, with only a bed pushed up against the wall and a dirty mattress on it. But that doesn't matter. I just start another story in my head—

Once upon a time . . .

—and reach under the mattress. I don't know if it's really there, or if it's only there because I believe it's there, but I pull out that old Ellen Wentworth storybook that I read and reread as a kid. The book where I first met Mattie through "Prince Teddy Bear"—the story Wentworth told about her.

I flip through the book, past familiar illustrations, then there it is.

The one of Mattie and her bear.

I reach under the mattress once more and this time my questing fingers find a pencil. I sit on the floor under the window so that the light comes in over my shoulder. Opening the book to the end, where there are some blank pages, I get to work.

Joe

"Honey was a city dog, wasn't she?" Jack asked as they approached the arroyo where Joe had met up with her earlier when it was still light.

Joe nodded. "Bred for the fighting pits."

"So what's she doing here?"

"I'd guess trying to put as much distance between herself and the crap that was her life."

Jack nodded. "Good point."

"Do me a favour," Joe said.

"What's that?"

"Play it cool."

"You mean with those dogs that are circling around us that we're not supposed to know are there?"

"They don't know you, and I'm not sure they really trust me."

"Can't I just give them the ghost of a scare? Shake up their lives a little?"

"Jack . . ."

"Hey, it's cool. I'm just mouthing off. Do what you need to do. I'm only here to watch your back."

Joe nodded. They were almost at the arroyo now, and the circling dogs used the cover of darkness to work their way closer, not realizing that the two canids could read scents from the wind as readily as they could. That their hearing was also as good, if not better.

Joe stopped and sank down to the red dirt, easing into a cross-legged position. Jack followed suit, keeping his back to Joe so that he faced the other direction.

"You let her know we're here yet?" Jack asked.

"Soon as we touched down in these badlands. She's on her way."

But before Honey reached them, a ghostly presence took shape in front of Joe. Looking at Anwatan brought Walker's face to Joe's mind. The sorrow of having lost a child that lay so deep in the cerva's eyes.

Can you come with me now? she asked.

"I'm kind of busy. I need to deal with my other problem before I get to yours."

Your sister.

Joe nodded.

"Who're you talking to?" Jack asked from behind him.

Joe hadn't realized that she'd only spoken to him.

"Anwatan," Joe said.

"Yeah?"

Jack started to turn, but then the dogs came out of the dark, circling around them.

This is where he is, Anwatan said, sending Joe an image.

Joe recognized the cliffs by the lakeshore that she showed him. It was the place where the deer people held their blessing ceremonies.

He'll be waiting for you when you're done.

"I'll be there as soon as I can," he told her.

Thank you, she said, and then she was gone.

Joe focused now on the dogs that stood watching him.

"You want to tell these boys we're the good guys?" Jack said.

You don't have to, Honey said.

She gave a sharp bark and the pack faded back into the night. But not far, Joe knew.

"You can turn around," Joe told Jack. "We're good now."

Jack scooted around so that he was also facing Honey.

"Hey, Honey," he said. "Long time no see."

I remember you. You were with Joe the last time we helped Jilly.

"Yeah, that goes back a bit, doesn't it? And here we are again."

I'm always ready to help Joe.

Jack nodded. "I know the feeling." He studied her for a moment, then added, "You've changed. You weren't near so articulate the last time we met. Next thing you'll be walking around on your hind legs like some five-fingered being."

I will never take human shape, she told him. *All it does is bring trouble into the world.*

Joe gave her a look of surprise. The last time they'd talked about this she'd seemed keen on the idea. Then he realized that seeing Del must have reminded her of the freak who'd run her in the fighting pits.

"I don't know," Jack said. "It's got its benefits."

I would rather be deaf and dumb again, than walk on my hind legs.

"Ouch."

"You about done here?" Joe asked.

Jack spread out his hands. "Just making conversation, Joe." He turned to Honey. "I didn't mean anything by it."

I know. I'm . . . She paused as though needing to find just the right word. *Unused to diplomacy.*

"No, it was my bad."

"I hate to break into the bonding here," Joe asked, "But what happened to Jilly? One moment I know she's back and safe, the next she's right off my radar again."

Honey explained, keeping it as brief as possible.

"Man, I thought *we* were busy," Jack said.

Joe nodded. "So you just let her go back?"

A low growl rumbled in Honey's chest, but when she spoke, her voice was calm in their heads.

There was no stopping her, Joe. She paused, then added, *This is something she needs to do. You know that. If she doesn't, she'll never be free of her brother's curse. You've said the same thing to her.*

"I never—"

The only difference here is that you didn't know the specifics.

"You're right," Joe said after a moment. "But I'm just so damned worried about her. Have been ever since the accident. There was a dimming of that light she casts after the car hit her, and it never really came back."

It has now, Honey assured him.

"Well, that's something."

I'm worried, too, Honey said, *but I also have faith in her. She will prevail.*

She seemed to believe it. Joe wanted to believe it, too, but he knew better than her how quickly things could go wrong in the otherworld. Especially in a situation such as this. A world that existed inside her own head? How could she possibly go there? The physics were improbable, even for the otherworld.

But that didn't mean it wasn't true. The problem was it was all new territory, new rules.

"The others are still waiting for her on the mesa?" he asked.

Honey nodded. *Joe, if there'd been another way . . .*

"I'm not laying blame on anybody," he told her, "except on me. I should have handled this differently. What was I thinking, setting some ordinary safety spell on her? If there's one thing I should have learned over the years, it's that Jilly's anything but ordinary."

"So, maybe she knows what she's doing," Jack said.

"Right. That's why, when she went back in, she was still stuck in the body of a child."

Have faith in her, Honey said.

"I . . ."

He was about to say that he did, but if that was the case, then why was he so worried?

"I'll try," he said.

He started to get up, but Jack put a hand on his arm.

"Wait," he said.

"Wait? For what?"

"Well, for one thing, to get centered again. I've never seen you like this, Joe. If you don't get focused, something *is* going to get screwed up."

"And how are we going to get centered?"

Jack smiled. "For starters, we're going to sit here a moment and let the night fill us. We're going to appreciate the beauty and the stillness. Then we're going to offer some smoke to the four directions and the Grace."

Joe gave a slow nod.

"And then," Jack said, "we're going to see what needs to be done. And if we need to kick some ass, we'll be ready for that, too."

He waited until Joe nodded again, then pulled out his tobacco and started to build a smoke.

"Pretty place you've got here," he told Honey. "I can see why it appeals more than where Joe first found you."

I wanted to raise my pups far from the stink and smell of that world.

"Yeah, well, it's not all pretty. No argument there."

Joe could feel Honey's smile in his mind.

But it's not all bad either, she admitted.

"I wasn't going to bring that up," Jack said. "But since you did, yeah. There are parts of that world that'll just take your breath away. I figure it's just like most of us. We've all got some good in us, we've got some bad."

Not all of us. There are some that are all bad.

"Or the same as," Jack agreed. He grinned at her, a feral coyote's grin. "And the ones that are like that, well, we just put down to make more room for beauty to grow."

He finished making the cigarette and handed it and his lighter to Joe.

"Do the honours," he said.

Joe flicked the wheel of the Zippo and a small flame sprang up from its wick.

"Light in the dark," Jack murmured.

Joe nodded and lit the cigarette.

"Light in the dark," he agreed.

Jilly

I write down the story the way I made it happen for Mattie, how every time Del came swaggering into my room, I put all the evil and hurt he did to me onto her so that she had to carry the weight of it instead of me. He would always say that I made him do those terrible things, but in my head, she was the one who made him do it. Not me. But all I really did was transfer my pain to her just so that I could get through the days and nights I had to live in that house of my enemy.

I don't sugarcoat the story now, or leave anything out, because it's not going to work if I'm not totally honest.

It doesn't matter that I didn't know what I was doing at the time.

It doesn't matter that I was just a messed-up kid myself.

All that matters is for me to find a way to make things right for Mattie.

So I sit there on the floor, working on it, filling the handful of blank pages at the end of the book with lines of tiny printing and little sketches.

After awhile I get up and take the book outside. I realize that this isn't the kind of thing I can finish in here. Not in this house, in *this* room.

It's where it all started, not where it should end.

It's still sunny outside and the humidity's completely gone. It's a perfect summer's day—the kind you'd get once or twice during the season back in the real Tyson County. I lean against the porch pillar to listen to a jay somewhere off in the spruce, scolding and raucous, then sit down on the top step and open the book again.

"Do you really think that's going to be enough?" an unfamiliar voice asks.

I suppose I should feel nervous, but I'm very calm as I turn to see who's spoken. I'm even calm when I recognize the newcomer as another character from the Ellen Wentworth book.

This time it's Tom Foolery, the title character from "The Scarecrow That Couldn't Sleep." Like Mattie, he looks like he simply stepped out of one of Wentworth's paintings. I could turn to the page of the book on my lap and find the same raggedy man with the painted cloth face and the bits of straw sticking out of his seams and from under his floppy brown hat. He's wearing a checkered shirt, old worn overalls, and a pair of rubber boots that are cracked with age.

"Don't tell me I did something to you, too," I say.

"No," he says. He waves a floppy arm out past the yard. "I was just hanging around out in the fields and got this sudden inclination to come back to the house."

I smile. "Literally hanging around?"

"Oh, no. I'm retired now. I was never much good as a scarecrow anyway. I like crows too much and, well, why shouldn't they have a share of the corn? They were here first, after all."

"Not in Ellen's story."

He takes a seat beside me. "Yes, well, that's the thing with stories. They only hold a little piece of your life, and even then, it's from somebody else's perspective."

"Unless you write it yourself."

He shakes his head. "No, the perspective still wouldn't be right. It would be an older you writing about a younger you, and memory has a knack of playing tricks on us, no matter how much we think we know better. Nobody remembers things the way they really happened, only how we think they happened."

"Are you talking about my memories of Del?"

"No, no. It's just . . ." He has work gloves for hands and spreads them between us. "You're getting the details right, but you're missing the big picture."

"I don't understand."

It's weird following the play of emotions on his face. The features are painted on, but they're still mobile like a real person's.

"The little girl who didn't know what she was doing, but still made Mattie's life miserable . . ."

"You mean me."

He nods. "The young you, yes. Where do you think she got the ability to do that?"

"What ability? I just couldn't face up to what was happening to me, so I pretended it was happening to someone else. That doesn't exactly require any special powers."

"Perhaps not. But then tell me this: what made it real?"

I blink in confusion. "Okay, I'm still not following you. What's real about this place? It's just inside my head."

"And yet here we are. Here we *physically* are."

"Someone said I'd probably created a hidden pocket world back when. You know, a few acres stashed away in the dreamlands, but parked just outside of normal access for anybody but me."

"And how did the little girl you were manage to do that?"

"Beats me. I don't know how I made it. I don't know how I pulled Mattie out of the book and invested her with all my bad memories. It just happened."

He nods. "Because of the light."

"The what?"

"Your gift from the Grace."

"Oh, that."

I've been hearing about this for ages. From Joe. From the White Deer Woman. From pretty much anybody with an ounce of magic in their blood. I'm supposed to be filled with this magical light which doesn't seem to do anything for me except make me an easy target to find in the otherworld.

"You're saying the light made Mattie?" I ask. "And I guess you?"

"Not the light. *You* brought us to life from the book. The light was only the fuel that allowed you to do so."

"Okay. Whatever. The light let me do it. So what's your point?"

"You didn't just make a nightmare for Mattie Finn. You made all of us, too."

" 'Us'?"

A floppy hand rises to point at the yard in front of us. I follow the movement and stare at the crowd of beings standing out there in the grass.

They approached the house so quietly, I never heard them, which, considering the size of some of them, means they're either really good at sneaking around, or I need to pay attention to my surroundings more.

There's the tubby hippopotamus Hank-a-Widdle and Frocious the lion from "A Circus in a Teapot." I look more closely and spot the Dancing Greasy Groos—a family of gangly-limbed monkeys—from the same story. There's a pack of Rackhamish fairies—all twiggy and leafed; the Prince and

Princess from "Speckled, My Egg"; Farmer Dorn, his wife Sarah, and the farmyard mutt Putsy from Tom's story; the nine sisters from "The Cakemaker's Magic Candlestick." And more, so many more.

There are traditional fairy-tale characters, too. Hansel and Gretel, Little Red Riding Hood and her grandmother, the seven swan brothers and their sister. None of the villains, but otherwise it seems as though every character Wentworth ever painted is standing out there in the yard. All the companions of my childhood that I used to people the stories I made up in my head.

I'd forgotten all about them, though how I could have done that seems impossible. But seeing them now fills me with a confused delight.

It's like finding a box of childhood toys that you haven't looked at in thirty years. You never think of them. It's like they never existed. But if you come upon that box and open it, the memories all flood back. Each toy you pick up, no matter how small and inconsequential, looms large once you hold it in your hand again.

Some things you can't forget. Bad things. Awful things. Sad things. When you've had a childhood like mine, you just try to put it all out of your mind. But seeing this crowd of memories come to life in the yard, I realize it's so important to remember that there were good things, too. Maybe they only lived on paper, or in my head, but they sustained me through those long, unhappy years.

"Without you," Tom says, "we wouldn't exist."

I turn to look at him. "So, you're like Eadar?"

Eadar are the inhabitants of the half world—what Joe calls the between. Beings created out of imagination, who exist only as long as someone believes in them. They're like my friend Toby Childers, the little man who was my companion the last time I got lost in the otherworld. Some are only wisps of beings—born from a daydream and fading quickly away. But others—like the beloved characters of favourite books—can become so real that they take on a life of their own.

Tom looks puzzled until I explain it to him.

"Exactly," he says. "We are Eadar, made real from the page by the power of your imagination."

I look out again at the crowd . . .

"But I haven't thought of any of you for so long," I say. "How would you all still be here if you need belief to exist?"

"You were that powerful. You *are* that powerful."

"Here," I say.

He nods. "Yes, here."

I'm trying to figure this out, but I must be totally dense because I really can't see where he's going with all of this.

"So, what are you saying?" I ask. "that you're . . . grateful?"

"Indeed," he says. "How could we not be? And we've come to you now to remind you that the child you were did good, as well."

"For you, maybe, but that doesn't change what happened to Mattie."

"No, of course not. But if you're going to write down the tale of what happened back then, you need to tell the whole of it."

"I don't think it's going to make Mattie feel any better. It's going to make her feel worse. You guys get to . . . do whatever it is you do, which I'm guessing is enjoyable because no one looks particularly ticked off. But all she got was my nightmares."

He nods. "But if you don't put our part of the tale in there, we might no longer have these lives of ours."

Now I get it.

"You're trying to get me to not make another mess of things," I say.

He nods. "And if we're still here, we can take care of Mattie when you're finished setting the world a-right again."

"You couldn't before?"

He glances back at the house. "Not so long as the Conjurer was in power. I won't say that we don't want to live, as well. We do. But we are not like him. And if you don't write us into the story, then the good you did when you were the child you were will be gone. Only the ugliness will remain."

Now I totally understand what he meant when he first asked me, *Do you really think that's going to be enough?*

"But I didn't *know* I was doing it."

"You didn't know you were hurting Mattie, either."

I look away from him and try to pick Mattie out in the crowd.

"I don't see her," I say.

He shakes his head. "She's not here. She's in the dark woods."

He points to the left, to where the spruce and pine and cedar grow thick, climbing up into the hills.

Once upon a time, I think.

Because that's how it is in fairy tales. You have to go through the dark woods before you can come out the other side again.

But what if you don't ever get to come out?

I see Mattie's face in my mind. The way she looked at me.

I look back at Tom. "I can't just 'once upon a time' this better, can I?"

I don't have to explain what I mean.

"In this place, you're the Conjurer," he tells me. "At least you are once more, now that you've defeated your brother."

It's funny. I never thought of it as defeating him. I just thought of it as surviving.

"You can do anything you want," Tom adds.

When he says that, I know how I can fix things for him and the rest of the Eadar my younger self pulled out of Wentworth's book. But that won't work with Mattie. Just as the healers couldn't fix my body until I dealt with the monster hidden in my head, I have to help Mattie do the same before I can work any magic for her.

Because some things—the deep, meaningful things that sit at the heart of our souls—can't be touched by magic. They can only be touched by the hurt or the love that we offer to each other.

That's the real measure of our worth: How we touch each other in a way that really matters.

Which, I realize, is what the Grace is all about.

I lay the book down on the step and stand up.

"I have to go to her," I tell Tom.

"I know," he says.

I walk down the steps and onto the grass. The Eadar open their crowded ranks to make a path for me, but they reach out and touch me as I pass by them. On my arms, on my shoulders, on my back. It's a curiously empowering experience. I don't have words for them, they don't have words for me. But we communicate our joy for each other's existence without them. That joy flows over us like a wave of light. Like the light that's supposed to be inside me that I can never see.

I can almost see it now.

I can certainly feel it.

The sensation holds all the way across the yard and follows me through the fields to where the forest begins. But once I'm under the dark boughs of the spruce, my footsteps swallowed by the carpet of needles under my shoes, I'm on my own. I may continue to hold their good will, but the deeper I go into the woods, the less tangible it becomes.

I don't worry about how I'm going to find Mattie, one small girl in all these acres of dark woods. We're in a story now—Mattie and I—and the story will lead me to her.

When I find her, she's sitting among the roots of a huge pine, holding the torn remains of her teddy bear. The pine's roots twine around a snarl of granite pushed out of the ground by frost.

"What did you do to him?" she asks. "I can't feel him anymore. Not really. It's just like there's a sliver of a memory left, but that's all."

"I wrote him out of the story."

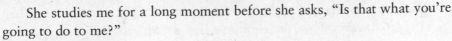

She studies me for a long moment before she asks, "Is that what you're going to do to me?"

I shake my head.

I hadn't even thought of that. But even if I had, it's not something I could ever do. Mattie's not my enemy, for all that I'm hers.

"You can't make it better," she says.

"I know."

"Nothing can make it better."

"Believe me, I know."

"So, why are you here?" she asks.

That stops me. I want to see her through to the other side of these dark woods. But is that really what I'm doing here? Am I here for her need, or my own? But if I'm expecting forgiveness, shouldn't I be willing to offer it to Del first?

Except I'm genuinely sorry for what I did to Mattie. Del doesn't know the meaning of the word.

She holds up the teddy.

"And look at Grath. Look at what you did to him."

I didn't do anything. That was Lizzie. But considering how everything that's happened here is because of me, she's not wrong.

But this, at least, I can fix. I only have to wake up the charm. Which, I know now, is calling up the light. The hidden mystery of the Grace that put the tiniest quiver of itself in my unworthy body when I was a child. But while I know I don't deserve it, that doesn't mean I can't use it.

Once upon a time . . .

And the torn teddy bear is mended like it was never hurt in the first place.

I guess I'm expecting her to at least be pleased with this. But her eyes are still cold when they lift from the mended bear to my face. She sets the teddy bear down on the grass.

"Kill her, Grath," she says. "Kill her forever."

And hard on the heels of those words, the teddy bear swells and grows and changes, from sweet toy to that giant grizzly I encountered when I first entered this world.

Tom Foolery said I was the Conjurer now, but it looks like I'm not alone. Mattie has enough magic in her to create a protector for herself.

What happens if I die here? What happens to Mattie and the other Eadar? Does the world end, or can it go on without me?

I think maybe it does. Go on, I mean. I'm not so egocentric as to think that it has to die with me. Maybe that can be my last conjuring, that the world goes on, no matter what happens to me.

Once upon a time . . .

The grizzly rears above, one enormous paw drawn back to strike me down.

Part of me doesn't want to struggle. Part of me believes that I should just let the damned bear tear me apart. That I deserve whatever happens.

And maybe I do. Or, at least, maybe I deserve *something*. I should have to pay something for what I did to her.

But I didn't give in to Del, and I'm not going to give in to this impulse either.

For all I know, it's a piece of Del that's making me think this. Maybe a small unending tremble of confusion and uncertainty is going to be his legacy to me, the bit I have to carry forever.

So I call up another piece of the story.

Once upon a time . . .

Once upon a time, there was a girl who went into a dark wood, but she wasn't scared of what she might find in there, she wasn't afraid of ghosts or ghouls or hungry beasts, because she was a ghost herself.

Just a Ghost Girl.

I flinch when the grizzly's paw strikes me.

Except it doesn't. It goes right through me instead, as though I'm made of air. As though I'm just a . . .

Ghost Girl.

The bear roars with frustration and attacks me with renewed fury. Branches and pine needles and bits of rock go flying in all directions because it can't touch me. It can only tear apart the ground I'm standing on.

Finally it stops and looks back at its mistress.

Mattie jumps up and runs to where I'm standing. She tries to beat me with her little fists, but they're no more effective than the grizzly's big paws and just go through me.

Mattie lets her arms fall to her sides. Her shoulders bow with defeat. But her eyes don't give up. They burn.

"What do you *want* from me?" she cries.

"Nothing," I tell her. "I just want to say I'm sorry."

"I know, I know, I know, I know. You're sorry. You were just a little girl yourself, and you didn't know better. But now you do. Now you want to make it all up to me. Now you promise everything's going to be better."

I shake my head. "No. I don't know that. I'm just sorry for what I've done to you. If I could take it back, I would. But I can't undo the nightmare. I can only tell you how sorry I am."

"Sorry doesn't do *anything*."

"I guess you're right."

"You're just saying it to make yourself feel better."

"I can't imagine anything making me feel better about what I did."

She turns away from me and reaches for the grizzly. When she touches his fur, he shrinks back down into a teddy bear again. Clutching him against her chest, she looks at me again.

"So, now you're back to pretending you're nice," she says.

"I don't think what I did was particularly nice. It was horrible."

"Oh, but you're nice now, aren't you? With that big light inside you, and anything you want you can just make happen, because now you're the Conjurer and I'm still nothing."

"If that's true," I tell her, "then it's not working."

"What do you mean?"

"I just want you to know that I'm sorry. That I'm here for no other reason than to tell you that."

"So what? Am I supposed to forgive you?"

I shake my head. "I'm not here for that."

"Then why *are* you here? And stop saying you're sorry."

I decide to come at it from another direction.

"What do *you* want, Mattie?" I ask her.

"If I could have anything?"

"If you could have anything."

"For you to be dead," she says.

"That's not an option," I tell her. "I wouldn't die for Del, and I'm not going to die for you."

"Then let me forget."

I study her for a long moment.

"Are you sure of that?" I ask. "I thought that was what I wanted, but all I did was make a nightmare for you. And the memories never really go away—not forever. Not for real. They end up festering away inside you and spoiling everything."

"Is that what happened to you?"

"Pretty much. But until I got here, I didn't know how badly."

She doesn't say anything, and I stop myself from talking. Instead, I change the story about the Ghost Girl and become who I was when I walked into the woods. I offer her my hand.

"What do you want now?" she asks.

"I just want to show you something."

"Maybe I don't want to see it."

"That's your choice," I tell her. "I won't make you do anything."

"But you could."

I look her right in the eye.

"I could," I say.

I'm still holding my hand out to her.

"And what if I do come with you?" she asks.

"Then you'll see the thing I want to show you."

"Why don't you just tell me instead?"

"It doesn't work that way."

She hesitates a moment longer, then holds the bear against her chest with one hand and reaches for my hand.

"This doesn't change anything," she tells me.

"I know," I say.

Except it does. How, that's still to be seen.

I lead her back to the house. She stares curiously at the Eadar gathered in the yard and almost smiles when she spots Tom Foolery, but she catches herself in time.

"Here, sit beside me," I say.

We sit on the steps, and I pick up the book and my pencil again.

"Can you read?" I ask her.

She gives me a withering look, so I turn to the end of the book where I've been writing. She reads what I've put down so far.

"And then what?" she asks.

With her looking over my shoulder, I write about the coming of Tom Foolery and the other Eader, of my going into the woods, and what happened between us in there. I draw a picture of her holding the bear, sitting in among the pine tree roots. When I get to the end, to us sitting here on the steps and my writing in the book, I turn to her.

"Are you going to finish it?" she says.

"No, you are," I tell her.

She looks out at the Eadar, then at Tom who gives her a wink.

"They're all innocent, aren't they?" she says. "They don't know what we know."

"They know," I tell her. "But they didn't have to experience it the way you and I did."

"Why did *we*?"

I hold her gaze. "I don't know why I did. But you experienced it because I was a stupid and selfish little girl. I wasn't brave enough to keep it to myself so I made you carry it for me."

"That's not true," she says.

I raise my eyebrows.

"You didn't know what you were doing."

"But that didn't make it right," I say.

She's quick to see how we're having the same argument we did before, except we're arguing each other's side of it this time.

"I . . . I just wanted to be loved," she says after a long moment. "By someone who didn't want to hurt me."

"Me, too."

"Did you ever find that?"

I think of all my friends, from Lou and Angel, to Sophie and Wendy, Isabelle and Mona. Joe and Cassie and Christy and Saskia and the Professor. But most of all I think of Geordie, waiting for me on a mesa somewhere else in the otherworld.

"I did," I tell her. "But it took me a long time, and it took me even longer to believe it could be true. And . . . and even now, I find it easier to believe that it's all just a dream. That it couldn't be real."

"I wouldn't doubt it," she said. "If I had people who said they loved me, I'd believe it. Especially if they didn't hit me."

I give her a slow nod. "I guess you're braver than I am."

She touches a finger to the blank half page that's still left at the end of what I've written.

"How does it end?" she asks.

"I really don't know. Like I said, you have to finish it."

She looks away then, her gaze going inward. She strokes her teddy's head.

I don't know how long we sit like that. Nothing changes. The Eadar don't move or talk. The light doesn't change—the sun just stays where it is in the sky.

"I want to grow up," Mattie finally says when she turns back to me.

"There's no reason why you shouldn't," I tell her. "It'd be up to you."

"Up to me . . ." Then she gets it. "Are you saying I could be the Conjurer now?"

"If that's what you want."

"But I don't want to hurt people."

"You don't have to be that kind of Conjurer."

"So, you'll just let that happen?" she asks. "You'll write it in the book and that's the way it'll be?"

I nod.

"What if once I'm the Conjurer I put you in the deepest darkest dungeon, and you have to stay there forever and a day?"

"I don't think you're the kind of person who would do that, but it's the chance I have to take. I just hope you'll look out for the others." I nod toward the yard. "They need someone to protect them and keep them safe."

"You mean me?"

"Well, I would think that's what a good Conjurer would do."

Mattie turns to look at the scarecrow.

"How would you feel about that?" she asks him.

"We just want you to be happy again," he says. "To be one of us."

"And . . . and the old Conjurer?" Mattie asks. "What happens to him?"

I tap the book. "This doesn't change."

She actually smiles now. "Because you're the Conjurer, too. You have to be, because all of this is inside you."

"So we'll both be Conjurers," I say, "though you'll probably make a better one than me."

"You're just saying that," she says, but I can tell that she's pleased, nevertheless.

"We already know you're braver."

She shakes her head. "I never could have done what you did." She smoothes a palm over the open pages of the book.

I take a chance, then.

"But you never made somebody else's life a nightmare," I say.

Her gaze clouds for a moment and I hold my breath. But then she shakes her head.

"No," she says. "I just tried to kill you whenever I could."

"So, shall I finish the story?" I ask her.

She nods, reading over my shoulder as I write the ending into the book. The last thing I do is draw a picture of her, but she's older in it. A young woman.

"Is that me?" she asks.

I nod. I close the book, lay it on the porch behind me, and put the pencil on top. I turn to her and open my arms.

She lets me hug her.

"You have at least one person now who loves you," I say into her hair. "And I won't ever hurt you again. I really would die before I'd let that happen."

Her arms come around me and hold tight.

"I was wrong," she says, her voice soft, muffled against my breast.

"About what?"

"It turns out things can get better."

I kiss the top of her head.

"Take care of this place for me," I tell her. "And make friends with the Eadar. I only pulled the nice ones from Wentworth's book."

"Will you come back?"

"I don't know that I'll ever be away, but yes, I'll come visit you."

"Why did you trust me?" she asks. I can tell from the look in her eyes that she's genuinely puzzled. "I'd just tried to kill you."

"I don't know. I can't explain it, exactly."

It was just something I knew I had to do.

"I think it was important to offer you trust and kindness," I say finally. "To make up for how I hurt you before. And it was really important for me to believe that you would do what was right."

"You didn't use magic?"

I shake my head. "Not for that. Never for that. It had to come from you or it would mean nothing."

"I think you *are* brave," she says. "I would never have trusted me."

"You would have, if you were me."

"That makes no sense."

I smile. "I often don't." I wait a beat, then ask her, "Why did you change your mind about wanting to kill me?"

"Because of what you wrote in the book. It made me realize that we both went through the same things, except you really did. I just thought I did."

"Didn't make it less real."

"No. But I understand better now. I might have done the same thing."

"Not knowing what you know now."

She shakes her head.

"Because I know for sure that I couldn't," I say.

I kiss the top of her head again and stand up. I wave to the Eadar, then my gaze goes to Tom. The scarecrow's painted features managed to look both solemn and cheerful.

"We'll take care of each other," he assures me.

Mattie looks up at me from where she's sitting on the top step. She makes her teddy bear wave at me.

"Bye, Jilly," she says.

"Bye," I say.

Then I let go of this world and allow myself to fall back to the mesa where Geordie and the others are waiting for me.

Joe

If Joe had stopped to think of the scare they'd throw into Geordie and the others arriving the way they did, he would have taken man-shape and called out from the trail before stepping up onto the mesa. Instead, two dogs and a coyote suddenly appeared right in front of them, landing almost in the middle of a campfire.

Geordie and Lizzie were playing a tune on their fiddles and stopped in midbar. Geordie cried out in surprise. He dropped his fiddle into its case and grabbed a stick as he stood. Lizzie was as quick to set aside her instrument, but she rose in silence and barehanded. Before the ground was steady under Joe's feet, she'd assumed a defensive stance that showed she knew what she was doing. Beside her, a knife appeared in each of the doonie's hands—Joe didn't see where they came from. The little man almost threw one before he recognized Honey.

Joe quickly changed back into a more familiar shape—at least more familiar to Geordie. Beside him, Jack did the same.

Geordie let the stick he was holding fall to the ground.

"A little warning next time would be nice," he said.

"Sorry about that," Joe told him. "We started to run here from Honey's den, then decided to just jump the distance while we were still in animal form. I wasn't thinking."

The doonie's knives vanished as mysteriously as they'd appeared.

"I am *so* ready to go home," Lizzie said.

Joe ignored her.

"Any word from Jilly?" he asked Geordie.

"No, and she's been gone for hours. I hate this."

"You and me both," Joe said. He turned and asked Honey, "Can you get me into this place where she's gone?"

No. Like I told you, it's a closed world And even if I could, I wouldn't. This is something she wants—she needs—*to do on her own.*

"I get that," Joe said. "But shouldn't she be back by now?"

We have no idea how long this will take.

"But if she's in trouble . . ."

Remember, Honey told him, *we need to have faith in her.*

Yeah, Joe thought. Faith. He had faith in Jilly, that she'd do her best. But sometimes your best just wasn't good enough. You could give it your all and still fail.

What if this was too much for her? What if she was facing something so big and terrible, the only way she'd survive was if someone had her back?

"I need to make this right," he said.

Jack put a hand on his arm. "No, you need to let go of the idea that this was your fault."

"But if I'd protected her better, she wouldn't—"

"And then you need to do like Honey says. Have some faith. Maybe pray, if you have anybody you pray to."

"This is going badly, isn't it?" Geordie said.

Jack shook his head. "We don't know that. We don't know anything except that Jilly told you she had to go back. By herself. I'm guessing that means she thought she could handle it, because she never struck me as the suicidal type, and the Grace knows she's had enough crap thrown at her."

Geordie gave him a slow unhappy nod. His gaze left Jack's face and drifted to the place from which Jilly had disappeared earlier.

You were playing music, Honey said to Geordie.

He nodded without looking at her. "I was trying to do something to stop myself from worrying, but it wasn't really working. I don't think I've ever played so badly."

"Yeah, well, your not so good is another person's great," Lizzie said.

Geordie started to turn, but then something happened in the air above the vortex. A dim glow appeared that suddenly burst into a flare of light. They were all blinded, except for Joe, who'd automatically closed his eyes. It wasn't that he'd anticipated the flare. He couldn't say why he'd done it. But because he had, he was the first to be able to see the small figure standing there when the flare died down.

Jilly.

She blinked in the firelight, obviously having come here from a place where the light was much brighter.

A wave of relief went through Joe when he saw she seemed to be all in one piece. But then he noticed something different about her. He took a step forward, then stopped when he realized what it was.

He'd always been able to see that light of hers—big and golden. He could see it as clearly as others took in her cheerful nature. But he could also see the shadow at the heart of it, that old piece of unhappiness that made it impossible for her body to be healed, because that shadow had to be healed first.

The shadow was gone.

"Wow," she said. "Check out the welcoming committee."

Joe started forward again but Geordie got to her first, wrapping her in his arms.

"Are you okay?" he asked. "Tell me you're okay."

"I'm totally okay," she told him.

"So you put that sick freak down?" Lizzie asked.

Jilly turned so that Geordie still had an arm around her shoulders as she faced them.

"In a manner of speaking," she said. "He's not going to ever bother anybody again."

"And that evil little girl?"

Jilly smiled. "I put her in charge."

"You *what?*"

"It's a long weird story."

She stepped away from Geordie to give Joe a hug.

"You look so worried," she said.

"Not anymore," he told her.

She let him go and went down on one knee to open her arms to Honey. The dog came to her and let her put her arms around her neck.

I'm proud of you, Honey said.

"You and me both. Putting an end to Del's threat wasn't the hard part. The hard part was making up for what I did to Mattie when I was a kid."

What do you mean?

"I didn't hold my hurt back then. I put it on her. I didn't know I was doing it, but all the awful crap Del put me through, I made it hers instead of mine."

"That's harsh," Jack said.

Jilly nodded. "Tell me about it."

"Who's Mattie?" Joe asked.

"An Eadar. I made a whole world of Eadar somewhere in my head, but she's the only one I hurt."

"You're right," Jack said. "This sounds like a long weird story."

Jilly gave Honey a last hug before she stood up and took Geordie's hand.

"I don't suppose you have some coffee to go with that campfire," she said. "I've got the start of a wicked headache from caffeine withdrawal."

Timony picked up the empty Styrofoam mug in which he'd brought Geordie a coffee earlier and handed it to her. By the time she took it from him, it was filled to the brim with hot, steaming coffee.

Jilly took a deep breath of its rich aroma before she had a careful sip.

"You are so going to have to teach me that trick," she said.

Jilly

It's weird being back on the mesa top. This is still the otherworld, but compared to that place where I left Mattie and the other Eadar, it seems . . . I don't know. Weightier. Like there's more gravity here, or presence, or *something*. It's not so much that I noticed a lack when I was in that version of Tyson County that lies inside my head. I just notice a *more* here.

I take a sip of the coffee Timony made for me, then something occurs to me. I'm still in the otherworld, and I've still got the light inside me. What's to stop me from working magic whenever I'm here? So I give it a try while we walk back to the fire and everybody's talking.

Once upon a time . . .

I'm thinking of just a small thing, only to see if I can do it. So I imagine the coffee is cocoa and that the fire is green instead of yellow and orange.

But, of course it doesn't work. It's only going to ever work in that one little piece of the otherworld peopled by a shiver of my brother Del and the Eadar from Ellen Wentworth's book.

I feel kind of relieved and disappointed, all at the same time.

"We should go back," Geordie says.

He and Lizzie have been packing up their fiddles. There's been conversation going on all around me, but I haven't heard any of it until this moment, when Geordie touches my arm to get my attention. I've been in a world of my own, like a person standing still in the middle of a hurrying crowd of commuters as they're getting on the subway.

"Jilly?" Geordie asks.

I nod, but going back is the last thing I want to do right now.

"Can I just have a moment to finish this coffee and catch my breath?" I say.

"Sure. It's just . . ."

"People are going to be worried," Joe puts in.

I look at Lizzie and Geordie. Of course. The band will be worried. And Cassie must be frantic about Joe.

"Maybe you should take them and then come back," I say. "I'll just wait here for you and let everything settle down inside me."

"I'm not going back without you," Geordie tells me.

"What's the real issue here?" Joe asks.

I don't want to tell him—at least not here, in front of everybody. They already know me at my worst from what I related about my history with Del and Mattie—I gave them the short version, but they all got the picture. I don't want them to know that I'm a coward as well. Especially not Honey.

But Joe's got that look in his eye—part worried, part curious, and all obstinate. If there's something going on with me, he's not going to let it go until I tell him what it is.

"Okay," I tell him. "The truth is I'm scared to go back and be, you know, the Broken Girl again."

Joe shakes his head. "It doesn't have to be that way. Since you got rid of the crap that was stopping them, the healers can fix you up now, good as new."

"So, it's like in the fairy tales."

"What is?"

"You know," I say. "Magic can't ever fix the real problems. In the stories, all the real problems are solved by kindness and pluck, or with a true love's kiss, with all that kiss means."

I find myself remembering a line from one of the Jewel CDs that Sophie often plays in the Greenhouse Studio while she's working. Something about how in the end, there was only kindness.

Kindness implied no expectation of reward, or even necessarily thanks.

It was simply the doing of it that mattered.

"But mostly the kindness," I say.

"Sure," Joe says. "I get that. But there's nothing wrong with using medicine when it can help. There's no good reason in turning down a helping hand, magical or otherwise."

Jack nods. "You didn't see Joe turning Anwatan down when she brought him back from the dead."

I just look at Joe, speechless for a long moment.

"You . . . you were dead?" I finally manage.

"Yeah, but it didn't take."

He's trying to be all jokey about it, but I can tell he knows it was as big a deal as I think it was.

"Anwatan brought him back," Jack says, "and the crow girls tidied up his death wound. They can fix you up, as well."

"But why me?" I say. "I can get around as I am. Why not go to the terminal ward of Newford General and help the people there? There are all sorts of people way worse off than me."

Jack shrugs. "I could say that maybe it has to do with preserving that light inside you—making sure it gets to shine on the way it's supposed to. Or maybe it's only because the crow girls like you. You'll have to ask them. But me? I'd just let it be done. Change the wheel I was on and get on a new one that makes sure I was worth the fixing up."

There's no shame in reclaiming the health you once had, Honey says. *You've had more than your fair share of suffering.*

"But I've had more than my share of good, too—like all the friends I've got. Some people don't get even one."

"Yeah," Joe says. "And somewhere out there, one of those people will get you for a friend, and it might just save their life. But they might not survive if you're not healthy enough to go out and make your rounds the way you used to."

Before the accident, I spent a lot of time volunteering at the food bank and the old folks home and anyplace else where I thought I might do some good. Joe's right. I haven't done any of that for way too long.

"And then there's your art," Geordie says. "I know how much you miss it. Maybe what you don't realize is how much everybody else does, too. I've talked to people who say it changed their life. Once a girl told me it *saved* her life. Having this poster on her wall from one of your shows reminded her every day of how important it was to connect to people, instead of hiding from them."

"You never told me that."

"Doesn't make it not true," he says. "And then there's—"

"Okay, okay. I get the picture. I'm a saint."

"You're no saint," Joe says, "but you're good people. Take the gift that's offered to you."

If you need to bargain with the idea of it, Honey adds, *consider this healing as payment for all the hurt that was done to you as a child.*

I give her a slow nod. "I guess I can do that."

Farewell and Remember Me

Geordie

It was so weird to be back in our hotel room in Sweetwater. Jilly sat in her wheelchair, the young twenty-something she'd been in the otherworld replaced once more by what she called the Broken Girl. Her gaze was on something on the other side of the window, but I don't think she actually saw anything out there in the growing darkness.

It was Monday evening. Hard to believe that it had been only a day since all of this started—or at least since Jilly and I fell down a rabbit hole into boganland and had our lives turned upside down.

Neither of us had much to say about it. We hadn't much to say about anything since we came up to shower and get changed. We were supposed to meet Lizzie and the others downstairs, but while we each had a shower and changed into fresh clothes, we made no move to leave the room.

In the old days, we could be together for hours and never need to say a word. Maybe we'd get that back, but right now the silence had a weight for me, and I felt I needed to break it. I stood up and came to stand beside her. The last of the day was leaking out of the sky, glowing a hundred shades of mauve and pink behind the tall pines.

"You must be relieved," I said.

Jilly looked up at me from the wheelchair.

"What do you mean?" she asked.

I shrugged. "You know. You've finally got the last of Tyson County behind you."

"It doesn't feel any different," she said. "Not now that we're back. It's . . . there's no magic here."

"Maybe not *right* here, but we both know it exists in this world."

She smiled. "It's still funny hearing you say that."

"You mean when I've spent so long denying it and finding more rational reasons for what couldn't really be explained except as magic?"

"Pretty much."

"Well, you know us Riddells. Bang either one of us along the side of the head with something for long enough, and we'll eventually sit up and pay attention."

"Yeah, neither you nor Christy is big in the change department."

"Some people would say that's part of our charm."

"Some people would only be you and Christy."

I smiled. "That was almost sassy."

"It was, wasn't it?"

I sat down on the bed, and she turned the wheelchair so that she was facing me.

"So, what was with that business back on the mesa?" I asked. "About your not wanting the crow girls' help? Ever since the accident, you've been all into self-healing meditations and alternative medicine to get your strength and mobility back. Why don't you want to try this?"

"I don't know. It seems too easy. Like I didn't earn it."

"Didn't you once tell me how wrong it was for people to think the only wisdom or help they could appreciate was if they paid something for it?"

"There's always a payment."

"You know what I mean," I told her. "And besides, if you're going to talk about things being earned, you didn't earn the crap you've had to deal with in your life."

"Everybody has that—to some degree or other," she added before I could say anything about how being abused as a kid, or crippled by a hit-and-run driver, doesn't exactly happen to everybody, thank God.

"But still . . ."

She nodded. "I know. I guess it's just some kind of weird guilt. Why me and not someone else?"

"It's not being offered to someone else."

"But *why?*"

She had me there. The difference was, for me it didn't matter. I wanted her to have everything that had been taken away from her. I wanted to see her dancing and running and painting and living large the way she loved to live. What happened to her as a kid—that couldn't be changed. But these physical holdovers from the accident. They could.

"Like Jack said," I told her. "You'll have to ask the crow girls that question."

She smiled. "Yeah, and off they'll go talking about cups of sugar and the colour of fish smiles or some such thing."

"But you're going to do it?"

"Ask them?"

"To see if they can heal you now."

"Absolutely."

We fell silent again. After awhile, Jilly reached over and took my hand.

"So all this talk about healing and the like," she asked. "Is that you circling around us talking about our relationship?"

"No. Yes. Maybe."

"If you're having second thoughts . . ."

She started to pull her hand away, but I tightened my fingers around it. Not hard. Just enough to let her know that I didn't want to let go.

"I did have second thoughts," I told her, "but that was only when you left us on the mesa. When we're together, I don't have the slightest doubt that being with you is what I want. What I've maybe always wanted, except I was just too blind or stupid or both to figure it out."

"Me, too."

"But when you went away, I got . . . scared, I guess is the only way to put it."

"Scared of what?"

"Well, neither of us is much good at making a relationship work."

"Though you're usually the one who gets dumped," she said.

"I know. But that was still because it wasn't working out."

"So you're afraid that'll happen with us?"

I shook my head. "I don't think so. It's just . . . what if it *did* happen? What happens to us being best friends? I can't even imagine a world without you in it. You know, when I first heard about the accident, I could feel a piece of myself just go so still inside me. It was like something collapsed in my chest, and all I could do was sit there holding the phone and wonder if I'd ever be able to breathe again."

Her fingers tightened on mine.

"We just have to make that not happen," she said.

"Can we do that?"

She smiled. "We can do anything—isn't that how it goes in the fairy tales? We've made it to the other side of the woods. All that's left for us now is our happy ending."

"I'd like that."

"Joe's always telling me," she said, "that there are some things you need to decide with your head, and others that you can only decide with your heart."

"My heart's definitely saying yes."

She lowered her eyes for a moment, and I realized that she was feeling shy. Jilly, of all people. And that shyness filled me with the courage to listen to my heart.

I stood up and helped her to her feet. She looked up into my face.

"You know what?" she said. "I'm tired of talking. I feel like I've been talking forever. To Del. To Mattie. To everybody."

I got the message and leaned down to kiss her. It was long and sweet and got a tingle started up way down inside me.

"Wow," she said when we came up for air. "How come nobody ever told me you're such a good kisser?"

I didn't answer. Instead, I scooped her in my arms and laid her carefully on the bed. Then I lay down beside her, my head propped on my arm so that I could look at her face. I reached out and followed the contour of her jaw with a finger.

"Maybe . . ." she started, her voice husky. "Maybe we should wait until the crow girls get me fixed up."

"I don't want to wait."

Those startling blue eyes of hers had a sheen, but she was smiling.

"Me, neither," she said.

And pulled me over on top of her.

Lizzie

"So," Siobhan said, "I'm guessing the lovebirds aren't leaving their room."

The band was sitting downstairs in the hotel's bar. They had commandeered one of the large booths—big enough for six—and they each had a whiskey and a pint of beer on the table in front of them. Con and Lizzie sat on one of the benches, Siobhan and Andy across from them.

Lizzie smiled. "You think?"

Con put his arm around her shoulders.

"Maybe we should all pair up," he said.

Lizzie pushed him away and punched him in the arm.

"Ow! What was that for?"

"Your endless flirting. You know, if it hadn't been for you, I would never have driven off the other night and none of this would have happened." He started to protest, but she held up a hand. "No, I just need to say this. If I ever decide to drive off by myself in the middle of the night again, you all know to just shoot me or something, right?"

"Except . . ." Andy began, but then he let his voice trail off.

"Except what?" Lizzie asked him.

"I don't know. It was all pretty amazing."

"Except for those of us who got pushed down the stairs," Siobhan said, "and had their arms broken."

"Sprained."

"But still . . ."

Andy grinned at her.

"Okay," she said. "It *was* pretty amazing. Scary, but amazing." She looked across the table to Lizzie. "Who knew that all those old fairy tales of Pappy's were true?"

"Pappy?" Con asked.

"My grandfather," Lizzie and Siobhan said at the same time, then laughed.

He nodded. "I keep forgetting you guys are cousins."

"Wait'll we introduce him to Timony," Lizzie said.

The doonie had gone back to the Aisling's Wood, but had promised to visit as soon as everything had settled down.

"Pappy probably already knows hundreds of fairy folk," Siobhan said. "I mean, just think about the way he told those stories."

"I just hope the ones he knows are all nice ones like Timony."

"No kidding," Con said. "Man, if you could have seen these buffalo guys. There were millions of them and talk about your heavy-looking dudes."

Andy nodded. "They made gangsta rappers look like boy scouts."

"I could do without ever meeting any of those heavy ones again," Siobhan said.

And then off the conversation went as they all traded stories about the various wonders they'd been witness to. At one point, Andy got up and fetched them all another round and while Lizzie knew the smart thing would be to not have another whiskey and beer chaser, what the hell? She'd earned it.

She knew she should be tired, but she'd never felt more wide-awake in her life.

While the talk went on, she noticed that Con had moved closer to her again. When he rubbed his leg up against hers, she turned around sharply.

"Okay," he said. "I get the message."

He started to scoot back along the bench, but she grabbed him by the shirt, pulled him close, and then kissed him. Seriously kissed him. Hard and long, like that fairy woman had done with Geordie on the mesa.

"What was that for?" Con asked when they came up for air.

Lizzie glanced at her cousin and Andy across the table. Andy looked surprised, but Siobhan had a smile in her eyes. Lizzie turned back to Con.

"You're always flirting with me," she said. "What do you *think* it was for?"

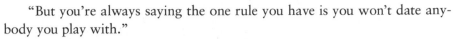

"But you're always saying the one rule you have is you won't date any-body you play with."

"So, maybe it was a stupid rule."

He shook his head. "No, it was a good rule."

"Are you turning me down?"

He grinned. "Hell, no. I like to break the rules."

Siobhan turned to Andy. "Looks like we're sharing a room, but I'll warn you right now. No funny stuff."

He gave her a look as though she'd just suggested he sleep with his sister.

"Oh, for God's sake," Lizzie said. "We're not going to . . ."

But her voice trailed off when she looked back at Con. He was so hand-some. Flirty, but always nice. And look where she'd ended up the last time she'd run away from him.

"Well," she added. "It might be nice to have somewhere private where we could . . . you know, talk about stuff."

Siobhan laughed. She downed her whiskey and slid out of the booth. When she was standing, she gave Andy a pointed look.

"What?" he said.

"Come on," she said. "I need a hand moving my stuff."

Lizzie waited until the two of them had left the booth and started for the door, before she turned back to Con.

"So," she said. "Do you want to go talk somewhere private?"

He laid a hand on hers and smiled.

"Wherever you lead," he told her, "I will follow."

"Oh, please."

But when he leaned forward to kiss her, she let him.

Joe

"I've just got one more thing I need to do," Joe told Cassie when the two of them and Jack got back to the city.

Cassie sighed. Before she turned back to him, she gave a longing look to the front of their apartment building. Which Joe didn't miss.

"I'm sorry," he said. "But it can't wait."

"Is it dangerous?" she asked.

"Don't think so. I just need to deal with the last of the bogans—the one those crow boys didn't find."

"Oh, Joe, you're not going to . . ." she began, then caught herself. "What am I saying? Of course, you wouldn't. You're just going to take him to Raven, right?"

He shook his head. "No, I made a promise to Anwatan to keep him away from the corbae. She says he's basically a good kid who got dragged along on the hunts against his will."

"Like there's any such thing as a good bogan," Jack said.

Joe shrugged. "I gave Anwatan my word."

"So that was the price for her bringing you back?" Jack asked.

"You know I don't work that way. Once she told me her need, once she explained about the kid to me, I would've done it whether she brought me back or not."

Jack gave him a coyote's grin. "Helps that you'd have to be alive to do that."

"I could've got around it."

"What's *that* supposed to mean?" Cassie asked.

"Spirits can get things done before they move on. Especially in the otherworld."

Cassie shook her head. "I don't believe you. What about me? What about us? How could I go on without you?"

Joe reached up and touched her cheek with his palm.

"It didn't play out that way," he said. "And we're still good, right?"

"We're still good. I just wish you didn't have to play hero all the time."

"It's nothing I choose."

"And would you still love him if he was any different?" Jack asked.

Cassie punched him in the shoulder. "No. That's not it and you know it. I just worry."

"You and me both, Cassie."

Joe looked from one to the other.

"If you two are done," he said, "maybe we can finish this and put it all behind us."

He reached for Cassie's hand.

"You want in on this?" he asked.

She smiled. "Sure. I've never seen a bogan before."

"Not much to see," Jack told her. "Ugly little buggers who—"

He broke when they stepped away, crossing back into the otherworld, and hurried along after them.

"A little warning would be nice," he told Joe when they arrived at the lakeshore.

He stopped and looked around. It was dusk back in Raven's world, but here, night had already fallen. A three-quarter moon sat in the sky above cliffs topped with tall pine and spruce. The moonlight gleamed on the lake water and made the sandy shore seem almost white.

"Hey, I know this place," he said. "This is where the cerva held Anwatan's blessing ceremony."

Joe gave him a curious look. "I don't remember you telling me you attended that."

"I didn't. I was watching from above." He indicated the cliffs. "It's where I ran into Grey."

Joe nodded. "Well, the kid should be around here somewhere. Let's start at the base of the cliffs, there in the middle, and work our way along both sides to see if we can pick up a scent."

"Is it part of your helping him to scare the crap out of the kid?" Cassie asked.

"What do you mean?"

"Well, what's he going to think? He's on the run from cousins, and here's a couple of tough old canids trying to track him down."

"Wouldn't hurt to give him a scare," Jack said. "Might help him remember the kind of trouble you can get into if you're not more careful about picking your friends."

But Joe was smiling.

"I'm guessing you've got a better idea," he said to Cassie.

"Does he have a name?" she asked.

"Rabedy Collins."

"What are you going to do with him anyway?" Jack asked.

"He can take dog shape."

"Really? I didn't know bogans could shapeshift."

Joe nodded. "Apparently Odawa was teaching them, but it only took with the kid."

"Well, he's got that much in his favour, then."

Cassie had already walked away from them, heading for the cliffs, so the two of them caught up with her.

"Give me a little space here," she said.

She walked on alone, softly calling the bogan's name, a coaxing tone in her voice.

After a few moments, a small shadow crept out from under an overhang and hesitantly approached her. The little black dog hung his head and had his tail tucked between his legs, but he closed the distance between them step by step.

"I don't like this," Jack said, his voice pitched low. "We don't know anything about that dog. How do we know he's not putting on the submissive act? If he goes for her throat, there's no way we can get to her in time."

Joe lifted his arm when Jack started forward.

"Cassie knows what she's doing," he said. "She doesn't just read cards. She reads people, too."

Cassie had one knee down in the sand and her hand stretched out, palm down. The dog sniffed the back of her hand cautiously, then let her pat him.

"You can come now," she called over her shoulder.

"They're not going to hurt you," Joe heard her tell the dog as they approached. "I know they look scary, but they're here to help you."

"Yeah," Joe said. "Anwatan sent us."

The dog's head lifted at the sound of her name. Joe didn't have to be part canid to read the hope in the dog's eyes.

"She's gone on now," he said.

Beside him, Jack stood with his arms folded, studying the dog.

"Let's see what you really look like," he said.

I . . . I don't think I should, sir, the dog said. *Anwatan told me not to. It's part of my . . . punishment, I think.*

"You don't like being a dog?"

I like it much more than being a bogan.

"Well, we're saying it's okay," Jack told him.

The dog hesitated a moment, then a shiver ran across his skin, from tail to head, and a bogan crouched there in the sand on his hands and knees. He sat up, his neck drawn close to his shoulders as though expecting a blow.

Jack continued to study him, then finally gave a slow nod.

"Anwatan was right," he said. "This kid's not a killer."

Rabedy cleared his throat. "What . . . what are you going to do to me?"

Joe sat on the sand beside Cassie.

"What do you think we should do to you?" he asked.

"You should punish me, sir."

Joe's brows went up. "What for? Anwatan said you weren't in on the kills for any of those hunts."

"But I was there. I didn't try to stop them."

"Why not?"

"I . . . was too scared."

Joe nodded. "Yeah, I've been there. Not a good feeling, is it, standing by when someone's being hurt?"

Rabedy's eyes went wide. "*You've* been scared?"

"Scared and stupid, just like you. And I didn't always have being young for an excuse, either. But then a day came when I realized I was either going to have to stand up for what I believed in, or really be the useless piece of crap everybody thought I was—even if it meant getting hurt or worse. Let me tell you, I've never looked back since. I can still get scared, but doing what I know is the right thing always gives me enough courage to get through it."

Rabedy had a look of astonishment on his face. Beside him, even Cassie looked surprised. But Jack only nodded and answered their unspoken question when Joe wouldn't.

"You try being a half-breed," he said, "trying to fit in with all the true-bloods. Some clans aren't so open-minded as we are, and they can be hard on a mongrel kid."

Joe gave the bogan a feral grin that made the light in his eyes seem crazier than it normally did.

"Everybody's got teeth," he said. "You just need to be willing to use them."

"I . . . I wish I'd stopped them, sir," Rabedy said. "I should have."

Joe nodded. "Yeah. You should have. And now you have to carry the weight of not stepping up. But the memory of what you didn't do can be the strength that lets you do the right thing, the next time you see somebody about to get hurt."

"I'll try. But I don't know that I'm brave enough."

"What you're really saying is that you don't think you're strong enough. You don't have confidence."

"I guess . . ."

"Well, I've got a friend who's going to teach you to believe in yourself. She's got the biggest and truest heart of pretty much anybody I know, but the thing is, you're going to have to do all of this in that dog shape of yours. She doesn't have much fondness for five-fingered beings."

"I really do prefer the dog shape, sir."

"Joe."

Rabedy blinked with confusion. "Sir?"

"Just call me Joe. When you say 'sir' I don't know who you're talking to."

"Yes, suh . . . Joe."

Joe smiled. He turned to Cassie.

"You want to see where Honey lives?" he asked.

"Even when she doesn't like 'five-fingered beings'?"

"You're cool. Don't worry about it."

"Then, sure," Cassie said. "But we're not completely finished here." She turned to Jack and asked, "Can you make us a cigarette?"

Jack nodded. When he pulled tobacco and papers from his pocket and started to build the cigarette, Cassie returned her attention to Rabedy.

"Do you know what this means?" she asked him. "Our sharing the sacred smoke?"

The little bogan shook his head.

"Three is sacred to fairy," she said, "but among the cousins the sacred number is four, because there are four directions. When cousins share smoke, they are offering it to the spirits of the four directions, which ensures that no spirit is forgotten, and they are asking the spirits to make note of the bond of peace and friendship that the smoke represents. If that bond is broken, it makes the spirits angry."

"And you don't want to see those old spirits angry," Jack put in.

"So . . . you want *me* to smoke with *you?*" Rabedy asked.

Cassie and the two canids all nodded.

The bogan couldn't seem to believe this.

"You would make a bond with *me*? But I'm just a useless bogan."

"You're not," Cassie said. "And we're none of us special. I'm human, Joe's a mongrel, and Jack . . ." She smiled. "Well, Jack's Jack. Individually, no one's really special. It's how we connect to each other that's special. How we can make something good come of that. So the smoke binds that promise and reminds us that we're not alone, even when we feel we are."

"I . . . I'm honoured," Rabedy said.

Jack responded for Joe, Cassie, and himself.

"So are we," he said.

He lit the cigarette with that old Zippo of his. He offered smoke to the four directions, then passed the cigarette to Rabedy.

It was closing in on midnight in the arroyo by Honey's den, but her pups were still playing down in the riverbed. Among them was a new foster brother, a black dog that was a little clumsy but his barks were the most joyful.

Cassie and Jack sat on stones close to the riverbed, tossing twigs for the pups, laughing to see the way they'd chase and have mock battles over the little lengths of wood. Higher up on the slope, Joe sat cross-legged in the dirt with Honey beside him.

"Thanks for this," Joe said.

Honey shook her head. *I would have done it anyway. He's a Child of the Secret, just like Jilly and me.*

"Yeah, I kind of figured that was the case. There was too much unhappiness in him for it just to have been caused by these hunts he was forced to go on."

The Secret pushes us into ourselves, closing us off from the world. The hardest lesson we learn is that it doesn't have to be that way.

"Not an easy thing to trust in when you've had a lifetime to teach you otherwise."

No. It's not easy, but it's worth the effort. Unfortunately, we don't learn that until after we've had the courage to reach out to accept the helping hand.

They were quiet for a moment, watching the pups playing. When Joe sighed, Honey turned to him.

What is it? she asked.

"You know Jack was right when he said it's not so bad to be a human from time to time. For one thing, it gives you another perspective."

Why should I seek that perspective?

"It's just good to have an understanding of the beings you interact with."

I don't have any urge to understand humans, any more than I do the ground squirrels or other game I hunt.

"You don't hunt humans.

She bared her teeth. *No. But there are some for which I'd make an exception.*

"So there's no other shape you'd like to try?"

Her muzzle rose upwards. *I think it would be . . . interesting to view the world from a bird's view.*

The crow in Joe's blood stirred at her words.

"I wish I could teach you that shape," he said, "but like I told you before, all I see in you is your canid blood."

And it is enough. It will be enough for my pups, so it will be enough for me.

"I wish it could be different. I wish we could all see the world through whatever eyes our hearts fancy. We're all so connected to each other, but most of us just can't see it."

I won't be convinced.

Joe nodded. "Don't mind me. When it's unfinished business, I always find it hard to let a thing go."

It's what makes you who you are.

"I suppose. But tell me. What was it that made you change your mind about this? Back when we started off to look for Jilly, you seemed pretty interested in learning to wear another shape."

Jilly's brother reminded me of everything I hate about that shape.

"I thought it was something like that. But if you ever change your mind . . ."

I'll know who to ask for help.

Joe nodded. But he thought that if that day ever did come, it was a long way from today.

What's going to happen to Odawa? Honey asked.

Joe shrugged. "Damned if I know. He'll probably be put down. They're having a big meeting about it at dawn—the air and water clans."

You won't be there?

"I don't have any interest in cousin politics, unless it impacts on those who can't defend themselves, and we're way beyond that now. The corbae and water cousins have it covered."

So, what will you do?

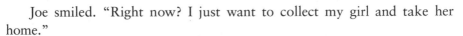

Joe smiled. "Right now? I just want to collect my girl and take her home."

It's good to have a home.

"Tell me about it. I didn't have one for so long, I thought I never would. But then it turned out I just needed someone to have a home *with*. Now it doesn't matter where we stay—so long as Cassie's there, I'm home."

That's how it is for me with my pack and my pups.

Joe nodded. "Jack might stick around for a few days—just to help you keep an eye on the new pup. I know," he added before Honey could interrupt. "You can handle yourself and your family. But we feel responsible bringing him here. We just want to make sure he fits in and doesn't try to hurt anybody."

Honey looked down the slope.

I have a good feeling about Rabedy, she said. *Anwatan was right to spare him, and you were right to bring him here. He has the potential to grow up strong and true.*

"That's all we can ask of anyone, darling—you and me included."

He stood up and brushed the dirt from his jeans.

You'll be back? she asked.

"Yeah, and I won't be so long about it, either—that's a promise. But you've got to promise me that the next time you get a hankering to walk in Raven's world and hang around outside our building, you come up to the door and let us offer you some hospitality."

I think I can do that.

Joe let a mock growl rise up in his chest.

"You do that," he said, "or I'll know the reason why."

She bumped her head against his thigh.

You're such a tough lone wolf, she teased. *How does Cassie ever put up with you?*

"With lots and lots of patience."

He started down the slope to join the others, Honey padding at his side, her laughter ringing in his mind.

Grey

The way Raven had talked about the air and water clans that were coming, I'm expecting a turnout of all kinds of different tribes of cousins, but when we get to the meeting field, the only air cousins are corbae. Oh, there's a big representation of the water clans, fresh and salt water, but the only birds are crows and ravens. Jackdaws, rooks, and magpies—local ones, as well as a pair of our mottled Australian cousins. I spy a few jays, but they're mostly blue and none of them are kin.

We all come as five-fingered beings as a courtesy to the water clans who might have had trouble travelling here otherwise, and we're now a couple hundred cousins gathered here on a peninsula not far from the city. The meeting field's a big expanse of flat rock, duned beach, and grasslands, surrounded by the lake on three sides and a forest on the remaining fourth.

Dawn's waking on the eastern horizon by the time everybody has gathered, and Raven's people walk Odawa out into the middle of the big circle that's formed. The trees behind us are black with crows and ravens and other blackbirds, sticking to their avian shapes. I wonder if the crow girls are among them, because I don't see them on the meeting field.

"You'll never find them at something like this," Chloë says when I ask her.

I'm walking beside her, the two of us making up the last of Raven's entourage.

"Why not?" I ask.

"It's too depressing for them. I know they can be serious—deadly serious—but they try to avoid being so as much as possible."

I know just how they feel. I've never seen so many grim faces all in one place before, and it's pretty obvious how this is going to go. But I feel I have to be here. I was there at the beginning, I owe it to my dead to be a witness at the end.

"I'm with them on that," I say.

"I suppose," Chloë says. "But we all have responsibilities to the greater good."

"Maybe theirs is to make the world seem a little less grim than it is. Or at least to remind us that it can be."

Chloë gives me a small smile. "Maybe it is."

Once everyone's settled, there's an immediate argument raised by the salmon clan, that this is a blood feud and so no one's business but that of those involved. Waninin, the chief of the salmon clan, makes the point that if anyone should be on trial, it's me, since I struck the first blow.

I'm willing to take the judgment on that, but there are too many predators present for the argument to go unchallenged. Lazy Lightning, an orca from a pod near the shores of my home forests, stands to glare at Waninin with an unblinking gaze. He stands tall—taller than any of the buffalo clans—and his shoulders strain against the fabric of his shirt.

"Since when does a hunt for food become a feud?" he demands. "We are predators. Or are you saying that we should forsake our natures?"

"Cousins don't hunt cousins."

"No," Lazy Lightning agrees. "And that was not the case here, either. Odawa himself has admitted that Grey only blinded him because he thought he'd come upon a dead salmon, half frozen in a stream. There was no malicious intent upon Grey's part. Odawa's retribution—that's an entirely different matter."

Tall and grave, a dark-haired woman I recognize as Moon Song of a Wave Upon the Coral, a rootwife of the dolphin clan, rises and waits for silence. She's dressed in a long dress the colour of the sea, which brings out the blue highlights in her own dark skin. I've seen her at councils such as this, back home, and while I know she can be patient, she doesn't suffer fools.

"Deciding the wrong or right of Odawa's blinding isn't our business today," she says. "We're here because of his dealing with fairy and the impact that has had—and could still have—on all of us."

"Better they were all dead anyway," someone says.

I can't see who's spoken, but Moon Song turns in the direction of a group of sea otters. The animosity between the otter clan and fairy selchie has never been satisfactorily resolved—at least, not so far as the otter are concerned. They have such friendly, round faces that it's always a surprise to me how dark and deep their anger can run.

But in that way, we're no different from humans. We have our differences—with other clans, with fairy and humans, and even with those who are members of our own tribes. Raven knows, I've carried my own for long enough.

"And that is not today's business, either," she tells the otters.

"*And,*" Raven puts in, "we have treaties in place with fairy, agreed upon by the chiefs of all gathered here, as well as by those who aren't with us."

It's the first time he's spoken, but his silence hasn't surprised me. I've come to see that Raven downplays the history that could make him an automatic leader of all the clans. It would be hard to argue with the one who brought the whole world into being, back in the long ago. I wonder if he ever plays that hand, or if he's always content to wander among us, his part in our origin mostly forgotten.

Moon Song nods in agreement with him. She's never been afraid to take on the role of leader if she feels it's required.

"Treaties that Odawa deliberately undermined," she says. "He wasn't simply taking revenge on Grey. He was trying to start another war with fairy. And tell me this, Waninin, and you, Yanei Ohka. Is a feud between two cousins reason enough to cause the deaths of the hundreds of brothers and sisters we would lose in another war with fairy?"

"You know that's not what I meant," Waninin says.

The sea otter that Moon Song puts the same question to, answers by changing the subject.

"I, for one," Yanei Ohka says, "would like to hear the specific charges being brought against Odawa. And I would expect some proof beyond the word of a few corbae."

A long, shocked silence follows.

Here's the thing about my people—one of the big differences between us and humans: our word is sacrosanct. We lie and cheat right up there with the best of them. But once we give our word, once we make a promise, we keep it to the letter. That's why Odawa's still here, awaiting judgment when you'd think he'd have fled as soon as Raven's people took him in their custody. He gave them his word that he would abide the word of the council, and here he is.

Our word is our honour. Without it, we'd have only chaos.

What Yanei Ohka's just said is enough to start a blood feud between our clan and his that could last a thousand years, because while we'll let a lot of things slide, the one thing that no cousin will do is question another's honour without a world of proof to back him up.

I can feel the corbae stiffen all around me. In the trees the blackbirds shift angrily. And then Raven stands up again.

He's different this time. Bigger, darker, his eyes fathomless.

"What did you say?" he asks.

His voice is quiet—like the hush before a storm, pregnant with menace.

Yanei Ohka's features pale. I'm guessing that he let his mouth run on ahead of his mind, and he's only just realized what he's said.

"I . . . I . . ."

"In the heat of the moment," Moon Song says, her voice soothing and mild, "we all say things we don't mean. Things we don't think or believe. Who knows what mad place inside our heads calls them up? But out they come, damaging and hurtful."

Yanei Ohka nods gratefully to her.

"I'm truly sorry," he says, directing his words to Raven. "That wasn't what I meant to say at all."

Raven's gaze never leaves his face. "And what was it that you did mean to say?"

"Nothing. Only that I'm ready to hear what Grey and the others have to tell us."

He sits down quickly and tries to hide among the rest of his clan.

Raven nods slowly. He doesn't seem to have done anything to effect the change—and I certainly didn't see it happen—but he's no longer so tall and forbidding. He sits down, as well, and the council goes on with more of the same. There are arguments and discussions, tempers flare, die down to a simmer. But it's been obvious all along what the final result will be.

I wonder how they'll choose to deal with Odawa. In situations such as this, there are usually two choices: death or banishment. The banished keep their lives, but nothing else, for they're allowed no contact with other beings—cousin, fairy, or human—and must give their word to abide by the constraint or be hunted down and killed.

Raven has already told me that Odawa will not give his word to abide by the conditions of banishment, but the council as a whole isn't aware of that. Raven has said nothing because Odawa might still change his mind, but considering how single-mindedly he's come after me through the years, I don't see that happening.

Finally, Moon Song rises to her feet.

"Will anyone speak in Odawa's defense?" she asks the gathered clans.

Odawa himself has refused to speak, and there's no one else. With the evidence laid before them, his own clan members know there's not a single reasonable argument they can make. The war Odawa almost brought upon us is too serious a matter, and it's obvious that while Odawa might not have tried to start a war with deliberate intent, he still acted with complete disregard for the hard-won treaties we've made with fairy and so put every cousin in danger.

And he certainly had a hand in the bogans' killing of a number of cerva.

The silence holds for a long space of time, but it can't hold forever.

In a moment, judgment will be passed and the punishment laid out.

In a moment, the deaths beginning with Mira and carrying on to so many others will finally be avenged.

In a moment, I'll finally be free of the curse Odawa has laid upon my life.

I'm not even aware of what I'm doing as I stand up.

"I will," I say.

The weight of all those gazes is heavy. I see surprise. I see anger.

The truth is, I've surprised myself. But I've been thinking of Mira, of how she would feel about this. She was like the cerva in that way—at least those of Walker's clan. She always saw the best in people. She railed against the injustices of the world and never believed that violence was a better answer than compassion and understanding.

Like Anwatan's response to Minisino, Mira would never have agreed to a solution that meant anyone's certain death—not even that of her own murderer.

"I don't excuse what he's done," I say, "but circumstances drove him to do what he did. Perhaps when I plucked out the eyes of what I thought was a dead salmon, I also damaged something in his mind because his single-minded pursuit of me over the years, the deaths he has caused, seem to me to be caused by madness, not the calm wisdom for which the salmon clan is known."

I don't look in Raven's direction as I speak, but I can feel his angry gaze on me.

"Are you saying he's guilty or not?" Moon Song asks.

"He's guilty," I reply, "but I don't believe either death or banishment is the answer."

"And what would be the proper punishment?" Raven asks.

I don't turn to look at him, keeping my gaze on Moon Song.

"If Odawa will promise to use his remaining days to make up for all he's done," I say, "we should allow him to do so. We speak of the gifts of the

Grace. Isn't compassion one of them? Would it serve our community better if Odawa was dead, or if he lived to help us make this a better world?"

"But if, as you say, he's mad . . . ?" someone begins.

I shake my head. "Single-minded, perhaps, and he was driven to a kind of madness. But if nothing else, his being held accountable today should make a difference. If he can take responsibility for what he's done and swear to make up for it, then we'll know that the madness was temporary."

Before anyone else can respond, Odawa finally speaks. He turns his blind gaze in my direction, and I swear he sees right into me.

"And what about you?" Odawa asks.

"I'll make the same promise," I tell him.

"That's easy for you to say. You already serve the community . . ."

He breaks off and gives a slow nod. "I see. That's the whole point of it, isn't it?"

"Is it such a bad point to make?" I ask.

"You weren't awoken from a frozen sleep to find the world gone dark."

"No, I wasn't. I can't pretend to know how that felt. But does another death help anything? Would it not be better for you to give your word to serve the Grace?"

"And you'll just forget all of this," he says.

"I will never forget," I tell him, my voice hard. "Just as you won't. But I'm willing to put it behind me because it's the right thing to do."

He shakes his head. "I say again, it's easy for you to—"

I cut him off before he can start.

"People I loved are *dead*," I tell him. "Don't you dare say this is easy for me."

The sightless gaze faces me for a long moment, then slowly lowers to the ground.

It becomes very quiet in the meeting field then, as though no one is breathing. I hear, as if from far away, the lap of the lake's waves against the shore, the wind soughing through the pines, the stir of a blackbird's wings in the trees behind me.

"Odawajameg?" Moon Song asks. "Will you give your word?"

Those milky-white eyes turn in her direction and he nods. "I do."

Moon Song looks about at the gathered cousins then.

"And does anyone disagree with Grey's suggestion?" she asks.

I wait for Raven to speak, but he doesn't say a word. No one does.

"Then let it be so," Moon Song says.

We came in ones and twos and small groups and leave the same way. There is little discussion, here in the meeting field, but I know cousins. They'll be talking about and arguing today's events for weeks to follow.

Odawa stands alone in the center of the meeting field, a tall silent figure. Still and unmoving. The only shifting about his figure is the slight billow of his robes in the breeze. The departing cousins glance at him, but no one tries to engage him in conversation. I'm not interested either. I'm done with him now. I'm done with all of this.

Or almost done, I realize, as I turn to face Raven's angry Buddha face.

Chloë, Brandon, and the others from the Rookery have already departed, but he's stayed behind waiting for me—a large, ominous figure, as unmoving as Odawa.

I start to walk by him, into the woods that separate the peninsula from the city, and he falls into step beside me.

"I don't want to talk about it," I tell him.

"That's not an option, little jay."

I glance at him, then shrug.

"So go ahead and talk," I say, "because I've got nothing to say."

"That fish killed Mira and only you know how many of your other friends and lovers. How could you even propose the thing you did?"

We're under the trees now. A few of the blackbirds remain, high in the boughs above us, but most of them have flown off now. Back to Stanton Street, maybe, or off to spread the gossip of what they've seen today.

Raven takes my arm, and I have no choice but to stop. He's an immovable force, and the grip he has on my arm almost pulls it from its socket when I try to keep moving. He lets me go when I stop. I refuse to rub my shoulder in front of him, however much it feels like it needs a good massage now.

"I know how you felt about him," Raven says, "and I certainly know how you felt about Mira. So I need to understand. How could you do this?"

"I've learned a few things from my recent association with humans and fairy," I tell him.

"And what would they be?"

"That we're not so different, for one. And that our similarities are worth celebrating."

"What does that have to do with Odawa? Up until ten minutes ago, he was still the enemy. He still murdered your wife and friends."

"But he wouldn't be an enemy in Mira's eyes. Just as the bogans weren't in Anwatan's. They could take her life, but they couldn't take away her pacific beliefs."

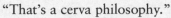

"That's a cerva philosophy."

"Does that automatically make it wrong?"

"No. It's just . . ."

Raven sighs. For a long moment I think he's going to leave it at that, but he gives a slow shake of his head.

"You never asked how Mira and I became estranged," he says.

"I didn't even know the two of you were close—not until Chloë told me yesterday. Mira never spoke of you."

"We had a . . . disagreement about my responsibilities."

I wait.

He sighs again. "She said if I brought this world into being, then it was my responsibility to see that it remained a fair and just place for everyone to live."

"That seems like a reasonable notion," I say. "If you are, in fact, that Raven."

"I am. But I'm also Lucius Portsmouth. Just like the crow girls, I don't usually remember my origins. I don't like to be reminded of them."

"Why not?"

"Because while I do see the wrongs and injustices that pervade this world, there's nothing I can do about them without causing more harm than good."

"But you made this world."

He shakes his head. "All I did was pull it out of a pot. Anybody could have done it—as Cody never tires of reminding me. The act didn't invest me with some great power."

"I've seen you . . ." I'm not quite sure how to phrase it and settle on: "become *more*."

"I didn't say I was helpless."

"Then why don't you do more?"

"Where would I begin?" he asks. "There's disharmony wherever one turns. I'm surprised that the Grace is even remembered anymore, this world has grown so distant to her gifts and teachings."

"Then just do what you can. Every little thing can make a difference."

"I see why you and Mira were together," he says. "That's exactly what she said. And I'll tell you now what I told her then: the only way to truly effect a change is to change what's inside a being. How they see the world. How they connect to it. But who am I to make decisions such as that? Who is anyone?"

"But surely—"

"Take Cody. How many disasters has he brought into the world? But he always means well and he has also done great good. Should I go into his mind and change who he is?" He pauses. "That's not the best example. I doubt anyone could make Cody be anything other than what he is. But do you understand what I mean?"

I nod. "I think so. Everyone needs to make their own choices or those choices don't mean anything."

He cocks his head. "Maybe you and Mira are more different than I thought. Because she wouldn't accept that. She said it was my responsibility to make things right—that the whole world was my responsibility, not just some small corner of it—and so long as I made no effort to do so, then we could no longer be friends."

I almost hear that conversation. Mira was nothing if not stubborn. But I also knew her as especially reasonable. How could she not have seen things from Raven's point of view?

I ask him as much.

He shrugs. "We all have blind spots. When it came to me, hers was that she'd decided I was supposed to mend whatever was broken, however it needed to be done. It seemed so simple and straightforward to her, such a fair and honourable solution, that my disagreeing with her could only be construed as a deliberate avoidance of my perceived responsibilities."

I think about how active he's been these past few days and compare it to the stories told of him, of how he distances himself from the world. How there are times when he *completely* withdraws from the world, sometimes for years at a time.

"I can see her side of the argument, too," I tell him. "Isn't it a part of the Grace's teachings that each of us has a responsibility to leave the world at least a little better than it was before we got here?"

Raven nods. "But Mira wanted me to put the world back into the pot and pull it out again, fresh and sweet once more—the way it was in the long ago. But you know, Cody tried that and all he succeeded in doing was almost destroying the world and the pot I brought it out of."

"I didn't know that."

Raven shrugs. "So you can see why I might be reluctant to attempt the global changes Mira insisted I make. I didn't want her out of my life, but she gave me no choice. I thought we would reconcile, eventually. But then Odawa killed her, and I was left knowing that we never would."

"You never went after him?"

"Oh, I did," Raven says. "But he's a wily one. I could never track him down, no matter how many of our kin I sent hunting him."

"I gave up hunting him," I say.

"Because of your guilt."

I nod. Mira wouldn't have died, no one else would have died, if I hadn't blinded Odawa in the first place. Saying I thought he was dead at the time—truthful though that was—was still no excuse. I'd still done the deed that set everything else in motion.

I look at Raven and see something in his eyes. It takes me a moment to realize what it is, where I've seen it before. The crow girls had that same look when they calmly told Raven to kill them so that they could go bring Joe back from the dead. It's the look of one living entirely in the Now. Not the Now of Zen philosophy, but a Now that precludes any memory of the past or consideration of the future.

There are people who consider the cousins to be spirits—guiding spirits. They say that we live outside of time, that the past, present, and future are all happening at once for us. Maybe that's true for some, but it's not for me. It might have taken humans to give time the forward motion it seems to have, but I've bought totally into it and the days pile up into years in my memory.

But Raven . . .

He's more like the crow girls than maybe he'd admit. Chloë said the crow girls avoid any consideration of their true nature, but I think they truly don't remember. Not unless someone, or some incident makes them. Then they can be fierce. Then they have power.

And Raven's like that, too. He doesn't avoid his past or the mantle of his history. Most of the time, he simply doesn't remember it.

Why didn't he continue to seek out Mira's murderer?

Because he'd forget to.

Why doesn't he mend the flaws in this world he's made?

Because he forgets to.

I don't doubt the truth of what he said. To truly mend everything, the world would have to go into the pot and be pulled out again so that everything could start over.

But unless he's reminded of it, I doubt he even considers it.

It's why he withdraws from the world. He doesn't *remember*.

When I think of how Chloë looks out for him, I realize that her solicitousness is born not simply of her affection for him, but also of necessity.

I turn to look ahead through the trees and sure enough, there she is, a large black raven perched on the low-slung bough of a spruce, preening her wing feathers while she waits for us to be done here.

I turn back to Raven. For a moment he doesn't see me, then his gaze, dark and old, focuses in on me.

"What will you do now?" he asks.

I shake my head. "I really don't know. I'd say go home, but I don't really have a home. I haven't had one since Mira died."

"You're always welcome at the Rookery."

"Even after what I did today?"

"I don't agree with what you did," he says, "but that doesn't mean it wasn't the right thing to do."

"You seemed so angry."

"I was. In many ways I still am. But it's done now. If I've learned anything over the years it's when and how to let things go."

Is it? I wonder. Or is that he forgets and it no longer looms large in his mind the way it would in another's?

"I'll see you again," I tell him. "But for now, I need some time alone."

"I understand," he says.

He hesitates, as though he's about to add something else, but then he simply nods and walks away, on through the forest. When he reaches the bough where Chloë waits for him, she drops down onto his shoulder.

I look back through the trees to what I can see of the meeting field. Odawa's no longer there. There are only some gulls, riding a thermal across the headland.

"I hope I did right by you, Mira," I say.

There's no response, but I wasn't expecting any.

Lizzie

The sun was just pinking the horizon in the hills behind the Custom House Hotel in Sweetwater when Lizzie awoke. It took her a long moment to remember where she was. Her dreams had been filled with elves and dwarves and people that were part animal and part human. Not like werewolves or monsters, so much, but in a way that seemed natural and unthreatening.

She turned her head toward the nightstand and looked at the clock. 6:14. Reaching behind her, she tugged up her pillow, then sat up and leaned against the headboard. It was only then, when she was sitting up, that she realized she wasn't alone in the hotel bed.

Oh boy, she thought, looking down at Con's handsome, sleeping face. He was turned toward her on the bed's other pillow, a half smile on his lips.

She'd thought that coming to her room with him had been part of the dream, too. Not to mention everything that had happened after they got to the room . . .

But obviously it wasn't.

Blame it on running around in bizarre worlds and all the unbelievable things that happened to her. Blame it on the whiskey, if nothing else.

But she didn't really need to blame it on anything. She'd been tipsy, not drunk, and Con had been lovely and sweet and very attentive—all the things she'd needed after the ordeal of the past few days.

It was so not a good idea to get involved with a band member, but the heck with it. Maybe they could make it work. Surely it had worked for other couples in the same situation, but she couldn't think of a single one.

Siobhan would know. Siobhan's head was filled with musical trivia that had no real use except for making introductions to songs when they were on stage, or at a moment like this, when you just needed to know some bit of arcane detail that your own poor brain couldn't call up. But she wasn't about to wake her cousin up to ask.

She sat there for a few moments longer, then slipped out of bed and stood at the window. There was a glow on the ridges of the hills across the river, pink and pale orange.

She couldn't remember the last time she'd seen the dawn—certainly not waking up to see it. Whenever she did, she was usually bumping into it on the way to bed after a long night of music.

It would be nice to be down by the river to watch the sun come up, she decided.

She tugged on a pair of black jeans, pulled a T-shirt over her head, and found her shoes. One was by the door, the other under the window beside her fiddle case. She sat on the chair and laced them up, one after the other, first the right, then the left, the way she always did. Standing up, she put on her jacket. She hesitated for a moment, then took a towel from the bathroom and slipped out the door, walking quietly downstairs to the lobby.

When she stepped out the front door, the air outside felt fresh and new— like it had in the otherworld, except the only enchantment here was the simple, ordinary magic of the sun bringing light to the darkness at the end of the night. It was magic that only happened once a day, but it happened every day.

A steadily growing chorus of birdsong followed her as she crossed the road and went down the steps to the pier. Its planks were damp from the dew, so she folded up the towel and used it to sit on as she watched the sun coming up. After awhile she lifted her hand to her mouth and traced the contours of her lips. She worked her jaw, opening and closing her mouth.

Such a simple thing . . . until you couldn't do it.

She let her hand fall to her lap.

She remembered Geordie telling them last night, before he went up to his room with Jilly, how they might forget all of what had happened to them. How it could seem like a dream that would slowly fade away as the days went by.

She didn't know how that could be possible.

If anything, right now *this* world felt like the dream. An early morning in the spring. Sitting here by the river, serenaded by the early morning birdsong.

The soft lapping of the river under the dock. The sky lightening, bit by bit, until what had only been a dark smudge was now the silhouettes of trees backlit by the morning light.

A lot of terrible things had happened since her car broke down at the crossroads on Friday night and she'd been pulled into a reality she had never even suspected could exist. Oh, there had been Pappy's stories, but they were always just stories. They weren't real like the music. Like sparring with Johnny at the gym. Like making love to Con last night.

But beyond the terrible things, something had opened up inside her, as well. Some great . . . potential for understanding . . . she wasn't sure what. Just that there was *more,* but she was still a part of it. Everybody was a part of it, even if they remained blind to its existence.

She didn't want to lose that.

She didn't want to forget.

She wanted to build on it.

It wasn't that she wanted to live in those otherworlds, or become one of the magical beings herself.

She just wanted to retain this open feeling in her head, the realization that anything could happen. That there were possibilities upon possibilities lying just at everybody's fingertips. People didn't *have* to experience them, but there was something at once comforting and worrisome that they might.

And for all the terrible things she'd had to undergo and do, they didn't hold a candle to the wonder she'd been allowed to experience as well.

To forget that . . .

"Timony," she said. "Timony Twotot. Can you hear me?"

"Always," a familiar voice replied from behind her.

She turned around and there he was, sitting on the stairs, the riser he was on bone dry while all the others were still wet.

She smiled. "I don't know if I'm happy or a little creeped out to know that you're always just a half step out of my sight."

"Oh, I'm not," he said. "Did you think I've been watching you, waiting for your call?"

She blushed thinking of what he would have seen in her room last night.

"I don't know," she said. "Are you?"

He laughed. "Not hardly. I've been back in the Aisling's Wood, setting things a-right. But I've had an ear cocked to hear you if you should call my name. Was there something you needed?"

"No. I just . . . I'm afraid I might forget everything, and I don't want that to happen. I don't want to forget you."

"What makes you think you will?"

"Geordie. He was telling us last night how people forget even the most amazing experiences like we had because it doesn't fit in with their worldview. That our brains think it's easier to forget, than to try to make sense of all this new knowledge and experience."

Timony nodded. "I've seen it happen. But only to those who *wanted* to forget. If you're determined to remember, you will."

"Do you think I'll ever go back over . . . into the otherworld, I mean."

"I can take you right now."

"Oh, no. I don't think I'm ready just yet."

"It doesn't all have to be all monstrous conjurers and evil bogans, you know. I can show you simple marvels that offer no danger except for how they will make your heart swell to look upon them. Bodach markets and the winged dogs of New Forthfallow and fairy dances with music that will make you dance whether you want to or not."

She nodded. "I'd like that. In time."

"Then why did you call me?"

"Just to make sure that you're real. To know that I could. I'm sorry that I took you away from what you were doing for no more than that."

"You gave my life back to me," Timony said. "You have only to ask me anything, and I will try to do it for you."

She shook her head. "I don't want there to be an obligation between us. I just want to be friends."

"We are friends," he assured her. "But the obligation remains whether you want it or not. It's the doonie way, and I can't change it any more than you can turn into a pony."

"How do you know I can't?"

He cocked his head and pretended to study her.

"You have me there," he said. "I don't. Shall we go for a gallop?"

"No. I should get back to the hotel. God, I slept with Con last night— can you believe it?"

He smiled. "I don't know. If you tell me you did, then I do. Is that a good thing or a bad thing?"

"It's just confusing. But why am I telling you this? You don't know him or anything about my life before we met in the wood."

"But I'd like to know more," he said. "And we'll have time for that, don't you think? And I really want to hear you play again, especially with your band."

"I'll remember to call you to me when we have our next gig."

"Is it long from now?" he asked.

"No, it's on the weekend."

She stood up and shook out her towel before rolling it up under her arm.

"I really should get back," she said.

He stood up as well.

"Just tell me," she added. "What's the best time to call you if I want to just . . . you know, talk."

"Any time is the best time. Now that I've been woken up again, I have days and hours stacked up all around me, just waiting to be used."

"Then I'll call you tonight."

He tipped a finger against his brow.

"Until tonight," he said, and then he took a step and simply disappeared.

"Oh."

Surprise made the sound just pop out of her mouth.

One thing was for certain. With everything she'd experienced, she certainly wasn't going to get used to this sort of thing anytime soon.

She took a last look behind her. The sun was up over the hill now and the water shone as though all the lights of fairyland were lit up under its surface.

Smiling, she started back up the stairs.

She hoped Con was still asleep, keeping the bed warm.

Jilly

I wake up snuggled against Geordie's side like it's the most natural thing in the world. And maybe it is. Maybe I've been out of step all these years, and I'm just now getting into the real balance of my life, coming at it all raggedy-ass backwards, the way I seem to do all too often, but so what? It doesn't matter how I got here because I'm here now.

I realize that Geordie's awake. Those soft brown eyes of his are open and looking right into mine. His face is so close to me I could just lean forward a couple of inches and kiss him.

So I do.

"Hey," he says around a smile.

"Straw's cheaper."

He groans, but there's laughter in his eyes. This time he kisses me.

I could stay here all day, just the two of us in the bed, in this room. Let the world go on without us. Surely it can do without us for one day. It can certainly do without me. It's not like I've produced one piece of art in years that I'd actually allow to be hung in a gallery.

I make some jokey comment about it to Geordie.

He sits up and leans against the headboard.

"You shouldn't say that," he tells me.

"Oh, don't go all serious on me, Geordie, me lad. I wasn't trying for the oh-poor-me vote. I was trying for the let's-be-cozy-here-all-day one."

"I know. But your art's such a huge part of who you are. It kills me to see you without it."

"Oh, pooh," I say. "I've gotten along fine without it. Look at me lying here, all bold and happy and with nary a paintbrush in sight."

We both know I'm lying, but I can't seem to stop with the bravado, even here, even now, where I actually feel safe lying naked beside a guy in a bed, instead of getting all trembly and turning into Anxious Girl.

"You don't have to be without it," he says.

"Do you have a miracle cure up your sleeve?" I ask, then I whip back the sheets. "Nope. You don't even have sleeves."

"I don't have a cure," he says, "but the crow girls do. We talked about this last night."

I sit up so that I can lean against his shoulder. I trace the bumps of his ribs with a finger.

"I know," I say.

"So let's just do it."

"Except we can't," I tell him. "I don't have the feathers anymore. I can't remember what happened to them after the crow girls arrived."

And I realize I don't mind. They were used for a good cause and I'd rather be in my present condition than not have brought Geordie back in the world of the living.

"You're just stalling," he says.

"No, I'm not. I really don't have them. I can't even guess where they are. And you know what the crow girls are like—they come and go at their own whim, never when you expect them to."

"Do you really think you need the actual feathers in your hand?"

"Maida and Zia sure gave me that impression when they handed them to me way back when."

"Maybe you just need to call them to us the way we did Walker."

I lean back a bit so that I can see his face.

"What do you mean?" I ask.

"Oh, that's right. You weren't here. Remember Walker told Lizzie he'd help her whenever she needed him? All she was supposed to do was call his name and he'd come."

"I remember."

"So when we didn't know what to do, we went into the woods and did just that, and sure enough, he just showed up out of nowhere. He wasn't so happy when he arrived, but he did come."

"Why would that work with the crow girls?"

"Don't you think they're expecting you to call them?"

I give a slow nod. "I guess I could make it out to the woods, so long as we don't go too fast and we don't have to go too far."

"Why do that? I'm sure we can call them from here. We only went into the woods to call Walker because—well, we weren't sure what exactly would show up, and it didn't seem so smart to do it in the hotel room."

There's no point in arguing, and I don't know why I am. I'm so sick of being the Broken Girl. Why shouldn't I take the crow girls' magical help?

I guess it's just ingrained in me to do it on my own. I'll take help from my friends because they're like my family—my real family, the one I chose—but I don't like reaching beyond them.

But I let Geordie—I was going to say win, or maybe, have his way, but it's not like that at all. He's so totally doing it for me. It's been killing him to see how I've been. It's been killing everybody close to me.

Oh, why am I pretending otherwise? It's been killing me, too.

But I know the real reason I'm fighting this. I don't want the crow girls to show up and then do their laying on of hands, or whatever it is that they'll do, only to find that they still can't fix me. That everything I went through with Del hasn't changed anything. That the darkness in me is like a set of those Russian dolls that fit inside each other.

First I thought it was Raylene. Then I found out about Mattie.

What if there's another shadow? And then another and another and . . .

"Jilly?" Geordie says.

I blink and look at him.

"Right," I say. "Time to stop stalling."

So we get dressed.

"Maybe we should call room service and ask for a couple of bowls of sugar," he says while I'm struggling with my T-shirt.

Sometimes it's just so hard for me to get my arms up over my head—especially in the morning when I'm the least flexible.

Geordie comes over and gives me a hand.

"Or sugar packets," I say. "I bet they'd love little sugar packets."

Geordie ends up going downstairs and comes back with a coffee for each of us and a handful of chocolate bars for them.

"Well?" he says when we've finished our coffees.

I nod and set my empty cup on the windowsill. I look out the window at the hills, the sun gleaming bright on the spruce and pine, shadows pooling under their heavy boughs. The light's amazing, still so focused and almost primal, the way it can be at the beginning or end of the day.

There was a time when I'd be just itching to get it down on paper with a pencil or pastels, yearning to capture that light before it changes, but these days, when the impulse comes to me, the first thing I do is push it away.

There was a time when I'd look out the window and feel the weight of the winter just past ease away because it's so beautiful outside and if it's not quite blossoms-spring-forth spring, it's not deep-drifts-of-snow winter any-more, either. I'd insist on us going out and tramping through the woods. I could be out there all day and relish every moment.

That's another impulse I push away, when it comes.

But if I could have it all again . . .

So I call their names.

Maida and Zia. Zia and Maida. Crow girls.

I feel kind of stupid, sitting in my wheelchair, calling to them. Geordie waits quietly on the bed, nodding encouragingly when I glance in his direction.

I call them again. The third time.

There's no response.

I look at Geordie.

"Once more," he says.

I nod and do it again, my gaze on him, watching him mouth their names with me.

And then suddenly they're here.

One moment, it's just Geordie and me, sitting in our hotel room, and in the next a tumble of black hair and black clothes lands on the bed in a tangle of limbs, squirming and giggling on the bedclothes, their eyes bright with laughter.

"Hello, hello," Maida says.

She flops onto her back and looks at me from an upside-down vantage. Zia, sprawled across her stomach, spies the chocolate bars.

"Oh, look," she says. "Bribes."

Maida sits up and grabs one.

"Don't be rude," she tells Zia.

"They're not bribes?"

"Why would our veryvery good friends Geordie and Jilly ever need to bribe us?"

Zia shrugs. "So that we'll behave?"

"Don't mind her," Maida says to me. "She was brought up in a tree by an old magpie."

Zia nods. "Oh, yes. Ancient and decrepit."

"Wheezing and bony."

"With long grey hair, tangled like a bird's nest."

"And there," Maida says, throwing out her hand in a dramatic flourish, "is where we lived."

They each open a chocolate bar and eat them in what seems like two bites. But while they obviously relish the chocolate, something about them changes when they're done. Sitting on the edge of the bed, kicking their heels against the box spring, they face me with suddenly serious eyes and solemn faces.

"So, is it time?" Maida asks.

"Of course, it's time," Zia answers before I can. "Look how she glows. All the shadows have been burned away."

Maida nods. "Except for that one."

She points at me, but I have no idea what she's pointing at.

"But that's only a shadow of a shadow," Zia says. "A memory, nothing more."

Maida slides off the bed and walks over to my wheelchair.

"This will probably hurt," she says as she stands on my right.

Zia joins her, standing on the other side of the chair.

"Not because we want it to," she adds.

Maida nods. "Because we don't."

"But because they are old hurts."

"Skin and bone and muscle has to be pulled back into shape."

"Fresh hurts are much easier."

"But messier."

They each hold one of my arms against the chair. Maida puts a hand against my chest, pressing me back.

"This is for the screams," Zia tells me, which is hardly comforting.

I don't know what she means until she puts her hand across my mouth. That's even less comforting.

I decide I want to talk about this a little more, but I can't move my mouth. They might look like skinny little teenage girls, but they're shockingly strong. Their faces lean in close to mine.

"Here we go," Maida says.

A sudden sharp pain, like someone chipping at the raw nerve of a tooth, tears through my whole body. My back tries to arch, but it can't move because of Maida's hand pressing me back. But I'm only dimly aware of that. Just as I'm only dimly aware of their murmured, "Sorry, sorry."

There's only the pain.

It feels like my arms and legs are being torn apart and whenever I think it can't get worse—that it has to end now—it only gets worse.

I don't think I can bear it.

I *know* I can't.

If Zia didn't have her hand over my mouth, I'd be screaming my throat raw.

I don't know how long it lasts.

A few moments.

Forever.

I think I pass out for one blessed moment, then the searing pain spins to a crescendo. My ears pop.

And then it's gone.

The worst of it's gone.

The crow girls continue to murmur their sorrys. They stroke my brow and push the wet hair back from my face.

I'm soaked with sweat and trembling from head to foot. My temples throb with a headache that seems mild and soothing after what I've just been through. I feel nauseous and weak and if it wasn't for them holding me, I'd fall right out of my wheelchair.

I realize my eyes are tightly shut and I open them slowly, wincing as the light intensifies the pain in my head. But as the crow girls continue to stroke my brow, the headache begins to recede, then goes away. The nausea fades. I'm still trembling, but it's for a different reason now. I feel filled with more excess energy than I know what to do with.

I see Geordie standing in front of me wearing an expression that's a weird mix of horror and worry.

"I . . . I'm okay," I tell him.

"Of course, you are," Zia says.

Maida nods. "You're veryvery brave. I've seen big old wolves wet themselves over less pain."

"I'm pretty wet," I say.

Though thankfully I didn't pee my pants. But my clothes and hair are soaked and plastered against my skin.

"Up you get now," Maida says.

She takes one hand, Zia takes the other and effortlessly, they pull me to my feet.

I stand there feeling wobbly, trying to adjust my balance. Everything feels wrong until I realize why that is. There's no more numbness. There's no more pain. My bad leg takes my weight without wanting to give way from under me.

The crow girls let go of my hands and I flex my fingers, delighting in the painless movement.

"Oh, god," I say.

Zia shakes her head. "That wasn't any old spirit that fixed you."

"It was a gift of the Grace," Maida says.

Geordie takes a step toward me, but I close the distance and throw myself at him, my arms wrapped around his neck. I swing there, banging my feet, first against the wheelchair, then against the end of the bed, but I don't care.

Geordie hugs me until I put my feet on the ground. He holds me a moment longer, to make sure I've got my balance, but he doesn't need to. I've totally got my balance.

"Oh, dear," I say and lift a hand to wipe at the big wet spot I've put on Geordie's shirt.

"Don't even think about it," he tells me.

His grin is as big as the one I can feel stretching my own lips.

I turn to the crow girls.

"I don't know how to thank you," I begin.

Maida steps up and lays a finger against my mouth.

"Shush," she says. "We've wanted to do this for ages, but we couldn't."

Zia nods. "There was a veryvery dark thing in you, but it's gone now."

"Gone, gone!" Maida cries.

And she begins an impromptu dance. She takes one of my hands, Zia the other, and we bang some more around the room, giggling and laughing until we finally collapse on the bed. I look up to see Geordie shaking his head, but still grinning. He pulls me up into a sitting position. I'm still snickering when I turn to look at the crow girls again, but all the merriment has left their faces once more.

They're solemn and serious. *Everything* feels solemn and serious, invested with a gravitas that's completely eluding me. The very air in the room seems to have an earnest weight to it.

"You should spend some time in the otherworld," Zia says.

Maida nods. "You really should. Both of you."

"The air of the otherworld is closer to the long ago than it is here."

"It will keep enchantment strong in your blood."

"So that you stay strong and your light will never pale."

"This world of Raven's . . . it has a funny hold on how things should be."

"Everything's harder here."

"Magic."

"Kindness."

"Remembering the Grace."

Then Zia winks at me, a quick smile in her eyes. "But it has better sweets."

Maida gives a solemn nod of agreement, humour dancing in her eyes, as well.

"This is veryvery true," she says.

They jump onto the bed and bounce up and down.

"Time to go, time to go!"

And just like that, as suddenly as they appeared, they're gone.

I feel breathless—the crow girls have the habit of making me feel that way. Only Lucius and Geordie ever seem truly calm around them.

Geordie sits down beside me. He takes what was the Broken Girl's hand and runs his fingers over mine. They're as healthy and flexible as his own, without even a hint of numbness or pain.

"Are you really okay now?" he asks.

"I don't think I've ever felt better," I tell him. "Except maybe last night."

He blushes, just a little, but he grins.

"I see they took the rest of the chocolate bars with them," he says.

I push him back onto the bed and straddle him.

"Oh, who cares about a bunch of old chocolate bars?" I ask him.

"Not me."

And he pulls me down, his hands going up the back of my shirt, his lips finding mine.

Matthew Garner's been my physical therapist since I got out of rehab, lo so many months ago. I don't see him every day anymore. These days, I only have an appointment every two weeks. But he knows my case. He knows my body's strengths and limitations. So when I come waltzing into his office, sans wheelchair or canes, a bounce in my steps and swinging my arms, he just stares at me with that classic slack jaw look that you're forever reading about, but never seem to actually see in real life.

It's been like that since we came down for a late breakfast at the Custom House in Sweetwater through to seeing all my friends. Wendy and Sophie and Mona and just everybody. Even dour old Goon stared in surprise and then actually grinned when I came skipping into the Professor's house after Geordie and I got back from Sweetwater.

I don't even have my scars anymore, and let me tell you, I don't miss them. Not because of vanity, since I've never been one for shorts or dresses. But because every time I looked at them, all I saw was the road map of my pain.

Geordie's waiting for me now outside of Matthew's office. He's sitting on the balustrade leading down to the sidewalk, his fiddle case open beside him while he plucks out tunes on his fiddle. I give him a kiss—just because I can.

"How'd it go?" he asks as he puts away his instrument.

I smile. "He so totally has no idea what happened to me."

"And wanted to run a million tests."

"Which I politely declined."

"As is your wont."

I shake a finger at him. "I'm the one who comes out with words like 'wont,' Geordie, me lad. Don't you go stealing my vocabulary."

"What's yours is mine," he says with a grin.

"Except we're not married."

"But we could be."

I stop and look at him, not quite sure what I'm hearing.

"Did you just propose to me?" I ask.

"I was kind of trying it on," he says, "to see how it would take."

"I don't know. It wouldn't be very boho of us. Don't all the good scruffs like you and me just live in sin?"

"We don't have to. I think it'd be nice. It would feel . . . complete."

"Plus it would let us avoid the whole girlfriend/boyfriend and significant other conundrum."

"And I love you."

I can't get enough of hearing those words.

"Say that again," I ask.

"I love you."

"You said it twice," I tell him, "but I still love you more."

Okay, so we're a couple of saps, but who cares? I've been in an endless freefall of happiness for days now and after the last couple of years I put in, I'm reveling in it. I give him another kiss and we start off down the street, holding hands like a couple of school kids.

"Do we have plans?" I ask.

"Not until tonight."

"Right. Dinner at Christy and Saskia's."

Geordie nods. "Christiana's supposed to be coming, too."

"That'll be fun. But I was thinking a little more long term."

"Such as?"

"Well, maybe we really could spend some time in the otherworld. I've only ever been there under duress. I'd like to just be able to explore it for once without having to think that my life's in danger."

"What about what Joe's always saying—you know, about how that shine of yours is going to attract trouble on the other side."

"We can go with Sophie and Wendy at first—or with Christiana. They can show us the ropes and keep us safe. Especially Christiana."

"No kidding. I think she's the definition of capable."

"And then there's always Joe."

He nods. "Except I can't go right away."

"Because you're still doing those gigs with the Knotted Cord."

"I promised, didn't I?"

I have to smile. The Riddell boys are like cousins and fairy in that way. When they give their word, you can take it to the bank and count on collecting the interest.

"Of course, you did," I say.

"It's only until Siobhan gets the full use of her arm back again."

I nod, but I could have kicked myself that morning in Sweetwater when we came downstairs and I saw her with her arm in a sling.

"We were so stupid to not ask the crow girls to help her, as well."

"I don't think it works like that," Geordie says. "I think it's got to be more serious than a sprained arm, or a cure for a hangover."

"We still should have asked."

"There's a lot of should-haves in both our lives," he says. "If we stop and worry about them too much, we won't have time to appreciate what's happening now."

I punch him in the arm.

"Don't go getting all philosophical on me," I say. "You know what I meant."

"I do."

"And Geordie, me lad?"

He turns to look at me.

"I'd love to be married to you."

That quick grin of his is so endearing that I have to pull him to a stop and kiss him again.

Like I said, we're a couple of saps. But we're loving every minute of it.

It's later that same night.

We're staying in my old studio on Lee Street because—hello? Stairs are no longer a problem for the new and improved All Mended Girl. I can get up and down the steep flight at the loft even better than I could before the accident. I have so much energy it's almost scary. I was never the quiet and demure type in the first place, but now there's a constant buzz in my every muscle and vein.

Maybe it's the light everybody's always talking about. I still can't see it, but maybe I can feel it now.

I sure feel something.

We picked up a DVD on the way back from dinner at Christy's apartment and started to watch it, except Geordie fell asleep halfway through. I turn off the DVD player and TV and sit there on my old Murphy bed for a while, watching him sleep. Finally, I lean down to give him a kiss, then scoot off the bed. I walk over to the window in my bare feet and look down at the street for a long time, feeling so blessed that there aren't the proper words to express my thanks.

But I send out thanks all the same. To the crow girls, to Joe, to the Grace, to Geordie and Raylene and everybody who helped bring me to this point where I'm so healthy and happy and alive. Right at this moment I'm not carrying any baggage. I feel vibrant and ready to be filled with new experiences.

After awhile I take the phone to the far end of the studio where I won't disturb Geordie, and call my sister.

I called her once as soon as I got back, just to let her know I was okay and say that I'd call her back later. This is the first chance I've had.

"So, what was up with that dream?" she says. "Except we decided it wasn't a dream, didn't we? Or if it was, you pulled me into one of yours."

"I'm sorry, but I really needed you there," I tell her. "You were my inspiration to be strong and stand up to the Del in my head, because you're the only one of the two of us who stood up to him for real."

"Yeah well, when you think about it, I didn't do such a good job. I should've cut his throat instead of just his leg."

"I'm glad you don't have to carry the weight of that."

"I guess." She's quiet for a moment, then says, "When we were there, you kept talking about how we were inside your head, but it felt just like the otherworld to me."

"I think it was a bit of both."

"I guess that's why I've been feeling this way."

"What way?"

"Well, ever since that night, I can't stop looking over my shoulder. I keep expecting to see one of those damned wolf boys, just a-gunning for me. They warned me pretty much point blank that they'd be coming for me if I ever went back."

Raylene's had her own experiences in the otherworld, but they didn't turn out nearly as well for her as mine did. You know how fairy tales have good guys and bad guys in them? Well, she was definitely the big bad wolf and the canids didn't take too kindly to what she was doing to their reputation. She's changed now, but cousins have long memories.

"I'll talk to Joe," I tell her. "He'll make them understand."

"Good luck with that because I don't. Understand, I mean."

So I tell her the whole story, everything I didn't get the chance to explain when we were sitting on the porch of that old homestead inside my head.

"I guess it all makes a certain perverted kind of sense," she says when I'm done. "Do you think you'll ever go back?"

I hear the yearning in her voice.

"I can't not," I tell her. "We'll probably go once Geordie's done with the last of his commitments to play with the Knotted Cord."

"So, Geordie's going with you?"

I smile, but she can't see it.

"Oh, yes," I say.

She laughs. "Someone's getting laid."

"It's more than that."

"Of course, it is. It's you and Geordie."

"No, I mean we're getting married."

"Oh, wow. I'd say 'so soon?', but you guys have been circling around each other for pretty much forever, haven't you?"

"I guess we have. Will you come to the wedding?"

"Is it going to be all mushy?"

"Come on, Raylene. Say you will. Say you'll be my maid of honour."

She waits a beat before she asks, "What about all those friends of yours? Wendy and Sophie and the one who draws the comics—"

"Mona."

"Whatever. Shouldn't it be one of them?"

"I want it to be you."

"Just a sec'," she says.

Her voice sounds a little funny, then I hear her put the phone down and blow her nose.

"Are you okay, Raylene?" I ask when she gets back on.

"Oh, sure," she says, with the usual sardonic tone back in her voice. "It's just allergies."

You big liar, I think. You don't have allergies any more than I do.

But I don't call her on it.

"So, say you will," I say instead.

"Of course I will. I can't not show up at the wedding of the only member of my family that I actually like."

"Careful," I tease. "You're being almost sentimental."

"Yeah, well . . ."

"I love you, too," I tell her.

I can almost see her do that little shake of her head she does when she's feeling uncomfortable. Just mentioning any kind of intimacy always seems to puts her off-balance.

"I'm glad for you," she says. "You really deserve some happiness after all you've been through this past couple of years."

"Everybody deserves happiness—including you, Raylene."

She surprises me. I know she carries a lot of regret over the things she's done in the past—things she can't ever change. She never talks about it, but I know she feels that there's no way she can ever make up for what she's done, that she doesn't deserve happiness because of all the pain she's brought into other people's lives.

But instead of brushing me off, she says, "I guess that's why I've got you in my life."

I can't help it. I start to cry.

"Oh, Jilly . . ."

"No, it's good," I tell her through my sniffles. "I'm . . . I'm actually happy. I'm so looking forward to seeing you."

"Me, too," she says.

I look out the window, at the strip of dark night sky I can see above the building across the street. I think:

Once upon a time . . .

Maybe fairy tales aren't the only place you can find a happy ending.

If I was writing one for all of us it would just go, Once upon a time, they all lived happily ever after.

Grey

I hear the music long before I see the pub. Some jaunty set of jigs comes spilling out the door and dances down the block to meet me whether I want to hear it or not. I've never really cared much for this sort of thing in the past. Irish and Scottish dance tunes. Fiddles and accordions and high-pitched whistles. It's all too busy and fast, with too many notes.

I follow the music the rest of the way up the block and it brings me to the pub. The sign hanging above the door says "The Tankard & Horn" with the appropriate imagery painted underneath the words, just in case you can't read.

Okay, that's just me being cranky and I've no reason for it. I pause to take a breath and work a crick out of my neck. When I start forward again, I try to do it with an open mind. And actually, when I give the music half a chance, I find myself smiling. Go figure.

Light spills cheerfully out the windows and door along with the music, falling on the half-dozen people who have come outside for a smoke. They're all shapes and sizes. A couple of punk kids in leathers and jeans, hair retro-spiked. A guy that looks like he stopped by on his way home from a mechanic's garage. Some old hippies, balding on top with thin ponytails. A tall woman in cowboy boots and hat who looks like she should be at a Hank Williams show. Their only commonality is their nicotine addiction.

One of the hippies nods to me as I walk toward the open window and I nod back, but I keep going until I can see inside.

Harnett's Point is a tourist town that's become a satellite community to Newford over the past few years. It's on the lake and close enough to commute, which makes it attractive, but I've never liked to watch this sort of thing happen. Prices go up, taxes go up, and pretty soon the people who have lived in a place like this for generations can't afford to even rent anymore. The people who do move in have no history—at least no history here—and therefore little appreciation for the way things were. So what they do is remake it all into something more familiar to them.

The main street is lined with coffee shops and restaurants, gift and souvenir stores, boutiques and pubs like The Tankard & Horn, all selling the same sorts of things you'll find in other towns where this has happened, all the storefronts looking the same.

I don't like it, but it's none of my business, and I don't want to think about it tonight. Tonight I just want to see Lizzie's band play and see if I can learn to appreciate the music. Though mostly, I want to make sure she's okay.

It's hard not to appreciate the skill of the musicians up on the stage and I find my foot tapping, all on its own. I smile as I watch Lizzie hamming it up with Geordie, the pair of them never missing a note. Lizzie's cousin is at the merchandise table.

I look for Jilly, but she's not sitting anywhere close. Then I realize she's at the front of the stage, dancing like a little tangle-haired dervish. I blink in surprise until I realize that Joe must not be the only one who knows the crow girls well enough to get some personal attention from them.

"Got a light?" someone asks me.

I start digging in my pocket for a packet of matches as I turn around, only to find Jack standing there with a cigarette between his lips.

"What happened to that fancy Zippo of yours?" I ask. "Did you finally lose it in a card game?"

He grins. "I don't lose at cards." He pulls the lighter out and gets his cigarette going. "I was just making conversation. You want one?"

I take the proffered cigarette and he lights another for himself.

"How's Joe?" I ask.

I haven't seen him since Anwatan and the crow girls brought him back from the dead.

"Being Joe," Jack says. "Last time I saw him he was back in Fitzhenry Park, doing his mystic Indian fortune-telling thing like nothing ever happened. But that's what I like about Joe. He falls into these big stories, but he never lets them take over his life. He just goes back to Cassie and that extended family of his, and it's all good."

"I'm glad. I like him."

"What's not to like?" Jack takes a considering drag from his cigarette, then adds, "Heard about what happened at the big meeting."

"You and everybody else. So, which side are you on? The one that thinks I've got a cerva's generosity of spirit, or the one that thinks I'm an idiot?"

"Neither. It's not something I'd have done, but that doesn't mean it was wrong."

"I just knew Mira wouldn't have wanted her own death answered with another."

Jack nods.

"But you don't agree."

"Well, that's the funny thing," he says. "I've just come back from a sort-of babysitting duty, watching one of Anwatan's killers prove that he's actually a sweet little guy."

"One of the bogans?"

"Yeah. Although he wasn't actually in on any of the kills, and it turns out he was coerced into even doing that much."

"Your point being?"

He shrugs. "Well, I would have just put him down and been done with it. But Anwatan made Joe promise to look out for him, and like I said, turns out he's really okay. Messed up from the part he had to play in those hunts, but determined to make up for it. That's not something I would have learned if I'd done things my way."

"Yeah," I say. "It's funny how these things turn out."

We finish our cigarettes and listen to the music for a while. The tune they're playing now is slower and has an almost tribal beat. I find I don't have to even try to like it. It just slips into me, as recognizable as my own heartbeat.

"Do you have much familiarity with this music?" I ask Jack.

"Me? Yeah, I love this stuff. But I hear you're not too fond of it yourself."

"I think I'm having a change of heart."

"With players of Geordie's caliber, I'm not surprised."

"Lizzie seems to be holding her own."

Jack nods. "You still sweet on her?"

"I was never sweet on her. I just knew she was in over her head and wanted to make sure she didn't get hurt."

"Whatever."

"Besides. I think she's got something going on with the guitar player. You see the way they keep looking at each other?"

Jack leans closer to the window and smiles. "Oh yeah. They've got chemistry, all right. Hey, is that Jilly dancing in there?"

I nod.

"Man, will you look at that shine of hers?" he says. "Makes you wonder about humans that they can't see something like that."

"Maybe they can't see it," I say. "But they can feel it. Look how the people close to her are all grinning and laughing, but the farther away from her you get, the less it touches them. They're still enjoying themselves, but they're not nearly so filled up with some good feeling that they could never explain if you asked them about it."

Jack smiles. "Seems like you're changing your mind about more than just music."

I turn to look at him. "What's that supposed to mean?"

"Well, come on, Grey. Everybody knows the hard-on you've always had for humans and fairy. I knew about it long before I ever met you."

I give a slow nod.

"I had my eyes opened, I guess," I say. "Turns out we're not all that different from each other. Except maybe some of the old cousin spirits."

His eyebrows go up.

"It's just. Well, take Raven . . . I don't think he's actually even *here* most of the time."

Jack grins. "You're just figuring that out? Man, all those old spirits are like that. Raven, Cody, Rosa, White Deer Woman. Oh, and let's not forget the crow girls."

"The crow girls seem *completely* here."

"Well, sure. So they look like a pair of teenage girls, and act like they're half that age, but you know they were here before Raven made the world. There's some say they *were* the long ago. Can you imagine carrying all those millions of years around in your head and not going crazy?"

I shake my head.

"Exactly," Jack says. "So, all of these old spirits have their own way of dealing with it. The crow girls and Cody, they're here and now. They don't fret about what's happened or worry about what's going to happen. Others, like the White Deer Woman, they become the wise old spirits people think they are, which is fine and does some good, I guess, but they end up with no life of their own. And then there are the ones like Raven, who just kind of shut down more often than not."

"What about you?" I ask. "How do you deal?"

Jack laughs. "Hell, I'm just a pup when it comes to them. Cousins like you and me, we're not even the gleam in our mama's and daddy's eyes in comparison to those old spirits."

I have to smile.

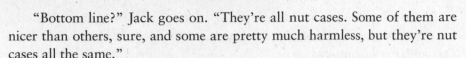

"Bottom line?" Jack goes on. "They're all nut cases. Some of them are nicer than others, sure, and some are pretty much harmless, but they're nut cases all the same."

"Even the Grace?"

"The Grace isn't a being, Grey. She's an idea. The state we find ourselves in when we're at our very best. She's an ideal. An inspiration."

"So you don't think she's real?"

Jack shakes his head. "But we can make her real. In here." He lays a closed fist against his chest. "But each of us has to do it in our own way. A group hug's not going to make it happen, no matter how good it makes us feel."

"How'd you get so cynical?"

"Hell, I'm not close to cynical. I'm hopeful."

Now it's my turn to raise my eyebrows.

"Think about it," he says. "Which is more hopeful? That we have to be led to the Grace by a shaman or priest or some nut case old spirit, or that we can find her in ourselves? I'm not blind to the worst in people, and maybe this sounds funny coming from a hard case like I make myself out to be, but man, I'm always striving to look for the best in them. In anybody."

I nod.

"Trouble is," he adds, "I get disappointed an awful lot."

"So, what do you do?"

He shrugs. "Try to live my life as an example—the way Joe does."

"And how's that working out for you?"

"I sleep nights. How about you?"

"Mostly," I tell him, "I feel cut off. Even though Odawa's no longer a threat to those I care about, I still feel like I shouldn't even be here. I should be out in the woods where no one can get hurt being around me."

Jack shakes his head and lays an arm across my shoulder.

"Let me buy you a drink," he says as he leads me to the door. "What you need is to see how that impulse of yours was on the money. Underneath our skins, we really are all pretty much the same. And that includes you."

"I don't know . . ."

But he won't let me finish.

"You just need to mix with people more," he says, "and see for yourself."

So I let him buy me a beer. We lean with our backs to the bar, watching the band. I see Lizzie's eyes widen when she spots us, but I just lift my bottle in a toast to her. She grins and gives me a nod, then puts her attention back into her playing.

I let my gaze wander. It drifts up to the rafters where I see a doonie sitting, banging his heels against the wood.

"I hope you're just here for the show," a voice says from beside me.

I turn to see it's that red-haired woman who stopped the buffalo from overrunning the fairy courts.

"Hey, Christiana," Jack says, leaning across me. "What brings you out to the sticks?"

She nods her chin at the stage.

"To see my brother play," she says. "What about you? If you're here to cause trouble . . ."

"Darling," Jack interrupts her, "I don't even know the meaning of the word."

She laughs. "Yeah, but somehow it finds you all the same."

"Not tonight." His gaze goes to the clock on the wall behind the bar. "And look at the time. I've got a poker game to get to."

He finishes off his beer in one long swallow and puts the empty bottle on the bar.

"You kids be good," he says.

And then he's walking off toward the door.

I watch until he steps outside before I turn back to look at Christiana.

"Did he set us up?" she asks.

"Not on my end."

"Because I wouldn't put it past him. Those wolf boys might play at being tough and hard, but they've got a romantic streak going through them a mile wide."

"Look, I'll just . . ."

"Relax," she says. "I don't bite. And we're just here to see the band, right? So we might as well do it together." She waits a moment, then asks, "Aren't you going to offer to buy me a drink?"

My first impulse is to leave. But then I remember what Jack said earlier. *You just need to mix with people more . . .*

It's safe now. Odawa's not out there, somewhere in the night—or at least he's not out there gunning for me anymore.

I can do this.

"Hello?" she says.

I smile. "Sure. What'll you have?"

"A margarita, I think."

I order her drink from the bartender and get myself another beer. When she has her margarita in hand, she taps the brim of her glass against my bottle.

"So, do you dance?" she asks.

"I can learn."

She smiles. "Now those are three words I like to hear from a man."